Facing the Lions

BY THE SAME AUTHOR

FICTION

Get Out of Town

So Fair, So Evil

Tears Are for Angels
(under the pseudonym Paul Connolly)

The Kingpin

The Devil Must

The Judgment

NONFICTION

Kennedy Without Tears

JFK & LBJ: The Influence
of Personality Upon Politics

Facing the Lions

TOM WICKER

The Viking Press / New York

First published in 1973 by The Viking Press, Inc.
625 Madison Avenue, New York, N.Y. 10022

Published simultaneously in Canada by
The Macmillan Company of Canada Limited

ISBN 670-30448-4

Library of Congress catalog card number: 72-11065

Printed in U.S.A.

TO MY MOTHER

Esta Cameron Wicker

Contents

The credit belongs to the man who is actually in the arena —whose face is marred by dust and sweat and blood . . . who knows the great enthusiasms, the great devotions —and spends himself in a worthy cause—who at best if he wins knows the thrills of high achievement—and if he fails at least fails while daring greatly—so that his place shall never be with those cold and timid souls who know neither victory nor defeat.

—THEODORE ROOSEVELT

Facing the Lions

The Professional I

Morgan was late. He was irritated too, because the wasted half-hour at the White House with Cockcroft actually had been the last part of a wasted hour. With the sublime indifference that transcended even his status as a Special Assistant to the President, Cockcroft had kept him waiting before telling him nothing. Morgan had expected that, but it still annoyed him because he regarded Cockcroft with the searing and unreasonable dislike of the self-conscious for the assured.

Morgan paused on the curb at K Street and looked apprehensively at the metallic evening glacier of buses, taxis, trucks, and private cars inching west toward Georgetown. An aged bus, spewing tangible pollution and listing to port under an overload of humanity, growled past; from its muddy windows, blank faces gazed at him unseeing. A spavined metal rack at his side bore an untidy heap of *Evening Star* late editions; PRESIDENT TO NAME NEW CIA CHIEF proclaimed the headline. That annoyed Morgan still more, mocking him not merely with Cockcroft's smug silence but with an insistent stirring just beyond the rim of recognition that limited his own memory; it was as if he were fumbling through numberless files for a document on which he could not quite lay his hands.

Inches from Morgan's foothold on the curb, a dusty station wagon approached hesitantly with a man and a woman in the front seat, a girl and a small boy wearing Confederate caps in the rear, luggage heaped behind them. The man craned his neck from a Hawaiian shirt to read the street signs while the woman pored over a large map; even in the oppressive heat of a Washington summer, she wore a scarf around her head, to conceal curlers. Morgan recognized the inevitable identification markings of tourists. As their car came abreast of him the lights changed; the pulsing mechanical herd halted on K Street, and another began to rumble and mutter up Connecticut Avenue toward Cleveland Park and Chevy Chase. Morgan walked behind the tourist car, feeling its noxious breath warm on his leg, noting its Missouri plates, and hurried across the street.

Morgan had a soft spot for tourist families; there was something moving, he thought, about parents who could ill afford the time and money bringing their big-eyed, trusting children to the capital of the shifting present in search of a comforting past. On just such a ritual childhood trip he had first seen the great white dome of the Capitol pure against the night and the godlike, brooding face of Lincoln, forever silent before the malice and charity of man.

Morgan was no longer a tourist in Washington. He felt himself at home —at least as much as he could be anywhere—in his chosen city of monuments and men. Surrounded by the impressive aura of the newspaper he represented, he moved with wary confidence in the capital's marble jungle of contrary interests, amid its careless dispositions of history and hope. He had few illusions about the ambitions that roved insatiably in its corridors, not least his own. He had not set foot for years in the Lincoln or Jefferson Memorials, but he knew quicker and better routes from one wing of the Capitol to another than the public course through the lofty Rotunda, with its guides and throngs. Even the tourists were more familiar than he with the view from the top of the Washington Monument; but Morgan knew what the Oval Office looked like and how to get there, and he could find his way through the State Department and the areas of the Pentagon where tourists were unknown.

Morgan knew who swung weight and managed matters behind the impassive stone façades of the Federal Triangle, the deceptively open glass of L'Enfant Plaza; and he had spent a good many years studying the currents of power that ebbed and flowed more relentlessly than traffic, from season to season, along Pennsylvania Avenue. He would break appointments to have lunch with some senators; others he avoided at cocktail parties; and if it was true—which Morgan rather doubted—that you could keep up with what was what in the House of Representatives by knowing only ten of its members, Morgan had learned the hard way that the real trick was to find out which ten, and he spent a significant part of his time keeping his own list purged. He cultivated certain deputy assistant secretaries and GS-18s who more nearly made things move or keep still—and who could tell him more about why—than cabinet officers and presidential assistants. Senators, congressmen, presidents, cabinet members came and went, not unlike tourists, but Morgan stayed on with the monuments and the bureaucrats. In a way, Morgan was both monument and bureaucrat, because, like the one, he had permanence and visibility, and, like the other, he had permanence and immunity.

But that damned Cockcroft, Morgan thought. Approaching the entrance to his building, he was assaulted by the piston noise and gasoline smell of life, and he was perspiring heavily in the sunlight that slanted at a low, brutal angle on the asphalt and concrete and metal and glass, on the hunched, hurrying humans around him. Other tenants were emerging as tentatively as divers tiptoeing along the board, reluctant to plunge into the heat and noise and odor, the thick summer evening waters of the city. Morgan felt a rising professional urgency at this evidence of the close of day, the onrush of deadline—an urgency as much a part of his life, after so many years, as any of his thousand familiar anxieties and competencies and attitudes; he even rather enjoyed—it was part of his notion of himself as unique—the reversal of his days, the way they built up slowly to tension and demand at the end, when sensible men were going home to martinis in the garden or to late-evening tennis at St. Albans.

I ought to have walked out on Cockcroft, Morgan thought as he strode into the lobby and the overpowering air-conditioning, at whose edge hovered two cheeping girls with fat exposed thighs and cascading hair. But it was not his style to be rude, even to deserving bastards like Cockcroft, with their impeccable lineage and imposing reputations.

"I spend half my life waiting for this goddam elevator," Morgan said to a janitor who was flicking a dirty mop around the fake marble floor of the lobby. "Man, *right,*" the janitor answered, not looking up. And the other half waiting for Cockcroft, Morgan thought. But he knew he would not punish Cockcroft or any of the other government stuffed shirts who liked to peer over distended nostrils at less exalted mortals.

The elevator and two lobbyists from the eighth floor arrived. "Ways and Means Committee," one lobbyist was saying as they emerged, and the other mumbled around a cigar, "Particularly this year," and both moved past, wrapped in smoke and their own concerns. Morgan entered, punched five, and watched the narrowing car doors pinch in on his view, like some new film technique, until the lobby and the indolent janitor disappeared.

It was not that Morgan—irritated anew by the lobbyists' lingering Cuban effluvia—was not powerful enough to make even Cockcroft respectful. In the first place, Cockcroft, as if by divine right, kept everybody except the President waiting; in the second, Cockcroft almost never agreed even to see any of Morgan's colleagues and rivals in the press. Nor was it that Morgan was necessarily too honest and ethical—like old Methodist hymns echoing from his youth, the words discomfited him vaguely—to use his own power for personal ends. Oh, he had never deliberately slanted his reporting, he would say at seminars; but he knew how easy it would be, and how effectively the slanting could be rationalized into truth, since truth in Morgan's world was, at best, uncertain and probably plural; and if that was the case, how could he be so sure about his own versions of it? But it was not that either; it was just that Morgan wanted most of all not to make too much of bastards like Cockcroft or of what they did.

Godard or maybe Welles pulled the vertical edges of the picture slowly back to the sides of the screen, revealing the lobby and janitor transformed into Janie at the office switchboard. Morgan emerged from the car, struck a pose, and announced, "They don't know to who they're talking."

Janie moved plugs and switches with hands like dying birds. "Kill 'em now or later?" she said to the switchboard.

"Kill 'em now."

Morgan and Janie shared a passion for Lotte Lenya, which they had drunkenly discovered in bed at her apartment, where he had intuitively ventured on a late night several years earlier, during one of his frequent fits of domestic despondence, and found Janie already damp in the dews of gin and lust.

"Sweetie, will you get me that son-of-a-bitch at the White House?"

"Ray Billings? Sure." He did not need to tell her he meant the President's press secretary.

Janie handed him a yellow slip. "Message for you."

Morgan took it with distaste. In all his years in the trade he had never overcome his dislike for the telephone, which constantly brought him news he did not want and carried precious bits and pieces of him where he did not want to go and where they were not welcome and from which they could not be regained. But life permitted few sensitivities. *Call Kathy Anderson.* The yellow slip informed him officiously that she was at area code and number.

"When did this come in?"

Janie shook her head. She was an execrable operator, but Morgan knew the work financed her hopeless voice studies, the grating results of which could too often be heard from the ladies' room. Besides, he knew, not without shame, that he could always go back to her apartment, even though he never had.

The newsroom was half empty, and he saw by the Western Union clock that he was even later than he had thought—and still bothered by some chimeric yellow slip undelivered from inept memory. He put the real slip in his shirt pocket and walked down the long aisle between littered desks and rattling typewriters toward Halperin's desk, wondering if it were Kathy or Hunt Anderson who wanted to talk to him. Recently, Kathy had been managing her husband's Senate office more than Hunt himself had been. It was probably Hunt, Morgan thought, and he was not in the mood to hold anybody's hand over long-distance; and lately, anyway, he had had more than he could bear of Hunt's long downward slide.

Halperin looked up at him and shrugged. "Zilch," he said.

"That goddam Cockcroft wouldn't give either." Morgan took off his light jacket; his shirt was clammy between his shoulderblades. "Not that he ever does."

"They don't even know who it is in the Armed Services Committee, and they're not happy about it either." Halperin was a Capitol Hill reporter; he had been a Capitol Hill reporter for so long that he not only looked like a congressman from Iowa, he thought like one, and therefore disliked presidents and the State Department on principle and took long vacations at Lincoln's Birthday.

Morgan sat in the empty chair at the next desk. "Well, I've got to write *some*thing. Joe!"

A man sparring with a typewriter at the front of the room looked back.

"Come back here and help me figure out what to write."

In the end, he knew, they would make too much of it, the way they always made too much of Cockcroft and Billings, the Armed Services Committee and the rest of the apparatus. In the end he and Halperin and Joe would make something resembling a story of it; they would make people think this appointment mattered, just as they had so often satisfied the need of yearning men to think a thousand other ephemeral events and persons mattered. That was what their work was all about, and they were good at it; they were professionals.

Joe came and leaned on Halperin's desk. He was lank, gloomy; after years in the Soviet Union, he now wrote about the State Department and kept mountainous stacks of *Pravda* and *Izvestia* on his desk. Morgan had just arranged for him to study Chinese at Berlitz on company time and expense, although the going joke around town was that even Joe's writing in English read as if it had been translated from the Russian.

"I've never seen one this tight," Morgan said. "Halperin says the committee doesn't even know, and I've been through the White House with a vacuum cleaner. How about your shop?"

"They don't know a word. They were asking me. Shelly just called in from the Pentagon and claims he can't get a line out of anybody that usually talks to him."

"What I don't understand is why the White House ever said the announcement would be tomorrow." Halperin picked up a malodorous pipe and put its bit in the slot it had chiseled in his side teeth; through long practice he could talk with the pipe in his mouth without letting it move a millimeter from the level. "Why build up all the suspense if you're going to keep it such a secret?"

"That's why," Morgan said. "And anyway this creep"—Morgan's phrase for the President—"this creep is probably enjoying the sight of the press running around in circles. They all do."

"Maybe there's some last-minute holdup," Joe said. "It's a sticky appointment. Maybe something's gone wrong." Years in Moscow had left him ever alert for conspiracy, mystery, unseen forces on the counterattack.

Morgan shook his head. "We'd have picked that up. Some of those White House pipsqueaks knew the name—I could tell they did when I talked to them. Longley told me the President had everybody terrified about a leak. I'm going to try Billings one more time but it won't do any good."

"It's the usual problem, isn't it?" Halperin took the pipe out of his mouth and gazed into its murky innards. "You don't pick a CIA chief every day. Either the conservatives or the liberals are going to foam at the mouth. The President probably doesn't want a head of steam building up against him on the Hill before he even sends the name up." To Halperin, a head of steam on the Hill was an irresistible force, opposed only by madmen.

Morgan stood up. "I can always write crap. TOP SPOOK CHOICE DUE. WASHINGTON SEETHES. If you guys can't find out anything to make me look good, what else can I do?" He clapped Halperin on the back, winked at Joe, despising his own empty joviality; he did not know any other way to deal with men who did not interest him.

"Billings on the line." Janie's voice, projected across the newsroom, menaced the windowpanes. "You want it there or in the office?"

Morgan pointed at his office and moved up the aisle. He touched Bill Watts's shoulder and murmured, "You're working too late." Watts had a heart condition.

Stopping for a moment by a girl with unbecoming eyeglasses, who peered anxiously through them at the paper in her typewriter, Morgan touched her shoulder. "If that reads as well as the piece you had this morning, I'll buy you a drink."

She looked up at him, her automatic smile stopping short of eyes made enormous by thick lenses. "You ought to have seen the other half of it," she said. "They cut the shit out of the color stuff."

"Bunch of bastards," Morgan said amiably, relaxed now in the comforting evening ritual.

He slung his jacket over his shoulder and moved on past the news desk toward his office. He pointed a finger in greeting to Keller, who was on the phone as usual. Those who live by the phone shall die by the phone, Morgan liked to say. Keller put his hand over the mouthpiece without taking the phone from his ear. "John O. Buckley in Oakland. He claims he's never even been contacted about the job and wouldn't take it if he was."

"Thank God," Morgan said.

In his office, by the big desk he pretended he could not keep cleared, Natalie stood holding the mouthpiece of his phone against her shoulder, her free arm across her stomach with its hand on her opposite hip; it was a characteristic attitude, and she was smiling the knowing quizzical hint of a smile that Morgan supposed she practiced daily—a smile that said she knew him so well, better than anyone, how could he deceive so many other people?

"Billings' office is holding," she said.

Morgan recoiled from the telephone and took time to hang up his coat. "I've talked to the son-of-a-bitch twice already," he said. "Let's go away to Jamaica."

"Make it Barbados and I'll think it over."

Morgan took the phone, which she had not moved from her shoulder. His fingers brushed her blouse; sparks jumped some ancient gap deep in his stomach. Nat moved away, secret female satisfaction on her readable female face.

"Hello, Ray?"

"Just a second, Mister Morgan. He'll be right on."

Morgan was pleased; it was one of his reverse snobberies never to play the Washington game of forcing the other fellow to get on the line first and wait. Ray Billings was one of the established masters of the sport, and, as Morgan had expected, he had time to get his tie and collar button loose, settle himself comfortably in his huge swivel chair, place his feet on the window sill, and gaze for a moment at the park across the street, deeper now in the shades of evening. Two Cubans in debate on a bench energetically conducted unheard symphonies. The rumble of buses, like artillery just over the horizon, underlay the wintry whisper of the air-conditioning.

On the floor by Morgan's typing table a stack of newspapers was pushed against the wall. They were issues that had appeared during a three-week trip abroad that he had taken after the election eight or nine months earlier; and he insisted, when Nat tried to move them, that he intended to read them all someday, catching up on the news he had missed while beyond the paper's reach. He would never do it, but Morgan's intentions had in his mind the virtue of deeds, and anyway, from the photo in the top paper on the stack, the belligerent, narrowed eyes of Paul D. Hinman rested in surprise—Morgan hoped—on Morgan at his desk. This pleasured Morgan immensely; it helped him write. Years before when Paul Hinman had been a governor and a presidential candidate, he had tried to have Morgan fired.

Just beyond Morgan's door, on Nat's desk, the other phone began to ring with the shrill insistence he considered uncivilized. Abruptly Billings came on the line Morgan was holding, speaking in the brisk, flat voice that never failed to suggest he was really too busy to be bothered. "I don't know a thing I didn't know two hours ago."

"Two hours ago you already knew everything I want to know now." Despite himself, despite his years in town and his status, Morgan felt a little rushed by Billings' manner; Morgan could never abide a suggestion— particularly on the accursed telephone—that he was intruding or foolish. "But we just got this shove from the managing editor on a name one of our best correspondents picked up out West." He could hear Nat's soft voice chatting with someone on the other phone.

"We're not prepared to make an announcement until tomorrow."

After less than a year in office, Billings already had mastered just the right government tone of boredom with what he wanted others to think were uninformed questions. Like that prick Cockcroft, Morgan thought; still, everybody in town must be pushing Billings tonight, and the poor son-of-a-bitch had to take Morgan's calls. Everybody had to take Morgan's calls.

"This name may make some sense," he said—too quickly, he knew at once. "John O. Buckley."

"Good Lord!" Billings seemed momentarily jarred out of his manner. "Who picked that up?"

"Well, he used to be in the Pentagon and he backed your boss last fall."

"Listen, Rich"—Billings switched momentarily into his sincere voice, as if offering to pick up a check—"listen, Rich, I'll lay it right out for you flat, if you won't tie it to me in any way. The President wouldn't have that bubblehead on a sensitive job. Maybe an ambassador in Africa or something, but, Jesus Christ, what kind of an administration do you think this is?"

"I'm not prepared to make an announcement until tomorrow."

Billings chuckled with repellent good humor. "Why don't you boys just give up? This one is locked up so tight radar couldn't find it."

Morgan hated to be lumped with "the press boys" or in "the newspaper game." Nevertheless, he realized, it had been a mistake to open the conversation with the hopeless Buckley ploy; that had only given Billings the moral advantage. "What I really need is some background, Ray. If I can't get an honest answer out of you pricks on the name, tell me anyway why the President is playing these games. He's got everybody running around on this thing, but he didn't have to say he'd make the announcement tomorrow. He could have just done it."

Billings resumed his government voice, ostentatiously putting the question in its proper perspective. "The President believes in making as much information available as he can. He just alerted the press and the public, that's all."

Up your goddam ass, Morgan thought. "Listen, Ray," he said, "I'm not asking for a public statement. I'm not trying to pin a damn thing on you." Morgan despised supplication. He was contemptuous of coercion. He tried to suggest the possibilities open to him without actually mentioning them. "I just want to be able to write a logical explanation for our readers, why this thing is being done in such a strange way. But of course if I can't . . . "

He let the implication hang somewhere on the line between them, maybe at about H Street; no more than he had in the case of Cockcroft would he make something out of Billings or of the issue by going further. He would see them in hell, he promised Hinman's insulting stare.

Billings quickly picked up the necessary vibrations; Billings was developing antennae.

"Rich, I'll always tell *you* anything I can, but Christ, the Boss's got the lid screwed down so tight it hurts. Listen"—Billings lapsed into the conspiratorial whisper he reserved for supposed leaks, not of course deceiving Morgan—"listen, just for you, if it'll help you any—and if you say I told you any of this I might as well catch the first plane back to Omaha—this thing is going to knock your ass off. The biggest surprise of any appointment the Boss has made, that he could get somebody like this particular guy for this particular job. So the Boss is going to have this little ceremony in the morning with the networks in and make the announcement himself in the Fish Room with this guy standing right there. And I won't say another goddam word."

"And this pre-announcement thing was just to work up suspense?"

"I didn't say that." Billings returned to suave boredom.

"You didn't have to. Okay, Ray, at least you told me he's not a woman." Morgan allowed himself a faint touch of sarcasm.

"You couldn't put a woman at the CIA," Billings said seriously. "But I've told you more than any reporter in this town knows." Billings actually was managing to suggest that Morgan remember his friends, despite having told him little he had not known or guessed.

"You're all heart, Ray. See you in the Fish Room."

Morgan hung up with a sense of relief; he had got through again without too much self-exposure. But, almost immediately, the insistent, forgotten something ticked fussily at the edge of his memory and went away. As he turned back to his desk Nat appeared in the doorway.

"That was Anne on the phone. She wants you to call." Nat never smiled her amused-lover's smile when they were talking about Anne. She had a realist's sense of the fitness of things. "And you're supposed to call Senator Anderson's wife."

He took the yellow slip out of his shirt pocket and studied the area code, but he simply didn't have the heart for it, not tonight. "Just last week I had lunch with Hunt Anderson and he didn't tell me he and Kathy were going down home this time of the year. Hot as hell down there."

"Is he any better?"

"No, and the way it looks, I guess he's not going to be."

"Well, shall I return the call?"

He dropped the yellow slip on his desk. "I don't think I've got time right now. Anyway, Old Hunt probably just wants to bend my ear some more. Keller!" He had a buzzer for the copy boy, an intercom telephone to Nat's desk, another to the little library at the rear of the newsroom; but for the copy desk and the staff, it struck him as more informal, comradely even, just to shout out the name of anyone he wanted. He liked for his colleagues to think of themselves as all working together with him.

Keller slouched into the doorway, and Nat squeezed past him going out. Keller was the most relaxed-looking man Morgan had ever known, but his ulcers were so malevolent that he lived mostly on melted ice cream. Keller wrote unread books about wildlife, working in the mornings before breakfast, and he and his wife rode rented horses on weekends. Their son stole automobiles.

"It's not a woman," Morgan said. "It's a big name. It's going to knock our ass off when we hear it. So put Halperin on all the hotels and see if that kind of character has checked in this side of Richmond. Like Lindbergh or somebody. Whoever it is is going to be in the Fish Room in the morning in person. Maybe the airline public relations people might even know something for once."

"Yeah." Keller's corroded stomach caused him to have a faraway look; he never seemed to focus on anyone in the same room. "Bert Bennett just had a little something on the T and V. Said it was going to be someone who opposed the President last year."

"Bert's not just one of those goddam announcers," Morgan said. "Who did he say told him that?"

"Political sources."

"Then feed that into Halperin too. If Bert said White House sources I wouldn't give you a nickel for it. Those guys are buttoned up tight and scared green."

"The desk up there is all over me, Rich." "Up there" was Morganese, adopted by all, for the newspaper's heavily populated home office, an unreal but menacing presence at the end of the telephone and ticker lines.

"Tell 'em I'm writing crap for the first edition."

Keller nodded and started to gather himself for the long slump back into his chair.

"And tell 'em"—Morgan grinned at him genuinely because Morgan felt no need to play games of any kind with Keller—"tell 'em up there it's not as if it really mattered."

Keller never smiled; when amused, he ducked his head and shook. "Eyebrows would be raised," he said and lurched out of the doorway.

Morgan reached for the phone. "Nat! I don't want any more calls." He dialed nine, then his home number.

Anne, sitting by the phone a mile away, picked it up on the first ring. "Who in the world were you talking to so long?"

"The President. I told him it was time to cut the comedy and start running the country."

"What did he say to that?" Anne had a literal mind; and she did not think it remarkable, any more, that her husband talked to presidents—it only set going something corrosive in her that Morgan never quite understood.

"Just kidding," he said. "It was Billings on this goddam CIA thing."

"What CIA thing?"

He sighed audibly, intending to sigh audibly. "The President says he's going to name a new CIA director tomorrow."

"I just asked. You don't have to get mad."

"I'm not mad. We've been going in circles all day trying to find out who it is."

"When are you coming home?"

He imagined her martini in one hand, her cigarette in the other; he was not sure how she was holding the phone. In nearly twenty years Anne had never been able to accept the simple fact that he had to work later and more irregularly than most people and that it was difficult for him to pinpoint his arrival for dinner; but then, *he* was always forgetting that she had her own problems of managing the house, feeding young Richie, all coming to a head late in the day. It was strange how this simple irritant had risen and remained between them like a constant threatening illness that might at any time carry one of them away.

"It'll be late as hell. I was just going to call."

"Oh, sure."

"Well, I was." I really would have this time, he thought.

"I'll go on and sit down with Richie then."

"You do that." Reciting memorized lines, he thought. "Don't worry about me."

"When you do get here, I'll probably be out playing bridge at Martha's."

"Have a good time. Stay as late as you want."

"I'm just going to play bridge."

"That's what you said."

"Well, I am. You can call Martha's if you don't—"

"Oh, shit," Morgan said. "Why wouldn't I believe you?"

"There'll be some chicken in the oven, but we're out of gin."

He was impatient now, annoyed. He had work to do, it was late, there was too much between them; he did not know any more what was lie and what truth and who ought to be angry at whom. "I'll get some gin," he said.

He could hear her breathing, then, "Rich . . . I'm left alone too much."

He wanted to beat his fist on his desk. "Listen, Anne . . . " He was angry now; he could hear himself being angry. "Listen, Anne, I am not down here for the fun of it. I am not down here working my balls off just because I love this life."

"I'm sorry. I'm *sorry*. I know you're not."

He closed his eyes, sorry himself, no longer angry, thinking it was probably Scotch she was drinking if there was no gin, wondering what he could do, what either of them could do.

"Good luck at bridge," Morgan said.

They hung up politely. Why this conversation, or something like it, had to come, as it always did, at the most awkward and tense hour of his day, Morgan had never understood. But then he understood very little, any more, about Anne or himself or what they had done with the years together —which was a hell of a lot not to understand.

Nat came in silently and put some unsigned letters on his desk. "Now it's the national desk," she said. "Hobart wants you to call him back right away."

Hobart always wanted Morgan to call back right away, but Morgan always put him at the end of the list. Hobart had bad nerves and hence was a natural target for the criticism and second-guessing of the managing editor and other superiors. Morgan knew Hobart would be less concerned with whether they had the CIA story than with whether someone else might get it, thus opening the national desk to official wrath.

"Screw Hobart," he said, glancing quickly at the letters.

"I'm going out for coffee. Want some?"

"So black it's got green scum on it. In a dirty cup."

"That's the way it comes." He could see that she could see it had been a bad call to Anne. "And since she can see he can see she can see," Morgan said, leaning over to speak to Hinman's obnoxious face, "she knows, does she not, that he could not possibly get along without her?"

"Phooey," Nat said. "She knows he could get along in a lion's den without anybody. And probably would rather."

"Then little does she know." He straightened and smiled at her. Nat never flayed him. If she accepted him not so much for what he was as for what she thought he was, at least she did accept him, and he could feel only remotely guilty about it. She was entitled to her misconceptions, and he had never really tried to mislead her, at least no more than he misled anyone else, and not at all in order to bring her to bed.

A black copy boy with an Afro hairdo brought in a message from the wire room. MORGAN WB, it read; LEADING PAPER YOUR SPOOK. NEED SOONEST. CHEERS WEINSTEIN.

Morgan handed the message to Nat. "Upchuck soonest," he said. "Weinstein hasn't even seen my piece and he's leading the paper with it."

In the newsroom, the deadline that was on top of him had imposed its discipline on the reporters, who were still writing for the next day. The musketry of typewriters, of the wire-service tickers flanking the news desk, came through Morgan's open door to complement the distant artillery of buses on the street; telephones alarmed the air, someone shouted "Copy!" and the Afro hairdo rushed out to pick it up. This was one of the largest news bureaus in Washington, for one of the nation's most powerful newspapers, and being its chief gave Morgan as much power—so it had been estimated in a turgid textbook called *Press and Power in Political Practice* —as a strong committee chairman or even a close adviser to the President. But it was power not so much quantitative as qualitative; it was not that

Morgan could get specific things done or not done—although, to some extent, he could if he tried, despising himself when he did—or, worse, telling himself he despised himself. As he often told the lecture audiences from which he received fees so inflated he secretly considered them obscene, the news was the atmosphere of events (he was quoting Woodrow Wilson, he always confessed, adding a touch of spurious scholarship to the dubious information he had been bribed to bring to some aspiring civic forum in some arid provincial city). And Richmond P. Morgan, possessing—*Press and Power* had fawned—the most prominent byline in one of the most influential publications in the world, was first among those who created, or at least colored, that atmosphere. What he wrote about men and events in Washington and the world had great effect on what other men thought, what other events might therefore follow—not so much on how the world turned, Morgan had been relieved over the years to learn, as on how men thought it turned and ought to turn. Fair game, he told himself uncertainly.

"Why don't I sell insurance for a living? At least"—Morgan knew he was playing Morgan to Nat's sympathetic secretary—"at least that's honest graft."

"You couldn't be a salesman. You'd just run down whatever you tried to sell."

"Whatever somebody's trying to sell you ain't worth buying." It was a specious Morgan thought but a useful Morgan line, and Morgan was particularly pleased that the "ain't" had for once been spontaneous; usually, when he pulled off an "ain't" or an "it don't" or produced some back-country homily with false attribution to his "Daddy" (Southern-born, drawling reporter Morgan, *Time* magazine had written in its poison-dart style, familiarly quotes Conrad, Camus, Faulkner. But when at day's end he unwinds with a third martini—seven to one, on the rocks—in the secluded garden of his tree-shaded, mortgaged house in neighborly, casually expensive Cleveland Park, he often sounds like a Dixieland combo of H. Rap Brown, Uncle Remus, and a Mississippi sheriff)—usually, when awash in the vernacular, Morgan was working at being Southern. Cornpone was good cover, he had found; it caused people to underestimate him, whether they were amused or shocked or both. Sometimes when he realized he really was Southern, syntax and soul, he felt redeemed.

"Why aren't you writing?" Nat had a small oval face, pale blue eyes, promising lips; at the end of the day she was always a little disheveled, like the little he knew—Morgan did not wish to be too involved—of her life outside their association.

"I'm writing, all right, I'm leading the paper, but I don't know what in hell with. Spent a whole damn day on it, and do you know for what?"

"Fame and glory," Nat said. "Lecture fees."

"Suppose I could choke this ridiculous spook's name out of that son-of-a-bitch at the White House. Oh, they'd be ecstatic up there, wouldn't they? Weinstein would say, you got to get up early in the old a.m. to get ahead of Morgan. So out comes the paper on the street at nine-fifteen p.m. Four minutes later the AP moves it. Richmond P. Morgan reported tonight that Granville R. Ambidexter is going to be blah blah blah. Not more than maybe ten minutes after that, the *Washington Post* replates with the AP lead, leaving Morgan out. So does every other newspaper in the Western world. All announcers put it on the eleven o'clock news, with or without Morgan. By tomorrow morning, the whole thing is going to be about as exclusive as a five-dollar whore. And you know the ultimate, palpitating truth of the matter, don't you?"

"Morgan speaks," Nat said, "but Morgan does not write. Why does Morgan not write?"

"The ultimate, palpitating truth of the matter is that the sum total of useful human knowledge and understanding has not been increased so much as by the hair of your chinny-chin-chin. Because tomorrow morning that son-of-a-bitch in the White House and the President are going to announce Ambidexter anyway, spread him all over television like deodorant, and all we're going to achieve by all this running around and all these telephone calls and all this pretending that we know something—all we're going to do is let people who don't much care find out a little earlier about a fact they're going to learn anyway and as soon as there's any real need to know it and without any help at all from Richmond P. Morgan. And even the fact they're going to learn is only the name of a new bureaucrat. Just information. Easy come, easy go."

"I don't have any hair on my chinny-chin-chin"—as, she was subtly reminding him, he had good reason to know. "Stop talking now and start writing."

"But I set out to be a storyteller," Morgan said. "What I'm trying to explain to you is that even if I had the name, I wouldn't have a story to tell. I could count on the fingers of one hand the number of times in this job I ever had a story to tell."

"But if you had the name you'd at least stop talking and start writing. Weinstein would be happy."

"Because I'm a goddam professional, too. Go get the coffee."

Nat turned to go, then looked back at him. "Is that so bad, Rich? Being a professional?"

Instead of a storyteller, she obviously meant. That was coming too close, and Morgan—faintly angered at her sudden reach toward his core—retreated instantly, effortlessly, into practiced flippancy.

"Beats working nights in a steam laundry," he said, watching her lips tighten momentarily in recognition of the rebuff. As she went out of the office he wondered—but then he often did—out of what profound but buried instinct he leaped so inevitably and so nimbly to cover his inmost self against even the most promising intrusions. Anne had said to him once, in the early euphoria of youthful marriage, that love would open him; and maybe, Morgan was fair enough to concede, love had burned itself out in the effort. But he never dwelled for long on such thoughts; he never seemed to have the time, and anyway he had no more wish to confront his own bedrock than to expose it to others; so, as always, he turned purposefully to his work.

He had been deliberately putting off what old Ray Phillips used to call the "ghastly moment," when a man had to stop thinking and maybe learning and start writing; everything frozen then on the page, as if thinking and learning had stopped forever. The delay was significant. It would be easy enough, though useless, to write *Washington Seethes;* it would be the sort of professional job Morgan had done often enough, and led the paper doing it too. Morgan the storyteller might know it did not matter, was not worth writing, but Morgan the professional could not concern himself about that; and Morgan the professional knew he was delaying because his instinct told him he had not yet discovered all the elements of even this poor thing; *go slow, look twice, think again,* Morgan's professional instinct said insistently.

He rolled copy paper into his typewriter and tapped at the top of the sheet "Spook (Morgan)." He gazed down at Hinman's fixed stare from the stack of newspapers at his feet. The phone rang with rude abruptness, and although it annoyed him because he had said no calls, Morgan answered quickly; one more chance to delay.

"You want to speak to Shelly at the Pentagon?"

"I guess so. But, Janie, no more calls after this one."

Shelly was already on the line. "I just had this idea, Rich. I thought I ought to pass it along."

"Yeah." Morgan had been the beneficiary of more of Shelly's ideas than he needed; Shelly believed in keeping him informed about everything Shelly thought.

"Well, here you've got this liberal new President," Shelly said, "and these gorillas I talk to over here are none too happy about him, believe me, and neither are the ones they do business with on the Hill. *You* know who I mean."

"Yeah, yeah." By now Morgan knew by heart the caption under Hinman's intrusive face: FORMER GOVERNOR DEMANDS CRACKDOWN ON MILITANTS.

"And a lot of voters feel the same way, as I surely don't need to tell *you*, Rich . . ." I might just fire this ass-kisser, Morgan thought. ". . . so what occurred to me was this. In making this CIA appointment, the President's just got to take all this into account." Shelly's voice hushed theatrically. "He just can't afford to appoint a liberal."

"Yeah, yeah, yeah." Morgan knew he would not fire Shelly or anyone else, not even Janie, even if the Newspaper Guild would let him; but one of his recurring daydreams had him picking up a tormentor by the scruff of the neck and the seat of the pants and giving him the bum's rush into K Street, the way Ward Bond would have done it in a John Ford Western. Shelly headed Morgan's list of prospects.

"What I mean is, he's got to put somebody in there who can take the heat, Rich. Somebody these gorillas I talk to over here can live with—"

"Thanks, Shelly, great hunch." Morgan hung up. Ass-kissers never failed to insult the ass kissed, in Morgan's experience, which was extensive. As if after fifteen years in this place, he thought, he was not supposed to have even the faintest notion of the politics of the CIA appointment. You guys, he muttered to Hinman, you goddam Yankees, you'll never learn about me. Morgan turned back to his typewriter, but as he turned, his eye fell on the yellow slip asking him to call Kathy Anderson. *Nine lives,* somebody said somewhere, sometime. He heard the words quite clearly, then he recognized the voice. Memory clicked into place, like the numerals of a speedometer turning over all at once to zero.

Morgan ran to the door of his office. "Nat!" She was coming through the newsroom with a paper cup. "Keller!"

He went back to his desk and pushed the buzzer for the library. A disembodied voice, not unlike the one he had heard in his mind, responded from the intercom speaker. "Get up all the biographical stuff on Paul Hinman and give it to Joe. Hurry!"

Nat put the coffee on Morgan's desk. Keller was standing in the door. "That's not a surprise," he said, "that's an earthquake."

"I'm not positive yet, but it makes sense, doesn't it? A liberal President and a non-political hard-liner. It even pulls both wings of the party together. And Bert Bennett said it was someone who opposed the President in the campaign last year, which Hinman sure-God did. Anyway, call up there and tell 'em to use wire copy to hold space in the first edition and be ready to replate with my lead. Have Joe put together a few hundred words of biographical background on Hinman to tack on to the end of my stuff if it pans out. Feed Hinman's name to Halperin for a hard check on the airlines and hotels—and I mean hard. Watts ought to get on the phone and start trying to find Hinman any reasonable place he might be if he's not in town. Turn everybody else back on their sources with Hinman's name and tell 'em I said to push like hell. Okay?"

Keller melted away.

"Nat . . . " Morgan took a sip of the coffee; it was hot and repulsive, the way he loved it. ". . . get me that son-of-a-bitch at the White House again. And, Nat, this time, just this once, sweetie, I got to have that prick on the line first."

"It'll be a pleasure." She hurried to her desk.

Hinman! He had had it in his head all along and had almost let it get away. Well, Shelly had been right. Morgan sipped his piercing coffee penitently. Shelly had not told him anything he hadn't known; Shelly had only turned his mind in the right direction at the right moment. Shelly had only made all the difference. Now I can't even throw the bastard out in the street, Morgan thought.

Keller materialized in the doorway. He never came in and sat down because standing in the doorway was a welcome relief from his chair with its surrounding battery of relentless phones; Keller said Morgan's doorway was the only spot in the whole office where it was not possible for a man to reach out and pick up a phone.

"A smash appointment," Keller said. "This new creep gives us one damn thing after another."

"What I like best," Morgan said, "is Hinman will eat Cockcroft for breakfast. Hinman is a tough little bastard."

"Never met him," Keller said. "He's been out of politics for so long."

"Better than ten years, but I can remember him like it was yesterday, the way he looked at Hunt Anderson when he was on the stand in the migrant investigation. When Hunt got through with him that day, Hunt knew, and Hinman knew, and everybody else knew, that politically Paul D. Hinman was as dead as Kelsey's nuts. The month before that Hinman was leading the Gallup Poll for president. It must have been hell to take, coming right between the eyes—pow!—like that. Hinman looked at Hunt the way you'd look at a sewer rat, but he walked out of there with his head up like he owned the goddam world. I'll say that for him. And I remember Hunt saying to me that night, 'Don't you worry about Hinman. A mean tough bastard like that is bound to have nine lives.' "

"Looks like it's turned out that way."

"I'm not positive yet," Morgan said, "but it feels right. All the corners fit."

Nat appeared beside Keller. "Billings on the line."

"Let the son-of-a-bitch wait," Morgan said. "I want him with the wind up. You get hold of Halperin?"

"He almost dropped dead," Keller said.

"I hope Hinman is in town tonight. I hope Halperin wakes him up about three a.m."

"Your source didn't know where he was?"

"I don't have any source. I was talking to Shelly and I just remembered out of a clear blue sky what Hunt said, all those years ago, and then it came to me what I ought to have remembered all day. Just about the first month this new creep was in office Hinman went in to see somebody at the White House, and they all said of course it wasn't the President, and anyway it was just about getting some guy on the SEC. So he'd been in touch anyway, and it just hit me all of a sudden that it was right, it fitted. But I'm still not sure. You think Billings is on there, Nat?"

"I spoke to him myself."

Morgan picked up the phone. "Hinman," he said, immediately, distinctly. "Paul D. Hinman."

He could hear nothing but Billings' breathing. The sighing sound of it went on for a while. It was all Morgan needed to hear, and he grinned at Nat and Keller.

'Well, of course," Billings finally said, "I'm not confirming any speculation at all."

"But you *are* steering people off the wrong names, just like you steered me off Buckley."

"I suppose"—Billings' miserable voice rose a note—"I suppose I am."

"You better call your wife," Morgan said sympathetically; at least Billings had not lied to him. "Tell her you won't make it home for a while. There'll be a lot of call-backs in an hour or so."

"If call-backs were all I had to worry about . . ." Billings' trailing voice left his other problems to distant, shuddering imaginations.

"I'll buy you lunch next week. We'll talk it all over." Morgan hung up. "If you're still here," he said to the inert phone. "It's Hinman all right," he told Keller. "I'm going to write it flat."

"That must have knocked Billings on his ass," Keller said. "Old Ray Phillips used to use that telephone gimmick."

"Where do you think I learned it?" Morgan pulled a memo pad out of his desk drawer. SHELLY, he wrote in capital letters. YOUR CALL GAVE ME THE LEAD I NEEDED ON THE CIA APPOINTMENT. MANY THANKS FOR YOUR HELP. MORGAN.

He tore the note from the pad, went around the desk, and handed it to Keller. "Read this and give it to Shelly when he comes in. And you better let them know up there I'm starting to file right now."

Keller read the note, clucked—whether in approval or dismay, Morgan could not tell, and was not meant to—and moved out of the doorway. The Afro hairdo came in with a slip of Assoicated Press copy. Morgan took it from him, saw his own name scrawled in the corner by the wire-room foreman.

"If you're going to be making more calls, I can stay late."

Nat's voice, as he read, suddenly was far away and hollow, as if she were on the intercom. Morgan felt the rapid ebbing of that sheer professional instinct that had seized him and carried him in its demanding grip to Hinman's name, moving him physically as well as mentally, like one of those automatic pilots in an aircraft. It was gone in a moment, as quickly and totally as it had come, and he stood there unmasked, vulnerable, a professional parted from his craft, his cover blown, no concealment in his illusory power, no comfort in his work that did not matter.

". . . if you're not, can you sign these three letters before I go?" Nat was saying; then, "Rich, what's the matter?"

"Anderson," Morgan said. "Hunt Anderson died tonight and I never called back."

The Storyteller I

About ten o'clock some final faraway pressure began at last to wring drops of moisture from the heavy summer evening air, humidity becoming at some indefinable point precipitation. The first big drops sizzled on concrete baked all day long by the August sun, and in the parks, on unpaved paths, little puffs of dust spurted briefly under the beginning sprinkle. Then the rain fell harder. An hour later it had become a gentle drizzle, and from the asphalt winding through Rock Creek Park rose wisps of steam, ghostly in the lights of automobiles.

"So I said to this buddy of mine," the driver was saying, "in this life they don't nobody hand me nothing on a platter that I can notice. So what do they think I'm gonna do, let 'em sit on their big black ass while I pay taxes to feed 'em?"

"Right." Morgan had been resigned for years to certain penalties levied on him for his Southern accent. Faces of black men would freeze in hostility when he said no more than "pass the salt" at a lunch counter. On the other hand, Klan types like this driver goon, in the absence of contrary evidence, invariably assumed he was one of them, which was good cover.

"Man works his ass off thirty years and all he gets for it is niggers taking over everywhere he looks . . ."

Morgan was not listening. It was strange, he was thinking, the way people were about funerals. Kathy knew how he had felt about Hunt. He didn't need to do anything now to prove it—couldn't if there was any doubt. There was certainly nothing further he could do about or for Hunt Anderson. Yet here he was, getting ready to fly off in the middle of a rainy night, when he disliked and feared the place he was going and the airplanes that would take him there and the barbaric obeisances of the living to the dead—all because it was important, in some imprecise sense, that he be there.

Even Dunn had thought so. Dunn and Anderson had had nothing to do with each other for years, and there was no conceivable gain for a "political leader" like Dunn in going to this particular funeral; once there might have been, but Anderson had lost all that long ago. Dunn had helped to break him, but even Dunn was going south to his funeral.

"What was it?" Dunn's assertive, clear voice never seemed to falter or hesitate. From hundreds of miles away, it had crackled into Morgan's receiver with the same authority with which it dealt with committees, conventions, legislatures. "His heart or his liver?"

"I don't know." Morgan had called the doctor and he did know. But Dunn could find out for himself, he thought bitterly.

"A lot of ability gone to waste."

"Maybe not to waste," Morgan said.

"The last time I saw him, just a glimpse at some damn reception back there, he looked sixty years old and crumpled up. I thought right then he wasn't too long for this world, the rate he was going."

"Listen, Dunn. Right now, tonight, I'd just as soon not talk about Hunt with you."

"That's why I called as soon as I heard it on the radio. I'm not going to let you feel that way."

"I just don't want to talk about Hunt, that's all."

"Well, I'll see you down there," Dunn said. "Why don't you come on out here with me when it's over? Just sit around and talk over old times for a day or so? The weather's great."

"It was his heart," Morgan said. "He just fell down and died in the goddam street with everybody standing there looking down at him."

". . . so the way I got it figgered out the real problem is how to stop all these nigger gals from having all these bastards on the welfare. Ain't that about it?"

"One problem, all right." Morgan relied heavily on an extraordinary instinct for dropping a yes or a no or a you-don't-say into some unheard dissertation at precisely the moment its author expected him to say something in response. Somehow he usually managed to convey the impression that he really cared about the views of any loquacious or aggrieved fool who might be buffeting him with gross notions or preposterous analyses—although it was not clear to Morgan himself whether this gift for saying something acceptably meaningless at the right moment derived from a profound contempt for the human race, an instinctive sympathy for its plight, or a cowardly refusal to mix it up with the bastards. Whatever the case, he had no need to listen to a taxi driver telling him about the trials of being white, a situation Morgan knew by heart. He refused to think about Anderson just yet, and the rain on the roof of the car, the swish of the wheels on the wet asphalt, the swatches of mist drifting past his window, the ritual mutter and mumble from the front seat—all seemed to set him apart for a moment in a murmurous floating world, warmly his own, tightly held against the surrounding dark.

Below P Street the taxi came out of the secluded woodland park. They passed beneath the bridges and lights of the city, and suddenly the Potomac lay blackly on the right, foul and beautiful in the rain—that dark American Rubicon over which Anderson and Morgan, each alone but together in youth and hope and yearning, had passed all those years ago; that thin, bridged gulf between them and a past that had shaped and held them. They had had to cross the Potomac many times since, going both ways; and seeing it now—seeing long shimmers of light streaking across its black mirror surface to Virginia, to the South, home—Morgan began at last to weep for his friend, and for his life.

They went on across the Memorial Bridge—Lincoln's monument behind, Lee's mansion ahead—and down the Virginia shore in the rain and the stabbing lights of oncoming cars. Morgan had felt alone in the world years earlier when his father had died; now he felt aimless. What had it all been about? He thought of his child and his work and his failures, and then of Anne, far behind him at the bridge table, and of the disapproval with which she had questioned why he should fly off in the middle of the night, leaving her once again. Anne had never understood him, or Anderson, much less the way some men rushed eagerly into life as into battle, where only the fortunate were struck down cleanly and at once. Anne had never understood anything, he thought bitterly, unfairly, his tears gone as quickly as they had come, the aching nostalgia and sentiment from which they had fallen overcome in the sour reflection of what was.

Morgan's driver was still ritually niggertalking as he nudged his way around the circle to the curb in front of the main entrance to the terminal. ". . . none of that crap down where you and me come from, ain't that right, buddy?"

"Right." Morgan tipped him heavily, ashamed as always that he had only pretended to take notice of a man and his angers. You and me, he thought, struggling out of the taxi with his small suitcase. And who knows who's who when the lights go out?

The terminal was crowded, steamy with damp clothing; the air-conditioning was overloaded. Morgan's ticket line seemed immobile, behind an elderly man who had insurmountable problems with his schedule. The PA system muttered incessantly of arrivals, departures, delays. Morgan perceived that he was going to lose his temper. He had stood in this line, at this terminal, at this hour—they were all the same in any case—so often that he could usually withdraw himself, leave nothing standing by his suitcase but the mortal hull, the shell of Morgan, to be assaulted by the world's indifference. Sometimes, in reverie, he transported himself to far places; more often he wallowed again with pliant women he had loved or had hoped to love; occasionally he made large, virtuous plans, and once he had actually begun a novel in his head while waiting for luggage at O'Hare, and had got well into the first chapter before he was told his bag was lost. But tonight the world would not let itself be thus suspended.

It was one of Morgan's weaknesses that he often suffered indignity and injustice too long, then became angry at the wrong time, for the wrong reason, when nothing could be done. Now he had nothing really to complain of, except the impersonality of things, but as if impelled he looked around for someone to hold accountable.

A lacquered girl in the abbreviated uniform of the airline stood nearby.

"Madam," Morgan said through clenched teeth, "is there any remote possibility that another ticket line might be opened?"

She turned vacant blue eyes on him and blinked enormous sooty lashes. "I just got off Two-oh-four," she said. "It's hotter heah than Houston." The lashes waved like a bird's wings.

Someone laughed behind Morgan, and he turned, really angry, feeling that he should not have to take so much, that on this night at least he deserved better of life and ought not to have to indulge in ridiculous behavior to get it.

"Throw some weight around, Rich. They can't do this to you."

It was the kind of remark at which Morgan had learned, over the years, to smile indulgently; and it was the kind of remark he always got in greeting from Charlie French, who was standing two places in line behind him. French was an able correspondent of Morgan's own age who represented a Midwestern newspaper and bitterly resented the greater prestige of Morgan's, hence of Morgan. Morgan respected French professionally, one reporter to another, but was appalled by French's willingness to show his feelings of resentment in public. Morgan did not know how to respond to such lack of wariness and dignity. As usual when uncertain, he retreated into joviality.

"This airline," he said, "flies Ford Trimotors. And its other operations are up to date too."

"Oh, come on now." The stewardess's blank bird-wing eyes fanned stale terminal air at him. "That's not fa-yuh."

French laughed again. "Honey, you better get another ticket line open for Mister Morgan. He might just put your boss out of business."

With expert male eye, Morgan searched for the girl beneath the lacquer and bird's wings. There appeared to be none—no flesh tints, no unbounded slopes or curves, no flaws, stray hairs, freckles. He guessed that she was little more than a child. If God created woman, he thought, man had surely created stewardesses. Just then she stuck out her tongue at him.

Morgan laughed out loud. "You see," he said to French, "this outfit can't even control its girls."

"Step this way, folks," a voice called from the ticket counter. A new line was being opened, and French moved swiftly to its head. Morgan managed to get third place.

"Now you see theah." The bird's wings flapped at him again. "Aren't you 'shamed of youah ole tempuh?"

It was the price he had to pay for his remark. "I sho' am," Morgan said gamely. "I might just die I'm so 'shamed."

Recognizing at last the mindless chatter to which she had been finely tuned by life and the airline, seeing all again right in the world as she grasped it, the child stewardess laughed with perfectly modulated glee. It sounded like highball glasses clinking. "Bye-bye now," she said, chipper as a parakeet. "Y'all have a nice trip with us, heah?"

Morgan hoped that she might show one more sign of unruly life, but she turned and marched away, her splendidly shaped haunches under resolute airline control.

French got his ticket, checked his bag, and stood by Morgan. "You going to Anderson's funeral too?"

Morgan nodded.

"Well, it wouldn't be a story for us except he won the primary in our state that first time he ran. Big upset."

"I remember." Morgan realized he was going to have to sit with French and talk. Once French's opening sarcasms had been launched, he was always decent enough, but Morgan looked upon transportation—the actual hours of conveyance from one place to another—as a time of welcome anonymity. He hated to have to yield these private interludes to the demands of personality, even in conversation that was easy to fake, about familiar things, with familiar people. He signed the credit-card slip, took his ticket, and moved out of line to join French. Morgan had an underseat bag that he did not need to check, and they moved off through the terminal toward their gate—naturally, the farthest possible.

A sepulchral voice murmured ominously through unseen speakers that Richmond P. Morgan was wanted on the telephone. French said something sarcastic about the President, and Morgan entered a glass booth reminiscent of dime cigars.

"The managing editor calling, Mister Morgan."

"Well, I've got to run. Put him on."

"I'm on, Rich. Where are you running to?"

Morgan told him.

"Rich, I know you and Senator Anderson were old friends, but this Hinman story of yours is pretty big. Congratulations on breaking it, by the way. All sorts of implications for this administration, don't you think? Worldwide too."

"Keller's in charge. Don't worry about it."

"Frankly I'd rather have you on hand. This smells to me like one of those stories that run on for a while, and I want to keep our best foot forward." The voice was bland, even, deceptive.

"Hunt Anderson was my friend," Morgan said. "What do you expect me to do, pay no attention when he dies?"

The voice on the line sharpened, turned a little screechy, as it always did in the heat of temper. "I expect you to put the best interests of the paper ahead—"

"Shit. You don't any more know than I do what the best interests of the paper are. Keller can handle things as well as I can."

Silence. Then, "Rich, some of us get pretty tired sometimes of the way you just do things as you please down there. Maybe you ought to think about that."

"I'll come up and we'll talk about it," Morgan said. "Right after I get back from the funeral."

"You do that." The screeching voice was almost cracking with anger, and the line went dead with an admonitory click.

Morgan felt both angry and penitent as he left the booth. It was petty harassment—he knew that. Out of long experience with the bureaucracy he worked for, and the compulsive need of its unknown, unseen administrative masters to discipline and restrain its public personalities, he had suspected what was coming before he picked up the phone. Possessive bureaucracy with all that pretentious nonsense about the best interests of something that had nothing but interests. Morgan liked to tell himself that he believed in rendering unto Caesar only after he had met the personal demands of his life. Yet he was uneasily aware, as he rejoined French, that he had done so only when it suited him. Anne, for instance, often accused him of being married to his work—"so screw it, not me!" she had yelled at him once when, after staying past midnight at the office, he had awakened her with a fumbling hand beneath her pajama top. In the broadest sense, therefore, Morgan knew he defended no real principle but only his own ox against a particular goring.

"What did the President want?" French asked, lumbering archness failing to hide his real anxiety.

"I told him to go on and intervene in the Middle East and stop bothering me about it." Morgan winked at him. French's strange devils were, after all, as real as his own.

They had been so long delayed in the ticket line and by the phone call that by the time they reached the gate passengers were boarding. As befitted its Southern destination, the plane was an old and weathered Electra, its four great propellers looming menacingly over the ill-lit asphalt. French and Morgan found seats side-by-side in the first-class compartment at the rear. Two slightly older and more hardened versions of the lacquered stewardess moved up and down the aisles, filling out mysterious charts.

"Look at the tits on the redhead," French said.

"Did you cover Hunt's primary campaign?" Morgan tried never to discuss women as if he were a spectator; to do so seemed to him to concede a vulnerability. Besides, since everyone else talked about women, he would not.

"They say these stewardi save it all for the pilots on the layovers," French said. "No, I was still on the Rotary Club beat in those days, and one of the boss's pets always got the good assignments. But I remember Anderson; back then he was really something."

"He was really something," Morgan said.

"I guess he learned his politics from Old Bull."

"He learned everything from Old Bull," Morgan said. In a manner of speaking, he thought.

"But the last time I heard him in the Senate you wouldn't have thought it was the same man."

"It wasn't." Morgan began to wish he had not brought up the subject.

A last passenger came aboard, far up the aisle, and the stewardesses wrestled shut the heavy door. Hearing the groan and clutch of its metal, horrid enough for a story by Poe, Morgan's shoulders tightened; now he was sealed up, strapped in, imprisoned in this gigantic self-propelled toothpaste tube, to be hurled helpless and without volition over mountains, rivers, states, continents. That grinding door meant that he had relinquished the little control of himself and his fate that life allowed, and this seemed a sin, even a sacrilege, against Morgan's sacred sensibility. He trusted nothing that could be calibrated, yet had to submit constantly to infernal technology.

Just let my luck hold one more time, he whispered to some inner creedless deities he held in reserve for takeoffs and landings. Just this one more time.

The last passenger moved briskly back to the first-class compartment and paused by French's seat. He was young, tanned, coifed; his bejeweled cuffs extended for precisely the right length beyond his jacket sleeves and along the back of well-kept hands, in one of which he held an attaché case of slim elegance. In the center of his forehead, at the hairline, there was a sizable patch of medical tape.

"Hello, Charlie." Pear-shaped tones. "Did you see the tits on the redhead?"

"I've been chewing the seats." French waved a languid hand. "You know the great Rich Morgan, of course?"

The plane began to move away from the gate, its feral engines roaring.

"Christ, no. How would I know Rich Morgan?" He put out his hand. "What you wrote about the March on Washington that time was the best, man, the best."

That article had brought Morgan a well-publicized journalism prize, after assiduous lobbying and bribery by his newspaper, and hence it was referred to frequently by people who knew little of Morgan or his work and who did not share his conviction that prizes, in the nature of the case, are reserved to the mediocre. Nevertheless Morgan took the smooth hand, which was barnacled with rings. "Thanks. And what's your name?"

"Larry Glass. With the Ben Blakey Show." Glass sat down across the aisle and bent to put the attaché case under his seat. There was another large patch of tape on the back of his neck.

"Glass used to work for us," French said, "before he went big time. What the hell happened to your head, Larry?"

Glass made a theatrical face; it ill accompanied his trained rolling voice. A wave of hair fell with precision over the front patch of tape and became a curl. "The producer thought my hairline was too high. He said the lights bounced off my forehead and made me look like Strangelove on camera."

The Electra crept through the night toward a distant runway. At least, Morgan was relieved to see, the plane was not overcrowded. It always seemed to him that if every seat were taken, the takeoff weight must be intolerable.

"So I had to have one of those little hair transplant jobs they can do now," Glass said. "Take a little patch from back here and move it right around to the forehead, and you don't even have to stay off the air if you get a chance to get on because they can cover up the tape with makeup. Of course, when I'm all done over, that frigging Blakey probably won't let me on the air at all for fear I'll get the whole slot."

"You mean they can make hair grow just for TV?" French looked at Morgan with comic incredulity.

"Man, you got to give up something to get something." Glass winked at Morgan. "Unless you can get away with it. You fellows going to the Anderson funeral?" Nods of assent. "I was working on that story of yours, Rich, and just when it was really breaking, the producer sends me off to the ass-end of the world."

French sat up straighter. "What story?"

"About Hinman." Glass stood up to take off his jacket. He wore brilliant red suspenders two inches wide, a denim shirt, and a polka-dot necktie.

"What about Hinman?"

"Man, I thought you had to know. Hinman got the CIA job, of all people. Rich here had it in his early edition, and we're spreading it all over the eleven o'clock news."

"I got to get the hell off this thing." But as French flicked off his seat belt, the Electra's engines boomed ominously, the huge plane swung in a half-circle, trembled violently, then lurched down the runway like an elephant going to its knees.

Just one more time, Morgan asked silently of his private gods. His rear teeth were clenched so hard his head began to ache just above his ears.

"Goddammit to hell!" French said. "A story like that breaking, and here I am on the way to nowhere for nothing. Why didn't you tell me?" He glared at Morgan.

"I didn't think about it."

French had no cover at all, but Morgan could not think about French. He could not even resent Anderson's funeral being called nothing. Trying not to look out the window, across which the rain scratched with evil talons, he was instructing the pilots fervently: Get this thing up. *Get it up.* But the Electra slewed and bumped on the runway, in the rain. It didn't feel right, Morgan thought, it didn't feel light enough to fly.

"I guess you get so goddam used to it," French said. "God, I'm sick and tired of everything in this town being leaked to one newspaper, just as if there weren't any others in the whole damn country."

It was all right, Morgan told himself grimly, if this was his time come round at last. It was all right. He had a whopping insurance policy for Richie. He had had a good run for his money, for a long time. Now would be as good a time as any to pay up. *Get it up!* he prayed nevertheless, and the Electra rumbled on in the rain.

"Hinman!" French said. "Those idiots let a story like that leak to one paper."

Anne would look after Richie. That was one thing you could say for Anne, she had always looked after Richie. Morgan felt the final reluctant struggle off the asphalt, the first shuddering turbulence, the hard bite of the propellers into the rootless rain and mist and darkness that now sustained his life. He stared at the back of the seat in front of him. *Get it up! Get it up!*

"Where's Big Tits?" Glass said. "We might as well open up the bar."

"Going to be rough," French said. "Those girls may never get their seat belts off."

Morgan forced himself to keep thinking of Anne, although there was nothing to think about her that he had not thought a thousand times. What bothered him most was her hostility; if she could just let well enough alone, accept it, her life and his, make the most of what they'd done, and let it go at that. But no—she had to keep flaying him, hurting him, tearing him down when she could. He deserved some of it, no question of that, but not all that bitter hostility; she knew how hard he'd tried, and he hadn't been the one who'd ever thought about leaving for someone else.

The Electra pulsed and bucked upward into relatively smoother air, and Morgan saw the seat belt sign go off. *Made it again, despite everything.* His body relaxed a little, and he realized that he was perspiring heavily. *Someday there'd be a price to pay.* French, to Morgan's relief, appeared not to have noticed his tension. French was not the kind of man who noticed much about other people.

"I ought to have told you about Hinman," Morgan said, as if there had been no break in the conversation, "but I guess I had my mind on Hunt Anderson, and it just didn't occur to me."

"Hell, you don't owe me a nickel. But I'm going to give Ray Billings an earful when I get to a phone."

"Funny it should break this way," Morgan said. "The night Anderson dies, Hinman breaks back into the news with a bigger bang than ever."

"Not so funny to me," French said.

The redhead bobbled down the aisle. "Y'all care for a beverage?"

Morgan admired the blatant fakery of her Southern accent—this second-rate airline, having little else to recommend it, specialized in mythical Southern belles. He debated whether to tell French that Billings had leaked nothing. That way Morgan might appear to be puffing his own professional prowess, but otherwise Billings would get blame he did not deserve. Still, if French thought the story had been a deliberate leak, it would be less of a blow to his vanity—it would even help maintain his notion of martyrdom to an overwhelming foe. Billings would just have to suffer.

"We-all sho' do-all," Glass said. "What's youah name, honey chile?" He double-faked a Southern accent in ludicrous imitation of her spurious drawl.

"Terry," She flashed a smile all around. Large, capped teeth.

"I'll have a vodka," Morgan said. "On the rocks."

"Scotch here, with soda." French was recovering his good humor by inspecting Terry's blouse at close range. He turned to Morgan with an open-eyed stare simulating amazement. Morgan looked out the window in embarrassment.

"Gin and tonic. Listen, Terry, can you serve us in the lounge?" Glass pointed to the circular cabin in the tail of the plane. "Come on, Rich, let's sit back there where we don't have to yell across the aisle."

It was bad enough to have to talk, Morgan thought, when he wanted to sit and be no one, but it was worse to be herded about by someone who used his first name in the first three minutes after they had met. Still, as he trooped obediently to the rear, unwilling to assert independence on such shallow ground, he was rather interested in Glass; Morgan was more impressed than he liked to admit by any form of self-confidence, and the two patches of tape bespoke what to him was an incredible feat of personal adjustment. Glass's hairline, high or low, meant nothing in itself, no more than the length of a woman's skirt; but to alter it was to admit the primacy of exterior over interior, appearance over quality, matter over mind. Did Glass not care what the producer had done to him? Or was he honest enough to concede that the producer was right? Could the producer even be right in such a case?

"What do you experts think—is this much of a story?" Glass asked. "I thought old Anderson was pretty much out of it all."

French shook his head. "He had a hell of a following at one time. But I'm only on it because he won a presidential primary in our state that year. Before your time, Larry. And he did come from a famous political family."

"I might even get on the air with a little of it, the producer said. He wants some local color—you know, an era passing, bullshit like that."

Morgan laughed. "Hunt Anderson was fifty-two years old. That's not much of an era."

Terry brought the drinks. As the Electra bumped heavily over a hill of air she twirled the tray expertly over her head, while balancing herself with one hand against Glass's shoulder. He stroked her ample hip and tried to skate his hand around on her bottom. "Sit right down," he said.

Terry recovered, pushed away his hand in due time, and held the tray in front of him. He took his gin. "You live in Washington, Terry?"

"No, Atlanta." She turned to French, giggling mechanically.

"Love Atlanta girls," Glass said. "I'm down there a lot."

French stared down the neck of her blouse, whose top botton was open, as she poured his Scotch over ice.

Glass assumed his exaggerated accent again. "Wheah 'bouts in 'Lanna y'all shack up, sugahplum?"

"Uh-uh. 'Ginst the rules to tell." She leaned over to offer Morgan the view inside her blouse. He took his vodka, looked into her hard, bored eyes, then turned toward French. It was as close as he could bring himself to a snub, and Terry went away rapidly.

"That's got an ass on it like a Pittsburgh madam," Glass said.

"Right after I got to Washington," French said, sipping his Scotch, watching Terry twist away up the aisle, "it was after Anderson's first presidential campaign, the real one. I was covering the Senate, and one day he came in to make a speech. You know how it is up there, they never listen unless they want to get the floor and ask a question. So there were maybe fifteen senators scattered around the floor when Anderson started to speak against putting a loyalty oath in some federal scholarship bill. I could hardly hear a word he said up in the gallery. Just talking along the way we are, was the way he seemed. First thing I noticed, though, McAdams got up on the other side of the aisle and sat down next to Anderson. Listening. You know you don't see many people listening in the Senate. Then one or two others. Before long every senator in the place had taken a seat right around Anderson and was sitting there listening to him, not interrupting or anything."

Morgan felt stinging tears far back in the interior of his head and steeled himself not to shed them. "With all they used to hold against him in the Senate," he said, "all the trouble they thought he caused politically, in the end he had a lot of personal standing. They learned he wasn't a fake."

Glass sipped his gin. "Did I hear you say he was only fifty-two?"

Morgan nodded.

"Then he must have swallowed the bottle these last years. He looked to me like he was ninety-eight."

"You never really had a chance to know him," Morgan said.

"What I always heard, if you know one senator, you know them all." Glass grinned and drained his glass.

The Electra rumbled on, into dark and rain, into the past that to Morgan was as tangible as the South itself—the past that Glass seemed not so much to disdain as to disregard.

"Where's that Atlanta broad?" Glass said. "It's thirsty out tonight."

Glass had begun to depress Morgan. If Glass had come to him for a job, Morgan would have rejected him out of hand, of course with the usual hypocritical Southern evasions and half-truths. Glass—the rearranged hairline, the false voice, the soft, affluent, ringed hands, above all the self-confidence that Morgan could see was finally mindless—Glass appeared to be precisely what Morgan most despised: uncaring, insensitive, holding truth cheap. Glass had no standard but gain, no guide but the producer. Like the bloodless television shadows in whose image he was being made over, Glass was artificial, ephemeral, without past or future; a turn of some numbered dial and he would vanish from the screen. Yet Morgan saw that precisely for these reasons Glass had a certain brittle American vitality; he could live with developments, even with the fingers on the dial, and adjust himself. He was oblivious to oblivion.

"Tell me about Hunt Anderson," Glass said. "I can use some backgound for the show."

Morgan was no longer perspiring; he did not notice the plane's bumps and grinds. Glass, he thought, had no more delicacy than life itself; there Glass sat, watchful and unavoidable, seat-belted in place, gin on his breath and a hard-on for the redhead, the plastic stigmata of contrivance and falsity on his face; there Glass sat, the picture of life on the way to the funeral. Glass lived, after all; he was in tune, in touch, and maybe that even gave him a kind of jurisdiction in Anderson's case; maybe on life as Glass represented it, Anderson had left his mark, or not at all.

But he need not think about that, Morgan decided. He would go back to his own seat, he thought; he would move safely, secretly, within himself, as he had so often done in self-defense. He owed Glass nothing, need yield him nothing—certainly nothing of that past which to Glass was only background for the Blakey Show. Or so Morgan told himself, in his grief and his loneliness and his awareness of failure.

"Not much to tell," Morgan said, standing up, carefully balancing his drink. "You could look it all up in *Who's Who.*"

But *Who's Who* would not give Glass much background for the Blakey Show or for anything else, Morgan knew. There was very little in *Who's Who* that told anything really useful about anybody, despite all the tightly packed facts in the neat rows of tiny type. Morgan resumed his old seat, let down the tray from the back of the seat in front of him, and put his drink on it. *Who's Who* would identify Hunt Anderson as a United States senator, for example, but that was precisely the kind of fact that was the most insidious enemy of truth—enemy even of that glimpsed, shaped, packaged version of truth that Glass could call background for the Blakey Show.

"United States Senator" was a fact that made truth seem simple, declarative and indisputable, without shadow or blood, as if truth were never more than a documentary record of births and deaths, weddings and vote counts. Where in that deceptive fact, Morgan asked himself rather complacently, as if he were the custodian of secret papers, could you find even Hunt Anderson himself, let alone the rest of a man's life? And how could such a fact distinguish between those who had shaped his days, like Kathy, and those who had touched him in passing, like old Zeb Vance McLaren?

Old Bull's Boy I

Zeb Vance had been Morgan's first and last hero in politics. He had not made much of a splash in Washington because by the time Zeb Vance got there nobody cared much for his kind at news conferences or on television or anywhere else where a man might make it big. In fact, the only national headline Morgan could remember Zeb Vance making while he was in the Senate concerned a speech denouncing the Ku Klux Klan.

All the wire stories had said Senator McLaren was "defying the South." Morgan was sure he knew just what had happened, although he had not personally heard Zeb Vance's speech. He could imagine the wire-service reporters in the press gallery, yawning and tired, bored with a lot of tariff amendments and minor immigration problems and ax-grinding special bills for the relief of somebody unimportant from something inexplicable, and occasionally some mumbled speech for the record on behalf of Turkey Day in Wyoming or Gold Star Mothers or prayer in the schools. There had been one old senator from the West who in those days had made so many speeches—all the same—on the price of silver that it was said he could empty the whole Senate chamber in ten seconds just by standing up and saying "Mister President."

So, in mind's eye, Morgan could see the wire-service men half asleep that long-ago afternoon, and how, recognizing man bites dog when they saw it happening, they must have sat up and got busy when Zeb Vance McLaren began giving the Klan hell—Zeb Vance in his shiny blue serge, his trousers not quite touching the tops of his clodhopper shoes, with his Southern molasses-drip of a voice rumbling around a lump in his jaw that anybody looking at him could tell was a chaw of tobacco (it would have been Days-O-Work, Morgan knew). Zeb Vance had been the last senator to use the old cuspidors in the chamber—which was a kind of immortality, and maybe as good as any other kind.

Zeb Vance had come up in politics when a man had had to get a crowd's attention any way he could, and he had therefore developed the kind of speaking style that never let an opponent or an enemy proposition off lightly. In the throes of oratory, Zeb Vance had been wholehearted. To him no man was a mere skunk; if it was worth calling him that, Zeb Vance always said, it was worth calling him a pusillanimous skunk, just as a bloodsucking banker might as well be a pussle-gutted bloodsucking banker, when a man was in the speaking way.

So when Zeb Vance went for the Klan, he didn't take it easy or watch out for his flanks, even on the Senate floor. He said straight out that the Kluckers were a bunch of no-account pool-hall guzzlers who had never done a day's honest work and, if they ever did, would collapse from the strain and go on relief. He said anybody who'd wear a Klan sheet would steal his mother's pin-money out of her sewing-machine drawer, and as for any Klucker protecting white womanhood or anybody else, why, he'd as lief have his sister protected by a cottonmouth moccasin or even a demented rapist, which he suspected some of these disease-bearing descendants of mongrel bitches probably were anyway. They didn't wear hoods merely to conceal the slope of their heads, and the only Klansman he personally had encountered recently had been unfortunately upwind and thus noticeable all the way across two pigsties and a four-acre tobacco field—which was as close as Zeb Vance McLaren wanted any of these bad-breath, cowardly, carcass-eating buzzards to come, now and certainly in the hereafter, where it would be extremely hot in their vicinity.

At the time Morgan had represented his state capital paper in Washington, and since Zeb Vance was from his state the speech obviously was going to be front page for him; as soon as he had learned of it from the ticker he had hurried off to Zeb Vance's musty corner in the old Senate Office Building. There he found the senator well into a bottle of Virginia Gentleman with Buddy Pruden, who had been the senator's assistant since they both got out of State Agricultural and Technical College, and J. Millwood Barlow, the clerk of the Tobacco Subcommittee of the Senate Agriculture Committee. Despite the stately appearance of a banker, Millwood owed this and every other job he had ever held, of which there were too many to count, to his marriage to the former Miss Pearl McLaren, Zeb Vance's sister and hostess. Zeb Vance was a lifelong bachelor—"to which disreputable fact," he would say, out of Miss Pearl's hearing, "I attribute a long prong and a fat wallet."

"Sit down, Scout," Zeb Vance said when Morgan had been shown in by a superannuated secretary selected by Miss Pearl. "Pour him a breath of life, Millwood." He moved one foot from its position on his desk blotter minutely toward the Virginia Gentleman; Millwood leaped for a glass from a mysterious region behind a black screen, where most of his clerkly duties seemed to be concentrated.

"No, thanks," Morgan said hopelessly. "I'm still working."

"Then pour him a real bazooka, Millwood. I reckon he wants to hear how I reached my politically courageous decision to risk my career by skinning the hide off the goddam Klan. We better help him gather hisself together for the ordeal."

It happened that the reason Zeb Vance was Morgan's first political hero was not that Morgan had first known him as a progressive governor and an honest one—and not even that, long before it was generally recognized that times were changing in the South, Zeb Vance had stayed away from racial politics. "Hellfire, Scout," he had said once to Morgan about this peculiarity, "they vote, don't they? Leastways in most of the state. I never won an election without nigger votes." Which was one way to look at the fact that he had appointed the first black members of the State Boards of Education, Welfare, and Hospital Control.

The real reason Zeb Vance had a special place in Morgan's heart was that the first important political story Morgan had written had been about him. It had been a disaster, and Zeb Vance had rescued him from it. Morgan never forgot that, although he knew Zeb Vance could hardly have helped doing what he did. It had been a year when Zeb Vance was running for re-election as governor, and he had come to make a speech in the little town where Morgan was working on the weekly *Citizen* as virtually the entire reportorial staff, proofreader, pressman's assistant, and Omaha-folder operator. In those days Zeb Vance's political friends referred to him as "the farmer-governor," and in the orotund lead Morgan turned out for the occasion he used that description routinely. Only when the press had turned for the last time and the ramshackle folder had done its job, in the early morning hours before Zeb Vance was to speak at noon, did Morgan notice that throughout the edition, in cold irrevocable print, his lead read: "Zeb Vance McLaren, the former-governor . . ."

There was nothing to be done. Rerunning the edition would have caused it to miss the mails and bankrupted the *Citizen* in newsprint and overtime costs; the story had to go as it was, and it did. When the hour of noon arrived and Governor Z. V. McLaren rose to the sunbaked, makeshift podium and gazed across the multitudes from the truckbed platform in front of the Sandhills County Courthouse, Morgan believed the governor's eagle old eye was unerringly searching out the culprit, where he lurked across the square in the hot, grease-smelling entranceway of the Purity Café.

"Friends," the governor roared straightaway, "it says here in your local sheet that old Zeb Vance is the former governor already and I didn't even know the election had been held."

Laughter rippled over the crowd, and Morgan slunk farther into the sidemeat odors of the Purity. "That story must have been written by the State Bankers' Association, or maybe even some red-nose chicken thief from the liquor lobby." Sandhills County was submerged in the Bible Belt, and this language drew a predictable hand. Morgan reflected bitterly on a career in journalism blasted before it had fairly begun.

"But I'm here to bring just one message to you good folks in Sandhills County," Zeb Vance suddenly bellowed, shaking his fist at malevolent skies. "Whether I'm the former governor or the present governor and especially if I'm the future governor, you and me, us branchhead boys together, we're going to keep on fighting the bloodsuckers and the special interests and the country clubs!"

That raised a rebel yell or two, and here and there in the crowd old fellows in overalls pounded one another's backs.

"And that's why I'm the present governor and why some folks want me to be the former governor," Zeb Vance declared, in tones that must have been audible all the way to the railroad station, "and why you folks gonna make me the future governor, and you know you are too!"

It went on like that for quite a while, and slowly it dawned on Morgan that Zeb Vance had turned a typographical error to his advantage. "I think McLaren's a fraud," a reactionary old editor had once told Morgan admiringly, "but, by God, he's a professional fraud!" Later, lunching on greasy barbecue at the Purity, Morgan felt a wild hope that perhaps the governor would not have him fired after all—which turned out to be understatement, because after the speech Zeb Vance sent for Morgan to talk with him in the governor's suite at the Henry W. Grady House and offered him a press-agent's job.

"The rest of this story you wrote is pretty good, Scout. You know some politics, it appears to me. I got some spies around here tell me you got sense enough to come in out of the rain, and never been known to steal anything but a cherry here and there. I need somebody who knows where the commas go, and my spies say you'll do. And besides, this former-governor thing, why, Scout, it's bound to be an omen, just like it's a godsend to a man in the middle of a campaign. I aim to quote it every day until election."

It took the better part of a bottle of Virginia Gentleman—which even then Millwood Barlow was tending—to make Zeb Vance understand that Morgan fancied himself a journalist and did not propose ever to accept the wages of a politician. He had had higher attitudes in those days, Morgan thought, sipping vodka, but he had never changed his mind about that.

"Even a politician that's going to be president," he had said to Zeb Vance at the Grady House, while peering through a glass as dark as if it had held iced tea, his second or third. "And, Gov'nor, if you don't mind my saying so, they'd whip your cotton-picking ass up North."

"Millwood," Zeb Vance said, "ain't this scout a piss-ant?"

So in Zeb Vance's Senate office almost eight years later, after one more gubernatorial term and most of one senatorial term for Zeb Vance, after an expanding reporter's career and a tour in Korea for Morgan, there had been a certain easy relationship, not at all stiffened by the glasses Millwood kept tea-colored.

"Now in the first place," Zeb Vance said, "I wouldn't let the Good Lord himself"—he tilted his glass to heaven—"say about me what those Klucking bastards said. Show him that clip, Buddy."

Buddy, of whom Zeb Vance said that he spoke only when queried by his family doctor or subpoenaed by constituted authority, silently handed Morgan a clipping from a down-home weekly. MCLAREN BLASTED BY KLAN SPOKESMAN, it said. At a Klavern Konclave—there was no trouble deducing the editor's membership from the deadpan seriousness of the article—the regional Kleagle, one Dr. Fred C. Brantley, a defrocked Methodist preacher who was at that time making political noises in the state, had called Zeb Vance McLaren an "atheistic Communist who ought to go on back to Russia where he must have come from."

"I don't mind the Communist and Russian part so much," Zeb Vance said, "but calling somebody an atheist down where we come from, that is about as lowdown as a man can do. Ain't that a fact, Scout?"

Morgan stopped himself, just in time, from telling in Millwood's presence the old one about committing nepotism with your sister.

"But that clipping ain't the half of it," Zeb Vance said. "These nightshirt pricks are talking me down all over the state. They fill my mail full of the worst stuff you ever read. I won't even let Miss Pearl see it. So I just thought I'd touch 'em up a little."

"But the Klan has been after you for years," Morgan said. "Brantley is new, but they were on your back when you were governor."

"Millwood," Zeb Vance said, "this scout always did question our integrity. Spice up his punch a little."

"Stay away from me, Millwood. So all this you're telling me is just for the record, right?"

"Now the rest you wouldn't want to print, would you, Scout, and disgrace an old man in the twilight of his career?"

"I won't say you said anything. I'll say a source close to you said it."

"They'll think that's Millwood."

"Then I'll say political sources."

"They'll think that's Miss Pearl."

"Then I won't attribute it to anybody."

"Now that way," Zeb Vance observed with satisfaction, "they ain't a soul to get mad when I deny it, if I do, and I probably will. The thing is, you know as well as I do, those sheets"—he waited for Morgan to laugh at the pun, which Millwood was already doing—"could swing about as many votes against me as your fice dog. They make noise, but the only folks poor enough and stepped on and beat up and mad enough to listen to 'em, why, folks like that back there at the forks of the crick, they been voting for me so long they might keep right on when I'm dead. They could do worse too. Fact is, the Kluckers can't hurt me with a stick of stovewood."

"So much for defying the South," Morgan said.

"But the fact is too, and I got to admit it, not as many folks live out in the country as used to." Zeb Vance removed a substantial residue of Virginia Gentleman from his glass and extended the glass in an enormous hand toward Millwood, who leaped out of his chair as if prodded. "Now your city folks never took much to me, grieve me though it might. So next year, if I run again, I just might be in a little trouble."

"But whoever might be damn fool enough to run against you," Morgan said, "by the time you get through hanging your ancient and natural enemy, the Ku Klux Klan, on *him,* why you ought to get enough of those sophisticated city votes added to the piney-woods crowd to give you six more years at the public trough."

"Millwood," Zeb Vance said, "I ask you to testify on the Bible if I've even decided to run yet."

Every morning he had lived in Washington, Zeb Vance had walked from the apartment in which Miss Pearl allowed him one cavernous bedroom and one untidy workroom, to the Senate Office Building; since the apartment was near the intersection of Massachusetts and Wisconsin Avenues, far out in Northwest Washington, it was a walk of several miles and one that could blister the heels of an amateur in half the distance. Not long after the Klan speech, Morgan's editor had assigned him to make the hike for a feature story.

"Little hike like this keeps me in mind of my youth, Scout. Millwood can't even make it to Rock Creek Park, and that's all downhill."

"I'm not sure I can," Morgan had said. "Before I collapse, just to pay your last respects, why not tell me why you voted against that amendment the other day?"

"Now what amendment might that have been?"

"You know damn well. The amendment on the highway bill to eliminate billboards."

"Oh, you mean that billboard amendment." Zeb Vance was loping along the sidewalk at an unvarying pace, his big shoes coming down squarely on the cracked cement, his hands in his pockets, his big alert head, topped by hair going rapidly gray, turning from side to side as he looked from the huge trees beyond the traffic flow to the lawns of the British Embassy just ahead. It was a long way to Capitol Hill, Morgan thought grimly.

"Well, now, Scout, I don't know that I'd want that vote carved on my tombstone. Ain't this traffic along here a crime?" He speared a telephone pole with a brown dart of Days-O-Work. Trying to understand information the way Zeb Vance gave it, Morgan had learned, could sometimes be like evaluating a captured document. It was not only hard to know what it meant but hard to tell if it was genuine.

"I don't like the goddam billboards any better than you do," Zeb Vance said vehemently. "Covering up the countryside with all that shit." He stopped to look with farmer's eyes through the iron embassy fence at the scraggly patch of the Queen's lawn. "You'd think them Limeys would know better than to fertilize grass in spring," he said. "Makes it fat."

Down the long hill toward Rock Creek Park, the green walls of the avenue, between which endless ranks of automobiles loosed their noise and fumes on the morning air, closed toward a patch of pale steel sky. They went on steadily, Zeb Vance setting a relentless plowhorse pace. It was hot, muggy, a day of Washington spring that could have passed for summer anywhere else, and Morgan slung his light jacket over his shoulder; but not a trace of perspiration showed on Zeb Vance's weathered face, despite his inevitable blue serge. He was looking at the sidewalk, and in the lax muscles and skin along his jaw Morgan could see more certain signs of age than the gray senatorial hair. On the bridge—even beneath which, on the parkway far below, inexorable booming traffic fouled the air—Zeb Vance paused a moment, leaning over the rail. The sun sparkled from the tiny black string of the creek far below; great trees lifted their green branches toward the bridge; and the air smelled of hot rubber.

"I don't know that I had much choice on that vote," Zeb Vance said. "The Judge deals hard." He spat over the rail and moved on.

Judge Ward—at that time "the Judge" could have referred to only one man in Washington—was one of the ranking members of the Public Works Committee and the chairman of the subcommittee that had handled the highway bill. He had bitterly opposed the so-called billboard amendment —not least, it was believed by radicals and cynics, because the oil company whose interest he fiercely protected was one of the biggest highway advertisers. If in those days Judge Ward had bitterly opposed the Book of Genesis, it couldn't have passed the Senate on a roll-call vote. Not that he alone was all that powerful; but he was one of those impregnable elders who, like a herd of mules in a circle with their rumps together, used to stand united and determined, across party and state lines, above issues and above the rules, foursquare for no principle whatever but their own iron and divine right of control.

Zeb Vance pointed across the avenue at the Moslem mosque just off the bridge. "You know they take their shoes off going in there? Scout, I believe us Christians could learn a few things from foreigners, if you won't say I said it."

"So next week," Morgan said, "when the Appropriations Subcommittee on Public Works starts to write up the pork-barrel bill, they're going to put the money in for that dam you want up the Croatan headwaters. Because Judge Ward is going to see to it that they put that money in for one of his friends that played ball with him on the billboard amendment."

"I wouldn't myself want to claim the Judge had any *friends*," Zeb Vance said. "Otherwise I can't fault that line of reasoning except maybe pork barrel ain't exactly the word I'd pick. I always tell Millwood, you got the makins of a statesman, Scout."

The sidewalk beyond the bridge was shady. Sprinklers lofted cool sprays of water above the immaculate lawn of the Venezuelan Embassy; and in front of the cobbled entrance yard of the Japanese, they had to stop for an impressive limousine nosing its way into traffic. Zeb Vance barely missed its departing bumper with a smooth jet of tobacco.

"Never know they lost the war, the size of that car," he said. "And giving us regular fits down home on blouses and flat goods."

They reached Sheridan Circle before Zeb Vance spoke again.

"The textile boys got me by one ball," he said, "and the city folks by the other. I got to do something on tobacco too. I tell you, Scout, if it ain't one damn thing it's another. You know this Matt Grant that used to be on the Agriculture Committee staff?"

"Never heard of him."

"If we don't get run over and killed between here and there, you'll meet him down to Dupont Circle, where I take my rest. Damnedest fellow for getting at a man."

It was Morgan who needed rest by the time they picked their way through Dupont Circle's two concentric rings of traffic into the park at its center. A cement-mixer truck with an open exhaust deafened Morgan from Connecticut Avenue, and a tattered wino rolled over in the grass and muttered something obscene at the impervious sky. A tall, cadaverous fellow with sturdy shoes like Zeb Vance's rose from a bench and put out a bony hand to the senator. He had a somber Lincolnian face from which deep-set eyes peered forcefully.

"Rich Morgan . . . Matt Grant," Zeb Vance said. "You boys can help each other, I expect, if you let up on me long enough."

"Mr. Morgan, I've been meaning to call you ever since you got to town but I didn't know where to reach you," Grant said, in the accents of Morgan's state, which Morgan could recognize in an instant. "I'm in the Agriculture Department, Tobacco Division, and I keep up with your paper."

"Call the Senate Press Gallery. They'll take a message for me any time."

Zeb Vance sank comfortably on the bench and crossed his legs. "Beats any office I ever had. Who's that rich Jew that does all his business on a park bench?"

"Baruch," Morgan said. "Mr. Grant, have you ever made this easy little morning jaunt with the Senator?"

"Just once. It almost put me in the hospital."

"And looking at that little thing bobbing along over there," said Zeb Vance, intently following the passage through the park of a black-haired girl with a large dog on a leash, "those things, I should say, why, I bet I could outlast the both of you in the screwing league too. But I don't know as I can put that bill in for you, Matt, now I've thought it over."

"Mighty kind of you even to consider it."

"I got to go a little easy these days. If I get the tobacco folks down on me too, I won't have a friend in the world except Millwood. I'm not saying there's not some sense in your bill."

"They'll come to it," Grant said. "There's no other answer."

"You take a right-down dirt farmer though, and you send a government man around to tell him how much he can actually grow—why, Matt, you got to admit you wouldn't want to be that government man, now would you? Think of your wife and kiddies."

"Not married. Besides, they'll come to it." Grant spoke humorlessly, with absolute certainty.

"What I thought," Zeb Vance said, "we might just sneak up on it."

"Pardon my ignorance," Morgan said. "What is all this?"

He and Grant were sitting on either side of Zeb Vance. Grant leaned around the senator and spoke directly to Morgan, who felt himself in the presence of a man intoxicated by an idea.

"You know about the surplus," Grant said. "You've written about it. Over seven hundred million pounds of flue-cured tobacco in government warehouses hanging over the market like a thundercloud."

Morgan had written reams about that surplus. Agricultural scientists, moving onward and upward as men will, had taken four varieties of tobacco seed and bred from them a single new variety, Chandler 159, which seemed to be the farmer's equivalent of perpetual motion. It was totally resistant to Granville wilt and blackshank, plant diseases that had frequently put tobacco farmers on welfare, and even without irrigation or special fertilizer Chandler 159 would produce at least 150 pounds to the acre more than any other known variety; watered and fertilized, it wouldn't stop producing. A couple of years after it went on the market, 60 per cent of all flue-cured tobacco plantings were in Chandler 159. The whole industry had come to the end of the rainbow, it appeared—except that, with the malevolent timing of fate, the cancer scare and the resulting filter-tip development was transforming the whole cigarette business. Filter-tips meant that cigarette makers wanted more flavorful and aromatic tobacco with higher nicotine content, and the only flaw in Chandler 159 was that, for all its disease-resistance and productivity, it grew rather pale, slick tobacco, with little flavor and aroma. Filter-tip makers didn't want it, and foreign buyers could buy pale, slick varieties for less in Rhodesia. The scientists had produced the perfect growers' tobacco, the farmers were growing it in huge quantity, and nobody at home or abroad would buy it.

"It gives me a perverse kind of satisfaction," Morgan said. "We just have to keep tampering with things in this country. Nature isn't good enough for us."

"Nature?" Zeb Vance said. "If that was all I had to worry about I could sleep late of a morning. But Matt here thinks I ought to be out of my mind enough to try to force the tobacco boys down home to stop planting that damn seed. Millwood would be scandalized to know I was even talking about it."

"It probably would have that effect on them," Grant said, "but more than that. I'm convinced—I know—it would be the start of a revolution in the farm economy. It would spread to every price-supported crop just as sure as the sun comes up. They're going to come to my plan, Senator, and this tobacco crisis is exactly the right place to start."

"Poundage controls. You think I could survive that, Scout? On top of billboards and those damn Jap flat goods?"

"They have to come to production controls, poundage controls," Grant went on as if to himself, as if Zeb Vance had not spoken, "because the kind of agricultural science we have now, any old farmer in this country can keep on growing more and more to the acre, and if that's the case, then the present system of acreage control is just moonshine." He sat back suddenly, as if his vision had been broken by one of the pigeons swooping to the grass. "But I know it isn't easy politically."

"Why, if I put that bill in"—Zeb Vance heaved himself to his feet—"I couldn't go home in a suit of armor."

"Oh, I can get it put in over in the House," Grant said, "but it won't go anywhere if the Tobacco Subcommittee won't buy it." Zeb Vance was the subcommittee chairman, as befitted a senator from a tobacco state.

The three men moved across the park in step with Zeb Vance's firm stride. A streetcar jangled down Connecticut Avenue and disappeared into the tunnel under Dupont Circle. "What I did think we might do, Matt," the senator said, "just not to pin anything right on anybody that's got to face an aroused electorate anytime soon, particularly me, I thought we ought to let it lie out in the yard awhile and see what dogs come up and pee on it."

The imagery, Morgan could see, did not appeal to Grant; Zeb Vance was speaking of Grant's child.

As they paused on the curb, facing down Massachusetts Avenue past the snobbish façade of the Sulgrave Club, Zeb Vance suddenly laughed out loud and clapped Grant's shoulder. "Maybe we can put it off on Offenbach," he said. "He don't even smoke."

Morgan drew his seat belt tight and handed his empty glass to the redhead. Tension gripped him again. No further smoking, somebody muttered. The Electra plunged down through dark and rain like a lost fluttering goose; and nothing down there but wet dirt, Morgan thought with whisky bravado, nothing but wet dirt and sodden life.

Glass and French had returned to their seats too.

"I don't guess there'll be time to sneak off and get an extra drink," Glass said.

"You don't know this flight like I know this flight," Morgan said. "They'll set this crate on the runway a good half-hour, probably more, but the only thing you'll get to drink down there is coffee or Coke."

Glass groaned. "I always forget there's nothing in this part of the world but Baptists and backwoods."

In spite of himself Morgan's indomitable Southern instincts stirred.

"And those guys that sing through their nose," French said.

But Morgan always refused to defend the South. If you had ever been a part of it, he thought, you felt it in your soul and bones, where it could have no defense because it needed none; and if you were not Southern, you could never have quite the right defense made to you, because no Southerner could ever be sure what the right defense was. He just felt it in his bones.

Morgan turned back to the window and the flecks of rain across it and the darkness made eerie by the flickering red glow along the wing. He tried never to think about landings, and he had no wish for further talk with Glass and French; he willed himself again into the reverie that had been broken by the seat-belt signal.

Adolphus Helmut Offenbach, Morgan thought, Republican of South Dakota. Or was it North? Either way it had been a splendid notion of Zeb Vance's that S. 1120 should be called the Offenbach bill; by soft-pedaling Grant's notion that all price-supported crops would someday be subject to his scheme and concentrating on flue-cured tobacco, Zeb Vance had persuaded Offenbach, who knew nothing about anything except wheat, hogs, and the Strategic Air Command, to sponsor the bill. At that, Offenbach probably understood it better than the third member of the Tobacco Subcommittee, Josiah W. Bingham, another Southerner, but one so preoccupied with defending the United States against nigras and the world against Communists that he had learned no more about tobacco—or peanuts, or dams, or textiles, or anything else relevant to his constituency—than his staff managed to stuff into him just before he had to vote or speak, usually the latter. He was best known for delivering, during a filibuster, a thirteen-hour oration entirely devoted to the constitutional theories of Edmund Ruffin of Virginia (except for a brief digression during which he declared that if one of these newfangled Soviet sputniks were to soil the sky over his home state, it would be the duty of the peace-loving United States Air Force to shoot it down).

With these official companions, Zeb Vance, soon after his and Morgan's meeting with Matt Grant in the park, set off on a tour of the tobacco belt to conduct public hearings on the "Offenbach bill." Zeb Vance planned to play, with Bingham, the role of a juror listening to the evidence. Offenbach's supposed proposals were to be described first by Grant as special consultant from the Department of Agriculture, and then would be supported or refuted by growers, warehousemen, exporters, politicians—anyone who had notified Millwood Barlow that he wanted to testify before the subcommittee. If the outcome was even close to favorable, Zeb Vance had confided to Morgan, he thought he might persuade Offenbach, who had no political stake in tobacco or the South, and even hornswoggle Bingham, who was basically uninterested in the matter, since he held his constituency not by serving its interests but by arousing its fears and prejudices, to make a favorable report on S. 1120.

"Which is why," Millwood said, as the party flew south in an Air National Guard DC-4 that Bingham—naturally, a colonel in the Air Force Reserve—had commandeered, "we flushed every possible witness out of the bushes. Some of them will just naturally say what Zeb Vance wants 'em to say, or what in some of those other states his friends want 'em to say. He used to get around a lot in those other states when he was roads commissioner and governor of ours, and he has got a lot of friends in them too. Which I tell you we are going to need every one that we can beg, borrow, or steal."

Morgan was the only reporter making the trip. As he listened to Millwood he was resolutely not thinking about the fact that he was going free, on a government aircraft, which would have violated his principles if he had let himself think about it. He knew that if it had been a commercial flight, his home office would have been too cheap to foot the bill; and he knew that by stretching a point he could argue that it was more important for the public to have first-hand reports than for him to maintain unsullied professional virtue—except that something told him that was just argument, not truth. Anyway, he had stifled his scruples and boarded the plane with the three senators, Buddy Pruden, who was looking mysterious and put upon, some subcommittee flunkeys, Matt Grant, and two rather pretty stenotypists, one of whom Millwood said he understood could be managed.

This was the first time Morgan had really felt the fatal lure of being on the inside of things, and in later years he had been thankful that his testing had come at such a relatively unimpressive level; he had learned early and at low cost that too long and too far on the inside of things would inevitably put you in someone's pocket. "Be neither in nor out," he ritually advised his bureau reporters in Washington, and each of them thought it was crazy advice until one day he found himself tied up too tight to breathe by some statesman he had thought he could trust.

"We got everybody on that witness list," Millwood prattled, "from big growers with blood in their eye to black-ankle farmers that won't even know what in hell this Grant is talking about, except the fertilizer dealers and the supply company tell 'em they ought to be against whatever it is. We got folks on there that wouldn't cross a creek to see three United States senators naked as jaybirds if one of 'em didn't just happen to be a German or a Swede or whatever he is named Offenbach, which I guarantee you there's nobody else named in the woods back where they live. We even got Old Bull's boy on that list."

"To testify? Really?"

Millwood chuckled. "Might turn out more in the nature of a speech. Zeb Vance won't sleep through it either."

At that time people around Zeb Vance's state had a better notion who was meant if someone said "Old Bull's boy" than if he spoke of Hunt Anderson, let alone his full name, Durham Hunter Anderson. The state knew vaguely that he was a child of Old Bull's late years who, as a little boy, had been whisked out of sight and of state by his mother, Old Bull's third wife, after Old Bull's assassination. Anybody concerned about it could have learned that later the boy had gone off to the Ivy League, but it was harder to find out that after taking a law degree with honors he had disappeared, at least as a public person, into one of those Wall Street firms with immense prestige and income, an interest in foreign trade, and considerable financial leverage on the Republican party. Morgan had taken the trouble to find out that much because a year or so earlier Hunt Anderson had returned to the state as quietly as he had left it. He had brought a Yankee wife with him, taken up the active management of the hefty Anderson estate, appeared on several important community projects, and taken charge of a few good works. They said around the courthouses that he looked like a man with an itch to run—Old Bull's boy indeed.

A name like Anderson's was sure to have a certain political potential, and it was not too long after his return before a rumor suddenly was around the state that Old Bull's boy was going to move into politics. More important was the knowledge available in newspaper circles that the rumor was being propagated by a so-called advertising agency in the state capital, a firm that did the bulk of a rather narrow-gauged business with gubernatorial candidates and the state administrations the particular candidates almost invariably came to head.

"You really think he'll run, Millwood?"

Millwood was not without a minor political expertise, if for no other reason than that Zeb Vance confided in him. He chuckled a little grimly. "The question is what for." Zeb Vance would be up for re-election the following year, and there also would be a gubernatorial election. Morgan regarded Zeb Vance as unbeatable, despite the maneuverings that made him appear to be apprehensive; Zeb Vance merely believed in taking no chances. "The only good opponent," Zeb Vance would say, "is no opponent."

Nevertheless, when Morgan could get away from Millwood without offending him, he drifted back through the plane toward Zeb Vance. Offenbach had appropriated one whole seat, pushed down the back of the seat in front of him, stretched his short legs on it, and was asleep, his porcine cheeks wobbling with each breath. Buddy Pruden was deep in the committee mark-up of an appropriations bill. Bingham had gone forward to log a little flight-pay time in defense of freedom, and Zeb Vance was relaxed, in his shirt sleeves with his shoes off, a stack of unsigned letters on a magazine in his lap.

"Sit down, Scout. Take my mind off the goddam Japs."

In those days Morgan had thought being invited into private conversation in such informal circumstances with a United States senator, even one he knew well, was no mean achievement; he had learned better, but even then he had refused to show that he was impressed. One way he often tried to show irreverence was with flip remarks. So he said straightaway, "Japs, hell. You'll really be in trouble if this Anderson runs against you."

Zeb Vance took the letters and stuffed them into a large, old-fashioned briefcase at his feet. He took out a small package and unwrapped its cellophane slowly, the blunt fingers of his country hands moving with precision.

"Have a fig newton," he said.

"God, no."

"Good for your liver."

"But not Hunt Anderson for yours."

Zeb Vance looked at Morgan with wide eyes, through the dark horn-rimmed glasses he wore for reading; Morgan could tell he was annoyed, one of the few times he had seen him so.

"Sorry I brought it up," Morgan said, "but I heard it from a pretty good source, and my editors want me to check your reaction directly with you."

"Those pricks would just love it if he did, wouldn't they?" Zeb Vance had been opposed at every step of his political life by the state capital newspaper Morgan then worked for. He looked at Morgan unwinkingly, put a whole fig newton in his mouth, and munched sourly, as if upon gall and worm-wood.

"Or maybe I'm wrong." The reporter's common tactic of blaming his importunities on absent editors had been a mistake, Morgan realized too late. "Maybe he can't get elected with a family history like his. Maybe Anderson couldn't beat you or even Caffey." Leonidas Caffey was a well-known hack who had been patiently and for years on what the state's politicians called "the Ladder," waiting his turn to run for governor. It would arrive the next year, as inevitably as winter weather.

"Long after everybody knew Old Bull was a crook, they voted for him anyway," Zeb Vance said. "Maybe it runs in the blood." Zeb Vance, in his youth, had done his first political chores for Bull Durham Anderson; Morgan had heard him tell fascinating stories of those days when, if you wanted to rise above township constable, you signed on with Old Bull, and then you took his orders and paid his dues. It was not that Zeb Vance was proud of the connection; to Morgan, it seemed more as if he wanted to get it into the open before opponents could throw it at him in their own way and at their own time. No doubt he had borrowed some of Old Bull's techniques, but there the resemblance ended; no one had yet accused Zeb Vance McLaren of lining his pockets. When Old Bull's will was probated it had run well into the millions of dollars, yet the only jobs Old Bull had ever held were on the state payroll. A lot of his take had come from bootlegger, gambling, and highway-construction payoffs, but there was also a standard 10-per-cent "deduct" from the monthly salary of every state employee, including, in a case that was documented in one of the frequent inquiries after Old Bull's death, a temporary chaplain of the State Assembly.

"I don't mean to say that crookedness runs in the blood," Zeb Vance said. "I don't reckon even Old Bull was born a crook. I mean he just understood folks, and they kept on voting for a man that knew what they wanted and how they felt and said what they wanted to say. I've known men with good sense otherwise that would swear on the Bible that if Old Bull stole a dollar he gave ten back in hell to the corporations. One time they accused him of having this indictment against himself quashed by some judge he owned in Union City. He went right out and made a speech about it. 'Of course I had it quashed,' he said. 'If they were after you, and you had the power, wouldn't you?' And they would have too, because as above the law and the landlords and the interests as Old Bull appeared to be, they all wished *they* were. After that crazy fellow shot him, some folks took on till you wouldn't believe it—like the only man they knew that couldn't be beaten by life or the system or anything else was finally hauled down by a lunatic."

"But why would they vote for the son of a crook?"

"Because some of them want Old Bull back, whether they know it or not, and they'll think this boy is him all over again. And some of them sure-God don't want Old Bull back, and they're going to be damn relieved this boy's not him. And what I hear is, he's not by a long shot, though I haven't met the gentleman myself. But he'll get a lot of votes both ways because folks always think what they want to think, and what I mean by running in the blood is, if he's even got one drop of Old Bull blood in his veins, that's exactly what this boy will let 'em think."

Millwood was coming down the aisle, and Morgan feared he would have to change the subject; but Zeb Vance had piqued his interest on one point. "Never heard you speak favorably of Old Bull before," Morgan said as Zeb Vance put the last fig newton in his mouth. "I always thought you considered him a disgrace to the state."

Millwood stopped in the aisle, grinning. "Must be six o'clock somewhere in the world."

Zeb Vance munched and swallowed calmly. "He was a disgrace. I just said he gave the folks something they wanted. Maybe needed."

None of this prepared Morgan for Hunt Anderson, whose appearance was scheduled for the third stop, in a small city near the Anderson home place. By the time the traveling party had reached it, Morgan had found out that Millwood had been right about the stenotypist and Zeb Vance had been right about the way the tobacco belt would feel about the Offenbach bill. The hearings had all followed the same pattern. Zeb Vance would call the session to order, introduce the other senators and the local congressman, turn things over to Matt Grant for a detailed presentation, and then everybody would sit back and listen to the ranting and raving. After the first session Morgan knew the Offenbach bill was as dead as Prohibition.

"That dog," Zeb Vance sadly told Matt Grant, "just won't hunt."

But the show had to go on. The third session of the hearings, at which Anderson, among others, was to appear, was held in the basement of the Mount Zion Methodist Church Sunday School building, which was big enough and, with its concrete floors and slow overhead fans, cool enough for the crowd of a hundred or more that turned out in everything from overalls to good church-going suits. Morgan sat at a press table equipped mainly with Cokesbury Hymnals; he was flanked by two local reporters. The three senators sat up front at the head of a long table; a witness chair was at its foot, and Grant assembled his charts on some tripods nearby. Millwood Barlow hovered over all, and the stenotypists flitted in and out of the big kitchen with their mysterious black machines.

"The meeting will come to order," Zeb Vance said, banging the gavel. "Now, folks, we'll begin the hearings on S. Eleven-twenty, a bill to authorize acreage-poundage allotments for flue-cured tobacco—what you probably heard of as the Offenbach bill, and I'm going to introduce its sponsor to you right off, but first, you know, this is not the real church, it's not Sunday, we are not going to have a collection plate, so it'll be safe for you to come up close, right down front here, and let's fill the seats."

Then he introduced Offenbach and Bingham and the local congressman, the Honorable Billy G. Melvin (". . . when I went down to the capital as governor, I wanted my old friend Billy to be on my staff, and so I asked him if he would take that job, and he thought it over a little and then he said, 'Z.V., I would love to go down there with you, but I am just not politically inclined.' ")

"Now in a minute I'm going to introduce Mister Matt Grant here from the Agriculture Department up in Washington, and he's going to tell you how Senator Offenbach's bill would work. Then we want to hear from all you RFD boys out there—I like to hear that RFD number because then I know you are home folks—but first we want to announce what you probably already have heard, that we are going to have a fish fry at noon and all of you are invited. This has been furnished through the courtesy of the Coffee County Chamber of Commerce and Farm Bureau, so let's don't get behind in our hauling, and we'll eat some fish at twelve o'clock. Now here's Mister Matt Grant and let's listen close."

Morgan could recall as if it were yesterday the evangelical intensity Matt Grant brought to describing S. 1120 and what it would do. He had believed in it so deeply, and he had been so sure it was the "future of the farm," as he once said, that it had been as if he were preaching the gospel.

"After all these years on an acreage basis only," Grant would say, pointing to his charts, "you can see that we have developed an actual supply of flue-cured tobacco of nearly four billion pounds, whereas a healthy supply would be approximately three billion pounds.

"So we now have a little over half a crop too much flue-cured tobacco. Why did that happen with rigid acreage controls? All of you know the answer is simply that yields have shot up very sharply in these last two years. And the scientists tell us that regardless of what we do, yields can be expected to continue to increase. Now high yields per acre are good if they can be obtained without sacrificing quality. But the surplus is only half the problem we are facing on flue-cured tobacco. The other half is the revolutionary change in demand. As a result of the cancer scare, the trend is toward the filter-tip type of cigarette with different grades of tobacco being used.

"We estimate that during the current year they will need about three hundred fifty million pounds of the heavier and more aromatic, more flavorful tobaccos for filter-tip cigarettes, and about three hundred forty million pounds of tobacco for non-filter cigarettes. Unfortunately many of the practices followed, such as close spacing and particularly these new varieties and so forth that go into increased yields per acre, also go into producing more of the light, neutral tobacco but less of your heavier-bodied tobacco.

"That also hits you hard in the export market, which represents about every third basket of tobacco you sell. Both the domestic industry and our foreign customers want the heavier-bodied tobacco, but our production practices are carrying us in the opposite direction. One reason why we are going in the opposite direction is that under our present system every time yields go up, acreages have to come down. So, as individual growers, you seek to increase your yield as fast as possible to protect your relative position. When you do that you tend to produce more of this neutral tobacco for which there is a declining demand.

"That leads us then to this bill that . . . uh . . . Senator Offenbach has introduced, which provides essentially for a different method of establishing acreage allotments. Something other than the kind of system we have now, under which you can have a drought year in Coffee County and this general area, as you had last year, and not increase your yields one iota and still take a twenty-per-cent cut, because yields went up somewhere else.

"By way of explaining the proposed new system of establishing acreage allotments, I have an example here on this next chart, using the case of a farm with a four-acre flue-cured allotment. For the sake of this example, we are using a yield of fifteen hundred pounds per acre because that is an easy figure to work with. So the base poundage allotment for the four-acre farm is six thousand pounds—four times fifteen hundred. That base would be permanent. Now, we will assume for the purpose of this example that you got a little above the average yield for the first year and you produced sixty-three hundred pounds. You can sell all of it just as you do now under the present acreage system. And under that present system, when yields per acre go up, say, an average of five per cent, what happens to the acreage allotments the next year? They are cut five per cent, as you all know.

"So, the first thing we do with this four-acre man is to determine that he sold three hundred pounds over his allotment. The three hundred pounds is divided by the fifteen-hundred-pound yield per acre, and we find he oversold the equivalent of two-tenths of an acre. In other words, he has overdrawn his share of the market by the equivalent of two-tenths of an acre.

"Now, if we are going into a system under which each grower maintains his own share of the market in pounds as well as acres, what happens to this farm's acreage allotment the next year? Does anybody want to call what it would be?"

And several men would always call out, like schoolboys, "Three point eight."

"Three point eight, that is right," Matt would say. "Under this system the man who caused the increase in yield takes the cut, no more, no less. So his next allotment, as you can see here on the chart, would be three point eight acres and therefore his annual poundage allotment would be fifty-seven hundred pounds, three point eight acres times fifteen hundred, which comes out to the same result as three hundred pounds subtracted from six thousand pounds.

"Now, again for the sake of this example, we assume that the second year he actually sells fifty-eight fifty against the fifty-seven-hundred-pound allotment, so he is over one hundred fifty pounds or the equivalent of one tenth of an acre. And now, we come to the crucial part of this proposal. What would the man's allotment be the third year?"

And somebody, looking pleased with himself, would call out, "Three point seven!"

"What else do I hear?" Matt would ask, and maybe one or two voices at most would answer, "Three point nine."

"I have a three-seven and I have a three-nine," Matt would say, auctioneer-style. "Do I hear anything else?" And he would get back loud conflicting choruses of three-sevens and three-nines.

"Well," Matt said, "he overdrew here in the first year three hundred pounds, or two tenths of an acre. But he has already paid that back. Now when you overdraw at the bank and you repay the overdraft, then if you slip and overdraw again a year later, you only have to repay the second overdraft. So three-nine is correct, isn't it? Because you always go back to the base acreage and poundage. The base remains forever, the yearly allotment is three point nine acres for the next year, and the yearly poundage allotment is fifty-eight fifty, which is three point nine times fifteen hundred pounds."

By this time Grant would usually have his audience hanging on his words, but after one or two exposures to his spiel those in the traveling party had the plan pretty well in mind. Since Morgan's job was really to cover the response, he was not listening closely that day. Zeb Vance was having a hard time keeping awake and Offenbach was not even trying; only Bingham's snapping blue eyes peered intently around the room, as if to spy out subversives and pacifists. Morgan began to notice one of the few women present, and not merely because she was showing a lot of sun-tanned leg. In fact, she didn't at first seem remarkably good-looking, although her legs were—she sat in the front row—and anyway, Morgan took her to be older than he was, because she looked more mature than he thought of himself as being (she turned out, eventually, to be two years older). At that time he was a firm adherent to the common American fatuity that only young girls are suitable sexual objects for he-men. What first took his eye, that day, was the way the woman with the good-looking legs was looking at Matt Grant, following his every move as he strode impatiently among his charts or banged his fist into his palm for emphasis. Morgan watched her for a long time, and never once did she take her eyes from Grant's lanky height; she seldom moved at all.

A slender figure, looking cool in the sunlit room, aloof in the shuffling, musky maleness of that rustic audience; short dark hair, a single strand of pearls at her neck, an expression on her face at once absorbed and faraway, as if perhaps her mind gave no real direction to the rest of her being, was not even concerning itself with what she seemed otherwise to be following so closely. That had been his first awareness of Kathy Anderson— those few impressions and, above all, a sense of the sheer intensity of her stillness, heightened, not broken, at one point, by the swift dark flicker of her tongue along her full lower lip. Morgan supposed that he had watched people more closely in those days than he did now; then, he had still believed he would put everything down someday, if he worked hard enough at it; he would come to see the world clear and whole, and then he would make it live, immortal and beautiful, in long hardened lines of type indelible on the page. Ah, how he had watched and listened! and noted down the odd small components of the great truth he knew he would someday make. (The great truth, Morgan thought, of which he now doubted even the existence.) But that day he had watched, as if transfixed, the long tanned legs in the front row while Matt Grant went into his final lines, which made what Grant thought were his most persuasive appeals, to the farmers' pocketbooks.

"Now, to illustrate that it works both ways, suppose this farm is hit by hail or drought during this third year and the crop is three hundred pounds less than the yearly allotment. Under the present system, you'd have no way to recover. But under this proposal, what would the acreage allotment be in the fourth year?

Voices: "Four point two."

"Right. And your banker ought to be interested in the fact that if you lose a crop in one year, you've got a chance to recover and pay out the next year. Suppose that first year in this example he had a hail or he had a hurricane that wiped him out, or suppose even that all his tobacco was gathered and then was all destroyed, but he didn't sell a pound. The next year he would get eight acres, because he has not drawn his share out of the bank.

"Are there any questions, Senator?"

At this point Zeb Vance would usually be ready to let go with a good long spout of Days-O-Work into a spittoon he kept at sporting range, as if to show the assemblage that he was clearing away for business. He had arranged at each hearing for some of his stooges to be recognized first, to ask friendly questions that Matt Grant—as Zeb Vance put it—"could pick before breakfast." Then the counterattack would begin. It was always as well planned as Zeb Vance's own approach, and it usually began with some of the "RFD boys" mobilized and coached to give the opposition a democratic down-home flavor.

There was one old fellow with hard huge hands like two weathered stones; while he testified he placed those hands flat on the table in front of him as if to hold it and himself firmly in place against fate. "I bought a farm last year that's been butchered up for a long time"—in a voice that came in an incongruously high pitch from his lumpish body—"and from the gover'ment I got a loan of fifteen hundred and I put twenty-seven hundred dollars in to buy it, all I been able to put together all my natural life, and I got good land there, but the gover'ment would never have loaned me money and I would never have put hard money in it, if this plan was in. Because I got only four point thirteen acres of allotment now, and the first year I have got eleven hundred pounds of tobacco and just about two thousand dollars income for the year, and there is no way in the world I can support a wife and two children and make a seven-hundred-dollar payment on that place each year on that kind of allotment and eleven hundred pounds. I could not even sell the place and get the money back on it, because nobody would buy it with that low poundage on it, if this was passed as a law."

And he was followed, as a theme is developed in a symphony, by another, better-educated farmer with a Masonic stickpin in his tie who described Grant's program as "a plan that says we better quit trying to do better in this world, and if you go ahead and use the blessings of Almighty God and Clemson College and these other people who have taught us how to have a good yield, then you are in trouble with Washington, and it is going to come out of your pocketbook, sure as shooting."

And there was always someone more clownish—a Farm Bureau committee chairman, perhaps, or a county commissioner, who had his own political interests among the solemn, hair-brushed farmers providentially brought within sound of his voice. "You just take that four-acre man right there in that Washington chart," he would say. "All right, the big shots from the Agriculture Department, they will let him sell fifteen hundred pounds to the acre. All right. So maybe one of the boys comes back from the service, and he is an energetic young fellow, and he does like the extension service tells him to do, and so he comes in and he tells pappy to step aside, he will take over. So all right, that is the American way. Now maybe just through favorable growing conditions and a little bit of hard work and good seed and fertilizer he gets twenty-two hundred and fifty pounds to the acre, and we all know of cases where it's been done. So it is cut fifty per cent next year, he is down to just two acres, and pappy, if I know him, he is going to say, 'Jack, you go on to town and get a job, and if we don't do so good next year we will get that two acres back, and you can come back and farm some of it.' "

They always saved the biggest gun for the last, and at that session the big gun was a peppery, rather short man in a dark blue suit, large pearl cufflinks, and a collar starched like whalebone. Everything fit him just a bit too tightly, not a speck of dust marred the mirror surface of his wing-tipped shoes, and as far away as the press table Morgan could smell his shaving lotion.

Zeb Vance all but tugged his forelock, welcoming him as "my good friend and yours."

He was no friend of Morgan's, who had seen him a hundred times—even then had been seeing him for years—making his way in the South, hustling used cars or bottled gas, collecting door-to-door on cheap insurance policies or renting shotgun houses in the back streets. But times had changed, and the little man in the tight suit had caught on fast to the new situations that opened up during and after the war. He had figured all the angles, made a quick dollar in wartime gasoline stamps and a beer hall for the troops from a nearby camp. Later he edged himself into part ownership in a soft-ice-cream franchise, and picked up the vending-machine contract in the new synthetics plant out where the state four-lane, put in after the war, approached the town. Then he got in on the ground floor of a new local bank stock, opened the area's first television dealership when the coaxial came through, and bought a piece of an old-line general store, which he turned into a discount supermarket. All those ventures had paid off, quick and big, in the mushrooming economic development of the South, in the cheap destructive boom of plastic, picture windows, vacuum tubes, freeways, and windowless red-brick factories sprawling across fields where small boys once flushed quail and set out rabbit boxes in the unforgettable vivid sunshine of their days. So the little man had prospered beyond his dreams, and now he owned the ground and buildings of the first shopping center in that area, with parking space for two thousand cars on the vast black zebra-striped cap with which he had sealed the fecund earth beneath it; now he lived in the town's newest, biggest housing development, in which he had substantial interest; he sat on the board at the bank and farmed a dozen tenants; his son would go to law school at Carolina, and his wife sat for the hairdresser twice a week and nipped gin in the bathroom before breakfast, perhaps in memory of some long-ago dawn with its sounds of birds in the clean piney air that used to be. Oh, he was tough and smart, all right, Morgan conceded that—a good man by his lights, come a long way on his own steam; he had learned to hire smart lawyers and clever politicians, and a good thing too; because lately he was a little scared of the way things were going. There were shadows in his head, strange fears in his mind, mystifying hints he did not fail to catch in the headlines and news broadcasts, and he had made up his mind that they were not going to take over if he could help it, not going to grab anything away from him, from what he believed he had achieved by himself. So he contributed to Joe McCarthy and listened to Fulton Lewis, Jr., and tightened his grip on everything, even though his accountants already were figuring his estate problem.

In this particular case Morgan could even remember his name. "A. T. Fowler, gentlemen," the man said. "I am A. T. Fowler of this city and I will not take too much of your time. It is my contention that we have not heard the speaker for the government tell us here this morning that whereas we once had a free enterprise system when one man on one side of the fence could plant what another man on the other side of the fence could plant, if he wanted to, now we are being asked in this S. Eleven-twenty to live under another control on our lives.

"Now these controls come from an increasingly more powerful centralized government, which today is trying to take over the schools and operate them and take over every step of our national affairs, and today we meet here not to determine whether they will do like we tell them, but whether they will create a situation where we got to go to Washington to determine whether or not we can plant our acreage.

"Now this gentleman here from Washington, he gets up and he says, 'This won't affect your poundage.' Well, what is the purpose of it if it is not a poundage control? It is to take the poundage right which we have. And so I say, they are trying to curb the initiative, the energy, and the ability of our individual citizens, and they are trying to make Russians or Communists out of them or Chinese citizens, that is what they want to substitute for a system of free enterprise which developed America."

Bingham was sitting at attention, beaming. Zeb Vance rang the spittoon with a good hard shot to the rim. "Now A. T.," he said, "there's no call to go that far."

"Well now, Senator," A. T. said, "you know and I know there was a time when we could get throughout the world a very profitable price on our export crop because we had a monopoly on cotton and tobacco. Well, the Chinese tobacco farmer, the Egyptian tobacco farmer, was able to profit by the prices that we created, and the Australian tobacco farmer is enjoying that today, where we have to curb the production and where we have the acreage control from our own government, whereas, we give them the green light to go ahead and produce tobacco to replace our tobacco.

"And this poundage limitation bill will continue the program of more scarcity without doing a thing about foreign production. It is absolutely socialistic in its tendency, because it holds you and me and everybody else down to the same level. And, friends, our good Congressman Billy G. Melvin there, a lot of you heard him say not long ago at the Coffee County Farm Bureau, that when you try to sell American commodities abroad the State Department steps in and says, 'We are hurting somebody's feelings.' Well, I for one am for telling the State Department to take our tobacco and just dump it into the ocean if it's necessary to do that, even give it away to our friends overseas—but I am absolutely and unalterably opposed to a policy that gives the Communist Chinese and the Russians the green light to come in and be competitive with us, and I say that this birthright and this inheritance that we had up until twenty or thirty years ago today is being taken over by a totalitarian, socialistic-communistic government."

Morgan could recall these last few little gems from A. T. Fowler practically verbatim. He could hear the little man's sharp-edged voice, see his jittery, nimble fingers shuffling among his reminder cards, even catch the faint recurrent waves of his shaving lotion washing across the Cokesbury Hymnals on the press table with each languid swish of the overhead fans.

Because it was at just that point in his fervid speech that Hunt Anderson entered Morgan's life with two words: "Mister Chairman?"

There was a mild Southern liquidity about his r's—"chay-uh-man"—but otherwise he had little accent. His voice was slow, timbrous, but Morgan was to learn that he never spoke loudly; that day he had difficulty hearing Anderson, as he was to have many times in the future.

Anderson had spoken first from his seat, but he continued to speak as he stood up. "I request the privilege of the floor"—he seemed to keep on rising for a long time—"for the purpose of addressing a question"—because there was a lot of him and as soon as one part unfolded something else would rise on top of it—"to the witness."

Hunt Anderson was six feet six inches tall, one of those men who seemed to eat and drink in Gargantuan lots, seldom exercised—Morgan came to know—but never gained a pound or an inch around the middle. All the years Morgan had known Hunt, good times and bad, a lot of each, Hunt had stayed lean, appeared strong, even when he came to look ten or fifteen years older than he was.

"Mister Anderson," Zeb Vance said, "if A. T. don't mind, I don't either, but I'll have to remind you your name's already next on our list."

But A. T. Fowler had not got where he was for nothing. He shied at shadows, but he was a competitor, he had gone to the mat with all he knew of the life around him, and he could not be faulted if he had thrived on luck and the times as much as upon guts and brains.

"Why, Senator," he said, "I never in my life ducked a man's question and I don't reckon I'll start now."

"Well, now, I know you never have, A.T.," Anderson said, "which is just exactly why I broke in the way I did." By the way the room had quieted Morgan would have known this was Old Bull's boy, even if Zeb Vance hadn't named him—an interesting political fact not lost on Morgan; the old pro had not had to have a potential rival identified by someone else. Long Tanned Legs sat beside Anderson, not looking up at him, motionless—undoubtedly the New Jersey girl he had brought back to his home state.

"What I thought," Anderson went on almost apologetically, "was maybe it ought to be on the record here, A. T., just what size your allotment is."

"Yeah. Well. I suppose . . . not in one farm, you understand . . . taken all in all, Hunt, it comes to a little better than a hundred, as anybody can find out any time they want to go check the county records."

"A hundred acres?" Anderson had some sheets of paper in his hands, and he looked around a little uncertainly, as if he had stumbled onto something he was not sure he could handle.

"There's plenty that's bigger'n that."

"I suppose there must be." Anderson looked momentarily toward the press table, and Morgan saw mild, myopic blue eyes behind horn-rimmed glasses, down a little over a rather prominent nose. "Now, A. T., what would you say your production's been running in recent years?"

A. T. swelled up a little. "Better'n a ton to the acre if you leave out that little biddy old worn-out rockpile my daddy left me with when I started out."

"I see," Hunt said. "Now, I call that real tobacco farming, A. T., especially with everything else you've got to do." There was something askew about Anderson: a hank of hair fell the wrong way across his part, another stuck out from the back of his head; his jacket hung strangely, as if one of his shoulders might be lower than the other. His face was oddly planed; not handsome, his might have been a head by some rather pretentious sculptor, and the angles of cheek and temple, of jaw and neck, seemed precise, edged rather than curved or blurred, joining parts carefully cast and assembled for some obscure effect rather than for mere representation. "Because, after all, you're not just a farmer, A. T. I mean, if the committee wanted it for the record, how would you list your occupation?"

"Everybody knows my business." A. T. sounded exasperated. "All these fellows here. Senator McLaren. You know perfectly well yourself."

"I just thought it ought all to be in the record." Anderson was speaking a little more loudly. "Like banking. Like . . ." He seemed to grope for a word.

"Well, real estate," A. T. said reluctantly. "Investments."

"Fertilizer," somebody shouted from the back of the room. "High-priced!" A titter of laughter broke the silence that had gripped the audience. "Fatback!" somebody else yelled, and the titter turned into a husky head-back laugh; even A. T., game and smart as he was, grinned a little and waved a quick, nervous gesture of surrender at Anderson. "Yeah, well, retailing too," he said when he could be heard.

"Mister Chairman." Hunt Anderson shuffled his papers and began to look behind him as if to make sure his seat had not been moved. "I apologize for this interruption but I thought the record ought to show that even with Communism and Socialism practically on top of us, even with all these controls out of Washington stifling us, I just thought the record ought to show that my good friend A. T. Fowler is the living proof that in this country where all men are born equal it is still possible for some of them to get a little more equal than others."

He had managed to get himself into his seat again by the end of these remarks, which rippled another laugh through the audience, and then, with remarkably greater speed, he rose to his feet again. "I did have one other question, Mister Chairman. I wondered if A. T. is at all in favor of any kind of production controls as such."

"Well, now," Zeb Vance said, "I don't want to put Mister Fowler in any kind of position that would—"

"Senator McLaren," A. T. said, "I been asked and I'll answer straight out. I think that in the world that exists today, with the pressure from the Communist countries, where they have absolute control over the individual, I am in favor, I think, of production controls—they may be a necessity, but I think they ought to be exercised so as to give the utmost initiative and privilege and impulse to the individual effort, rather than to a strong centralized government, which stabs at the vitals of every citizen."

"So it isn't a question of controls as such but of what kind of controls? One kind might be necessary but not one that would hurt, say, the fertilizer business?"

"Well, that's not exactly what I said." A. T. saw too late where he had been led. But Anderson was already back in his chair with another muttered *"Thank you, Mister Chairman"* to a rather bemused—Morgan thought— Zeb Vance, who was seeing too late that what ought to have been his scene had been neatly stolen.

A. T. quickly cleared out of the witness chair, rather as if it had been suddenly electrified, Anderson's name was called, and Millwood Barlow showed him to the committee table with a bit more flourish than the occasion demanded. As Anderson moved away—he walked the way he stood up, in sections—Long Tanned Legs looked after him, breaking for almost the first time that stillness—it was not repose—the intensity that Morgan had been watching more closely than he realized. As her husband began to lower himself into the witness chair like one of those lofty construction cranes dipping and lurching over the steel vertebrae of a new building, she looked toward the press table with slow, disinterested eyes of a color that, at that distance, Morgan guessed to be the smoky lambent blue that drifts mistily on soft Southern mountains. Suddenly those eyes were gazing straight into his, a fixed and demanding stare, as if to say, why should I not watch you as you have been watching me? Morgan did not evade that still intentness; it had discovered him lurking behind the hymnals, and he grinned at her, a little sheepish, a little flattered, and she looked away and was still again.

". . . pleased to have your distinguished views on this important matter," Zeb Vance was saying.

"My pleasure to be here, Mister Chairman."

"But just first"—Zeb Vance leaned forward, looking owlish and innocent
with his horn-rims lower on his nose than Anderson's, his hair a little
tousled as somehow it had not been only a few minutes before, his big rough
hands fumbling among papers for something apparently misplaced—"I
reckon we ought to have it in the record too, just what your allotment is
out there on that mighty fine farm your daddy left you."

Morgan knew he had found his lead: *Next year's political campaign
opened here today,* etc.

Anderson was ready. "Why, Senator, like my good friend and yours,
A. T. Fowler, and I want to say he is my good friend, I reckon I'm a large
grower, though not as large by any means as Governor Anderson used to
be. When the tobacco program started, according to our records"—he
produced a piece of paper from somewhere, leaned over it, and traced
figures with a long, thick finger—"we farmed just over one hundred sixty-
five acres of tobacco on the Anderson place, and now after all the cuts over
the years that we've all taken, my flue-cured allotment is seventy-eight,
which doesn't quite put me in A. T.'s league but pretty near, and we produce
about what he does to the acre, right about a ton, the Lord willing. I ought
to add that this year there's a total of eleven families—my own and tenants
—involved in that seventy-eight acres of tobacco and to some degree dependent on them. As for other interests, why, I'm like A. T. again, numerous investments, but I don't have any active business interests like his, in
this city or area, except my farm."

That made Round One a draw on Morgan's card. Zeb Vance tried
another light jab. "Why, I thought I recollected the Governor used to own
about everything worth owning downtown here along Live Oak Street."

"We retain," Anderson said, hitching around a little in his chair as if to
include Long Tanned Legs behind him, "just what he was most devoted to,
the land and the home place."

That was about like saying that Jesse James had only cared about his
horse or Pierpont Morgan his brownstone. It was so outrageous that there
was some laughter behind Anderson, the kind you hear among fisherman
or golfers when somebody gets off a whopper. And when Anderson himself
grinned amiably at the preposterous size of this response, the laughter
became general.

Round Two, Anderson. Zeb Vance fumbled among his papers and leaned
back to study his man a little more closely. Offenbach, like a slumbering
hog stirring its fat barrel under the pinpricks of bottle flies, heaved himself,
puffing and blowing, an inch or two nearer the table.

"Just one more point for the record," Offenbach grunted. "If the witness . . . uh . . . Mister Anderson . . . uh . . . would be good enough to give us the answer to the same question he asked Mister . . . uh . . . Haytee . . . does he—"

"Fowler," Anderson said. "A. T. Fowler."

"Fowler. But do *you,* sir . . . uh . . . believe in these controls that, like Mister . . . uh . . . Fowler said, any way you look at them they hold back your . . . uh . . . incentives?"

"Two ways to look at incentives, Senator Offenbach. One is increasing your yield so that you are getting an increased share of the total market and getting into a race with other growers, without regard to the effect upon the market or the quality of your product. If that is your definition of 'incentive,' then this method proposed in your bill reduces it. If, on the other hand, you want to follow such practices as will enable you to concentrate on quality and cost per pound instead of pounds, then this proposal certainly gives you greater freedom to exercise your management prerogatives and skills."

"Uh," Offenbach said and lapsed gratefully into torpor, his day's work well done.

"You're supporting this bill?" Zeb Vance sat up a little straighter.

Beyond him, Millwood Barlow's face rose beaming from the palms that had been clasping his jaws above knee-braced elbows; Matt Grant hitched his chair forward; and from the corners of his eyes Morgan saw the tiny movement of Long Tanned Legs turning her head to watch Grant again.

"Unlike your good friend and mine, A. T. Fowler, I'm supporting this bill," Anderson said, trying for a point or two in the process of losing Round Three by a mile. A raspy whisper of "Godamightys" and "Jewhearthats" rose above the scraping of feet and creaking of seats in the background.

Zeb Vance, obviously considering the bout ended with this fatal mistake by his adversary, settled back comfortably.

"You just take all the time you want, Mister Anderson."

"Thank God we're taking off at last," Glass said.

Morgan, feeling himself pinned against his seat as the Electra plunged down the runway, the familiar tension clutching his stomach, watching in spite of himself the redhead's big tits bounce as she hurried along the aisle, growled at Glass, "It could have been worse. Sometimes they take twice as long."

"Hey, Red," Glass called, "how's chances for some extra drinks in the caboose? Morgan here can fix it with the CAB." He grinned at Morgan with idiot familiarity.

"That's the stuff," French said, but the redhead was buckling herself into a seat far up the aisle, and the plane was rumbling and shaking as if in a fierce storm. To hell with it, Morgan thought, forcing his thoughts away from the takeoff, pushing himself as if bodily into memory.

Anderson had started in a slow voice, almost uncertainly. "Senator McLaren, this is an issue which goes to the livelihood of every farmer throughout this area because we all produce tobacco. They started this acreage program a good many years ago and we all have seen the fruits of it, and I am not one to say it is a failure.

"But even when you have something that has been going along good for years—it is like when you go to church, sometimes when you go and join a church, you backslide a little as you go along and we get to the place where we have to have revivals. Maybe we need to have a little bit of revival in this tobacco program. Not too many years ago you could take fifty dollars an acre and grow a crop of tobacco, and if you made a hundred dollars an acre then you were making a profit, but today you have to have eight hundred or nine hundred to get a profit, and there aren't enough who can do that. I hate to be one of those who say we need a change, but I have seen the handwriting on the wall. Senator Offenbach, I say that fundamentally, basically, I believe your acreage-poundage bill is sound."

So far Morgan was not much impressed. The low, timbrous voice was as hesitant and its words as rambling and loosely collected as those of the farmers who had preceded him, and Anderson had produced nothing to win attention to his argument. Was this the best Old Bull's boy could do?

"Now we know," he was saying, "that for the past four years we have taken a forty-seven-per-cent reduction in acreage—and they came out in the *Capital Times* the other day, and I understand Mister Morgan is down here today from that great paper we all read—there were articles which stated that the soil bank would take this year voluntarily from this state's farmers an additional eight per cent, which would run our total reduction up over the past four years to fifty-four per cent.

"Now there comes a time when you can't go any further and still continue to operate. Oh, I suppose I could, and Senator McLaren, your good friend and mine, A. T. Fowler, he could keep right on even with another big cut in his acreage, but I'm talking about growers who don't have that kind of allotment to take it out of. In the last five years forty thousand farmers in this state have had to give up their farms because economically they could not produce. There's a figure for you. That is a serious and tragic problem."

The reference to Morgan confirmed, if anything was needed, that Hunt Anderson was planning far enough ahead to check up on press coverage and knew when he set foot on Zeb Vance's turf that he was making news. Morgan scored him another point on the favorable reference to the *Capital Times;* actually, in that part of the state it was a highly unpopular paper, but it circulated throughout the state, and the favor of its editors was not a small asset to anyone running for statewide office. It also set Morgan up a little to be mentioned, and there was some craning of necks toward the press table. But Morgan noticed that Long Tanned Legs did not move at all.

"I believe," Anderson said, "that we must get back realistically and produce that which we can sell. I think this proposed program is sound. We grow acres, but we sell pounds, pounds of tobacco is what is used in making cigarettes, and, after all, pounds in the final analysis is the word we must use. This program goes in that direction, and I believe it's time."

Morgan followed the direction of Long Tanned Legs' gaze and saw Matt Grant sitting forward on the edge of his chair, elbows on his knees, his big hands clasped in front of him, his head up. There was something glowing in his usually saturnine face, and he listened to his own doctrine being preached—for the first time of any importance in all the hearings—as if he were some lanky country boy almost persuaded at a tent meeting. It occurred to Morgan that Grant was watching Hunt Anderson with the same intensity that Long Tanned Legs was devoting to Grant.

"One other thing we all ought to consider," Anderson was saying. "We as growers have got into this rut of knowing we have so many acres year after year, and we have worked ourselves to the bone to produce every pound that we could produce, and we all know that we have forgotten quality in many instances. If this proposed legislation is given the right chance, I believe it will lead us back to quality tobacco, and that would be a good thing all around. There are too many processes and activities in American life that debase value and destroy quality, and it is tragic for agriculture to become one of them.

"Now if some of you think it's easy for a grower like me, with seventy-eight acres, to come out for stronger controls, just think about that a minute. You'll see that if we cut the acreage any more, then the small farmer trying to support his family is through. And if we produce more tobacco, we *are* going to cut the acreage. And if we do that, we are going to let large growers like me and your friend A. T. Fowler, Senator McLaren—just as sure as God made little apples, the big grower with his irrigation system and expensive fertilizer is going to take over the market and put the small farmer out of business. And the way not to do that is to control poundage."

He was picking up speed. Matt Grant was still rapt; the audience was listening more closely than it had. Anderson's words took on point and bite, and his sentences began to shape themselves and roll with a bit of rhythm. He had, Morgan could see, the makings of a speaker. Anyway, Morgan knew by then that he had a page-one story, and in those days—he thought, staring through the plane window into the night—he would have raped his grandmother to get on page one.

"Now let me add a final point, Mister Chairman, and I'll be done because we all want to get to that fish the good ladies are frying for us. I think this is more than just a matter of income for this state. I believe the idea of production controls ought to be applied to other crops too, and for more than economic reasons." Offenbach's eyelids began to flap. "Planned production, in my opinion, is an attainable goal once you begin to approach it in broad terms rather than on the traditional seasonal basis. And that's important for the whole world . . ."

Offenbach was now sitting up, breathing in quick, shallow puffs, a habit he had when under stress. Beside him, Matt Grant was grinning broadly, almost in wonderment; he had found a man who not only understood his doctrine but who shared his vision.

". . . we must not delude ourselves, Mister Chairman. In the immediate future, in the lifetimes of many of us here today, the possibility plainly exists that some of us are going to watch on television while people starve in India or Latin America, the way people used to go to see the marathon dancers, if we do nothing now to prevent that. Mister Chairman, if our nation stands for anything, it must stand for a better world than that. It must work for a better world than that. Mister Chairman, I believe we have to organize ourselves and other producer nations to feed the world, not as a mere duty but as a matter of survival for us all."

Now he had Bingham listening too; Bingham knew a one-world do-gooder when he heard one, and his alert, glistening eyes had stopped roaming the audience and fixed their stare hotly upon Anderson, as if to melt him in his softness. Morgan saw that Anderson had managed to turn two members of the subcommittee against him by talking too long and unnecessarily.

Ultimately, Morgan had come to know that Hunt Anderson had a long view—foresight, not prescience. Anderson had been only postulating, that day, from good solid evidence; in that Southern Sunday School room with an audience of dirt farmers and tradesmen and maybe one or two people who knew something of the world beyond that part of the state, and before Morgan had ever heard any other politician mention it, much less make a speech about it, Anderson had talked knowledgeably about what everyone soon came to know as the population crisis.

In those days Morgan had thought he knew everything there was to know about the South; at the least he had thought he knew damn well there were no Southern votes to be had from charitable talk about starving Hottentots, who were sure to be as black as the ace of spades.

But even then, as Morgan looked over the still head of Long Tanned Legs at those rows of lined, sunburned, rigid faces, those eyes looking back at him from the land and the weather and the years and the poverty and the sameness, those eyes that could look on impassively, hopelessly, while a crop wilted or a child died or a house burned—as he looked at them, Morgan realized that while many a Southern politician, like Bull Durham Anderson, had known exactly how to light those eyes with the rockbottom hatred they knew was down there dormant in the soul and gut of every poor Southern son-of-a-bitch, he had never before seen a Southern man doing to Southern men what Hunt Anderson was doing in his slow, even voice, and his testimony that few of them were likely to have understood, and fewer to have liked if they had. Morgan had never seen those faces of his life lit before, kindled not with hatred but with—surely not with hope, for Anderson was not even talking about them or their lives; and surely not with love, for they had poured the last of that, long ago, into all the things that had left them hopeless. Whatever it was, Morgan saw that day that Hunt Anderson had the gift of making people believe in him; maybe it was because he so obviously believed in himself and in what he was saying.

There was no applause when Anderson finished, but the sounds of life came back into the room, the coughings and mutterings and foot-scrapings, the squeak and clatter of the seats, a door banging somewhere at the rear; the stillness while Anderson spoke, Morgan realized, had been the loudest applause a man could have.

Anderson started back for his seat, after first shaking hands with the three senators. Bingham looked repelled by the experience. Later that day, to Morgan, he dismissed Anderson with a bitter epithet: "An idealist!" Zeb Vance began the adjournment routine, and Morgan hurried around the press table, catching up to Anderson just as he lowered himself by sections into his seat. Morgan stooped between him and the long tanned legs carelessly crossed beside him.

"Morgan, *Capital Times,*" he whispered. "Thanks for the plug. Can you say anything about these rumors you're running for governor?"

Anderson took his glasses off and got his face down close to Morgan's. The blue eyes were weak and blinking, all right, but they were pleasant too; they were kind, Morgan thought.

"Damn if I know what to do," Anderson said. "I want to run for something, but tell you the truth, I'm not sure for what."

"Atta girl," Glass was saying as the redhead appeared with a round of drinks they were not entitled to. "Atlanta broads are the cat's ass."

French, on his way to the magazine rack, paused long enough to take his Scotch, and the redhead leaned over Morgan with vodka in an airline plastic glass. "You didn't order, but I just sort of . . ." The Electra lurched over a bump of turbulent air, and she braced herself with a hand on his shoulder.

"Thanks." Morgan took the glass, and even in the midst of the memories that had absorbed him he did not fail to notice, as she straightened, the momentary unnecessary flutter of her fingers on the side of his neck.

"The ass end of nowhere," French said suddenly, loudly, over her shoulders. "Whole story of my whole goddam life."

The night after the hearings the touring senatorial party and its hangers-on had been invited to a barbecue at the Anderson farm, a local showplace. Except for burning-eyed Bingham, who made some excuse to get back to Washington ("It must be his turn," said Zeb Vance over one of Millwood Barlow's iced-tea-colored glasses, "to stand guard at the Unknown Soldier"), all were driven out in cars furnished by the local Ford dealer—like A. T. Fowler, one of Zeb Vance's major contributors.

The Andersons—Long Tanned Legs was introduced as Kathy—had invited some local guests, and tables were spread under the trees, with tubs of cold beer and watermelon; hickory smoke rose blue and thick from a barbecue pit, over which a pig was in the final stages of preparation. It was just a reserve. A supercilious black man, obviously conscious of his art, was chopping up another pig, already barbecued, with an ancient cleaver. A white-coated bartender was doing a flourishing business under a spreading oak.

"Millwood," Zeb Vance said, viewing the scene with appreciation, "we ought to send Miss Pearl a postcard."

Morgan made immediately for the bar, spurred a little by the undeniable fact that Long Tanned Legs, interrupted in a conversation with Matt Grant to be introduced, had shown about as much interest as if he had been one of the blaze-faced Herefords that had peered solemnly at the cars moving along Anderson's private road from the highway. Morgan was not pleased at being snubbed by a handsome woman. He obtained a glass of Scotch, which Millwood might have poured, and kept to himself, looking around. The house was the kind he most passionately hated—pillared Tara-style, white as the cleavage of a Southern belle, under trees, atop a low hill, with lawn and pastureland rolling away, and black servants in profusion. In fact, the house was not so old and was not so much out of *Gone With the Wind* as out of Old Bull's deduct box, out of the pockets of people like Morgan's father, bilked and milked by the political kingdom Old Bull had created and so long sustained on their blood.

Morgan drank quite a lot of Scotch, ate some good hot vinegary barbecue, hushpuppies light as marshmallows, and cole slaw in which the cabbage had been chopped so fine it was almost granular. He drank some more Scotch, still keeping away from people. The dark came down, lanterns were hung in the trees, and servants roamed around fighting mosquitoes with spray guns. Zeb Vance held court on Tara's lower veranda, telling political stories, while Millwood plied steadily between him and the bar. Grant and Hunt Anderson sat on the steps, deep in conversation.

At one point Morgan went past them into the house; Kathy Anderson nodded absently as he crossed the porch. Inside, he found a telephone and reversed the charges on a call to Anne in Washington. As he had expected, a baby-sitter answered. No, she didn't know where Miz Morgan was, or sound like she cared, but she'd tell her Mister Morgan had called, for what that was worth. Morgan wandered out on the porch and listened to Zeb Vance for a while. People moved around. Morgan headed for the bar again.

A figure came into the lantern light, head down, plunging toward the house. It was Matt Grant, and Morgan had to catch him by the arm to stop him. "What's your hurry? You liked to knock that tree down over there."

"Oh, Rich. Some work to do. I got to get back to town. You ready?"

Morgan thought briefly of the manageable stenotypist; but once to the well with a girl who bit collarbones was quite enough. "I'm ready to go," he said, "but not back to town."

"See you later then."

Grant loped off again, toward the house and the waiting cars. Morgan waited awhile, where he stood. Kathy Anderson came out of the darkness, and he walked toward her.

"Nice tonight," he said. "Where do you order your weather?"

"We get it wholesale." She stopped, her hands in pockets placed low down on her light dress, below her waist. That pulled her shoulders together a bit, giving the impression that she was hugging herself. "Are you having a good time, Mister Morgan?"

"Better than Matt Grant, I reckon. He just went by here like a fullback. On his way to town, he said."

She looked at Morgan coolly, calmly, obviously reading him, her shoulders hunching a little nearer together. He suddenly felt as if he were transparent as a child.

"He had a good time," she said. "I believe he had a good time, Mister Morgan."

"Well, I didn't mean . . ." Caught in his own ineptitude, Morgan ground to a halt, a little sullenly; until that moment he had not fully realized what an impact she had made. He thought bitterly of her in the dark with Matt Grant, of the goddamned baby-sitter, of his own traitorous tongue, exposing himself to her amused contempt, as he supposed it must be. Anger rose in him, but before he could say anything else someone called, from toward the house, and a tall figure ambled toward them.

"Detour," Hunt Anderson said, grinning amiably in the lantern light. "On my way to the bar."

"You look like you know the way, all right." Kathy nodded toward the house. "Are the senators still here?"

He might easily enough have said that it should have been her business to know, but he either chose not to make a point of her absence or had not noticed it. "Offenbach looks ready to leave, but Zeb Vance is going strong."

"I'll go play hostess then," Kathy said. "Shouldn't you maybe switch to Coke about now?"

"Sooner be caught dead." He seized Morgan by the arm and abruptly propelled him to the bar, seeming to take no further notice of his wife. Morgan was easy to guide toward the Scotch, especially after his humiliation—even more especially because Long Tanned Legs obviously was more interested in Matt Grant than in him. Matt Grant! Morgan thought, angry still, years later. All that clod knew was flue-cured tobacco.

"Been wanting to talk to a political expert like you," Anderson said. "What do you think I ought to do about running?"

"Take that good-looking wife and all your money and go way off somewhere and live the good life and never come back or even think about it again."

The bartender had departed, leaving numerous bottles. Anderson went behind the bar and uncorked one. "That's what I used to think. I never wanted to bother with this place even." He swung a long arm in a vague arc, endangering other bottles, then poured Morgan's proffered glass more than half-full of Scotch. "I used to sit in that bloody law office in New York and think about California. You ever think about California?"

"No more than I can help."

"Then I would think about Europe."

"That's more like it."

Anderson carefully poured his own glass nearly full, added ice, recorked the bottle. His eyeglasses had slipped down his nose, and he peered comically over them. Morgan came to know that Hunt Anderson was never above striking a little pose; sometimes it was as if he were really mocking himself.

"Girls would ruin a man. European girls screw you to death."

"I am told," Morgan said, focusing on that, "they make an art of it."

"Specially Italian girls. Italy during the war."

"Well, if you were a war hero, screwing poor little homeless girls for a goddam Hershey bar, maybe you ought to go ahead and run. That's the kind it takes."

Anderson took a drink, looking warily over the edge of the glass. "You take a man like me, Morgan, what's he going to do once he's screwed his Italian girls? Everything downhill. Or maybe up, the way you put it."

"And after he's got enough money," Morgan said. "Some of it stolen from my old man."

"Goddam right it was." Anderson came around the bar and peered at Morgan's left shoulder, then his right. "Can't see the chip, but even if I could I don't aim to knock it off. I'm too old."

"I'm sorry. That was a lousy thing for me to say."

"Exception'ly lousy," Anderson said, "mostly for being true. The money and the Italian girls too. But why I didn't take your advice long ago . . . You see, I couldn't get far enough away. Couldn't see any good life that would be good enough or built on anything but that same money. So here I am. Except I've managed this place until it manages itself. Investment brokers coming out my ears. A man can't go through life fixed like that."

"So you think you'll run for governor just to break the monotony?"

"There you go again," Anderson said. "I didn't say necessarily governor anyway."

"Well, I don't know what you expect me to say." Morgan put his glass down hard and Scotch spilled over a little on his hand. He had been excited and humiliated by Anderson's wife, he was jealous of Matt Grant, he had exposed his uncertainties and resentments to a man who was virtually a stranger; as if something were pouring out of him to the ground, Morgan felt his self-control ebbing away. "I never had a pot to piss in, and you stand here in the middle of a movie set and give me this poor-little-rich-boy bullshit."

"That chip is a lot bigger than you think it is," Anderson said quietly, his kind, weak eyes steady. Morgan knew, suddenly, that Anderson was not drunk, not even tipsy. "How old are you, Morgan, if it's any of my damn business?"

"Thirty. And feel about seven right this minute." It was one of the worst moments Morgan could remember, in a lifetime of some bad ones. There was a burst of laughter from the porch, and Morgan was sure for a second that they all had witnessed his debacle, that the whole world was snickering at his disclosure of himself.

"Is that old fart always that comical?" Anderson said.

Morgan seized the chance to recoup, re-establish some cover. "That way, people don't realize how serious he is until it's too late. Or how smart."

Anderson adjusted his glasses and looked at Morgan closely, as if again searching for the chip on his shoulder. "Just thirty, huh? I'm thirty-eight, Morgan, and I'm here to tell you there is just one hell of a lot of difference between thirty and thirty-eight. I remember thirty pretty goddam clear because I got married that year and that marks things for a man."

For a moment his strangely planed face was brooding, shadowed in the yellow light from a lantern hanging over the bar. Marrying those legs would have marked me, Morgan thought.

"I had the goddamnedest chip on *my* shoulder you've ever seen."

A white jacket, under a black face, approached them. "Miz Anderson say the senators leaving now."

Hunt Anderson put down his empty glass and seized Morgan's arm again. "But not you, Morgan, not yet. We've got some serious drinking to do."

Offenbach and Zeb Vance were climbing somewhat shakily into the back seat of one of the borrowed Fords, with the benevolent dealer himself at the wheel. Millwood Barlow was in the front seat. Kathy Anderson stood alone on the steps. One or two other cars were starting up or moving away; no guests remained on the broad porch.

"Here comes our star reporter," Zeb Vance said as Morgan approached with Anderson. "Jump up there with Millwood, Scout, and let's go get some sleep. Long day tomorrow."

"Sleep?" Anderson said. "Why, it's hardly good dark yet. And Morgan here's got me talking politics."

Zeb Vance looked at Morgan sadly and put his big hand out the window of the car to Anderson. "You fixing to do it, are you? I can always tell when a man is down bad with the running fever."

"Why, Senator," Anderson said, "I reckon it sort of goes with the blood. I might run for governor, I guess, if I thought you'd support me." He took Zeb Vance's hand.

"Now that scout there will tell you there ain't many things I love to do better than give a promising young fellow a hand up. That a fact, Scout?"

"You might not kick him in the face," Morgan said. "Not unless he was running against you." He spoke almost absently because he was trying to guess what Anderson wanted to talk about.

"Dolphus," Zeb Vance said to Offenbach, "they just don't understand us public servants, do they?"

Offenbach muttered something Teutonic. Morgan learned later that the barbecue had upset Offenbach's Midwestern stomach; which proved again what Morgan had long known, that the South exacts its revenge in many ways.

"But if you're bound and determined," Zeb Vance said to Anderson, "you just remember what the old nigger said to the little boy. 'Don't play in the bushes,' he said. 'Dey's rattlers in dere shedding dey skins, and sonny, dey's pitiless.' "

Hunt chuckled. "I'll remember that," he said. "I'll even steal the story."

After florid assurances from Zeb Vance that it was the most splendid evening of his life, and after the Andersons, with matching hyperbole, described the senators' presence as the most notable honor ever to befall their poor household, the Ford dealer drove into the night, rather more like a king's coachman than what Zeb Vance privately described as a "bankroll."

"Glad that's over," Kathy said. "I thought they'd never leave."

Morgan, still shaken by his earlier defeats, tried to be carefully pleasant and meaningless. "You'd better get used to it, Miz Anderson. At the table and at the bar, politicians are worse than preachers."

"Oh, Hunt isn't running for anything yet." Her tone of voice disclosed nothing of whether she wanted him to or not.

"Old Zeb Vance can spot running fever pretty well." They moved up the broad steps to the porch.

"Well, you know the old story about the boy crying wolf. Hunt talked about running for governor last time but . . ." She shrugged eloquently.

"Timing," Hunt said, "is ninety per cent of the battle. I keep trying to tell you that."

"And what's the other ten?" Before Anderson could answer, she spoke again, putting out her hand to Morgan. It was cool, firm, like her gaze; its touch excited him, not vaguely. "I'll leave you two to talk about it, if you don't mind, Mister Morgan."

"I don't blame you," Morgan said, bitterly disappointed, amazed and puzzled to be bitterly disappointed. "I won't keep him up late."

"You won't have much to say about it, if I know Hunt." Her hand tightened, for the merest part of a second, in his. "I missed saying good night to your friend Mister Grant. Will you tell him I'm sorry?"

Her smile was bold and certain. Morgan let go her hand abruptly. "It's his fault. He had something important to do in town."

"Good night, Mister Morgan. Hunt." As she turned away Morgan thought her face was positively triumphant; or maybe it was just his own feeling of inadequacy.

Anderson seemed scarcely to notice her departure. As the screen door slapped behind her he folded himself down into a big padded porch chair. There was no apparent hostility between them, Morgan thought, just nothing alive or reaching. But how could that be possible? In his experience marriage was just the opposite—a hot, small room, stifling with the blood odors of intimacy, a closed chamber in which love and hatred circled each other endlessly, closing warily for the kill.

A white jacket appeared from the house and put a bowl of ice, two glasses, and a bottle of Scotch on the table between them. "You go on to bed now, Jodie. I reckon this'll hold us." Hunt began putting ice into glasses. Jodie faded away; Morgan had forgotten how Southern blacks could make themselves all but invisible.

"We better get one thing straight right away," Morgan said, doubting that Anderson could want his company as much as he wanted a reporter's ear—and because he was still off balance and trying to recover a professional manner. "Is this going to be on or off the record?"

"Goddammit." Anderson poured Scotch without even looking up. "I drink liquor with people for fun, not business."

That made Morgan feel silly, so he became angry again. "I can leave," he said. "You don't have to drink with me at all."

Anderson handed him a glass. "You're just mad at yourself. Here, this'll cure you and practically anything else."

The glass was cool, moist, darker than Millwood Barlow's best. Anderson lifted one as dark and grinned—that wide, slow smile of his that so lit his strange, planed face.

"Ah, hell," Morgan said. They clinked glasses and drank awhile in silence. It was quiet beyond the circle of light on the porch too, and cool in the evening. Morgan could hear crickets, and a bullfrog far off, another answering. There was a clean smell of pine resin in the air, and sometimes a whiff of hickory smoke from the barbecue pit. Morgan had lived in Washington hardly a year, but the night made him placesick for the South; he thought briefly how it never left its children, never fled their imaginations and their dreams; how some small thing—a frog's croaking, the sight of an old black washpot, a lined and patient face, maybe just redbud by the road in spring—could, for anyone who loved the South, bring it flooding back like a river of mind. Morgan tried to think of something decent to say and fell back on a reliable move.

"Your wife is a handsome lady."

"Fit for a gentleman."

"But I couldn't be quite sure a minute ago whether she wanted you to run or not."

"I couldn't either." Anderson did not sound as if he cared. He drank some Scotch, set the glass down, took off his glasses and rubbed his eyes with the knuckles of his forefingers; it was a gesture Morgan came to know well. His eyes were terribly weak, and he said they would literally get tired of seeing. Morgan could remember a piece of newsreel film that showed him doing that during the third roll call, the one that counted, at the convention.

That night on his front porch, Anderson put his glasses back on and looked at him rather sternly. "What you said about stolen money, Morgan. That used to be on my mind all the time. Everywhere I turned there was the money, and there was some evidence of where it came from and how Old Bull collected most of it. So let me ask you this, and you tell me what you think. What was a poor little rich boy supposed to do about it?"

He finished his drink and reached for the bottle. Morgan had finished his too, and Anderson poured both glasses full.

"Why ask me?"

"Because you remind me a little bit of myself, back then. Because you're angry way down deep, the way I used to be. Because you keep your guard up, the way I used to do."

His perception disconcerted Morgan. "I'd put some of it back where it came from."

"Bullshit," Hunt said. "Oh, I set up something called the Dixie Foundation all right. I even started to call it the Old Bull Foundation and then I figured that would be ludicrous." His voice sharpened, and a queer contortion of muscles momentarily wrenched his face out of shape in an expression of profound distaste. "But don't give me that kind of bullshit, Morgan. I mean, what was a poor little thirty-year-old rich boy going to do about the situation—not just the money? You can get rid of money, but how can you change history?"

"You can rewrite it. You can't change it."

"Rewriting is changing. History is only what people think it is, Morgan, only what they know most about. That's a big difference in thirty and thirty-eight. You come to see that. Then, I just wanted to hide away, go off somewhere like you said, where they never heard of this state or Bull Durham Anderson, give most of the money away, and pull the hole in after me. That didn't exactly suit Kathy." He made an unexpected humorous face, drank some more Scotch. "So I had to face up to it. I practiced law and then I managed this land, and all the time I thought about the situation and myself and tested out an idea or two, and now I believe I'm ready to change history, Morgan, whether you believe it or not. The truth is, I don't have a thing to lose."

Morgan drank Scotch and looked at him, his anger gone. Morgan was away from center stage, and they were talking about Anderson; that meant Morgan could retreat into his profession. Personally, even then, he had considerable doubt that politics mattered. He placed higher value on knowing what men did than on having the power to cause them to do it. It seemed to Morgan that the largest questions to be explored, the greatest gambles to be taken, were within oneself, not in the arenas of society. Yet, professionally, he was fascinated by the politician and his subtle art, his not inconsiderable risks of self and material, the visions and urgings that drove him. And professionally too, Morgan could see that whatever Hunt Anderson was— fool, visionary, guilt-ridden zealot—he obviously was not the simple man of good will he had played so adeptly that day in the witness chair. Among other things, he had a hard head for whisky; his latest glass of Scotch was going as fast as Morgan's own. And in those days, Morgan thought, I could drink a mule under the table.

"Well, you weren't so bad in there today, everything considered. You had them listening, and that's at least something."

Anderson laughed out loud. "They came to see Old Bull's boy politicking, Morgan, and what I had to do was to make sure they saw him." His face lit up again with his remarkable smile. "A bunch of old boys like that, you have to set them up a little. I don't care how mean a man's life is, Morgan, he wants to know there's something a little beyond him. He might be kicking hell out of somebody down below, but he still wants to look up and see somebody who talks a little better and knows a little more and lives a little higher; not somebody untouchable, you understand, not somebody who's kicking *him*. He just wants to know that it's possible to do a little better in this world than he's done. Like going to church; maybe he won't ever get to heaven but he wants to know it's there and he's got a chance."

Morgan remembered Zeb Vance's remark that *as above the law and the landlords as Old Bull was, they wished to be.* "If I were you," he said, "I wouldn't count on changing history with the support of Zeb Vance McLaren."

"Hell, he can't support me if I run for governor, I know that. Caffey supported him twice. That doesn't leave him any choice, the way that crowd plays the game. I was just buttering the old boy up a little. He doesn't have to work against me."

"He told me you might beat Caffey."

"But you don't believe it. You think I'm an amateur. The son of a man a lot of good folks are ashamed of. No organization. But it takes two to make a horse race, and if one's got the blind staggers the other is likely to win."

"Caffey isn't much. But then most of our governors haven't been much, except maybe your father and Zeb Vance. But you won't be running just against Caffey, you'll be running aginst all that courthouse bunch. What you got to do is get yourself on the Ladder, which with your name and at your age ought not to be any trouble at all, provided you're not in too much of a hurry. But running against Caffey is just exactly the one way you know damn well it can't be done."

"I haven't got time for their damned Ladder," Hunt said. "The world is changing, and they'll have to change with it. Some ways, Morgan, I'm really Old Bull's boy. Let them play my game is what I say. Just what he always said."

"What'll you do for an organization? Where'll you get the money, outside your own checkbook?"

"That's the part I'm surest of. I've spent a lot of time roaming this state, Morgan. I belong to every damned civic club there is and I don't miss a state meeting. I've been up and down and forward and back in the last few years, and there's one thing I've found out that *they* don't know. In every town and county, there's a crop of men like me—younger fellows that don't want to wait on any damned silly Ladder for all these old duffers to get out of our way. So even if I don't do it, sometime soon, somebody's going to stand up and say to all those young, smart, concerned guys that believe we're too near through the twentieth century to keep on living in the nineteenth— somebody's going to say, 'Follow me.' And they will. Look here, Morgan, I read your stuff and it's pretty good. I concede you know the state pretty well, but you listen to the old farts too much. What makes you think they know anything about politics? Have you ever asked yourself what would really happen if one of those courthouse hacks that's been home-free all these years ever had an opponent who really knew how to run for office in the twentieth century? Even Zeb Vance?"

Morgan groped for a professional answer, but Anderson was warmed up and going strong.

"They're living on borrowed time. I give old McLaren maybe one more term at most, and he's the best of the breed. But you take a man who thinks it's still good politics in this state to spit tobacco juice all over the sidewalk, I tell you he's just waiting to be taken."

"Caffey chews Brown's Mule," Morgan said.

"And what does old McLaren chew?" Anderson said. "Being governor in this state is a horse's ass job."

The level of the bottle kept getting lower and lower, and of the voices higher and higher, the words more and more basic. Before that evening was out, before there was even much light at the top of the bottle, Morgan had decided Anderson was a political natural. Old Bull's boy to the bone.

With Anderson's gift for seeing where things were going, what he had seen most clearly was the way things were changing in the South. People knew all about it now, Morgan thought, they wrote books in the universities about what Hunt Anderson had talked about that night—increasing industrialism, the new managerial class and suburban ethic, population draining out of the countryside, the decline of the farm economy ("Why the hell is Matt Grant down here with his bill except to try to save their necks?"), higher educational standards, even a subtle shift in the race issue.

"Still basic," Hunt said. "It is everywhere and will be for your lifetime and mine. But old Jackass Caffey, for instance, about the only thing he's learned is not to say nigger in front of one or call a black lawyer 'boy.' Shit, man, you can't just go on saying the same old things more politely. Too many business interests here that don't want trouble. Too many modern industries that need educated personnel. Too many young folks coming along that want to get on with other things. Any man who sounds too much like he's going to close down the schools in this state to please the rednecks is going to get his ass whacked in the cities and suburbs. But you watch, Caffey is going to promise to close 'em."

"And what'll you say when he does?"

"If I'm running against him I'll say I'm going to provide a good education for every child, black, white, and polka dot, in this state, and no damn closed schools. And I'll say I can do it because there's not going to be any school integration around here to amount to anything for another five or six years minimum, no matter what I say or do or what Caffey says. You go talk to the black people, the way I do. They can't be turned around that quickly, not after what they've had to live with, not the way they look at us. Over there in town, we'll get exactly two black applicants for the white high school next year, and some of us have had to go out and recruit them on the sly, to keep the courts out of our hair. These black people love their kids just like we do. They're not going to send them off to some white school to get hit with rocks, which is what they believe for damn good reason is likely to happen. But Caffey doesn't know that. The only black skin Caffey has talked to in forty years is his cook, and she probably lies to him like everybody's cook does."

Anderson had it in mind, that night, to be the first important candidate in the state to make a major campaign on television, and Morgan had found out there on his porch over the Scotch bottle—the only thing Anderson put off the record—that he'd already started his planning with a New York advertising agency; and back then, most television sets in the state still had round screens. Oh, Anderson had been a strange one, Morgan thought, the oddest mixture of Old Bull and idealism, modern ideas and old principles —an original, maybe too good to be true. At one point, Morgan had suggested in Zeb Vance terms and out of a slight excess of Scotch that if Anderson let himself get caught on the wrong side of the school issue, Caffey would not hesitate to nigger him to death. "If you want to go out there and throw yourself in the volcano and go up in a blaze of molten lava," Morgan said, "go right ahead. But that won't change history."

Anderson adjusted his glasses for a better view, but by then, as the Scotch level had fallen, he had dropped lower and lower in the porch chair, his knees rising to frame his face. "Why, Morgan, damn your eyes," he said, "you are now going to tell me that I can't do anybody any goddam good at all unless I can get elected. Isn't that what comes next? What good is a defeated hero? What use is a dead martyr?" A sudden upsurge of energy through his sprawled limbs brought him to his feet in two or three spasms, and he leaned forward, wagging a long forefinger inches from Morgan's nose. "I say bullshit, Morgan, bullshit! I know all those lines by heart. If I listened hard enough I could prob'ly hear my daddy crooning those same old lullabies when I was in the cradle, and I'll tell you something else, Morgan, goddammit, that's the whole story of American politics. That's what's wrong with this fucked-up country. That's what's ruining us, all this self-serving, idiotic, yellow-belly crap! Morgan . . ." He folded back into his chair with remarkable precision, his knees coming up ludicrously beside his head. "I tell you, the minute a man decides it's better to be a live politician than a dead hero, the second he begins to believe the only way he can do any good is to get elected, right that instant he's sold out, he's as dead as Kelsey's nuts, only he doesn't know it. He might go on and squeeze a few drops out of the turnip, like old Zeb Vance and his dams and roads, but he won't change any goddam history, Morgan, put your money on that."

"If you'd stop trying to feel up that redhead," French said to Glass, "maybe she would bring us some more booze."

"Old Morgan's asleep," Glass said. "He's had too much already."

"I'm not asleep," Morgan said. And I could drink your ass right into the baggage compartment, he thought, wondering at what point he would no longer be able to act civilly toward Glass. To this day I could put you under, just the way I'd have put Hunt under that night if finally Kathy hadn't raised a window somewhere in the darkness above us and pointed out that it wasn't so bad for a pair of drunks to wake up her children, but if they were going to wake them up with all those four-letter words they ought to go on out to the barn with the other animals. I can hear the window coming down now, with that decisive crack, like a judge's gavel.

"Mad," Anderson said. "She might be down here any minute with a bucket of water."

"Water?" Morgan said. "We can't switch to water now."

It was funny, Morgan thought, that he could remember those exact words after so many years. Just a typical, unfunny drunk joke. But he could remember that particular joke because, in the condition he and Hunt had been in, it had sent them off into howls of laughter, and they had rambled across the porch and out through Anderson's acres of grass, still laughing. Anderson had thrown an arm over Morgan's shoulders and they had laughed some more. And when they had finally stopped laughing, they were standing together, far out in the night, with the sounds of crickets all around, behind them the mellow light from the porch, overhead a high and winking sky. For a moment they had been isolated from the world, Anderson and Morgan, set apart from all its forces and terrors, all its ancient lures. Morgan could remember precisely the way it had been at that moment—the air clean and cool with approaching dew, the smell of grass, and the stars far above, blazing and untouchable, like the dreams of men.

"I tell you I'm going to do it," Anderson said, softly. "I've got to do it. I was born to do it."

He was looking at the stars too, Morgan thought, and perhaps it had been the enveloping, protective darkness, the isolation, the sounds and smells of fields, earth, creatures, outside the clutter and tangle of men—maybe it had been just that brief, clean moment; far more likely, it had been only the whisky in both of them. Morgan had not even been sure exactly what Anderson was going so surely to do. But for that moment Morgan had believed he would do it.

"Maybe it's worth a try," Morgan said. "Whatever it is. Since there's nothing to lose anyway."

Anderson lifted his huge hand and clapped Morgan's arm. "Morgan," he said, "let's go tell Old Bull." And suddenly he was running—that big, shambling figure was lunging past, long arms and legs seeming to fly outward, heading more or less in the direction from which they had come. Morgan could hear his big feet pounding away in the grass and his voice calling back, "Let's go, Morgan! Let's go!"

Ordinarily there was nothing Morgan hated more than being forced into doing something foolish or undignified because some idiot had left him no choice. Even as a child he had hated dares. But that night, not knowing or understanding why, he was running too, running after Anderson. Morgan was out of shape and full of Scotch, and in the darkness he had no notion where he was going, what lay under his feet, why he was running or there at all in the star-slashed night. He ran on after Anderson's high, lunging shadow; in the damp grass his pants cuffs were quickly soaked, and once he stumbled and nearly sprawled full length, but managed to fend off the ground with one hand, regain his balance, and run on. It was exhilarating, strange, incredible; he had never known what it was to yield, let go, run free. And I'm not sure I ever have again, he thought.

That night, as he ran somewhere near the lighted porch, other lights flicked on, headlights, pointing to his right. A motor roared. He saw Anderson folded around the wheel of an old Army jeep, his long legs poking up like broken stilts on either side of the steering column.

"Jump in," he called, racing the engine. "Let's go, Morgan, let's go!"

Morgan managed to get one foot into the jeep and his rump partly on the seat; then Anderson yanked a lever, let in the clutch, and the jeep leaped ahead like a rearing horse. Morgan clung to the windshield brace and somehow hoisted the rest of himself into the seat; by that time they were bounding and bucking out of the barnyard area toward a dark loom of trees, the jeep roaring as if to wake the dead—which, in a sense, Morgan thought, proved appropriate. It jounced along a two-track road Anderson was more or less following, and Morgan had to hang on every second. Anderson let out a kind of whoop that Morgan knew to be from high spirit suddenly freed. Something rose in Morgan's own throat, unbelievably, and he was yelling too, turning loose; he threw back his head and whooped at the beckoning sky.

"Heads down!" Anderson yelled as the jeep dashed straight at a wall of trees. A startled Hereford stood a moment, transfixed by the two beams of light bearing down on him, then broke moaning off to the side of the road. There was an opening in the trees just wide enough for the road, and the jeep slewed into it, branches whipping at them from the side and above. Anderson had somehow coiled himself down behind the windshield. At undiminished speed they crossed a little brook, and a sheet of water rose from the front wheels, glittered a moment in the headlights, and sprinkled down on their heads.

As quickly as it had seized Morgan, exhilaration vanished in the slashing trees, and he was frightened. He had the impulse to jump, to separate himself from this careening madness, this driving, driven man; but the tall pine trunks reared up so closely on either side of the road that he could no longer jump, and, in any case, he knew he had to hang on, once put to the test; that was part of his creed. Morgan shut his eyes and clung grimly to the windshield and frame. Once again, somewhere far into the woods, Anderson whooped, a wild, exuberant yell that made Morgan think of an animal escaping his cage.

Then he could tell by the changed sound and the absence of clawing branches that they were out of the dark woods and covering open ground. He opened his eyes and raised his head. They were climbing another low hill like the one on which Anderson's house stood; but there was nothing on its crest, against the starlit sky, but a few old trees, round and black and massive. The jeep slowed, skidded a little going over the top of the hill, then slid to a hard-braking stop just short of one of the trees. Anderson killed the engine at once, and silence dropped like a falling wall. In the unwinking glare of the headlights there was a wrought-iron fence, a gate with an ornate metal arch above it, tombstones beyond.

"Bull!" Anderson's low-pitched voice rang out and bounced back from the dark. "I'm going to do it, Bull!"

He swung his long legs out of the jeep with amazing agility for so large a man and ran toward the gate. Morgan sat where he was, his fear gone, as with his exhilaration before it. He was not sure he wanted to follow any more, that he wanted to go on to wherever Anderson's path would lead. Anderson stopped, looking back. The headlight glare flashed brilliantly from the lenses of his glasses, and his big body suddenly seemed lean, hard, menacing.

"Morgan, come on!"

Then it seemed to Morgan that if he had come at all, followed any part of the way, he had to go on with Anderson. He swung down and went after him again, through the arched gate, between the old stones ivory in the beam of the headlights. A breeze had come up, rattling drily in the trees above. Crickets clicked and whispered, and although the grass in the graveyard had been recently mowed the dew was heavy by then; Morgan's feet swished noisily in it, and his wet cuffs were chilly against his legs. Anderson was breathing heavily, as if he was only now beginning to feel the effects of the long run through the meadow to the jeep.

"The old bastard's over here," he said.

At the far end of the graveyard, a little out of the direct glare of the headlights, a white marker rose well above the top of the guardian iron fence. Solidly set upon a heavy blocky base stood the stone figure of a man, with arms outspread as if to bless and comfort those below. The whole thing was at least ten feet high, and the looming figure itself was life-size.

"They brought in a stone for him to look at years before he was shot." Anderson stopped near the grave, and Morgan could see him adjusting his glasses, as if to make sure of what he was seeing. "He had this notion about picking out his own grave and his own marker, so they brought a big one for him to see, the kind they thought he'd like. Jesus with his arms outstretched, suffering the little children to come unto him. My mother told me Old Bull looked at it awhile and then told them he liked the shape and size of it but he didn't want any damn Jesus standing over him with a disapproving look on his face for the rest of eternity. Get that Jesus off there, he said, and put up a likeness of Bull Durham Anderson in just that same Jesus pose, and see how the bastards like that."

"Does it really look like him?"

"Not much like his pictures. I hardly remember what he looked like in the flesh. The main thing I recall is a big shock of white hair and a kind of harsh voice. And he had rough, strong hands. He'd pick me up out of bed and throw me up in the air and catch me. I remember that, all right. It would make me cry sometimes, and he'd get mad. I remember his voice when he was mad and the way his hands squeezed me. But this stone has kind of puny-looking hands. Jesus hands."

Morgan went nearer and peered at the base. The light was too dim to make out the lettering, except for the big block capitals that said BULL DURHAM ANDERSON.

" 'Eighteen sixty-nine, nineteen twenty-three. Four Times Governor. Always a Man.' He ordered that put on there too." Anderson seized Morgan's arm, pulling him half around. "That one over there," he said, pointing with a long, rigid arm toward a smaller marker on the right side of Old Bull's grave, as they stood at its foot. "That was his first wife. He was always a man, so he fucked her to death. I mean literally. She had eight miscarriages, but he kept right on knocking her up and the last time killed her."

"I don't want to hear all this," Morgan said. "This is your burying ground, not mine."

"Well, it made you angry to think he stole a few miserable dollars from your father, didn't it? And that wasn't even direct, just part of the general corruption he spread around like manure. So if that makes you mad, what do you think having Old Bull's blood did to me, Morgan? When I was thirty like you? A long time ago, maybe about then, maybe a little before, one night when I was drunker than I am now, down home on leave from the Army, I came out here on a bright moonlit night and pissed on his grave and on that statue too. Don't worry, I wouldn't do that now. Another difference in thirty and thirty-eight."

"Goddammit, then, let's go. This is none of my business."

"I'm trying to tell you it is." Anderson was speaking gently, as if to a child. He wheeled Morgan back toward Old Bull's marker; in the grip of his massive hand, in the power of his words, Morgan was seized, helpless. Except for the wind and the crickets, there was no other sound, and from beneath the trees Morgan could not have seen the stars had he looked. He felt enclosed in the night; the iron fence seemed too high and near, insurmountable; and the artificial light behind them flung queer, derisive shadows past the sprouting tombstones, as if to mark out dark places for other graves, other lives.

"Always a man," Anderson said. "That's the point of it. I can live with that. I even wish I hadn't pissed on his grave that time. It's not personal any more, because he *was* always a man. Not a superman, but a man like you and me. Every vicious thing he did, every law he broke, every man he bought and cheated and ruined, all that power he used for his own ends, the barnyard of corruption he made out of this state—just like it says on there, he was always a man. He did the things men do. He debased everything he touched. Someday I'm going to have two more words chiseled under those."

He waited, his head a little over on the side, his weak eyes intent on Morgan's. Morgan said nothing.

" 'Like You,' " Anderson said. "That's what I'm going to carve on there someday for everybody who comes here to see. 'Always a Man—Like You.' "

"Then why do you think you can change history?" Morgan said. "If he just did the things men do?"

"Because I want to chance it. I can't put back the money he stole. I don't want the kind of power he had. What I want is just not to corrupt people or cheapen anything. To show you don't have to do it. I just want to show the best in a man instead of the worst. Maybe in the long run I just want them to remember me instead of Old Bull."

"Don't you know the bastards will stomp you?" Morgan said. "They could take Old Bull but not what you're talking about." He was the one who felt older then, wiser, far more schooled in the ways of men and the great world. Anderson smiled, that slow, delighted smile that transformed his angular face, softened and sweetened it; that night it made him young and eager, and so it made him beautiful; and just as Morgan had in the meadow, under the illimitable stars, he thought fleetingly, he could not help thinking *maybe it's worth a try*.

"They won't stomp me," Anderson said. "I'm Old Bull's boy. I've got his blood."

They walked slowly back to the jeep and climbed in. Anderson sat still a moment before starting the engine. "And when I've done it to my satisfaction," he said, "I really am coming back out here and carve those other two words on there."

Morgan looked back at the dim figure of Old Bull with his arms spread. The momentary illusion was gone, and he was cold. He was glad that in the strange and ominous shadows he had not been able to see the hard stone face, to read in the marble eyes what they would do to his boy.

"The way he sounds to me," Morgan said, "he'd rather have you piss on him again."

Anderson started the engine. As it crashed in the night like thunder coming down, above the deafening snarl of the exhaust, Morgan could barely hear him shout, "I never said he wouldn't!"

The Storyteller II

When the fasten-belt sign came on, Glass was asleep across the aisle, his face quite young and blank, even with the tape like a badge of surrender on his forehead.

"Have I got time for the john?" French asked the red-haired stewardess. She nodded and pointed toward the front of the plane. French rose unsteadily and strode with purpose between the seats.

The overhead lights had been dimmed long before, and in the shadowy cabin Morgan could see the other stewardess, far up front, checking the seat belts of sleeping passengers. The redhead had followed French, briefly; then she reappeared, leaning over his seat.

"You might as well have these," she said, slipping several miniature bottles into Morgan's jacket pocket; the faint clink of glass was swallowed in the engines' steady rumble. "Just a few left of your brand. It's more trouble to pack it up, you know?"

"Thanks." Morgan looked at her tired face; she was a broad-shouldered girl, tall, who would soon run to flesh. The red hair was a little disheveled, and the automatic smile was gone. He tried hard to remember her name and fell back on one of the few small-talk openings he knew. "Where you from originally?"

It was obviously a question she had answered a thousand times, but she perched on the arm of French's seat and appeared to consider her answer. "Bowling Green," she said finally. "You know, Kentucky."

"This goddam airline." Morgan could already feel his stomach tightening for the coming landing. "Why do they make a nice Kentucky girl fake up that terrible cornpone accent?"

She smiled, and even in the near-darkness of the cabin he could see that it was not the bright, rigid grimace designed for passengers. "It's kind of fun, you know? Some people really eat it up. You and your friends getting off here, aren't you?"

"I'm happy to say."

"So are we. A different crew takes the plane on to Birmingham and Jackson."

"Hell of a place to lay over," Morgan said. "They don't even run the late show on TV."

"Well, we're always so tired anyway. And the motel's not bad. It's got a pool shaped like an ell, you know?"

"That's the best one." Morgan knew by then, remembering the butterfly fingers on his neck, that it would be a snap, if he decided he wanted to accept the opening. But Anderson was dead. It had been a long day, a long night, and tomorrow would be worse. Tomorrow he would see Kathy. In the dim light he could barely see French emerge from the toilet cubicle, far up the aisle. "Thanks for the vodka, Red."

The girl looked down at him steadily. Morgan thought she was going to touch him again. "You're not like those creeps you're with, you know?"

Morgan chuckled. "Not," he said, "in any way I'd let you notice." He was disappointed she did not touch him again.

She made room for French, who slumped heavily into the seat. "Glad to get off this clunker," he mumbled rather thickly. The redhead went away, tall and swaying.

"Damn glad." Morgan looked out the window at the lights of the city beneath him. It was a smooth approach, the rough air, the rain, having been left far behind. He dreaded the landing, not just because of his usual fear and distrust of flying, but for what awaited him. It was always hard to come back to the South; it always hurt to feel again its fatal grip, relentless as time passing; but this time it would be worse because Anderson was dead. The lights below seemed dull and listless; they had no sparkle, no leap. Along some invisible highway out from town, tiny headlights moved toylike; but in the dark and the disorientation of flight, Morgan could not tell if they were moving toward the hilltop house beneath whose spreading trees he had first known Hunt and Kathy Anderson.

It was strange coming back to the South with Anderson dead—as if one more link that had bound him had fallen away, abandoning him nearer the perilous edge of freedom. For years Morgan had felt a vague, hurt sense of having been cast off by the South; he carried the knowledge like a psychic wound that while his own life went on changing, so did the life he once had known, to which—no matter how far he had wandered—he longed in his heart to fasten himself as to a rock. He had had a right, it seemed to Morgan, to think of the old life, its manner and values, as unchanging, as the rare permanence on which every man needed to believe he could depend. But ugliness and haste, concrete and steel, plastic and neon, were overwhelming gentleness, largeness, the old sure sense of land and place; and Morgan knew, just as some men could feel a thunderstorm making up on a windless June afternoon when even pine boughs hung still and quiet, that a world was swiftly coming in which even in the South there would be no knowledge that each day was a part of the seasons turning and the sun going round, of something going on so endlessly that in the final dust it made no difference whether a man had run hard or at all or had slept in the blessed shade.

Morgan knew that world was coming; his own life had disclosed it to him; Anderson's death only made him the more certain. And whom had they to blame but themselves? For no one had fled the old life more swiftly than they, reaching, as they had, for—what? A sense of being *there,* Morgan thought, at the center of things. But more than that . . .

In the drab and dusty town of his childhood, Morgan had been a paperboy. For years, in the freezing dawns of Southern winter, as in the dewy summer mornings when even before the sun rose above the rooflines the heat of the coming day could be felt boiling up from the earth, he had expertly wheeled his rickety bicycle along the rutted streets and unpaved walks—Morgan could remember with special thankfulness the summer the WPA men laid down paved sidewalks; they had made his route much easier —no hands on the handlebars, rolling as he went the thin, ink-smelling pages into the tight missiles he could sling with either hand and unerring accuracy across the straggling lawns and the green guardian hedges—slap! —against the gray porch floors.

Morgan's route took him all around the town and to most of its houses, before school in the winter, before the long summer days of baseball and swimming and mowing neighbors' lawns and reading on the shaded porch of his father's house. On Saturday mornings Morgan made his collection rounds, meticulously entering payments and debts in the record book the newspaper provided him, and at his father's insistence handing out receipts from the book of blanks he bought at Rose's five-and-dime. Morgan was paid twenty-five cents on the dollar, so he was an assiduous collector, returning doggedly to doors that did not answer his knock, especially to

those where he had reason to believe he was being deliberately ignored—
Mrs. Ada Ingram cheated every way she could, hiding in the kitchen,
forging receipts, claiming no deliveries; Mr. and Mrs. Cotty Walker were
usually too drunk or hung-over to get out of bed on Saturday mornings; the
Widow Bowen would not come to the door if she was entertaining, as she
often did, Mr. Crocker, the high-school manual-training teacher, whose
wife was in the lunatic asylum (for no real reason, everybody said, except
to let Mr. Crocker and the Widow Bowen indulge their sordid passion
undeterred); sometimes old lady Lila Bennett, who was rich, would not
answer the door out of sheer meanness, and Morgan had known her to fling
down his money from a second-story window, so she could cackle angrily
at him while he scrambled for it in her nandina bushes; and then there was
Doctor Miller, with his sad brown eyes, who everybody knew was a dope
fiend—what unspeakable iniquities Morgan could imagine within, when
Doctor Miller's sagging old backstreet clapboard house gave back nothing
but echoes to a timid knock!

But there was never any trouble collecting from most of Morgan's customers, who knew he would ruthlessly cut off the paper—leaving them, as
like as not, stranded in the middle of a Dick Tracy adventure—if they fell
two weeks overdue. Many of them would ask him in for a glass of iced tea
or Kool-Aid in the summer, or to warm by the fireplace in winter, while
they rooted in pocketbooks or cookie jars for the payment. Morgan was as
familiar in most of the houses of the town as Amos 'n' Andy on the radio,
or Alf P. Reeves, the cheerful weekly collector for the Metropolitan Life
Insurance Company. Alf had helped Morgan by giving him detailed
briefings on certain households where it was better to do business at the
back door. Among them, Alf had advised Morgan, was that of the Claude
J. Goingses.

"That Miz Goings," Alf said, "is mighty queer folks. Not that Claude
J. ain't too. She ain't ever been known to walk through the front parlor to
the front door, I reckon for fear she might stir up dust."

So on those Saturday mornings large with the promise of twenty-five
cents on the dollar and a double feature in the afternoon, Morgan would
peddle down the Goingses' driveway, which no automobile tire had defiled
in years, lean his bike against the corner of the locked garage, which no one
had ever seen opened, and knock on the black screen door at the rear of
the house. Under oak trees, the house stood low to the ground, its clapboard
a weathered gray—a closed house, at whose windows there was not a touch
of color; by eight-thirty every night, winter and summer, it was dark and
quiet as the brooding sky, and from it at six every morning, as regularly as

sunrise itself, first light showed yellow from the kitchen panes. Six days a week, at seven-thirty—so precisely the neighbors had given up noticing—Claude J. Goings came out of the back door in neat blue overalls and set off for the coal yard where he worked, and from which at six-thirty in the evening, as if he were the sun in its inevitable rotation, he came home to the back door, begrimed, powdered with the black dust of his trade—an angular man with his lunch pail, his head slightly bent, as if he did not even wish to see those he passed, to whom he never spoke.

"I'd sooner try to talk to a fire hydrant," Alf P. Reeves would say of Claude J. Goings.

Morgan knew the door beyond the screen would open as soon as he knocked; he always wondered if in some way he could not fathom Miz Goings had watched him coming down the driveway, parking his bicycle, walking to the door; because almost instantly, through the single pane of glass in the door, he would see her staring out at him. She was tall like her husband, and as angular and silent, a plain, worn, gray woman with no expression or light in her eyes. She would be seen maybe once a week, plodding to the City Grocery, picking among its cans and meats and produce; and once more, on Sundays, at the First Baptist Church with Claude J. Goings, she in lank and shapeless black, he in shiny gunmetal gray. Otherwise no one ever saw her except at her back door—least of all Morgan. She would open it, push the screen ajar, and thrust his money—always the right amount—at him. "Morning, Miz Goings," Morgan would say, handing her the receipt he always had made out in advance; and she would nod at him, once, not looking at the receipt, not really looking, Morgan sensed, at him. Then the door would close softly, as if it had rubber edges, and she would not be standing beyond its single pane.

No one knew the Claude J. Goingses, or what Miz Goings did in the long days, the still house, or why they lived so mutely in the town. No one remembered for sure where they had come from, although there were old-timers who knew the Goings house had been the Judson place, until Buck Judson got struck by lightning while playing second base on the Rodeheaver No. 2 team in the county textile league. Buck's wife and four kids had had to go to her family in North Florida, and the Goingses had next turned up in the house.

"Durn if I know," Morgan's father had said when asked. "Maybe twenty year ago. Buck Judson never left his folks a cent." On his face, Morgan could see undimmed by two decades the utter contempt in which his father had held such men.

Morgan never lingered after Miz Goings had closed the door. He did not like the Goings house, or Miz Goings' face, or her musty smell he knew he mostly imagined. As the years went by, and the Saturday-morning ritual repeated itself as unvaryingly as Claude J. Goings' trips to and from the coal yard, the gray house under the trees began to cause Morgan a special fear —nothing Gothic, he thought in later years, after he had read "A Rose for Emily"; he had never thought even in childhood that there was anything grotesque or haunted about the Goings house. But *not that*, he would always think, peddling out of the Goings drive. *Not for me . . .*

Now, moving swiftly in the great plane down toward the Southern earth, watching the lights of his past rising relentlessly to meet him, Morgan knew well enough what he had really feared, in those moments at the Goings door, what profound aversion had been planted deep within him by that closed house, that locked garage, those removed lives. But he knew too that, in the end, the house of Claude J. Goings had been merely the dramatic symbol, the force in his mind, of the invisibility he feared above all; and that it was not so much from the symbol as from the life that somehow had shaped it that he had fled so far.

As for Anderson—Anderson had finally stopped running, stopped reaching, but it had cost him more than his life. And anyway, Morgan thought again, in the fatalism that rises from awareness of death, we had nobody to blame but ourselves.

"Bigger place than I thought." French craned to see past Morgan, at the lights below.

"Growing fast." Morgan looked across the aisle at Glass, sound asleep, untouched by Anderson's life, unmoved by Anderson's death, or anyone's. Morgan wondered if in a world in which image so easily became value and shadow could exist without substance, Anderson's death might be a sort of last rattle for truth—if, in fact, truth might not already have been cheapened out of Glass's vacuum-tube world.

The Electra's wheels touched down with a bump, the plane bounced slightly, then plowed along the runway, snorting and popping sparks. Morgan was in touch with earth again. The cabin lights came on brilliantly, while outside the engines screamed into reverse, thrusting him forward in his seat. French shook Glass awake, and they lined up in the aisle behind the few other passengers. The plane jerked to a halt, the redhead swung open the door, and a hot whiff of Southern night, tainted with exhaust fumes, impinged on the frigid cabin.

"One thing about life on the Blakey Show," Glass mumbled, shaking his hair exactly into place. "You learn to sleep anywhere."

"Bye now," the redhead was saying, like a telephone recording, as sleepy passengers stumbled past. Her brittle cheer bounced off the gloomy night outside. "Bye-bye. Hope y'all had a nice flight'n'fly with us again. Bye now." Expertly she evaded Glass's hand reaching for her bottom. "Bye now. Y'all fly with us again."

Morgan filed past her, the last man off. "Sweetie," he said, "there must be something better in Bowling Green."

She dropped the accent. "Not that I ever found."

"Go look again." Morgan went on down the steps. He turned to wave to her, but she had already disappeared into the cabin; maybe he had misread her after all, he thought, not much caring.

Across the blacktopped apron, the new glass terminal, with its slanting roof and concrete tower, its stark interior and plastic seats bolted to its chill, impervious floor, rose garishly against the night, like a small-city skyline. It was at this airport, if to an older terminal, that Morgan had come with Zeb Vance and the Tobacco Subcommittee years before, when he had first met Anderson. So it was somehow right, Morgan thought, to return on this occasion, even to see Matt Grant standing just inside the gate.

They shook hands solemnly, as befitted the moment. They saw each other often enough in Washington; yet, Morgan reflected, Anderson's death and their meeting here, far from accustomed places, made it seem as if he and Matt had not seen each other for years. He found himself studying the other's gaunt, sallow face for signs of age and change, and felt himself the object of the same scrutiny.

"Hell of a reason to come back South," Morgan mumbled.

"We'd been here a few days." Grant held his hand longer than necessary, almost as if he were comforting Morgan. "Kathy thought maybe if we got him away from Washington awhile it might help him get going again. He was really drifting, these last months, kind of aimless."

"I know. We had lunch last week."

"Then you do know."

Grant and Morgan looked at each other dumbly. They had never really talked except by semaphore and significant silence about what had happened to Anderson. Morgan knew that Grant, too, must have been thinking of the day when they had first seen him, tall and slow and compelling, turning Grant's plan for managing tobacco surpluses into an idea for feeding the world. Grant must be remembering that, as well—Morgan thought a little ironically—as so many other things.

French, standing next to them, cleared his throat. "When's the funeral? Has it been set?"

"Tomorrow at four-thirty p.m. Miz Anderson just didn't want to wait any longer."

Morgan made brief introductions. "Matt's been Anderson's administrative assistant for—how long, Matt?"

"Ever since he came to the Senate."

"Listen," French said, "can we get a taxi? I'm beat."

"Right out the main entrance there. I'd give you fellows a ride but . . ." Matt hesitated, looking at Morgan. "There's one or two things I have to talk over with Rich in private, if you don't mind. And Rich, they were paging you a minute ago." Grant looked at a pocket notebook. "Call Operator Three-two-eight, New York."

"Oh hell," Morgan said, and French looked anxious. "Where's the booth?"

It was between the flight insurance stand, closed for the night, and the ticket counter for Stonewall Jackson Air Taxi, Inc., also closed. Touch-Tone dialing had come to the South, and Morgan listened to eerie whistles and pings as he read scratched graffiti on the rear wall of the booth. *Area Code 303–687–5124 puts out.* Names were giving way to numbers all over.

Operator Three-two-eight duly delivered the calling party, who turned out to be a copy editor on the national desk in Morgan's home office. "Oh yeah, Morgan," he said. "Let me see here." Much background chatter ensued. "Uh . . . yeah, Morgan, nothing much." They were always casual, bland, Morgan thought, while they tore a man's work apart. "You say here in the second add, third graf, 'the choice of Mr. Hinman was the most surprising of the President's several surprise choices for high office.' They want to know who says it was the most." No one person ever wanted to know anything in Morgan's home office; inquiries always came from unseen, unnamed higher powers, of menacing portent—"they." He imagined "them," grave, gray, passionless, gathered in the board room.

"Well, Jee-sus Christ," Morgan said automatically, just to register. "You mean those pricks want a source for *that?*"

"Well, not a source exactly, just some authority."

"Tell them it's my authority then."

"Uh . . . well . . . would you maybe mind . . . suppose we could just say *'Observers thought* the choice of Mr. Hinman was' et cetera et cetera and so on?"

"I don't know if any goddam observers did. I only know *I* thought it was."

"Uh . . . yeah." The voice was beginning to sound anxious, as if a crisis suddenly were recognizable where none had been expected.

Morgan knew "they" would never accept his argument, impeccable as it was, or they would never have raised the question, mindless as it was. They were not passionless, Olympian, at all. They were tired men in shirtsleeves with ulcers and authority. Once they had acted, they saw no alternative but to carry their point; authority never did. In any case, it was not the hapless copy editor's fault.

"Oh hell," Morgan said, "just make it read 'the choice of Mr. Hinman was *considered* the most' blah blah blah. That'll fix it."

"Yeah, great, great." The copy editor was relieved to be out of the middle; he knew, as Morgan did, the meaningless change would be acceptable. It met the meaningless requirement.

While he had the booth Morgan called his house in Washington. "How was bridge?" he asked when Anne answered.

"Won three dollars. Where are you?" Her voice was thick with alcohol and sleep.

He told her. "Is everything all right? Richie all right?"

"Asleep. We're both asleep."

He pictured her in bed, cool in the air-conditioning; she never wore anything sexy and transparent in bed, but suddenly the notion of her lying there, the darkness of the room, the cool flowing air, the imagined scent of her, excited him. He thought of her small hard breasts, and how, long ago, before Richie, she had once put lipstick on them for him. "Listen," he whispered fiercely to the mouthpiece, "I wish I was there."

"Good," she mumbled. "'S nice."

"Do you know what I'd do if I were there?"

"Oh God," Anne said. "Don't mention it."

It was an echo of words he had heard a hundred times. A thousand times. "Forget it," Morgan said. "Go on back to sleep." Maybe she didn't mean to hurt him. Maybe she didn't, every time she did it. They chatted on a minute before he hung up with a cool good-by. He should have known better, he thought. Why did he keep on doing things like that?

Charlie French was hovering at the door of the booth as Morgan came out. "Just a minor fix," Morgan said. "Relax, Charlie."

Grant left them at the outdoor baggage claim, under a cantilevered steel shed thrusting from the terminal proper, and went in search of a taxi; Morgan knew Grant's Southern instincts had been distressed by his polite refusal to drive French and Glass to the motel. They waited in silence until the baggage arrived.

Grant reappeared, followed by a taxi. "Take these fellows right to the

Bright Leaf," Grant said. He turned to French and Glass. "Sorry again but . . ."

"No problem," Glass said, "One thing, though, my crew's coming in in the morning and I want to lay out the day for them. What's your TV arrangement?"

"Well, we hadn't really thought . . ."

"They'll be all over the place," Morgan said. "From the state capital anyway, and if Blakey's people sent in Glass here there may be more from the other nets too."

"I'm sure Kathy doesn't want TV."

"She probably won't have any choice, Matt. You know they don't give anybody any choice. You better get James in here right away." Ralph James had passed in recent years for Anderson's press secretary, although he had had little to do lately, and did that badly.

"He's here already."

"You call Ralph James first thing in the morning," Morgan said to Glass. "And, Matt, you better warn Kathy."

They stood a moment on the curb, under the baggage shed, looking after the taxi. "TV," Grant said. "Somehow I just never thought I'd be setting up TV for his funeral."

"Neither did he," Morgan said. "That was part of the trouble."

Grant led the way to his parked car. They drove off silently, two old acquaintances under the constraints of death, their whole relationship necessarily in a subtle new context, now that part of the old context was gone, now that Anderson was dead. Morgan thought, suddenly, that the Andersons had been the only real link he and Grant had had to each other; and he wondered if, now, there could be another or if they would find themselves set loose from something that had not been personal anyway.

Grant pointed to the scaffolding and masonry rising in the darkness to their right. "New airport motel." He turned onto the highway. It was three lanes, the third having been added to the side. "So traffic is going up for the new terminal, and it'll go up more for the new motel when it's finished, and finally we'll have to four-lane this death-trap. Nothing ever seems to get finished."

Except a man's life? Morgan wondered. And even that went on affecting people.

Years before, when he and Zeb Vance and Matt and the Tobacco Subcommittee had driven in from the airport, there had been open fields, gradually giving way to suburban litter, along this road, then only two lanes wide. He had been along the route many times since but had never really noticed the extent to which the cracked concrete with its asphalt apron on one side now ran between endless belts of service stations, restaurants, cheap motels, shopping areas of all sorts—laundries, banks, variety stores, bowling alleys, skating rinks, remnant stores, groceterias, auto supplies. Every few hundred feet there was a used-car lot, garishly lit, its strings of bare bulbs mercilessly exposing the tinny monsters crouched on the graveled or blacktopped earth; these days, too, there were frequent "mobile home" lots.

"I wouldn't mind things changing so much," Morgan said after a while, "if they didn't get uglier all the time. Do you realize what we've done to this continent, Matt? Do you realize what we had here and what we've done to it? Look at that goddam incredible neon monstrosity over that dinky little ice-cream stand! All that red and green and winking on and off and higher than a pine tree and for what? For an ice-cream stand that isn't even open and to make people buy something they don't even need."

"What I wanted—" Grant started to say.

"And the worst of it is," Morgan went on, consciously putting off whatever was to be said, "nobody needs a single one of those hundreds of stands like that all over the country, and those ridiculous signs don't serve anything remotely resembling a real purpose. They're just made up and stuck in the ground, like so many damned toadstools, just as parasitic and twice as ugly. And we tolerate it."

"Hell," Grant said, "we encourage it. Rich, did Hunt know about Kathy and me, all those years ago?"

Christ, Morgan thought. Worse than I figured. "These recent years, Matt, I don't much think he would have cared if he did know."

"These recent years there hasn't been anything for him to know. I didn't think I had to tell you that."

Now why did he think he didn't have to tell me that? Morgan thought. "As for what Hunt might or might not have known before, he never talked much to me about Kathy." It was not much of a lie, Morgan told himself; it was, in fact, literally the truth that Anderson "never talked much" about Kathy. "Hell, you and I never really talked about it before this."

"I think he knew, Rich. He never talked to me about it either, but I think he knew. But whether he did or not, I know he knew I worked for him because I believed in him and admired him. I *know* that, Rich." He braked to a stop at a traffic light. "Don't you think I'm right?"

You poor son-of-a-bitch, Morgan thought. How do you or I know what Hunt Anderson thought about either of us? Or Kathy? All you want is somebody to tell you it's all right, that you didn't hurt him. And maybe you didn't. How do we know that either? How are we ever going to know anything about him now?

The red light turned green, and Grant drove on. An enormous truck thundered out of the night toward them; loud as the Electra, it brushed past them contemptuously, and Morgan felt Grant's car sucked toward it, toward destruction. In the night, the exhaust pipe over the truck cab spewed sparks high into the air, and the earth shook beneath monstrous wheels that cared nothing for life. They sped on.

"You must not think so," Grant said. "You're not saying anything."

"No, that's not it." Morgan had never before heard anything like emotion in Grant's voice. Grant's normal attitude of quiet capability had given way to a nervous search for reassurance that was somehow touching. With some surprise, Morgan discovered that he had always thought of Matt Grant as needing no help. But Morgan had discovered to his sorrow that everyone needed help, sooner or later. And what had Grant done anyway? If anyone had been guilty, wasn't it Kathy, who had known what she was doing, and done it only as long as it suited her? "I was just trying to think of what to say. Hunt thought a hell of a lot of you. He thought you were his good right arm, I heard him say so a hundred times. He thought you were indispensable to him, and you were, right from the start. I'd say—you know you could use the word talking about Hunt—I'd say he loved you. Now whatever he might have known about what you're talking about, I never saw anything to make me think it made a difference in what he thought of you. So why don't you stop worrying about it?"

"Because I betrayed him." Grant's voice broke. "You know it and I know it and Kathy knows it, and I reckon it must have been a miracle if he didn't know it. That's why I can't stop worrying about it."

"That's a big word," Morgan said. "That's a lousy word. The whole fucking world betrayed him, for that matter. Maybe he even betrayed himself. How do you count who betrays who? What makes it so important whether you did?"

"Because it *is* important to me."

Morgan thought of his father, suddenly, and recognized with a hard, tight smile in the darkness of the car that it was the talk of betrayal that had reminded him; he had never got over the uneasy feeling that he was not what his father would have wished—that he was not honest enough, much less virtuous. He never thought easily of the proud, harsh Puritan who had dominated so many of his years; and sometimes in the early morning, when he could not sleep, it would seem to him that he could hear his father moving about the house, as he so often had roamed in the grim dawn hours of Morgan's childhood.

"And I guess I have to confess," Matt said, "I wouldn't want you or Kathy to think of me as a hypocrite."

"I don't think that, and I doubt she does."

"Because you see . . ." Grant hesitated, then spoke with an edge of excitement in his voice. "I've made up my mind to go for Hunt's seat."

"Well," Morgan said, maintaining professional equanimity.

"I just took the bull by the horns," Matt said. "Maybe it'll seem callous to you, but I called the Governor tonight."

"Moving fast, aren't you?"

"But so will everybody else. The Governor may even want it himself, but I think I made him a couple of good points, and he seemed to listen."

"You certainly know more about the office and the problems than anybody else could. You even hired most of the staff."

"That was the first point I made to him." In the light from the dash Morgan could see eager animation in Grant's usually calm face, and he was speaking a little more loudly than usual. "The second point, I told him I hadn't been political, and he said he knew that. It means he could claim not to be making a political appointment, you see, just putting in a man who knows the job better than anybody, knows Washington. Then when the special election comes up next year, if I hadn't locked it up for myself by then, it'd be my own fault."

"But maybe he wants to make a political appointment. It's a political job."

"Well, I'll tell you one thing." Matt's voice was suddenly snappish. "I deserve the appointment, you'll have to admit that, Rich. I've worked all these years for Hunt Anderson, practically ran the whole show by myself. And I never asked for a thing for myself, you know that. Some people might think it's pushy to move so soon, and maybe some people think I was just Hunt's water boy, but—"

"Nobody thinks that, Matt."

"Well, I've been treated that way sometimes, but I don't care what people think. I deserve that appointment and I'm going to do everything I can to get it." Matt drove on. Morgan had seldom heard such vehemence from him. "I don't think Kathy thinks much of the idea, but too bad. I've sacrificed a lot of my life for her too, the way I did for Hunt, and now I think it's my turn."

"Well, I hope it works out for you."

"That was the other thing I wanted to talk about." Matt drove awhile in silence, then words burst suddenly from him. "You could help, I hate to ask you, but you're so well known down here, they're proud of you even when they don't agree. If you put in a word for me with the Governor, he'd—"

"I'm sorry." Morgan hated saying no even when he did not want to do what he had been asked. He always feared it would make him seem harsh and uncaring, that others would not see how generous and understanding he really was. "I'd love to see you in there, but I can't play that kind of politics, Matt, even if I thought it was right. They'd can me quicker for that than anything else, and they ought to."

"I thought you'd feel that way but I just took a chance. I thought it'd be all right if I asked."

Morgan saw that, as usual, he had not needed to apologize—a lesson he learned often, and as often forgot. Grant was, in fact more anxious than he was to make amends for what Grant saw as his own importunity.

"And that's why I started out about Kathy the way I did," Grant went on. "I didn't want to sound hypocritical to you."

"Last thing on my mind," Morgan said, pleased to give absolution. Nothing made him feel better than his own generosity.

"I understand your position, Rich, I really do. I know you newspaper guys have your own kind of ethics, although sometimes, I don't mind telling you, they're kind of hard for me to follow. And the one thing I really want you to know, whether I get the seat or not—and I'm going for it, I'm calling everybody I know—I was for Hunt all those years, not for Kathy. Maybe I betrayed him a long time ago, maybe there was something there shouldn't have been with her for a little while, but in the long run it was Hunt I believed in and worked for and tried to help."

"What I think," Morgan said, "is that everybody betrays everybody, because in the end everybody does what they think they have to do."

"That's a good try, that would help a lot to think, but I can't let myself off that easy, Rich." Grant's voice was calmer, as if having nerved himself to a distasteful task he had come back with a kind of relief to his usual self. "I can't forgive myself that way."

"Well, if Hunt did know," Morgan said, "he would have."

The Bright Leaf Motel was located at an intersection of the airport road and an interstate highway, a giant concrete river that slashed through part of the city, dividing one third of it from the rest, splitting its nature and personality. Around each of the connecting tunnels and bridges that spanned the highway river, new clusters of expressway business had sprung up like weeds. All were linked to mobility and speed—glittering service stations, chain restaurants with uniform national food, automobile dealerships and repair shops, prefabricated glass-and-plastic motels.

Grant had a room at the Bright Leaf too, and the two men entered the lobby just as French and Glass were disappearing down a corridor that led to a wing of guest rooms. Morgan signed in with the blue-haired desk clerk, somebody's widow who was at once, he saw, house mother and house detective. He asked if the restaurant were still open, and in a voice suggesting that decent people were already in bed she said that it was.

"I'm going to turn in," Grant said. "I could talk all night, Rich, but it's been rough here today."

"Glad it was you and not me." Then he realized that neither of them had mentioned Kathy, at least not as part of Hunt Anderson's death. "How's she taking it, Matt?"

Grant shrugged. "It's obvious it's a relief. But then, of course, it's a shock too. As for whether or not . . ." He broke off abruptly. "Kathy was always tough as hell. She's made all the arrangements, just as efficient as a secretary."

"His wife is a better man than he is," Morgan said, and they both laughed. It was an old political joke against Anderson, circulated at a time when Kathy had been most active politically and when opponents were trying to picture Anderson as soft on everything from Communism to currency. "I always thought Dunn started that one. I forgot to tell you he called me tonight. He'll be here tomorrow if he can get here."

"Hypocritical bastard," Grant said.

"Oh, Dunn always had a kind of funny thing about Hunt."

"Well, if you call it funny to put the knife in somebody's back. There's a congressional delegation coming in too."

"There's your real hypocrites. They all knew what Hunt was, and they still turned their backs on him until too late."

Grant nodded. "Enough blame to go around, I reckon. Are you expecting Zeb Vance?"

"Don't ask me. I haven't seen him for years." As Grant surely knew, Morgan thought. But in the best of people there were strange, flashing streaks of cruelty, or perhaps just the desire to set others on their own plane. Morgan knew he was himself no exception, so he took no offense.

"Kathy wants you to come out as soon as you can," Grant said without expression. "She especially wanted you to know that."

"Right."

Morgan headed for the restaurant just as the airline party entered the lobby, the two pilots following the redhead and the other stewardess. The redhead smiled at Morgan, eagerly, immediately, and at once he made up his mind. He went across the lobby, and the tall redhead, still smiling, watched him coming with obvious satisfaction. To Morgan's surprise, the pilots and the other girl paid them no attention.

"I'll buy you a cup of coffee," Morgan said, as always a little sheepish on the approach.

"And some bacon and eggs?"

He nodded.

"Sign me in, Carol," she called to the other girl, and as if to the blue-haired desk lady, "I won't be long."

"The hell you won't," Morgan said, deciding at once to establish the point. He had never deluded himself that he was merely a neglected husband, if he was that at all; he loved women, their company, their attentions, their laughter, their clothes, the touch of their skin, the beauty of their hands, the softness of their bodies, and he actively sought their affections, drawing the line, he told himself, at deception. He had little tolerance for flirtation or dalliance; he had too strong a need to know his own worth, which could understandably be accepted or denied by a woman, according to her tastes, but which he could not let be placed for long in question. Feeling so, he refused to practice the male variety of sexual trickery—or, again, so he told himself.

"It's just for Carol's sake," the redhead said. "She'd be embarrassed in front of that old bitch, you know? If I didn't say something to take her off the hook."

Morgan decided that she was as direct about sex as he believed he was, which pleased him. They went across the chilly air-conditioned lobby with its slippery tile floors, its waxen artificial ferns, its chrome and leatherette fixtures. The most warm and colorful spot in the room was a wallrack of folders for other motels, other pools.

"Sweeta-pah," Morgan said, "they's jes' one li'l one thing Ah got to say. Iffen Ah heah so much as one li'l ole word of that theah big ole Suth'n acksent, Ah'm gone whup yuh sweet ice. Heah naow?"

Laughing, they went into the restaurant, where music came in loud and clear from undisclosed sources, heavy on violins. The waitresses wore fairly conservative imitations of Bunny costumes, with black tights. A few scattered people were eating or just sitting in the darker areas, and Morgan saw, with the start the sight never failed to give him in the South, a well-dressed black couple eating a few feet away from two white men.

A bored maître d' with sideburns found them a table, then went back to his own dinner. A pseudo-Bunny sullenly denied that breakfast was being served. Popping gum, she took an order for setups and cheeseburgers.

"That's one thing I'm glad about being a stewardi," the redhead said, watching most of the waitress's bottom wobble away. "We don't have to wear anything like that, you know?"

She moved comfortably on the seat beside him and settled her long, heavy leg warmly against his. Getting her head a little closer than before, she looked up at him with large painted eyes. "Hello there," she said softly.

Oh, for Christ's sake, Morgan thought and pushed away the electric candle that was burning before them in a fake kerosene lamp chimney. Suddenly he did not want to be seen, even by people who did not know him. He thought of walking away, just walking away. That was prevented when the pseudo-Bunny came back with remarkable speed, bearing glasses, ice, ginger ale, the inevitable limp Southern setup lemon, and water. Morgan took two of the vodka miniatures from his pocket and made drinks, going light on the redhead's ginger ale.

"Skoal," the redhead said. "To us."

"Yeah, right, right," Morgan said, shuddering. He wished her perfume was more subtle.

"Mmmm, strong. You know, funny thing—I mean me a stewardi and all, I've only been drinking since last spring."

"Not continuously, I hope."

"No, silly, you know. I mean I just somehow never took it up, not that I thought it was wrong morally or anything, I just didn't want to, you know? Until this one night in Mobile, this pilot, I don't mean he forced me to or anything, but this drink he fixed for me, it was so good. It had pineapple, you know? I got high as a kite."

"I understand," Morgan said confidentially, guiding the conversation through this opening to the main matter, "from my friend French that stewardesses usually save it for the pilots."

"Save what?"

"French didn't say."

"Is he the one with the tape?"

"You don't think I'd call *him* a friend."

"Real grabby," the redhead said. "Some stewardi maybe, and some pilots *maybe,* but not these old creeps on this shitty airline. They swing like your grandfather or somebody, you know? But you know what attracted me to you right away? I mean, you know, seriously and all."

"It couldn't have been the company I was keeping."

"I'll say. It was the way when they were teasing me, you know, about my bosoms, you wouldn't."

Morgan began to doubt that he could go through with it. "Honey," he said, "how old are you? I mean, you know, seriously and all."

"Old enough. Twenty-four."

Old enough, he thought, tired, depressed, feeling every day of the two decades longer he had lived than she had. What was he doing there, in that ridiculous place, with this banal child, exchanging these empty words? But he knew quite clearly and bleakly what he was doing. It probably was true that, this particular night, he wanted to bury some of his hurt and grief and failure in what she offered him, no doubt in the fatuous belief that by some human miracle he out of all the crowd really cared about it, and thus about her. But that was merely true. The deeper case was that like a dog with a bitch he was reaching for something, blindly, mindlessly, that he could not even define, did not even want so much as he merely had to have it.

"What you were talking about on the flight. You here for some kind of funeral or something?"

"Senator Hunt Anderson died today. He lived near here."

"Never heard of him. I hate funerals, you know? So sad and all."

"I hate funerals too," Morgan said. "I hate weddings, births, graduations, bar mitzvahs, lynchings, and Christmas. So sad and all."

She pouted, but her lips were too sensuous and full for the gesture. "You're making fun of me." She moved her leg away.

Since making fun of her was exactly what Morgan had been doing, her remark shamed and therefore angered him. "Put your goddam leg back," he said, and she obediently put it against his again. "I wasn't making fun. I really do hate lynchings."

"And *Christ*mas?"

"The fact of the matter is," Morgan said, "I hate practically everything but screwing. Why doesn't she bring those cheeseburgers?"

"Oh my," the redhead said. "Such language. I believe he's impatient." He felt her breast full and warm against his arm. "I told you I was old enough." It might have been her hand that touched the inside of his thigh, and was gone. "I meant old enough to make it worth waiting for."

Morgan loved explicit sex talk with a woman as much as he hated it with men. "Make what worth waiting for? You've got a specialty?"

He got no answer because at that moment Glass made his way through the semi-darkness to their table. "Swingin' scene," he said with theatrically curled lip. He pulled up a Spanish antique chair. "Can a man get a drink in old Dixie?"

Morgan took another vodka miniature from his pocket. "Only from me." He set it in front of Glass, who examined it, then smiled knowingly at the redhead. He pushed the lamp chimney to light up their faces.

"I'm breaking something up." But Glass made no move to leave.

"Don't flatter yourself." The redhead flounced in her seat, which was not easy, and Morgan could tell she was pleased with her swift rejoinder.

Morgan was not particularly upset that Glass had broken up anything; in the first place, he had not necessarily done so as yet, and in the second, Morgan rather hoped he had. It would solve things neatly to have the choice of lust or dignity taken out of his hands by circumstance. But Morgan *was* upset that Glass *thought* he had broken up something, and therefore might think Rich Morgan chased airline stewardesses. He watched Glass's sharp eyes glitter and turn from one to the other of them as he poured vodka over ice and flooded it with ginger ale.

"Couldn't let these go to waste." Morgan put the last two miniatures on the table. "Not after Red here stole them for us."

"I didn't steal them exactly. It was sort of like public relations, you know? I've got some more in my pocketbook."

"You chose the right man." Glass winked at Morgan, the tape going up and down on his forehead. "You know this guy is the biggest thing in the business, don't you?"

"What business?" The redhead suddenly was all sooty eyes and breathlessly parted lips.

"The media."

"Oh shit." Morgan was old enough to use four-letter words sparingly, if at all, before women. This time it had been unpremeditated. "I work for a newspaper and he's in TV."

"TV," the redhead said breathlessly. "A producer?"

"Not exactly," Glass said. "Speaking of TV, Rich, what I came down for wasn't to break anything up—"

"You didn't."

"—but I was on the horn to the producer and mentioned you were here, and naturally they want to know if you'd give us maybe a minute or two on film tomorrow about Anderson."

"I don't do TV."

"Well, I mean since you were such friends and knew his background so intimately."

"That's why I don't do TV," Morgan said. "Not about my friends."

"You can put me on TV any time," the redhead said.

"Topless you might be a smash."

"Even topless would beat that shitty old Electra."

The pseudo-Bunny brought the cheeseburgers, and Glass ordered one too, settling in. He watched them while they ate.

"Maybe you could just talk about the little things, the human side. I mean, like you said, I never got to know him."

Morgan set his glass down carefully. "Look, Glass, Hunt Anderson was a good friend of mine, not just some politician I wrote about. I'm not about to go on TV and talk about him and tell a lot of 'little things,' as you put it. Little things are the big things."

"If he doesn't want to, you can't make him, can you?" The redhead was noticeably friendlier to Glass since his television connections had been disclosed. "Me, I'd love to go on TV."

"Everybody would love to go on TV. Everybody but Rich Morgan. He's different."

Morgan looked at the hard, eager glitter of Glass's eyes, saw the nervous movements of Glass's soft hands, and knew that he was not so different. "Oh, I've done my TV," he said. "Over the years."

"I don't think I ever caught any of your stuff," Glass said, professionally patronizing.

And Anderson, Morgan thought. Had not Anderson reached out too, for what everyone wanted—one moment in the lights, when all would see, all would cry out in recognition? And when the moment was in reach, had even Hunt Anderson sacrificed everything to it? Morgan knew he didn't know, but maybe Glass did; maybe Glass knew things like that instinctively. Maybe Glass was one of those people with a sixth sense for winners and losers.

As if sensing Morgan's stare, Glass looked at him over the rim of his glass, the tape rising inquisitively on his forehead.

"I'll bet you read Myrtle Bell's gossip column, don't you?" Morgan said.

"I can't start the day if I don't."

"I thought not," Morgan said. "I figured you couldn't."

Old Bull's Boy II

Myrtle Bell too had an instinct for winners and losers, which was what had brought her to Morgan's mind. Say Myrtle had a typical little item about some distraught hostess whose dinner party had almost been spoiled by the late arrival of the guest of honor. No educated Myrtle Bell reader would put that guest down for mere bad manners. He had to work late, which meant he was big, because that was a difference between government and business—the big pricks worked late in government; and it meant he was on the come too, because he'd been noticed by Myrtle Bell; which, in turn, meant he probably had some spin on the ball, enough to know which hostess was on top of Myrtle's source list that season or that month.

That was something in itself, because it was not all that easy to keep posted on the way Myrtle's pigeons came and went. So he was a big one and he knew the moves. You might as well open a file on him, Morgan thought, if he was also youngish and presentable and in one of the stylish agencies. The White House was best, of course, and the CIA, but State and Defense were all right, and Justice was still in there; you could do worse than Treasury too—for instance, Agriculture or FTC or, God forbid, the VA.

You had to say for Myrtle that she had absolute pitch for a guy like that. She could pick up the kind of notes he sounded and hear them the least bit flat or sharp in the middle of the Marine Band playing "Hail to the Chief" outdoors on a windy day. Of course she had to, because any night in Washington, in any year and in any administration, at maybe one round dozen black-tie affairs from Constitution Hall to Thirty-fifth Street in

Georgetown—not to mention the Virginia suburbs and Montgomery County, out beyond the smell of the ghetto—there would be maybe twenty such smart-ass tacticians on the prowl.

There would surely be a deputy assistant from State carrying one of those electronic beepers under his cummerbund so that it could signal him by prearrangement in the middle of the rare beef filet from Ridgewell's, and his hostess wouldn't mind at all when he had to take the call upstairs, particularly since he had had her figured from the start for a Myrtle Bell tipster.

Or before the action at the Waltz there might be a high-interest-rate type who would let it drop that he couldn't stay late, he was off to Zurich in the morning to see the gnomes. He'd love to say what it was all about, but, frankly, it's like that delicious story about the international monetary system, the only people who understand it are an obscure GS-12 in Treasury and an ancient "clark" in the Bank of England, and they disagree. And whether or not that turned up in Myrtle's column, under her occasional heading "Capital Cracks," attributed to High Interest Rates on the eve of his trip to Zurich, depended largely on whether he had accepted the right invitation and whether he had known just whom he was talking to at the table.

The most renowned off-tackle smash of recent years had been executed brilliantly by a certain national-security speedster with granny glasses, who had caused a gap at a subcabinet dinner table by rushing away during martinis, audibly explaining that he had left a top-secret folder out of the safe. Everybody read about that one, naturally, in Myrtle; because in every way that particular ace had become one of the hottest pilots Washington had had around since the Roosevelt administration, and through all those stunting black-tied men-to-watch and all those catered-affair hostesses on the morning telephone circuit from Wesley Heights through Spring Valley to Georgetown (with occasional side calls to the horsey types in McLean), Myrtle Bell could sift her way as unerringly as the FBI fingerprint machine and come up as precisely with the exact whorls and patterns of behavior she looked for.

But Myrtle was tuned in on another band too, Morgan conceded to himself; Myrtle was an intelligent, cynical old broad who had made it flat on her back during the court-packing fight, when a certain amorous senator had nightly filled her in on the latest inside details. She had got the message early that human performance is intricately and intrinsically linked, like one sweaty body with another, to the copulative instinct.

As if she were a scout for a baseball team, Myrtle was always beating the bushes for new talent, and what Myrtle looked for first of all, she had once told Morgan, one pro to another, after too much champagne at an embassy ball of such unrivaled boredom that even Myrtle's sharp little purple-lidded marmot's eyes were glazed with alcohol and stupefaction—what Myrtle looked for first was the swing of a pretty woman's hips when she left a room full of men, and the predatory male flash in the eyes that inevitably followed —some eyes anyway. "Absolute rule," Myrtle had mumbled boozily through the considerable distance by which her cantilevered front separated them as they stumbled among throngs of bouncing drunks foxtrotting to some reedy offshoot of Meyer Davis. "Absolute rule. Any politician that can't get it up is a clunk all around."

This revelation had been offered to Morgan years after a particular Myrtle Bell column in which he had been interested to discover that she had located a new pair of interesting rookies. He had been a virtually unknown young reporter in Washington, and Hunt Anderson had been in the Senate only a little over a year. That morning, in her overblown style, Myrtle was telling her readers:

> To the harassed committee of the Capital Marching Society, the stunning Mrs. Hunt Anderson presented a delicate last-minute problem the other night before the CMS dinner-dance. Her husband, one of the serious new breed of hard-working younger men in the Senate, was off suddenly to a fill-in speech for an older colleague, who lay ill. Could Mrs. Anderson, a leggy brunette whose figure makes most Senate wives weep in frustration, be escorted by the Senator's bachelor AA? The committee could find no rule against AAs, and the two danced away the evening with the other CMSers, casting no pall at all on the customary gaiety of that renowned group.

That had been well down Myrtle's column, Morgan remembered, but the significant thing was that it was in the column at all, conspicuous by its very nonentity among the more widely recognizable events and persons that surrounded it. There could be three explanations, the first of which—that Myrtle was doing or paying off a favor, which was of the essence of her art —Morgan had dismissed over the boiled eggs Anne had cooked too long, as usual; the Andersons had been in town too short a time to move any goods at that sophisticated level.

Or Myrtle in her insatiable appetite for names could have spotted Hunt Anderson as a winner. Morgan at first leaned toward, but finally rejected, this second possibility; on the trolley going past the White House toward the Capitol, he decided that Hunt Anderson, while he no doubt had his own tactics, was not really of the Myrtle Bell school of talent. Besides, Morgan was reasonably certain that if Myrtle had merely been putting her early stamp of approval on a promising new boy, she surely would have found or manufactured an item casting him in her favored role of a hot rookie reaching for the first string, rather than as a grubbing substitute for some sick old windbag.

Instead, Kathy Anderson had presented an already harassed committee "a delicate problem." Senate wives, most of whom would not yet have noticed Kathy Anderson, would notice from then on, Morgan decided, and the next sound anyone would hear from that direction, if not weeping and wailing, would be at least the gnashing of teeth.

All of which, by the time Morgan got off the trolley on Independence Avenue in front of the old Nicholas Longworth office building, recommended to him the third possibility—that Myrtle Bell in her infinite wisdom and her vigilant watch on rumps' progress had seen not Hunt but Kathy Anderson as the kind of new talent Myrtle always liked to boost along toward stardom, the better to claim the credit for the fruits of success.

But it had been none of his business at the time, not directly. Not long after Zeb Vance McLaren had decided not to run for re-election, opening the way for Hunt Anderson to run for his Senate seat rather than for governor, Morgan had got his big break too—if that's what it was, he thought, pouring vodka. He had left the *Capital Times* to cover Congress and politics for the big-city newspaper he still worked for, and that meant that the senators and representatives from his state became just faces in the congressional crowd, and not very important ones at that.

So Morgan had not paid much attention to Hunt Anderson in Hunt's first year in Washington; he had been too busy settling into his own new life. He had gone by the cramped office they'd given Anderson in the old Senate Office Building, just to say hello, and he had spoken to Anderson a few times off the floor and at parties and other casual meetings, and he knew Matt Grant was running Anderson's staff, but a new senator from the South seldom figured in the assignments Morgan worked on or coveted. So far as he knew, Hunt Anderson was buried in the usual concerns of a freshman in the Senate—finding his way in that peculiar institution, meeting the insatiable demands of a parochial constitutency; if he was able to devote any time to the problems of the larger world, neither Morgan nor anyone else had been able to detect it. He had certainly not been able to do anything more with Matt Grant's acreage-poundage tobacco bill than Zeb Vance had.

Myrtle Bell's bitchy item, cryptic as it seemed, was the first thing about the Andersons' life in Washington that had roused in Morgan any interest at all, and it had set him thinking of Kathy Anderson, not Hunt, just as it was meant to do.

Still, that morning, with the paper folded under his arm, he had decided to walk across the great East Plaza of the Capitol to the old Senate Office Building, the green roof of which could be glimpsed through the trees along Constitution Avenue. Someday, he had explained to himself, Hunt Anderson as a progressive Southerner might make a good political source, so there was no sense in not developing the acquaintance.

They had been building the new East Front of the Capitol in those days, making it the kind of cheap fake we like best in this country, Morgan thought, like manufactured antiques or ranch-style houses or the kind of brittle new skin that's called a "model change" on last year's or last decade's automobile. But even with the scaffolding up and an endless brigade of cement-mixer trucks roaring through the East Plaza, which had itself been turned mostly into a parking lot—even though he was by then something of a blasé veteran in Washington—Morgan loved the place, loved the familiar graceful length of the Capitol with its dome and the Goddess of Justice standing pure against the sky, out of reach; he felt comfortable with the old bronze lampposts, left by some miracle from the carriage era and topped by old-fashioned milky globes; and it somehow reassured him to see, beyond the lawns and trees and the iron grillwork benches, the Greek Revival portico of the Supreme Court, the dirty old stone pile of the Library of Congress.

In front of the central section of the Capitol itself, over which the flag waved, he could look past brick pillars down the tree-shaded vista of East Capitol Street, the same view that presidents had had on Inauguration Days, before they started blocking it with a tower for television. Morgan never crossed that Plaza, then or later, not after all his years in Washington, even with the cars and tourists swarming over it like beetles and the false front rising past the three great flights of stone steps, without a certain romantic excitement, a sense that here was where Lincoln sought to bind up a nation's wounds and Roosevelt dared fear itself and the Bonus Army marched to its sad, harsh fate. It seemed to him that a great deal of what Americans were had been both praised and shaped in that place, and sometimes it seemed he could hear it all—everything that had happened there had happened to Morgan.

It had been beautiful too, he remembered of that spring day—beautiful and ominous the way spring sometimes is in Washington, with its trees and parks paying spurious tribute to nature from the feet of the huge white rooted buildings and the monuments looking permanent on the earth. Morgan believed that spring, blooming matchlessly green in Washington, brought there as nowhere else its recurring, ignored reminder that something existed, something "flawless as truth and harsh as justice" functioned and repeated in nature, and had since long before man with his tools and his machines and his sciences began to shape and soften and restain everything, began to make the whole world fit his needs as he in his tiny genius saw them. In the process man had diminished that world's natural given value to something approximating the value of man himself, which was given too, but ephemeral. So Morgan believed that spring in Washington, in its sad, magnificent blossoming, gave warning of the ugly truth that, not content with defiling the East Front, which after all was only man's work to begin with, man was hacking at the earth itself, debasing even the nature that spawned it, in the ultimate act of destruction but one, which would be man's own, the final solution to be devised by his demonic instinct—and a fitting irony too, since man loved nothing more than himself.

Glass was droning on in interminable monologue about the daily iniquities perpetrated by the unspeakable Blakey. The redhead moved her fingers on Morgan's leg, murmuring past moist lips dark in the electric-candle glow, "You're not talking any more. And I love the way you talk. So confident and all."

Morgan thought, yes, yes, but what does talk matter? Talk was the surface of a story, not the story itself, which might be something else entirely. Even the smell and the taste of a thing or a moment could delude a man who remembered them, or thought he did, or remembered them the way they should have been rather than as they had been—just as, in that moment with Glass and the redhead, Morgan could remember the long-ago day in the East Plaza as of a particular sunny brilliance, as if it were every spring in his memory, or as if it were one of those days that marked something so unforgettable or so important in his life that it took on a special tone and an artist's quality of light; but in fact he did remember that nothing special had happened. You couldn't trust memory any more than life, you had to check it all the time, but it was all a storyteller had to work with, and it would do if you watched it, rationed it, fed it sensibly with imagination.

"Sorry," Morgan said. "Sometimes I just feel talked out."

Hunt Anderson had not been in his office that day. A receptionist, in one of those Southern drawls that blondes can make interminable, told Morgan he was somewhere out West, on a trip for the Agriculture Committee, on which he also had taken Zeb Vance's seat, as a senator from a tobacco-growing state. Matt Grant was around somewhere, she said, as if it hardly mattered. Morgan found him in the back third of an office that once had been a single room, behind one of a pair of frosted glass partitions that made it more or less into three. Freshman senators had less office space than influence.

"If you can find room to stand up," Morgan said, peering around the edge of the partition, "I'll buy you a cup of coffee."

"That's a deal." Matt tossed a thick sheaf of papers on his cluttered desk. "I'm going blind sitting here."

"I see by the papers," Morgan said as they went down the long corridor, heels echoing from its marble floors, "they've already got old Hunt running around on the rubber-chicken circuit."

Matt's pace quickened a little toward the elevator. Far down the corridor, with its tall brown doors and its single, marching line of white-bulbed ceiling fixtures, an archway opened into the rotunda. "That fool woman had it all wrong. Old Hughes wasn't sick. It was a fund-raiser, and the campaign committee found out they hadn't sold a hundred tickets. They needed some sex appeal, and about the only guy under seventy who could get loose to go was Hunt."

Typewriters clattered away in offices on either side; the brown walls closed in darkly, and for a moment someone's silhouette appeared in the archway, black and menacing against the lighted rotunda. On one of Morgan's first days in Washington, he had seen just such a silhouette far ahead, entering one of those dark, echoing corridors. The silhouette and he had walked toward each other, the hollow crash of their heels on the floor merging, growing louder, until the silhouette was not shadow or dream but a man—a little hunched over, his hands in his pockets, his eyes on the floor, shambling along unsteadily. When he was about ten feet away the man had raised his face and looked at Morgan with bleary eyes from a broad, unshaven face; and with a shock half-fear, half-thrill, Morgan had recognized Joseph R. McCarthy of Wisconsin, trudging along alone in his last lost days.

Morgan had hated what McCarthy stood for, had never seen him before, would never see him again, except occasionally as one of many on the Senate floor. There had been nothing to say and no need to say anything, but something in Morgan had spoken anyway. "Hello, Senator," he said, and he would always be glad he had; because he could still remember the way the sagging face pulled itself together for a moment, the way the shambling frame seemed to straighten, just to have been recognized, addressed civilly, in the same corridors where not too long before it would have been impossible for him to have moved without an adoring crowd reaching for his touch, seeking his smile.

Morgan was to learn that the silhouette he had seen that day in the corridor of the old Senate Office Building was what power in Washington came to. But it had taken Morgan time to find that out; it had taken years; and it had never occurred to the young reporter who walked along another corridor with Matt Grant to ask why men sought power, because he had not known then how likely they were to be destroyed in the search. Instead, he had taken Matt's arm confidentially and said, "Myrtle Bell seemed to think it was somebody else with all the sex appeal."

The elevator doors opened, and they stepped in among giggling page boys and one corpulent lobbyist—or maybe he was just a real-estate operator in from Indiana to put the heavy hand on some quivering senator. They rode down silently and emerged near the entrance to the gray tunnel that bored through the ground across which Morgan had just walked in the spring sunshine.

"Let's stretch our legs," Matt said and led the way along the railed ledge above and beside the little Senate railroad track. That was before they dug the new tunnel, laid new track, and put in ritzy cars with rubber tires. Then, the old "Toonerville Trolley" still clanked and screeched along on its iron wheels, and the careening ride was worth the inevitable wait. Matt plunged ahead rapidly in his long stride, reminding Morgan momentarily of Zeb Vance; but he did not like to think about Zeb Vance.

"The fact is, Rich, that woman must have made that crazy piece right up out of her head, I mean the way it read, when all that really happened was I just filled in at the last minute for Hunt the way he filled in at the last minute for Hughes. Will you tell me what's news about that?"

"Sex appeal. Kathy Anderson's got lots of it, as I expect an old country cocksman like you might have noticed. Myrtle Bell sure did, because out of all the other senators' wives around here, a one-armed man could count on his fingers the ones you could say that about."

A rather sheepish grin lit Matt's dark face. "It's just the last thing I expected, a little bit of nothing like that being in the papers as if it was something big." Morgan could see that Matt was not really displeased.

The trolley screamed past, laden with tourists and office workers and one of the more oafish senators talking volubly in the rear seat to a middle-aged woman, who strained for his words as if they were pearls. The trolley banged and clacked down the tunnel behind them, the echoes of its wheels volleying back for a long time; when they died away Morgan put in one last needle, a quick probe in the nether regions.

"Old Hunt," he said, "he's a busy man, I reckon, but that Kathy looks to me like a powerful argument for staying home at night."

He knew instantly that he had hit a vein. Matt looked up sharply, slowing his pace perceptibly. "What's that mean? Have you heard something?"

Morgan stopped altogether. Along the tunnel ahead, a group of gray flannel suits carrying briefcases approached slowly. "What do *you* mean? All *I* meant was she looks like she'd break a man's back in bed." That was pushing him hard, and Morgan wished he hadn't said it as soon as he did. He knew that, whatever professional or journalistic interest he had in the matter, there was too much personal curiosity involved to do him any credit.

Matt Grant normally had the kind of face that was almost impossible to read; it scarcely even showed the obvious emotions. That day it was as if, suddenly, he put its muscles and nerves under a control so rigorous that the effort became visible. It was only in his eyes, in the quick flicker of his glance past Morgan's head, before it met Morgan's gaze, that he might have been evasive. "Let's forget it," he said a little sharply.

"I didn't mean to offend you, if I did."

"It's not that, Rich, it's just . . . hell, they're good friends of mine. Besides, Hunt has such a terrific future. I mean it'd be a damn shame if something personal got in his way."

Talking as much to himself as to me, Morgan thought.

They began walking along again, and the gray flannels moved into single file against the rail to let them pass. "Is this the right track to Brooklyn?" one of them said, with the joviality that passes for wit among most American men; all the others guffawed mindlessly. Matt looked over his shoulder, grinning. Morgan quickly took his arm and pulled him along, not wanting the quarry to slip off the hook.

"To be perfectly goddam frank," he said as they moved into the little terminal area under the Capitol, toward the short flight of steps leading to the elevator corridor, "it did cross my mind when I saw what you call that little bit of nothing in the paper that it wouldn't have been there at all unless this Bell bitch had some reason for putting it there. So you tell me, is anything wrong between Hunt and Kathy?"

Standing before the elevator and in the car going up to the ground floor, they were surrounded by people; and as they walked along the colorful tile of the Capitol corridors the spring tourist flood made conversation impossible. Drifts of school boys and girls in Confederate caps babbled past, trampling beneath their relentless feet the canned history being offered them by glazed guides. Matt had plenty of time to think over his reply, and it was not until they were seated at a small corner table in the Senate Dining Room that he spoke.

"I didn't mean to suggest there was anything wrong. It's just that I've known a lot of politicians in my time, and I'm no psychiatrist, but the way I see it a politician looks at a woman the way he does a poll or an issue. Will it help him get where he's going? How should he handle it? A politician begins to get all mixed up between himself and his public face. You take Hunt—it's remarkable the single-minded way he goes after things that interest him, like this investigation. So I just wonder sometimes if he doesn't take Kathy for granted a little. Hell, I'm not a married man and you are. Why should I try to tell you what that can mean in any family?" Indeed, he did not have to. "And a guy running for office needs family trouble like a hole in the head."

One of the obsequious black waiters the Senate then kept around to remind itself of the good old days was bowing and scraping and pouring coffee for the white folks. Morgan had seized the moment—oh, I didn't miss much in those days, he thought, sipping his vodka, feeling the redhead's leg against his; even then I was getting to be a real goddamned professional, slick as a goat's ass. And I was hungry, reaching. Back then, it seemed, I was always reaching.

"What investigation?" he had said, pouncing. "What's Hunt Anderson up to out West?"

"Well, well." Matt grinned, not even trying to conceal his relief at having the subject changed. "We didn't know you cared any more now you're so far up there in the big time."

"Yeah, yeah, but what investigation?"

"And you don't mean to tell me that big important sheet you work for now ever even heard of the Agriculture Committee, much less have any interest in anything it might do?"

"Listen, you comical prick," Morgan said. "A year or so ago, the first day I worked in this building for the *Capital Times,* I didn't know a soul or even where a men's room was, let alone what I ought to do or even who I ought to ask what to do. I remember coming down from the gallery and along that corridor out there with the tourists. I looked into this room at that press table right over there, and there they all were—the reporters from the big-time papers, the friends of the great, the ones who knew the ropes, guys who'd campaigned with Roosevelt and Truman and picked Dewey, people who could make and break politicans. There they all were, lined up at their own private table in the middle of the United States Senate Dining Room, and there I was, standing outside the door looking for a place to sit down. Listen, Matt, I was afraid if I came in and sat down somebody would look at me and say, 'What right have you got to be here with us?' "

"That bunch?" Grant said. "Most of 'em couldn't find their ass with both hands."

"But I didn't know that or anything else. They were the heroes of my profession, you see? Big men. And I just stood there and sweated and fidgeted and finally somebody stood up—I can remember who it was, that AP know-it-all with the bad breath, Billy Gattling. When he went out there was a place where I could go in and sit down, but I still just stood there. I believe it was the hardest thing I ever did in my life, to make myself go in there and sit down among all those people who knew they belonged there when I didn't know I belonged anywhere."

"You always seemed to me like the kind of a guy who barges right in."

"Good cover. But what I just told you wasn't so long ago. So do me a favor. Come off that big-time stuff, will you?"

"Hunt always says you're as touchy as a virgin, and damn if I don't believe it."

"Sensitive," Morgan said, "is the word we literary men prefer. Now what the hell is Hunt doing on the West Coast? Got a girl out there?"

"Oh, well, you know old bleeding-heart Hunt—we had these hearings on migrant workers, and there was some testimony about hungry children. So the chairman got tired of Hunt banging on the table about that and just to get rid of him he wangled some kind of a select committee with Hunt as chairman. Doesn't amount to much. He got just about enough money to go out to the Coast and down South a couple of times and hire a little staff. I reckon he'll be putting in a report after a while. Maybe hold some hearings first."

"But what's he think he's doing way off out there when he's got his own voters to work for?"

"That's just Hunt. In fact, that kind of thing is the main reason I went to work for him. I didn't have to switch and I never really thought of myself as anybody's staff man."

Morgan poured him more coffee from the pot left on the table. Matt stirred it idly, leaning on an elbow, his shoulders hunched, his deep-set eyes pensive.

"After that hearing down there where you and I met him, we exchanged some letters on the acreage-poundage thing, and then one day he called me up. Zeb Vance was quitting, he said, which I knew from those stories of yours, and Hunt was going to run, which I didn't know. So why didn't I come down and help out, and then, if we got along, manage his staff in case he won and came to Washington? It made some sense because even if I didn't know much about running for office, I knew one hell of a lot about the state and Washington and the bureaucracy and Congress. But the thing of it was, what was in it for me? The only answer I really had, then or now, was whatever it is that's got him out West worrying about hungry children. I just got the feeling that if I was ever going to be able to do anything about things that meant something to me, maybe I could do it better through Hunt Anderson than any other way. It appeared to me he was a politician all right, he might even go somewhere, but for some reason, maybe the way he felt about his father, he wasn't as self-serving and shortsighted as most. It struck me he was a fellow who could take a long look, see beyond his nose, maybe even stick his neck out a little. All of which he's doing out West right now, so maybe I was right, for once."

He had talked on for a while, telling Morgan a good bit more than Morgan had thought he needed to know about the problems of migrants. But Morgan had not really been listening; because Morgan had known a good deal more than Matt had thought he did about how Matt had come to be Hunt Anderson's second man—more, Morgan remembered a bit guiltily, even after so many years, than I had any business knowing.

"Now, Morgan here," Glass said, sucking a cube of ice from his drink, "they'd never treat Rich Morgan like they treat yours truly. That's the difference in having a big name and just being on the way to the top like me."

"I never knew a really big name before." The redhead was warm and pulsing at Morgan's side. "I mean they don't usually fly those crates of ours, you know? Not the really big names."

"Well, I like to go among the people," Morgan said solemnly. "It keeps me humble. Glass, I advise you to do the same if you want to get anywhere in this business." The redhead nodded her approval, but Morgan did not really care. He was remembering Kathy, Geraldine, Hunt in the old days, the long-ago campaign that once had been such an event in his life.

Just before Morgan had departed the *Capital Times,* its political editor had called him back from his Washington assignment to cover the state campaign. Hunt Anderson was then just beginning to show himself to the voters, all of whom knew his name but not yet his face or voice or style. Later Anderson would appear mostly on television, putting together the first thing like a statewide network the state had seen; but he had wanted to give the voters at least one good look at himself and he also wanted to give himself a clearer view of the state and its people.

So he set up a series of rallies, widely spaced and strategically located, and to get from one to another—it was a solid three-week effort—he chartered a bus, had some of the seats taken out, put in a desk or two and some typewriters, a mimeograph and a sound system, hung a couple of banners on the sides, and started off. There was nothing particularly new about any of that, but the first political tour of Old Bull's boy proved to be a surefire draw everywhere. Since Anderson turned out to be a good, confident speaker and also brought along a country music band called The String Beans, the rallies gave him a smashing political debut.

Morgan joined the traveling party in a little town down in the east where they packed pickles and staged, in those days, an annual fall mob scene when the old white high school opened 99 per cent white and 1 per cent black, the 1 per cent under court order and reluctant police protection. Morgan arrived one bright spring afternoon; from the bus station, carrying a light suitcase and a typewriter, he walked up the hot glaring street— midsummer temperature arrived in April in that part of the state—the sound of the "Game of the Day" coming staccato and sharp from the open door of a barbershop but fading gradually into the deeper boom of Anderson's loudspeaker.

The crowd in front of the courthouse was spilling over its lawns and sidewalks and out into the street. He was just in time to hear Hunt Anderson handle the bitter, root issue of Southern politics, and, looking at all the faces grim in the late-day sun, Morgan thought it wasn't a bit like sitting on the porch at midnight and theorizing over Scotch.

" . . . so what I have to say in answer to my friend's question out there"—Anderson had the theory that people did not like to be lectured and wanted to take part in whatever was happening, so question-and-answer periods were a regular feature of his rallies—"is that I could make you a lot of promises but I couldn't go up to Washington and keep them. So what good would that do you, or even me, as soon as you found out I couldn't keep all those promises?"

A man in a druggist's jacket stood just in front of Morgan. Turning to a woman beside him, he shrugged and started to speak, but she was intent on Anderson, a lanky figure halfway up the courthouse steps, as alone against the stone background as the pigeon-limed Confederate soldier on his pedestal to Morgan's right.

"So I make you folks just one promise on that subject, which I don't discount for one second as the gravest and most difficult problem we face. Just one promise, and one I can keep, and that's to work for the best education we can possibly provide for the children of this city and this state —and I mean white and black children alike, because you know and I know that education is the only hope there is for their future and for the future of America."

"Talk, talk, talk," the druggist muttered audibly, and in the silence that greeted Hunt's words the mutter carried far. Faces, unsmiling, impassive, turned toward the druggist. Abruptly he began pushing off through the crowd.

"You may not think mixing the two in the same school is the best kind of education," Anderson went on just as Morgan thought he'd finished, "but you know closed schools mean no education at all, and just remember the court only said 'desegregate'—it didn't say 'integrate.' That's a mighty big difference."

And back then, Morgan thought, with schools being closed and legislatures passing nullification acts and the big mules braying about massive resistance and the mobs just waiting to march, that wasn't so easy to say in a Southern campaign, particularly in the Black Belt.

That long-past day, hearing the almost total silence that followed Anderson's statement, watching the druggist march off militantly through the crowd with a number of grim-looking men drifting in his wake, Morgan had feared it was going to beat Hunt Anderson, as it already had beaten so many; nigger politics would haul him down before he could even begin. As if he felt it too, Anderson abruptly brought on The String Beans, who appropriately closed out the rally with "Cold, Cold Heart."

Morgan detested man-in-the-street interviews, but there was no way out of it that day; he had explicit orders. A man in a striped railroad cap was standing beside him, his hands thrust in the pockets of greasy work pants. As the Beans faded into silence, Morgan turned toward him. "Think this fellow can win?"

The railroad cap moved a little up and down as the man silently thought it over. "Don't make no difference," he said at last. "All a bunch of bastards." Which, by and large, Morgan thought, I consider sounder judgement now than I did then.

He moved on to an elderly woman in a flowered hat, opened his mouth, and got a look from her that made him close it rapidly before she could call the police. A man in a business suit turned out to be an insurance agent who was delighted to talk to the *Capital Times* and just felt like from what his policy-holders was saying that they thought this Anderson was a slick one like his old daddy that you'd never catch letting on anything he really had up his sleeve, and that was about what he felt like himself. Then Morgan found a woman clerk from the dime store who didn't know a thing about politics but just felt like whatever most folks felt like she ought to do would be all right with her and she would say that her son sure did feel like things were pretty bad these days. As for the auto dealer next waylaid, he said he would be in hell with his back broke before his kids would go to the toilet with niggers and as for this Anderson he just felt like a big talker like that probably didn't know peaturkey about a durn thing.

By that time Morgan had worked his way pretty near the Anderson campaign bus, with its speaker horns like antlers on its roof, and he shouldered on through the diminishing crowd, past a sheriff's deputy with a belly bulging over his belt and knee-high riding boots on fat legs. Obviously a veteran of the high-school mob scenes, the deputy eyed Morgan's suitcase dourly and the typewriter with loathing. Morgan hastily put both aboard the bus, swung in after them, and found himself face-to-face with Kathy Anderson, who sat leafing through a newspaper on top of a desk incongruously placed just behind the driver's seat. Her marvelous legs were marvelously crossed, Morgan did not fail to notice.

"Ernest Hemingway here. Mind if I join the safari?"

She looked up from the newspaper, smiling. "I do if I have to call you Papa."

"Daughter, you can call me Ishmael."

She laughed and slipped elegantly to her feet. "We heard you were coming," she said. "Hunt's secretary is all agog."

"Ah, my reputation precedes me."

"In more ways than one. Did you hear Hunt speak?"

"Except I thought for a minute it was Earl Warren."

"You certainly are in a gayer mood than the last time I saw you." In the warm bus, even with the remnants of the crowd going by and cars growling and snuffling in the street outside, Morgan caught the scent of her, felt in the pit of his stomach her nearness and her intensity, as if she were of some radiant material. She could make him feel enclosed with her, as if they were in a room getting smaller all the time, until in the closeness he wondered if he could breathe or live.

He was, definitely, in a gayer mood than when he had first met her. He knew he would be moving up from the *Capital Times* right after the campaign—up, among other things, to nearly twice as much money and to permanent assignment in Washington, free of any danger of rotting unknown in the South; and because, Morgan thought, he had believed then that all *that* had value, that his life at last was going well, so that soon he would pull it all together, all that he knew and was, all he had done and would do, in the big effort, the work that would stand for him against time. So he had been gay and younger than he thought, and although it had not occurred to him then that his life might touch Kathy Anderson's except peripherally—he had thought of her as an Older Woman to be impressed, not as a person with whom he might involve himself—he had wanted her liking and approval.

"You look great," Morgan said. "Campaigning must agree with you."

"I wouldn't call it my idea of fun. I'm still too New Jersey—I don't know much about this state and I never knew there were so many colored people. And so poor. I never knew there were so many problems that don't interest me. I heard a lecture this morning on hog prices from some men Hunt had in here. He's always studying something or being briefed or calling up his main office for more material. Or out there shaking hands in quest of greatness. It can get tiresome."

Through the open door Morgan could see Hunt Anderson, Matt Grant, and another man moving slowly toward the bus in deep conversation. Even as Anderson talked, he was reaching out with both arms, his big hands in constant motion, seizing all hands around him. He had had a kind of genius for that, Morgan remembered. Anderson could talk normally to people while shaking hundreds of hands, and seem to be giving personal attention to every person he touched or to whom he spoke; in a crowd he could create warmth, like a small personal sun. But Morgan had not yet recognized, that day, the strength of Anderson's impact on people.

"You're lucky to have Matt," Morgan said. "What did Hunt do to get a fellow like that to take a chance on a political campaign?"

He turned partially away from Kathy, but he felt her move nearer, felt the rising intensity of her presence, heard the faint feathery sigh of her breath. "Oh, we persuaded him," she said softly, almost absently, and Morgan turned and saw her looking at the approaching men too, with that same still regard, that close and pointed interest, that—almost as much as her legs—had first made him notice her.

Other than The String Beans, who traveled in their own station wagon, Anderson had had only a small entourage at that stage; even later, running for president in the state primaries, he had believed in traveling light—and had to anyway, for lack of money. There had been in that first campaign party Geraldine, the thick-ankled secretary-typist-mimeographer who obviously was not agog at Morgan's arrival and who convinced him by her mere appearance that she was made of more Puritan stuff than Zeb Vance's hard-biting stenotypist of the year before. There were also a couple of advance men who showed up in brief alternate spurts of activity, only to blaze on ahead to arrange still more crowds around yet other courthouse steps or within some dank school auditorium; and four other reporters from whom, in smug satisfaction, Morgan withheld the news of his new stardom in order not to despoil their envy when ultimately they would read about it, he hoped perhaps on the front page of the *Capital Times*. A bus driver who doubled as baggage handler and bodyguard in the bigger crowds, a sound technician, and an official photographer completed the roster. The number of reporters varied—some would come along just for a day or a particular rally. Also in the bus as it moved from place to place was nearly always a variety of local political types who wanted to get in on the ground floor, to scout the new man running, or to cadge some free exposure to the voters.

That day there was a long run from the town where Morgan got aboard to the one where the next morning's rally was scheduled, and where rooms had been reserved in the local hotel—on which subject, Kathy Anderson assured him, she had become a ranking expert and could count on the fingers of one hand the number of hotels in the whole benighted state where one could get, in the same room, a private bath, a telephone, and a full-length mirror. The party stopped somewhere for a leisurely, mostly inedible dinner, then drove on, with no one very anxious to arrive at what Kathy said was sure to be another former Civil War barracks.

Morgan had just a moment alone with Anderson as they strolled across the restaurant parking lot to the bus. "Is it different from what you thought?" Morgan asked. "Are things working out?"

Anderson went on for a few long strides, then stopped, his hands thrust down in his trousers pockets, his head thrown back as if he were baying at the sliver of moon that pierced the sky. "I like it more than I thought I would. It scares me I like it so much sometimes."

"Like what? All that grab-ass in the crowds?"

"Oh, I do like reaching out to people, I guess, having them reach for me. It never ceases to amaze me, Morgan, how people want so desperately to be noticed—just to catch somebody's attention for a second or two, be some part of the world before it goes by." He started walking toward the bus again. "I like that, all right, touching people that want to touch and be touched, but more than that—something happens to me when I'm up there talking. Maybe it's a sense of power. Whatever it is, I'm up there, and I'm talking, and they're listening, and I see them looking back at me, and right then I seem like more nearly me than any other time I can remember. I feel like myself, I'm home, in tune, even when they're not listening or not believing, because you see, Morgan, it's not them I'm in tune with so much when I'm up there as with myself."

They reached the bus door and stopped again. Sam Joyner, the bus driver, was racing the engine a little, and in the glare of the desk light the earnest, pudgy face of thick-ankled Geraldine was bent over her transcripts and mailing lists. Behind, in the dark of the parking lot, Matt Grant suddenly laughed aloud, his deep voice rising in the kind of gaiety that, from him, seemed alien and forced, as if someone were tickling his ribs.

"Not me," Morgan said. "I look at a crowd and I see them cheering on the lions."

Anderson's long arm came out of the darkness and a big hand closed tightly on Morgan's elbow, shaking him gently. "Exactly," he said. "Exactly. But wouldn't you like to be one of the Christians, Morgan? Wouldn't you rather be in the arena than in the crowd?"

"Hell no. Morgan sits in the pressbox."

"Because in the arena"—Anderson's voice was low, unhurried, as if he had not even heard Morgan's reply—"in the arena, among the Christians, that's not common. That's not ordinary, is it, Morgan? Isn't that really something down there facing the lions?"

Oh, they're going to tear him to pieces, Morgan thought as Sam rolled the bus sonorously through the darkness, down the moon-traced highway slashing like a firebreak through the great pine forests; they're going to eat his liver and lights and toss his bones in the air. And Morgan smiled cynically, aloof and disdainful in his seat near the rear, his colleagues having been chilled by his visible preference for his own company, his own silence. Up front the desk light was off, and Geraldine was sitting primly upright and alone, a Bible clenched, no doubt, between her pudding thighs. Hunt Anderson, his long body buckled into odd planes and angles like a piece of equipment half dismantled, slept in a seat behind her and part of another across the aisle.

Headlights rose and fell in the night, and the bus rolled on. Houses occasionally flickered past. Sometimes a glittering expanse of asphalt, advertising, and gas pumps floated past like a modern magic carpet; and far away, once when briefly the tall trees gave way to the rich, flat earth, train lights strung like beads moved for a few moments in exact cadence with the rushing bus and slipped one by one into darkness. Morgan slumped lower in his seat, tucked his old raincoat under his head, and slept fitfully. It took only the sound of a voice to wake him. For a moment Morgan could not think where he was, or who, and then, like a surreal flash of weird imagination, a lurid imprint of neon glared redly at him from the black screen of the window: CHICK'N STEAK DINER. It disappeared, except from his seared subliminal vision, and the bus rolled on. The voice that had waked him spoke again.

". . . just don't think it's the place for me, that's all. It just isn't working out."

It was Matt Grant's voice, and it brought Morgan awake enough to see in the dim interior of the bus the back of his head over the seat just in front. Then Kathy spoke, and the sound helped Morgan discern the outline of her head near Matt's in the aisle seat. Morgan didn't know when they had moved from the front of the bus, but they could hardly have sat down, he thought, without seeing him in the seat just behind. Probably they had thought him asleep, as he had been.

"We'll make it work out," Kathy said.

I could always cough if the going gets rough, Morgan thought. On the other hand, that would be embarrassing all around. He closed his eyes and tried to go back to sleep, hoping they'd speak too softly to be overheard. But although they seemed to be almost murmuring and Kathy's head was quite close to Matt's, something in the smooth accustomed hum of the bus, the particular resonance of their voices, and Morgan's involuntary awakening sensitivity to them—as if to a dripping faucet or the creaks of an old house—combined to make their words audible.

"You don't understand," Matt said. "It's not anything anybody's done or not done that can be put right. The more I see of Hunt, the more I think he's an extraordinary man. If he can win this thing, and I'd like to see him do it, he'll get to be somebody in the Senate, that's for sure. It's just that *he's* going to do it, it's his ability and talent and brains, it isn't Matt Grant that's going to get elected to the Senate and be somebody. And nobody can do anything about that."

"No." Morgan opened his eyes. The dark outline of Kathy's head was shaking vigorously. "You don't understand. Hunt needs you, Matt, he really does, for all sorts of things, but mostly to keep his feet on the ground. But if you think it's all one way—"

"I didn't mean that."

"I know what you meant. You want to be Matt Grant, not Hunt Anderson's man, no matter how great Hunt might get to be."

"That's it exactly. It's arrogant, I reckon, but I've got things to do in this world too. He's not the only one."

Her head moved nearer Matt's, her voice became even more murmurous, and Morgan was ashamed to find himself straining to hear. He closed his eyes again, as if the pretense could redeem his offense.

"But you could never be anybody's man. I'll tell you something you may not know yet, something I see that you can't see yet." Morgan opened his eyes to see Matt's head turning a little toward hers. "In some ways, Hunt is going to be *your* man, if you stay. Oh, I know him so well, Matt. You say he's wonderful, but he can be vain and foolish too. He's got this romantic notion of himself righting wrongs and making up for his father, and it's going to get him into trouble, you know it is. And he can charm anybody, and sometimes he'll try to get by on that. Sometimes he's like a child playing a game, pretending he's a great man. But you could handle him, Matt, you could shape him in so many ways he'd really in a sense be something you created."

"But I don't think that's what I want either."

"Well, if that isn't enough, if you don't see how you could do the things you want to do by making him what he could be but maybe never will be if you don't make him—then, please, Matt, I need you. I can't let you leave now."

"You're on my mind all the time," Matt said in a rush as if something had broken loose in him. "On my conscience, in the air I breathe. But you're his too." His voice quivered with misery and exaltation. They were silent for a long time then, so long that Morgan thought one of them must have moved away, and he opened his eyes, ready to stand up and so warn them he was awake. Before he could do so, in the dimness her head rose from beyond Matt's shadowy outline, and with a piercing sexual thrill that struck right into his groin Morgan realized she had had her face against Matt's chest—or out of sight—for a long, long moment. He was gripped, enthralled even, by that small evidence of intimacy in the dark; and his own desires rushed through him, lush and rapacious, as if *he* had been electrically touched by those hands moving on him, that head against his pulsing veins, that soft breath touching his shivering skin.

"Poor Matt," she whispered. "Poor sweet honorable Matt."

"Honorable." The word was ecstatic with shame. "Kathy . . . don't . . ."

Lost the game, Morgan thought, intoxicated, writhing. He's lost it all.

"No, no . . ." Swift as thought, something moved, touched Matt's face, was gone. "No more, if it bothers you. It's not even what I meant."

"But it's why I've got to go. The main reason."

"No, you can't go, Matt, not if what I want means anything to you. Because when I said I needed you I didn't mean for what you must have thought. I meant I needed you to help Hunt get where he's going, as long as he's bound to go. I need you to take the job off my hands."

"But why? I'd think you'd want . . ."

"Because it isn't my job." Kathy said. "I never asked the big fool to be a great man."

So Morgan had had his own thoughts that morning in the Senate restaurant, with Myrtle Bell's snide tale in the paper at his elbow, and Matt's earnest voice describing the iniquities of California ranchers and Florida orchardists and Long Island farmers and all the others who were exploiting the migrants. Somebody was always exploiting somebody, Morgan thought, so screw that; and he was wondering how much Matt's protestations of admiration for Hunt Anderson were genuine and how much they were rationalizations for his own behavior.

"It's one of those situations where the interests and the politicians get so tied up together it's hard to tell who's doing what to whom." Matt looked around, leaned forward, lowered his voice. "Hunt picked up one little trail from some ex-secretary that even looks like it might just possibly lead to Paul Hinman."

Suddenly migrants seemed a far more interesting subject than Morgan had believed. "You mean to tell me Hunt Anderson is private-eying around Hinman?"

As if remembering suddenly for whom Morgan worked, Matt looked a little guilty. "Now don't go writing anything even close to that," he said. "It's just a hint, just a possibility really, and when Hunt looks into it, it may not even be that."

Hinman was governor of his state then, and being governor of that state was not peanuts; moreover, Morgan knew that since the old boy then in the White House couldn't succeed himself and had made no real effort to pick or promote anyone else as his successor—he would let the dogs scramble for the bone, he had remarked inelegantly but accurately—Hinman's governorship made him the second biggest man in the party. Hinman had "task forces" at work on the issues—he could already command the academics in obedient droves, a sure sign of the front-runner—and every Sunday he was batting slow balls out of the park on one of those TV interview programs, which were just then the big new thing. Mostly because of these appearances, everybody said Paul Hinman handled himself like a pro, like a president.

That, Morgan knew, was half the battle, once people started saying that.

With Hinman or any other winner, it wasn't so much looks, although looks did matter, and it wasn't so much words, although press agents and speech writers could not get a man through a news conference, and it certainly wasn't issues, although if any candidate seemed baffled by the issues he was finished. No, more than any of those things, it was manner that Hinman had. It was something that made people think he could do it—handle the job, make the decisions, set the examples. If a man didn't have the manner he couldn't fake it, not after television began to look at him with its red, relentless eye. Hinman had it, and people—including Morgan—thought he was going to be the next president. That was his major asset, the main reason he led all the polls three years before the election. Three years was a long time, and reporters always wrote cravenly that of course "anything could happen," but most of them did not really believe it.

So that morning over the coffee cups in the Senate Dining Room, Morgan's reverie about the night on the bus during Hunt's campaign, even his interest in Myrtle Bell's little bitchery about Kathy and his speculations about Matt, all disappeared at the sound of Hinman's name. With that single word ringing in his professional ear, he was thinking fast. Even Matt Grant, straightforward though Morgan thought him to be, was an old hand. He knew the game, he and Hunt had their interests. Had his tongue slipped —to mention Hinman in such a way to a reporter, even to one who was something of a friend? Morgan doubted it. Was it a deliberate leak, with which Morgan was expected to rush into print to boost Hunt politically? Morgan guessed it would do just the opposite, as Matt would know, because freshmen senators were not encouraged to cast suspicion and obloquy on their party's next president. Besides, Matt also would know Morgan's newspaper well enough to understand that it would hardly print what he himself had called "just a possibility" without a thorough investigation.

"Why, you goddamned fox," Morgan said, "you're trying to get me hooked on your lousy migrant story."

"A mere slip of the tongue. I know you'd never take advantage of it or of me."

"Of course not. I guess I'll just forget you ever said a word."

Matt grinned cheerfully—for him. "Well, now, I wouldn't go that far," he said. "I believe I'd keep it in mind if I were you."

Until then, Hunt Anderson had been interesting to Morgan primarily as Old Bull's boy, who—rather dreamily, Morgan thought—was hoping to clean up the family name and do great deeds; as an intelligent and unusual man who nevertheless would come around in the end to the routine political progression from promise, through the centrism imposed by the play of interests, to, at best, a competent and dedicated professionalism in managing and balancing those interests. This sad American political odyssey that Morgan had seen so often represented, it seemed to him then, the best one could hope for in a sprawling and variegated democracy that had no time and no room for excellence or grandeur, let alone the eccentricity of genius or the light of virtue. Morgan had thought Hunt Anderson probably would make it on those inexorable terms, once he had successfully bypassed the Ladder system in his state—which, anyway, was less rigid for senators-to-be than for those who aspired to be governor. The mere hint that Anderson might come into collision with Paul Hinman was, for Morgan, the first suggestion that Anderson might actually be different, might actually tempt fate and the odds. It seemed clear to Morgan's cynical political understanding that any freshman senator who got into an investigation of his party's leading presidential candidate was not progressing from promise to professionalism so much as risking oblivion.

A few days later, with something more than the rather gossipy interest in Kathy Anderson that had led him to seek out Matt Grant, Morgan decided at the last minute to go to a cocktail party the Andersons were giving at their rented house in Georgetown. It had a tiny garden enclosed by a brick wall; a fringe of grass sprouted like a monk's hair between the wall and a brick patio. French doors from a big, airy living room opened into the garden, and between the two spaces guests ebbed and flowed from the bar inside to the rear wall, against which a short, scrubbed industrialist from Anderson's state had braced himself in wary suspicion of the Washington liberal crowd. That morning the industrialist had been through a confirmation hearing—the occasion for the party—on his appointment as ambassador to a Central American backwater, and was no doubt feeling ill used because some do-good senator had rather sharply questioned whether his having made a fortune in asphalt qualified him to deal with the revolution of rising expectations.

After a dutiful, moist handshake with the guest of honor—whom Morgan had known in his previous down-home incarnation as a heavy political contributor—Morgan was free to make some cocktail-party moves. He did look around for his wife, whom he had telephoned to meet him at the Andersons', but there was no sign of her and no way of knowing if she really would appear. Anne, who did not like cocktail parties, had demanded in acid tones to know what she was supposed to do at the last minute for a baby-sitter, a problem Morgan tended to regard as hers.

After a desultory look around and a quick visit to the bar, he found himself in something resembling conversation with the unintelligible mustachioed wife of the ambassador from the backwater to which the asphalt man was going. It did not really matter that her English was minuscule but loud and Morgan's Spanish non-existent, because while they made noises at each other she kept her eyes steadily on what Anne called "the bird on your shoulder"—that is, she never looked at Morgan but just beyond his shoulder to see who might be more influential and interesting. After Morgan managed to convey to her with much wiggling of fingers that he worked at a typewriter, her eyes promptly glazed over, and she moved past him to chatter her fractured syntax into the ears of a State Department type who cultivated his eyebrows.

Morgan next talked a little Americanism with a congressman from Texas who wanted to know whether his newspaper realized the extent to which the country was fed up with the subversion of liberty and religion by the goddamned Supreme Court. After Morgan assured him treacherously that it did, he found the tipsy wife of a lawyer out of the last administration, a man who had stayed in Washington to make a fortune during the present administration, and flirted with her for a minute or two, mostly for the hell of it but also because he had decided at an earlier party that she was bored enough to be possible.

After that, having spied past the bird on *her* shoulder one of the men being touted as the President's choice for national party chairman, Morgan introduced himself and elicited what little the potential chairman wanted Morgan to know of his views on the next congressional elections. But Morgan was still something of a rookie in that league, and just as he was becoming aware that the bird was back on *his* shoulder, the potential chairman moved abruptly around him, a beatific smile dawning on his powdered jowls, and seized the limp hand of a White House assistant known to have something to do with patronage and fund-raising. Morgan waited patiently to be drawn into their conversation, but nothing happened. He was too Southern to barge in, too green to know how to insinuate himself, and too unimportant to take their notice.

Finally, Morgan just stood there in the warm, crowded room, sipping watery Scotch and perspiring, watching all the confident noddings and wavings and puffings of smoke; around him, tangible as tobacco fumes, hung the noise of laughter and talk, ice and glass and pouring liquid, shuffling feet and slithering cloth, and from beyond the postage-stamp garden the underlying tones of home-going traffic struggling up Wisconsin Avenue to Bethesda. For a moment it was as if from some vantage point on an unseen staircase the child he had been crouched low and, unbelieving, peered down to see, in an unimaginable future, himself at the party. It was a strange, lonely moment in which Morgan was not quite sure whether he *was* on the staircase or there among those loud women and overstuffed men, much less which place he belonged; but then he knew with sad certainty that even if somehow he really were on the staircase, even if the greatest reality lay always in the experienced past, he was nevertheless inexorably on his way to that party. He could not escape it because he could not escape himself.

At that moment, across the room, he saw Anne, her small, lovely face framed between the blue shoulder of an Air Force colonel and the bald head of a deputy assistant from the Treasury; smiling a little tentatively beneath the rather short cap of dark hair she had worn that summer, she was looking up with her hurt eyes at a man they knew, whom Morgan had not expected to be at Anderson's house. She was so rapt, so entirely taken up in what he was saying, even if her uncertain smile suggested she was not sure she should be listening, that Morgan knew if he called and waved she would not in that packed room even be aware of him. He turned and edged toward the French doors and the garden.

Even then, when they were young and Richie still a child, Morgan had known their life together had gone wrong. She had not let him touch her for months and he knew from experience that when she relented he would come too quickly and she would call him a selfish bastard and turn her smooth, cool back. After too many drinks, she would ask him how he thought anyone could love a gloomy bastard like him, always slaving at his goddam typewriter like there was nothing in the world but words, words, words.

Still, pushing through the crowd, seeing from the corner of his eye the curve of a woman's breast in something clinging, he thought of Anne's hard breasts and narrow hips, her flat stomach; and in something like despair he sensed, as always, the treacherous lift of desire.

So maybe even then he should have left her, Morgan thought, hardly conscious of the redhead at his side, of Glass across the table. Maybe he should have left her even before she had told him just once too often that he had never brought her off, and never would, it was never going to be any good between them; even before he had shouted back that if that was the case she ought to go and find a man she could make it with; certainly when she had answered without hesitation, "I already have."

Much of it was his own fault, he knew that, had conceded it to her; but he knew, too, that a man or a woman should pay only so much in dignity and pride and self-esteem, even for the hope of love. He had paid too much for too little, Morgan knew; he had been a fool, but at least he knew why. Because I took her any way I could get her, he thought, so that someday maybe I could have her the way I wanted her.

"I always dream like a son-of-a-bitch," Glass said to the redhead, his voice slurred, his eyelids sagging. "I mean the minute I put my head on the pillow, even when I'm shacked up with a broad. The wildest things you wouldn't believe, like Disneyland or something."

The redhead nodded sympathetically. "I couldn't even tell you my dreams, I'd be so embarrassed and all. I can't explain but it's like that every night with me."

Morgan laughed bitterly. "The worst kind," he said, "are when you're awake. The kind you come to think are true."

In the garden Morgan saw a girl he knew from the Majority Whip's office. She spoke pleasantly, but she had a disfiguring birthmark, and Morgan moved cruelly on. Somebody said the Vice-President was coming to the party, but Morgan knew better than that; and somebody else said through him to an unknown presence in dark glasses that USIA was in a bigger fuckup than usual; and Morgan said to the asphalt man it's hot and the asphalt man said it was hotter still where he was going and Morgan said next or finally? But the asphalt man didn't get it and turned to his wife, who was smashed and mumbling, her first time up in the big leagues. A television man and Morgan talked political shop over the head of a syndicated columnist who was trying to live above having just lost his Washington outlet, until the television man spied the White House man still talking to the national committee candidate and bludgeoned off through the crowd to merge his prestige with theirs.

Someone touched Morgan's arm, and Hunt Anderson's voice said, "That empty glass looks funny on you."

"It wasn't empty a minute ago."

"Mine either," Anderson said. "I'll show you the bar, since I know you'd never find it by yourself."

They made their way toward the French doors. Anderson patted a pretty girl's back, very near the fanny, and she kissed his cheek swiftly. There was nobody around them but a member of the House from their state who was lecturing the Texas congressman's wife on textile imports, and still a third State Department type who was discussing Chad with a black in flowing robes.

"How about Hinman?" Morgan said. "Did you nail him?"

"Nail him? We're not even close—not yet. But give us a little time," Anderson said. "Your nose is trembling like a bloodhound's."

"*I'm* not the bloodhound."

"Sweetie, you look great," Anderson said to a willowy girl swishing in at ten o'clock. She whispered something in his ear, laughed, and went on. "Bert Fuller's new receptionist," he said, looking after her. "Fucks like a mink, they say. You know how Bert is."

Morgan did not know how Bert was, apparently, since he had assumed Bert to be one of those Western senators preoccupied with sugar beets and Air Force bases.

"Where did you get all these people?"

"The State Department creeps are the desk people for Mister Ambassador back there. Senators from the subcommittee. Some of our delegation. The rest are one or two acquaintances like you and some people who've been nice to Kathy and me. Is your wife here?"

"Over there." He saw that Anne was still talking to the same man.

"She looks better every time I see her," Anderson said.

"Yes."

They were still holding empty glasses, and Morgan held his up and turned toward the bar. They pushed through the thickening mass of people in the living room, and Morgan caught a glimpse of Kathy Anderson in the hallway beyond, holding out her hand to the state's senior senator, a classic bore who told jokes. He edged with Anderson through a conversation about the Middle East to the bar, replacing at one end of it two serious young men who moved away in earnest conversation staccato with statistics.

"Don't let anybody tell you these academics all live in ivory towers," Anderson said. "Those wizards there are sociologists, which I always thought was about the sorriest thing a man could be, but some work they did at Harvard got them interested in migrants. They came down to testify on a wetback bill, and I guess I was the only senator they could get really interested. So after I got the select committee together I hired them, because practically nobody else knows anything about the subject." His face darkened. "Or cares."

"I didn't know you did."

"Hell, they come right through our state by the thousands, picking crawl beans and strawberries. Did you know that? Do those guys you used to work for at the *Capital Times* know that? Or do anything about it? Every year, thousands of them, living like animals and working like dogs. Never in one place long enough to put down any roots or for the kids to get any schooling or their parents any kind of political power. The best we know, they don't average a thousand dollars a year." His fist clenched on the bar in front of them. "We can't nominate Hinman, Morgan."

"You just watch."

"Not that man. It has to be stopped. Listen . . ." He paused until the hired bartender slopped Scotch into their glasses and went away. "It isn't just that he hasn't done a goddam thing for them, and his state has one of the worst problems of all. I can't prove it yet, but I *know* it—that arrogant son of a bitch profits from them."

"Hunt, it's none of my business personally, in fact it looks like a damn good story, and that ought to be all I care about. But are you sure you know what you're doing?"

"Well, I went into this thing—I'll be frank with you—mostly because it looked like an area I could stake out for my own." Anderson had the gift of speaking in such a way as to be quite clear to someone close yet inaudible only a few feet away. "I got this committee the only way a freshman could, by finding something obscure nobody else cared about and hocking part of my soul to a couple of chairmen. One thing good about it is the other members don't give a damn, and so it's all my show. I've traveled some and seen for myself—I've got hold of a remarkable character named Adam Locklear to head the staff, you've got to meet him—and I've found out it's a goddam shame on this country, the way we let those people live, and a crime, I mean a *crime*, the way we profit on hungry children and old women breaking their backs in the beanfields. Its just one jump ahead of the slave trade, that's all in the world it is, and I believe Paul Hinman's in it up to his ass. If I can prove that . . . you're gooddam right I'll know what I'm doing."

"All right," Morgan said, "then I'd like to be in on it all the way. My editors will shy off like scared rabbits, but when the stuff's solid they'll print it. I'll say that for the bastards." Morgan did not need to tell Anderson that he was offering him a lot. If Anderson was taken seriously by Morgan's newspaper, he would be taken seriously everywhere.

Morgan did not know, looking back on it, whether he had been merely hungry for the story, the first one for his new paper that promised to be big, or whether he had been seized again—as he had been that night in the meadow, looking at the stars—by something compulsive, some sense that maybe here was a man at last who would do it—do what, he couldn't quite say, then or now. Maybe just hold fast. He suspected he had been moved by both currents, the ignoble ambition to promote himself, the profoundly moral desire to believe in something, even if only a man. It wouldn't have been the first time that his motives were so mixed, or the last, let alone anything unique to Richmond P. Morgan.

Anderson touched Morgan's glass with his. "Then let's keep in touch, Rich."

"Hunt," Kathy said behind them, "here's Senator—"

"B.D.!" Anderson exclaimed, his face lighting up as if he were really glad to see his senior colleague, although no one ever was. "I thought you were tied up."

"Got loose sooner than I expected," B.D. said in thunderous courtroom tones. He was a former prosecutor who made speeches against the Fifth Amendment. "Came right on down soon's I could." He had his arm around Kathy, pulling her tightly against him. "Can't stay away from this little filly of yours, Hunt, damn'fi can, damn'fi can." His ancient face beamed down at her idiotically.

"Here's a drink." Anderson grabbed something tall from the bar.

B.D. was known to drink anything, although not usually before eight a.m. He seized the glass and swigged heavily at it, crunching Kathy closer, his hand groping at her breast. He knew he was too old for anyone to hit him.

"Listen," Anderson said, taking B.D.'s free arm. "I've got to talk to you. This interstate highway route, what do you—"

"Right down the middle," B.D. said, finishing the drink. "Right smack down the middle is the only way, and damn the torpedoes."

"But that's right through the old battlefield, B.D. The Historical Society will go up in smoke . . ."

Gently Anderson pulled him away. Reluctantly, with a final apish grope of his thick hand, B.D. disengaged from Kathy. They moved into the crowd, Anderson clutching B.D.'s arm as if it were a mule's ear. "Full speed ahead," Morgan heard B.D. cry out, before the Air Force man drowned him out with a fusillade of laughter at something essayed by the lawyer's tipsy wife.

"That man," Kathy said, "every time I have to be around the old goat I wind up black and blue."

"A lonely old gentleman, deprived of love."

Kathy laughed. "Hunt always finds some way to pull him off of me before the rape. Every woman has the same trouble, I'm told."

Morgan raised his glass gallantly. "With less cause."

"Stop that and get me a drink if you and Hunt have left any. Gin and tonic."

Morgan speared a watery one from the bar and held it out to the bartender for ice. "You've been in the papers," he said to Kathy.

"Wasn't that silly?" She sipped the drink. "I've never even met that woman."

"Myrtle's eye is on the sparrow."

"She must have something in it, then. Poor Matt Grant was embarrassed to tears."

"Poor Matt." He had been about as embarrassed, Morgan thought, as the pauper mistaken for the prince.

"There wasn't any problem at all. I never even really asked the committee, I just notified them, and nobody said a word. The only thing that woman had right in the whole thing was that Hunt was out of town."

"He's working like hell, they tell me."

She made a face. "So what else is new? Always following the Grail."

"So Matt Grant is a lucky man."

"Matt! He's just as buried in his work as Hunt, just as single-minded. I was lucky that night at the CMS that Matt wasn't off somewhere too, or working late at the office or something."

"A good team," Morgan said. "A matched pair."

She looked coolly at him above the rim of her glass. "Hunt couldn't do without Matt. He doesn't really know what he's doing yet. He relies so much on Matt. Sometimes it's hard for me to tell which one is the senator."

"Be careful then. Some people, Myrtle Bell, for instance, could get to thinking you really did have them confused."

"It's nice of you to worry," Kathy said. "You worry about it a lot, don't you?"

Morgan wondered, in quiet despair, why he had let it come to this point again—in fact why he had driven it to this point, as he seemed always to be doing with her. Before he could blunder on she smiled and moved nearer. "You like your new work," she said softly. "I can tell. You like being somebody." Her eyes never left his, as if she did not want to miss the impact of her shift of topic.

"Am I somebody now?" Morgan felt helpless, floundering on ice.

"Well, you *know* you're somebody now."

"All right," Morgan said. "You put that one right in to the hilt. Right under the ribs."

She leaned ever nearer, still smiling a little, sipping lightly from the gin she had barely touched. "You stop doing it to me, Rich Morgan, and I'll stop doing it to you."

He seized the offer eagerly. "Why has it been like that ever since we met?"

"Because you're so damned sensitive and because I don't play the game the way, deep down, you think women are supposed to. You must give your wife a hard time too."

"That's a two-way street. Isn't marriage always?"

"Then what I'm saying is, I'll be your friend if you'll be mine. Maybe we both need a friend."

Morgan took the glass out of her hand, put it with his on the bar, put his hands on her shoulders and kissed her cheek. "The best deal I ever made."

"Then tell me for openers," Kathy said, "what's all this mystery Hunt thinks he's up to?"

"Oh, well now . . ." She was wasting no time taking advantage of a new friendship. Kathy was always very direct, very New Jersey. "He hasn't really let me in on any mystery." Morgan was not sure whether even a brand-new friend had any business telling Anderson's wife something Anderson obviously hadn't.

"You're a liar because I know Hunt Anderson." She smiled at him, taking the sting out of her words. "Not that I really care. You men and your politics—what's more boring?"

"Sometimes it isn't. Sometimes it's as fascinating as a love affair. Or a hanging, like Mencken said."

"But look at this crowd . . ." Her cool glance around the room dismissed them. "Nitwits, bores, and frauds."

"Which one am I?"

"Never a nitwit. A bore when you get so angry at things. Sometimes a fraud like the rest of us. How can anybody be real in politics, when the whole thing is to make people think what you want them to think?"

"You're real. Hunt's real."

She made a quick, wry face. "I'm trying not to be in politics any more than I can help. And it's just one more of the games Hunt plays."

"That's a funny thing to say. I think Hunt's one of the few people I ever met in politics who's serious about it."

"Oh, he's serious, all right. But I can remember when he was serious about practicing law, then about farming. Once he wanted to go into archaeology. He thinks he's serious about politics, I agree with that, but it isn't going to be enough for him, just being an unimportant junior senator among all those old men like B.D. It's already boring him, which is why Matt is so important to him. Sooner or later Hunt will go charging off looking for something else. You wait and see."

"You know your husband better than I do, but I'll bet you're wrong."

Kathy laughed. "Wives often are. It's part of the trade."

"Because I think he's hit it. He's found what he's looking for and he's going to take off now."

She looked at Morgan seriously. "The big mystery again." She smiled wickedly. "I'm going to ask Matt. I can find out anything from Matt, don't you think?"

Which, Morgan remembered telling Anne with boozy relish on the way home, could only mean that even if Hunt Anderson was fool enough to pay no attention to his good-looking wife, she had Matt Grant where she wanted him, prone or otherwise. Anne, who in the late stages of the evening had also been mauled by B.D., pointed out a bit thickly that when it came to paying no attention to wives he had no goddamned room to talk because he had made no attempt to rescue her from that old gorilla son-of-a-bitch. Morgan said he had had no reason to believe she was relying on him for rescue since she had not bothered to speak to him on arrival or to look him up later.

"I take it," Glass said, "you'll be taking the redhead to the sack with you, so a lowlife like me needn't even bother to apply." The redhead had picked her way unsteadily among the emptying tables toward the ladies' room.

Morgan opened the last of the redhead's stock of miniatures, controlling himself. "I'm taking her to *her* room." The cover story came as easily as breath. "Poor thing's too drunk to fool with."

Morgan had gone to Matt Grant's office early the day after the Andersons' party. Adam Locklear was on a trip, but Matt called in the two wizards from the migrant labor committee, and Morgan started learning. He did not realize then how important the subject was to become to him. Sprock & Berger, the wizards, were apt teachers—humorless pedants who struck Morgan as having less interest in the plight of thousands of people than in the charts, graphs, averages, medians, grosses, and nets by which they had quantified the situation; but, like anyone who knows more about a subject than anybody else, they were eager to talk about their knowledge of it. Finding in Morgan as devoted a learner as, apparently, Anderson had been, Sprock & Berger, in the course of an interminable summer, in innumerable long afternoons in their jammed cubbyhole near the subway tunnel in the old Senate Office Building, poured their limitless facts into Morgan's reeling brain (there were 450,000 migrants who did farm labor in 900 counties of 46 states, working about 85 full days each for a yearly total of about $900 per capita income; Sprock & Berger estimated that 20 per cent of these workers were functionally illiterate and put their median educational grade level at 7.2 years).

Equipped with several notebooks full of such facts, Morgan accompanied Hunt Anderson and Adam Locklear to some migrant camps and saw for himself their conditions of misery and degradation. Once he and Anderson even tramped the long rows of a beanfield in their state, then went down on their knees together picking snap beans, trying to get a sense of what it was like to crawl along in the dust, day after day, under the pitiless sun, stripping the plants with aching fingers and tossing the beans into a bushel basket that seemed as if it would never fill; when it did, after an endless hour of backache and thirst, they got a yellow ticket from the crew leader. The ticket was worth a dollar at the end of the day, minus the crew leader's cut. It was a bad field, a second crop coming in skimpily after heavy rains had ruined the first yield, and a seventy-year-old black woman with sunken cheeks and pads on her knees told them that even the good pickers, who could ordinarily bring in twenty bushels in a ten-hour day, were making only seven or eight. "This work will keep you in shape," she said, "but if the other fields keep being bad like this one, I'll tell you what I'm going to do, I'm going to quit and draw them checks."

When Morgan reported this on-the-spot research to Sprock & Berger they nodded in unison, and it almost sounded as if they spoke that way when one of them—Morgan never learned to tell the difference—said, "You grasp, of course, the fact that the ticket system works for the owners. For instance, it penalizes the worker even for going for a drink of water." And the other chimed right in on cue, "Because if he wants to make ten bushels, he has to keep right on working. So if the owner just puts in one spigot or a barrel way off at the edge of the field, he discourages them from drinking water and not only cuts his cost but increases his productivity." They were as fascinated by this device, and about as outraged, as if it had been a table of statistics.

It was mainly due to Sprock & Berger that—with some confidence and to the wary relief of Morgan's editors, who grudgingly had let him put a lot of time into a project they did not fully understand, since he had told no one of the possible involvement of Hinman, and they were therefore understandably unable to connect his interest to his customary political reporting—he was able early in the fall to file a lengthy story, of which he still kept a tattered old clipping in his wallet:

WASHINGTON, Sept. 10—Senate hearings on the problems of nearly a half-million migrant farm workers will begin here tomorrow, with some of the testimony expected to provide "political dynamite."

That phrase was used by Senator Hunter Anderson, the chairman of the Select Committee on Farm Labor Migrancy, which has been conducting for six months an investigation of the use of migrant labor on American farms.

"These people are the single most exploited group of Americans," Senator Anderson said at a news conference today. "They have no money, no power, and no place. The minimum wage doesn't protect them, they don't stay in one locality long enough to vote or to own property or to send their children to school, and many of them aren't even eligible for Social Security because they don't work long enough for one employer.

"The federal government has practically no program to help these people, and the worst of it is that state and local officials sometimes actually profit from the system."

Senator Anderson, who said the purpose of the hearings was to devise practical federal legislation to protect migrants from exploitation, declined to identify in advance any "state and local officials" who "profit from the system." He said he would "let the evidence testify for itself."

Sources familiar with the investigation said later that the names of several state governors might enter the hearings—including, it was suggested, that of Gov. Paul D. Hinman . . .

Morgan had had a call from his editors as soon as they reached that graf. "It seems to us," they huffed on the other end of the line, "that that ought to be more strongly sourced, Hinman being who he is, and if you *could* beef it up a little, Morgan, why, then, it seems to all of us here that Hinman is the lead. Don't you think?"

"Well, no, I don't think. You see, if I could beef it up I would have already. But since I can't, I put Hinman down there in the sixth graf. I don't want to bear down too hard on the basis of nothing but informed sources."

"Then maybe we just ought to let the Hinman angle go till you can peg it down tight. It'll hold, won't it?" They always thought something someone had worked on for months could "hold."

"Of course it won't hold. These Senate characters are floating that name to work up interest in their hearings. Hell, *they* want me to go hard on it too, but they won't give me any red meat. So I'm not in any doubt about it but I just refuse to hang Hinman up in the lead with no more than I've got on him at this point. But if we pass up that angle altogether, Anderson will just leak the name somewhere else."

They had printed it, still shaking their heads and clucking; and their instinct had been as sound as a gold tooth, because the first edition had scarcely hit the streets before Governor Paul D. Hinman was on the telephone. He had pulled the publisher—so Morgan later learned—out of one of those groups of suffering males who, having just sat stiffly in their black ties through a formal dinner, were sinking with sighs of gratitude into easy chairs, cigar smoke, and cognac. Having thus ruined the only passable part of the publisher's evening, Hinman had proceeded to ruin his own case by demanding that Richmond P. Morgan, whoever he was, be fired.

"Because, you see, that was the one thing the publisher couldn't even think about," an assistant managing editor told Morgan afterward in faintly reproving tones, as if it had been a little too much for Morgan to delay the publisher's cognac. "Not that the unions would let him fire anybody around here anyway for anything short of stealing one of the presses. But I mean the publisher couldn't have that kind of interference from the outside, even from a governor. Where Hinman made his mistake, he ought to have asked the publisher for a golf date or at most made a denial and demanded a retraction. If he'd been reasonable you might have been up to your ass in trouble."

But there had been no hint of any of that when, for the first time since Morgan had been his employee, the publisher called him a few days later. They chatted amiably for a moment about politics or maybe the Middle East—perennial things. Then, without mentioning Hinman's call, the publisher said Morgan's story was "most interesting."

"You'll want to bring out all the details," he said, "as time goes along."

"I'm told there are a lot of them, but I'll do my best."

"Exactly," the publisher said. "I know you will. Because we'd be doing less than our duty, it seems to me, if it turned out for some reason we didn't print substantial detail to support a serious charge like that."

Morgan had no trouble deciphering that. "Don't worry," he said fervently. "We'll back that story to the hilt."

"Oh, I'm not worried, Mister Morgan. All of us here have great confidence in the work you've done for us. It's just that we've all learned that once a charge is made, it's hard for some later refutation to wipe it out of people's minds. The damage tends to be done even if the charge isn't true."

That was a rule a newspaperman ought to have engraved on his brain, but Morgan hadn't known he was under even that gentle pressure the morning his Hinman story first appeared.

He read it with satisfaction as the trolley rattled down M Street and into Pennsylvania Avenue; they had given him only a one-column head below the fold, but Hinman's name was in an eight-point subhead, and Morgan knew it was going to leap off that page and into every political eye in Washington. He believed that story was bound to be money in the bank for Richmond P. Morgan, and so it had turned out to be, which was why he still carried a clipping of it in his wallet, close to his expense-account greenbacks.

It was, therefore, in a euphoric mood that Morgan arrived early for the first day's hearings, wrote his name on a sheet of copy paper and placed it on a good seat at the press table. He knew there would be few reporters at first, but his story would bring out a few more than would have appeared otherwise, and he wanted to stake out a front seat before attendance and interest began to build, as he believed they would when the full case was disclosed. Anderson had tried and failed to get the huge Senate Caucus Room, and believed he had been turned down precisely because the Senate leadership wanted the affair as muted as possible. He had been given a musty little chamber on a lower level of the old Senate Office Building; it boasted an impressive chandelier, a few US Code books scattered in a glass-front bookcase, a horseshoe-shaped rostrum for august senators, and chairs for perhaps fifty spectators. The plaster on the walls was bright as tobacco juice, the pompous rostrum was a dark walnut, and even the chandelier could do no more than push ineffectually at the gloom of the decades, gathering there where men's interests and ambitions had vainly clashed for so long and so obscurely that probably no one except perhaps some minor historian grubbing away in the stacks of the Library of Congress any longer knew what the room's original purpose had been.

Only a few other reporters and one or two spectators—Senate hearings, like trials, have their inevitable buffs—were there when Hunt Anderson came in, stooping a little in the doorway, although he did not need to; Senate doors were built oversize, to fit mythical senators. He had a single folder in his hand. Morgan went to the rostrum past the stenotypist setting up his black box, and leaned his elbows on the dusty walnut. With the usual effect of a collapsing scaffold, Anderson descended into the high-backed chairman's chair.

"So now it begins," Morgan said. For the first time in his Washington experience he was feeling that heady confidence that comes from the surety of knowing more about a situation, being able to develop it more fully, than any conceivable colleague. He was a mile out front on the story; he was certain it was going to be big, it would matter, and in his professional newspaperman's world that was not only money in the bank, it was pride and excitement and the sense of arrival, of doing at last what he had known all along he could do, and better than anyone else.

"The public part begins anyway," Anderson said.

"I didn't mean the hearings so much. I meant the process of changing history."

Anderson grinned, his odd, planed face looking a bit sheepish. "It just might at that, in ways I didn't foresee."

"When will you get to Hinman?"

"Might not ever in public." He looked past Morgan to make sure no one was listening. "That story of yours threw the fat in the fire."

"What did you expect?"

"What I'm getting. More pressure than you'd believe."

"So if they pressure you out of mixing up Hinman in this mess, who changes history?"

Anderson shook his head emphatically. "They won't pressure me out of it. They might hogtie me some way I don't expect. No matter what happens here, I figure one way or another Hinman's bound to be exposed, now that his name has been in your paper."

"Don't bet on that, not if you mean the free press of democratic America will inevitably sniff out the evildoers. You better do the job yourself if you want to make certain."

Another reporter joined them. "Is it true what we hear, Senator, that you're going to call Governor Hinman?" He had the wire-service man's blank truth-machine manner, which paid no deference at all to the fact that what "we hear" was what Morgan had written that morning. At that moment Morgan knew for certain that he had arrived in the trade.

"Oh, well now," Anderson said. "Governor Hinman certainly knows a lot about the subject of these hearings, and I suppose it might be that he'd want to be heard before all's said and done. Let's let that work itself out."

"But you're not going to call him?"

"Not unless it's necessary. Governor Hinman is a busy man."

The truth machine went away, apparently satisfied with this soft soap, since it would give him a lead for the early PMs, one of the few commodities that had any value in his life. Matt Grant had appeared behind the rostrum and was unpacking a stuffed briefcase. Sprock & Berger flitted about, emitting pipe smoke and statistics. Adam Locklear, who was not yet playing a public role in the investigation, was away in the Southwest.

"This way," Morgan said, "you're going to force a showdown with

Hinman, and you know it. Surfacing his name and then just letting it lie there. No wonder the pressure's on."

"I've been studying that guy." Anderson held up a book Hinman had written, *Creative Bureaucracy.* "Also his record, his speeches, everything about him. And you know why I believe we're going to get him?" He raised his eyebrows. "Because he's an overbearing son-of-a-bitch. He won't even believe we're here until we've got him."

Matt moved closer, a little importantly. "And don't worry about pressure, Rich. That's what we don't get anything else but, and we're used to it."

"Oh, you guys are tough guys all right. After all, I remember the April Fool poll."

Anderson laughed a little too heartily. "That's exactly the point. There's more ways than one to skin a cat, just like there was then."

The April Fool poll was not a comfortable memory for Anderson. It had taken on that label during his Senate campaign, among those of his entourage who knew about it, and it had marked, Morgan believed, the point at which the crushing realities of trying to lead and persuade fallible, obstinate men had come home to the perceptive rationalist, the engaging speaker, the human being who loved to touch and be touched in the crowds.

Anderson had by then opened the obligatory elaborate campaign headquarters in the state capital, and one afternoon late in March, just about a month before the primary voting that would be decisive, Morgan went there with a story in his pocket for Anderson's comment. Anderson had taken over the mezzanine ballroom of the Piedmont Hotel, an establishment so long and so completely politicized by its biennial infestation of state legislators that its lobby reeked permanently of cigar smoke, the cuspidors it had only recently abandoned, and what in other surroundings was known as courthouse disinfectant. In a certain hallowed parlor on the ninth floor, political insiders knew, had been struck the deal that made Jess Workitt the Speaker in '39, in exchange for a gubernatorial nomination three years later for one Clyde R. Blucher, who turned out, before he could accept it, to have been a draft dodger in World War I. Down the stairwell in the northeast corner of the seventh floor, Old Bull once had suspended a whore by her ankles until his wallet, along with everything else not snapped on, had been shaken from her flapping clothes and fallen through her echoing screams to some far-below floor, whereupon Old Bull had allegedly availed himself free and on the stair rail. And down the fire-escape on the rear wall had crept an entire Appropriations Committee in ignominious flight from an irate band of American Legion Auxilliary ladies who had arrived outside the committee's secret-session room, each brandishing a large hammer with which, their placards said, they intended to "nail down" a bonus bill.

Anderson's headquarters was a ballroom that only six years before had been Zeb Vance's HQ. It had been so often occupied before and since by would-be governors and senators that it always seemed incongruous between primaries to see white-jacketed high-school boys dancing there with girls in chiffon, or ladies in flowered hats drinking tea for a cause, or the Kiwanis Club at its annual dinner, sawing at its roast beef through thunderous claps of uplifting oratory. As Anderson's headquarters, it was understaffed by past standards, and Morgan encountered no obstacle among the letter-folders and envelope-stuffers and button-pinners until he reached the faithful Geraldine. She sat guarding Anderson's inner sanctum as if it were her virginity, although it was no more endangered.

"See the boss," Morgan said.

"In conference," Geraldine said, locking her knees.

By that time Morgan had been a part of the Anderson entourage long enough to feel more or less at home in it; he had some confidence the others would not humiliate him in some way. He raised his voice. "If he's taking his afternoon nap to sleep off the Scotch he swilled before lunch, wake him up and ask him if he wants to see the press."

"Mister Grant," Geraldine said with finality, "is with Senator Anderson."

"Well, wake them both up." His voice was loud enough to be heard over the movable partitions that formed the office and that were nicely symbolic of the elusive nature of most political campaigns—nothing that lasts, nothing that will remain of any value, just old handbills, fading in the rain on a row of telephone poles.

"I'm not even putting calls through." Geraldine glanced apprehensively at the closed office just as Matt Grant, looking glummer than usual, opened the door and beckoned Morgan in.

"Thanks, Geraldine."

Later on, when Geraldine went to Washington with Anderson, she lasted just two weeks before fleeing home, irreparably shocked that a black man smelling of whisky had touched her knee with his on the Cabin John trolley. But she had been devoted to Anderson, and that day, as Morgan entered his little office, from the walls of which stared an immense poster of Anderson's angular face over the slogan HE CAN DO MORE, Morgan saw that he and Grant were indeed in serious conference. Anderson eyed him without speaking, almost as resentfully as Geraldine had.

"Thank God I'm not bringing bad news. You look like you might have me beheaded."

"Ump," Anderson said, or something to that effect, still staring belligerently.

Morgan learned that that was a tactic Anderson sometimes tried—to stare a visitor down, make him ill at ease, and thus get the moral advantage of him. Anderson never became good at it, however; he was too kindly, too instinctively sympathetic to the plight of another, to take advantage of him. Morgan knew, because he had once been stared down by a president who was an expert at it.

It happened to be the first time Morgan had had a private interview with that particular president, and the appointment was a sudden response, late one afternoon, to a request he had almost forgotten; so that when he had trotted panting and sweating to the White House through a hot summer twilight, and been shown in past the secretaries' desks between the Cabinet Room and the Oval Office, he was out of breath, disheveled, and unprepared. The President was having his hair cut; he sat in a chair in the middle of his office, under a striped barber sheet, with his head a little pushed forward by an anonymous man who was trimming his neckline. Morgan thought momentarily of how many clearances must have been required before that anonymous man had been permitted to hold a razorblade against the neck of the Leader of the Free World; but he did not long pursue that fascinating notion because from under his brow the President of the United States was staring at him contemptuously; and in the spell that office cast, the sense it imposed of history and responsibility crowding down on its occupants, in the absolute solemn quiet of the nerve center of things as a reporter in Washington knew them, under the weight of that unwinking stare, which evinced no more concern for Morgan than if he had been the barber or one of the two cream-colored sofas that then flanked the fireplace, Morgan was not merely imposed upon by man and surroundings; Morgan was beaten. Still the president stared and kept on staring, until Morgan even began to mumble. He thought of falling to his knees and had to stop himself. It was only later, after the president had relaxed and started telling political yarns, that Morgan understood how ruthless the man had been, how he had deliberately reduced another man, how—with the sure understanding of his kind of the ways in which men can be made to react—he had used his power to make Morgan less than Morgan was, himself more than he was. Which, Morgan believed, is what power does, and why those who momentarily have it are always, at root, dangerous men, and merciful only when it is tactically sound.

Anderson had never learned to be good at that sort of thing, although he had understood the principle very well. He had always been uneasy with power, an attitude that could be fatal to those who seek it; Morgan knew you had to seize it by the throat if you wanted it. That day at Anderson's headquarters, Morgan was not really bothered by what seemed to be Anderson's hostility because, despite it, Morgan knew he had value in Anderson's eyes.

"Actually," Morgan said, "it's good news. The *Capital Times* poll." Before every major election the newspaper ran a statewide poll—not very scientific, more of a random straw poll than a profile test, but it covered a broad sampling of readership, had a reasonably good record, and sometimes affected campaigns. More important, it always got the paper a lot of publicity and maybe even boosted circulation.

Anderson raised an eyebrow. "Good news?"

"You're running behind, but just barely. The story goes April first, and if you'd like to allow for our readers as how it shows you'll take him in the stretch, why, I'm right here to record your words for a waiting populace."

"April Fool's Day? Are you trying to kid us, Morgan?"

"Look at the figures." Morgan held out a galley proof. "April Fool's just a coincidence."

"It's not a very damned funny coincidence to me when Matt here has just got through convincing me I'm getting my ass whipped. Not that I didn't know it anyway. So take your silly goddam figures and get out of here."

"Wait a minute now, let me get your exact words. You say you're getting what whipped?"

"My ass," Hunt said. " 'Hunt Anderson, candidate for United States senator, said tonight he was getting his ass whipped and was thinking of withdrawing from the goddam race.' Write that, Morgan, just that way, and see if that rag of yours will print it."

Beneath the profanity Anderson was serious, distraught. It was the first time Morgan had heard him even suggest that he could do anything but win. He had not been a braggart candidate—his style was understated, that of a good neighbor and good citizen concerned for the public weal—but in public he had an unmistakable air of confidence and conducted himself as if he had no opponent and no problems. In private Morgan had heard him speak only of how he planned to overcome certain obstacles, meet certain issues, take advantage of certain breaks. With a little over a month to go, the *Capital Times* straw poll presented what seemed to be a reasonabe picture of the campaign—as a newcomer Hunt was running a little behind, but he had started with good name identification and now in a well-organized and well-conceived campaign he was coming on strongly. Recognizing Anderson's unmistakable dejection, Morgan realized that despite his own misgivings he had been assuming—perhaps since the night at Old Bull's grave, perhaps since Zeb Vance's retirement—that Anderson would win.

"Show him our poll, Matt."

Grant eased a piece of paper out of his breast pocket as if it were too hot to be held in sensitive fingers. "Off the record?" He raised his eyebrows.

"Not on your life," Morgan said. "I've been tied up by experts. You amateurs haven't put anything off the record here so far."

Anderson laughed a little bitterly. Suddenly he sat up straight, his big frame dominating the room. "He's right, Matt. I've been popping off like a damn fool."

Grant put the paper back in his pocket.

"Listen, Rich, let's get the business part over with. Geraldine!" She appeared like an overweight genie, her pad ready. "Here's what I'll say on the record: 'The *Capital Times* poll is a welcome sign that our campaign is in a strong position for the kind of finish we've always planned—all-out and no holds barred.' Okay? Will you see that the wires get a copy of that, Geraldine, on hold for release?" She went out, clutching the pad as if it were his will. "All that part about getting my ass whipped," Anderson said, "the exact quote, I'll leave on the record too, yours being a family newspaper. That part about withdrawing was a bad joke, which I retract. Now, you want to see that piece of paper off the record?"

"Not if it was the Russian war plan," Morgan said. "I'm not deaf, stupid, or for sale. My lead tomorrow is you're convinced you're losing at this point, statement or no statement. If I let you two slickers tie me up on your actual figures I won't have any right even to say you've got a bad poll. This way, I can say honestly you've got a bad poll but won't release the actual figures. Which is just what I aim to do."

"Fair enough." Anderson looked ruefully at Matt. "I goofed, old buddy, and our prickly friend here has got himself a story."

"Two stories," Morgan said. "What's this about no holds barred from a gentleman campaigner like you?"

"All right then, can we finally go off the record? I'd as soon fill you in as have you guessing, and I wouldn't mind having your reaction, but it can't come from me."

"Who's it going to come from?"

"Off the wall."

"So you can deny it. But it's a deal, this one time."

"Your straw poll is so much bullshit. At a good guess I'd say it's bound to represent a lot more city circulation than countryside, for one thing, and for another, it only measures one newspaper's readers and at that those that care enough to send in your coupon; all of which weights it my way. And I'm frank to tell you my people around the state have been mailing them in by the ton. So has the other side, and I'm still running a little behind. The fact is, we got the best private poll-taker in the business in here and paid him a lot of money for a professional job, and what he found out is not only that I'm dead in the water, which confirms my own instinct, and Matt's too, but why."

"You must be getting niggered," Morgan said. "I was afraid it would be that way."

"Oh, that's one thing. In the east, where they buy your newspaper to hang in the outhouse, I'm in bad shape for that reason. But we can beat that by running well everywhere else. The worst thing is all over the place, and I'm a stupid jerk not to have realized it all the time. They don't think I act enough like Old Bull's boy." (*Some of them want Old Bull back whether they know it or not,* Zeb Vance had told Morgan the year before.) "So what this poll says to Matt and me, and I've spent the day checking out the notion with the best county leaders I've got, is that I'm doing well with all of what you might call the anti-Bull vote, the ones who want a serious candidate to talk about the issues. But I'm nowhere with most of the Bull types, the ones who want a candidate to raise hell and call names—of which there are a good many. And I've got just a month left to do something about it."

"No holds barred?"

Anderson looked at Matt Grant. Matt lifted his shoulders in a helpless gesture that made clear what all three knew, what the long silence that fell on them made dramatic. Only Anderson could answer. Morgan was the youngest of the three but by circumstance had seen more political campaigns in operation than either of the others, and he thought he knew what they were going through. They thought, but they couldn't be sure—so Morgan guessed—that they had to come down off the level they had set themselves, save the campaign by tactics that were not their preference. But it was always tough to change a battle plan in the heat of the action; inevitably it meant you had been wrong once and maybe you would be wrong again.

In hindsight, Morgan knew he had had no real idea of what was happening, and neither had Anderson or Matt. They had been faced—in the final analysis, Anderson had been faced—for the first time with the real necessity for choice, which was what politics and life always came down to. That was what Morgan had learned; he supposed Anderson must have learned it too.

Choices got made—even not making a choice was a choice—and what separated the men from the boys was whether you tried to make your own or let circumstances make them for you. *I tell you,* Hunt Anderson had said to Morgan in that long night of talk and hope, *the minute a man decides it's better to be a live politician than a dead hero . . . right that instant he's sold out.*

Morgan had come to see that that was only true. It didn't explain the greater truth that, even in politics, a man seldom had to make one decisive all-or-nothing choice, either to go down in flames or to bed with the devil. Instead a man had constantly to make lesser choices, the meaning of each of which was not clear at the time he chose. And then suddenly all those incessant, troubling choices became together the one big one, and a man had gone round the bend before he knew it, with the damage all done—not in some romantic instant of clear-eyed knowledge that had at least the dignity of comprehension, but inch by inch, step by step, day by day. So Hunt Anderson was beginning, that day in the Piedmont ballroom, the long process in which he would ultimately become a live politician or a dead hero.

"But Morgan's married," Glass argued, clutching the redhead's hands. "Why screw around with a married man when I'm free as a bird?"

"Well, you know what they say." The redhead extracted her hands from Glass's without rancor. She looked at Morgan with bleary eyes. "He may be married but that doesn't mean he's dead, does it?"

"No holds barred," Anderson said, "this side of libel, mayhem, and pornography. Old Bull's boy fights hard as hell but almost fair. Puts on a good show, don't he, but underneath it all sometimes he even talks sense. Just a good old boy but knows how to handle the big boys, dang if he don't. Sharp as a tack but too rich to steal. City suits but common as a cotton undershirt. That's the new image, and God help us."

"The problem is," Matt—ever the technician—said in his serious way, "we've got a good base of support with the more sophisticated voters and we have to hold on to them while we double back and cut in on the old Zeb Vance crowd. Rich, do you think Zeb Vance might come out for us after all?"

"How would I know what Zeb Vance might do any more?"

"I guess you wouldn't," Matt said. "Anyway the one thing we've got going for us is that our voters don't really have any place to go but us, no matter what we do, not with a jerk like Johnson for an alternative."

Morgan refrained from saying that a jerk like James T. Johnson made a pretty good candidate in that state—and perhaps in any other. Johnson was a self-made man, naturally, and his literature proclaimed that he believed in God, free enterprise, hard work, and low taxes, and while he was certainly not a racist he did not believe in moving too fast or too far, the way the extremists wanted to do. Down the middle of the road was the right way for good old James T. Johnson, a man of property, a man of responsibility, a man of unimpeachable integrity, a man of experience in government (as chairman of the highway commission), who believed schools and hospitals cost too much, welfare was immoral, and the duty of government was to be inconspicuous. Johnson stumbled through lengthy speeches prepared by flacks from the bankers' association and the state Chamber of Commerce, dispensed campaign buttons that said GOD, COUNTRY AND JIM JOHNSON, hired campaign workers by the herd, began each rally with the Pledge of Allegiance, closed it with prayer, and was running nicely ahead.

Such a candidate made Anderson's problem all the tougher, Morgan thought the next day, as the campaign bus rolled through flat farmland toward the rally where the new image was to be unveiled (rather as if it were a piece of sculpture or a redecorated storefront). James T. Johnson, he reflected, was a hard man to attack, just as it was hard to fault your old mother; she might be an unconscionable crone, but in America the presumption was in her favor.

As Anderson began to speak that night he seemed little different from the serious campaigner with whom the state had become familiar. The echoes of The String Beans twanging away on "Great Speckled Bird" and "Fireball Mail" seemed to hang in the thick sweet spring air above the courthouse square in Denton, one of the small towns in an area where Anderson's private polls showed him lagging behind Johnson. There were yellow antibug bulbs behind the frosted glass atop the old wrought-iron lampposts in the parklike square, and in their mellow glow a good but quiet crowd was lined up comfortably on the slatted benches that had been assembled for the rally. Quite a few people sat on the grass too, and some boys were clinging precariously to an equestrian statue of General William Dorsey Pender. Dogwood blossoms and redbud floated in the darkness above the crowd, and in a well-tended circle around the statue, flowering almond and forsythia and rich dark winelike clumps of azaleas sprang from the rejuvenated earth.

Anderson's rostrum was not, as it would have been in most towns, on the steps of the courthouse, which was on one side of the square. Instead he spoke from the broad first-floor porch of the King Cotton Hotel, a ramshackle old brick building that roamed down the opposite side, and from whose columned front political candidates had been making speeches since the second Cleveland administration. Old Bull had known it better than Hunt did, Morgan thought a little ironically as he settled back in his chair at the rickety press table behind the speaker stand.

Kathy had not made this trip as she was entertaining, not very happily, a group of Anderson Girls at a tea arranged by Concerned Women for Anderson, a group Kathy irreverently called Harpies for Hunt. By then Morgan could find little excitement in the campaign anyway, and her absence made the evening seem more of a let-down, despite the promised new developments.

Matt Grant was standing unobtrusively at the rear of the porch with some local men, one of whom, in stentorian tones, had just—on instructions — bellowed an introduction of Anderson as "a real chip off the old block, when it comes to a fight," which was a new line altogether. The other men around Matt—mostly those young lawyers and businessmen of the area who, like Anderson, were eager for a new kind of politics in the state— looked glum. Gradually, as no doubt they had been warned to expect, a strange new tone began to be heard in Anderson's calm voice. For the first time in the campaign, for instance, he mentioned "my opponent," and the two words dropped into the still pool of that spring evening with heavy splashes, signaling that everything had changed.

". . . my opponent likes to say that if he's elected he'll vote to keep taxes down. That's the kind of promise my daddy used to say wouldn't get you a cup of coffee unless you put a nickel alongside it."

Another first—no one had heard him mention Old Bull publicly.

"Now it takes a dime, and in the first place, folks, a United States senator doesn't have anything more to do with all these state and local taxes you pay than your old hound dog does; and as for federal taxes, the only way my opponent would know how to vote to keep them down would be if somebody showed him which way is up . . ."

With smooth timing Anderson broke off as a ripple of laughter moved over the crowd at this none-too-veiled allusion to rumors that James T. Johnson was something less than a mental giant. He let the laugh play itself almost out, then quickly picked up the mood.

"Why, they tell me my opponent even has some kind of plan where he's going to get farm prices raised and acreage allotments increased all at the same time, and I want to tell you folks, if he can do that, you ought to elect him because he can make magic—maybe he can even get those banker friends of his that are spending big money to finance his campaign and pull his puppet strings to stop gouging you on production loans. But, friends, you know he can't do that because my opponent's no magician . . ."

The pause for a laugh did not get much response this time, and Morgan thought that Zeb Vance might spit on the sidewalk but he could certainly pull off this kind of thing a lot better than Old Bull's sophisticated boy.

"He's no magician, and I'll tell you what he is instead—he's a congenital prevaricator who's going up and down this state spreading lies and treating good hardworking folks as if they're too dumb to know that any man who tries to tell them he can cut taxes *and* give them better schools and roads and hospitals has been out in the sun too long without his hat. You're smarter than that even if he isn't."

A weak round of applause spread limply from a group that looked like shills Matt and his local organizers had planted in the crowd. It soon died away, and Anderson, after pausing a moment—rather desperately, Morgan thought—plunged on.

"I'll tell you just what my opponent can do for you—just how smart he is. He's been highway commissioner for almost ten years, he tells us that a hundred times a day on the radio and the TV, paid for by his big-money buddies. As if neglecting the roads down here in this part of the state to keep his millionaire friends' taxes down has anything whatsoever to do with what a United States senator needs to know about foreign policy and the national economy and the A-bomb and Soviet Russia, but never mind all that, we concede he's been highway commissioner all those years. But just today, folks"—he began fumbling in his inner coat pocket—"before we started down here to Denton, I thought I remembered something, and I got out this old diary my daddy used to keep years ago when he was just starting out in life and, sure enough, there it was . . ."

He had found the paper and was peering at it in his uncertain way, his big frame looming up incredibly over the rostrum, even with his shoulders slumped as usual. "I'm going to read you the entry. Now here it is, right out of my old daddy's diary when he was a young man. 'June ten, eighteen ninety-one. Train to Denton to call on Rose.' Now think of that, folks, all those years ago. Miss Rose McNeil, later she was Old Bull's first wife. 'Train to Denton to call on Rose. Walked to Red Springs, eleven miles.' Miss Rose was from Red Springs. I bet a lot of you folks know her family, there's a lot of good old McNeils living right out there in Red Springs still, and I'm glad to say they're every last one supporting me. Now the diary goes on here: 'Red Springs, eleven miles. Two hours thirteen minutes. Made it for dinner.' That's what it says, right there in Old Bull's diary, and I'm here to tell you, folks, eleven miles in two hours thirteen minutes flat is pretty good walking time, especially in June heat and on the dirt roads they had back in ninety-one, all those years ago. And you know what, folks?" The story had them listening, and Hunt paused, dramatically this time, looking from right to left, drawing himself taller, his shoulders straightening. "That's the same road out there from Denton to Red Springs, the very same road Old Bull walked in two hours thirteen minutes flat, *and to this day it's still not paved.* That's what my opponent has managed to do for you good folks down here, just pour a little gravel on the same old dirt roads you always had, and that's about all he'll ever do for you in the United States Senate too. Old Gravel Roads Johnson—you send *him* to Washington and you put a dime beside *him* and they won't even give you a cup of coffee."

As Anderson roared through to the climax, his voice rose powerfully above the laughter that came fully and freely for the first time, and when he fell momentarily into silence there was a hasty round of applause and one or two people—not Matt's shills—even rose to their feet.

"In fact," Anderson continued after a moment, rolling along in good form, suddenly at ease in his new style, "in fact, I'll bet you there's not man nor boy in this crowd, or any of the ladies either, that right tonight, all these years later—I'll bet there's not a soul in this square could go out there tomorrow and beat Old Bull's time to Red Springs. Because, I've checked it myself, and, if anything, the road's worse today than it was in eighteen ninety-one. Anyone who doesn't believe that's what old Gravel Roads Johnson has let happen to the roads in this state, you just go out there tomorrow in a good pair of walking shoes and you start out at the Esso station and if you can make it to the Red Springs crossroads in less than two hours and thirteen minutes, I'll give you a prime bull calf right off Old Bull's best pasture."

"How 'bout you?" somebody yelled from beyond the statue. Morgan learned later that Matt had had a man set to ask that question but he never got a chance before somebody raised it honestly—life transcending art.

"I'll be there," Anderson shouted back. "I might even get on the phone and see if I can get old Gravel Roads to come."

And the next day there was the big shambling figure of Hunt Anderson leading a party of fourteen men—boys were in school—and two women, with about as many photographers and reporters—alerted in advance by Matt Grant—along eleven hot and dusty miles of dirt road, through worn-out farm country and piney woods, to the lost and dying community of Red Springs, where there might have been a lot of good old McNeils supporting Hunt Anderson but where nothing was to be seen but a few decrepit farmhouses and barns across the fields and low against the pines.

At the crossroads there was only one old clapboard general store, long in need of paint and perched on four spindly brick shanks, its silvered walls plastered with tin signs for Six Six Six, Hadacol, and Goody's Headache Powder. This enterprise was run by a Gothic old lady in a faded print dress, bewildered and none too pleased to have so many men crowding around her counter at once, to buy beer and soft drinks. Later the Anderson campaign organization had to set up and manage a refreshment stand across the road, from which the old lady got the profits although, not a good old McNeil, she remained to the end a Gravel Roads Johnson voter.

Of that first walking party, led by Hunt himself, only one, a spry old retired mailman with a cocked eye, could beat Old Bull's record. Morgan came in last, limping and disgruntled. In the afternoon, a second group, made up of schoolboys, tried the walk, with two of them winning bull calves.

The Great Bull Calf Walk, as the *Capital Times* and other papers soon began to call it, was on. Entrants came from all over the state—at first drummed up by the Anderson organization, but later on their own—because those were splendid bull calves Anderson was giving away, because the publicity was good and so was Anderson's promotion, and no doubt because something in man loves a good show and a good challenge. One of the state's new television stations sent a truck to film the Walk on the third day, and that put the show over more than anything else; entrants kept hoping TV would come back and show them making the Walk and winning a calf. A national newsreel came the day Anderson made the Walk a third time and finally beat Old Bull's time by a shrewdly managed thirty seconds; whereupon, since he said he could hardly give himself a calf he already owned, he said he would instead ship a chicken to old Gravel Roads, who steadfastly ignored the whole thing.

Which was probably all Johnson could do, Morgan thought, but it cost him dearly, because in the closing weeks of the campaign the Great Bull Calf Walk from Denton to Red Springs came to dominate the state's headlines and screens. Among other reasons, the press in its follow-the-leader fashion took up the story shamelessly; the campaign had been dull otherwise, the Bull Calf Walk revived memories of the state's most famous political figure, and it also had plenty of what editors in their mindless way call "human interest"—as if that were a commodity that could be packaged or even defined. Day after day there would be two or three groups of walkers going down the road in clouds of dust under the hot pale spring sky, and there would be Hunt Anderson in the headlines and photos giving away another calf, maybe to some glowing 4H-er, or in one case to an armless veteran, and in another to an elderly black man who told hovering reporters he had once tended the yard of James T. Johnson for ten cents an hour and as a result of this business relationship was surely going to vote for Mister Hunt Anderson. A calf went to the star quarterback from the university, after he trotted the whole eleven miles in track regalia amid swarms of puffing sports reporters. The lieutenant-governor of the state won a calf, and so did the state commander of the American Legion, who didn't hurt Anderson a bit by ungraciously announcing that he was still going to vote for "a real American," Gravel Roads Johnson. The state commander didn't use the nickname of course. He didn't have to, because the Great Bull Calf Walk hung it on poor Johnson forever. (Just recently, Morgan had seen it used in a clipping somebody sent him that reported old Gravel Roads had spoken out against pornography.) And the one thing a solemn-ass candidate like James T. Johnson couldn't stand was ridicule.

The name caught on, and Anderson kept giving away calves and making fun of everything from Johnson's intellect to his political backers to his record in office. Johnson twice lost his temper in public, and once, red-faced and ludicrous, even stalked off a speaker's platform. He demanded peevishly that this Anderson stop giving the voters a good time and get serious. Suddenly the front-runner had been pushed clearly on the defensive; Morgan and the other reporters could feel the campaign change shape. For one thing, whatever closing kick the people behind Johnson might have had in mind never broke through the Great Bull Calf Walk headlines, although Johnson himself began to talk more and more about desegregated schools and dangers to womanhood and the Southern way of life; but the kind of racial charges and innuendo that might have strung Anderson on the rack between his conscience and his prospects failed to make any real public impression.

That was one important function of the Walk, but there was something else, perhaps of greater importance but harder to define. The Anderson campaign just began to move. Politics is a thing of hidden sparks and hair triggers. A candidate one day or one week seems to take charge of things. People who paid him no attention suddenly listen. Workers who were going through the motions for reasons of their own actually get down to business. Then a lot of money comes rolling in—too late to be budgeted into the campaign but an excellent mark of progress to workers, backers, and the candidate himself, and in plenty of time to pay off debts. Crowds get bigger, happier, for no apparent reason. Everything is suddenly electric, speeches crackle with good lines, bands get snappier, the enthusiasm around even the smallest campaign office is infectious. Victory becomes tangible, on one's fingertips; everything is there for the taking if everyone will just work a little harder, put in one more phone call, another round of late hours, one last swing through this county or that city.

And so, on primary eve, Hunt Anderson was back in Denton, this time in the hot white glare of television lights illuminating across the state the first live program ever to originate from the hallowed porch of the King Cotton Hotel. And he was in. Morgan *knew* he was in, everyone felt it; there could be no mistaking the way the Great Bull Calf Walk had touched the match to the tinder, set it all on fire.

In his final speech Hunt Anderson became again the man of the early campaign, the thoughtful expositor of issues—after a final thrust at Gravel Roads Johnson, who had at last, but too late, found the way to deal with the Great Bull Calf Walk by refusing to make the final Primary Day walk on the surprisingly good-natured grounds that his feet hurt. That was bound to be the result, Anderson said in his opening lines, of keeping them in his mouth through the whole campaign.

Otherwise Anderson did not try to be a showman that last night. With clarity and brevity, imposed by expensive television time as much as by inclination, he summed up the issues he had emphasized—improved education and therefore, by implication, open schools, citizen responsibility, and what he called "a balanced economy" as an alternative to the heavy-handed industrial development the state had been pursuing since World War II. He made ritual promises to keep his office door open and to return often to the state to keep in touch with its purifying airs and attitudes—as against the city cesspools of the North. Then, peering a little more at the cameras than at the crowds before him, he closed on a note that took Morgan back to the night by Old Bull's hilltop grave.

"My friends, this has been a long road for me and a journey on which I've learned, I think, a lot about you, and during which, undoubtedly, you've learned something about me. I've asked to serve you and I believe that tomorrow you're going to confer that honor on me." He paused for the kind of cheers a winner can always get for that kind of statement. "If not, it'll still have been a great thing for me that I tried, that I've had the warm reception and the intelligent attention you've all given me, all across this great state of ours, this land that means so much to all of us, that comes down to us from our fathers as a charge to this generation. And if I am to be allowed to serve you for these next six years, I aim to be worthy of that charge. I aim to be worthy and, my friends, I aim to call upon all who love this state, all who revere its great history, to join with me in making them worthy at last of the liberty and the humanity to which we and they pay homage."

These were a bit more than the usual words of uplift due at the end of a campaign. Morgan analyzed them in the story he phoned in that night: Anderson was still dealing, boldly but subtly too, with the Old Bull issue; by invoking fathers and history, he had identified himself once more with his own; and by the suggestions reverberant in *worthy at last* and by the tone of the peroration, he had also called upon himself and the state to rise above their own pasts, to some greater future.

That tone had permeated his whole campaign, he reminded Morgan later that night, even if "the big trick" had been turned by the Great Bull Calf Walk and by the new role of folksy showman that he had slipped on like a comfortable suit of tailor-made clothes—finding in that role and the response to it, he further explained, something of an extension of the warmth and human feeling he got from handshaking, at which he had continued to perform prodigies throughout the campaign.

"It just came to me that night in Denton when we kicked off the Walk," he said, "if you make them laugh, make them think you care, make them think you know a little something about how life is for them, give them a little fun, how is that any less respectable than giving them a lecture on the Gross National Product?"

"It isn't," Morgan said. "But, on the other hand, does it get anything done on civil rights? On the minimum wage?"

"Well, the first thing a leader has to do is to get other folks to follow. Rich, you know damn well I haven't changed my position on a single issue, including civil rights *and* the minimum wage. I've made the most serious campaign this state has seen in this century. Like my speech tonight. It's just that I've also given away some calves rather publicly and the folks happened to get interested."

"Forty-nine bull calves, to be exact." They were riding together in Anderson's bus on the way back from his final speech. Outside, the countryside was green except for the plowed earth lying rich and promising in the moonlight. Morgan held in his lap the bottle with which they were frequently replenishing their paper cups. "And that's a lot of bull and a lot of money, even for you. Can I ask you one last shitty question, strictly off the record?"

"Shoot."

"Was that entry really in the diary?"

"What diary was that?" Anderson said.

Oh, Anderson had been on top of the world that night, Morgan thought.

He had known he had won, had pulled everything together when he needed to. It was only later that he would sometimes get a little edgy about the Great Bull Calf Walk.

"You can't fool me," Glass said, rising with wobbly scorn. "Five minutes after I'm gone you'll be balling her ass."

"You're *aw*ful!" the redhead insisted, not angry enough to speak too sharply to anyone in television.

And the funny thing is, Morgan thought, watching Glass weave away, indignant, in the gloom, I don't think even *I* could do it now. Tonight. After everything.

On the morning the migrant hearings opened, Morgan was not surprised that Anderson turned away, a little too pointedly, from being reminded of the Great Bull Calf Walk. It had not been, after all, the way he had expected to win; it had not created exactly the image he had hoped to convey. But Anderson's momentary annoyance, if that was what it had been, was soon lost in the business of the hearings; and while some bookish Assistant Secretary of Labor was droning through the basic statistics and legislative history of the migrant labor problem in America—material Anderson wanted in the record at the outset as a frame of reference for what was to follow—the door opened and Kathy Anderson came in, moving almost furtively to a seat near the rear of the chamber, a folded newspaper under her arm. She was inconspicuously dressed—a light raincoat, perhaps something dark and decorous beneath that—but nothing, Morgan had thought at the time, watching her to her seat, could conceal the beauty of those long legs that he had first noticed, or the grace with which she moved; and nothing could be more striking than the hard, motionless intensity into which, at once, as in his first glimpse of her, her body and consciousness seemed to compose themselves.

Morgan looked then at Anderson, who was studiously following with bent head and a huge blunt forefinger on the page the assistant secretary's monochromatic tones. Matt Grant was in whispered conference with Sprock & Berger. Morgan left the press table, made his way down the side of the chamber past the other scattered witnesses and buffs, across the rear, and sat beside Kathy. Not until he was that close did she appear even to notice his movements.

"You're too early," he whispered. "No fireworks today."

She inclined her head to his side, and her perfume touched him with sly fingertips. "I'm not going to miss a minute." It was not exactly a whisper;

some women have the gift of speaking so softly they need never whisper.

"This could go on for weeks."

"It better. We need to let it build."

Something about the remark puzzled him until he realized he had never before heard her identify her own interests with Anderson's politics—indeed even speak with political content. It was also remarkable how even this exchange seemed not really to break her concentration on the room, the scene, the assistant secretary's dronings. Her replies seemed managed, as it were, separately, from some other motive center; like blinking one's eyelids, they seemed not to need really to be thought about. Morgan had the impression that if his words or presence were to demand of her that she break the direction of her intensity, if she were to have to deal consciously with him, she simply would not have responded. She had the capacity to draw about herself a still circle of consciousness, from which she excluded everything upon which she was not focused; and Morgan had a moment of despair in which he feared that that circle would never draw itself close and embracing about him.

As abruptly as she had settled into her stillness, she broke from it, twisting toward him, fixing him with cool, pale eyes. She wore no makeup but a trace of lipstick and perhaps some light powder, and again her perfume touched him insidiously.

"It's going to make him," she murmured, something for once impassioned in that soft voice that had seemed always so indifferent. "If he does it right, it's going to make him at last." The newspaper lay on her knee, and her hand moved featherlike to touch the headline on Morgan's story.

"And that's what you want?"

"If he's got to be a great man. If that means so much. With this, he can be." Her hand touched the newspaper again, clenched suddenly, and there was in her voice an edge of ferocity Morgan had never heard.

"It could break him," Morgan said. "Playing with Hinman is playing with dynamite. And it'll be hard to make the case and make it stick."

"I like a gamble when the payoff is big. This big."

"A big payoff or nothing," Morgan said.

"Hunt will finish him." She looked at Morgan steadily, fixed on him as never before.

Interested, Morgan thought. Caught up at last.

Kathy leaned closer. "I've been through it all with Matt, every scrap of the evidence. There's enough for Hunt to finish him."

"Maybe you're right at that. Maybe Hunt and Matt will finish him. Then what?"

She ignored the question, still staring at him. "Matt's good. Matt's a wonderful staff man."

Morgan heard the words fall one by one; there were wicked, wanton tremors in his heart. "A great second-man," he said, "that's Matt."

She nodded slowly, seriously, her eyes steadily on his. "But *Hunt* will finish Hinman." And just as the heat of her intensity became uncomfortable, almost physical, she smiled, her full lower lip barely touching the perfect white edges of her teeth. "And then they can't stop us," she said.

As suddenly as it had come—before Morgan could even ask "stop you from what?"—her attention passed back to the chamber, in which, at that moment, as if bees were alighting to succor themselves, the assistant secretary's drone dropped into silence.

"Now, Mister Secretary"—Anderson's low but carrying voice in a moment filled the room—"that was a most comprehensive statement indeed and the subcommittee thanks you for it. It gives us . . ." He went on for a moment with Southern and senatorial fluency to suggest that the subcommittee simply couldn't have done its work without the assistant secretary's brilliant contribution, which had put most of those in the room to sleep.

Morgan went back to the press table, from which he could see Matt Grant searching the room. When Matt discovered Kathy, his gaze lingered on her a moment, troubled, Morgan thought, then suddenly indulgent, a little fatherly and forgiving, as if in her unobtrusive dress and rear-row seat she had assumed for him some station of penance. Morgan could still feel the intensity with which she was listening, following the play, joining in at last, waiting for that shining moment that would finish Hinman and make Hunt Anderson.

And what would it do, he wondered, for Kathy Anderson, who had never asked Hunt to be a great man? What burned in her now with such consuming heat, changing her attitudes, and leaving Matt Grant no longer in the circle, not even anywhere near it, poor fool. Poor Matt! Poor man! No more to her than staff, who even in betrayal had been betrayed.

The Storyteller III

Morgan, awakening with the sun in his eyes, sensed at once that he had done something he would wish he had not done. He had not had enough sleep, but he always woke early, no matter how late and debauched the evening had been. Morgan could get along for days on little or no sleep; then, one night, he would collapse for twelve hours or more. He hated waking in dark, enclosed rooms and habitually threw open shades or draperies before going to bed. Even more ritually, he carried inside himself a small secret notion, an ultimate arrogance, that what might be permitted to others was not necessarily allowed by the fitness of things to Richmond P. Morgan. This omnipresent consciousness was most insistent in the waking moments, which Morgan knew from long experience brought him not a sense of fresh beginning but a quicksilver repetition of the day and night before. So he was used to waking in strange rooms reproachful with sunlight, in the sour aftermath of drink and lust, with a sense of having sinned against the true self concealed beneath his careful cover. For a moment he was not sure who lay beside him, whose great Renoir haunch rose like a monument beneath the sheet, whose heavy legs clasped one of his, whose torso lay across his throbbing arm. He sniffed tentatively, but any telltale perfume was drowned in the odors of sleep and sex. Then he saw lank strands of red hair inches away on the mangled common pillow and, remembering all, groaned aloud in despair and anguish.

As if on cue, the haunch rolled massively over. His leg and arm were released. In the one blurred glimpse he allowed himself before closing his eyes, like a child who believes that if he cannot see he cannot be seen,

Morgan saw that her makeup was gone, replaced by a smile of terrifying cheer spread across teeth he had not realized were so prominent; and even in his self-imposed darkness he could not avoid the ripe smell of liquor that hung near her lips.

"*Good* morning, glory," she said, breathing heavily, and plastered her damp mouth on his.

Let me die now, Morgan prayed to the peculiar gods he summoned *in extremis.*

She released his mouth noisily and thrust her head back, smiling again —he knew without looking. Her hands strayed over him. "*Ohhh,* you!" She got hold of him with her fingertips and wriggled closer, pushing billows of flesh stickily against him.

"Careful," Morgan muttered into his lumpish pillow. "It's about to fall off." He recognized, in this lapse into the joviality that ritually marked his cover, the faint stirrings of self-preservation, and hated himself the more.

"Oh, the poor little shriveled-up thingums," the redhead whispered lovingly. "We wouldn't let that happen, would we?"

"Let go of me and get your ass up," Morgan said, deadly serious but managing to speak lightly. Reluctantly he opened his eyes. A foot away, her broad face beamed at him with what was unmistakably a motherly kind of pride.

"Not since my very first time," the redhead whispered. "After that, I mean, it was just blah, like I was all frozen up inside or something, you know? I mean just nothing, like a side of beef. And then *you!*" He sensed the liquor, then felt her mouth like a suction cup on his, and barely stopped himself from pulling away.

"You don't mean it," he said, when he could.

"Not a thing for years. And then twice just in one night, you know? I thought I'd die!"

"I'm not sure I didn't." He tried to remember their thrashings and groaning in the night. She had not let go, and in disbelief he felt himself rising in her hand. Suddenly, in the old familiar compulsive cycle, desire was at war with disgust, and for a moment, even in the closeness and heat of the bed, the dampness of their bodies together, he shivered all over, his legs jerked out straight, and—helpless, despising himself—he felt himself sinking into his weakness and need.

"Was it so good?" she murmured, stroking. "So good for him too?"

The inane little girl voice, the sheer emptiness of what she said, despite the narcotic intimacy of what she was doing, wrenched him back from the dark gulf of sensuality over which he knew his life hung by the frayed thread of his self-regard. Abruptly he swung his legs over the side of the bed and stood up. "I give up," he said. "You win the silver fucking cup. I concede."

At the bathroom door he looked back. She lay on her back, the sheet pulled modestly to her waist, her hands behind her head, her breasts beneath her armpits, her face broad and quivering with satisfaction and pride and mother-love. "Oh *you!*" she cried, and he fled to the shower.

It worked its magic quickly. At least, he thought, hidden in the steam and spray, he was not hung over. Aside from a certain dryness in his mouth, he was free of charge for all the drinking, and now that the ghastly moments of waking were past, perhaps the highest price had been paid for the redhead. Standing, head down, with the water stinging and scalding his shoulders and neck, he tried to recall how much Glass knew, examining his memory for whatever cost in self-respect that would levy. A sudden draft speared him between his shoulderblades, the sound of the water changed, and strong, soft hands moved on his ribs.

"What's a stewardi for if she can't wash a fellow's back?"

"Christ," Morgan said, going rapidly over the side of the tub, "I'm steamed like a clam." He was toweling himself vigorously before he looked back to find her soaping one wobbling breast in each hand.

She pouted her underlip at him. "Wash me then."

"Wouldn't know where to start." Morgan bolted for the bedroom, slamming the door behind him.

It seemed to him that he had never known a woman, except Anne, who could understand that at some point the game was over; in her cool detachment, Anne demanded even more than mere attention, petting, lover's deference. Whatever it was, it was precisely what he had never given her, what he perhaps never could, yet would sell his soul to lay at her disdainful feet. Or would have, at a time when it might have made a difference.

He fumbled in his small bag for shorts, got them on, found a pair of socks. In a sense, Anne only proved the point that the male might be the aggressor but the world of the female was a sort of Russian steppe that a male invaded at his peril. He would be drawn in, trapped, destroyed; there would be no retreat, and no hiding place, once he set foot on the deceptive, enfolding plain of sex.

For the first time in years Morgan thought of his Cousin Liza; and even in the harsh morning sun, even among the pieces of plastic furniture and the cheap modern prints and the gaudy thin carpeting of the Bright Leaf Motel, he could see again in mind's eye his Aunt Octavia's huge, dim kitchen, the dark corner beyond the wood range, the patterned linoleum, the round oaken table on its pedestal in the middle of the floor; he heard the sharp slap of the screen door behind him as he fled the big old gloomy kitchen to the wide back porch.

The last red glare of the sun was going down. Long streaks of salmon cloud climbed the enormous sky, and the night's first bullbat sent its raucous racketing cry to the ends of the drab Southern earth.

"Liza?" he called. "You out here, Lize?"

"Don't you call me Lize," Liza said, coming around the corner of the house. "It makes me sound like some old darkie."

He went down the steep back steps and took her by the arm.

"Where we going?" she asked.

"To my hiding place." He turned to make sure no one saw them. Eight windows and a door looked out from the house on the backyard, and the glass in each of them blazed and glittered with the final suspended orange light of the sun; as he watched, they all went as one into blackness and the sun was gone. The old house loomed up vengefully in the night.

Liza was skinny that summer, skinnier than in all the summers they had been visiting their Aunt Octavia, the only times they ever saw each other. She was a year older than he was and beginning to put on airs about it. Sometimes she would lash out at him in obscure fury, then run to her room and stay there for hours.

"Dark out here," Liza said.

They had reached the hiding place, and he pulled apart the branches to show her the way.

"You mean this old grapevine is the hiding place you've been bragging about?" Liza leaned past him, peering into the dim little cave. The vine grew from a twisted central root clump and spread out over the rotting stumps and rafters of the frame that had held it aloft in its bearing days. All around the root clump was a hidden cavern the sun had never touched.

"Aunt Octavia wouldn't want us in there together, Richie. It's not nice."

"She won't know about it if we don't tell her." He had often—and easily —deceived his father, who seldom even noticed his presence, and his sister Estelle, who was too busy keeping house to keep up with him, but even the notion of hiding something from his aunt was vaguely disturbing. "God cares about the littlest thing you do," she had told him in her sad, tinkling voice. "He marks the sparrow's fall." He was sure God and his Aunt Octavia went hand in hand. Sometimes he would mix up the face of his aunt with the picture of his mother on his father's dresser; the things he remembered most about his mother were the way her voice sounded when she sang "Mighty Like a Rose" at his bedtime every evening, and the single scream that had awakened him the night she died, and so did the little brother he would never have. Sometimes it was easy to confuse both his mother's picture and his Aunt Octavia with the angels pictured in the Bible. Now that he was old enough to visit her by himself he would have dreams in which his Aunt's soft, plaintive hands swooped like mourning doves about his pillow, while the scent of tea rose clung about her hair and her sweet, reproachful face hovered over him.

Liza peered dubiously into the opening. "It sure is dark in there."

"Dark won't hurt you." He put his hand against her rump and pushed gently. She gave a faint, startled gasp, then crept into the hiding place. He followed.

Liza's groping hands found his arm. "I'm scared, Richie."

"Nothing to be scared of." He pulled Liza down beside him. Her knobby little knee gouged into his thigh, and he put his hand on it. "Swear you won't tell."

"I swear." Her whisper was almost lost in the faint rustle of the leaves of the vine, in the ghostly breeze moving across the backyard. "Richie, you aren't going to do anything, are you?"

"Do what?" His hand was still on her knee, and he noticed suddenly that her skin was hot and sticky.

"You know, what boys do." Liza's hand touched his. "Please don't do anything bad, Richie. Please don't scare me."

Before he could ask what boys did, he realized it was not just the breeze rustling the leaves of the vine. Before he could move, a beam of light caught them in a bald, pitiless circle. Liza screamed, and terror filled his whole heart, rushing soundless from the far rim of darkness. It seemed that all his life he had been waiting for something like this—something awful—to happen to him.

"You filthy little beasts!"

There was no sad sweetness, no gentle reproach, in that voice, but he knew it was his Aunt Octavia's. He looked up then, and the light wavered; beyond its single fierce eye, at the edge of a white-hot circle, he saw her, immensely tall and jagged, only a shade darker than the unconcerned sky.

The phone rang in the motel room, mercifully snatching Morgan from the relentless past. He picked up the receiver and mumbled something.

"When can you get here? I hoped maybe you'd come last night."

"Kathy," Morgan said. "Kathy, goddam it."

"It's all right. I'm all right, except I wanted you last night."

"I tried to call back. It was too late."

"I got the message. It's all right."

"I cried in the taxi," Morgan said.

The redhead came in from the bathroom, naked, beaming. She saw him holding the receiver and made elephantine gestures of silence to herself.

"There was this old colored woman," Kathy said. "She held his head in her lap."

"On the sidewalk?"

"I knew you'd want to know that," Kathy said. "Come out right away. I couldn't sleep last night. I wanted you with me then."

"As fast as I can," Morgan said. "Try to relax."

Kathy hung up as abruptly as she had come on the line, and Morgan looked dumbly at the receiver, appalled at its inadequacy, which matched his own. He thought of Hunt Anderson down on the pavement, his head in an old black woman's lap.

The redhead was posturing gaily before the full-length mirror on the bathroom door. "There may be a lot of me," she said with satisfaction, "but it's all woman this morning."

"Look, sweetie, that was an old friend, and I've got to get the hell out to that funeral right away. You'd better dress."

"A hell of a lot of woman." The redhead leaned forward to examine more closely her mirrored billows. "You made me feel like a lot of woman, you know?"

"Great." Morgan had a shirt on and sat on the bed to pull socks over his feet. The redhead pranced to the dresser, fumbled among her scattered things, went back to the mirror with her hands at her neck.

"Better." She admired the effect of the strand of pearls on her nakedness. Morgan tugged at his socks. The redhead came to the bed, put her belly close to his face, and tipped up his head with both hands on his cheeks. "You like my pearls?"

Morgan sighed. It was pathetic, he thought, that she had no other resources, had never seen the need for any other, than her body. She nuzzled him. Morgan lifted the one foot he had encased in a sock, put it flat against her belly, and pushed her gently away. "You're the greatest, Red. But I've got to get moving."

"Was that somebody on the phone you're in love with?"

"I'm not in love with anybody." She was more perceptive than he had thought, and he knew that now the trouble was coming.

"Well, have I done something wrong then?"

Morgan reached for his other sock. He could not look at what he suspected would be her quivering lips. "You did everything so right an old fart like me couldn't take any more of it even if he had the time, which I don't." He winked at her, knowing she was on the thin edge of tears. "Anyway, you've got to save a little something for the pilots."

She laughed bravely, went back to the mirror for more assurance, and finally began to fumble with clothes. "I dress from the top down," she explained confidentially, stuffing a blubbery breast into boned lace.

Morgan, pulling on his pants, refused to be drawn into intimate talk. He wanted to be out and away, primarily because Kathy was waiting for him, but also because, as always, the probing morning sunlight had reached into and activated the deep controlling cells of his self-esteem. He flinched from the redhead's vacuous chatter, her gaucherie, her ponderous playfulness, her overwhelming flesh in the pitiless sunlight, all of which—he told himself —robbed him of the simple exuberance of love-making, the lusty, uncomplicated enjoyment of his body and hers. But try as he might to push the awareness beneath conscious recognition, he knew with chill certainty that this was an evasion; the truth was that he despised himself for wanting lusty exuberance, uncomplicated enjoyment, yet denying them to himself—because what might be fit for lesser mortals could not loosely be indulged by Richmond P. Morgan, was only a reproach and an embarrassment to the self-esteem that led inevitably to self-contempt, and to the exact depressing knowledge that, like any weakling, he had used his sensuality and the body and spirit of this sad, hoping girl to numb his damaged sensibility, relieve his glands and nerve ends.

Morgan finished putting on the sober lightweight suit he had brought for the funeral. The redhead, still dressing from the top down, had somehow managed to stay bare below the waist. He went across the room, wobbled her bottom with a gentle hand, and kissed the back of her damp neck. "Nice to know you, Red."

She turned to face him, flinging her arms around his neck.

"But I've really got to run now." He suffered a lingering wet kiss, the surge of her belly against him.

"Will I see you on the flight back tonight?"

Morgan had not thought of that. He was appalled. "I don't even know when I'm going." He kissed her cheek, disengaged, and retreated rapidly. As he went out the door, carrying his bag, he saw the redhead slumping barebottomed on the rumpled bed, young, alone, stripped. But his spirits lifted immediately; he was out of it, he thought meanly, he was in the clear. His luck had held again, and damn good ass to boot.

The elevator came, bearing a sour tourist couple ridiculous in shorts. Morgan followed them into the glass and tile lobby, where Dunn was just turning away from the registration desk. Dunn looked neat, crisp, rested, as though he had not flown all night, as Morgan knew he must have; but Dunn always looked as efficient and in-place as a drill press in a workshop. In addition to the green-tinted lenses that concealed his eyes, the way he had of seeming functional in all circumstances was a large part of his intimidating effect. Dunn was a man to whom persons cast adrift in a lifeboat would instinctively turn, in fear as in hope, since he obviously would not hesitate to throw the weaklings overboard to right the ballast. Morgan had never seen Dunn not in control of things and himself—just as Dunn now registered no surprise at all upon seeing Morgan.

"Going in for breakfast," Dunn said. "Come on." They fell into step, heels clicking through the echoing lobby.

"How was your flight?"

"Unspeakable. Then I had to rent a car and drive two hours."

Morgan started to ask if Dunn had slept on the plane but stopped; of course Dunn would have slept on the plane, or anywhere. They were at the door of the coffee shop, and a doleful lady, corseted masochistically, waved them in with a large menu, as if it were a fan.

"But I had to come." Dunn took a seat with his back to the wall. "I know what people think, but I liked the guy. How's Kathy?"

"Haven't seen her yet." Morgan did not feel quite ready to talk with Dunn about Anderson or Kathy, but there was little help for it. "You'll get the headlines anyway. The famous political boss. They'll resurrect all the old convention stories now that you're here."

Dunn put down his menu. "I never thought of that. Maybe I shouldn't have come."

He seemed older than Morgan remembered—more gray in his hair, more lines in his neck, his hands boned and veined more prominently—but the thin mouth was as sharply etched as ever in his dark face, beneath the green lenses.

"What does it matter now?" Morgan said. "The old convention stories, I mean. Why shouldn't you have come?"

"I wouldn't want to upset Kathy. But I suppose nothing I could do would be likely to upset her. She doesn't give me the time of day. Not when I've seen her in recent years."

And never really did, Morgan thought. But Dunn did not know that. Or maybe he did. Dunn had not managed things over the years, ruled the party in his state so effectively, by being indifferent or insensitive. Dunn was hard —callous, some said. Once at a state convention, when Dunn had determined to put a new man on the ballot for state auditor or some other minor office, Morgan had seen him tell the stunned incumbent that he was finished, with no more emotion or concern than he might have displayed in trading a used car or taking a small poker loss on a bluff hand. "Look," Dunn had told Morgan later, "I didn't want to do it, much less enjoy it, but the guy was going nowhere in politics. Now he can practice law and get rich on the connections I gave him. The other guy has some style, and if I don't look ahead, pretty soon I'm out of the ball game. The new man will be governor in four years." The "new man" was now the governor, and as with most of Dunn's choices, he was even a good governor.

Dunn did not play the game for money, if only because he apparently had plenty of that, and made more every year as a heavy stockholder in an unrelated family business. Precisely why Dunn wanted political power, when he already had money, Morgan did not know; except that Morgan believed most men wanted power, one way or another, judging themselves either immune to its fatal erosion or deserving of its rewards. It was not clear to Morgan whether Dunn was either, neither, or both, or thought himself any of the three. But Dunn was efficient, too smart and too rich to steal, and he thought for himself—all qualities rare enough in Morgan's political experience for him to value them.

Matt Grant came in, saw them, hesitated, then walked to their table. He and Dunn spoke coolly, but when Morgan asked him to sit down, Grant, holding up a folder, said he had some papers to go over. He took a table nearby.

"One thing I have to say for Hunt Anderson," Dunn said, "his people are really loyal to him."

"I wasn't one of Anderson's people."

"Not when he was alive. Why don't you let yourself be now?"

"Maybe you're right," Morgan said, after they had ordered. "Sometimes a man just can't keep his neutrality, I suppose."

"Neutrality?" Dunn sipped coffee as if to clear his mouth of the word. "You reporters talk about neutrality as if it's integrity. Or honor. But it's bullshit, is what it is. Nobody's neutral."

"But don't you see a certain terrible attraction to it, Dunn? Impartiality.

Isn't there something Olympian, a kind of imposing beauty, about that?" Dunn was one of the few men Morgan had known in politics or for that matter in life—Anderson had been another—with whom Morgan could talk abstractly, in concepts, whose intelligence was not limited to or narrowly focused on operations and issues.

"I see that." Dunn's green lenses peered at him. "To be above the battle is to be too good for it. Neutrality as purity. But the question is whether you mean the issue that causes a particular fight isn't worth your Olympian concern, or whether fighting itself, taking sides, choosing, is beneath you, no matter what the issue."

" 'Was John Milton to conjugate Greek verbs in his library when the liberty of Englishmen was imperiled?'—Anderson used to quote that. *He* believed in the battle, at least he did until . . . As for me, sometimes I don't believe the battle makes a damn bit of difference."

"Then that's not really neutrality," Dunn said. "That's detachment, maybe even indifference. Neutrality as arrogance."

"Exactly. That's what I meant about the attraction. The notion that it's not for you, all that blood, sweat, and tears, it's for lesser beings, grubbing along."

"Is that the way you look at life? Isn't that really setting yourself apart?"

Morgan drew within his cover, feeling Dunn move in too close. Morgan did not know Dunn that well. They shared no real intimacy. On the level of abstraction, Dunn was one thing; but Morgan was not sure he wanted to offer Dunn or anyone any part of himself on any other level. He flinched inwardly, thinking momentarily of the redhead.

Outwardly he shrugged. "I'm a reporter. A privileged spectator."

Dunn's tinted lenses seemed suddenly to flash. His finger jabbed the air in front of Morgan and disappeared. "Spectators are interested in the spectacle. Nothing detached about that, much less Olympian."

Morgan was obscurely angered, but before he could say anything the waitress brought sallow eggs lumpish on the plate, flaccid bacon, a travesty of biscuits, hard and heavy, and a circle of waxen grits with a glazed brown pool in its precise center.

"Christ," Dunn said, "now I know I'm down South."

Morgan chuckled, holding his cup for the waitress to pour coffee. "You Yankees are never going to get through paying for Appomattox."

"Probably not. Listen, I don't know this governor down here. Who might he appoint to Anderson's seat?"

"I haven't seen the paper to get the speculation. Hell, Hunt's been dead less than twenty-four hours." There was no point, Morgan thought, in mentioning Matt Grant's aspirations; let Matt do it if he chose.

"I can tell you the phone started ringing in that governor's office twenty-four seconds after the news got out."

They talked politics desultorily as they picked barely edible particles from their repellent breakfasts. Morgan asked Dunn what he thought of the Hinman story.

Dunn made a face. "I never thought much of Hinman. That wasn't why I didn't support your friend Anderson." Dunn himself was as opaque as the green lenses. "The trouble with Hinman, at least in the old days, was that he was such an overbearing bastard. If he hadn't tried to face out that migrant labor scandal and make Anderson look like a nitwit or a schoolboy, he might have come out all right. But he had to go ranting and raving around and getting into a fight he couldn't win. Looking back on that, to tell you the truth, I'm not exactly overjoyed to think of him with all those spooks to order around. All those godless, atheistic Communist governments to overthrow. But things aren't quite like they were in the old Cold War days, are they?"

"In fact," Morgan said, "things have changed so much—I know it's easy for the living to say, but in some ways maybe it's almost better Hunt's dead. To be alive and out of things was too goddam cruel. It was a burlesque, his getting re-elected again last year just because they couldn't find anybody but pipsqueaks to run against him. I think he knew he was really out of it, whether he quit or not. That's what made this last year the worst of all. Hunt always knew himself pretty well."

Dunn moved his plate away. "I'm not sure I agree."

Briefly, Morgan thought perhaps Dunn was going to talk, would tell him at last, now that Anderson was dead, what really had happened at the convention. But at that moment Glass came to their table, grinning knowingly at Morgan, the tape on his forehead like a leering third eye.

"Were they real, lover?"

"Were what real?" Glass was bad news, Morgan thought ruefully; Glass with his crude drive and his groin instinct and his disdain of value would pursue him, now that he'd been given license, as relentlessly as life itself.

"The redhead's boobs, as if you didn't know."

Morgan introduced him to Dunn, reluctantly, and tried a half-truth halfheartedly. "I told you the redhead was stone blind. She could hardly stand up."

Glass sat down uninvited, grinning and winking at Dunn. He jerked a

thumb at Morgan. "A swordsman you'd never believe. Don't let that innocent face fool you. And a hollow leg in the bargain."

Dunn's face was inscrutable. The green lenses peered at Glass. "Have
some breakfast, Mister Glass."

Morgan was grateful. Dunn would, of course, note the matter in whatever
mental dossier he maintained on Morgan, Richmond P., political correspondent, VIP. But Morgan could not help that now; Dunn would think
what he would think, but he had at least quashed Glass's public invasion
of Morgan's sanctuary.

"I ordered breakfast in the room," Glass said. "Looked like a dog was
sick on the plate. Can I catch a ride with you fellows to the Anderson
place?" He regaled them with the story of his dealings with Ralph James,
who, naturally, had not expected and so had not thought of television
coverage. As a result, Glass's camera crew, cursing the heat, had gone ahead
in a rented station wagon. "But I thought I'd try to ride with one of you
guys that knew Anderson well."

"I didn't know him so well—or so long." Dunn buttered his toast carefully, precisely to its edges.

"But well enough." Dunn's not going to get off the hook that easily,
Morgan thought, seized suddenly with the old impatience to know what had
happened between them. "What was the thing that struck you most about
Hunt?"

"I took him to be a man"—Dunn chewed a piece of toast, the green lenses
maddeningly blank—"who thought he could do anything." He shrugged.
"I suppose there was more to it than that. There usually is."

But had there been? Morgan wondered. He knew resentfully that he did
not know. He, not Dunn, had known Anderson well, but Dunn, not he, had
the keystone of the arch, the piece of the puzzle without which there could
be no whole. And Dunn would not part with it, had refused steadfastly and
for years even to talk about it.

The corseted woman walked with excruciating care through the coffee
shop, calling, "Mister Morgan, telephone for Mister Morgan."

"Be right back."

The woman saw Morgan rising and, without interest, pointed vaguely
toward the lobby. By the door to the coffee shop French was watching him
anxiously.

"Fill me, if it's important," he said as Morgan went by.

"It won't be, at this hour."

But it was, Morgan knew as soon as he heard his publisher's voice on the line. "Rich, I was sorry to hear about Senator Anderson. I know how close you were."

"He was special."

"I know."

He probably did know, Morgan thought, because the publisher made it his business to keep as closely in touch as he could with the people on whom his business depended.

"When are the services?"

"Late today."

"I was wondering . . . Something's come up. Do you think you could get up here in the next day or so? I mean, after you're not needed there any more." Which was meant to tell Morgan that the publisher was not in sympathy with the managing editor's criticism of the night before; or if he was, he wanted Morgan to believe he was not. Actually he probably cared mostly for keeping the peace and had no doubt mollified the managing editor too.

"No problem at all," Morgan said.

"Maybe we all ought to have a little chat."

"Maybe we should, but to tell you the truth . . ." Morgan liked the publisher because you could tell him the truth, even though he was often too cautious or too committed to act on it. ". . . I doubt we can improve things a damn bit." Morgan did not have to be told that the managing editor had again taken his perennial complaint about Morgan's independence to the point of ultimatum. He had done it before, and sooner or later one of them would have to go.

"Oh, well," the publisher said, "it never hurts to kick things around, sit down at the table and talk a little." He had a deep-seated faith that if people would only say straightforwardly and to other people's faces precisely what they thought, most of the world's misunderstandings would disappear. Morgan was profoundly skeptical of that proposition; in his experience people who ostensibly said exactly what they thought seldom really did so, but nevertheless caused most of the world's wounds and animosities with the things they did say.

"You name a day and I'll be there. I know this kind of thing must be a pain in the ass for you, with all the other stuff you have to worry about."

"What I'm paid for," the publisher said with paid-for cheer. "How about the eighteenth?"

After Morgan hung up he noted the engagement on his pocket calendar. It was a dreary prospect. Not for the first time, it occurred to him that he should strike the publisher for a fat salary increase and a request to be kicked upstairs. Maybe the time was ripe to get out before he was forced out, before the pricks could get their satisfaction.

French, who was chatting with Dunn and Glass when Morgan got back to the table, looked at Morgan anxiously. "Home office bullshit," Morgan said. "They'd track me down in Ouagadougou. Sit down and have some breakfast."

"You guys are finished," French said. "I'll go keep Matt company."

Dunn offered to drive his rented car to the Anderson place if Morgan would point the way. Glass and Morgan went with him across the sunbaked parking lot—Morgan anticipating the air-conditioning he knew would be available in any car rented by the efficient Dunn.

"I'm really pleased to meet you at last, Mister Dunn," Glass said as they settled themselves in the car. "I tried to get an appointment with you once, during the last campaign out there. They said you weren't seeing the press."

"How do you think he got to be the best-known and the least-quoted boss in the country?" Morgan said. "Have you ever sat still for an interview. Dunn?"

"I see friends, and friends are always off the record."

He was the only political manager Morgan knew who never demurred at the word "boss."

"Interstate North or South?" Dunn asked.

"North."

"Put me on your list," Glass said.

"No list. Just a few friends."

Anyone but Glass would have dropped it, but Glass was impervious. "Maybe a documentary sometime. How a political machine really operates. That could be pretty great, you know?"

"Dull as dishwater." Dunn turned out of the parking lot onto the entrance ramp to the interstate.

Cars began to thunder and whistle around them. The changing city fled past on either side, baked, strangely contorted. Behind chainlink fence, ranks of brick duplexes in a geometric public-housing tract appeared and disappeared. Gigantic cloverleaf intersections ripped enormous holes in the city. Urban renewal had blown down an area Morgan vaguely remembered as a poor but lively block of shotgun houses and one-man stores, and had left a vast, empty sprawl of brick-strewn space where, a billboard proclaimed, the Futurama shopping center soon would be built.

"You remember about the plow that broke the plain?" Morgan said as they passed a tremendous new civic auditorium—steel, glass, concrete slabs, a saddle roof, in the middle of an endless blacktop parking lot. On that land there had been block after block of neat, middle-class housing, trees, lawns, little boys on bicycles—all gone, now, Morgan supposed, to the suburbs that were in themselves new cities. "In the end, you had the Dust Bowl. How do we know this isn't the same kind of thing? All this uprooting, tearing down, driving people away to make room for cars."

"We don't. It's like being on one of these interstate highways," Dunn said. "We're going like hell and there's no way to stop or turn back, and if you break down you just wait for somebody to tow you away."

"If Hunt had made it, if he'd been elected president, could we have got on some different road in this country?" It was the growing emotional stress of Anderson's death, together with the new-morning view of a city pulled apart, left gaping and broken, in grim disdain for serenity, stillness, the primacy of living things, that caused Morgan to ask such a question; and he answered himself before Dunn could. "I suppose not. A president has to go along more than he ever leads, so probably neither Hunt nor anybody else would have made much real difference. Still, he had a personal sense of things. It interested him, the way people lived. Hunt really cared, and when I see the world gone so gigantic and impersonal, I can't help wondering if he wouldn't have made a difference. I don't know how. I just think he might have done it. What does a president do anyway, except set a tone?"

"But Anderson didn't make it," Glass said.

Morgan took no notice of him. Morgan shook his head sadly, slowly, as if to rid his eyes of old visions like cobwebs, his ears of old sounds, like water in their tubes. *I took him to be a man who thought he could do anything,* Dunn had said, and that much was true, that had been his magic, and its loss had been his true death, perhaps in Morgan's eyes—Morgan had to admit—as well as Anderson's own. But now that the tall body was literally stilled, even the dull light of recent years gone from the kind, weak eyes, now that the undertakers no doubt had done their futile best, the only thing real, all that was left, was the remembered spirit. In memory, the old magic suddenly lived again and worked its spell; and Morgan's eyes burned with tears to have recovered in death his belief in his friend.

"And I gather," Glass said airily, with that absence of sensitivity that gave him his appalling vitality—Glass was a life portrait, Morgan thought, a flawed masterpiece, terrifying in its immaculate but soulless representation—"I gather that you're the main reason Anderson never made it, Mister Dunn."

Dunn did not turn the green lenses by an inch from their fixation on the road. "I switched delegates to someone else on the crucial ballot."

"Another thing about Dunn . . ." Morgan felt himself upset, knew he ought to say nothing, but there was a rush in him, an urgency; he had a passionate desire to bring things to a head, even though he knew that was almost always the worst thing to do. ". . . Dunn can't be bought. Can you, Dunn? Not even by a presidential candidate."

"I've been bought—one way or another."

"Every man has his price." Glass sounded approving of this fundamental wisdom.

"So what was your price, Dunn?" Morgan's voice was insistent even to his own ears, even though it galled him to echo Glass. "What would it have taken?"

"What I always heard," Glass said, "was that Anderson offended the party bosses, and they screwed him at the convention."

"Oh, sure, that's history, but Dunn was different. They might not have stopped him without Dunn, and Dunn was different, weren't you, Dunn?"

For a moment the green lenses turned toward him, the tight mouth flexing a bit, then turned back to the road. "The reason Anderson didn't make it was I thought he wasn't the right kind of man to be president. So I put my delegates behind somebody else."

"Jee-sus," said Glass.

Morgan said nothing for a moment, reflecting sourly that, as usual, bringing things to a head, forcing an issue, had proved to be worse than letting it lie. Dunn was confirming exactly what Anderson had told him— as far as Morgan knew, what Anderson had believed right to the end there on the sidewalk, to that moment when the world was going dim and the last impulses flared and guttered in the doomed, valiant brain. So, plainly, that was the truth of it; there was no longer any reason to believe anything else.

"Except I don't believe it," Morgan said.

"Believe what?" Glass thrust his head forward eagerly over the back of the seat.

Morgan ignored him. Dunn did not turn or acknowledge Morgan's remark, unless the small wrinkles that suddenly contracted near his mouth were the faint traces of a suppressed and ironic smile. Morgan hated Dunn then, not for whatever he had done to Anderson, but for knowing what had happened and keeping it from Morgan. Or, worse, for *not* knowing, if that was the case. Because Anderson was dead, and if Dunn didn't know, no one did, and neither Morgan nor anyone else ever would.

"The thing was," Morgan said after a while, "back then, we all had this sense of a golden touch. Everybody around Hunt got the feeling that everything he touched and did would turn out right. That's why it's always been so hard to understand what finally happened, because from the day he took on Hinman we all thought Hunt Anderson had the golden touch."

Old Bull's Boy III

Of course there was Adam, Morgan thought. I guess if there was anyone who held back it was Adam Locklear. But then Adam never expected too much from anyone; he had his side dealt to him a long time ago and that settled everything. That laid down the rules Adam Locklear played by.

It was a peculiar set of rules, in Morgan's view, but then Adam was not an ordinary man. Hunt Anderson had told Morgan how he had found Adam, on the first trip Anderson had made to look into migrant labor. Sprock & Berger had given him Adam's name and what they thought was his address. It wasn't, but the launderette operator who had taken it over thought he knew the new one, and so on through several references until Anderson finally found Adam in a bare little office in the backroom of a shotgun house out on the edge of some hot Southern farm town, the kind around which the fields begin at the city limits. Adam sat listening, smoking one cigarette after another, his feet propped up on a window sill, an old electric fan squeaking back and forth in one corner, while Anderson told him what he had in mind.

"Is it going to be a whitewash?" Adam asked as soon as Hunt had finished.

"How do I know? It isn't planned to be. Not by me anyway."

"What is it planned to be?"

"A basis for legislation to protect these people."

"Who'll enforce the legislation?"

"The law," Anderson said.

"Then you mean protect the growers."

"Of course not. I mean the workers and their families."

"Then the law won't enforce anything. The law protects growers and senators, not fieldhands."

"Well, then," Anderson said, "why don't we see if you and I can change the situation?"

Adam had laughed, Hunt told Morgan, but not bitterly, rather as if he had heard a fairly good joke. "Can you repeal man, Mister Anderson?"

Anderson stood up then, as if that was enough. Morgan could imagine the way the two of them—Hunt tall and angular, Adam blocked out like a building stone—would have filled that steaming room with its yellowing flowered wallpaper stripping away at the seams, its creaking floors, and the single bulging filing case at a careless angle to the wall, where Adam could reach it from the old library table he used for a desk.

"They told me you were a loner, Mister Locklear, but I thought it wouldn't hurt to try you out."

"Why didn't you write me a letter? Save yourself a trip to the provinces."

"I was coming down here anyway. I aim to see things for myself."

"They'll bullshit you to death."

"No," Anderson said, "I don't reckon they will."

So Adam stood up too. "I can spare the afternoon to get you started."

Adam told Morgan later that if Hunt *had* written him a letter, in the kind of foggy federal prose that usually comes with letterhead and frank, he might not have given him the time of day. Senators meant nothing to Adam Locklear. But Anderson had gone down there by himself—not anonymously, but without staff or pretensions either. "He just showed up and said he aimed to see for himself," Adam said, "and I got the idea he was going to do it, one way or another."

Though he had wondered, Morgan never got out of Adam any more about why, finally, he had agreed to be chief investigator for Anderson's committee. Not because he had any special feeling about Anderson, Morgan thought, any sense that Anderson had special qualities. There was nothing that romantic about Adam. More likely he had seen that the job would give him a little more scope, teach even him a bit more of what he needed to know if he was to meet his own commitments; and then, too, it would have paid him fairly well. Most likely, in fact, Adam Locklear had made more money working for the migrant committee than he ever had before, or since. And a man like Adam, Morgan thought, would have seen immediately that it was money that need not tie him up, that would be useful for a long time on the small scale of living he allowed himself.

Dunn's rented car purred smoothly along the interstate. Even Glass had fallen silent; and the hiss of the air-conditioning defied the angry white sun. They raced on toward Anderson's house, toward that unexplained past of which, it sometimes seemed to Morgan, he could see everything but its truth —as he could see clearly another hot day, in the late summer before the migrant hearings, another rented car, another oncoming road, and yet could not make out how or why the glittering future toward which that other road had surely led had dissolved, finally, into nothing more than the common-place of the last darkness coming down around a big head cradled in an old black woman's lap.

Adam Locklear had been driving that other day, rather too swiftly as usual, along a narrow blacktop strip between wide fields that stretched away on either side. Morgan was beside him; in the back seat Hunt Anderson, in unsenatorial denim and heavy shoes, was poring over some new material Sprock & Berger had sent along. Not quite two hours earlier the three had caught a taxi to National Airport from the old Senate Office Building.

"Most of your do-gooders," Adam was saying, "what they really do is shoot the wounded after the other guys are through fighting. The trouble with that is the fighting goes on all the time. You're in it or you're out, but it goes on." He lit a cigarette from the stub of another.

Adam Locklear was unique in Morgan's experience, although in his youth Morgan had seen one or two labor organizers run out of town, one clad in tar and feathers. They had been evangelists basically, sustained by the conviction that they were going to right the world's wrongs; they saw light eternally at the end of the tunnel, held aloft by the NLRB. Adam Locklear suffered from no such illusion. He never doubted the race was to the swift, the battle to the strong.

"Which is why I'm not in it to win," he would say. "I'm in it because I belong in it."

Morgan knew he did, if anyone did. Adam was the son of migrant parents, a part-Indian father and an illiterate white girl, who—before either was twenty—had been killed with nine other migrants at an unmarked grade crossing somewhere in Georgia, when a freight train smashed the old truck in which they were riding. Fourteen others were injured, several critically. No one had any insurance, and the railroad denied liability and got away with it, since none of the survivors knew enough to sue and the railroad bought off the shysters who tried to get up a case. The truck driver, who had been high on wine and who went to the chain gang for life, was one of only two uninjured persons in the truck. The other was Adam

Locklear, aged two, who had been thrown clear. He was found, scratched, bloody, and screaming, among the broken bodies and the few sad scattered remnants of six families and everything they owned.

To judge from all Morgan had seen of Adam, that might have been the last time he cried about anything. His parents' death, he would say, had got him out of the hopeless migrant cycle, which might or might not mean that in the long run they had done something with their lives, but anyway, he insisted, nothing less drastic would have saved him, or would save any such child as he had been then or ever.

"Not that that's what matters," he would argue. "When you start thinking that the main thing is to get a guy out of migrancy or poverty or whatever it is, make some kind of new man of him, you lose sight of the only thing that counts, which is the man the poor son-of-a-bitch already is. And the chances are, he always will be. What he needs most is a buck or a break right then and there."

In Adam's case, a family in a nearby town had taken him in after the wreck, got custody, raised him meanly and used him hard. But at least they let him finish school in return—beginning in his tenth year—for the wages of seven straight summers of six-day weeks in the watermelon fields and peach sheds around the town, and for the earnings of each Saturday of his every high-school year, from six a.m. to nine p.m., in the local A&P. That was in addition to the hours of daily chores at home, from lugging in wood and building fires to clearing the chicken pen and swilling the pigs—all, of course, before his homework. But the old man razor-stropped him for being no-count only once or twice a week, and the last two years even let him eat at the table with the other children.

The day after he got his high-school diploma, Adam methodically beat up his two foster brothers in a fifteen-minute fight, then left town with his last Saturday's wages from the A&P, and all his possessions in a paper bag. He got a job in the Buttercup Ice Cream plant in a nearby city where there was a one-horse teachers' college, put himself through in three years, and was graduated with what they called honors just in time to get his greetings from Uncle Sam. Three months after Pearl Harbor he was sent overseas; six months later he refused officer's training, instinctively identifying rank and privilege with owners and growers, and even then knowing certainly on which side life had cast him. Two Purple Hearts and a Bronze Star later, he went to night law school in Nashville on the GI Bill, emerged first in his class, and told the best law firms in the South to get lost when they came recruiting.

Anderson leaned over the back of the seat, the voluminous fruits of

Sprock & Berger's labor spilling out of his lap in the paperwork mess he never failed to create around himself. "Now, Rich, you don't want to let Adam convert you. You listen to him long enough, you'll come out thinking there's nothing for it but the Ark and two-by-two again, mankind excluded."

"What he's got is the perfect system for the big mules." Morgan winked at Anderson. "Growers on the one hand and fieldhands on the other, and nothing to be done about it."

"Not a damn thing about *that.*" Adam wore a short-sleeved shirt, and dark hair was matted along his forearms, in the vee at his neck. His dark, smooth hair glistened. "I don't say you can't improve conditions, but there's always top and bottom."

That notion had left him lots of room in which to operate. He had simply identified himself with the bottom—"with my origins," he said—totally and finally, and set about doing what he could to improve the conditions in which it existed and, he believed, always would. From the bare little office in which Hunt Anderson had met him—and others like it where in his restlessness he set up shop before and after—he had roamed the back roads, the migrant camps, the tenant farms, the black slums in the growing Southern cities and the quiet little towns beneath their peaceful, deceptive oaks. He would show up in jails, demanding decent food or clean blankets for the winos and vagrants or even habeas corpus for the occasional hopeless innocent swept up for whatever reason of chance or illogic in the arbitrary and unfathomable clutch of the law. He would appear at school board and county commission meetings with questions no one could answer and charges few could refute. He drew no line between black and white— suspecting, no doubt, as his foster family surely had, that there was more than Indian in his swarthiness—and had made himself as familiar in the unpainted, unpaved niggertowns, in the rickety old AME Zion churches and fish-sandwich cafés, as in white pool halls and beer parlors and barbecue joints, or the eroded farms and the sweat-shop textile mills and fertilizer plants where the rednecks eked out their stony lives.

He tried criminal cases when he had to, filed suits, represented groups before indifferent political structures, gave counsel to anybody who needed it, and stood up to sheriffs and garnishee men and the kind of furniture stores and loan sharks that created a more binding slavery than the Confederacy had ever conceived. He goaded welfare and public health and extension offices, read the law in a sort of relentless underlying drone to heedless sanitation departments and employment services, and generally made of himself what the mayor of the warehouse-and-supply-store town where he had grown up called "an ungrateful agitator bitin' the hands that fed him" —although that was the one community within whose city limits Adam refused absolutely ever to set foot.

What sent its mayor to the boiling point was a damage suit Adam slapped on him after two men working in the mayor's pack shed out in the county were beaten up and discharged for demanding a guard rail around a dangerous belt drive. Ultimately the mayor bought off the two men for legal costs and fifty dollars each, but the next season the guard rail went in. That, and maybe a new storm sewer along some darktown street, or better bus service for country kids at a county high school, or grudging county medical care for poor youngsters with strange diseases like hypoglycemia—that was the kind of progress for which Adam Locklear was an agitator biting the hands that had fed him.

He went back regularly to the migrants in their desolate camps and their old station wagons and dilapidated school buses and flatbed trucks, with their callused knees and supple fingers, their wary, hostile eyes, their scabby children and wormy dogs. A couple of seasons, as if something in his blood drew him, the way fish come back to their birthplaces to spawn and die, he even went up the stream with the migrants, driving an old ambulance he had found somewhere. A couple of families he had picked up during the winter vegetable harvest in Florida went with him through the lush spring fields in Georgia and South Carolina and a few weeks of strawberry picking in North Carolina to the hot summer acres of asparagus and lettuce and cucumbers in Delaware and South Jersey; then back south in the early fall in time to crawl through long, dusty rows of late snap beans before returning to Florida to rest up and blot out life on cheap red wine and loud music and the lumpish bodies of drink-sodden women—wives mostly, but sometimes sisters or daughters or mothers, if the wine was strong and the mattress crowded and the world more overpowering than usual. For who cared?

Adam knew the route. He could strip a bean plant with one hand and make twenty bushels a day on a good field. He knew all the ways the crew chiefs would cheat a man when they calculated his wage deductions, and he had taken a slick insurance agent to court for selling what he said were life policies to one migrant family, none of whom could read enough to know that they were, in fact, buying three collision policies on one car they did not own. He had seen traveling workers who complained—about wages, food, housing, life itself—jailed without charge or trial by local deputies subservient to the growers' association upon which some town or county thought its interests depended. He had been in crews lured hundreds of miles on the promise of work but actually in order to create a labor surplus that drove down wages and set men to scrambling for jobs like rats for shreds of cheese dropped carelessly on the floor. He knew how many boxes of oranges or bins of apples a skilled man could harvest in an hour or a day, and he was not fooled by advertised piece rates set so that fat wages could actually be earned, but only by the best and strongest pickers, going up and down the ladders from dawn to dusk and into the night, up and down the ladders as endlessly as Sisyphus pushing his rock, living dead whose living hell commanded their souls up and down the ladders forever.

But he was out of the stream for good by the time he and Hunt Anderson joined hands, because by then Adam had been blacklisted as a troublemaker by every growers' association from the Everglades to upstate New York, and the mere sight of him around some camp would be enough to bring down the state police on everyone existing in its tarpaper shacks, among its rusty spiggots and clogged toilets.

"Bad law in this county." Adam glanced at Anderson in the mirror. "You sure you want to do it this way, Chief?"

"If they know who I am in advance, they always clean things up a little. This time I want the full treatment."

"In this county," Adam said, "nobody wants the full treatment, believe me."

Some packing sheds appeared to their right, and in a field between these and the road a scattering of men and women worked bent over, shuffling forward on the flat, baked earth. "Asparagus." Adam threw away his cigarette. "That kind of stoop labor breaks your back. The camp's on the right beyond the curve. I got run out of there by state cops three years ago."

What could be seen of the camp from the road looked almost pleasant, Morgan thought—a few small houses in a grove of sparse trees, a flash of white where something hung from a clothesline. Adam turned into a dusty, rutted drive and pulled up at an open gate in a high chickenwire fence. A man was tipped back in an old kitchen chair against the gatepost on Morgan's side; he wore khakis that might once have been Army and a dirty old blue cap that gave him a vague appearance of authority, like that of a bus driver or a toll taker. From under the cap's cracked black bill, he peered at them suspiciously.

"Private road," he mumbled, not moving.

"Mind if we look around?" Morgan tried to sound casual. He thought his work clothes were a little too new and unsoiled to be convincing.

"Nothing to see." Still the guard did not move.

Adam leaned over toward Morgan's window. "We just lookin' round." His voice was startlingly changed, the words coming out slurred, slovenly, carrying Morgan back to the voices of the poor and the ignorant he had heard so often in his youth. "From over round Glos'ter 'n' we got to set up a place for a buncha goddam nigguhs comin' in next month. Boss say you folks got a pretty good camp over here."

The kitchen chair tipped forward. The man stood up with painstaking precision and adjusted the cap with dignity. He came to Morgan's window, bracing with thick fingers against the door, and peered in with unfocused eyes. His sweet-sour breath washed Morgan in wine fumes.

"Say from Glos'ter?"

"Over that way." Adam lit a cigarette. "Lookin' round a little."

"Thought you was Com'nists or sump'um." The guard opened his mouth to laugh at his own joke. Nothing emerged but the wine smell and a choking sound. Mogan flinched from the window.

"Shit, man, whachew talkin'?" Adam leaned farther toward the window, grinning inanely. "Over round Glos'ter we ain't fuckin' round with no Com'nists, I mean we don't *fuck* withum."

The face under the bill swayed back; the man reeled away from the car, regaining his balance by a miracle. He waved an arm in the general direction of the gate, mumbling something like "gone in." Adam drove quickly into the camp. Morgan looked back in time to see the guard lurch into his chair, with the aid of the gatepost.

"That shit." Adam was looking in the mirror. "Last time I was here he was man enough to crack me in the balls with a hoe handle while some troopers held me down. Looks like the wine bottle's got him."

Adam braked to a sudden stop as a child, black and naked, dashed across the road. The child stopped, staring with wide, hostile eyes, then ran around the corner of the nearest shack.

Morgan saw that the camp was not at all pleasant, as it had momentarily appeared from the road. The near shack's weathered clapboard had had one coat of paint, years before. Its single window was broken, and glass lay in muddy shards on the ground beneath it. The first step was missing from the stoop, from beneath which a mangy-looking dog peered at them with drooping eyes. The shed roof was of tarpaper, on which some thin strips of lath had been nailed here and there where the paper had been torn by the wind, and roughly patched. Along the two-track road ahead of them about twenty similar structures were scattered on either side.

"This the Saugus Camp Number One or Two?" Anderson's voice seemed professional, almost toneless.

"Number Two." Adam killed the engine, and in the sudden quiet they heard a bird singing cheerfully. He could fly away from Saugus Number Two any time he wanted, Morgan thought. "Number One is a bachelor camp and this is for families."

"It says here"—Anderson was shuffling through sheaves of Sprock & Berger— "a cabin at Saugus Number Two rents for five seventy-five weekly or twenty-eight dollars monthly, no toilet, no running water, electricity when it works is extra. One of the best camps in this area."

"There's only bad and worse," Adam said, puffing smoke in clouds. "Let's look around before the goons show up."

They went to the steps of the first cabin. The door hung half open, on one hinge. Anderson stepped over the broken step and knocked; no one came. As he pushed open the door, the smell was overpowering. Hunt went in, then waved to the others, and they followed. The floor was a dingy sea of thin, torn mattresses. Some dirty clothes hung on nails around the walls. In one corner an orange crate was turned on end as a counter for a two-eyed hotplate on which stood a black skillet caked with grease. A single light bulb hung from the middle of a ceiling that was bare plank rafters and tarpaper, some of which hung in dank black stalactites above the mattresses. Around the walls, where these met the ceiling, cardboard stripped from boxes had been tacked up to make something resembling a firm joint against rain and wind. A baby lay on one of the mattresses, away from the open window but flecked with flies. The baby's legs were thrust through two holes in the bottom of a paper bag, tied around its belly with a string, a makeshift diaper that obviously needed changing. The stench was also from the bedding and the walls and the tarpaper and the grease, from the clothes hanging on the wall, from the stringy hunk of fat on which the baby was sucking.

"We've got to get that child out of here." Anderson's voice was still toneless, rigorously controlled.

"No right to take somebody's child." Adam went out on the steps. "Hey, bud!" The naked boy appeared instantly, as if something in Adam's voice might have reassured him. "You looking after your bubba?" The boy came into the room silently, his thumb in his mouth, his eyes wide, wary, fixed on Adam. He nodded. "Your momma show you how to clean 'im up?" The boy shook his head, his thumb still in his mouth. "I'll show you then." Adam took the boy's hand. They picked their way across the mattresses.

"Hunt," Morgan said, "I got to get out of here."

Anderson was right behind him. They went to the car, and Morgan leaned against the front fender.

"Sons-of-bitches," Anderson was whispering, but not to Morgan, not to anyone, just over and over. "Sons-of-bitches. Oh, those sons of bitches . . ."

After a while Morgan's stomach stopped heaving. Adam came out of the shack, lighting another cigarette, and the three men started along the track between the other houses, all of which were similar to the one they'd been in, each perched on four stilts of concrete block. One had a whole clapboard missing, and the open strip was patched with cardboard; another had no steps at all; none had an unbroken window; a frayed strand of electric wire, like a loop of exposed viscera, weakly connected the shacks. A few listless children played in the spaces between them or ran aimlessly in the road. The premises were littered with junk—old refrigerator bodies, broken chairs, a bottomless washtub. Beyond one house an ancient car sat among the weeds on wheels without tires; it reminded Morgan of the old Ford his father had propped up on sawhorses in the backyard, after selling the wheels and tires for Hoover carts. But even when his father had been out of work so long, even when at Christmas or Thanksgiving the church ladies had brought the food baskets and the faded hand-me-down clothes and the thin bag of cheap candy from the five-and-dime—even then, with his father's face rigid and white as the old china his mother had left in the glass-front cabinet in the dining room, with the charity smell of the church ladies as tangible in the house as their starched smiles and flowered hats—even then, Morgan had not been poor, not the way the people of Saugus Number Two were poor. Morgan hoped that, somehow, his father had known that too; but he doubted that he had.

"These families may not have anything, and they have to go to the fields and leave the children because there's nothing else to do with them, but they're close," Adam said. "It'd surprise you, Chief. They're good families, most of the ones I've known. If we'd tried to take that baby out of there, that big kid would have been on us like a wildcat. Next year they'll probably take him to the fields."

By the time they were halfway along the camp street other children had come out from the cabins and from among the junk in the weeds and were following them—perhaps ten or twelve altogether. Some were naked, others wore little more than undershorts; among them there was a sad variety of runny eyes, distended bellies, skin sores, stunted and twisted bones, and the stained teeth that Morgan knew from Sprock & Berger meant a deficiency of fruit and vegetables in their diet. Typically the migrants spurned the rich crops they picked in favor of starchy foods—canned corn, fatback, potato chips—as if they resented the harvests on which they depended, that kept them in bondage.

"But why do they stay in it?" They had come, at the end of the street of shacks, to a somewhat smaller building, and Morgan was not getting at all used to the smell or to the silent, following children. "Why does anyone put up with conditions like these?"

"How they going to get out?" Adam spat into the dirt of the road. "They never make enough money to make the break, and if they did somebody would cheat 'em out of it. And if that didn't happen, what would they do? Where would they find a job? No skills except field work, no education except in surviving. And any town where they might stop and try to settle just doesn't want low-class people like these, or their children in the schools. It's really another kind of slavery, except in the old kind down South at least the owners had a stake in keeping their slaves alive and healthy because they were valuable property. Migrant slavery, the owners just use the bodies a few weeks of the year, get what they can out of them, and get rid of them when the season's over."

The building at the end of the street was obviously a toilet. Its door hung open, and the smell of human waste was overpowering. Outside and a few yards to the left, a faucet topped a shaft of rusty pipe that rose from a sprawl of mud and water eight feet across. A plank that might have been part of a clapboard from one of the shacks bridged the puddle to the foot of the pipe.

"That's the water supply for everybody." Adam jerked his head at the outhouse. "And that's the toilet, as you can smell. Don't stick your head in there if you want to eat tonight."

Something moved near one unpainted wall of the outhouse, a rat as big as a cat. Morgan picked up a rock. "Look at that big son-of-a-bitch. Hunt, you see that monster?"

"Too big to run," Adam said. "How'd you like to wake up with one of them biting your kid?"

Morgan threw the rock as hard as he could, missing the rat by a foot. The rock made a hollow thump against the outhouse. The rat moved sluggishly into the weeds.

"Feel better?" Adam grinned at Morgan, not humorously; in his dark, impassive eyes there was a glitter as if of fever, or desperation, or hatred.

"Not a damn bit. Can't we put somebody in jail?"

"Yeah, some of the people that have to live here. Anybody raises a stink to the law in this county—zap. They'll put you away for a week or so before they even tell you the charge. The growers *are* the county in these parts, so naturally they're the law too."

With the air of a man going into battle, Anderson walked toward the door of the outhouse; Morgan had no choice but to follow. They stood silently, looking in. It was a two-seater, but it was obvious that neither of the cracked commodes worked. They were overflowing. Flies buzzed. There were brown piles on the floor, brown smears on the wall. Another rat bared long teeth in one corner.

"The growers will all tell you"—Adam had come up behind them—"that these people won't take care of anything. Break windows, break refrigerators if they have them, make a mess like this in the can. And in a strange, reverse way, it's true. The growers think they're just savages or animals, but the doctors call it hostility. Mad at the growers, mad at the crew leaders, the cops, the storekeepers, mad at everybody that gouges them, mad at life itself. Hell, I've felt it. I've broken windows, shit on floors. After a while you have to take it out on something."

"Let's go," Anderson said. "I've seen enough. Too much. Every one of these places I come to, it seems that much worse."

"What about this guy Tobin you wanted to find?"

Before Anderson could answer, there was the sound of an engine and a pickup truck came rattling between the shacks. The children scattered, rather more swiftly than the rats had. The pickup rumbled up too close to them and stopped, a little cloud of dust settling behind it.

"Trouble." Adam hitched up his pants. "You want to play out the game or 'fess up, Chief?"

"See how it goes." Anderson took a big step backward, leaving Adam a little in front.

A big man in clean khakis got out of the pickup and walked toward them, truculence in his stride. He pushed a billed hunter's cap back from his sunburned forehead; a little strip of white skin ran across it at the roots of his graying hair. "What's this shit?" He put his hands in his hip pockets.

"From over round Glos'ter," Adam began.

"Shit you are. I know all the growers round there. Ain't a one setting up no camp and they'd know how if they did. What you want round here?"

"Well, I didn't see any point in riling up that wino on your gate." Adam put a cigarette in his mouth. He spoke in his natural voice but he squared around a little toward the man in khaki and hooked his thumbs in his belt. Morgan thought of two cats bowing their backs. It all seemed a little ridiculous, as belligerent men always did to him.

"Some kind of inspectors, huh? Or maybe just agitators?"

"Some kind of." Adam lit the cigarette. "You the owner?"

"One of 'em, if it's any of your business, which it ain't. Now whyn't you get your three asses off this private property and be quick about it."

"Private property regulated by state law. Supposed to be."

"I know the law well as you do, mister. You want to show me some kind of papers or badges before I call some law of my own?"

"How many square feet per person?" Adam spoke softly, but the man heard him all right.

"Lissen"—the man hitched himself a step closer—"I asked you politely. Was it just the one of you, I'd throw his ass off myself. Since it's three, what I aim to do in about ten seconds, unless you get out some papers I don't think you've got, is go down the road about a hundred yards and call the law to throw some trespassers in jail."

"And if I showed you some papers you might do it anyway, mightn't you?"

"I just might at that." For the first time something wary sounded in the rough voice. "The law round here don't hold with outsiders messing in our business."

"I'll bet not. You go on down the road and call."

"That's right." Anderson stepped forward. "Tell them you want them to arrest a United States senator for trespassing." He held up something from his wallet. "Chairman of the Select Committee on Farm Labor Migrancy. Go on and make your call."

"Well, whyn't you say so all along?" The man in khaki was almost whining. "I thought you was Reds or sump'um, the way this fellow's acting." He put out his hand. "I'm sure honored to meet you, Senator."

Anderson eyed the hand with distaste, and the man put it in his pocket.

"You're Thompson?" Anderson asked.

"Jack Meechum. But me'n' Ben Thompson own this camp." He added hastily, "Ben looks after it mostly."

"How many square feet per person?" Adam said.

"Why . . . uh . . . whatever the law . . . uh . . . the law says."

"You ever go in there"—Adam pointed without looking—"and take a pee?"

"These people here," Meechum said, "I swear you wouldn't believe what me'n' Ben put up with. You give them everything. Toilets, stoves, mattresses, roof over their heads. They don't take no more care of a thing than a baby would or an animal in the jungle."

"When did you paint last?"

"Well, now, you see, I wanted to paint this year, but Ben, he convinced me, and I got to admit it's true, no matter what you do, they just don't take care of it. They just won't. You fix up and they tear down."

"When was the last state inspector here?"

Meechum looked puzzled. "My daddy brought the first niggers in from down South in I think it was nineteen twenty-six or so, and we never yet had any state inspectors around that I know of. We pretty much take care of our own business, this part of the state."

"I bet you do." Anderson's voice was rising a little. "You run things just the way you want to, and if anybody doesn't like it, he doesn't have to come back. If anybody complains, throw the son-of-a-bitch in jail or beat him up and teach him his place. And no interference from upstate, by God, not so long as you and Ben and the other growers kick in every four years. Right, Jack? That the way it works, Jack?"

"Well, now, maybe you don't understand exactly, Senator. We got to harvest these fields or go broke, and folks won't eat either. So we got to have labor, and we got to have it when we need it, and the only labor we can get when we need it is these people that come in. And no matter how we try to do something for them, they just tear down and loaf around. All the same, they must like the wages we pay and the housing and all. They do keep coming back, don't they?"

"Now that's interesting." Anderson looked at Adam. "Isn't that interesting, Adam? Don't you think that's so interesting we ought to let Jack here tell it to the committee?"

"In open hearings, so everybody can understand his problems."

"Wait a minute here, now. I never volunteered to go and talk to some committee. I never said—"

"You just volunteered." Adam put a subpoena in Meechum's hand. "You won't be lonely 'cause we got one for good old Ben too, if we can find the bastard."

"And another thing," Anderson said. "Is there a man here named Tobin? Lonnie Tobin?"

Meechum nodded miserably, peering at the paper in his hand as if it were a wound. "Crew leader. Comes in every year."

"And goes on up to the potato fields?"

"I reckon. None of my business where he goes."

"None of it is any of your business, is it? If they live like animals." Anderson's voice was sharp, loud. "If they get cheated. If they're sick and hopeless. Not your doing, is it? Your conscience is clear, isn't it? When you sit in church on Sunday you're in the clear. You never made the system."

"Well, goddammit, I didn't." Meechum raised his head defiantly. Anderson had penetrated to the man's core, touched on the idea that permitted Jack Meechum to traffic in misery, that defended him against himself. "Folks got to have food, don't they? How they going to get it if I can't plant crop and get labor to harvest it? You think I'm getting fat down here? Senator, all them rich folks eating asparagus up there in New York City that was grown right here"—he pointed with a jabbing finger at the ground beneath his feet—"they got things a hell of a sight better'n Jack Meechum, and I don't hear them hollering about it either."

An old school bus grumbled into the camp with a whine of gears and stopped, as if expiring, midway down the rickety lines of shacks. People got off and moved listlessly away. Children appeared again. A youngish man and woman went into the nearest house, a little girl trotting after them. Almost immediately there was a burst of loud music from the inside.

"You see"—Meechum gestured toward the sound—"they even have fun out here. You ought to hear what goes on Saturday nights."

"Plenty of wine?"

Meechum made a face. "By the gallon."

"Who takes the top cut on the price? You and Ben? Or Tobin?"

Meechum glared at Adam. A man sitting behind the wheel of the bus got out and came toward them. He was black, neat, smiling, not very tall. He wore a straw hat with a jaunty band and he walked with a jaunty step, as if with an ear cocked to the music.

"A gathering," he said. "A congestion practic'ly is what we got in old Saugus. Room for one more in the crowd?"

"We could squeeze over." Adam moved a step to meet him. "You'd be Lonnie Tobin, right?"

"In the flesh." Tobin looked Adam over with eyes not nearly so merry as his voice and step. "I had the pleasure? These old eyes seen you somewhere, Big Cat?"

"Could be. I been around the track."

"Jail in Birmingham," Tobin said. "Springing some cat."

"Or what would you say to Agri-Packers? You run a crew up there when you leave here, don't you?"

"Now that would be 'taters. But not where I seen you before."

"Right." Adam handed Tobin a subpoena. "Don't blow your nose on this."

Tobin spat on the ground between Adam's shoes. "Got it now," he said. "Last time I seen you, Big Cat, you was wearing a night stick twixt your nuts out there by the gate."

"A hoe handle. But I could forget that." Adam scuffed dirt over the blob of spittle. "I could forget all sorts of things I know. I could forget practically anything, under the right circumstances."

"Like which circumstances?" Tobin took off his hat and tucked the subpoena like a feather in its band; his opaque eyes did not leave Adam's

Adam fished a crumpled cigarette package out of his shirt pocket and held it out to Tobin."Like if we were doing business."

"Business"—Tobin put the hat back on and took a cigarette—"is my business, Big Cat."

"Why do they lay 'em away so fast down here?" Glass said, rousing from torpor. "He only kicked off yesterday, didn't he?"

Morgan had almost forgotten Glass, so intense had been his recollection of the day at Saugus Number Two. He looked back at the grinning face, the patch of tape on Glass's forehead, astounded at what seemed Glass's infinite capacity to be offensive. It was tempting to think there was something symbolically right about it—that a man who made a living by the intrusion of the world's red and unblinking eye into the affairs and despairs of anyone fate might momentarily expose would have to be as relentlessly insensitive as Glass.

"It's the heat," Morgan said. "As in everything else, Glass, these people down here are years behind in embalming techniques."

"You're putting me on."

Morgan ignored him. If Glass had known Kathy, he would have expected her to get the funeral over with as soon as decency permitted. But Glass did not know Kathy; he did not know much of anything except that the main chance lay somewhere before him. Which maybe, Morgan thought sadly, is not so different from the rest of us—not from me, not even from Hunt.

Adam and Anderson had been elated, as they later sat at dinner with Morgan in a hotel dining room in a city not too far from Saugus Number Two.

"Because I'm roaming around down South earlier this season, and there's this old boy laying off a year with something in his lungs and he complains a little about the way this Tobin treated him last year at Agri-Packers." Adam paused while a waiter brought drinks. "Since the chief here is so interested in Agri-Packers, I prick up my ears and talk the old boy into signing a statement, with witnesses. Then I work my way around some more." Adam patted his vest pocket. "Now I got four signed statements about how Mister Lonnie Tobin does business, which is not altogether on the up and up. Mister Tobin is a smart cookie who is going to read these statements over, when he and I have our little chat tomorrow, and he's going to get real anxious real quick to tell me everything I want to know."

Up to the point, only a few weeks before the hearings were to begin, when Adam and Anderson had found Tobin (and even crew leaders in the migrant stream are not so easy to track down—"We go everywhere but we don't belong nowhere," one morose young apple-picker, had told Morgan), they had been fearful that not much of a case could finally be made against Paul Hinman.

"We traced Hinman's interest in Agri-Packers, all right." Anderson said, "but he could always claim he didn't really know about conditions out there in the camps; at the worst, you might pin some sort of moral obtuseness rap on him. That wouldn't help him politically, but Madison Avenue could live it down for him. But Tobin has been bringing his crews to Agri-Packers for years, and Adam's sworn statements show that it isn't just bad housing, terrible as that is. That company has been systematically cheating these people and letting Tobin cheat them, and that's a good deal more than moral obtuseness."

"But maybe Hinman didn't know about the cheating either." Morgan was contemplating the menu with no great relish. As Adam had predicted, Saugus Number Two had left them all with impaired appetites. "At the very least, he's going to claim he didn't know, and to tell the truth even I can't believe Paul Hinman ever actually dealt with a pimp-type like Tobin."

Adam laughed. "Pimps exist so men like Hinman don't have to get their hands too dirty."

Anderson signaled a waiter for another round of drinks, although he was the only one who had finished his. "Sometime in the past, Adam thinks, Hinman may very well have dealt with Tobin. Neither Madison Avenue nor anybody else could wipe that off the record, if Tobin confirms it."

"*If* he confirms it," Morgan said. "But I concede that for a presidential candidate it would probably be bad politics to fall back too often on an 'I didn't know' explanation. Neither did all those Nazis we tried after the war. And who wants a president who can't even keep up with what's going on on his potato farm, much less clean it up?"

"Not me." Anderson took a pull at his second drink. "We're going to knock that son-of-a-bitch so far out of the White House he couldn't even get in with the tourists."

"Don't be so gay about it. It's your own party you're talking about, you know."

"My party, all right, and it'll be better off if we can strip the hide off that bastard before we're stuck with him. Which is what we're going to do."

"Sure we are." Adam flicked his menu as if brushing away insects. "We'll burn the bastard at the stake. And what else will we do, Chief?"

"That's a lot. Unless you want Paul Hinman to be president."

"I don't give a damn who's president."

"Oh, come on, Adam," Morgan said. "That's pretty strong even for you."

"You go elect Mahatma Gandhi president. Elect Senator Anderson here. Elect Jesus Christ. What's he going to do about Saugus Number Two?"

"Clean it up." Anderson sipped his drink. "At least if it's Anderson. I can't speak for those other two fellows."

"You'd pass a law, I give you that, and they'd comply. They'd slap a coat of paint on the outhouse maybe, fix the johns so they'll work for a week or two, and go about their goddamned business. You'd think you'd done something."

"Well, I would have. I'd do more than you admit and at least I'd have tried."

"Bully for you. You'll go to heaven for trying, and Hinman won't, and Saugus Number Two will go on forever. But why should I give a damn whether a president goes to heaven or not? You got to have a president to drop bombs and make foreign policy and worry about the economy. Presidents don't have a damn thing to do with Saugus Number Two."

Anderson picked up his glass, held it out toward Adam in what might have been a toast, then finished his drink. "This one will, " he said, "if he can knock Gandhi and Christ out of the primaries."

Everybody laughed, and the evening became a bit gayer, and there was nothing more to suggest that Hunt Anderson had any serious intention, or that Morgan should infer it; but, turning it over in his mind, then and later, Morgan believed he had heard something important. Anderson was a freshman senator, a Southerner at that, practically an unknown and getting ready to run headlong into his own party and its biggest names; yet Morgan knew—somehow he had no doubt after that night—that Anderson was thinking about "the brass ring," as Morgan later heard a president himself refer to it.

Morgan had not then realized how many public figures thought constantly about that ring. He knew from history that even Lincoln had once confessed that the taste of the presidency was in his mouth a little, but experience had not yet taught Morgan that the taste of it on the tongue was hard to wash away. He had not known, in those early years of his Washington career, that behind almost any important roll call in the Senate could be found some driven hack without a prayer—no money, no personality, no distinction—casting his yea or nay in the inexplicable conviction that when the great bell sounded and the skies parted and the moment arrived, some mystical force would find him "available." Nor that at any national convention, no matter how foreclosed and foregone, there to the end, against every conceivable notion of interest or reality, some second-rate governor, high on illusion, would be likely to hold his howling delegates uncommitted until all their blandishments and threats and supplications had been swept away in the roar of the crowd for the inevitable victor— the cheers for someone else that would mean ruin and derision for a man who had been sure he had a chance.

It took Morgan years to grasp the fact that all over the country, almost anywhere he looked, there would be a tycoon or a college president or a big brain who wrote books on the new capitalism or on managing technology, or maybe even a mayor whose city hadn't been blown up or strangled, yet —and if any one of them were asked if he were a candidate he'd have said of course not. But if any one of them were asked if he'd refuse to serve, if elected, any one of them would have said that would be presumptuous, wouldn't it? Because the taste of it would be in his mouth a little. Because he believes he could do it, Morgan thought, remembering Anderson, watching Dunn's thin, strong hands on the wheel. There's always some poor fatuous human son-of-a-bitch like Anderson who comes to believe that in the crunch he's got more of what it takes—the guts, the integrity, the intelligence, the public confidence, the charm—than anybody else. Some hopeful sap that comes to believe he's God's gift, a chosen man, he's got the golden touch. And that's what makes him run. That's what makes him think in the end he's entitled to do anything—anything in the worthy cause of giving himself to the world.

When Hunt went off to the men's room that night, Morgan said to Adam, "You hit him where he lives."

"You think he'll stick this thing out?"

"They'll squeeze him hard but he won't cave." Morgan realized as he said it that he had come to believe it.

Adam shook his head. "I know that. I'm just afraid he'll chase the rainbow, the way that wife of his eggs him on. This business started out as an across-the-board investigation of conditions. Now she's got him thinking about TV, all kinds of things, putting too much emphasis on this Hinman when there are a thousand as bad, maybe worse."

Adam's bitter tone surprised Morgan. "At the moment, chasing Paul Hinman is more nearly chasing a buzz-saw than a rainbow, and it does dramatize the issue."

Adam snuffed out another in his endless chain of cigarettes. "That makes political sense, I reckon. It's just that I've got my doubts what politics ever accomplishes."

"Damn right." By then Morgan was on his third drink. "So have I. You changed the goddam diaper, not Hunt. Not me either. I wouldn't have touched the stinking thing with a ten-foot pole, any more than Hunt would. Which is the trouble with politics. Politics is a federal program. It takes you up on the mountain. Politics won't wipe a baby's ass."

"That's not what you write in the papers."

"Hell no. I'm a professional. But I'll tell you something, if you want to hear it. Someday I'm going to write it. That and a hell of a lot of other things."

"Why not now?"

"It's a funny goddam thing to me, Locklear," Morgan said, "that you don't remember your mother or father or know anything much about them, and you've written off the place where you grew up, and yet you seem to know who you are. It's like what fucks up all the rest of us never touched you. So maybe we do things all wrong in this world. Maybe in some screwball way you had it better than the rest of us."

"Don't you know who you are?"

Morgan was saved from having to answer by the waiter, who arrived with a new round of drinks. Hunt came back and they ordered dinner, and they talked about the investigation while they ate it (avoiding specific recollection of Saugus Number Two), then about life, money, women, food, sports, politics, automobiles, homosexuality, dogs, fishing, history, and dreams. Adam didn't drink much, but Anderson and Morgan did, and that night for a good reason.

Every now and then in life—not too often, for no one could stand it— it seemed to Morgan that the curtain was pulled aside and the scenery pushed back; the lights were beamed down brilliantly, and there, center stage, was the world in its corruption. It was only a glimpse anyone was allowed, just enough to make out the flies crawling on the dried blood; then, mercifully, the curtain fell and the lights dimmed and someone began to play a waltz in the background. Ultimately the mask of the world would deceive and pacify the viewers again; but for a long time they would not be the same. For a long time laughter would have to be induced, because they would have to laugh or shriek. So he and Anderson drank, that night, and induced themselves to laugh perhaps too loudly, and it was not until Adam Locklear stood up to leave that they came back to the questions raised earlier.

"Don't think I didn't get the message," Anderson said, looking up at Adam's chunky figure by the table.

"I wasn't carrying messages, Chief."

"Sure you were, and I got mine okay. You needn't worry. We're in this for one thing only, Adam. We're going to do something for those people out there at Saugus. We're not running for anything. We're not running from anything. We're going to bring out the truth, and we're going to get some legislation on the books and maybe even help somebody make a living or get a square meal." This was the first time Morgan heard him use the "royal we."

"That's why I'm here." Adam was smiling. "That's what you said to begin with."

Anderson spoke slowly, tapping the table occasionally. As he went on, the words came more rapidly, but he did not raise his voice. "It's what I still say, more than ever. I tell you, I'm no damned Pollyanna, I only have to look back at my father to know something about what kind of world it is, but every time I go to one of these places like we saw today, every time I see kids in that kind of squalid condition, every time I see some mean bastard like Meechum or some con man like Tobin profiting from human misery and helplessness—I tell you, Adam, it makes me sick inside, ashamed to be a human being. Then I get mad because, whatever you say, I know the world doesn't have to be like that. I get to feeling the Old Bull in me, and when Old Bull got his blood up he could whip the ass off a catty-whompus. Maybe we can't do that, but I guarantee you they're going to know we were here. They're going to feel us, Adam."

"For a while," Adam said. "I'll give you the works on Tobin tomorrow night." He gave Morgan a quick salute and turned away, touching Anderson lightly on the shoulder. It was as near a gesture of affection as a hard soul like Adam Locklear knew how to make. Later, Morgan thought that maybe it had been more than that; maybe Adam had sensed something of what was impending; maybe he had known that somehow the seeds of disaster always sprang from the fruit of triumph.

Adam had a bleak view of human possibilities, Morgan knew that. Adam lived, he once had said, in fear of the moment or the circumstances that would break him, believing absolutely that it was bound to come; and he lived in even greater fear that he would not know it when it did. Perhaps believing, that night, in the sincerity of Hunt Anderson's professions had only made Adam foresee a harder fall; and so perhaps it had not been so much affection but sympathy that caused him to touch Anderson's shoulder —a gesture of solidarity.

After Adam left, Anderson and Morgan sat rather quietly, talked out, not quite drunk, still somewhat off balance from the day's experience. Anderson refused an after-dinner drink when Morgan ordered one.

"Better not. Somebody from the office is supposed to get in late with a batch of stuff I've got to know about on the floor tomorrow. Listen, in that bunch of kids following us out there today—how many were white and how many were black?"

"Didn't notice."

"Neither did I. Pretty remarkable for a couple of Southern boys. Misery even wipes out the color line."

"But has it occurred to you, my friend, that most of these migrants in the East Coast stream *are* black—and the growers are white?"

"So what?"

"So maybe it's a good thing you're not running for office down home for another five years."

"I'll worry about that when I come to it."

"On the other hand"—Morgan looked at Anderson over the rim of his drink—"about the only way a guy with a Southern accent could reach for the White House was if he'd managed to get the goddamned race issue off his back up North."

Anderson laughed, watching Morgan carefully. "You're smarter than that, Rich. I'm just a frosh."

"Well, if you blow Hinman up the way you're getting ready to do, all of a sudden there's going to be one hell of a big hole where the next president of the United States used to stand."

"And a good thing too, since it's Hinman. But they're hardly going to fill the hole with the guy who blew him up."

"It won't make you any friends in the party, but it's going to make an awful lot of headlines. It's going to get you on a lot of TV screens. It's going to give a lot of people the notion that you're riding around on a white horse, smiting evil. And after Hinman, right now, there's not really anybody else. He's shut everybody out."

"You're out of your mind. You know damn well that—"

"If drafted, would you refuse to run?"

"Oh, the hell with you!" Anderson was grinning, pleased, a little embarrassed.

Morgan knew then he had been reading Anderson's own thoughts back to him. "Well, let me give you some advice. The next time you visit one of those hell-holes, take a photographer along."

"I'm already planning that, but just for the evidence. Oh, here she is now." Anderson waved across the dining-room.

A willowy girl carrying a thick folder of papers hurried between the tables. She was tall and smiling, and Morgan had seen her before.

"You made it," Hunt said. They both stood up, and Morgan swung over a chair from another table. "Alice Rogers . . . Rich Morgan."

"We've met, I think, haven't we?"

Alice sat down and crossed her legs. She put the folders on the table. "I used to work for Bert Fuller until a few weeks ago. Maybe that was how we met."

"It must have been. Good old Bert."

"Look at that stack of stuff!" Anderson shook his head in mock despair.

"I'm looking at it," Morgan said. "It'll drive me to drink, so I better shove off."

Anderson cut a wickedly amused glance at Morgan. "Maybe we could have one more before—"

"No, thanks, I've had more than enough." Morgan tapped the papers. "And you'd better get to work."

"Good night, Mister Morgan."

Alice Rogers was as coolly impersonal as if she thought Morgan really believed she had come all the way from Washington just to bring the mail. Briefly, leaving the room, Morgan envied Hunt; then he was annoyed with him for taking political chances; then he thought about Kathy and felt his blood race a little. So it's that way, he thought.

But Alice Rogers—Alice had proved subsequently to be a Seven Sisters type who needed her salary only for mad money and her job for kicks (it was *exciting* to be really *in* politics and to *really* know the inside of things) until the right Yale man took her off to Westchester County, where naturally she would cheat on him with upper-class blandness—Alice was long gone and no doubt often replaced before the migrant hearings had ended and Hunt Anderson went on to bigger things. As well as Morgan had come to know Anderson, he never knew much about Anderson's relations with Alice, or any woman. Some years later, Morgan got the impression that Anderson was frequently visiting, with and without Kathy, the Southampton beach house of a certain interesting woman whose three husbands each had left her a fortune as, one by one, advanced age shuffled their decrepit souls off this mortal coil. But Anderson had insisted she was only a big campaign contributor.

Besides, Morgan had learned that the kind of man who could publicly declare himself for the highest titles and honors and responsibilities, who was willing to risk all his privacy and all his hopes on the uncertain response of millions of people he could never see or know—that kind of man was not likely to become deeply and closely involved with women, or a woman; he was seldom personal enough. He could not see a woman, even his wife, as a complex human being, with her own dreams and involvements and needs. He could hardly see anyone that way. By ordinary standards he might be decent, humane, generous, but he was bound to be too single-mindedly bent on his mission, on achieving the place for which he knew in his heart he had been chosen, to enter promiscuously into demanding human relationships. How could he, if he believed he'd been chosen, see other people as having needs equal to his, possibilities of achievement as splendid as those that lighted his days? Like an artist who values nothing but his art, a politician who hears the highest call knows only that he must answer.

And something else; that night at dinner, after the visit to Saugus Number Two, Morgan had asked Anderson why he thought a man with Hinman's prospects had not put so much distance between himself and Agri-Packers that no one ever could have connected the two—why, in fact, he had got into such a risky project at all. Why had a man who planned to be president left this small entanglement lying there to trip him on the threshold?

"I don't know, except I'll tell you this," Anderson had answered. "A guy like Hinman, or maybe Old Bull, maybe any politician who gets anywhere, maybe even me, you always think you can pull it off. You can come from behind, get the votes, find the gimmick, say the right thing at exactly the right time. So maybe you come to think you can get away with something too—whatever it is. But you always think you can pull it off or you wouldn't be in the business. It's what makes a politician different from a shoe clerk."

So Anderson himself—Morgan sometimes speculated—might or might not have accepted love and homage from many women; he could have considered that his due, or at least a necessary occasional diversion or renewal, and he would not have concerned himself with the political liabilities, since chosen men did not so much calculate the angles as make demands on fate. Morgan doubted that sex ever meant to Anderson what politics did, and that if Anderson ever gave his heart to anything it was, in any case, to some shining ideal of public behavior and personal dedication that he saw as his guiding star.

Anderson would have had, moreover, no problems with Kathy because he had a good political marriage—at least until after the convention—and Morgan knew there was only one basic pattern for that. A good political wife, as he came to know many of them, might be a private source of strength, seldom seen or heard but holding the great man together, not least by massaging his ego and salving his wounds; or she might be a public asset who could campaign like a candidate, give important dinners, and persuade the opposition with tough talk as well as sweet smiles; she could even be both public *and* private. In every case, however, the one thing that made her a really good political wife was that she never made real demands on her husband, none that pushed, pulled, or nagged him away from the main matter—his mission, his destiny—because she knew that, for him, the mission was the motive.

Morgan was not so sure why Kathy Anderson, in particular, became a good political wife, but he knew when. As the migrant hearings brought Hunt Anderson increasing notoriety, something seemed to change or accelerate in his wife. His Senate campaign and his early months in Washington had rather bored her; Morgan knew she had not entirely believed in any of that, or in him. Perhaps at some point she just got the presidential bug. Morgan was to learn that the taste of it was in her mouth a little, but he never believed that was anything like the whole truth. She would have made a fascinating First Lady, he insisted in later years, good-looking as she was and with so much flair and intelligence and candor; but the prospect had never seemed to arouse in her more than a certain amusement, and she would certainly have been neither the Social Queen, titillating the world with her parties and gowns, nor the Ministering Angel, visiting the poor and beautifying the parks. She would have been something unique, Morgan told cocktail-party audiences, but whatever it would have been—he did not say —she had never thought much about being First Lady, or cared—he was sure of that. Nor did she, to Morgan's knowledge, ever crave the sort of remote-control political power some wives exercised through the duped or indulging authority of titled spouses; she would not have given a damn, in his opinion, about who was appointed to the Subversive Activities Control Board or whether the FCC gave the time of day to an acquisitive friend who coveted a TV channel or a favorable ruling. Morgan had never heard her express the faintest interest in social causes, except migrant labor, and that for expedience. So he knew that whatever made Kathy Anderson become a good political wife was more personal, ran far deeper into her soul, than any of the usual reasons. It might have been, he thought briefly, that she came to believe in Hunt Anderson in ways she had found impossible before;

or maybe she had begun to see the possibilities of political power; more likely, he believed, it had been her own time of reaching, her own struggle toward the sun. Whatever it was that had happened to Kathy, it had been invaluable to Hunt Anderson.

Day after day, Kathy attended the hearings, obscure in the rear row, listening with that exclusionary intensity of hers, sometimes taking notes, sometimes seeming asleep or indifferent, seldom more excited or tense in the moments of drama and disorder than in the hours of droning dullness. Inevitably, her faithful attendance, her looks and demeanor, attracted attention, and eventually, as part of a picture story on the hearings, *Life* ran a two-page spread of her, a photo on the left showing her quiet and unmoving as all around her people jumped to their feet, craning to see Hunt Anderson restraining an irate lettuce farmer who was trying to take a swing at Adam Locklear for outlining how the farmer—a former Okie who owned two Cadillacs and a private plane—had trucked Mexican laborers hundreds of miles to break a strike in the Salinas Valley; and a photo on the right showing her in virtually the same restrained pose, alone among a sea of empty seats as some low-ranking bureaucrat from HEW mumbled empty excuses as to why there were no federally funded health, education, or welfare programs for migrant laborers.

Both photos, of course, showed Kathy's splendid legs, discreetly hemlined and crossed. Although in black and white the readers could not see the misty blue of her eyes, both photos caught the special quality of her face, framed in dark hair she was then wearing a little longer than when Morgan had first met her. Her face was well formed, not mobile or highly expressive, rather doll-like in its routine prettiness, with no dominant feature unless it was an imperious chin; but it was a face with an oddly wary quality, as if she were always about to break from repose into laughter or frown. She seemed constantly on the verge of a changed mood, which would of necessity alter things also for those around her, so that they found themselves the more eager for her rare smile, more apprehensive of her infrequent frown. Together with the intensity she could gather about her like a cloak, this made her something of a dominating figure, of whom others in a room were quickly and strongly aware. She did not smile or frown often but rather conveyed what repose always does—a certain inner calm, a cool knowledge that while there might be much to fear, there was little to be done.

The *Life* photos set off, as such things do in the incestuous world of journalism, a round of publicity for Hunt and Kathy Anderson—"which you know better than I do," Hunt told Morgan, "you don't get unless somebody suggests the idea to some editor while holding him in an armlock, and then cooperate like hell while they take one million pictures and ask one thousand silly questions. I suppose it's worth it, depending on your purposes, but it's strange how near a 'political buildup' is to just plain blowing your own horn. I get uneasy about a process that almost requires a man to brag on himself to get anywhere."

Look also did a picture story on the hearings, which featured a special section on Hunt and Kathy at home. There was a "People" item in *Time* about Kathy's being given a lift downtown in one of Washington's multi-passenger taxis by a man who did not know that the pretty lady was the wife of the senator who had just questioned him sharply about the size of the federal subsidy (about $100,000) to his cotton farm, on which the wages paid his hands averaged less than fifty cents an hour.

On a morning television program Kathy talked with authority about the plight of the migrants and how her husband intended to so something about it, particularly about the children, and she was widely quoted when she said rather sharply, in response to a banality from the glamorous female idiot who was interviewing her, that "the reason they're hungry is that people don't pay them enough money and cheat them out of what they do get. It's ridiculous to say that we should teach them how to stretch their money. They're already experts at that." This sort of thing—or the article in the *Evening Star* about her Southern recipes, or the piece in *McCall's* about Senate wives that prominently featured her—added a kind of interest (an editor would call it the "woman's angle") to what might otherwise have been either too statistical or too crushingly depressing.

Dunn slowed at Morgan's gesture and turned the car into the ramp curving down to the paved county road that eventually would take them to the private drive into Anderson's place.

"Have you talked to Kathy?" Dunn said.

"Just for a minute."

"Is she much broken up?"

Morgan did not know how to answer. He did not know how much Dunn knew about Kathy and Hunt, how much Kathy would want him to know. Then he realized there was nothing, anyway, that he could conceal from Dunn longer than it would take them to arrive at Anderson's house.

"What you'd expect," Morgan said. He could not tell from the faint stiffening of Dunn's lips whether that had told him anything or not. It would depend, he thought, on whether Dunn ever had broken into the still, hot circle of Kathy's attention—not Dunn the leader, but Dunn the man.

The notice that came to Kathy, as the hearings continued, was as nothing to the national "exposure" in press and television that fell on Hunt Anderson. Methodically he worked his way through the hearings toward the climactic involvement of Paul Hinman; and it was in another way, Morgan came to know, that Kathy—more and more the expert political wife—made her greatest contribution. Sitting each day in rapt attention to the grim facts of migrancy as they were unfolded in dreary progression, she became something of a critic of the performance, a knowledgeable audience-symbol against whom Anderson could test new ideas or check the reaction to whatever had happened. It became their habit each night to discuss in detail the day's events and what from her place among the listeners he had seemed to accomplish. Then they would talk about the next day's strategy and the over-all position. These nightly conferences—sometimes Morgan sat in, sometimes Matt or Adam, sometimes all of them, but always the two of them talked—became part of the ritual of the hearings. She could spot holes or conflicts in the testimony, not merely from expertise but because she listened and put herself in the place of the uninformed.

"What they're not getting enough of is an idea of how it is in the fields and the camps," she said over dinner at L'Espionage one evening, in a crucial period. "I mean all the Sprock and Berger has to be in the record, but you really need to bring out more dramatically the way it smells and the way they must feel after all those hours on their knees in the beanfields or the cornfields or whatever."

That led Hunt to a decision to put real migrants and crew leaders on the stand far sooner than he had at first planned. He consulted Adam Locklear, who promptly produced the necessary witnesses—among them, a Navajo named Fred Tedeahby, whose account of law enforcement in the small-town Southwest impressed Morgan.

"The farmer we worked for there, he has one of these barracks, I believe it is what they used during World War II. They cut them off in sections, which is not no bigger than this corner of the room up to the table here, for my wife and myself and our oldest daughter and my three boys. And we had one outhouse—for the men, the women, and the children, only one."

"How many workers worked there?"

"We had somewhere between twenty-five and thirty. Some got discouraged and they leave."

"What sort of crops does this particular farmer have?"

"Broom corn. It has a tassel that is pulled by hand and put in bales and used for brooms. This one particular instance I went to town to call some of my people in Gallup, and after I had made my call I went back and sat in the pickup, and I seen these two Indian ladies coming down the street. Where they had been or where they were going, I don't know, but I seen this man, the constable in the town pulled up right beside them, talked to them for maybe two minutes. He opened the back door for them and put them in. They had what they called a detention or what you call a jail. He took them there and put them in and then he drove off.

"Pretty soon he parked next to me and asked what I was doing in town, and I told him, and he said, 'Just as soon as you get through, you get out of town and get back to the farm where you are supposed to be working.' I said I would go after I finished my call and after a call had come back to me. I asked him why am I being treated like that?

"He said, 'Well, we have been told by the Broom Corn Growers Association to keep you people back on the farm.' I told him that I had a privilege and the right to go wherever I wanted to when I wanted to. He told me then, he said, 'Not in this town, you don't.'

"I asked why not? I said, on the north end I seen the sign that says the town of one thousand friendly people. I said, 'Where did that friendliness go to?' And he said, 'Well, we have a standing order to pick you people up and take you in and call your bossman, and he in turn will come in, and if there is any fine to be paid he will pay the fine and take you back out, and you work that fine back out at one dollar an hour.' That is what we were getting paid."

There was also a young black named Carl Wiggins, who spoke with the slow and brooding sullenness of a rage that went so deep there could have been no words to express it if he had tried. Morgan had thought, listening to him, that someday that rage would come pouring out of him, volcanic, uncontrolled, if it didn't kill him first or smother him in hopelessness.

"They ask us this one place we go and pick celery about the children to go to school," Wiggins said. "Most of us people, the children they don't have the right clothes that they need to go to school and get lunches, and anyway we don't know how to put them in that school because we got to have health cards. They want to know if your children are vaccinated and for what, and all them that they require to get in we don't have. No matter what shots we got, it ain't the right ones."

One old woman, vast and puffy in a tentlike cotton print so faded it appeared almost to be cheesecloth, detailed the economic facts of life in the stream. "In this one town where we goes in the spring, they's just this one store, but we try not to buy there. They's a bigger market in another town twenty miles away, and that's a long way, but where we stay, it is just a privately owned store by a man that lives there, and it seems like when we come in, ev'rything just goes thew the roof. The products are not marked. We don't know what we paying. We might even pay eighty-five cents for a five-pound bag of sugar, maybe even more than that. We always ask them the prices and things jump so high, it is not funny."

When Hunt Anderson asked her if the migrants ever tried for better conditions and wages, she shook her head slowly, and her whole body seemed to sway mournfully in her chair. "One time my son he ask for a little higher wage someplace, I recall maybe he wanted one dollar an hour, and the man he say, 'Yes, we can give it to you. We will give you just what you think you are worth, but we will have to charge you what it's worth for your house and your lights and the fuel that you uses.' So they will deduct what they give you and you are no better off."

After Kathy's suggestion, Anderson and Matt—Hunt was usually the only one of the committee members present—developed a sort of counter-punching technique. Every time some sun-broiled sugarbeet rancher would testify to the difficulties of getting decent labor and a crop to the market for anything less than highway-robbery wages and all sorts of handouts and bonuses, then from Adam Locklear's voluminous lists would be produced some nervous, ill-dressed, half-literate black or Mexican or Indian or Puerto Rican, sometimes even a white from the lowest, most hopeless ranks of that ordinarily fortunate and domineering color of animal. Whoever and whatever he was, he would be uneasy in the occasional TV light (if it was a slow news day elsewhere in Washington, and a crew could be spared for a low-level operation like the early migrancy hearings) and would have to be sympathetically drawn out by Anderson, whose easy manner with such witnesses occasionally led to bursts of passion or simple eloquence or shocking fact that might otherwise have been lost in the intimidating surroundings.

One county commissioner from the black belt, indignant at the shiftlessness of migrants who wintered in his jurisdiction, testified: "Why, one time we were shorthanded in the road department, we sent a representative over to White River with instructions to hire twenty people. We were going to furnish transportation and offering to pay them a minimum of fourteen dollars a day, which is in some places very small but a lot better than the welfare. We were able to get five of these people to work."

He was followed, not by accident, by a jumpy little black man who kept looking around like a cat over a bowl of milk, as if he feared what might be coming up behind. "Well, in this potatoes where we was working, you were supposed to get a dollar an hour, but the farmer says let's do it this

way and you are going to make some money. He says, I am going to give
you seventy-five cents an hour to go on. He says, at the end of the job you
will have twenty-five cents saved up for every hour that you worked, and
he says, by the time you get through here, you will have a fistful of money
—he calls it. But a day and a half before the job was supposed to be finished,
there was something went wrong somewhere. We got cut off, so there went
my bonus out the window, and there I was with no money. So I borrowed
from a man in town, this particular man that I go to, a barber. I pawned
my car title to him for enough money for a tank of gas."

That particular witness had his wife with him, a big mahogany-colored
girl with a heavy sullen mouth and haunches like a black Angus. Anderson
asked her if she worked in the fields all day and then came home and cooked
for her family.

"I gets up along about four in the morning and cooks for my family and
we goes to the fields. Later in the morning when it gets hot, we stop in the
fields and rest. I can run back and pick up my daughter and let her come
and help us awhile because we can't work her no more than eight hour a
day. She only fo'teen, and they's always somebody somewhere maybe sittin'
off the side of the road, just waitin' for you to break some law or sump'um."

And just often enough—without any particular planning that Morgan
could learn about—some AP photographer would catch a good shot—as
one did of that sad, beaten pair, the last lingering traces of mutiny etched
on her face, the shivery nerves of her husband hunching up his shoulders
a little, as if against inevitable blows, and between their timeless heads the
county commissioner, still sitting in the front row, his face creased in a wide,
callous grin around a huge cigar. He hadn't even been listening to the
witnesses, just to some flip remark from whoever was sitting next to him,
but no one could know that from the picture; and the next day that scene
hit every front page in the country because even picture editors—Morgan
grudgingly conceded—were not blind enough to miss that kind of drama,
those three heads of humanity—rapacity, stubborn courage, final surrender
—from the same blind and capricious sculptor.

As the slow point-counterpoint of grower and migrant, society and out-
cast, exploitation and dependence, continued in the musty old chamber,
there came to be just enough drama, just enough moments of passion and
truth, with just enough of them frozen in time by the camera, or broadcast
indiscriminately by the wonders of radio and television, that like a Broad-
way show the hearings became a "hot ticket." This particular show caught
on first with the liberals, some college students, academics, women. Lots of
clerical collars began to appear in the long lines that queued up in the

hallway outside the cramped basement chamber. Then came everything from button-downs to "beat" kids. Most remarkably, even other members of the committee began occasionally to appear. Sometimes those waiting outside for a seat to empty could hear a burst of applause or the sharp rapping of the gavel, and once the angry shouts of a grape man from the Imperial Valley could be heard clearly in the corridor. Adam Locklear had produced the facts on the grape man's illegal importation of wetbacks into virtual slavery, and the grape man was accusing him of the theft of his records—which Morgan suspected might well be true.

"That's a hell of a show," Senator Jack Styron told Morgan one day over breakfast in the Senate Dining Room. Styron was considered one of the senators most sensitive to the gentle throb of the public pulse; he was the sort of senator who could make a blistering two-hour speech on the waste and favoritism and political payoff in some pork-barrel appropriation bill and then be the only senator to vote against it—having known so well all along that it was inevitably going to pass that he had slipped an appropriation or two for his own state into the fine print, "Maybe I missed the boat," he told Morgan. "I could have been on that damned committee of Anderson's but I passed it up. Now I don't know. All that free TV. But he's not really going to drag in Hinman, is he?"

The national press interest doubled, trebled. Morgan was no longer lonely at the press table and had the delicious experience of being miles ahead of late-coming colleagues who could never catch up and, in the time-honored tradition of the craft, would have to fake and bluff their way or take a "fill" from him. The demands of television and radio and the big magazines became so onerous that Anderson reluctantly did what he had never thought to do—he brought in a Madison Avenue operator named Danny O'Connor to handle public relations and what O'Connor called—Morgan had never heard the expression before O'Connor appeared in his gray flannels and rep ties—"the media." Through blarney and blandishment O'Connor arranged for an hour a day of the hearings to be carried live on the smallest network, which had a big ironing-board audience of bored housewives. That was enough to make Anderson's face and voice familiar to millions in the space of a few weeks. Besides, no one had to arrange the nightly segments he now was getting on the big news shows on all the networks. In the ultimate accolade of the build-up business, *Time* sent a reporter to dog his footsteps for a possible cover story, the actual appearance of which, Morgan knew, would depend on the confrontation, if any, with Hinman. "Being interviewed by *Time*," Anderson said to Morgan, "is like being in bed with a cobra."

Day after day the hearings went on, a shocking parade of the callous and their victims, almost—Morgan thought at the time—as if they were masters and slaves, caught and held together in some eternal grip, dependent on one another. Almost as if it had all been staged by a master director, day after day would come the kind of person in the kind of moment that nice ordinary people came to see and hear, out of their own inexplicable fascination with misery and evil and the victimized. Once it was a sixteen-year-old Puerto Rican, with eyes dark and soft as wine, describing in a voice so devoid of tone that his words sounded more like a ritual chant, an incantation to absent gods, how he had been arrested for vagrancy after demanding back wages due him, kept in jail for three weeks without a trial, and repeatedly gang-raped by the sots and thieves and degenerates with whom he had been caged in one dank cell. Another time there was a white father who told how his eleven-year-old son had died in agony because an insecticide spray had remained acutely toxic in a heavy dew lying on the fields, and the boy, who had had nothing to eat that day or the night before, had sucked nectar from a morning-glory flower. Naturally there was nothing the grower could do in compensation, or had to.

On the most memorable occasion of all, Senator Hunt Anderson rose slowly to his full height and stood a moment, towering over the dark rostrum, a fearful sight in the barely controlled anger that had drawn his long body more rigidly than usual into lines and planes. He glared down at a stocky, freckled man in a shiny suit and yellow shoes who represented a farm association that employed thousands of migrants every year.

"I've tried to understand you," Anderson finally said in his low but resonant voice. "We've taken a lot of time listening to what you have to say. We understand you have to have labor to harvest the crops on which we all depend. Now you say you don't have anything more to add to what you've said. Well, I have a little something to add. I think until I heard what you had to say here this morning I never really knew how hardhearted and selfish and blind men can be. No—no, let me finish, you've had your say; you had nothing to add. It shocks me, when members of this committee see the conditions in which human beings have to live and work, and then when we face a good man like you, a community man, a family man, who I suppose goes to church and worships God like most people do, and you say you have no responsibility. You say there's nothing you can do or ought to do. Well, sir, I tell you flatly, because I want you and the people of this country to know it, you and your kind are criminals. Just as if you stole money from a bank or shot somebody in cold blood."

"You just don't see anything like that very often," Danny O'Connor said, late that day over drinks at Wearley's, across the plaza from the old Senate Office Building. "I mean someone just saying what moves him rather than figuring the angles and worrying about his timing and his profile. I mean the camera angle was all wrong, you know, and the lights in that lousy cubbyhole. But it was natural action, passion, life, tension. Great TV. I wouldn't change a second of it."

Kathy looked thoughtfully into her martini. "You don't think it was maybe too rough? That somebody might think Hunt was bullying that man? It could be awfully easy to create sympathy for somebody who looks like an underdog."

"Just what I mean. You're figuring the angles, being careful. What made it such great TV was that it was the real thing."

"I doubt the bully business anyway." Morgan was studying his notes. Anderson had spoken so slowly and with such emphasis that it had been easy to take his speech down verbatim in longhand. "The big thing, it seems to me, is the American people are for the underdog, it's part of the myth, and they don't want to think of themselves as being any part of a bunch of slave-drivers like these grower goons. They think they're above anything like that when in fact it's just they're in a different position. They can afford to be above it. So they associate with Hunt, is my guess. Not so much with the migrants, shiftless bums like that, but with the white knight. They sit there and nod their heads and say 'give it to the bastards,' feeling righteous and unguilty. And if practically any one of them raised celery for a living, he'd be in there gouging and cheating with the best of them, because that's the way people are and the way things are done."

"You think these growers are different from the rest of us? Worse people?" Adam put the question to Kathy bluntly.

Her eyes narrowed, turning a little darker than usual. Morgan thought she seemed almost hostile.

"Not different fundamentally, not in human nature. I guess I agree with Rich about that although I'm not as misanthropic as he is." She cut her eyes mischievously at Morgan, then was quickly serious again. "But, yes, there's something in all this that seems worse than what you'd normally expect, even from people. A banker that cheats, a crooked politician, a bribed policeman—somehow, bad as they are, it doesn't seem to me the same order of evil as letting children go hungry when you can see it happening and could do something about it. Then telling yourself it wasn't your place to do anything. I think that's worse."

Adam punched Morgan's arm. "You know this lady is smart some-times?"

"But not smart enough to know why it is," Kathy said.

Adam finished the concoction before him. Morgan had never seen him drink anything but high-school stuff—rum and Coke, or bourbon and Seven Up, or once, before Morgan could stop him, Scotch and ginger ale—because he had an almost morbid fear of the Indian's supposed weakness for fire-water.

"The worst thing that can happen to a man," Adam said to Kathy, "is to be somebody's master. Pretty soon if you're a master, you find yourself beating up your slave, or taking his woman or starving his kids, just because you can do it. Because you're free to do it, and if you are, you can't help doing it. And then you begin to do it to him because you like to do it to him. You like the freedom to do it even more. And the next thing you know, you're as much a slave as he is. You're dependent on him for your freedom just as much as he's dependent on you in his slavery."

"Caligula," Kathy murmured, and Adam looked puzzled. Danny O'-Connor set his glass down with a little slap. "Five million Jews." He grinned without mirth. "Or was it eight? Adam's right. That's what slav-ery leads to. That's what I keep thinking about, every new witness we hear."

Morgan knew that Anderson, partially owing to Adam's influence, had reached similar conclusions about the peculiar nature of the grower-migrant relationship, their spiritual interdependence, which had its visible counterpart in their economic linkage.

"Let's face it," one grower had told the committee, "our farms are to a great degree dependent on a good stable source of workmen. Labor to us is as important as capital, as farmland, as management, or even as owners themselves." And an angry young schoolteacher from Florida had pre-scribed his own drastic remedy: "Burn down all this shameful housing. Right to the ground, everywhere. If there's no place for the migrant, he won't come and the crop won't get picked, in which case these growers won't have any economy. So you can bet your life there'll be steps taken to put up decent housing so the crops can get picked."

After Anderson's denunciation of the growers as criminals, it was not so much his understanding of migrancy as his political tactics upon which he had to concentrate. As Morgan predicted, a flood of letters, telegrams, and calls, overwhelming the Capitol facilities, placed the public heavily behind Anderson. There was also a barrage of angry responses from growers' groups, chambers of commerce, local politicians, and other assorted parties at interest.

Two days after Hunt's outburst, a band of farm-state senators took an hour on the floor to denounce the upstart Anderson, with what was generally known to be the support of a number of other senators, not a few from his own party, who resented the fact that he was "stirring up people" and causing "a lot of trouble over a few migrants." Anderson sat coolly listening, disdaining to defend himself against any particular remark; but when the farm-staters had completed the attack he rose—whereupon most of his attackers rather ostentatiously left the chamber—to set forth unemotionally and with adequate quotations and statistics the few facts, derived from the hearings and investigation, that he said were necessary to sustain his use of the word "criminals." He concluded in a manner that Morgan, listening in the gallery, knew was intended to move the hearings toward the dramatic conclusion for which Anderson had been maneuvering.

"Mister President," Anderson said, "if for my recent remarks I should be thought intemperate—and that is apparently a mild word for what my distinguished colleagues consider me—then let me say that intemperance itself would be a mild remedy for the abuses our committee has encountered. Mister President, under what circumstances should a man who knowingly breaks or evades the law *not* be called a criminal? If he is our neighbor, is he any the less a criminal? Or if he is otherwise a respected citizen of our community? If he is some ignorant black man or Indian, unable even to read vagrancy laws, is he any the *more* a criminal for breaking them in his ignorance? No, Mister President, none of my able and distinguished colleagues from the farmland states"—Anderson looked around, smiling a little—"some of whom, I see, are no longer present, but if they were, none of those gentlemen would maintain that a lawbreaker should be judged not by his offense but by his place in society or his standing in the community. Mister President, I can only conclude therefore that my distinguished colleagues believe me wrong on the merits of the case, wrong on the facts, wrong on the law—although I listened in vain this afternoon for the evidence which would point out the errors of law and fact that they must have discovered but that are not as yet apparent to the committee and the staff that have labored for the better part of a year on this painful matter. Now, Mister Preseident . . ." He paused to shuffle some papers on his desk in the rear row, his tall form bent nearly in half, his big hands fumbling aimlessly, and his hair, as always, in some disarray, a large hank shooting up straight over one ear as if he had slept on it.

The notoriety of the migrancy investigation, magnified by Anderson's sensational remarks, was by then great enough to fill the galleries, an unusual sight. Around Morgan, the rows of press seats were also crowded, which was seldom true for floor debate. In the family gallery he could see Kathy, still as always, wearing dark glasses, sitting quite alone, although other senators' wives were nearby. The floor was also better populated than usual, despite the fact that not many senators had taken any interest in the migrancy problem; what had drawn them was the conflict in the Senate itself and, on Anderson's side of the aisle, within party ranks. Rather suddenly, a considerable storm was breaking around a freshman who was causing trouble in a body that always hoped to avoid it, and in a time when new senators were expected to be quiet and vote right. There were not many in that chamber who had not realized, with their political natures, that Anderson had taken dead aim on Paul Hinman; so he had an audience all right—not sympathetic, not quite hostile, wary, gauging him.

"You see the problem is," an old pol had once told Morgan, "ever so often you have a little something somebody wants and you got to decide whether to throw it to him, and what you want to know is can he manage it? What does he know and who else is with him, and when somebody up there decides to separate the men from the boys, is he going to have what it takes? Because, if not, you could go down with the ship."

That was what his colleagues were studying, that afternoon, about Hunt Anderson, whom many of them had only started to notice.

While Anderson was fumbling at his desk, one of the senior senators, a border-state cutthroat whose power over the Finance Committee was at that time nearly total, rose from his desk across the aisle. "Will the distinguished Senator yield for a question?" He was a renowned cut-and-thrust debater who had only to rise amid the general mediocrity on the Senate floor to send through the working-press rooms the anticipatory call: "Old Ed's up!"

"Without losing my right to the floor, certainly," Anderson said.

"Senator yields," sang out the chair, at that moment the most junior member, formerly a Western state governor, who had appointed himself to a vacant seat and who was therefore known derisively as the "instant senator"—an appellation that in the campaign he ultimately had to face helped sink him without a trace.

"I thank the able and respected Senator." Old Ed—one of those beneficiaries of the seniority system who, despite the fact that his state had little population and was losing most of that, had been around long enough to control Finance, influence two other major committees, and arrogate to

himself the privileges and attitudes of a sultan, with approximately a sul
tan's deference to the popular will—Old Ed came around his desk and
leaned against it with folded arms, a posture that the Senate press corps had
learned over the years he assumed only when he anticipated slicing some
helpless victim to ribbons. "I am sure the distinguished senator"—Old Ed's
voice dripped with sarcasm—"will be able to tell me what legislation he
intends to propose as a result of these rather spectacular hearings he has
been conducting." The emphasis was on the "he" in order to place the
responsibility elsewhere than on good, respectable senators, and Old Ed
who had never been noted for humility, kept turning his head a little, as if
trying to see his colleagues' certain approbation. What few empty seats
there had been in the press gallery had been filled within moments after Old
Ed had put his first question.

"Well, let me say to my esteemed colleague . . ." Anderson continued to
fish through the papers on his desk, not looking up, an act of calculated
insult to a senator of Old Ed's pre-eminence and vindictiveness. Morgan
knew Anderson well enough to know it was an act—a dangerous one, he
thought. ". . . our committee is preparing a report. We anticipate making
lengthy recommendations to the Senate. The able and experienced Senator
will understand, of course, that until the committee reaches its conclusions
the chairman is not able to state what those conclusions will be."

"Well, will the able and . . . uh . . . dedicated Senator yield for a further
question?"

"Without yielding my right to the floor."

It all had a certain ritual quality, Morgan thought; a good presiding
officer with a sense of rhythm and drama sometimes seemed like a rabbi in
the synagogue (a simile the Senate would not have appreciated).

"While of course I understand that the dedicated Senator may not as yet
be able to disclose legislation in detail, if he ever will be, could he not
confirm for me the rather obvious deduction that it is likely to be labor
legislation?"

"Some of it." Anderson straightened from his papers at last and lounged
against his desk, as if not to be outdone in casualness. "That *is* rather
obvious."

"Labor *organizing* legislation?"

"Well, I will say to my good friend, and let me assure him that he is my
good friend, that the committee has taken much testimony, which I com
mend to his attention when our report appears, that attests the farm work
ers' need for more bargaining power. And the experienced Senator does no

ʌeed me to tell him that in our society such bargaining power traditionally ʌas been derived for wage workers through labor organization."

"Exactly!" Old Ed's voice was sharp with triumph. "And so would the *dedicated* Senator"—he was bearing down a little harder on the "dedicated" every time he used it, as if he had found just the right word with ʌhich, in good senatorial fashion, to damn Hunt with the faintest of praise —"would he agree with me that if and when his committee brings any egislation to this eagerly awaiting chamber"—the slightly nasal voice did ʌot bother to conceal the sarcasm—"it will surely be an effort to put one ʌore segment of what used to be free American labor and one last strongʌold of free American enterprise—I am speaking of farm workers and the ʌreat agricultural institutions on which the strength of this country is built —an effort to bring them under the yoke of the giant unions and the NLRB ʌnd the closed shop?"

"Well, now, Mister President, my amiable"—with a straight face Anderʌon emphasized the word—"colleague is making a little speech, which I ʌouldn't mind except that I yielded only for a question."

"It was a question, Mister President." Old Ed turned his back and ʌranced up the aisle a step or two, waving one arm high in disdain and in ʌnderson's general direction.

"A have-you-stopped-beating-your-wife question. But I would never ʌuibble with so distinguished a colleague, so I will just say to him, Mister ʌresident, that while his state, which is not normally thought of as a farm ʌtate, maintains its present right-to-work law, which I understand was ʌassed many years ago during its beloved senior Senator's distinguished ʌenure as governor, it seems to me it need not worry unduly about a closed ʌhop for the"—suddenly there was a three-by-five card in Anderson's thick ʌand—"for the more than two thousand migrant farmhands who annually ʌork in its potato and vegetable fields and who live, Mister President, in ʌhat much testimony before our committee and to our investigators shows ʌo be about the most miserable and inhuman conditions of any migrants in ʌhe Eastern stream—"

"Will the Senator yield!" Old Ed was not walking away from Anderson ʌny more, and it was not a question he shouted but a command.

Anderson paid him no notice. "I will of course make this testimony ʌmmediately available to my distinguished colleague, who naturally has not ʌad time to attend any of our hearings—"

"Mister President!"

"He will be particularly interested in the evidence our committee has that his state's code on migrant housing, which as a former governor he will surely be familiar with, was being openly violated last summer in more than a dozen migrant camps visited by our investigators."

"Will the Senator yield?" Old Ed was shouting almost into Anderson's face; his own was red and furious, conditions he was more accustomed to induce in his victims than to suffer himself.

A few of his colleagues, even some of the Senate's elders, were looking a bit amused; but that was deceptive. They might not mind at the moment seeing hard-bitten Old Ed scratched up a little; but what would stick with them was that it had been done by an upstart who'd better be put in his place before he visited similar indignities on them. In the long run, the old Senate mules would always recognize that their own interests demanded solidarity among them even when they despised each other—as many of them despised Old Ed, and for good reason.

Anderson's temerity also was making something of a stir in the galleries. Reporters were scribbling; tourists were on the edge of their seats; in the family section, Kathy sat alone, appearing unmoved behind her dark glasses, except to those who knew of her nearly total immersion in the hearings.

"Mister President," Anderson said mildly, "I'd be glad to yield a third time to my amiable and distinguished colleague, even for another speech and even if I have answered his pointed and well-stated questions, except that I'm due in a matter of minutes at an important committee meeting. I regret I have no more time to spare, but in any case I'll soon yield my right to the floor. Now, Mister President . . ."

"Good show," muttered the reporter sitting beside Morgan. He was an old Senate head. "But bad politics in this place." He shook his head sadly. A veteran reporter, he had, like an insect that takes on the color of its surroundings, fallen into a more senatorial outlook than most senators.

This sort of assimilation was a hazard of the trade. Morgan could be around any reporter who'd had the same Washington assignment for, say two years—the White House, or the Treasury, Capitol Hill, politics—and in not more than five minutes deduce exactly where he worked. A reporter who spent all his time and intellectual energy discovering the White House view of things began to think in Executive Branch terms—to consider Capitol Hill, for instance, a faraway place full of provincial obstructionists. A State Department reporter was likely to regale dinner-table companions with the same talk about the Bloc or the Chinats or the Subcontinent or the Cables as would the foreign-service types from whom he had picked up the jargon. The old Senate head sitting next to Morgan that day called all senators by their first names or nicknames and gravely discussed with the Leadership on Both Sides of the Aisle whether there could be adjournment ("Can we get out of here?" they would wonder) by November 15 or whether the session would have to "go over" to November 17— a weighty matter on the Hill. He could always tell you without consulting his discreet notebook the exact status of every appropriations bill—"They're still holding out for a ten-per-cent cut in development assistance but the administration is too bullheaded to give. We won't be out of here till Christmas, the way it looks now."

As Anderson continued to speak, that particular old Senate head sighted along his pencil at the floor; he was always eager to point out Taft's desk or Huey Long's. He said wisely, "Look at Old Ed down there. When he gets through, Anderson'll be lying there in the aisle in little pieces wishing he'd kept his big mouth shut."

"Ump." Morgan was trying to listen to Anderson.

"And wait till the next time Anderson wants some highway or hospital money out of this place. Old Ed will run his balls up the flagpole."

"Ump, ump."

"But these kids, these new guys come in here, I've seen a lot that never do learn how to operate in this place."

"If you want to get along," Morgan said, "go along."

The old Senate head looked at him with deep respect. "The only way. The sooner they learn it the better, in this place. But some never do." He pursed his lips and shook his head gravely.

" . . . indeed does constitute criminal behavior," Anderson was saying, "and if the states, who to this point in time have the only applicable statutes, care to prosecute in any case, the committee can furnish much evidence that will be of assistance. We will forward, of course, our reports to the proper state officials. But, Mister President, I fear the states will *not* act. The disgraceful truth is that the states have not acted in the past, and with far greater investigative and enforcement powers at their disposal than our committee staff has had. We have found so few instances of states acting to enforce their own housing and health codes—where these even exist in any way that effectively applies to migrant labor—as to be negligible. The same is true for state investigations of conditions in the fields and in the camps, including, I am sad to say, the state of my good friend with whom I have just engaged in amiable colloquy. Now, Mister President, why should that be the case in *any* state?"

His voice rang out a little on the question, and Morgan noticed that the other senators in the chamber were attentive, especially Old Ed, who sat glowering and beetfaced. In the rear, from a sofa just by the cloakroom door, Adam Locklear and Matt Grant watched Anderson closely, rather like parents seeing an offspring off to school.

The Senate could be interesting—humanity on display—but to Morgan it was usually an antiseptic chamber, as seen from the press gallery. The speeches tended to sound alike, and the bills were all reminiscent of other pieces of timid legal prose, and the men who moved about buttonholing one another looked to be of a size. Or maybe, he thought, the gallery was just a bad vantage point from which to see; maybe it foreshortened men and events to look at them from above. Down on the floor, he was certain, the Senate could not be such a pallid spectacle, but was, rather, a formally organized version of the ancient human struggle to emerge from the pack.

"I think we can only conclude, Mister President, that the states do not want to act to protect migrant labor. They don't want to interfere with conditions imposed by large grower and packing interests. They don't want to tamper with their farm economies, inefficient though they may be. They don't want to attack the status quo. After all, who among the migrants votes? Which of them pays taxes, has any influence, holds a union card? Most of them are not even white, or English-speaking. Many are not literate. No, Mister President, I greatly fear we cannot look to the states for needed action, not when those who would be benefited are so powerless and those who think they would be injured are so powerful. And I also fear we must not look to the states for the reason that so much testimony before the committee shows so much involvement of so many state officials in the migrant system itself. Mister President, I mean to say—and I assure this chamber that I choose my words carefully—I mean to say that we have reason to believe some state officials not only condone the exploitation of migrants but profit from it."

Morgan could feel the tension tighten in the chamber, like a rubber band slowly being stretched toward breaking. "That fool is going to do it," the old Senate head muttered. Even Old Ed was looking at Anderson expectantly. Morgan knew Hunt was about to take a step that would have large political consequences, but suddenly he was not thinking of that. He was thinking that Hunt Anderson was about to bring down on himself—far more than he already had—the great floodtide of the American publicity machine. He was about to open himself to the buffeting and acclaim of the curious and the concerned and the awed and the outraged and the star-struck. That was more than a big step; it was a lunge. No matter what happened, Anderson was going to be forever changed. Kathy would inexorably be drawn along with him, and changed too. Morgan wondered if

Kathy, still and attentive in the gallery, was concerned, whether she still believed breaking Hinman would "make" her husband—or whether, in fact, making him would finally be for good or ill, by her lights. But she gave no sign.

Abruptly Anderson named Hinman's state. " . . . for instance, has in peak months about fourteen thousand migrant laborers in its vegetable and potato fields and its apple orchards. But in that state, anyone with a strong stomach and average eyesight can in a day discover literally hundreds of violations of what rudimentary state codes there are. The committee investigators have done so—I have done so—and very thoroughly, I may say. But no state action has been taken or threatened, nor—so far as the committee can see—will it be. Mister President, we also have evidence from that state of wholesale exploitation by unscrupulous crew leaders and calloused growers and local officials. We will show, I believe, a new kind of fraud—in an area of human life where one would have thought all possible frauds had been long ago devised—a new fraud stemming from the recent extension of Old Age and Survivors' Insurance coverage to migrant workers. I might add that is about the only action ever taken by the federal government to help these people, many of whom can claim no state, let alone a community, for their own. And now even that small act of compassion and concern is being perverted by cheating employers.

"Mister President, I have asserted that the states are so lax in enforcing their own laws because they have no interest in changing the system. In this particular state, one of the biggest users of migrant labor, Mister President, there appears in fact to be a high-level interest in maintaining the system."

There were audible gasps from the gallery. "Ape," the old Senate head muttered. "He's gone *ape*shit."

"When the governor of that great state"—Anderson plowed as steadily into his climax as if he were reading an editorial on motherhood into the *Congressional Record*—"is himself a major though unacknowledged owner of a corporate potato farm and packshed known as Agri-Packers . . ."

A wire-service man at the central desk on the first row of the press gallery quietly picked up a telephone with a muffler attachment and began talking over the direct wire. As Anderson continued, the wire-service man, his voice inaudible two feet away, kept dictating his story—produced almost effortlessly by the supreme skill of his trade, by the professionalism that passed in his life for value. The story was already moving on the wire even before the speech was finished.

" . . . which comprises more than a hundred acres, each with a crop value of more than three thousand dollars in a good crop year, and when . . ."

A youngish senator stood up and stalked into the cloakroom. He represented a major Lakes state and was honorary co-chairman of Help Hinman,
a "volunteer" committee Hinman's staff had bought and paid for to manage
their man's national political interests in advance of his actual campaign.

" . . . when Agri-Packers' fields are harvested each year almost entirely
by migrant workers housed in camps maintained—to the extent that they
are—by Agri-Packers . . ."

Around Morgan, reporters were jabbing at their notepads or at the yellow
sheets the Standing Committee of Correspondents made available in the
press gallery. Two more senators, one of whom was said to have his eye on
the State Department in the forthcoming Hinman administration, left Anderson's side of the aisle and went to the cloakroom. Someone, Morgan had
no doubt, would already be on the phone to the White House, where the
hard-shelled old pinochle player who lived there would see immediately
that he would have to emerge from his pose of neutrality, either to help
rescue Hinman or to produce a salable substitute if that became necessary;
neither of which courses would amuse him. Someone else would by then
have an open line to Hinman himself.

" . . . then the governor of that state can hardly be considered disinterested," Anderson concluded, adding florid assurances that he was only
citing one rather typical example, not trying to make a particular instance
of it.

The old Senate head next to Morgan was right when he mumbled something about the futility of trying not to sit down after a man had blistered
his own tail. He and Morgan both knew the fat was in the fire; and when
Morgan emerged into the working rooms behind the press gallery, he found
them a bedlam of men shouting into phones and at each other, of furiously
clacking typewriters and jangling teletype bells. Morgan hurried around to
the family-gallery entrance, but Kathy had left immediately after the speech
—followed, a guard told him, by a man with four cameras festooned around
his neck. Morgan went across the East Plaza in sharp autumn air to Anderson's office suite, which, small and crowded, was also a bedlam. Probably
never going to be any bigger, Morgan thought with grim amusement, not
after the Leaders get through with Anderson.

Morgan was well known on the premises, and guardian Geraldine was
long gone from the dangers and shocks of the capital; a quick check on the
intercom by a busy secretary sent him right into the inner sanctum, the only
room of Anderson's suite not jammed with desks and filing cabinets. There
was a desk big enough for table tennis, a baronial fireplace, carpeting to the
metatarsals, a brown leather sofa and two matching chairs, a telephone

console winking like a jukebox, and over the mantel a rather undistin-
guished pastel of Kathy and their two children. Anderson had not then been
around long enough to collect many of the signed, smiling photographs and
the overwritten plaques and framed tributes that covered the walls of most
politicians.

Kathy and Matt were there; Anderson was on the phone.

"I know it gives you problems," he was saying. "I understood that all
along. It gives me problems. But I think the President will agree I gave the
governor every chance to get it off his back before it came to this."

"White House." Morgan did not need Matt's low mutter to understand
that.

Anderson listened for a long time. There was a sense of unseen powers
on the other end of the line, menacing shades, imposing presences. Finally
Anderson grinned, held the phone away from his ear as if it were red hot,
and listened some more; then, "Well, tell the President, naturally I'm sorry
he feels that way. Tell him I'll do anything I can to . . . repair the situation.
I don't want to hurt the party any more than he does. But, Charlie . . . You
know this is a matter of principle, and it's too late to turn back anyway.
. . . I know, Charlie . . . Now you know that's not so, Charlie. . . . No, there
wasn't any other governor I could pick on, none involved this deeply.
. . . I *kept* you posted, Charlie. . . . Well, you tell the President I regret it
as much as he does. . . ." There was more in that vein for two or three
minutes.

When Anderson hung up he looked more cheerful than he had in months.
"Got the pricks jumping," he said. "How'd it go, Rich?"

"The wires are screaming."

"Matt, see if Hinman has put out anything."

It was said with more authority than Anderson usually displayed, and
Matt promptly left the room. Morgan had the impression that Anderson
was in a sort of ecstatic shock, the way he had seen other men, even in
Korea, just after an ordeal, physical or mental, they believed they had
weathered well. Anderson was garrulous, exuberant; he strode rapidly
about the room, touching things, bending to kiss Kathy, sitting down in one
of the leather chairs but quickly rising to walk about again.

"Old Ed," he said. "Bastard tried to touch me up. Did you see me pull
those figures on him? And those farm characters, like a herd of goddamned
bull elephants on the way to the graveyard. Sweetie"—to Kathy—"did you
hear it all, did you make it for the whole show?"

She assured him she had, he had done well, putting down Old Ed was
the best part, better than Hinman.

"Right," he said, "right, because Old Ed, he really thinks he runs this goddam place and, man! is he going to ream me a new one first chance he gets." It was as if he relished having defied them, as if he felt true to his idea of himself. "You know something, Rich?"

Morgan raised his eyebrows.

"They were listening. All the old farts were sitting there listening to me. You should have seen the way they looked at me up close. That was something, Rich."

"And one thing," Kathy said, "if Hinman comes on, they'll have to give you the Caucus Room. It'll be a mob scene."

"Bet your sweet ass they will."

The phone buzzed. Anderson snatched it up, listened. "TV? I'll see 'em all at once"—he looked at his watch—"in twenty minutes. Get that makeup man in here."

"Makeup?" Morgan said when Anderson hung up. "Are you kidding?"

"I hate the goddam stuff, but O'Connor tells me my cheekbones make these big shadows under my eyes, so I look like Boris Karloff without it. That O'Connor drives me crazy."

"Yeah," Morgan said. "Me too."

Matt came in with a yellow piece of wire copy. "Hinman bit hard."

Anderson grabbed the paper, read it, handed it to Morgan.

Morgan leaned over Kathy, noticing her perfume, and they read the story together. She was warm; Morgan heard her light breathing, his arm touched her shoulder. The story said an angry Hinman denied everything but the Agri-Packers interest, which he said was in blind trust with his other interests. What mattered was that he demanded to appear before the committee and refute the charges personally.

"We've got him!" Kathy's voice broke a little with eagerness. She had not even noticed Morgan was beside her, touching her. No one had to tell Morgan that. He moved away, toward Matt.

"By God," Anderson said, "I never really believed until this exact second the little son-of-a-bitch would bite. I never believed he'd be that foolish."

"Matt"—Morgan had a story of his own to write and was on the way out—"better tell that makeup man to hurry."

Just outside Anderson's suite he met Adam Locklear walking along head down, his hands in his pockets, his chunky body bull-like in the echoing dimness of the long corridor.

"Well, Five-Star, you've got a big story at last," Adam said. "I suppose you'll even be running him for president now."

"Should I?"

"If he pulls off the Hinman trick, I guess so. You're the political expert."

"If, you said. Hunt talks as if it's in the bag."

"Talk's easy. That cold-blooded snatch has got him believing he can do anything, but I'm not so sure. Hinman's a big mule." His obvious bitterness at Kathy must have made Morgan's face appear startled. "I'm sorry, Rich, I shouldn't have said that. It's just that Hinman is really such a small part of the whole picture I'd hate to see the Senator get the whole investigation discredited, or let it be diverted into some smelly political fight, by going wrong on this one part of it."

"Hunt won't let that happen. You know how he feels about what's been happening to all those people."

"If I didn't," Adam said, "I'd be off for the canebrakes by tomorrow morning."

Morgan's taxi had to fight traffic along Pennsylvania, and the driver made the mistake of trying to go up Fourteenth to K, so he was late reaching the office. Keller, the news editor, was waiting at Morgan's desk.

"They're screaming for a start up there. You're on top of page one and they've blocked out a buck and a half just tentatively."

"Tell 'em to make it two. What about text?"

"We'll tack on the right excerpts from Anderson's stuff at the end of your piece so don't take too much space on quotes. They'll take care of the Hinman crap up there, so just give 'em a high reference. I need short takes at this hour." Keller turned away, then came back. "Good payoff for you." He gazed at Morgan kindly. "They're happy up there. I can tell, even when the bastards are screaming for copy."

A good payoff for us all, Morgan thought as he worked. He knew that what Anderson had most feared was that Hinman would simply ignore the charges. By such a lofty course. Hinman would suffer minimum damage, hold the notoriety of the story within limits, and leave the committee in the position of swinging wildly at a target that refused to act like a target.

"Except that I don't personally think he'll do any of that," Anderson had explained to Kathy and Morgan over dinner at La Salle du Bois, the night before he implicated Hinman on the Senate floor. "This is an arrogant man, you see, a very hot boy who's never had anybody stand up to him anywhere along the line. He must be straining at the leash already, and when he hears what I'm going to say, I just don't believe there's going to be any holding him back. Damn the politics of it. You can't say that kind of thing about Paul Hinman—especially not if you're an upstart like me that nobody ever heard of. That's what I'm banking on. He's going to come roaring down here like a freight train ready to run right over me. It isn't even going to occur to him that the smart thing to do is to lie low. The Paul Hinmans of this world don't think they're required to do the smart thing, they think it's a little beneath them."

Hinman did come back as predicted, swinging hard, so that there would be the confrontation Anderson wanted most—rather as if, it occurred to Morgan that night, "the smart thing" somehow was beneath Anderson too. Suddenly, above the clatter of his typewriter, he could hear Adam Locklear: *I'm afraid he'll chase the rainbow.*

"In one way," Morgan said to Dunn quietly, as if he did not wish Glass to hear, "I suppose you could say I made Anderson a presidential candidate."

The green lenses barely moved as Dunn's head nodded almost imperceptibly.

"How's that?" Glass brayed from the rear seat.

"The night he dragged Hinman into the migrant mess . . ." Maybe even Glass could understand some things, Morgan thought, at least Glass was in the trade. " . . . I was writing the story, and I put in a high graf to say that since Hinman's had been almost the only name mentioned for the nomination, if the Anderson hearings knocked him out of it there could be an open convention."

"And that being the case," Dunn said, "the next thing you had to do was to list all the possibilities. Right?"

"Right. Now you understand it made no difference that I'd have to attribute the names to political analysts or 'informed sources.' All those frauds would only be Richmond P. Morgan in disguise. And it didn't make a damn whether my colleagues on the other papers would list Anderson with all the obscurities and hopefuls and perennials *they* might envision in Hinman's place, if it finally came open. Because the truth is, it's not really news until it's in our paper. At least it wasn't in those days. So I wrestled with it a little while but not for long.

"A presidential candidacy begins, in my opinion, not in a lot of publicity but in the 'speculation.' All that gossip, insight, fact, fancy, prejudice, and propaganda that political writers like me pass on to the nation—which is just to say *our* sense of a situation and its possibilities. Usually we're remarkably near unanimity, since we all feed on each other's thoughts and writings, and dredge those up from about the same sources—what we see and hear and filter through our experience of politicians; and, more important, what politicians want us to see and hear and report; and, last but not

least, our personal likes and dislikes. I don't know about you, Glass, but
I've seen reasonably good men never get off the ground, either because they
couldn't get themselves into our speculation or couldn't maintain it when
they did; and I've seen some nothing-balls jump into it overnight because
of one speech written by somebody else, or maybe a newsy press conference,
or even just a lavish buffet dinner with useful press handouts. And there's
nothing like an efficient campaign organization—never mind if the candidate's any good—to catch the attention of the political press."

"Not a bad system," Dunn said. "You guys are a sort of nominations
committee acting for everybody else. You can't all be fooled all of the time,
and damn few of you can be bought. Your biggest weakness is that too many
of you want to believe in people and things you're too lazy to question. But
in my experience your committee does manage to weed out the culls. Every
now and then you do go wrong and put a good man down or a bad man
up—how is that different from anything else in life? And the truth of it is
that a man who can get himself into what you call the speculation and turn
it to his advantage is likely to be the kind of man who can make the
presidency; on the other hand, if he can't even manage the speculation, he'd
better stick to his law practice. I think political writers provide a pretty good
test of whether a man's got it or not."

But got what? Morgan thought. Aloud he said, "When they can push
themselves away from the bar. Except that reporters tend to fight the last
war, like generals. They depend primarily on experience, and as fast as
things move nowadays, nothing deceives a man more. Anyway, I put Hunt's
name on my list that night. Analysts here credited Mister Anderson with
a brilliant but dangerous political gamble, blah-blah-blah. By wrecking Mr.
Hinman's chances, Mister Anderson could wreck their party's chances, and
perhaps his own future in that party, and so on and so forth. But on the
other hand—there's always another hand in the speculation—the national
attention Mister Anderson is receiving and his unique situation as a Southerner defending Negroes could catapult him into the presidential picture,
et cetera, ad infinitum.

"Of course, that part about Southerners and Negroes was solid stuff, and
I got to tell you, none of the other political hacks got that point at all, the
one that was really necessary to make Hunt a believable candidate. That's
why my story really was the beginning of his campaign, and the funny thing
is, I didn't have to write it—and not even a psychoanalyst could tell you
or me why I did. Because I liked Hunt, liked Kathy, liked his political style?
Because I believed in his character? Let's face it, I stood to gain professionally if a friend became a candidate, particularly if he became president. I

enjoyed having the power to validate him in the speculation. I could even work up a little outrage at men like Hinman and the migrant system, and I always tended to support the newcomer against the settled situation, that's in my blood. I think maybe I must have been a little romantic too. I remembered something Hunt had told me when we got drunk one night. *'What I want is just not to corrupt people or cheapen anything'*—he actually said that to me."

"Christ," Glass said, "just think what you could have done for him with thirty seconds on the tube."

"Maybe you were just a pro." Dunn's green lenses turned for a second toward Morgan. "Maybe you just knew a solid political angle when you saw one."

For whatever reason it had been written, Morgan knew, that story really had been one of the things that had led Hunt Anderson on, just as it had been one of the things that had led the public to accept him as a presidential possibility. Nothing affects a man more powerfully than what he thinks about himself, and Morgan's few words, in such a forum, working on Anderson's concept of himself, had both confirmed and stimulated that shining ideal that, Morgan believed, had beckoned Anderson always. Anderson had been a politician; so he had believed the glowing things he read about himself, even when he had helped contrive them; and it never occurred to him that Morgan might have written that passage out of some obscure or mixed purpose of his own; because everything concerning Anderson derived from Anderson's own worth. Not, Morgan remembered, that Anderson had conceded a thing; in fact, the next day, looking rather as if he had just had a sumptuous meal, he had chided Morgan for being "premature."

"That's not the same as inaccurate," Morgan said.

Anderson laughed. "For your information, I'm making a strong denial of candidacy at noon."

"You'd better. You can't admit a thing—in fact, you don't even want to, not yet, not until you've sunk Hinman in a mineshaft and filled it up with concrete."

Morgan had encountered Adam Locklear just after that day's hearings. Adam was looking no more dour than usual but said right away, without preamble, "So the Chief's off and running just like I thought he'd be. Now the whole thing will turn into a sideshow, you watch. Those two tomcats will scratch either other up, and that witch will sit up there in the gallery egging him on, but who gives a damn for some poor bastard with a backache and hungry kids?"

"Adam, dammit, that's not fair. Not about Kathy and not about Hunt. He cares about that poor bastard, and you know he does. If he did happen to make it, he might even know enough, and have enough guts and fire-power, to get something done for a change."

Adam nodded glumly. "But, you know, Rich, a man starts down that political road, he goes where it leads him. Especially with a woman like that to please."

"Maybe this road won't lead far. Maybe you're right and we underesti-mate Hinman."

"I don't know whether he's underestimating Hinman or not," Judge Ward told Morgan the next day. "Personally, I never took to Hinman much, the few times I've dealt with him. But I can tell you the White House is boiling mad and around this place there are a lot of us who happen to think this Anderson is putting himself pretty far out ahead of the party. That might be one thing if he'd earned the right over the years, but who the hell does he think he is?"

"Judge, I hate to say it about a man, but I think Hunt Anderson may be about ninety-eight per cent sincere."

"Sincere?" The Judge looked at Morgan as if Morgan had body sores.

They were sitting in the ornate President's Room, just off the Senate floor, where senators came when a reporter to whom they were willing to speak sent in a note. Morgan thought the medallion portraits of Washington and his cabinet, the Brumidi cherubs, the gilded mirrors and chande-liers, the black leather couches, and the baize-covered Lincoln's Table in the center of the room provided exactly the right surroundings for Judge Ward, one of the last senators who dressed the part—high, detached col-lars, old-fashioned suits, watch chain, gold-knobbed cane, lengthy cigar, always a white flower in his lapel, and all this beneath long flowing blue hair and a pink cherubic face with pince-nez. From the galleries, the guides would point him out to the tourists, and in the corridors of the Capitol he could be seen genially showing dazzled schoolchildren from Terre Haute the stone staircase up which the dastardly British had charged during the War of 1812. Of course the Judge's appearance was more than mildly deceiving; as he had been when he coerced Zeb Vance McLaren into voting for highway billboards, the Judge was an authentic Senate potentate, one of those voracious old sharks who rarely made more than ceremonial appearances on the floor but operated with razor-sharp teeth and abrasive hide behind closed committee doors. Willful and over-bearing in his senatorial habitat, deluded by his standing in it, he had once sniffed after the presidency himself, until party leaders tactfully let him know that his connection to the oil companies just couldn't be explained outside his grateful and adoring home state.

"Sincere?" he said again. "Everybody's sincere in this place, young man. Everybody's got to be sincere about his own interests and his state's. That's why we're here."

"I meant sincere about helping these migrants."

Judge Ward made an expansive gesture. "Oh, that's all right about the migrants. Nobody objects to doing a little something for them. But this Anderson—he didn't clear with anybody around this place. He's just gone off on his own."

Kathy laughed when Morgan told her of Judge Ward's indignation.

"It's no laughing matter if Hunt's expecting to have a future in the Senate," he said.

"No, it isn't." She watched Morgan carefully with her calm eyes; they were having coffee in the Senate Dining Room, and she had laid aside her dark glasses.

"But then Adam says you're driving Hunt on to run for president."

"I'm driving him?" She smiled over the coffee cup, a bit thoughtfully. "Why does Adam think that?"

"Mainly he seems doubtful Hunt has a strong enough case against Hinman. He'd rather not have stirred it all up."

"Well, he's right about one thing." She set her cup down with a little clatter. "Unless Hunt can back up what he said about Hinman, Hunt won't be running for the Senate or president or anything else."

The day Hinman finally appeared in the Caucus Room, Morgan was afraid for a moment that Anderson really might have underestimated him. The huge room—where Joe McCarthy had made and lost his reputation and Estes Kefauver had exposed the big-time criminals—was jammed with people. There was scarcely space at the press table to move an elbow, and the television cameras and lights were ranked down the far wall in a grotesque jungle of legs and cables and reels and men. In front of the committee table, photographers ("the stills") swarmed like flies but far more noisily.

By then, and with Hinman to appear, the migrant hearings had developed not merely political but social status. All over Washington that night, at dinner tables from Capitol Hill to Spring Valley, people would either have been there or they would be out of the conversation. Here and there in the audience, old hands could spot some of the most fashionable hostesses in the city, as well as a number of well-dressed women who sought to be seen by the hostesses. Lobbyists, downtown lawyers, political types sweating through an out-of-office term, a few students and others from the original hearing audiences—all were there. The wife of a former president was there too, a formidable crone animated and sibilant under a wide-brimmed hat that blocked the view of those behind her, who dared not protest. Two rows away the French Ambassador's wife appeared in something expensive from Paris, the sort of display for which, it was suspected in cynical circles, she was well rewarded. A few cabinet wives, looking uniformly righteous and unsexed, also were to be seen, and Myrtle Bell fluttered between the press table and a flock of her pigeons who had good seats near the entrance. Senators' wives were everywhere, and even a few diplomats were on hand for the strange American show.

The first of Anderson's colleagues on the committee to arrive, knowing the early bird got the photographers, was a Westerner named Updyke, with the face of a choirboy and the soul of a rug merchant. Updyke and Anderson, ostensibly, were members of the same party, but Updyke had been designated by the Senate Leaders to represent theirs and the party's interests against the maverick Anderson. There was no hope of prying one of even such facile loyalty as Updyke loose from this commitment, since the Leaders also were guaranteeing him approval of the development of a big hydroelectric site by a power company that had bought him so dear even he had stayed bought.

Next, blinking sleepily and lumbering along like a tank car, was none other than Adolphus Helmut Offenbach, he of the porcine aspect and drowsy temperament, in whose foreign name Zeb Vance had vainly clothed Matt Grant's acreage-poundage bill three years earlier. Offenbach was followed by the other minority member, who wore a gay vest and was known colloquially in the press gallery and the cloakrooms as the Senator from the Dominican Republic, owing to the flamboyant zeal with which he advanced the interests of the great Caribbean democrat, Rafael Leonidas Trujillo, who as a result never failed in those days to secure an American sugar quota or to provide vacations in the sun and a sizable campaign fund for his benefactor.

In the prickly matter of Hinman, if not on other questions facing the committee, Hunt could count on Offenbach and the Senator from the Dominican Republic for the impeccable reason that they would be delighted to ruin their party's prospective opponent in the next presidential election. But Hunt's own political heresy would be made to appear the worse if he had nothing but opposition-party support, and for that reason he regarded the last senator to enter the room as the most important of what, in senatorial style, he called "this august body."

The latecomer was a sharp young patrician from New England, Warren Victor, who was serving by appointment and was already in the late stages of a remarkably brief tenure. Victor's problem was that he could not conceal his contempt for most of his colleagues, including the Leaders, who as a result were systematically blocking or killing the few projects he had deigned to seek for his home state. In the long run this did not really matter, since Victor could not conceal his contempt for the voters either, and they were soon to show theirs for him, given opportunity. As he entered the Caucus Room that day, wrinkling his Puritan nose at the crowd, Warren Victor represented the support Anderson needed most against Hinman; he was the only member of the committee majority who could save Hunt from having to rely entirely on the opposition party.

"But the bastard just looks at me with those codfish eyes and says he prefers to reserve judgment," Anderson had said. "He thinks people like himself, and I suppose Hinman, have some kind of god-given right to run things for the masses. On the other hand, he's so damned ethical I'm afraid to buy him a drink. I don't have any idea what he'll do except he'll act like an abolitionist."

Anderson himself, his sense of timing well-honed by Danny O'Connor's coaching and by the long weeks of the hearings, was the last to appear past the great doors from the stairway off the Rotunda of the Senate Office Building; as he entered there was scattered applause from standees outside. In the Caucus Room there was much stirring and murmuring until the photographers, descending with shouts and flashes of piercing light, blocked Anderson mostly from view, although his odd head, with its hair in the usual twists and cowlicks, could be seen turning courteously as directed.

Morgan caught a glimpse of Kathy, entering just behind her husband; later, he would remember that something had seemed to impel him from his seat. He left the press table and shoved his way down the crowded middle aisle to the seat a Senate functionary had been holding for her in the accustomed place near the rear. Gradually, the hubbub around Anderson died, and he moved through the pack of photographers to the rostum, pausing for a moment to chat with Victor, then again for a whispered head-to-head minute with Adam Locklear, then posing with the gavel for the insatiable stills. Kathy came along the aisle, heads turning to follow her; far to the front, Myrtle Bell was craning to see what Kathy was wearing Kathy gave Morgan a small, impersonal smile, sat down, and put on her dark glasses against the television lights.

"How's it going to go, Coach?" He knelt beside her, sensing, as always, her gathering intensity.

"You tell me. Is he here yet?"

"You think that guy would let anybody top his entrance? Kathy . . . something I wanted to say." Morgan was surprised at himself. Years later, he still was.

She was craning a little, trying to get a view of the doorway through which, at any moment, Paul Hinman would appear. Without turning her head she touched Morgan's forearm as it lay across his knee.

"Hunt's going for the brass ring if this goes right today," he said.

She looked at him then, her fingers still, tense, on his arm. "Did he tell you that?"

"No, he's got to play the game with me. But I know."

"Is this the time to talk about it?"

"I just wanted to say that wherever the road goes, I'll try to be there if you need me. Or if Hunt does."

It had not then been clear to Morgan why he said it; he was rather amazed that he had. Much later, after long thought, he realized he could not have said it to Anderson because, from a political reporter to a potential president, it would have been suspect, and from man to man it would have blown too much of his cover, and maybe of Anderson's. He could not have waited, because if all went well with Hinman it would sound merely as if he were climbing on a bandwagon. So it had had to be then, it had had to be to Kathy, and it had had to be said—not because Morgan knew or even sensed what was going to happen, but because he didn't, could not have known anything but that Hunt and Kathy Anderson were going to pay a price whatever happened.

So he had said it, astonished at his own words; but before she could reply —other than for a faint momentary tightening of her fingers on his arm— the doors opened and Paul Hinman entered.

Hinman was not a large man, but he had vitality and confidence, almost too much of both, and they gave him presence. Before Morgan had even seen him, past the tall doors, he could sense him in the sudden hush. Then Morgan saw him and knew he was going to be hard to handle. Hinman had the kind of swing in his stride, strong movement of his shoulders, forward setting of his head—rather handsome, lean-jawed, with wavy hair—that could win a debate or a battle before it started, by impressing an opponent. He looked as if he expected to win, merely wanted to get it over with quickly so he could turn to something important. Not that he was nonchalant, or gay, or even smiling; Hinman was too solemn to take easily any slur on his notion of himself. Yet Morgan thought he conveyed, as he marched toward the seats reserved for him and his party, that he was really present to accept surrender. Behind him, not quite in step, was an unsmiling troop of gray flannels, sober ties, and briefcases.

Hinman's entrance naturally created another commotion, set off more flashbulbs and photographers's cries, and a small crisis; Hinman could be seen shaking his head vigorously, and as Morgan made his way back toward the press table he asked Eddie Bontemps, a wire-service photographer, what was happening.

Eddie breathed beer fumes on him. "Bastard won't pose with the chairman."

Morgan laughed. "Can you blame him?"

"Bastard." Eddie had seen them come and go and ranked them all a subspecies.

But Anderson had been an infighter. Hinman had taken a quick lead by entering the Caucus Room like Napoleon after Austerlitz, and set a hostile tone by refusing to fraternize with the enemy. Almost before Morgan could get back to his seat, the gavel was cracking, the din subsided somewhat, and Anderson spoke.

"The Select Committee on Farm Labor Migrancy will come to order." He paused a moment, peering toward the photographers still clustered around Hinman. In other circumstances it would have been the moment for a courteous word of welcome to a distinguished state governor. Morgan looked toward Hinman too. "The committee calls as its first witness this morning Mrs. Jonelle Everett of Hartford, Connecticut."

Morgan was looking directly at Hinman, and at the sound of the witness's name Hinman's head jerked up—Morgan could not tell whether because of the name itself, or because Anderson had snubbed him by calling another witness, unmistakably signaling that Hunt was not at all intimidated. Hinman stared for a second at Anderson, then made a dismissing gesture to the photographers and began talking rapidly to the gray flannel on his right.

Mrs. Jonelle Everett was a well-girdled woman with a sharp, disappointed face, a skimpy fur piece, and a DAR hat. Hinman did not look up as she came forward, in a buzz of surprise from the audience, and took her seat. Hunt was explaining something in a whisper to Updyke as Adam Locklear gingerly elicited Mrs. Everett's name and address.

"And what is your occupation, ma'am?"

"Housewife." Mrs. Everett was not one to leave any false impressions.

"The late Doctor Everett, of course, was in the healing arts. The dental profession, to be specific."

"I see. Now, ma'am, were you once a professional person yourself, before you married Doctor Everett?"

"For many years, yes, I certainly was."

"An executive secretary?"

"For a number of leading executives. Hiring, firing, everything."

"And did you ever work for Governor Paul Hinman?"

"Not"—Mrs. Everett's voice rose, sharpened—"after he entered politics. He said *then* that he preferred someone . . . younger." She hesitated; her mouth opened; then, abruptly, she was silent. For once she had resisted the temptation to expand on fact, to explain circumstances, and it left her last sentence hanging there, bitter, unreconciled, reverberating in the Caucus Room, as if she had described the whole episode, recounted every moment of the years spent in brooding memory.

Hinman sat unmoving.

"And were you ever the secretary and a stockholder in a corporation known as Agri-Packers?"

"I certainly was and I still own one share of that stock. Not that it's worth so much."

"How did you come to be the corporation's secretary?"

Mrs. Everett half turned her head toward Hinman, and Morgan thought he glimpsed on her face the fine glow of moral retribution.

"When I was executive secretary in Mister Hinman's law firm, he organized a corporation to buy a farm and packing operation. He called me in, told me I was to be secretary of record, and there wouldn't be anything to it, but anyway I was to have one share of stock." She cleared her throat contemptuously. "I believe the law required that the secretary be a stockholder."

"And when did this happen?"

"Eight years ago. I remember it was the year I met the late Doctor Everett at the dog show."

"Now, ma'am, do you know why you were made secretary of Agri-Packers and given a valuable share of stock?"

"Never made me very much, I must say. The late Doctor Everett, had he not died so suddenly . . ." She could not resist telling all, that one burst of eloquent brevity had exhausted her capacity for restraint. ". . . was going to sell it back to them if he could. Oh, I suppose they just didn't particularly want a public connection with it, I'm not sure why. It was all perfectly legal, of course."

"And how long was your tenure as secretary?"

"Until I left the law firm." Her mouth was open to go on when Hunt began thanking her profusely. She left the stand without looking at Hinman; firm beneath her girdle, her powdered face looking—at least to Morgan's imagination—faintly relieved of its sharpest edges, she went back to Hartford.

She was not even out of the door before Hunt banged the gavel again. "Committee calls Mister Lonnie F. Tobin of Immokalee, Florida."

There was another disappointed buzz in the Caucus Room as the unknown Tobin's name was called and as he came forward. Tobin was looking sharp in an electric-blue suit, and he was apparently feeling sharp; he walked to the witness chair with the same nearly dancing step Morgan had last seen at Saugus Number Two some months earlier. He sat down as if he were taking a seat in a poker game among drinking companions.

Peter Butcher, a news-magazine reporter across the table from Morgan, made a face and whispered, "Another goddam sob story to set the scene?" Butcher's identification ploy was to be more hard-nosed even than the Pentagon bureaucrats.

Updyke, despite his supple character, was something of a fighter, and this time he leaped right into the breach. "Well, now, Mister Chairman, I should think, in all courtesy, maybe now we ought to hear the distinguished Governor Hinman, since I'm informed he's here at considerable personal inconvenience."

"The chair appreciates the able Senator's suggestion, and the chair is sure the distinguished Governor does too. The chair thinks, however, that it will become apparent in the interest of orderly procedure why we should first hear Mister Tobin—who, I assure the able Senator, is also here at considerable . . . ah . . . inconvenience."

Morgan noticed with foreboding that Victor's thin nostrils quivered more disapprovingly than usual.

Adam Locklear again conducted the questioning, from his place between Hunt and Updyke. "State your name and address for the record, please."

"Lonnie Tobin, Immokalee, Florida, when I stays put."

"Occupation?"

"What they call crew leader."

"And what is that?"

"I supplies labor. Get a crew together, keep it together, look after it, take it hither and yon to the fields."

"You take crews north in the East Coast migrant stream?"

"Don't know about that. Florida, Georgia, Carolina, Delaware, Jersey, Long Island, all up and down there."

"And in the course of the year," Adam said, "have you ever taken a crew to a potato farm known as Agri-Packers?"

"Every year, just about."

Hinman was now listening attentively. A little starch seemed to have gone out of him, but that could be for no more reason than that Hinman had been keyed up to tear into Hunt and, instead, was being made to wait until Tobin had testified.

"Now, Mister Tobin," Adam said, "as a crew leader, do you know about Social Security regulations for farm workers?"

"Yeah. Law say these cats work for one person twenty days in one year, they covered. Or they earn more'n hunnerd fifty dollars from any one 'ployer, they covered that way too."

"Do you have to keep the records, Mister Tobin?"

"Got to do everything for these cats. Law say the crew leader the 'ployer if he provide the labor and some cat work for him twenty days or make a hunnered fifty off him."

"The way it works, then, the grower pays the crew leader for the labor, but the crew leader actually pays the hands, and the law says the crew leader is the employer of record."

"Reckon that about it."

Butcher passed a note across the table. WHAT'S THIS ALL ABOUT? Morgan shrugged and crumpled it up.

"That means," Adam said, "the crew leader has to deduct the OASI tax for any of his hands that are covered?"

"What that?"

"Old Age and Survivors' Insurance—what you probably call Social Security. You have to deduct the withholding tax for each of your hands that's covered?"

"Yeah, man, I does that, all right."

"And then as the employer you have to match that amount out of your pocket and send it to the government. Right?"

"What the law says." Tobin spoke with infinite weariness.

"It's a matching program, isn't it, the workingman paying half and the employer paying half?"

"It's a mess, I knows that."

There was some laughter in the crowd, and Tobin looked as if he had drawn a third queen to a pair.

"Why is it a mess, Mister Tobin?"

"Well, you see now, these cats don't know much about nothin', and they always goin' hither and yon like I told you, and so don't many of them know the numbers."

"Social Security numbers?"

"If they got one, maybe they lose the card. Always something like that. Seem like I just can't keep up."

"But you always make the deduction from the wages of the covered hands, don't you, Mister Tobin?"

"Law say I got to."

"The law also says you have to send it to the government with your matching contribution, doesn't it?"

"Yeah, but if they don't know the numbers I—"

"I offer for the record an affidavit from one J. D. Jackson of the Social Security Administration," Adam said. "It states that since OASI was extended to farm workers, no payments of any kind have been received from a crew leader-employer named Lonnie Tobin."

Tobin was silent.

Butcher was scribbling another note.

"And it further says that, since then, no payments for farm labor have been received from Agri-Packers, Incorporated, except for the permanent staff that had been covered all along."

Butcher slid the note across the table. I SEE SAID THE BLIND MAN. Morgan winked at him, feeling superior in his knowledge.

"I think this affidavit ought to go in the record at this point, Mister Chairman."

"So ordered," Anderson said. "I wonder if the distinguished Governor would like to have a copy of this document?" He peered with elaborate concern over the rostrum.

There was a hurried conference around Hinman, in which he ostentatiously took no part, gazing steadily at the back of Lonnie Tobin's head. There was a curious buzz in the room, and a gray flannel stood up. "We would, Mister Chairman."

Hunt passed a piece of paper to a page boy who came running.

"Now, Mister Tobin," Adam said, "letting go for the moment what your obligations are under the Social Security Act, as amended, have you ever had any discussion with Agri-Packers about whether or not you're obeying the law?"

"Naw, man. They just wants taters dug." There was enough laughter at that to cause Anderson to tap his gavel.

"Yet you as the crew leader are the middleman who relieves Agri-Packers of the legal responsibility for these workers' Social Security payments?"

"Reckon so." Tobin's voice resigned him to his fate. "They don't worry me none about it."

"Who do you deal with at Agri-Packers? I mean mostly?"

"White cat name Derounian, he like the field manager out there."

"And is he the one who pays you, so you can pay the hands?"

"He the one."

"But Derounian has never mentioned Social Security to you?"

"Not that I knows of."

"Isn't that worth right much to you then?"

"Much?" Tobin was incredulous. He stiffened in something like outrage. "Considerin' all I got to do for these cats that mostly ain't worth killin' ?" He shook his head sadly. "Man like me is always behind the eight ball, see? Always livin' from day to day 'cause you never make enough to pay the bills or anything. Them deduct pennies don't seem like much to me when these cats don't even know the numbers."

Adam's voice was curiously gentle. "Dog eat dog—is that the way you see it, Mister Tobin?"

"I ain't saying that. I only know *I* got to eat."

"Any questions, Mister Chairman?"

Morgan was surprised that Hunt had none. Victor used a few moments to express moral indignation at Tobin, who blinked and nodded. The other senators looked blank, and Tobin was dismissed. There was a shuffle of anticipation in the Caucus Room.

"Now let's get down to business," Butcher said out loud.

Hinman was sitting forward in his seat, obviously ready to rise.

"Committee will now hear from Mister Allen F. Winston."

Hinman's face went red, whether in anger or embarrassment or both Morgan could only guess. He heard a TV cameraman swear in frustration. One of the gray flannels got up and made his way toward the front of the room, just behind a tall, burly man, a little paunchy, who looked like a former Green Bay Packer; in fact, he was a political science professor who had been elected to the legislature in Hinman's state, owing to a scandal in the other party, whose candidate was charged with molesting a child.

As Winston took the witness chair, Updyke protested once again that Governor Hinman should not be kept waiting. Once again Anderson explained that the reasons why other witnesses were being called first would become apparent through their testimony.

"Are you still a member of the Assembly?" Adam asked Winston.

Winston smiled. "I only lasted one term. In my field, Mister Locklear, those who can, run; those who can't, teach. I'll be teaching from now on."

This drew smug laughter from the politically oriented audience, secure in its knowledge that the real thing was different from what the eggheads thought.

"And during your one term did you sponsor any legislation?"

The gray flannel suit was conferring with Anderson. He was making vigorous gestures, and Anderson was nodding with exaggerated Southern politeness.

"Quite a bit. It's easy to introduce bills."

Winston got another laugh with that one. He was flattering Washington with his recognition of the intricacies and hazards of its main preoccupation, not to be fathomed by a mere amateur.

"And what happened to yours?"

"One passed."

"And the others?"

"Rocked," said Winston, "in the cradle of the deep."

There was more laughter, which is never hard to evoke when you make fun of yourself. The gray flannel went back to his seat with an air of injured righteousness.

"What did the one that passed have to do with?"

"It wasn't quite revolutionary. It required more comprehensive testing and regulation of school-bus drivers."

"Did that go right through?"

"Oh no. You see, it put quite a few local employees out of jobs, or at least required them to meet higher performance and physical standards."

"So how did you get it through?"

"I wouldn't have without Governor Hinman."

Adam did not look surprised. "He supported that one of all your bills?"

"Not at first, not that I knew of. Nobody did, except some other do-gooders."

Winston had the right touch in that crowd; another laugh. Butcher was scribbling furiously, and some of the little red lights had come on. Winston was scoring; maybe, Morgan thought, he would become one of those TV personalities who make it big by deriding their own attainments or watering down their knowledge. He looked just right for a late-night talk show, or one of those witty little panel groups that comment wryly on State of the Union messages.

"Then the Governor called me in one day. I must say I wondered how he had learned of my talents." Morgan saw the trace of a smile above

Hinman's knotted bow tie. "He said he liked me, hoped I enjoyed politics. He wanted to help. My bus-driver bill had merit. It needed doing and he thought he could swing it through."

"And what did you say?"

"I asked him who he wanted kidnaped." Even Anderson grinned at that one. "But he said it was nothing like that. The calendar was cluttered, and the leaders wanted to clear away for adjournment, and for reasons of his own that year, the Governor wanted the leaders to have their way. But they were all afraid that the minority or even some of their own people would slip something through in the confusion if a lot of bills came up at the last minute. They just wanted to clear some of the underbrush off the calendar."

"Including your other bills?"

"Including literally hundreds of other bills, maybe thousands. It wasn't unusual, I knew that. And I agreed with the Governor that the bus-driver bill was the most important one of mine.

Adam consulted his notes, whispered something to Anderson, then asked, "Could you describe some of your other bills, Professor?"

Adam had not seemed amused by Winston's quips. Morgan knew Adam was not one to depreciate education, advantages, opportunity; only those who have had them do.

"Liberal stuff. Reforms. Most of them impossible, I suppose. Like tuition-free state colleges."

"Anything about migrant labor?"

"One bill. It would have made it mandatory for employers of more than five farm laborers in any calendar month to provide at least fifty square feet of housing space per person. I didn't think that was exactly communistic. Fifty square feet is only a little bit bigger than the top of a pool table."

"What interested you in migrant labor?"

"Oh, up in my part of the state, they come through to pick apples and they live like dogs. Worse than dogs. I wanted to help if I could, and that seemed one way to start."

"Now did Governor Hinman mention that particular bill to you? The day he called you in?"

"I discussed several of my bills with *him,* including that one. I remember because I thought it was reasonably important. But he said the bus-driver bill was the only one he could put through for me, so I had no choice."

"Any questions, Mister Chairman?"

"Just like to say to Professor Winston, if he ever comes to my state to run, I hope it's against somebody else."

Victor looked disapproving of this levity but passed, as Updyke did. The

Senator from the Dominican Republic wanted jovially to know whether Winston's speech writer was available for employment by the other party. Offenbach's Bavarian cheeks wobbled with jollity, but he had no questions.

Winston left the stand and walked into a broad sea of smiling faces in the Caucus Room; he had risen perfectly to the occasion. Butcher passed another note: NO GLOVE ON PDH. Morgan passed one back: BUT SWEATING? He thought Hinman looked less assured and domineering than he had at his entrance; but the change, if any, was nothing specific, nothing traceable. Sitting there among the gray flannels, barricaded by their briefcases, he merely seemed a little smaller than he had before. Morgan saw suddenly that Hinman was, indeed, quite short; usually, his presence kept anyone from noticing. Morgan wondered if he stood on anything when he made a speech.

"Committee calls Irby Cullen of Immokalee, Florida."

Audible murmurs of disappointment swept the audience, and the gray flannel who had conferred with Anderson spoke angrily to Hinman. Hinman shook his head, his thin mouth tight; he was not to be surprised again. Updyke, watching him closely, also decided to say nothing.

Irby Cullen, an elderly black man who had been going up the stream since childhood, told in a listless voice how he had been recruited the year before by Lonnie Tobin for field work and had gone north with him in the old school bus Tobin drove. Ultimately they had worked the fields at Agri-Packers. Drawn out by Adam's questions, Cullen said yes, he reckoned Tobin had taken the Social Security out of his pay. Didn't know if Tobin had sent it to the gov'ment. Oh, yessir, he'd been paid by Tobin all right, eighty cent an hour. 'Cept on top of the Social Security, Tobin took out twelve cent an hour. Can't say just what for, 'cept all the crew leaders, they took out maybe that much, maybe more. Maybe for just letting you work, a sort of commission? Reckon so.

Made it hard on a man 'cause he still had to pay for a bed and sump'um to eat. Well, as for the bed, he paid Tobin for that, leastways Tobin took it out. Best he could remember, three dollars a week for the bunkroom, three dollars blanket fee, and kerosene extra if it turnt cold. Hard to say on account of, nosir, they wa'nt no chits or nothin'. Food now, Tobin took that out too, 'cause he run the lunchroom in camp was the onliest place to eat. Food draws from maybe twelve or thirteen a week right on up, they ain't no tellin' 'cause it depend on how much a man eat and drink. See, the lunchroom don't provide no bev'rage, you got to buy your bev'rage extra, twenty-five cent a pop.

"What about wine?" Adam asked. "Didn't you have wine in camp?"

"Sometime."

"How much?"

"Well, a dollar a pint, if a man had cash, but Tobin he would charge it up to the lunchroom for a dollar'n' a quarter and deduct if a man was busted. Yessir, you could get it for fifty cent in town but, trouble with that, how you goin' to get to town?"

"Now did you get paid cash, Mister Cullen?"

"After Tobin taken hisen out. Like I say, he don't give no chits but he always know what to charge."

"He takes out all his deducts, the lunchroom and the blanket fee, the Social Security and all, and gives you what cash is left?"

"Ain't much either."

"And then when you start home to Immokalee, Mister Cullen, how do you get there?"

"Tobin drive the bus."

Adam nodded, as if he had known it all along. "And what does he charge for the trip home?"

"Twelve-fifty last year."

There were no questions from Updyke, but Victor again used free TV time to fulminate against evil. He did it well, but everyone in the immediate audience had heard him do it so often that a buzz of conversation rose and Hunt again had to gavel for order.

Offenbach heaved himself an inch or two forward and asked, "Can you . . . uh . . . say to the committee . . . uh . . . I mean . . . why do you let this Tobin . . . uh . . . treat you that way?"

"Got to work," Cullen said. "Got to eat. What else I goin' to do?"

"Um . . . mmm." Offenbach lapsed backward, as if to think that one over.

"Committee will now hear from Mister Leon Derounian."

This time, Morgan could see, Hinman had not even expected to be called. He looked more casual now, unworried, although the gray flannels were grim with disapproval, and Morgan wondered if Anderson was stretching the suspense too far.

Derounian turned out to be a slender, surly fellow in a suit from which his arms and legs stuck out a little too far. No, he had no idea whether Tobin paid in the Social Security to the government. That was Tobin's responsibility. No, Tobin ran the camp, that was the usual arrangement. Crew leaders ran the camp, provided food and beverage. Agri-Packers owned the housing, all right, but when the workers came, Tobin managed the camp at his own expense. That was all Tobin's responsibility, part of the system. He provided the labor, Agri-Packers paid him for it, and that was all Derounian knew. The rest of it was none of his responsibility. Of course, Governor Hinman and the other owners knew nothing about any of this. Why would they?

Adam asked, "Now what would you say, in those camp houses and bunkrooms where the men live, how much space per man?"

"Wouldn't know."

"Well, you gave one of our investigators the plans from which the bunkrooms were built. Any changes since then?"

"None except patch the roof and put in some window lights they broke out. They always break out the window lights."

"Then it's still got about five hundred square feet of floor space?"

"Whatever it comes out to on the plan."

"And maybe twenty-five men in there, day in and day out in season. What's that come to, Mister Derounian?"

"I don't have a pencil."

"Comes to twenty square feet a man," Adam said. "You don't need a pencil for that, Mister Derounian. How much is twenty from fifty? Here's a pencil."

"Thirty." Derounian ignored the pencil that Adam tossed in front of him.

"Thirty is right. Now one other thing. Irby Cullen said he was paid eighty cents an hour at Agri-Packers last year. What was the prevailing wage on the other farms around there?"

"About that, I reckon. Must of been."

"You don't know for sure?"

"We paid eighty. I know that."

"That's strange. According to the state labor office—and I offer this affidavit for the record, Mister Chairman—the prevailing wage in that area on hourly rates last year was one dollar even. How'd you get workers for eighty cents?"

"I don't know about prevailing wages. The crew leader brought men, we were offering eighty cents, and they took it. I thought they seemed glad to get it."

Again, Hunt had no questions. Only Updyke spoke up, grilling Derounian on the wage question, as if he wanted to know the secret for himself, then leading Derounian once more through a strong denial that Hinman had any knowledge of how Agri-Packers was operated day to day.

As Derounian left the witness chair Anderson said, "The committee will be pleased now to hear from Governor Paul Hinman."

"But the press can't do everything," Dunn was saying. "You could have
eculated until you were blue in the face and nothing would have happened
Anderson hadn't knocked Hinman out of the box. He had to do that for
mself, and I have to say he did it well. I was glued to the TV set that day,
d what I couldn't get over, watching it, was that Hinman never seemed
realize it wasn't his legal position that mattered. He never understood
at with the cameras there it wasn't a trial, it was a debate. It wasn't fact
at mattered, it was manner."

"Which was what Hunt counted on," Morgan said, "right from the
rt." He pointed to the private entrance. "Turn there, it's just a mile or
from here."

The between-witness chatter in the audience died at the sound of Hin-
an's name. Hinman did not move. The gray flannel who had conferred
ith Anderson stood up, looking thunderous.

"Mister Chairman, I am Harold B. F. Ogden, representing Governor
inman's trust managers in this extraordinary matter. In view of the dis-
urtesy of this committee in scheduling other witnesses ahead of Governor
inman, who is here at considerable personal inconvenience, and in view
the brevity of the time remaining before noon, I suggest that the commit-
e adjourn for lunch and hear the Governor this afternoon."

Hinman had never served in Congress or he would not have allowed his
wyer to criticize the whole committee; Morgan knew that, if it now came
a vote over this request, all the members would have to support Hunt,
en Updyke, because the one thing that would hold them together—no
atter where they stood on the basic questions—was anything non-congres-
onal that seemed to question their congressional authority or the propriety
'its use. If Ogden had confined his remarks to the chairman, he might have
ade his point. As it was, Anderson was in a position to take a strong stand,
owing the committee would have to back him against an attack on it.

"We'll hear the Governor any time he wants to speak," Anderson said,
ut I would think since his time is so valuable he'd be better served to go
ead now."

"But it would be most awkward if his testimony had to be interrupted
r lunch."

"Oh, we'd go on, Mister Ogburn. I don't think—"

"Ogden."

"Ogden. I don't think the Governor is going to need all day, do you?"

"Of course not, but—"

"Naturally, if the Governor needs a little time," Anderson said, "in view

of what's been brought out here, to prepare his defense, why, we wouldn
want to rush him."

"Now, Mister Chairman," Updyke said, "I just have to object a little b
right there at that particular point because I don't think that was at all th
point of what Mister Ogden was trying to say."

"Indeed not," Ogden said. "Mister Chairman, this is not a court of la
and Governor Hinman is not preparing a 'defense' of any kind. As h
representative, I am compelled to say that we have heard this morning
reprehensible tissue of innuendo and supposition and very little fact that ha
the slightest relevance to the Governor."

"Well, he's not here under subpoena, Mister Cogden. He's—"

"Ogden, Mister Chairman."

"Excuse me, Mister Ogden. The Governor's here voluntarily, I was goin
to say. Now the committee is going ahead with its work. We have othe
witnesses, some of them here at considerable personal inconvenience too
If the Governor has been surprised by what we have brought out and wan
to take an hour or so to prepare a defense, it's all right with us. We'll b
here whenever . . ."

Hinman stood up then, and whatever else Anderson said was lost in th
sudden stir of the crowd. Butcher put another note in front of Morgan: II
THE GUT. Hunt had gone right to Hinman's weakness. Hinman was arro
gant, overbearing; he could not abide the suggestion that he was surprise
or confused or had to work up a "defense." He wanted to brush Anderso
aside, contemptuously dismiss the charge against himself, and stalk out th
master of the situation. It was what people expected of him; more than tha
it was what he expected of himself. The attempt to put his appearance ove
to the afternoon had been a rather petulant rejoinder to Anderson's tacti
of making Hinman wait; it had backfired, and Hinman was smart enoug
to know it.

Ogden looked surprised as Hinman pushed past him and stalked towar
the witness chair. In some confusion, clutching his briefcase, Ogden fo
lowed and seated himself beside the Governor, whose stiff back now wa
turned to Morgan and the others at the press table. Hinman did not eve
wait for Anderson or Adam to begin but quickly stated his name and titl
in tones icy with disdain.

"Well, we're glad to have you here, Governor." Anderson's voice ha
become a little more Southern, his unruly hair a bit more tangled.

Two networks were carrying the proceedings live that day; all ove
America, Morgan supposed, housewives were peering over their ironin

boards. The photographers milled and cursed and clicked in front of Hinnan; and Anderson waited patiently before signaling them away.

"What I suggest, Mister Ogdill," Anderson said, "is let's just let the Governor proceed any way he wants to, and if the chair or the committee isn't clear on anything, we'll just ask a few questions when he finishes and maybe even interrupt if it seems useful at some point."

Ogden looked at Hinman with raised eyebrows. Hinman paid him no attention. "Mister Chairman," he said in his arctic voice, "my inclination, as I listened this morning, was to leave this chamber without comment, trusting to the intelligence and the sense of fair play of the American people to see this situation for what it is—an outrageous attempt to smear me, for obviously political reasons, with the greedy behavior and possible law-breaking of this . . . this person who described himself as a crew leader, and with the deplorable conditions he apparently created at the worker camp at Agri-Packers, Incorporated. That was my inclination, Mister Chairman, and it still is, but I will say this much. Although I did purchase a financial interest in Agri-Packers, all such interests are in trust for the duration of my term, and I therefore have no knowledge, none of any kind, of any of these activities this committee has been exploring. And now I bid you good day, Mister Chairman."

He rose to his feet, as if jerked upright by invisible attachments to his shoulderblades. Ogden rose too, more clumsily. Neither had turned away before Anderson said, apparently unruffled, "Thank you, Governor. I think you might like to answer some of the questions the committee needs to put to you, and I'm sure you'll want to hear the rest of the testimony we expect to take today."

"No interest whatever in your testimony or your questions, Mister Chairman." Hinman turned away with the air of a man tried beyond endurance.

The room was quiet. The former president's wife was staring intently at Hinman. The cameramen were peering through their red-eyed machines.

"Well, Governor, you're not sworn, and as I told your defense counsel a moment ago you're not under subpoena. I doubt seriously this committee of Congress would seek to subpoena a state governor, even if you do choose to remain silent."

The more Anderson explained that he could not compel Hinman to testify, the more pressure there was on Hinman to do so voluntarily rather than have it appear he had hidden behind technicalities and legal devices.

"But I feel in duty bound to inform you that testimony we expect to take later in the day is going to raise grave questions of propriety about your involvement in this matter and about your statement a moment ago that you 'have no knowledge of any kind' of what we've been discussing here."

That sent murmurs across the room, and Anderson tapped his gavel gently.

"Mister Chairman, I really must object," Updyke said again. "Governor Hinman has already made a very full and straightforward statement, and I congratulate him on it. I see no reason for harassing him further."

The trouble with that was that Hinman had done nothing of the kind, which everyone knew, and which made Updyke's conclusion patently empty.

The patrician Victor chose that moment to intervene. "We must never forget in this body," he said in his pedagogical manner, "the presumption of innocence."

Morgan realized immediately that this had stung Anderson. Anderson knew well the difference in a congressional committee and a court of law, but it was not in his ideal of himself that he would take advantage of the former to abuse the rights of a witness.

"No conclusions have been drawn here," Anderson said. "I'd remind my able and distinguished colleague that the very reason I have suggested that Governor Hinman submit to questioning is so that he can clear up, if that is possible, the serious questions that have been raised."

Ogden set his briefcase on the table with a defiant thump. "The conclusions of the chairman appear all too plain to me," he said. "In view of your own reported political ambitions, and Governor Hinman's high responsibilities, I believe this is the most outrageous and unprincipled proceeding I have ever witnessed. I demand—"

"No." Hinman's icy voice stopped Ogden as if a tap had been turned in his throat. Hinman sat down again, as starched as before. "Ask your questions, Mister Chairman." He made it sound as if he would be a reluctant witness to obscene rites. There was not a quiver in his voice, not a hint of uncertainty.

Hinman was dead game, nerveless; he must have known by then that he was playing on Anderson's field, by Anderson's rules; he had seen that his adversary was not to be brushed off with a show of disdain; the early witnesses must have suggested to him that Anderson knew a great deal about his entanglement with Agri-Packers. Yet Hinman had silenced his attorney, spurned his legal escapes, and there he sat, driven to the end of the line by Anderson's goading, but still confident, cool, even arrogant. He could be that way for the same basic reason that he had allowed himself to get into the Agri-Packers imbroglio and to be drawn into such a confrontation; it simply would not have occurred to him either that he had done anything for which he ought to be held accountable, or that any adversary, in the long run, could get the better of him. He had had too much success, for too long; he had come to believe that he had the golden touch. So he would not concede an inch; and in a sense, therefore, he had Anderson as much at bay as Anderson had him. The match was to the death, and Morgan sensed that there would be no holds barred.

"I'd like to establish a basic point first. Mrs. Jonelle Everett testified that you first acquired your interest in Agri-Packers, Incorporated, eight years ago. Is that correct?"

"To the best of my knowledge."

"Why have you tried so hard to keep it a secret?"

"I see, Mister Chairman, that you have learned your lessons from your colleague Senator McCarthy."

A murmur swept the chamber. Anderson's face reddened. "The answer to that," Hinman continued, "is that I did not attempt to keep it a secret."

"Well, you had your private secretary listed as the principal officer of the corporation, didn't you?"

"A business convenience, and not an uncommon one."

"But isn't it a fact that there was never any publicity of any kind, no public knowledge of your farming interests?"

"I invited none. I concealed nothing."

"Can you seriously contend, Governor, that if it had been public knowledge that a corporation in which you were an owner made extensive use of migrant laborers, the miserable conditions in which those laborers lived and worked would not have been a political issue?"

"That's a complicated and iffy question, Mister Chairman. I was not in politics at the time of the purchase. And quite obviously I don't know as much about political issues as you do."

"Well, you knew you were going into politics, didn't you?"

"I may have. But I resent your suggestion and repeat that this was purely a business matter."

"Wasn't it a rather strange investment for a lawyer?"

"No. It was good property with a good earning record, available cheaply from an estate. I organized a corporation and bought it for that purpose."

"Five years before you became governor?"

"Yes. I was inaugurated three years ago, Mister Chairman, at which time Agri-Packers, along with all my other holdings, were naturally placed in a blind trust." Hinman went into lawyer's detail about the trust, and how impossible it was for him to influence the worth of his holdings, or even to know what they were. "In fact, I am only assuming that my interest in Agri-Packers has not been sold by the trustees, which would be their right to do if they saw fit. I have no idea whatever of the present value, if any, of that holding."

"Were you perhaps assuming that it had been sold when you influenced Assemblyman Winston to drop his migrant housing bill?"

"Ooohh," someone murmured audibly from across the press table. "Below the belt."

"Maybe it was," Anderson said late that night, when he dropped by for a late drink at the house Morgan had bought in Cleveland Park. "By courtroom standards, I mean, or in some ordinary case. But we weren't in a courtroom and the case wasn't ordinary. It's hard to hit a man like Hinman too low, and I thought it was important for the country to see what kind of man he was, to know what he was capable of, before we made him president. If I had to shake him into losing his temper and blowing up, well, that was what I had to do."

Morgan squinted at his nearly empty glass. "Isn't that saying the end justified the means?"

"I think it's saying the means made the end possible. That's what I thought was important, and I still do."

Morgan was on his third or fourth drink and went a little further than he had intended. "And what's the end? To knock Hinman out of the White House or to put yourself in?"

Anderson put his drink down and stood up. "I'd have expected that from some people but not from you."

"I'm sorry." Morgan stood up too. "I only meant that sometimes it's too easy to lose sight of one's own motives. Sometimes they get disguised as principles." Morgan knew something about that; he knew how a man could fool himself, and often did.

"Oh hell," Anderson said. "I can't help it if what tears down Hinman also happens to build me up. I still have to do what I have to do. What I think is right. Besides, a mean, tough bastard like that is bound to have nine lives."

Morgan walked out with him. It was a cool, quiet night. Above them, the Cathedral spire stood whitely lit against the sky; far down the hill there was a faint rumble of traffic on Connecticut Avenue. The house was dark behind them—Anne out somewhere, little Richie asleep, a light burning only in Morgan's littered office downstairs.

"You don't pull your punches, do you?" Anderson paused on the side-
alk, looking down at Morgan.

"Some of them. Maybe lots of them."

"It wasn't any fun for me today, you know."

"Doing what you think you have to do usually isn't."

"Especially," Anderson said, "if there's any doubt at all in your mind
at it is the right thing. You have to put doubt aside."

He had certainly shown none that day, nor had Hinman conceded him
n inch; he had waited a full thirty seconds before answering, while he
ared coolly at Anderson. "I assumed nothing. I had no knowledge at all
at Assemblyman Winston was sponsoring such a bill, before I conferred
ith him as he has described. He made no great point of it to me even then.
o hearings had been held on it, not that I know of. Thousands of bills are
troduced pro forma in our legislature every year and are never seen or
eard of again. I had an agreement with the legislative leaders. I merely
sked the Assemblyman to help us clear the calendar, which he did."

Anderson sounded incredulous. "You had no knowledge before he told
ou of a bill that would have forced you to better than double the migrant
ousing space at Agri-Packers, and cost you thousands of dollars? To say
othing of what it would have cost all the other growers in your state?"

"I do not," Hinman said, "keep up with all the minor legislation intro-
uced by minor legislators."

The measure of Anderson's tactics and the seeds of Hinman's destruction
ere in that exchange. Morgan knew Anderson and Adam Locklear did not
ave any evidence that Hinman had deliberately maneuvered to kill Win-
on's bill, which could have been buried in any of a thousand ways, state
gislatures being what they were. But in view of all the testimony so far
ken on the plight and exploitation of the migrants, Hinman's contemptu-
us attitude of not having known what was happening at Agri-Packers was
amaging; and for him to refer to Winston's bill as "minor" was nearly
isastrous. His reference to Winston himself would have seemed discourte-
us and ungracious in any case.

Anderson seized the opening "What about *major* legislation, Governor?
ave *you* introduced a program that would stand a chance, that would aid
igrant workers or improve their living and working conditions?"

"That is hardly one of the major priorities of our state, Mister Chair-
an."

"Well, at peak season you have as many as fourteen thousand migrants

at work in your fields and orchards. Have you got another fourteen thou
sand people as badly off as they are?"

"They are not, of course, our citizens or taxpayers, in most cases. But th
committee can rest assured, Mister Chairman, that my priorities research
ers and program planners will recommend to me what may be necessar
when it becomes necessary, and it will be done if it is within the resource
of our state."

"I wish it was that easy around this place," Anderson said. "Are we
understand that your experience with Agri-Packers has given you no idea
of your own in this field?"

"I have never acted as operating head of that corporation, Mister Chai
man. I might point out"—Hinman was swinging along in fine style, soun
ing confident and competent, the way he did on *Meet the Press*—"tha
although there was testimony earlier today suggesting the possibility
fraud in the collection of Social Security taxes from laborers at Agr
Packers, the federal law extending OASI to farm workers did not take effe
until two years ago; a full year after the trust took over my interest i
Agri-Packers—which is not in any case and by your own testimony th
employer of record."

"So you're in the clear on that too?"

"I am 'in the clear,' as you put it, entirely, Mister Chairman. But surel
even you can see that the Social Security matter is particularly irreleva
to me."

"During the five years that you owned Agri-Packers before becomin
governor," Anderson asked, not conceding the irrelevance, "did you eve
visit the property?"

"Occasionally."

"The migrant camps?"

"I suppose so. I don't recall specific occasions."

"And what did you think of conditions?"

"Well, of course, Mister Chairman, one doesn't expect the Waldorf
such places. I am not among those who believe such people as migrants ar
incapable of taking care of things or bettering themselves. But they a
itinerant, and that can lead to . . . ah . . . irresponsibility, and I suppos
growers have to take that into account when they provide housing."

"All right, but I asked what you thought of conditions in the camps
Agri-Packers."

"I believe they were rated as good as any in the area."

"How many square feet per man?"

"I object to that question," Ogden said sharply, as if he had been seek ing an opportunity to break in and earn his fee. "Unfair, irrelevant, misleading—"

"Withdrawn. Did you understand, Governor, that the crew leader ran the camp?"

"In a general way. As I said, I never acted as operating head of Agri-Packers."

"So here's your position, Governor, as you see it, and correct me if I'm wrong. When you bought this property and concealed your interest in it, that wasn't political, that was just business. When you became governor, you didn't know Mister Winston had a bill in to improve migrant housing. No responsibility for killing that, much less supporting it. The Social Security law was changed after you put the property in trust, so no responsibility for that either, even if the people who in fact work for your corporation are defrauded of their OASI. As for the camps, the crew leader ran them and Agri-Packers' are as good as any others. No problem there either. And if there were, none of it is your business. Does that state your position, Governor?"

Hinman obviously had a sense, by then, of having set his foot wrong, but he had not got where he was for nothing. He went smoothly, toughly, to the offensive.

"Well, Mister Chairman, if I sat where you sit, and you sat where I do, I suppose that's about the way I'd describe it. If I wanted to destroy someone for political purposes of my own, that might be the way I'd try to do it. If I wanted to smear someone, I could hardly do better than to go about it just as you have. If I had the kind of political ambitions you're reported to have, I might possibly see my way clear to the kind of course you're following. But none of those 'ifs' are true, Mister Chairman, and so I think the way *I* would describe my position is that I find these charges of yours totally unfounded, irresponsible, and politically motivated."

The Caucus Room was so quiet that at the press table some of the TV crewmen could be heard muttering among themselves, oblivious of what was happening or of anything but their lights and reels and dollies. Butcher shook his head, for what reason Morgan could not say. Morgan, looking back along the middle aisle, saw Kathy sitting forward in her seat for the first time since the hearings began, her air of calm remoteness vanished, her dark glasses in her hand at her side.

"That was the moment," she told Morgan years later, "that was the time I was most scared Hunt would quit. That was when he had to have iron in his backbone, more than I was sure he had, if he was going ahead, because all those things Hinman said were exactly the kinds of things that would disturb Hunt the most, attack his idea of himself, make him question what he was doing. That was the moment I knew was coming sooner or later, when Hinman would put it that way, and then Hunt would either go on or back off. And I couldn't be sure which he would do."

"Let's just look at one more point then, Governor," Anderson said. "You heard the testimony, did you not, that Agri-Packers' wages ran twenty cents lower last year than the prevailing wage in that area. Can you explain that?"

"I have stated and restated, Mister Chairman, but you seem incapable of understanding, that I have absolutely nothing to do with the management of Agri-Packers. Nothing, Mister Chairman. It is an absolute word."

"But what about five years ago, Governor? Eight? Right before your trust was set up?"

"I had very little to do with the management of Agri-Packers then and I have nothing at all to do with it now."

"You just take the profits?"

"And the losses, if there are either."

"Did you ever know Lonnie F. Tobin?"

Hinman turned his head, as if from a disgusting object. Then he snapped it back toward Hunt and bit off his words curtly. "Certainly not."

"You're sure of that?"

"Not only sure," Hinman said, "but extremely tired of having my word questioned in this manner."

"Then as far as I'm concerned, that'll be all." Anderson suddenly sounded almost uninterested. "Any other questions?" He looked in either direction.

"We . . . ah . . . well, personally, Mister Chairman," Updyke said, "I thank the distinguished Governor for coming here and discussing these matters with us so fully and frankly."

Hinman, already standing, nodded at him without smiling and turned away. Ogden, as if reassured that the world was round, drew himself to full Wall Street dimensions and said, "I repeat, Mister Chairman, that I have found this proceeding extremely distasteful and I—"

Anderson's gavel cracked like a rifle shot and he rose to his feet, for once in a smooth, swift motion. His eyes were narrowed, and he leaned forward, menacing in his height and manner. "Do you think I haven't?" he said in a low, strained voice, as if through clenched jaws. "Do you think I like this kind of thing? To hear what we've heard today? To say what I've been forced to say? To hear myself called what I have been called for trying to reach the truth about a matter of human misery? I'll thank you to remember, Mister *Og-den,* this is a duly constituted committee of the Congress of the United States, going about its business of finding fact and developing legislation. The Governor was given every opportunity to say anything he wanted to say. No doubt you and he are going to find this distasteful too, but this committee now recalls Lonnie Tobin."

Hinman spun around and stared at Anderson, then slowly resumed his front-row seat. As Lonnie Tobin came jauntily forward again, Ogden, his shoulders hunched a little, sat down next to Hinman.

Anderson did not even try to gavel down the commotion in the room. Morgan could see Myrtle Bell squawking like a myna bird to her fluttering companions. In the rear of the chamber Kathy had returned to her customary composed position. She was wearing the dark glasses again.

Anderson finally cracked the gavel, the photographers drifted away from Tobin and Hinman, and the Caucus Room fell silent. The red eyes glared. Adam Locklear rose from his seat and leaned against the wall behind Anderson.

"Mister Tobin," Anderson said, recovering the calm voice in which, for most of the time, he had questioned Hinman, "when did you first take a crew to Agri-Packers?"

"Eight years ago, best I can recollect."

That sent another murmur over the crowd, and Hinman said something to Ogden. Butcher raised his eyebrows and bent to his notes.

"And who did you deal with that first time?"

"Mostly Derounian."

"What did he tell you?"

"Said he was new, the owners was new, everything new, and they wanted new crew leaders, new hands, start a whole new thing out there."

"He wanted you to bring up the hands?"

"He say he gone make it worth my time."

"How was he going to do that, Mister Tobin?"

"He say come on round here tomorrow about this time and see the boss . . ." Another murmur; Hinman did not move. " . . . so I goes round there, and Derounian and his boss, they waitin' for me, all right, and Derounian he say do I want the contract? And I say, man, they all want old Lonnie to bring 'em a crew 'cause I don't cause 'em no trouble when I do."

"Did he make you an offer?"

"He say—"

"Who did?"

"Derounian. He say, look man, forget them others, we gone pay you five cents per hour for every hour your hands work for us, and you gone take a potful of money out of here in December. And I say, how you gone do that? And he say that what he gone do if I bring 'em in there for lessen what he got to pay somebody else. And so that year they was payin' seventy-five around there and I let Derounian have a crew for fifty-five."

"So by the time Derounian paid you a nickel an hour, he was about fifteen cents an hour ahead on his wage bill?"

"Good deal all around," Tobin said. "Gone back there every summer since, same deal. 'Course the rates gone up."

Morgan moved his foot, and every person in that room could hear it scrape along the floor. It was hot under the lights, still. Adam Locklear moved to get a better view of the witness, and his slight motion took every eye.

"Mister Tobin." Anderson fiddled with his papers for a moment. "You said Derounian's boss was with him when you made that deal eight years ago?"

"Stood right there. Derounian, he say to 'im, 'This way we not only save but Tobin, he'll see to it we get good hands when we need good hands.' "

"And what did Derounian's boss say to that?"

"Nothin' one way or 'nother that I can recollect."

"Now after eight years, Mister Tobin, can you remember what Derounian's boss looked like?"

"Don't fergit many faces."

"Is he in this room? Derounian's boss?"

Tobin swiveled around and pointed directly at Hinman. "Big as life. That cat over there."

Hinman stood up, the sound of his chair scraping beneath him the only sound in the huge room. As if at a signal, Ogden and the other gray flannels stood up, grabbing up briefcases and topcoats. Everyone watched them. Nothing else moved, except the hungry, turning cameras.

"Mister Chairman"—Hinman was staring directly, coldly, at Anderson, his voice as firm and icy as ever—"this is a tissue of lies and deceptions to which I refuse any longer to be a party, however innocent. I bid you good day."

He was heading for the big doors, the gray flannels falling in behind him, when Anderson's voice crackled through the room. "Do you wish to respond to this personal identification by an eyewitness, Governor?"

Hinman stopped, spun on his feet as if executing a military maneuver, glared a moment at Anderson, then focused malevolently on Lonnie Tobin who still sat half turned in the witness chair. "You may take your choice," Hinman said clearly. He seemed to choke, then spat out his words. "My word . . . or the eight-year-old recollection of this . . . colored person."

Morgan looked immediately at Victor. Shock and distaste flashed on his face—Hinman had lost him; Hinman had lost everything with those few words. Morgan looked back as Hinman resumed his march toward the doors. Ogden and the gray flannels fell in obediently behind him. Their footsteps clattered martially, defiantly.

"Let the record show"—Anderson's voice sounded drained, tired, almost hurt—"that the witness, Lonnie Tobin, pointed to Governor Hinman in response to the question of the chair."

Morgan caught Adam Locklear's attention and lifted his eyebrows. Adam shrugged; it was a weary gesture, but Morgan could read little into it.

Someone opened the big doors. Flashbulbs were popping. Hinman went out of the room with dignity, unhurriedly, without looking back. At his disappearance, the stillness of the Caucus Room was broken; excited voices began to rise. The gray flannels followed Hinman, one by one; as each man went past the door, the noise level in the big room rose steadily, until there was an uproar.

Anderson began banging the gavel; the flashbulbs turned toward him. Adam Locklear had disappeared. People began leaving the Caucus Room in considerable numbers, making a noisy crush near the doors. The former president's wife sailed splendidly out beneath her hat. The show was over.

Anderson finally obtained enough silence to conclude. "Mister Tobin, has the committee offered you any inducement of any kind?"

"How's that?"

"I mean have we paid you any money or promised you you wouldn't be prosecuted or anything of that sort?"

Morgan thought he knew why Anderson seemed, at last, so listless, almost uninterested. It was more than emotional exhaustion; he was beginning to wonder whether it had been worth it, how it all squared with his lofty self-image, that ideal of himself that was so much of his life.

"Ain't promised me nothin.' Ain't nobody ever give Lonnie Tobin nothin' he didn't hustle for hisself."

"Then why tell us all this? Some of it obviously may tend to incriminate you."

"Yeah," Tobin said. "That big cat up there"—he pointed to where Adam had been standing—"he say do I keep my mouth shut they gone throw it all on me. He say I better tell the whole story like it happen or they gone try to throw it all on me. Just like they done."

"I see." Anderson brooded a moment, then said, as if to remove any doubt, "Did you ever recruit any of your hands for Agri-Packers through the Farm Labor Service?"

"Some."

"Well, did you know that the law is very specific on that? I have to inform you that no person may use the Farm Labor Service, which is federally financed, if he charges a fee to either employer or the employee."

Tobin shook his head miserably. "Sure is lots of laws."

Morgan got up and started through the stream of people moving quietly toward the doors. A strong hand seized his arm and held him a moment against the flow of the crowd. Adam put his face close to Morgan's and murmured, "Now we know who won't be the next president. But who will?"

"Was Tobin lying?"

"How do I know? Except that everybody lies, everybody helps himself. Why shouldn't Tobin?"

Morgan pulled away and went to sit by Kathy, just as he had the day the hearings had opened, all those months before. "You called it the first time. Hunt's finished him, all right. Hinman's exit line did it, if nothing else."

She took off her dark glasses with one hand, seized his hand with the other. Her grip was strong, hot. "Now what, Rich?" she whispered. "What comes next?"

But Morgan knew no answer was needed; he knew she scarcely saw him through whatever wild surmise danced mad and enticing before her blue elated eyes. He watched Adam Locklear leave the room.

The Storyteller IV

Several cars already were standing in the gravel drive in front of Anderson's house—freshly painted that year, Morgan saw, and romantic as ever atop its hill, under the trees that shaded its lawns. Morgan hated it still, hated all it suggested, but it had been the right house for Hunt Anderson; Morgan had to concede that. It was a house out of legend, a monument to a dream not unlike the one that had taken up Anderson, led him on, dropped him at last, not so much broken as defrauded; just as the fairytale vision of a big white house on a green Southern hill could not stand much historical investigation, so Anderson's dream had not sustained the application of a man's life.

State troopers were on hand, ready to direct cars into the meadow across which Anderson and Morgan had walked laughing beneath stars. Dunn followed their hand signals meticulously and stopped. Morgan stepped warily out of the car's air-conditioning into the sun, white and merciless in a ceramic sky. The long exhaustion of summer had left limbs and shrubs, even the meadow grass, drooping, rank, coarse as women painted against the fading of the seasons; and that too, Morgan thought, was just right for the day of Anderson's funeral. He walked reluctantly between Dunn and Glass, as if to his own obsequies. Dust from the drive drifted pallid and stale in the still air. He took a futile swipe at the tiny insects swirling about his head from the rich surrounding fields.

"Beautiful place," Dunn said.

They walked toward the house, passing occasionally through shade from the trees patient in the sun. A man came out on the porch, looked at them, then came down the steps.

"Hello, Ralph," Morgan said. "Glass, this is the man you want to see."

They shook hands briefly. Ralph James was effusive in his greetings to Dunn, and Morgan suddenly realized that James was out of a job. He might hang on briefly with Anderson's successor, but most senators wanted their own assistants, personally chosen.

"Your crew's here," James told Glass. "They set up around on the patio." He waved vaguely toward the side of the house. "There's another crew down from the state capital and they're out there too, and I'll try to steer the senators and the Governor and so on, when they arrive, right back there for whatever you want."

"Yeah, well, sure," Glass said. "What I was really hoping for was to get a look around the place, some local color stuff maybe. Like the graveyard where Old Bull's supposed to be buried."

James cleared his throat. "Uh . . . well, yeah, but the graveyard . . . fact is, Mrs. Anderson just told me a minute or two ago absolutely not. No TV at the services."

Glass looked stunned. "But I mean for the Blakey Show. Doesn't she want the services on the network?"

"I'm doing everything I can," James said. "I really worked on her. But maybe a shot or two out there before the services or something."

Dunn chuckled. "If she said no TV, Mister Glass, she meant no TV, I can assure you."

"Mister Sam was buried on TV," Glass said. "I was there myself. They bury presidents on TV, don't they? What's so different about this guy?"

"He's not going to be buried on TV," Morgan said. "That's one difference anyway." Suddenly he was impatient to see Kathy.

As if anticipating Morgan's thought, Dunn said, "Where is Mrs. Anderson, Mister James? Can we see her?"

"I think so. You know, she really looks fine. Bobby, her son, got in from school last night, and he's around somewhere too, and one of the morticians. Why don't you just go on in? There'll be people all over the place before long."

A black man was coming down the steps. He was older, slower, but Morgan knew him. Morgan went to meet him and took a big limp black hand in both of his own. "Jodie, dammit, what we going to do now?"

Jodie's sad, stern face crumpled a little, and he squeezed Morgan's hand; or Morgan thought he did anyway. "Got to git on somehow," Jodie said. "Don't feel much like it today."

For years Jodie had taken care of Hunt Anderson, there and in Washington, shepherding him through the worst times, wary in the background during the best. "If there was one living soul in this world he loved and counted on," Morgan said, "it was you, Jodie."

It was true enough, but Morgan felt cheap and false saying it; like many people brought up in the South, he feared that blacks peered with cynical vision through his determined and transparent good will to his indomitable white core. Morgan tried so hard not to be racist that he knew it was no use. It would never die within him, that racial consciousness, rank and taunting down there where it had been grafted to his soul; and only in the highest euphoria could he even delude himself that, as with a fearful man overcoming his fear, the greatest blow to racism was to recognize and stifle it. Jodie would know he was doing just that; they all knew he was doing it, Morgan thought, every time he did it.

Jodie took his hand away and shook his head. "Mister Hunt always made me feel like some *body,*" he said. "Miz Anderson seen y'all coming out the window and she ask me to bring you right up, Mister Morgan."

That, Morgan thought, would put Dunn and his goddamned green glasses in his place, but Dunn was talking as easily with James about flight schedules as if he had not heard, even though Morgan, following Jodie up the steps, was certain that he had heard.

Then he forgot Dunn. Until he actually reached it—until, in fact, he could smell its heavy sweetness inches from his face—Morgan steadfastly had not let himself see the white spray of flowers by the door. Until then Anderson's death had seemed real, permanent, a fact, only in short bursts of odd realization—there would be no more wordless Sunday rambles in Glover Park or along the Canal towpath or to the Saint-Gaudens in Rock Creek Cemetery; nor would they again come upon each other unexpectedly, as upon a rescuer, at some stupefying smoke-fogged embassy reception where they would retire to a corner to look boozily around on the entangled aspirations and pretensions prancing before them; for sure, there would be no more of the long, disjointed telephone monologues in which Hunt Anderson in recent years had alternately fascinated and bored his intimates; and at last Kathy could give up any pretense of interest in the Senate Wives Club. The spray forced realization of a different order; it evoked no subliminal blaze of mere memory or regret; once recognized, the spray was threatening as truth. It put the mark of death blatantly on Anderson's house—sly triumph and ominous warning, all at once, serving unctuous but insistent notice from the living to the living. Going past the spray, still looking away from it, Morgan thought that only man in all the universe had the courage and the cruelty, the arrogance and the understanding, the subtlety and the gall to celebrate his momentary survival and proclaim the waiting darkness with a single perfumed symbol.

In the cool hall lit dimly by the fanlight over the door, Jodie turned back to him, his face indistinct above his white jacket. "You want to see Mister Hunt first?"

"See him?" Suddenly Morgan was confused; things were too much for him. The question seemed to belie the day, the white spray by the door.

"Look just as natchel as I do. 'Cept now he look more like he look ten years ago." Jodie stepped back and held out his arm toward the door into the formal sitting room. Beside the door there was a small stand with a shaded light over it. A book stood open on the stand.

"Oh," Morgan said. "In there you mean?"

"Brought him home this morning early. I said to Miz Anderson, I said when I seen him, they was peace in his face again."

A slender man in dark blue came out of the sitting room. "Do come right in," he said. "We're viewing until three p.m."

"Oh . . . uh . . . I suppose," Morgan said, "later maybe . . . I mean, maybe later would be better because I'm on the way up to see Mrs. Anderson." It had not occurred to him that the coffin would be open; it seemed unlike Kathy to permit it.

"Of course." The slender man picked up a pen chained to the stand and held it out to Morgan. "The family will want you to register so they can know you were with them in this sad hour."

Morgan eyed the pen with loathing. But he took it and meekly signed his name; no conditioning was more powerful than whatever it was that decreed that an undertaker could not be defied in the presence of his work. Beyond the open door Morgan could see a bank of flowers past which, he supposed with obscure resentment, was the open coffin.

"Miz Anderson's bearing up just beautifully," the undertaker whispered. "She is a source of real strength to the family."

Morgan hastily followed Jodie up the curving staircase. As he came round the bend he saw Anderson's son sitting on the top step, staring at him. Morgan put out his hand. Old Bull's grandson took it reluctantly.

"Well, Bobby." Morgan knew as he spoke that there was nothing to say. "You're the man of the family now."

"You're going in to see her." Bobby pulled his hand away and stared past Morgan. He was thin, tall, but as he sat hunched and tense on the steps he seemed no more than a child to Morgan, who could remember him bouncing and scrambling on Anderson's lap.

"I can find my way from here, Jodie."

The black man nodded and walked down the hall toward the back steps. Morgan touched Bobby's shoulder. "Why don't you come along with me?"

"She sent me out so she could talk to you."

"All right. We'll talk later then."

"There's nothing to talk about."

Morgan could not dispute this. He thought of his own son, several years younger than Bobby. I've got to take more time with Richie, he thought; I owe him more of my time than he gets. He touched Bobby's shoulder again and went past him.

"Don't you stay long," Bobby said. "Don't you stay long in there with her, you fucking bastard."

Morgan stopped, turned. He had known all along, he realized, what the trouble was. But what was there to say, even so? *Sorry, wish it hadn't happened.* That would be worse than nothing, he thought, staring down at the rigid, miserable back, the thin, long neck, the head that had never seemed so much like Hunt's. How was living to be explained to anyone? And even if you could explain it, you couldn't justify it with words. Living was its own justification, or it had none, and when it brushed you aside or knocked you down, you had to get up and go on to your own knowledge of it. Not even a storyteller could make a substitute for that.

Morgan went on down the familiar hall and knocked on the door. His heart was pounding heavily, as it sometimes did when he had not seen Kathy for a while. Hearing her call, he fumbled with the knob that for years now had turned too loosely in its fitting. Then the door opened and he went in.

Kathy was standing by the window in the hot morning sun, with her back to him. The air in the room was cool but not chill with air-conditioning, the way she always kept it. It was as much a sitting room as a bedroom, and on a low table before a sofa there were a coffee pot and cups, with a single rose in a stem of crystal on a silver tray. There was a pink coverlet on her bed, but the room was not overly feminine; books were scattered about, and there were family photographs on the wall and an exercise bicycle in a corner.

Morgan walked without sound across the thickly carpeted floor. "You ought to get that doorknob fixed," he said, as he had so often said before.

She turned and came fiercely into his arms. She was wearing a loose quilted robe that fell to her feet, and she was without makeup or perfume. There were too many lines, now, near the corners of her full mouth, and the shadows under her eyes, pale blue in the morning light, would never again be mysterious or suggestive; but Morgan did not care. He knew the range and depth of her, the richness of her body, and the strength of her presence; all combined, for him, in a beauty that would never fade, never cease to draw him into its unending vitality and variety. He held her tightly, his heart still pounding; her forehead was hard against his shoulder, gouging him, and he felt her strong arms squeezing his waist.

"Hold me, Rich!"

Morgan bent his knees, slipped one arm below her waist, and picked her up, although she was not small or light. She moved her face from his shoulder to the hollow beneath his ear and took the skin of his neck between her teeth. He began to twist from the waist, rocking her gently. He rocked for a long time. She was not biting hard, but to him it seemed that she was penetrating him, sinking herself into some deep and vital place. Eventually she moved her mouth to his ear.

"But I'm alive, Rich . . . I'm alive . . ."

Morgan murmured into her hair. "We're both alive."

"They called me . . . some policeman called me. He mumbled and I didn't understand. Then I did understand. The first thing of all, the first thing I thought was, I'm still alive."

Her lips moved along the line of his jaw, and he turned his head and kissed her avid mouth. For a long time, desperately, their lips and tongues searched for the life in each other. Then she moved her head an inch and spoke against his cheek, into the moist place at the corner of his mouth.

"After that, it was awful. After that, I thought about Hunt and all the years. I called Bobby, and there were a lot of things to do, and everything was awful, and blue. Along about ten o'clock I got away from people and went out in the field somewhere and lay down in the grass and cried."

Morgan rocked her again and she curled a bit in his arms, and his chin fitted exactly over the top of her head lying softly against his chest and neck.

"But every second of all that, down under everything else, I was thinking, I'm alive, I'm alive! Was that bad of me, Rich? Wrong, just to keep thinking of my own life, that it wasn't over, I still had breath and sight, I could still do things, there was time. Was that wrong, when Hunt was dead?"

"How could that be wrong? It's just the truth."

"And then later, when I was alone in here, still thinking all that, I wanted you." She lifted her head, and her mouth butted fiercely at his, her teeth sawing his lip.

Morgan let her slip through his arms, her robe rising along her legs, until her feet touched the carpet. Her hands came behind his head, and with his own on her hips he pulled her against him.

She barely moved her lips from his when, finally, she spoke again. "Why didn't you come? Why weren't you here when I wanted you so much?"

"I didn't know." But that was not good enough for the moment, so Morgan lied effortlessly, with the practiced skill of long life. "Matt gave me the impression somehow I'd maybe just be in the way, and anyway I thought maybe you'd think I was pushing it if I came along in the middle of the night."

"Pushing it? You liar." She moved against him. "I was lying here aching for you but you weren't aching for me."

Kissing her, Morgan did not try to lie again. She pushed her hands between them and opened her robe at the top and her thin pajamas beneath it, and he lowered his head and put his lips eagerly on her breast.

"You love that," Kathy said, touching the back of his neck. "You love that better than anything else. That's what I wanted most last night, to have you doing that so I could really know I was alive." She moved quickly away, smiling wickedly. "I wanted everything else too, but you've never been as good at that. And now all these people around, there's no time."

"That goddamned Matt should have told me to come out here." Reading her new mood, the kind of flashing change he had so often seen in her, which gave her so much of her power, Morgan went to the coffee table and poured himself a cup. "You want some hot?"

"No, thanks, I've had gallons." She had gone back to the window. "Matt's broken up, isn't he, Rich? He's taking it as hard as Jodie, even if he does have this notion about the seat."

"Harder than you and me." There was always, he thought even at the best of times, the thinly veiled urge in each of them to hurt the other, to hit hard at exposed places.

She struck right back. "Because they don't think about themselves as much as we do."

"That may be. Mostly because they were more wrapped up in him, their lives had got dependent on his. They looked after him."

She turned to look at him, suddenly not fighting. "And our lives went the other way. You're right. Poor Matt was always afraid that was what would happen to him."

"He talked to me last night but not about that."

"About me?"

"Why about you? About wanting the seat. Mostly about Hunt. Matt says he betrayed Hunt."

"It wasn't all my fault," Kathy cried out bitterly, defiantly. "Once Hunt got in politics, everything had to revolve around that—Matt, me, the children, everything. It was Hunt's fault as much as mine, and Matt wasn't so high and mighty about it either."

"I know he wasn't. I don't think it was anybody's fault."

"It was mine." She sat down beside him so childishly contrite he almost smiled. "Back then, Hunt and Matt were so much alike. They both looked through me as if I weren't there. Hunt decided to be a politician, and at the same time he decided I'd be a politician's wife, and that was all there was to it. I knew Hunt, there wasn't anything to be done about it with him. He was . . . reaching for something. It wasn't me—he thought he *had* me. So I made Matt look at me, not through me. Matt wasn't as hungry as Hunt. I could make Matt do what *I* wanted."

"And it wasn't too difficult?"

"Difficult enough." She took his hand and held it to her cheek. "But then it was like the things you used to want so badly for Christmas. Once you had them they didn't matter after all."

"I wouldn't know much about that," Morgan said.

"I don't think I'm a bad person, Rich. Not about Matt, not about you. Anyway, you can take care of yourself, even with that little peach you married. I used to worry about Matt, but not any more. It's funny. I needed Matt, and then it turned out Hunt *really* needed him, and maybe that's the way the world works." She was stroking her cheek with Morgan's hand, gazing past him with absent eyes at, he supposed, the irredeemable years. "A long time ago I told Matt it might work out that Hunt would be *his* man, not the other way round. And that's the way it happened, didn't it? These last years, I mean. Matt's had to be everything but a senator himself."

"Everything but."

"Which is why he wants the seat for himself. But I'm not going to think about Matt any more. I'm not going to think about Hunt either, not until they sing 'Abide with Me,' and that'll tear me up, but I'm not going to think about it until then."

She was strung as tightly as a rubber band doubled over, and Morgan let her talk on, not interrupting. She took his hand and put it on her leg and held it there, touching it insistently, moving it, toying with his fingers, never shifting her gaze from its focus on old shadows.

"I can't go downstairs, the coffin's open. I couldn't go near it. The only reason I let that fag undertaker do it that way, Bobby said he wanted it.

Bobby said it didn't matter who looked or didn't look, the damned body-snatchers weren't going to close his father up until they had to. I think Bobby may hate me, but the worse Hunt got, the more Bobby worshiped him, as if the more Hunt refused to deal with life, the more Bobby saw him as a hero. Some sort of lone eagle. Isn't that wild? I suppose Bobby won't deal with life either. Or can't." She paused, pulling gently on his fingers.

"I wouldn't say that." Morgan pulled her against him. "And he doesn't hate you. He's only a boy, and it's all been hard on him." He and Kathy had been especially hard on Bobby, he thought; he did not dare ask her, on this day, if she understood how much Bobby knew about then.

"Hard on him. I know. The night little Kate went to the hospital Bobby was already asleep, and I had to come home in the morning and tell him Kate wasn't coming back. So Bobby went to bed with a little sister and woke up without one. Last night I told him he didn't have a father any more. That other time, his father was out in New Mexico, that's wild too. Talking to some delegates. Imagine being in New Mexico and back home your little girl dies in convulsions. I had to tell him, I always bring the bad news, it's my fate. Hunt said to me on the phone, I think I've got the delegates but what good does that do now? Of course that didn't last for either of us. After Kate died we both threw ourselves into it harder than ever, but you know all that. I don't suppose Bobby understood why, or any of it. I think he may even blame me about Kate because I was the one that was there. The way some things work out is really wild. And when it mattered most, everything was for Hunt. . . . Stop feeling me, Rich, I don't want to get in the mood again."

Morgan left his hand beneath her robe. "Why wouldn't it be a good idea if I carried you over there to the bed and tucked you in and pulled the shades and sat with you while you sleep a little? You're going to break like a pane of glass."

"The hell I am, I'm not going to break. Hunt broke, but I didn't and I won't. Besides, you just want to make love and there's no time."

There was a knock at the door, and Morgan took his hand away, sick with desire and his own clumsy duplicity. She went to the door, and he watched what he could see of her body moving under the robe. Suddenly it came to him that everything was going to be changed; there would not be merely an absence of Anderson, but all his presence had caused and affected would be different. Bobby would be the man of the house in fact. And Kathy was not ageless, nor was he. The years lay bleak and empty around him; the air-conditioning whispered obscenely.

Jodie was at the door. "The Governor on the phone for you, Miz Anderson." There was no awe in Jodie's voice; he had for years lived among governors, senators, cabinet officers, served them unobtrusively, sometimes put them to bed, suffered their indifference.

"Oh, I'll take it here." Kathy turned away, and Jodie pulled the door to, his old eyes looking impassively at Morgan.

He knows too, Morgan thought at once, sure of his instinct. Or perhaps, after Bobby, it only seemed that everyone knew. Kathy went across the room to the phone. "That son-of-a-bitch better not try to weasel out of coming." She pressed a button, picked up the receiver. "Hello?" Her voice suddenly weak, exhausted, the voice of bereavement. Morgan could hear a faraway quacking, as of birds flying over.

"So good of you to call again . . . Hunt would have appreciated that. . . . Yes, I suppose I'm fine, tired of course, but everybody's been wonderful and I'm all right." More quacking. "I'm afraid it's an imposition, Governor, I don't want you to feel . . . Well, of course Bobby would be so pleased, and knowing how busy you are I can't think of anything that would have pleased Hunt more."

The interruption had succeeded in pulling Morgan back from the dizzying edge of his insistent sensuality. Listening, he felt weak with relief, as if spared a fearful pain.

Kathy hung up and came back to the sofa, nothing absent about her eyes or voice. "Do you know much about that man?"

Morgan shook his head, edging away as she sat down. "Run of the mill is my impression, but I don't really pay much attention to state politics nowadays."

"Oh. I don't think Hunt liked him, but I can't remember why. Anyway it's for Bobby, not for me. Now get out of here for a while, I've got a thousand things to do and I don't want to think or talk either. I'm going to have too much time to do both from now on."

Morgan kissed her cheek as sexlessly as if greeting an old lady at teatime. Her mood had shifted again, sliding effortlessly as a child's sled on snow into intense fixation on things to be done.

"Send that fag up, and Rich, be a dear, give poor Ralph James a hand if you can, he hasn't got a clue. Did I see you with that unspeakable Dunn? I suppose I'll have to see him too. Tell him I'm changing right now . . ."

He was eased out of the room as efficiently as if he had been a subscription salesman.

Down the hall a door closed. Bobby was gone from the steps. Morgan wondered how often the boy had watched his mother's door from his own, narrowly opened; how often he had waited in the quiet house, the long night. Morgan shook his head; the boy needed affection, assurance, but then didn't most boys? One way or another, the adult world that dominated them was hard, lonely, crushing . . .

Like my birthday cake, Morgan thought, as he often thought, as if it had been yesterday. The long hot summer afternoon, the dry squeak of Estelle's rocker, the occasional dusty car speeding by on the highway, far down the block the whir of a lawnmower. Estelle sat sewing, not even looking up, the line of her jaw as rigid as the corner of the house. When his sister was angry she never raged or lifted her hand; she froze into a disapproval so over-whelming in its air of violated probity that he wanted to grovel, confess his worthlessness, beg her forbearance. But Estelle would disapprove of that too. That morning, in the flush of a year's completed growth, flamboyantly displaying his new wallet with its secret compartment, he had bought a box of candy at the drugstore and taken it to a neighbor lady who had the same birthday and who, as usual, had given him a pair of socks to mark the occasion.

"A dollar!" Estelle said when he told her of his manly gesture. "For *candy?* You could of got a hanky at the dime store for a quarter."

That had begun it. By the end of the silent afternoon, in miserable contrition, he had calculated a thousand items with which he might, for a dollar, have eased his sister's intolerable burdens. He was crushed; he despised his improvidence and callousness. And there was something else of which he was uneasily aware that he should not even be thinking, toad that he was; finally he could help himself no longer.

"Estelle," he said and waited for a sign. There was none, and he plunged desperately on, hating himself. "What about my birthday cake?"

"In the kitchen. Cut yourself a piece, I don't care."

He rose from the porch steps. A June bug buzzed in the nearby shrubs. "You going to eat some of it with me?"

Estelle did not look up. "I'm busy. Don't make too much mess in the kitchen."

Morgan could still taste that cake, feel it dry and lumpy in his throat; he could hear the hot, disapproving silence of the kitchen as he sat alone at the table, staring at the Coca-Cola calendar on the wall. Years later the memory of the cake with its red candles never lit, the single triangle he had sliced in it, could bring the sting of tears to his eyes; and it did, as he went downstairs, brooding, and hurried past the open parlor door and the flowers beyond.

Morgan found Jodie in the rear, told him Mrs. Anderson wanted to see the undertaker; then, overcoming his hatred of the telephone, called his office from the wall phone in the pantry. Janie mumbled something about lots of messages, then switched him to Nat.

"Nothing really important," Nat said. "Billings wants to talk when you get back. Your broker about Xerox. Hobart to say nice work on the Hinman story. A speaking invitation in Kansas City. Senator Barstow wants to have lunch."

"Work that in next week. He wants to talk about this feud he's got going with that con man at the Pentagon. What's the Kansas City fee?"

"I told them two thousand and expenses. They didn't bat an eye that I could tell."

"Then okay provided it's half q and a, and you can work out the date, but no goddam cocktail parties with any old ladies."

"Just young ones. Is it awful down there, Rich?"

"You know what funerals are, a laugh a minute. Kathy's fine though." A slight pause. "Mrs. Anderson," Nat said, "is a strong person."

Morgan knew when to change a subject. "I expect to be in tomorrow but maybe late. If I don't get back tonight I'll call in first thing and let you know, but I don't expect that."

He hung up, then called Anne. She said he had caught her going out the door to the hairdresser.

"Then I won't keep you but a minute. It's just I got away so quick last night, and then you were half asleep when I called, I don't think I ever said I was coming home tonight." Suddenly, he thought of the redhead waiting for him on the plane and nearly changed his mind. "That is, as far as I know now."

"Fine," Anne said. "I guess not for dinner though?"

"Oh no, it'll be late at best. You go on and do whatever you had in mind. I just wanted you to know I was planning as of now to be back."

"I didn't have anything in mind, I'll be right here."

"Well, I just wanted you to know."

"All *right.* I stand warned."

"Oh, for Christ's sake, I didn't mean—"

"I didn't say you meant anything. I just stand warned you're coming home late, that's all."

Morgan was silent a moment. "Kathy's holding up well," he said. "I think it's even kind of a relief."

"Of course it is. Tell her I'm thinking of her, will you?" But not much, her voice suggested.

"I'll tell her. Don't forget you're out of gin, I forgot to bring it home."

"Oh, I'll do something about *that.*" She laughed with what sounded almost like amusement. "How have you been getting along on your manuscript?"

"What manuscript?"

"You know, that novel you've been working on for so long."

I could just hang up, Morgan thought—she knew there was no manuscript, only talk—but he had hung up too many times, stalked out of the room too often. It was good theater, even momentary therapy, but it never changed the situation unless to make it worse. "That's one of the cruelest things you've ever said to me, Anne."

"I just thought maybe having to go down there was interfering with your writing, and I know you get so little free time for it anyway."

"Oh hell," Morgan said. "I'll be home tonight."

"All right. Rich, you're not . . . I mean I know what Hunt meant to you but . . . don't be too gloomy." It was one of her favorite words, to which by subtle shadings of voice she could impart an infinite variety of meanings, all negative.

Morgan took it, and her abrupt change of tone at that moment, as a reminder that they were probably about even-up in words as in life, and as a plea for him not to fall—as they both knew he sometimes did—into the sort of prolonged depression that she always seemed to think was less a mood than a petulant response to hurts or disappointments. That usually irritated Morgan because he tended to see himself as melancholy, sensitive, borne down by his preception of a demonic world. This time, as if avoiding battle that would be too intense, he decided to concede peaceful intent; he knew there were times when she really was concerned for him—if for no other reason, out of long familiarity, partially shared lives.

"I'm all right, I'm not gloomy." His voice was a little sharper than he intended, but for once, as if she too were warier than usual, avoiding conflict, she did not pick it up—or perhaps she did; in any case she let it pass.

"Don't rush back, Rich, if there's anything you can do for Kathy. We're all right here."

For once they hung up almost amicably.

Morgan sat for a moment on Jodie's high stool, staring at the rows of glasses, all shapes and sizes, in the orderly wall cabinets. He had meant to ask especially about Rich Junior, but of course he had forgotten. In the incessant guerrilla warfare of marriage, children were the most frequent victims. I've got to stop this running around and all this bloodletting with

Anne, he thought; but he knew he was not really going to submerge his own life and needs in anyone else's, not even his son's.

The pantry door swung open, and Myrtle Bell strode in behind her imposing prow. "Why don't you get off the goddam phone and give somebody else a chance, big boy?"

"Why, you eavesdropping old bitch," Morgan said. "I suppose every word I've said will show up in your column tomorrow."

"It would if you'd said anything interesting." She gave Morgan a bear hug. Perfume and powder odors swamped him.

"I didn't expect to see you here, Myrt." And why are you? he wanted to ask, but she would be too sharp to give away her reason.

"You weren't the only one who loved Hunt Anderson, big boy. I was never so broken up in my life as when Kathy called. I caught the morning plane and here I am."

Morgan reviewed in his mind which senators might be coming to the funeral; Myrtle could be chasing something on one of them. Or did Anderson's death raise some flashy news possibility of which he had not thought? Something about Hunt he had not known, an old love affair perhaps. Maybe the Long Island beach-house woman was coming. That was the kind of story on which Myrtle was unerring. He gave no thought to the possibility that she had merely come to Anderson's funeral; he knew her too well.

"Why, Myrt, you know that really moves me?"

"The ends of the earth, that's how far I'd go for Hunt Anderson. Not to speak of Kathy. Where *is* Kathy?"

Morgan pointed vaguely upward. "Managing things. Does she know you're here?"

"Not yet. Let me get at that phone, big boy, I've got to call those shits in my office."

Morgan abandoned the stool to her. As he was leaving the pantry Myrtle called after him, "Doesn't Hunt look wonderful? Better than he did alive!"

Morgan wandered out to the front of the house. Jodie was managing a party of helpers under the trees; they were covering several long tables with white cloths. A number of other cars had arrived, and a steady trickle of viewers was moving solemnly through the sitting room. Matt Grant had arrived, and he and Ralph James were circulating, rather like hosts. Dunn was in earnest conversation with a burly red-faced man in a suit too heavy for the weather and too tight for his body; Morgan recognized him as the state party chairman.

It was remarkable, Morgan thought, that the scene was almost festive; but a funeral, after all, was as much a celebration of life as a mourning of death. And there was always in a funeral throng a peculiar intimacy; old friends would find each other again on Anderson's lawn, old wounds would be healed, and old truths perceived briefly. Once the body had been viewed and the register signed and the closest among them had murmured grave, loving words to Kathy or Bobby, they would all be free to talk, laugh, eat the food of life that would be set out under the trees, reminisce, mourn a little for what had been, and would never be, and in that way love one another truly, if only in passing. As for the dead, as for Anderson, Morgan thought, going down the steps, seeing the line of viewers—move on, folks, keep moving.

He walked across the lawn, past one knot of men talking baseball and near two large women in hats who were clucking over the drought and by a group of student types in long hair and ill-knotted ties—Bobby's school delegation, no doubt—who fell abruptly silent as he came within earshot. Just beyond them Dunn and the state chairman were still talking.

"Message from Kathy," Morgan said to Dunn. "She's running in circles right now but wants to see you just as soon as she's got a minute."

"Ummm." Dunn adjusted the green lenses. "A short minute, I'll bet. You know Gil Brock, don't you?"

"From way back."

"From Zeb Vance days." Brock eyed him without welcome.

"Those were the days," Morgan said. "Oh yes, those were the days."

The green lenses peered from one to the other; like a referee parting boxers, Dunn smoothly slipped idle conversation between them. "Gil was telling me that the President looks in bad shape in this part of the country . . ."

Dunn had the one thing no politician could get far without, Morgan thought, the ability to pick up vibrations and give them meaning. This was something Morgan had known well enough, but abstractly, in his years of dealing with Dunn; not until that moment had he applied it to the conundrum of what had happened between Dunn and Anderson at the convention, behind the locked door of the bathroom in Suite 1201. Strange that even that number had stayed with him—he could still see the fake antique chairs in his mind's eye, the bed covered with papers, briefcases, coats, the carpetbag stickers plastered on every mirror, the huge poster on one wall proclaiming ANDERSON'S IN! and the drooping dried chrysanthemums mournful on the dresser. Yet the central thing that had happened there, the one fact that mattered, still was unknown to him; and now one of the only two men who had been behind that bathroom door was dead and the other was bland, wary, close-mouthed, if near enough to be touched.

". . . but the suburban vote," Dunn was saying, "I mean the close-in, middle-class suburbs, not the big rich, I don't think they're conservative so much in any economic sense as they're resistant to change socially . . ."

Kathy had called Dunn "unspeakable," but Morgan knew her voice, her inflections. The word had been a signal not a description, a suggestion to Morgan that Dunn was of little consequence to her one way or another; but she would not have bothered even to make the suggestion had it been true, had she not for some reason wanted Morgan to think it was true. Vibrations, Morgan thought, vibrations everywhere. Men lived, died, by them, became president or failed, on the pulse of a moment, by the way other men felt it, or did not. There lay the secret of Dunn and Anderson, and Morgan despaired more than ever at the possibility of learning it; because history, unlike life, was made of words, not vibrations.

Morgan, half listening to the political talk, watched Jodie come across the lawn toward them. Kathy was ready for Dunn, he thought. But Jodie's message was not for Dunn. "Mister Brock, Miz Anderson, she say could you step up to see her just one minute please?"

"Why . . . umph . . ." Brock hitched up his trousers, which were already high and tight on his thick body. "Why, anything that little lady wants, yes sir, I'll be right glad . . ." He followed Jodie importantly.

"Little lady," Dunn said, "with well-filed teeth."

Morgan touched his neck self-consciously. "She's kind of in a state, you can imagine. Rigorously not thinking about Hunt but it keeps breaking in. And the little girl. I hadn't heard her talk about Kate for years. And she's worried about Bobby, he's so angry and withdrawn. But Kathy's still managing things. Drawn down fine but still managing things, most of all herself."

"Witness Mister State Chairman Brock's summons to the presence."

Glass appeared abruptly at Dunn's elbow. "Those sons-of-bitches," he said. "Do you know what they've done now?"

"I don't blame them. I wouldn't let you film the body either." Morgan was faintly discomfited by his own remark, but he told himself it was the sort of deadpan line Anderson himself might have delivered and appreciated.

"I don't mean them. It's that mother of a producer of mine that's really fucked me up." With loud gasps and small shreaks, several elderly ladies hastened out of earshot. The thin old man who was with them took a tottering belligerent step toward Glass.

Glass did not notice. "Got me all the way down here with a crew and now they don't want any film at all."

"That's crazy." Morgan watched the thin man hesitate, then hasten after the gasping ladies.

"Big goddam deal. They've got this frigging fashion film out of Paris, a six-minute piece, and the producer decides he wants it on the show tonight. So out goes Anderson and out goes you know who."

"I'm not surprised," said Dunn, ever the calm analyst. "It's really astonishing how fast a man can fall out of the public eye these days. Anderson went up so fast, he came down even faster, accelerating thirty-two feet per second, and then there were all his personal problems, and frankly, I doubt if many people watching your show tonight will ever even have heard of him."

"But I could have been doing the Hinman story," Glass said. "The pricks will be on the air with that one all right."

"You can catch an afternoon plane." Dunn always had schedules on hand, agenda in his heart. "One change right into DCA."

"I might just do that." Glass threw his arms wide in a comic gesture. "Old Morgan even got the pussy last night. I struck out all around."

First Bobby, then Jodie—if only in his careful eyes—and now Glass; Morgan thought that whatever his sins, he had endured more than he should have to. As he saw no point in the mortification of the flesh, he saw no use in indecent exposure of the life within the flesh. Sin, if it existed, demanded only expiation, a private and internal matter. "Glass," he said. "Don't take the afternoon plane. Stay for the funeral."

Glass shrugged. "Nothing in it for me. My crew's already packing the gear."

"But *you* stay."

"You mean I might learn something?" Glass was grinning, but the tape on his forehead moved a bit up and down, as if his skin were flicking nervously, as if he might be aware at last through his concentration on self that he had struck a wrong note. Glass, of all people, would not be long unaware that a vindictive Morgan could hurt him in the profession; and he could not be sure whether or not Morgan was vindictive.

"No. You won't learn anything and I doubt if you'll get any pussy either. But stay anyway. You owe it to Anderson."

"I'll stay if you want. I don't have to be back until tomorrow. But what do *I* owe Anderson?"

"Respect." Morgan turned away, toward the steady, penetrating focus of the green lenses and the lean jaw and tight mouth beneath them. Beyond Dunn, Jodie's helpers were beginning to bring food from the house— heaping plates of potato salad and cole slaw and sliced tomatoes and biscuits and corn on the cob, several large hams, immense platters of chicken; frosted pitchers of iced tea were placed at either end of each table, and the gathering crowd of mourners began drifting together around the abundant spread. Matt Grant and Charlie French came across the lawn.

"I was just saying to French here"—Matt made them all an elaborate wink—"if I ever saw a crowd that could use a drink before lunch, this looks like it."

"Lead on," French said.

Matt gestured with his head toward the house and started off. Dunn and Morgan fell in side by side. Glass hurried past them and began chattering to French.

"Respect?" Dunn did not look at Morgan as he spoke. "Why should you think Glass should think Anderson deserves respect?"

"Doesn't every living thing? And the dead for having lived?"

"Even Glass himself?"

"Of course Glass. He struggles too."

"Well, if you respect everything that struggles," Dunn said, "I don't think respect means much."

"Sure it does. After a while it gets so hard to give."

They went up the porch steps behind Matt, who led them past the open sitting room, with its banks of flowers, its straggling lines of viewers moving in and out, to a big dark room deep in the recesses of the house. It was, like Kathy's, a combination of bedroom and "office"—as Hunt had called it—where he had worked when at home. It was sparsely furnished: a big library table that served as a desk, a double bed, a soft leather chair with a floor lamp behind it, a wall of bookcases stacked as much with old magazines and newspapers and Senate documents, several coffee mugs, some meaningless plaques given Anderson in lieu of speech fees, a rack of pipes he had once used and abandoned, as with books, to which he had not been much addicted.

"I don't have much patience with reading just for reading's sake," he had once explained to Morgan. "I guess I want to be told what I need to know at the moment, and straight out, like the size of the defense budget or how many school dropouts we have or what the labor factor is in steel prices. Just abstract reading, just taking myself out of the real world into Madame Bovary's farmhouse or somewhere, hell, it bores me stiff except the sex parts."

That was one of the limitations of the political mind, Morgan thought —it confused steel prices and the defense budget with the daily realities of lonely, reaching people, finding their way. But what else were politicians

emselves? It was the essential falsity of their lives that, sharing as they
d the clay of humanity, they nevertheless concerned themselves with
cieties and economies, laws and institutions, which could be made to
nction only by those who measured things in head counts, who made
dgments according to the greatest good for the greatest number, and
ministered affairs by due process. So perhaps only if you did consider the
ovary farmhouse an abstraction, not real, could you also think politics was
ore important than personality, identity—could you think, as no doubt
politician had to, that politics changed things any more than the shuffling
out of furniture in an over-elaborate parlor.

Matt stood back to let them enter Anderson's room. Morgan was last,
d as he went past, Matt murmured in his ear, "Brock's got his own man
it he says he won't veto me."

Morgan nodded and went on in. He gazed nostalgically around the room
nile Matt went to preside over a well-stocked liquor cabinet that stood in
corner, with glasses and an ice bucket on its counter top. Many a night,
ese recent years, Morgan had sat in that room talking and drinking with
nderson, until Jodie came; and then he had gone upstairs to Kathy. And
Bobby knew that and Jodie knew that, then probably Anderson had
own it too. Now that Anderson was dead, Morgan rather hoped so—he
alized that he had always hoped so—because if Anderson *had* known, he
d given his tacit approval by his silence. There would be no other way
look at it, Morgan told himself—not, he hastily conceded, that Ander-
n's approval or disapproval could have changed it.

Dunn, as if by natural right, sat at Anderson's littered table. French
propriated the easy chair. Glass, for once seeming anxious to please,
ssed around the drinks Matt prepared. Beyond glass doors opening to the
ar lawn they could see Jodie's white-coated helpers moving back and forth
tween the tables and the kitchen. Morgan went to the wall upon which
ng Anderson's extensive collection of inscribed political photos.

"I was looking at those this morning," Matt said. "They'll take you back,
ch."

"There's that silly Lundy. Old Sneakers Lundy, the Senator from the
ate of Forecourt. Always two sets before the morning hour. What's he
ing in Hunt's gallery?"

"Don't knock Old Sneakers. He kicked in big for Hunt's campaign."

"The hell you say. And look at this one of the old Speaker. Why, he hated
unt's insides, but listen to this: 'To an esteemed colleague of the other
dy.' "

Matt pointed to a framed photograph somewhat larger than the others.

"That's Hunt riding in from the airport the day the convention opene Look at that crowd! Man, I almost thought we had it made, that day. Litt did I know."

Glass gave Morgan his vodka and stood with them, looking at the pi tures, the framed pens with which presidents had signed parts of the names to bills in which Hunt had been interested, and the original cartoo concerning Anderson that he had requested from the cartoonists.

"I'd sort of forgotten the way they used to draw him so tall," Morga said. "Those guys, when they're good, they really make a point. He towe over everybody in all these drawings. Look at that Herblock there." Morga shook his head; there had been no Anderson cartoons for years.

"I can recognize most of these characters, but who's that guy?" Gla pointed high on the wall to a photograph of the smiling, rather jowly fa of a young man; it was inscribed in a script too florid to read.

"That's the way Danny O'Connor used to look before he got fat ar famous," Matt said. "Danny's the biggest in the business now, but he real got his start with Hunt's campaign. Fair enough too, because Hunt's car paign was nowhere without Danny's spots. Not that you'd ever know it, tl way you boys in the newspaper game like to tell it . . ."

Old Bull's Boy IV

"... I mean every four years, when they have another primary up there," Matt said, "somebody drags out the old clips and writes a feature story about the big upset. I'm no word man, but actually I believe I could write one of those stories myself if I had to. Seems like they all start off with some fellow slogging through the snow and he looks up and there stands this tall guy with his hand out and he says, 'I'm Hunt Anderson and I'm running for president and I need your help.'

"And all those stories always go on to say that what won the big upset was Hunt getting out and shaking hands personally with so many voters. Actually it did help a lot, I admit, but the real truth is Danny O'Connor was the reason Hunt won that primary, and Hunt was always the first to admit it. Not that Hunt was exactly one to hide his own light under a bushel.

"Hunt found Danny during the old migrant hearings when he needed somebody to sort of handle TV for him. Danny was an Irish cop's kid who started out in radio doing singing commercials and switched to television early. Only he was the kind of a guy who never could make it with one of the networks or an ad agency because they wanted these big moneymakers who never rocked the boat. But Danny—all the big producers had fired him at one time or another, mostly for causing them trouble or screwing their wives or spending money or telling them they were fools—Danny was convinced the industry was gypping him out of the Jimmy or the Emmy or whatever it is, even though he'd just had this one series of his own they put on at 7:30 a.m. on Sundays, where he just used the camera without any words or music or explanation because Danny's basic idea was that TV was visual, so the nearer you came to no words at all the nearer you were to perfect TV. That's the kind of crazy ideas Danny used to have. He actually did a show on the Battle of the Bulge without words or sound effects. That was the one Hunt saw and decided to hire him, but Danny's series was taken off after three weeks because of a show he did on garbage disposal. Danny was pretty funny about it—he said even at 7:30 a.m. Sunday he wasn't commercial enough, and I can believe it, although he's in the big money now from political TV.

"It was actually Kathy who talked Hunt into going for a TV man, and he was one of the first politicians to take on a guy just for that, even if it wasn't his idea. Every night Hunt would come home from the hearings, you see, and there'd be Kathy telling him he wasn't getting enough mileage out of the tube, they were missing the best stuff, or putting on the dullest, or not giving Hunt the exposure he deserved. She never missed the hearings, and then she'd sit down at night and make notes on whatever there was on the seven o'clock news and the eleven o'clock, and then she'd be up early the next day to watch the morning shows too, and I tell you one thing, she had a sharp eye. Sharp as a tack. She just never let up on Hunt until he agreed to bring in somebody to improve the TV. Kathy can be hard to argue with . . ."

I'll say she can, you mealymouth prick, Morgan thought, silently sipping his vodka under the picture of Danny O'Connor, listening as if he could not have remembered it all himself—every word and moment of it. Yes, by God, hard as hell to argue with when you're crawling into bed with her, you pious hypocrite.

Morgan knew that was not worthy, was really only the lingering trace of the trembling passion that had seized him in Kathy's room. Worse, he thought, it was sick evidence of the latent jealousy he still felt whenever he thought of Matt Grant's having been chosen before him.

". . . so Hunt checked around and a few people came in," Matt was saying. "Outright flacks mostly, and then one day Danny O'Connor showed up carrying the Battle of the Bulge in a can, and Kathy and Hunt sat down and watched it. They took him off to lunch, and Hunt put him on the payroll that day. I'll bet anything it was Kathy who decided it, even though she told me Danny tried to feel her up under the table. Hunt handed him over to me, and Danny said in that careless manner of his, 'Well, let's make that big redneck famous, huh?' I never did find him a desk, but Danny worked pretty much out of his head anyway.

"Now, off the record, he didn't do so much for us as you might think during the hearings because he didn't come aboard until about the time I had them going so good newswise that we didn't need him all that much. He knew all about angles and zooms and prime time and Nielsen and stuff like that—and girls! Danny O'Connor was unquestionably the most indefatigable chaser I ever met. He scored too, to hear him tell it, and he spent a lot of time at first finding out who would and who wouldn't among all those girls working in the Senate Office Building. 'I'm dead and this is heaven,' he used to say.

"But at first he didn't know his hat from third base about politics, especially the running-for-office kind. Pretty soon he started learning. He went back to Hunt's state campaign and got out all the TV and ran it over and over, like a football coach studying his team and their opponents before a game. Then he went down there and spent a lot more time in the local stations, going over all their old news film, and then he got some stuff one of the agencies he'd been fired from had made for a lot of other candidates, and he studied that too, when he wasn't making out in the file room. That whole year and a half, between the migrant hearings and Hunt's announcement, Danny just sort of drew his paycheck and went about his business, and if you'd asked me what he was doing I'd have probably said 'nothing but screwing, he doesn't even have a desk.' That shows you the kind of bureaucrat I am—first things first.

"But Hunt always ran a loose ship, only it turned out Danny knew about as soon as any of us that Hunt was definitely going to run, and when we went into that first primary up there, it also turned out Danny was the only one ready. I'd been running the Senate office practically singlehanded while Hunt rambled around the country lining up supporters and delegates and money—not enough of any of 'em—and I didn't have a clue what Danny had been up to.

" 'Okay,' he says at the first staff meeting for the primary campaign, just as if he's in charge. 'Now here's what I need.' I was going to be campaign manager, I'd just found out, and I'd never set foot in that state, which was typical of the way Hunt organized things, but I doubted if Danny O'Connor could tell us much about it, so I sort of frowned at him. But he went right on. 'The spots are in the can,' he says. 'The only question is where are we going to show them?'

" 'What spots?' I said.

" 'The campaign spots. Now this agency in New York I got spies in tells me we only got to have a couple of channels to cover that state like long underwear. Here's the rate cards, and I'm figuring five spots a day for two weeks on both only costs us seven or eight thousand, which is a Brink's job.'

"I jumped right out of my chair. 'Are you nuts? Seven or eight thousand for television spots in one little state?' That may not sound like much now, but back then it was a wad even for TV.

" 'Not counting the last week,' Danny said, not turning a hair. 'Then ten a day and five in prime time. Maybe ten thousand more, but what's money?'

" 'Whatever it is, that's a lot of it,' I remember Hunt saying, which was understatement if I ever heard it. But then Hunt always acted as if campaign money grew on trees.

" 'And what about longer shows?' I said. 'What about a closing speech the night before the primary? We'll need fifteen minutes at least, maybe on both channels if we can get them.'

" 'Speech, smeech,' Danny says. 'Lay down my spots on two channels on this schedule I've got, and you can go lie in the sun somewhere, Boss, and play diddles with Kathy. Who listens to speeches any more? Not me.'

"Well, to be perfectly frank, that was probably pretty close to the truth although, at the time, I went right down the line for just a few spots and putting what TV money we had into a couple of setpiece speeches near the end of the campaign. It seemed more presidential to me.

" 'I'm with Danny,' Kathy said—Kathy always sat in on the staff meetings after Hunt started running. "We brought him in here to give us good TV, and I think we ought to go along with him. I don't listen to speeches either, and I don't know anybody that does.'

" 'But I won't go lie in the sun.' Hunt had his feet up on his desk, the casual way he liked to look, studying the rate cards. 'At these prices I couldn't afford it. What do you say to half that budget, O'Connor?'

" 'If you don't put it into any lousy speeches.'

" 'No speeches at all, not on TV. We're going to shake every damn Yankee hand in that state, do some street-corner stump-speaking, and if they're as good as you say they are, we'll show those bloody spots till we're bankrupt. If that won't do it we'll come back to the Senate and forget it.'

"And that's the way we planned the strategy for the big upset. We cut back Danny's spot schedule a little, not touching the final week prime time, and actually, I'll have to say this, when I finally got a look at the spots I sort of changed my mind and wished we'd booked more time slots for them —not that we had the money. But at that point it seemed to me we were going to need everything we could lay our hands on."

"I guess I was still in college," Glass said. "In college the only thing you
bthered about was pussy and basketball. But I can remember the headlines
bout what a big upset that primary was."

"But in retrospect, I mean looking back on it," French said, "you can
e what a setup it really was for Anderson. It's a wonder some of us didn't
e it at the time."

"I'll bet some did." Morgan's voice rang savagely in the room. "I'll bet
unn saw it."

"No." The green lenses moved slowly side to side. "I was as fooled as
l the other so-called experts. But that's the way you learn things. Being
oled."

"A lot of ideas people just take for granted in politics nowadays," Matt
id, "they really saw for the first time in that campaign. Like Danny
'Connor's spots—nobody had seen anything like them before that pri-
ary. I guarandamtee you that. And people in those days still thought
olitical organizations counted for more than anybody thinks they do now
-maybe that was the real key to it. Or maybe it was more nearly that it
asn't until about then that it began to look like old men couldn't get
ected any more. And don't let anybody tell you Hunt Anderson himself
asn't surprised the way it turned out, at least the size of it.

"One thing for sure, from the President on down, the party bosses just
lain underestimated Hunt, and so did the press experts too—even Morgan
ere, for instance. Hell, I've got to admit it, I had to be convinced myself.
ven after he blew Paul Hinman out of the water, even after the *Time* cover
ory on what they called 'The Darkest Horse,' quite candidly, when he told
e he was going to move around the country and actually see if it looked
ossible, you could have knocked me over with a feather.

"Not long after the migrant hearings ended, there were congressional
ections that had to be gotten out of the way, you know, before anybody
ould really pay attention to a presidential election two years off. All the
ublicity put Hunt in demand as a speaker and fund-raiser, and he cam-
aigned all around the country for senators that had to run that year, mostly
r the younger, more liberal ones that he felt at home with and that he
ould possibly later expect some help from. That was a good year for the
arty, if you remember, and Hunt's candidates did all right, so by and large
e came out of it in good shape, pretty well known, with some due bills in
is pocket, some friends scattered around, and looking like he had some
oattails.

"But with a year still to go before the first presidential primary an almost two to the election, the big problem—other than his youth an inexperience—was the opposition of the regulars in the Senate and th party. I mean, that was tough. Hinman was out of it but he was sti governor and still had some power; and people who'd made commitmen to him and people who'd expected to go up with him—there wasn't a chan that any of them would forgive Hunt. I don't need to tell you guys that th went double for the President, because all those others that were so dow on Hunt were mostly the party people the Old Man depended on the mo and stood up for the strongest. And while I wouldn't want to be quoted o it, I'm not sure Hunt cared all that much how they felt. He wasn't one t sit back and let somebody else do his hauling for him, and in those day he thought he was destiny's child, you know. They all do. He just ke moving around, making speeches, shaking hands, telling people that if h ever ran for higher office he sure would appreciate their help. That was th kind of stuff he was good at, while I was back in the Senate working m ass off on his migrant bills.

"The first big break Hunt got was a story Morgan wrote that a coup of the big civil rights organizations were looking favorably at Hunt. Th was important, Hunt being a Southerner, and it showed how the migra hearings had got the colored issue off his neck. Then, of course, he ha friends here and there, from the Ivy League and his New York lawyer day and the old home-state organizations and some new people he'd natural picked up during the congressional campaign and after the hearing brought in so much publicity. Pretty soon there were these Anderson fc President clubs going to work all over the country—off the record, with little stimulation from the head man. Danny was promoting him on the T shows all over the place, even the game shows, and Kathy too. Danny sa Kathy was very exposable.

"In the fall of that year all the clubs gave these twenty-five-dollar dinne —they didn't want it to look fat cat, the way a hundred-dollar dinner alway does—and what they all put on the plate was just one hamburger. That Kathy's idea, not Hunt's. A lot of people came to those twenty-five-dolla hamburger dinners, and they raised a lot of money, but what was real important was the publicity and the way they dramatized Hunt as a so of poor man's candidate running against the bosses. All of a sudden, it jus sort of dawned on everybody that without anybody really noticing, an without any formal announcement of any kind, Hunt Anderson was ou front of everybody. And he hadn't even been in the Senate quite thre years."

Morgan said, "Out front, but then nobody else was really running."
"That's not fair," Dunn said. "It's true but it's not fair. Anderson was
putting political capital in the bank. I could see that from where I sat. He
didn't have any of the pros with him, but nobody else was doing anything.
I told the President that myself. And there were lots of others telling him
if he didn't get a candidate in the field, Hunt Anderson was going to be hard
to catch."

"That was it," Matt said, "you put your finger right on it. That was what
Hunt kept saying when he was in the office long enough to talk about how
it was going. Everybody else on the list of possibilities was holding back,
waiting for the President to make his choice, each one hoping the Old Man
would point the magic wand at him.
    " 'But the one thing sure is he's not going to lay his dirty hands on us,'
Hunt used to say with that crazy self-confidence he had back then. 'Because
even if the old bastard would take us,' he'd say, 'he couldn't get any of the
other old bastards to go along, and some of the Hinman types probably
would take a walk all the way out of the party. So put that together with
the fact that, after the hearings and the elections last year, we're the best
known of the whole list, and there's the big issue right there—bossism. Old
Bull's boy beat the bosses down home, and stood up to them on the Hinman
thing. So we're the people's candidate, but the leaders are going to come
up with some other guy and try to ram him down the people's throat, and
that's going to play right into our hands, you wait and see.'
    "Personally, I was never that sure it was so good to have all the powers
against him, and of course I turned out to be right. But I'll be damned if
when the President finally did make a move he didn't do just what Hunt
expected. By then, it was only—let's see—maybe a month or so before the
first primary. Maybe two months. Joe Bingham had started making his
move down South—not that he had the chance of a snowball in hell but he
saw the vacuum after Hinman. He and the other Southern leaders were
putting together the Southern delegations, all except ours, behind Joe as a
regional favorite son to swing some real weight at the convention. Naturally, most of the Southern boys weren't too keen on Hunt, he even had
some trouble in our delegation, after he began to build up his civil rights
backing and reach for the big-city colored vote. And of course Joe Bingham
started getting big ideas maybe he could actually make it. They all do.
    "Funny how the Bingham thing used to get under Hunt's skin. He
wanted it all, and it rankled him that he didn't have the South too. Particu-

larly the South. 'I'm Southern,' he used to say. 'I'm twice as damn Southern as Joe Bingham ever thought about being.' It was silly, but he never conceded that the colored issue had really shut his water off down there, except where they sort of had to support him in his home state, and particularly with Joe Bingham in the field.

"Joe was a fire-eater and he had the Southern delegations in line, and there again, you see, the President had to take a hand. The Old Man couldn't stay out of it after Hinman collapsed on him, because if anybody was going to shake any of those Southern delegations loose from Joe for anything less than a price nobody could afford to pay, it wasn't going to be Hunt, it was going to be the President. The Old Man maybe wasn't popular down South, but at least he had some old-time ties to some of the Southern leaders and he knew how to play that kind of a game, you can bet your bottom dollar on that. So that put the ball in his court too, and before long you newspaper boys were writing a lot of stories about how everybody was waiting for the President to point his finger. The way things go, when one or two big columnists printed that, every one of 'em chimed right in like sheep, they always do, and then, by golly, people who hadn't even given it a thought really did begin waiting to see what the President wanted to do. To be perfectly frank, half of what happens in this world probably wouldn't happen at all, in my judgment, if there weren't any damned newspapers. But don't get me wrong, I'm not knocking you boys personally.

"So finally at a news conference one day that winter, a month or so before the first primary, some half-ass reporter gets up and puts it to the Old Man straightaway. Who did he support for the nomination? Why, he says, grinning a little, there was a long list of good party men—and he bore down on that a little—that he thought would make a good president. Well, Senator Anderson was active, was he on that list? And the Old Man just grinned some more and said a lot of people were on it. Well, then, who were some of them? So he toys around with that, mentioning no names anybody believed, and then some smart guy hops up right at the end and says, 'Mister President, is the Vice-President on your list?' "

"That was planted," Morgan said. "I was there, and they had the son-of-a-bitch that asked that in their hip pocket. I can't stand a reporter that plays ball."

"But some do," Matt said, "I grieve to say. Anyway the President answers right off that the Vice-President was not only on it but at the top of

e list, and you can bet that sent the boys running for the phones as hard
 they could go. And of course the Vice-President, they hardly got that on
 e wires before he comes out with the kind of statement they always make
–he wasn't running, he wasn't seeking the nomination, but if the party saw
 to turn to him, why, naturally he'd serve the great American people any
 ay he could with his great experience and dedication and so forth and so
n.

"So right away that made the Vice-President the front-runner, not Hunt
 y more, and right away the Vice-President began going around the coun-
 y acting like a candidate and drumming up some crowds. The President
 uldn't have picked a more popular man, and for a while there I'd be less
 an frank if I didn't tell you that even Hunt was knocked off his pins."

"Popular," Dunn said, "but I never bought the Vice-President for one
 inute, and I doubt if any of the other leaders did. It was obvious to me
 at the President was just holding the fort until he could find his real
 ndidate. Why was the Vice-President popular when you got down to it?
 ecause he'd spent the best part of sixty-nine years being a back-slapper and
 good old boy and going across the street to keep from making anybody
 ad. The old gentleman would rather have climbed a telephone pole to
 uck a fair question than stand on the ground and answer it. It wasn't just
 olitics with him; he was a genuinely kind man, one of the few I ever knew,
 aybe the only one, and he knew the truth was likely to hurt, so he avoided
 . He liked people and he wanted them to like him, and that was how he'd
 ade his way up. But that kind of thing comes to an end somewhere, and
 it isn't sooner it's certainly at the White House. Governor, senator, even
 ce-president, all that was fine. But none of the pros could buy the old
 ntleman for president."

"Well, I can tell you one thing, maybe it looked that way to you," Matt
 id, "maybe *you* didn't think he was much of a candidate, but the way it
 oked to us, he was a humdinger.
"The first poll that came out he was so far ahead, I said to Hunt, that
 st about does it, I guess. And he thought so too, I could tell, but he kept
 sisting that a poll was one thing and a polling booth was another. Which
 true, but he was pretty down, Hunt could never fool me.
"After that news conference, after the Old Man put the Vice-President
 , Hunt got a sense of what they could do, the power they had. It took the
 ge off his self-confidence, and it made him think about the hard road
head, the long way he had to go. Just candidly and not for publication,

I think he might even have chucked the whole thing if his little girl hadn died. After that, he just wanted to keep busy, and so did Kathy. It was hard . . ."

Morgan was thinking in exasperation, No, no, that wasn't it. Which why you didn't and couldn't last with her, why you're not ever going to t a storyteller even if you do remember the facts or anyway most of then You're no good on the vibrations. Because it wasn't just what Zeb Van used to call running fever that had hold of Hunt Anderson. Oh, it had hi by the pecker—he had had the golden touch long enough that all of sudden everything seemed possible, and he was reaching out as far as l thought a man could. But that wasn't all of it.

Kathy, for one thing. Morgan had known, if Matt had not, that she w *with* Hunt at last, the way she'd never really been with him until t hearings, the way she'd never be again after the campaign. She believed i the golden touch too and urged him on—manager, cheerleader, and disc plinarian all in one. She got him all the way off the bottle and on a diet th melted ten or fifteen pounds off his waistline; she hauled him off to churc on Sundays; she threatened him with mayhem if he so much as winked a girl or breathed a four-letter word in an empty room.

"It's still a Puritan country," Kathy liked to say, "even if most peop go to church with a hangover. So control yourself."

"I never knew you had to be a monk to run for president," Hunt on complained, about half in earnest. Morgan thought Hunt was secretly little proud of himself for the sacrifices he was making; it appealed to h romantic sensibility, to his notions of virtue and commitment.

"Some monk." Kathy ran her hand along his jawline.

Morgan could remember thinking that she was not given to many ge tures of affection; the thought of her touch made his stomach constrict

They were having lunch in the Senate Dining Room, and Anderson ha rather ostentatiously recoiled from the low-calorie special diet just place in front of him.

"Danny says if you can take off one more chin he'll be ready to shoot t horseback commercial."

"*Spot,* goddam it. You and O'Connor act like I'm a new dog food."

Kathy had also become an operator in her own fashion. She had had lot to do with the club activities, and she began getting around to speak the kind of women's groups she had previously scorned. She had a flair fc publicity, when she wanted it, and she began appearing regularly on th *Post* and *Star* women's pages, not as the sexy swinger of that first Myrt

ell column but as fashionable hostess, clotheshorse, and do-gooder—even
ace as a French cook (which made Morgan laugh out loud). The little
eorgetown house and the postage-stamp garden were well in the past that
inter, and the Andersons played the big reception-small dinner game from
a imposing brick pile on California Street just off Embassy Row.

"I could have bought up two counties down home for what she paid for
ais carbarn," Hunt told Morgan proudly, as pleased by the house as by his
ew asceticism. And if anyone had studied Kathy's dinner lists closely, they
ould have been seen to be jammed with big para-political names: potential
ontributors, influential editors, columnists and network executives, ex-
abinet members, Washington lobbyists and lawyers, the kind of bank
residents who had made it big and rich from political appointments to the
reasury or the Federal Reserve staff or the Council of Economic Advisers,
ternational affairs buffs from the Wall Street law firms and the better
oundations and institutes, some academic in-and-outers—the types who
ook high-visibility political or government jobs and held them until their
aves-of-absence were strained, then went back to the campus to write a
ook and teach any course they couldn't avoid until they had served enough
me and penance to rate another LOA and could swing another deputy
ssistantship or White House staff slot.

Those were the kind of people who had to be made to take Hunt seriously,
Morgan knew, if he was to get together money and backing for a credible
residential campaign. Kathy stage-managed it nicely; she knew how effec-
ve it was to corral nine or ten of them in Hunt's study, submerge them
a good brandy, strong coffee, Cuban cigar smoke, and leather chairs, then
et Hunt started (usually, she later told Morgan, by planting a question or
topic or a hint of inside information on her dazzled dinner partner, who
ould be sure to follow up later when the men were by themselves and
olemnly discussing Affairs) on the kind of long, astute, genial discourse—
onologue almost—of which he was a master.

It exasperated Morgan that Matt Grant hadn't yet explained that Hunt
as best at close range; Hunt had language, wit, a mobile face, expressive
ands, he was tall and forceful enough to dominate a room—an important
atter in presidential politics; mousy men needn't apply. He was doing his
omework too, and while Morgan had never been included in one of those
noke-blowings, he had heard echoes of them and he could imagine Ander-
on—articulate, informed, frank, sometimes, as befitted a Southerner, con-
ulsing the group with funny yarns, even some raunchy Old Bull stories,
ut always appearing solid, trustworthy, moderate. The public renown of
ne Hinman hearings had been all very well; but it did not necessarily

convey the respectability and reliability the big-time president-watcher demanded. Running against the bosses was all right too—it was even advan tageous if not carried too far—but Hunt already had the reform vote, an these men would have shied from a really hot-eyed idealist, who would b certain to have his head in the clouds.

Morgan knew it must have tried Kathy almost beyond endurance t retreat with the ladies to their crème de menthe frappés, when she woul have wanted to watch the show she had produced; but if she suffere woman's lot not gladly, he never heard her complain of it.

So that's one point you're missing, Matt, Morgan thought, how muc they were in it together. They began to travel together on some of thos early forays after delegates; and wherever she went, local newspapers an TV stations frothed over her clothes, hair styles, skirt lengths, words, advic to the housewife, the lovelorn, and the working girl. It was only luck tha she was at home, rather than with Hunt in New Mexico, the night Kate' fever went up. And there's where you really miss something important wit that simple-minded notion of yours that after that they had to keep bus and not think about Kate.

The morning Morgan had heard what had happened, he had been sittin on a bench in the Macomb Street playground, watching little Richie playin on the swings and wondering what he was going to do about Anne—ju sitting there bundled against the cold and the gray bulging sky and th heavy lump of bitterness and sorrow and puzzlement inside of him. Excep for two or three older boys mishandling a basketball on the windswep court, there was no one else in the park but Richie, and Morgan could hea his tuneless, happy humming as he went up and down in the creaking swin; unaware, secure in his little world, thinking no harm could come, when was all around him, malignant and implicit in every human face. Whateve else might be true, Anne really had no right to take Richie, Morgan tol himself, but then he had no more right to keep him, and possibly not a leg; leg to stand on. He looked up, and Anne was coming down the steps fror the sidewalk in that light, hurried way of hers, with that air of hurt innc cence, and he thought that she must have made up her mind at last, sh was coming to tell him, and he felt his shoulders hunch up around his necl But that wasn't it. Kathy had called; the doctor had not been able to sto the convulsions. Morgan and Anne went over to Richie and hugged hin and then Morgan went to the Andersons' big brick house to see what h could do.

Of course there was nothing. Bobby was with school friends. Morgan sa Kathy only briefly; that time she wasn't thinking about herself, wasn't ju;

glad to have survived. She was as near broken as he would ever see her, but not really, not even then. Even before Hunt got in from New Mexico late that night—there had been no jet flights in those days—everything was being managed, all arrrangements were well under way. Morgan met him at the airport, not by her request but by his own. Hunt snuffled a little in the car on the dark drive to his house, in the cold and the drizzling rain that had finally oozed from the morning's cheerless sky. Morgan said what the hell, a man was entitled to put his head in his hands and cry out loud for his children. But Anderson straightened then and blew his nose vigorously.

"I keep thinking of the two brass buttons on the back of that navy blue sailor coat she wore," he said. "When we bought her the little bike, I didn't believe in training wheels, I thought they kept you from learning, I was a big goddam busybody about it. So I kept putting her up on the bike and she'd ride a little way and fall off, and I'd pick her up and put her back on and she never even whimpered. She kept falling and then she finally got it going, right around the house, and there she sat, straight as a ramrod, pedaling along in that little blue coat, and I can still see those two brass buttons on her straight little back going away from me. Just last week, out at the shopping center, there was one of those merry-go-rounds in the parking lot and she wanted a ride. When we got there, just at that moment there weren't any other children, but she wanted to ride anyway, and I put her on. So she went round and round by herself, with her little back just as straight as always, and there were those two brass buttons going away from me again, and I thought about the bicycle and how I had made her get up and keep riding every time she fell. Christ, I thought she was all right when I left yesterday."

Later, when it was over, they came one evening for drinks—Kathy never made an objection again when Hunt had a couple of Scotches—and Anne was gentle, the way she could be when she wanted to be, and it was pleasant by the fireplace.

Morgan asked Hunt what came next.

"Why, we're going on," Anderson said without hesitation. "It won't be as much fun, but it would be worse than ever to lose now or give up."

That was a puzzle since, at age six, Kate had scarcely known or understood what her father was up to, much less expected anything but warmth and protection from him. But then Kathy said, "Life seems empty enough now," and Morgan had understood.

So you can say they just needed to keep busy and not think about Kate, if you want to, Matt, but that wasn't what they meant. They meant having lost one child, one part of themselves, they couldn't stand to lose another.

    With his facility for hearing conversation without really listening, Morgan knew Matt Grant was still talking . . .

    ". . . but after the child died, we had to gear up the staff because there wasn't any further doubt about it, Hunt was going in the first primary, Vice-President or no Vice-President, come hell or high water, and actually, just here in this room, I suppose there probably were some sympathy votes in it although Hunt never said a public word about Kate or played it up in any way. What he did do at about that time—maybe you remember, Dunn—he went to see the President and laid his cards on that table. Then he came back to the office madder than hell. What had happened was, first Hunt assured the President that if *he* could have run again Hunt wouldn't have dreamed of challenging him. He tried to explain that what had happened to Hinman was Hinman's own doing, not Hunt's. And he said he was a good party man, always had been a good party man, had proved it in the congressional elections the year before, and that all he wanted was a fair shot, the same as any other candidate—not to be shut out in advance.

    "But that Old Man was hard as nails—you know that, Dunn. He sat there stone-faced, hardly even speaking, and when it got down to the nut-cutting, he took off his glasses, blew on each lens, polished them with his handkerchief, put the glasses back on—all that was engraved on Hunt's mind, and after Hunt told me about it, it was on mine—and said, 'When a man acts like a billygoat, he's got to expect some folks'll think he smells like one. I've already made my commitments.'

    " 'To the Vice-President?'

    " 'To the party. You want some advice, Senator?'

    " 'From you, Mister President, I sure do.'

    " 'Play up that bossism bullshit. It always reads good and it's the only shot you've got.'

    " 'Just so you know it's nothing personal, Mister President.'

    " 'With me either. But with some of my people in the Senate and the party, it's a different story. You know that. And you know I got to stick with my people.'

    " 'All right,' Hunt said. 'I understand.'

    "But he was spitting mad. He went right out and told the reporters the President had 'other commitments' but he would make up his own mind and not let the party bosses stop him from running if he thought the people wanted him. Off the record, of course, he never had any intention of not

running, not even if the President had asked him not to. So he went on and
announced pretty soon after that, and then it was February and there he
was—just over three years in the Senate of the United States and just
forty-three years old, running in a presidential primary against the Vice-
President of the United States, who'd been in politics about a half-century
and had shaken more voters' hands in all those years than there were people
in most countries. But that was the kind of windmill Hunt Anderson
thought in those days he was born to charge. And I'll tell you one thing,
it was right about there that Danny O'Connor and his TV spots turned out
to be money in the bank.

"There were two series that we used up there. One we called 'Strong
Silent Man.' They were Danny's favorite kind of stuff, without sound of any
kind, half-minute or sixty seconds. Remember that long shot of Hunt
coming up the Capitol steps toward the camera with the Supreme Court
building in the background? He kept getting bigger and bigger and finally
it was just that honest-looking face of his right in the camera and right then
Danny froze it and the slogan came up—'On the People's Business.' And
then Hunt's name and that was all. Another one showed him in a crowd
shaking hands, head and shoulders over everybody, still no sound, and all
the people trying to grab his hand, with Hunt smiling. All it said was 'Let
the People Decide.'

"And the best one, I thought, had the slogan 'His Own Man'—it showed
Hunt getting up from his desk and walking alone down one of those long
corridors in the Senate Office Building, and then on the old Toonerville
Trolley, still alone, and finally walking into the old migrant hearing room
and picking up the gavel and banging it down once, like he was splitting
a rail. The emphasis was all on strength and independence—character, you
see, and just in all candor, if Danny had known a damn thing about politics,
if he'd been what they call a pro, he probably wouldn't have fallen back on
anything that simple and that effective. Not that I've got anything against
the pros, Dunn.

"The other batch of spots was more on issues but they were original too.
When Hunt had gone up there a couple of months before the primary
campaign broke out, Danny went along with a cameraman and a sound
technician, and Hunt got some students and professors in a conference
room somewhere and let them go at him for all one afternoon. And there
were Danny and his people, getting every bit of it on film and tape. Then
Danny edited the parts he wanted into spots of Hunt talking informally
about anything under the sun they'd asked him. And he got lots of the kids
in the film, which put the emphasis on youth because by then they knew

the Vice-President was running, and he was older than God and looked it. And I'm here to tell you that Hunt Anderson may have had his faults, and I've got good reason to know most of them, but nobody ever was better than he was in that kind of setting, a small room and a few people and no holds barred.

"Back then, nobody had ever seen that kind of political TV, certainly not the Vice-President. So I'll tell you one thing, those spots hit that state like a whirlwind. Danny just might have been right, that Hunt didn't even need to go up there at all. But nobody had campaigned in that particular primary in years, and the Vice-President had already made a big speech saying that the dignity of his office would not permit him to "barnstorm." Joe Bingham was busy down South. So Hunt saw another chance in that.

"Two weeks to the day before the primary, he appeared one morning on a street corner and started shaking hands. That afternoon he was in another town, and the next day two more—and the state papers were blanketed with stories about the presidential candidate who'd personally come up to that backwater state, saying he was looking for help. And the *next* day, the papers carried his delegate slate, and it was just a plain damn shocker. One of the opposition papers said they must have been just folks he met shaking hands, and hardly anybody outside their home towns had ever heard of any of them; and that made a hell of a point when you lined up all those unknown names beside the Vice-President's slate, which had every big name you could think of in state politics, from the governor and two senators and a couple of congressmen right on down through the highway commissioners and some county sheriffs."

"You know damn well where he got those people," Dunn said, "and it wasn't on the street corners shaking hands. He got them where he got his people everywhere he went. They were the ones who'd been trying to get into politics, who wanted to try new things and shake up the state, or who just wanted to push the old crowd out and take over themselves. They scared the organizaton to death, so it shut them out. And so they were sitting there waiting for someone to come along and lead them, and Anderson did. I wasn't there but I know, because that's what he did everywhere he went."

"That's exactly what happened in our state later on," French said, holding out an empty glass to Matt Grant.

"Hell, he started out that way in his own state," Morgan said.

"Of course," Dunn said, shaking his head when Matt tried to take his glass too, "most of those people who cracked the old organizations back then, if they did now, they are the organization. I could point you out a lot of regular party people in this country today, including some you wouldn't trust with the tax receipts, that got their foot in the door going against the bosses with Hunt Anderson."

"I could too, but you won't find many of them who'll admit it," Matt said, reaching for Morgan's glass. "Anyway, Hunt's being up there in the flesh and having that slate of unknown delegates—you can see he hardly even had to state the case that he was the people's choice running against the bosses. So there he was, all over the streets and in the headlines, and the last week he brought in Kathy. She started working the women's clubs and the church circles and the department stores. But not taking anything at all away from Hunt and Kathy, what I still think was really the clincher was all those TV spots Danny had running practically all the time. A blizzard came up four days before that primary, and it didn't hit that state half as hard as that TV blitz and the Anderson campaign. Hell, they were prepared for snow! . . ."

Taking his second drink from Matt's hand with nostalgia, as if for youth, as if for a time of hope and even belief, Morgan was remembering for himself: More nearly a circus than a campaign because nobody knew the route from one place to the next and so the schedules were usually off, and even when they weren't, Hunt couldn't keep to them—one more hand to shake, one more burly old bastard in a red-checked shirt to be assured that the Communists had to be stopped, by God. Like as not no driver, or not enough drivers if there was a caravan, so some pimpled teenager would have to be pressed into service to take the car careening over the frost heaves and ice patches to another quiet white town or another grim block of houses clustered around the edges of a decrepit red-brick mill. Sometimes the old mill stood there idle, useless, and the old people sat by their fires, useless too.

Or to a civic club luncheon in a larger town, and Hunt invariably late; or maybe an evening rally in some overheated school gym or town hockey rink, Kathy getting the biggest hand, sometimes because she was the only speaker, since Hunt might be held up twenty miles away by an impromptu street-corner debate or a snap decision to drop in on a church supper.

Never reluctant to break in on some flustered backwater disk jockey to "say hello to your listeners out there in this great state," or to put his big feet on some country editor's littered desk for five minutes' easy talk about the old virtues. Never failed to ask audiences if anyone had seen the Vice-President, which would usually get a laugh, whereupon he would say in mock amazement, "You mean the Vice-President hasn't been to South

Waterford?" or Grove Corners, or whatever flattered village he happened to be working.

In one grimy neighborhood of a withering old industrial town, warned by some tomato-faced priest in shiny serge that the prospective audience for the night would be playing Bingo instead, the candidate pulled out his wallet, bought up the evening's cards, and told the priest to round up his flock for the speakin'. And going down the production line in the antiseptic new electronics plant off the superhighway just thrown across the state he posed in coveralls—it was strictly for the photographers—at the controls of a baffling array of dials, needles, and flickering lights; but making his way through a dark, barnlike home for the aged, peopled with wisps and ghosts and frail, forgotten old particles of life, the tears in his eyes were not available to the camera.

"Because back then," Matt was saying, "it was just too much for the press boys to believe that a practically unknown senator could even come close to knocking off a big wheel like the Vice-President, who had the whole party with him. Of course, somebody around that smart old bastard in the White House—maybe he was the one himself—finally got the wind up. And as if he felt something coming and was trying to guard against it in advance, at his last news conference before the primary the President tossed off one of those remarks of his that everybody always remembers. 'Primaries,' he said, 'are bunk.'

"Up there in the snow, the next morning, somebody read that out of the papers to Hunt. 'That means we're in,' he says, but those smart-ass reporters still didn't believe it. They never do.

"Actually, the first thing any of the experts saw that made them think something was up was the turnout on primary day. There was snow ass-deep most places, but you should have seen those lines in front of the polling places. I remember a couple of the press boys came to see me and asked what I thought it meant, and I told them it meant they had egg on their face and it looked good on them. They wouldn't admit it even that late. And Danny O'Connor was sitting there with me while I talked to them, and Kathy too—Hunt was somewhere still shaking hands, he never stopped working that state till the last polling booth was closed—and when the boys left, still looking puzzled, I remember Danny made this kind of a gesture like sweeping trash out of the room. 'Those guys,' he says, 'they're out of business because of my spots and they don't even know it yet.'

"And Kathy went over and hugged him. 'You big old mackerel-snapper,' she says, 'can we do it? Are we really in?'

"And naturally, Danny being Danny, he grabs a little ass while he can, but fortunately I'm standing there too, and damn if Danny didn't put his other arm around my shoulders and pull me into the huddle and give us both a big Irish bearhug. 'Sweethearts,' he says, 'are there lots of broads in the White House?'"

Morgan's relentless memory prodding him again: That was the night coming back through the white stillness of the countryside, birch stalks gleaming in the moonlight, old farmhouses and attached barns stretching back from the roadside, through the woods maybe the bare expanse of a pond, frozen, snow-covered, stark as death. The campaign over, the polls closed at last, Hunt on the way back to his hotel headquarters miles to the east, behind him the last long walk along some dim winter evening street, shaking hands.

They were being driven by a young lawyer who had helped run the campaign; beside him was the only other reporter who had covered Hunt's final trip, a taciturn local who had forgotten more about that state than Hunt and Morgan would ever know.

"Have I got it won?" Hunt asked him.

"Ay-yuh."

"If it's close, can they steal it?"

"Won't be close."

"Well, for god's sake, why didn't you write that, Ab?" The lawyer showed his exasperation, and his youth.

"Paper's out against your man."

Morgan laughed. "Hell of a way to run a newspaper."

Hunt was slumped far down in the seat, a gangling form beside Morgan in the darkness. "I don't think it's close either. But if it was, they'd steal it."

"Ay-yuh."

Morgan thought of all the Abs in his trade, or anybody's, obscure, wasted, plodding on.

"Well, they can't stop you now." The young lawyer looked momentarily over his shoulder. "Senator Anderson, I'd like to stick with your campaign all the way. Can you use me? I don't care how minor a job. I've got some savings, I don't ask to be paid."

"Sure, I'll tell Matt Grant to sign you on. I need all the help I can get, and many thanks." The ungainly form moved, a slow, tired heave. Morgan could barely hear his voice. "But don't you believe they can't stop me. There's a long way to go." And after a while, "A long way to go."

And while the young lawyer was parking the car, Ab off to his office, Hunt and Morgan creaking up a rear service elevator smelling of fish toward the sounds of celebration already audible from Anderson's headquarters suite, Hunt said suddenly, "It's not as much fun as it was. It's all too complicated. All the money it takes. So many people getting involved, like that young fellow using up his savings."

"And in the end," Morgan said, "he'll want something from you."

Hunt stared at him, weak eyes more tired than usual. The elevator jerked to a stop. He took his glasses off and rubbed his eyes with his knuckles. "It'd be better," he said, as the doors began to open on the victory, "if a man could just depend on himself alone."

"'Scuse me, Mister Grant," Jodie said from the doorway of Anderson's room, "Miz Anderson like for you to come up a few minutes if you don't mind."

"Tell her Dunn's here," Morgan said, rubbing it in.

"She knows that." The green lenses turned with maddening deliberation toward Morgan, then away, as Matt Grant hurried out of the room.

"But what I don't understand," Glass said as he looked at the pictures on the wall, "is why if Anderson was all that good they didn't hold their noses and accept him just in their own interest of having a winner."

"Because they couldn't be sure," Dunn said. "In the first place, political leaders are good haters, and Anderson threatened them all when he ruined Hinman. So they had it in for him. But even if they could have swallowed that, they thought they couldn't afford to let an upstart knock their heads together. They thought they had to demonstrate who cracked the whip or they might not be able to hold their own people in line.

"But the worst problem was they weren't sure about Anderson. They didn't know him. He was a maverick type; he didn't come to them for help. They couldn't be sure what he would do or how he would do it or who with. Politicians want to know where they stand, and with Anderson they couldn't be sure. When he began to look like a vote-getter, that just scared them more. Including me."

"Then you must have been mighty scared after that first primary," Charlie French said, "because I remember Hunt Anderson looked like a vote-getter then, if anybody ever did. Our state held the next primary, you know, and when Anderson made his next swing through, he really had some momentum going for him.

"At that time I was just a young local, of course, not a big-timer like Rich here, but I was trying to break into the big political stories and I'd have given an arm to get the Anderson assignment. I worked like hell on it, read up all the background, but we had this ass-kisser the managing editor thought was the hottest thing since Walter Winchell, and naturally he got the assignment. But I was used to that, even then. I only got to do one real story about Anderson because teacher's pet had a cold one day and they sent me out in his place. But it turned out to be big.

"You see, after the big upset in that first primary, the way I remember it, the other guys switched tactics. The President had called the shot when he said 'primaries are bunk,' and that was their line from then on. Of course they never let the Vice-President go up against Hunt Anderson or anybody else, not in our primary or any of the others, and they kept insisting that primaries didn't necessarily mean anything, didn't prove anything, wouldn't matter at the convention, where the party would make a real democratic national choice that everybody could agree on. But they kept doing their damnedest to beat Anderson anywhere he ran.

"In our state they put up the Governor as a stand-in candidate, and of course he had the whole state organization behind him and anybody he wanted from Washington. A regular parade of bigwigs coming in. But Anderson started right off the same as he did in the first primary, with a delegate slate of unknowns, a blast at the bosses, and lots of TV. But I'm probably boring you experts."

"Not me," Morgan said. "That was the one primary I didn't spend much time on." Because, he thought, with unabated bitterness, right about that time that son-of-a-bitch was fucking up everything, including Anne, but I'm not going to start brooding about all that again.

"Everybody always thought they'd promised the Governor second place on the ticket," French said, "if he could win as a favorite son and knock Anderson off then and there. The Governor knew the state better than Anderson, but on the other hand the state knew him too, and the voters hadn't exactly been thinking of him as presidential timber. So I guess it started off about even-steven.

"The way that particular governor figured things the guy who won elections was the guy who hit the hardest in the most exposed places, so he waded right in on Anderson. First he pulled out the carpetbag issue— what the hell right did somebody have to come in from outside and run against a state's favorite son? But Anderson just kept talking about bossism and shaking hands and showing those TV spots. He'd had all that publicity as the man who had beaten Hinman one way and the Vice-President another, and a lot of people by then actually thought that Hunt Anderson was maybe going to be president, although frankly, as for me, I never believed things go that well. And you have to remember that in our state people are usually against the ins, and for damn good reason. Besides, the Vice-President hadn't looked so hot in that first primary and nobody took a cornpone like Bingham seriously. The only other guy anybody thought about in those days was old Stark, and he didn't enter our primary."

"Or any other," Dunn said, "because he only had one chance and he knew it. Stark had that big liberal name and a lot of due bills, and the minute he let people know he was available he picked up a lot of Hinman's old liberal support—people who didn't necessarily follow the President's lead and were too hot about the issues to back the Vice-President. Some of them probably wouldn't even have been against Anderson if he hadn't been the one to shoot down Hinman. So Stark could have some strength on the floor all right, but he was a stick of wood with that long Brahmin face and that Yankee accent, and if he'd ever wandered into a primary against Hunt Anderson he'd have been clobbered. The one chance Stark had was to wheel and deal at the convention and hope the President would swing behind him. Or that he could make a deal for Number Two."

"It's all pretty dim in my memory," French said, "except what happened in our state. It must have been confusing as hell for Anderson at the time, I mean trying to run in so many states all at once. They don't come one after the other in orderly fashion. And the way I recall it, in one state they'd have a write-in going against him for some congressman who wasn't even a candidate. And somewhere else they'd put up just the delegate slate against him with a lot of big names but nobody on top of the ticket. Of course Stark and the Vice-President could always say they weren't running, because neither of them ever announced formally until after the primaries. The only guy who could lose a damn thing in one of those brawls was Hunt Anderson, because he was the only one who couldn't duck any challenge. He had to run everywhere and keep winning.

"Anyway, while Anderson was out of the state, campaigning somewhere else, this big-ass governor of ours got loose and made this crazy speech. Says he's going to play Twenty Questons with the carpetbag candidate, pulls this sheet of paper out of his pocket, and roars out the twenty questions like the announcer at a heavyweight bout, which was just about his speed. I don't remember them all but you don't have to guess hard; the first one was something like, 'Why should the people of this great state think that your youth and inexperience qualify you to be president?' Then they got worse. I remember one was, 'Will you use the same McCarthyite tactics in this campaign as you did in smearing Governor Hinman?' And 'In view of your attacks on party leaders, can we expect you to remain loyal to the party if nominated?' And when he'd read off twenty questions like those, the Governor stuck out his belly and brayed into the mikes, 'Now if the carpetbag candidate dares to come back to this state, I want the answers to all those questions and I want them straight!'

"Well, it happened that the one day the office sent me out on the Anderson story was the first day Anderson came back to the state. There was a big crowd of press and supporters at the airport. TV cameras all over the place. One of the Catholic school bands was playing—you see, the public schools were so afraid of the Governor that Anderson's advance man couldn't even rent one of their bands. There were these rumors that the state police were going to make it hard for the Anderson motorcade to get around, and I knew for a fact that the Governor had passed the word around to the state employees that if anybody turned up missing from work while Anderson was in the state he'd better have an ironclad excuse.

"So there were some who were saying that Anderson might as well write that state off and get on to some other primary—including some of his own local backers, I just happen to know—but that morning at the airport I knew the minute he came out of the plane to the top of the ramp that he wasn't going to do it. Because he stood there waving with one of those long arms of his, and in the other hand he was holding up the biggest, gaudiest carpetbag you ever saw."

"That's when it got to be his campaign trademark," Morgan said.

French drained his glass. "Of course you were there too, I guess."

"No," Morgan said, "not that time, I had some personal business to tend to." Personal as hell, sitting home four days in a row waiting for the phone to ring or mail to come or the door to open or a time bomb to go off or something, anything, to happen—just sitting there with the badly typed capital letters of the note burned like a cattle brand in my eyes, my brain. RICH—IVE GOT TO FIND OUT SOMETHING. DONT EXPLODE WILL CALL SOON OR GET IN TOUCH. ITS MY LIFE I THINK. ANNE.

"Well, of course," French was saying, "the crowd really loved that carpetbag. Anderson got a lot of TV out of it too. They put him on a little stand the advance men had provided and introduced him, and a lot of housewives were going through the crowd, passing out buttons shaped and colored like Anderson's carpetbag—no slogan, just the button. And then it got quiet, and Anderson stood there a minute, holding the carpetbag.

" 'Well, folks,' he said at last, as if it had finally come to him what he ought to say, 'we're glad to find so many of you don't mind our coming back to your great state.' And they all cheered that, because people in this country will always cheer something they feel a part of, like their high school or college, even if it's something as big and shapeless as a state. Maybe there's so few things you *can* feel a part of.

" 'We've been surprised to learn,' Anderson went on, 'that apparently your governor thinks your state is some kind of an exclusive club, like the one he belongs to over on top of the Midtown National Bank building.'

"Somebody had done some good research for him, you see. The Governor's membership in a no-Jews, fat-cat luncheon club had become public knowledge since his election, but no one had had a chance to use it against him in a campaign.

" 'Or maybe he thinks now that you've put him in public office that that gives him some kind of right that everyday people like you and me don't have—some kind of right to say who can and who can't come here and talk about the people's business.' He put the carpetbag on the rail in front of him, and the boobs were shouting, 'No, No!' and yelling and whistling and jumping up and down like idiots.

" 'But you don't believe he's got any such right and we don't believe it.' More stomping and whistling. 'That's what this campaign's all about, here and in every state. The Governor isn't a real favorite son, he knows it, you know it, we know it. He's a sort of department-store dummy standing there in place of the Vice-President, and the White House pulls the strings on both of them.' I remember that line almost exactly. 'Well, we're just not going to let these self-appointed bosses and leaders dictate to us who we can vote for.'

"He'd been fumbling with the carpetbag, and while the morons yelled some more he finally got it open and pulled one sheet of paper out and held it up over his head. 'Now, folks, we've been handed a list of questions . . . twenty questions.' Lots of hooting and jeers and laughing. 'We've been studying them on the flight out here, and it appears to us that what they all say, one way or another, is "Senator Anderson, have you stopped beating your wife?" '

"And when they'd stopped laughing like that was really funny, he waved the paper at them again. 'Well, there's only one way we can answer that question, folks . . . *here's* my wife . . . Kathy, come on up here.' And she came running up the steps behind him to stand beside him, holding some roses and waving, and if they'd been cheering up to that point, they really just erupted then. She was the kind of looking girl in those days that right away everybody in that audience knew it probably wasn't beatings Anderson gave her, not with the legs on her and the way she was built. So for a long time the two of them just stood there waving, with the crowd roaring. I looked around at the cameras, and sure enough the little red eyes were burning away. And I'm thinking the Governor must be getting himself an eyeful.

" 'Your governor said he wanted straight answers,' Anderson finally went on when the boobs got quiet. 'Now even if Kathy here is the best answer we can give anybody, still the Governor seems to want us to play by *his* rules, the way he wants to lay down *his* rules about what you folks can do and what you can't. Well, we've thought it all over and we've decided that if he wants straight answers, we're going up to the Capitol right now and give him some!' And of course that had them screaming like nitwits, which crowd types practically always are, and they went off even louder when he managed to make them hear that he was inviting them all to come along to see the Governor."

"Now I never heard that story before, but that was absolutely characteristic Anderson politics," Dunn said. "One thing he taught us all was to confront problems head on instead of bobbing and weaving. Or at least appear to. With television, what comes through strongest is the impression you make, not what you actually do or say, and Anderson was the first big-time candidate to catch on to that."

"Well, he never got to face up to the Governor that day," French said, "but it wasn't for lack of trying. It took them some time to get organized —the advance man was the local Episcopal rector, and hopeless. By the time they got the motorcade moving they'd lost a lot of the crowd, and sure enough there was no police escort and they had to stop for red lights and creep along through traffic. After that, incidentally, any time Anderson was in our state, he'd announce that he wouldn't take a police escort and he'd make a big thing of how he wasn't going to hold everybody else up in traffic just so he could get around. Of course that made the Governor look sillier than usual when he'd drive someplace with a dozen motorcycles howling out front.

"But that particular day it took Anderson a good hour to get to the Capitol, and when he got there only a dozen or so cars and a busload of press and cameramen and campaign workers were still following. Even so, there were maybe a hundred people all told, and when Anderson led those troops up the long steps to the Capitol portico—the delay had given the TV plenty of time to set up at the top—the half-dozen fat cops out there weren't able to do a thing. You can guess the kind of cops they were—unemployed cousins or brothers-in-law of somebody important who'd cadged them a spot on the state payroll. One of them waved his stick at Anderson's advance man for about thirty seconds, and then the whole crowd just moved right on past and through the rotunda, and the tourists either cleared out of the way or joined up to see the action.

"We went thundering down the corridor toward the Governor's office with the cameramen scrambling to keep in front and the writing press shouting questions at Anderson and everybody in the rear shoving up behind the people in front. It was a good-natured crowd, but I don't mind saying it was a little scary. That kind of thing can turn ugly in a flash, and I kept thinking somebody was going to get trampled. Of course today we've all been through that kind of crunch and worse a hundred times. I don't understand what's happened to make people march and demonstrate so much. I'm just a reporter instead of an analyst like Morgan and some of the others, but it was my one day with Hunt Anderson that I got my first taste of it.

"Anderson was up front, so tall you could see his head over everybody else. When we got near the door of the Governor's suite he took a long jump forward, got a yard or so out in front of the mob, turned and held up his arms and shouted something, I never was sure what it was, maybe just "hold up a minute!" or something to that effect. Whatever it was, mostly those long arms going up, it seemed to have an instant effect. Everybody came to a stop and got quiet. So don't let anybody tell you Hunt Anderson didn't have magnetism.

" 'Let's keep it down,' he said, 'let's let everybody hear and nobody get shoved.' And for the next few minutes you'd have thought you were in church. A couple of TV cameramen with those big monsters on their shoulders got through the door first with their sound men, and then Hunt and the advance man followed them into the Governor's suite, and some of the writing press got in too. I was just outside the door when some wire-service son-of-a-bitch shoved his fat ass in ahead of me even though I'd been in front of him all the way down the corridor. But I could hear every word even if I couldn't see anything. 'Like to see the Governor,' I heard Anderson say.

"There was this growl. Anybody who'd been around our state knew right away it came from Cappy Webb, so-called the Governor's AA but in fact his brains, to the extent he had any. Cappy was handling maybe his third or fourth governor by then, and there were reports he had warned Washington before the primary that this particular number wasn't exactly a racehorse; and one night after the Capitol correspondents' dinner, which natually is always a monumental drunk, Cappy had a load on and I heard him say myself the Governor was too dumb to sell ass on a troopship. But Cappy wasn't a fool or a coward, maybe not even personally much of a crook, and any reporter who ever worked with him will tell you he never lied to you without tipping you off that he was lying, so you wouldn't crawl out on a imb just on his sayso.

" 'Not here?' I heard Anderson say. 'Then we'll wait.'

"This time I made out Cappy's growl. 'Gone for the day.'

" 'But right here in the paper,' Anderson said, 'his schedule shows lots of appointments right in this office we're standing in.'

" 'Schedules change.' Cappy was not a man to be intimidated by mere acts.

" 'We'll wait anyway,' Anderson said. 'Where is he?'

"Cappy cleared his throat with the sound of a bulldozer. 'At the university. Regents' meeting.' The university was two hours' drive to the south, and the governor had never been known to attend a regents' meeting unless here was a football game the same day.

" 'That's not on this schedule in the paper.' Hunt's voice had risen a little, and the crowd behind me was beginning to buzz with the news that the Governor had gone out the back door. 'Don't you fellows know what you're doing around here?'

" 'We're flexible,' Cappy growled. 'We don't get ourselves all locked up ight like some people, Senator.'

" 'Flexible enough to send the Governor to the other end of the state when he sees on television that we're coming to give him those straight answers he wanted in person?'

" 'Senator,' Cappy growled, unruffled, 'you don't maybe have any idea ow flexible we can be around here.'

"Later Cappy told one of our Capitol reporters that he was thick with, hat if he'd had his way the whole Twenty Questions bit never would have come up. But after it did, no matter how bad it made the governor look to ug out, Cappy said sending him down the fire escape was better than facing im up to Hunt Anderson in a television confrontation. 'Anderson would ave bounced the slob off the walls,' Cappy told our man, and he'd made ure it couldn't happen.

"So there was a surge back out into the corridor, and I managed to get a good hard elbow into the ribs of that fat-ass wire-service prick. Then Anderson's tall figure blocked the doorway. 'Folks,' he said in that relaxed voice of his, which still could be heard down the narrow Capitol hallway, 'looks like we've got to play Twenty Questions all by ourselves.' That about brought the house down and the yelling almost deafened me. But he held his arm up and got them quiet again. 'So if you'll all go on outside and gather round, we'll let the good folks that work here get back to their jobs, and we'll let the TV people come out there with us and play the game by *our* rules.'

"Well, you can see what a story that was for me, that one day I was on it. I led the paper for once, and actually Cappy may have been right, but I still think that day was the reason Anderson won our primary going away. Everybody in the state saw him on the TV news that night, answering the Governor's questions on the Capitol steps, without a sign of the Governor anywhere in that vicinity. And from then on, every appearance he made in our state, every time he stood up in front of a crowd, Anderson put an empty chair right beside him. And then he'd open up the carpetbag and take out the Twenty Questions and invite the Governor to come up, have a seat, and 'get your answers straight as your bourbon.'

"But of course the Governor never showed. Cappy had decided to play it the other way, and Anderson would always say, 'I guess he's too flexible to come.' And I don't know what you experts think, you're the ones that know, but I call that hard stuff to beat."

"Damn right," Morgan said. "What happened to the ass-kisser that missed a story like that, Charlie?"

"He's managing editor now."

"The way you guys tell it," Glass said, "I'm getting the idea this Anderson was the greatest thing since the wheel."

Which is exactly what lots of people were beginning to think about then, Morgan thought, brooding, the past to him as alive in the room as Glass restless under the pictures. Except that it was clear, if you looked closely enough, that step by step Anderson was burning his bridges behind him and separating himself that much more from the party and the leaders. First Hinman; then the Vice-President; then that hack governor; and all the while that constant attack on the "bosses."

Even in hindsight, Morgan did not consider that Anderson had had any real alternative, but his campaign had cost him dearly; it had meant that in the long run Anderson was relying wholly on popular support and putting himself completely in opposition to the interests and institutions and personalities that order and manage the customary politics of democracy. And Morgan had known even then that nothing scared those interests and institutions and personalities as much as the notion that ordinary, run-of-the-mill people were about to run away with things. But that was what they'd have been doing if Anderson had won; or so it must have seemed. So the fight had grown rougher every day.

It had taken its toll, too, even on Hunt Anderson. When Morgan had finally got out of Washington again that spring and joined Anderson down South, he could see lines of fatigue around the corners of Anderson's mouth and eyes, which looked weaker, more tired, than ever; he fancied there was more gray at Anderson's temples, a more pronounced stoop to his tall figure.

"What the hell are you doing in this god-forsaken swamp?" Morgan said, trying to sound cheerful. "You couldn't beat Joe Bingham down here with a bullwhip. God himself couldn't beat Bingham down here."

Anderson chuckled, without much amusement—which he had started to do more and more as the campaign wore on. They were riding together—sometimes, looking back, it seemed to Morgan as if in that campaign he had spent more time with Hunt Anderson in the back seats of automobiles than anywhere else—after a morning of touring the hot streets of some stark, packshed town where the people on the sidewalks looked at Hunt's outstretched hand with glum suspicion, toward a Rotary Club luncheon in another town that would not be much different, certainly no friendlier.

"I'm not trying to win," Anderson said. "It won't cost me much to lose to Joe Bingham in his backyard, everybody expects me to do that; but if I'm running against the bosses and the interests, and playing for the black vote, I've got to run everywhere and take them all on, the South in particular. Everybody's white knight, that's Old Bull's boy this year."

"Listen," Morgan said, "they're going to whip your migrant education bill while you're white-knighting around this sink-hole."

Anderson took his glasses off and rubbed his tired eyes. "I'll be there for the debate. We're not beaten yet."

"It's more than the debate and the vote. You need to be there now. Matt's good but Matt's not you. Matt can't get the vote together by himself."

"It isn't," Anderson said carefully, "as if I were off in the Caribbean getting a suntan. Running for president is important, it used to say in my civics book."

"But do you have to shake every redneck's hand in the whole country?"

The car sped along the humped two-lane blacktop. In the flat meadows stretching beyond the barbed wire on either side, mangy cattle cropped at thin grass.

"We set up a migrant health service last year. We put a code of conduct on the crew leaders and got some Social Security adjustments. I put in a lot of time on those bills, Rich."

"Which is what you need to do on the education aid."

"Don't you think I know it?" Anderson's voice cracked with anger; but Morgan knew it was not directed at him. "I can't be everywhere at once. Besides, a president might be able to do more for migrants than a senator. I tried to explain that to Adam before he quit, but he wouldn't listen either."

"I don't mean to needle you."

"Every right." Anderson rubbed his eyes again. "You know, I did get to wondering the other day where the issues went to in this campaign."

"Bossism is an issue."

"That's what the President said. He sounded delighted I'd raised it. The only shot I've got, he said. But doesn't it seem to you there ought to be something more than that in all this agony and play-acting and rat-racing? I mean the shape the world's in, the real problems in this country, I'd like to talk about some of those things—I even think I could maybe do something about some of them if I were president—but it always ends up I'm talking bullshit about how I'm for the people and not for the bosses. I'm actually beginning to feel like one of O'Connor's goddam spots. It's getting so sometimes I don't recognize myself, much less what I set out to do."

"What you need is a rest, that's all."

"Well, I can't rest. There's not enough days left for all I need to do."

"You're doing all right so far. It'll look a lot better to you the first time you take a weekend off and get some sleep." Morgan had known better, but he saw that Anderson needed cheering.

Or maybe, he thought, listening to Glass's professional voice, watching the waiters outside on the lawn, maybe I was being a professional, and just wanted to keep him talking. A professional could never be sure about things like that, because the essence of professionalism was to do your work well without having to think about it.

"Don't kid yourself." Anderson had slumped lower in the seat; he propped a long leg over the back of the front seat. "I have to keep stirring up my people all the time. They think we've got it made because we've won a few worthless primaries. I just look good right now because the other side hasn't got a horse, and you can't beat a horse with no horse, like Zeb Vance used to say. They can't take Bingham. Stark is a certified ass. They're just

ropping up the Vice-President until they can produce somebody halfway
ecent. Like Aiken."

"Aiken's all right," Morgan said. "A pretty good governor as they go,
ut nobody wets their pants when he stands up."

"But in the end he'll be their man—you watch. When you consider all
he other guys, Aiken's by far the best they could do, the toughest for me
o take. Listen, some of the bastards even tried to resurrect Hinman, did
ou know that?"

"I heard the President helped to shoot that down himself."

"But not until the civil rights leaders went up in smoke. Anyway the polls
howed Hinman was running behind Undecided. They were actually willing
o consider that bastard—anybody but me—until they saw he was dead and
one."

"Aiken is hardly even known outside his state. If he's really the best they
an do, you've got a better shot than I thought."

Hunt chuckled again, in the same dry, mirthless way. "Thanks for the
ompliment. How's Anne?"

"Fine, I guess."

He sighed. "With a fine piece like that around the house, you're chasing
ne around the country. Something's wrong with your priorities, Rich."

"That's not exactly an ogre in *your* house."

"But Kathy's never home. My God, I don't even know where she is
oday, not even what state she's in. She's running harder than I am."

"And neither of you has to do it, not like the poor old reporters that have
o trot along behind you."

Some of Anderson's depression had rubbed off on Morgan. Not that I
eeded much influence to be depressed in those days, Morgan thought,
ipping vodka. Anderson's reference to Anne had startled him, that day,
ntil he realized Hunt had been away so much and so busy he couldn't have
ad an inkling of what had happened. But then, few people did. Anne so
esolutely lived at the side of, rather than as a part of, Morgan's professional
ife that most of his colleagues in the Washington press and political world
new little more of her, then or later, than what she looked like and a few
dle conversations.

Anderson had not pursued the subject. "You know that guy from the first
rimary? The one we were riding with that asked to join up? You said
ooner or later he'd want something?"

"I'll bet I was right too." The car was slowing carefully for the outskirts
f the town where Hunt was to speak. Its old frame houses and baked streets

looked harsh and unforgiving of those who had managed to live elsewhere

"Well, I don't know about him, I mean specifically—there're so many like him now in so many states I lose track. But I've thought a lot about what you said." His eyes were closed, as if he did not really want to see another town. "It's true, isn't it? Everybody wants something. That's what it's always been about, in Old Bull's time and now."

"And ever shall be," Morgan said. He was still thinking about Anne. There had been a time when he was always thinking about Anne, reaching for her. If I had ever known what she wanted, he thought, maybe I could have found some way to give it to her. But that presupposed that what Anne wanted was finite, describable, even to her; when in fact, the day she had come back, she had answered his agonized question with cruelly casual generality.

"Why, Anne? What were you looking for?"

"For something to happen," she said. "But nothing did."

And Morgan could see precisely what that meant in her finely boned face, in her hard, distant eyes. She had wanted something to happen that had never happened with him, and she believed it never would.

"Everywhere I go," Anderson said, "everybody I talk to, it all comes down to what they want. Textiles wants quotas and oil wants offshore wells and cotton wants bigger loans and cattle wants no controls. The Negroes want jobs and the whites want their own schools and neighborhoods. Steel wants higher prices and the big contributors want lower taxes. I guess I could cope with the interests though, if it weren't for the ordinary people. They all want something too. The other day some character lobbied me for his local post office, and I'm already getting applications for the custom houses on the Mexican border. The defense workers want contracts and the government employees want raises. I've won a couple of primaries, so already I've been hit up for highways, bridges, dams, sewage plants, cabinet offices, inaugural tickets, and Annapolis appointments, and there's one delegation I could have on the first ballot if I promised to let the Air Force build a new bomber—in their state, naturally. The press wants a hot new story every day. The TV wants interviews. The photographers want just one more. People try to pull your buttons off, or your cufflinks, or even your shoes. I got a letter here from a union leader who wants me to wear a hat to stimulate jobs in the hatters' industry. Sometimes I fall into bed at night saying, 'I'll see what I can do.' Then I ask myself, 'What's a president for anyway?' And I wonder if there's anybody in the world who doesn't want something for himself, first and foremost. You ever met a man like that?"

"Not even you. You want the presidency."

"Maybe me least of all," Anderson said. "Listen . . . I figure now I've
ot a chance to win, Rich. Just a chance."

The driver stopped and asked a woman with dewlaps how to get to the
otel. She lifted a fleshy arm languidly and held it out in the direction they
'ere going.

"A long shot," Morgan said as the car moved on. "If all the pieces fall
ato place at the right time."

"Is it worth it, Rich?"

Morgan thought about that for a block or two, but he knew before the
heels turned twice that he couldn't answer. And I wouldn't have known,
e thought, pondering the question still, wondering if Anderson ever had
arned the answer, I wouldn't have known even if I had been the one who
'as going to have to pay the particular price. How do you measure what
thing is worth, or know precisely what thing you want? In the matter of
ving your life, Morgan had learned, famous brands could deceive you, and
ie consumer reports were vague. That long-ago day Anne was going about
teir house as before, in her blue jeans with martini glass, the ashtrays were
verflowing again, and in a few days it had even become possible for
1organ to resume quarreling with her, and to wrestle vainly with her in
ie bed, in the black and despairing night. Incredibly, it seemed, life was
oing on as before she had left him, and returned, and what cost-accounting
ystem could cope with that, much less with Anderson's question? When
mattered, the only useful standard of price was what the traffic would
ear.

Anderson's car had come to a stop in front of a whitewashed building
'ith a sagging marquee.

"A long time ago," Morgan said, "out there in the graveyard, you told
te you wanted to change history, but you never mentioned the price."

Anderson had his feet under him and the car door open. He looked back
t Morgan, scowling. "You never forget that, do you?"

Morgan retreated instantly from any risk of self-disclosure. "In my trade,
pro is never too drunk to remember what he needs to remember."

Anderson struggled out of the car, his big body barely making it through
ie door. The driver was already on the sidewalk, conferring with someone
1organ took to be the advance man.

Anderson stooped to look back at Morgan through the open door. "I
ever said I wanted to chance being President, did I?"

He stood aside and Morgan got out too. The unmistakable odor of a
aper mill drifted putrid in the air.

"But the other thing," Morgan said. "Showing the best in a man. What's a better way to do it or at least a bigger risk to take? Selling ladies' shoes?

Members of a Rotary Club welcoming committee—instantly distinguish
able by enormous round name badges—were being ejected one by one fror
the revolving door of the hotel and forming formidably under the marquee
Anderson stared at Morgan, the beginning of a smile touching his mout.
and eyes—the first real humor Morgan had seen in him that day.

"You're a funny goddam kind of professional, you are," Anderson saic
He touched Morgan's arm and turned toward the welcomers.

Fatigue disappeared instantly from his carriage; as if it were electricity
energy seemed suddenly to flow through him, and he took two long stride
across the sidewalk, his big hand outstretched.

"I'm Hunt Anderson," Morgan could still hear him saying. "Mighty nic
of you fellows to let me speak."

". . . politicians are a bunch of sheep," Dunn was saying, "look alike
sound alike, think alike. I never thought the public had any idea whethe
Anderson was much good—or cared, for that matter. But they knew he wa
different because he was doing and saying so many things nobody else ha
said or done. Whether that's good politics in the long run is another thing
but if you're as shut out as he was it's a good way to break down door
I—"

"Look who's here," Matt said. "I found the old cocksman himself in th
hall, probably looking for a girl."

"Why, Danny"—Morgan stood up—"it's been a long time. Charli
French . . . Larry Glass . . . this is Danny O'Connor, TV genius an
lady-killer, that Matt was telling you about."

"And you know Dunn, don't you?" Matt's tone was not quite hostile

"He's elected some of my people," Dunn said. "I thought you'd be here
Danny."

"Wild horses wouldn't keep me away, only I was somewhere out Wes
making a speech and I got the word late. Not too much water in that Scotch
Matt."

"Dunn, you're supposed to run up to Kathy's room a minute," Matt said
"Door's open right at the top of the stairs and she's expecting you."

Morgan, watching Dunn leave, wondered if behind those green lense
there was a man who liked to have a woman bite his neck; but one of Dunn'
powers was that no one knew anything like that about him.

"I'm telling you it really took me back," Danny O'Connor said, loosenin
his tie. "That particular state, I mean, getting the word out there that Hun

as gone. I wanted to howl like a dog, not because he was a great man, or anyway almost a great man, but just because he was my friend. You know, he and Kathy gave me a chance when nobody else would. And I especially remembered that particular state where I was from the campaign, since he actually put me in charge out in that region. One of those states you can ride across all day at sixty-five miles per hour and not a person in sight, maybe one or two cows and a windmill. So they've got a primary? So maybe there's not enough voters out there to get your money back, I told Hunt.

"But you know him, if there was someplace to run that year, there he was, running like hell. Out there we could put a couple spots on two or three channels and hit everybody. So he decided to do the whole bit on the tube rather than campaigning personally, except the one day he went there to announce his candidacy. Some ex-congressman sees the main chance and leaps in to run stand-in for that flannel-mouth Vice-President, and he even gets the notion in his fat head he's going to win and be the favorite son, and maybe somewhere on about the ninety-ninth ballot lightning's going to strike. And him the kind of a guy that could fuck up a two-car funeral. Anyway, this fathead goes around debating an empty chair, which is older than George Washington, but pretty soon I can see it's maybe just possibly some trouble for us.

"Anderson's off somewhere else, and Fat Head is making time with that simple-minded gimmick, you get the picture? So maybe a week before the primary Kathy comes in for a day—we were putting her into places Hunt didn't have time to go, because that girl had the real pizzazz for the yokels, those tits and that spectacular ass. Worth a first-class mailing to every voter in the state, I used to tell her. So after I grabbed the usual handful and got my ears pinned back—with her its always worth it—I told her I was worried about Fat Head and his empty chair. Too goddam bad we should lose the all game in the cactus country, I said. So she gets on the phone to Anderson—"

"No, no, it was me," Matt said. "I remember she said you had the wind up and she asked what we could do and I said I didn't know. Funny thing, that was about the first time I realized how much she was taking charge. Because she said, right away, 'All right, then I'll tell *you* what we'll do.' "

"A real tough broad," O'Connor said admiringly. "She would knee you right in the crotch. Anyway, the night before the voting out there, Fat Head hires the biggest auditorium they have for people, although I believe they got some bigger ones for cows. He sets up his goddam empty chair and the

local TV is all over the place—you get the whole fucking picture? Fat Hea
figures a ten-strike; I heard he put fifty per cent of his whole TV budget i
that one big night, which shows what a fat head he really was. And just on
minute after he gets on the air, he's turning to point to the empty chair, an
right that minute Hunt Anderson walks in and sits down in it. Fat Hea
turns into a grease spot right there on the floor—can you see it? He fall
apart so hard Hunt just takes over most of his air time, and I'm back i
my hotel room watching the tube and throwing the blocks to some cowgir
—I always had a hard-on for three days after Kathy came to town—an
I'm laughing so hard this cowgirl says to me, 'If you think everything's s
goddam funny, why'n't you just pull that little bitty old weenie of yours ou
of me.' Only I'll tell you the god's truth, I wasn't laughing out there las
night when I got the news."

"It was pretty sudden," Matt said.
"Not to me." O'Connor finished his drink, held out his glass. "To me
he's been dead a long time, maybe since that goddam convention."
"Oh, come on," Morgan said. "A man's not dead just because he
stopped running for his life. Anything but."
"Anderson was." O'Connor nodded, lost suddenly in Irish gloom, his big
soft hands coming up to touch his face. "Dead these many years, Rich
Dead these many years, and what a hell of a man he could have been too."

"Well, now, I just don't know so much about that," Matt Grant said. "I'
leave the philosophy to you intellectuals, although it's a fact that after tha
campaign and the way it turned out, Hunt never was the same again. A
downhill, I'll give you that, Danny, and a hell of a disappointment to m
personally. Sometimes I think about Hunt the way I guess a father feel
about a child he's sacrificed everything for, and the child throws it all away
But what your story really makes me think about was the incredible shoe
string way we had to run that crazy campaign.

"I'm here to tell you fellows, there never was another one like that an
probably never will be. Hunt Anderson went farther on less, he got neare
being president without any of the things a candidate's supposed to have
than anybody in modern times. Right, Danny?

"I guess I was the over-all manager, dividing my time between the Senat
office and running the downtown shop, an old townhouse we rented o
Seventeenth Street, facing Farragut Square. They were going to tear it dow
to put in an office building, so we got it cheap on a month-by-month lease
and staffed up mostly with volunteers. After good old Curly Layton cam

n with us, we had a solid man to run the delegate operation in the field, because Curly had some experienced troops of his own that he could use. Curly might look a little bit Hollywood with that hair of his and those ce-cream suits, but he was a real pro; he made the operation look more professional than it was.

"Just the way we got Curly tells you something about the way we had o do things. About Kathy too. It never has come out to my knowledge, but she just went to Curly, he was governor then, and laid it on the line that f he wanted to control his own delegation he'd better get on the Anderson bandwagon publicly and right away. Otherwise Hunt was going to break he unwritten rules and come into the state primary and beat the hell out of Curly on his home grounds.

"When Curly scoffed—he told me this himself—she pulled a private poll out of her pocketbook and threw it in front of him. Of course it was hypoed o hell and gone, but Curly's just happened to be a state with a high percentage of black voters and poor people, and she figured Curly would ake one look at that poll and think back to the big crowd Hunt had drawn n a public appearance there the year before. And we knew Curly didn't much like the President anyway. Sure enough, Curly said all right, he got he message. Which is how we lined up at least one important governor. As t turned out, Curly became a genuine admirer and the Anderson floor manager and main delegate-hunter at the convention.

"A long time later I asked Curly how an old head like him could fall for a cooked poll, and he kind of laughed. 'It crossed my mind at the time,' he said, 'but how often does a man get the chance to get himself conned by a lovely little mockingbird with legs like that?' I think Curly just took one ook at Kathy and was ready to be had, and she was the girl who could take him.

"But in fact, after Hunt and Kathy themselves, we didn't have but two real assets, Danny's TV and a lot of public interest. You mentioned Sneakers Lundy a while ago, Rich. Do you fellows realize he was the only political eader of any stature at all that helped us without having his hand forced n a primary or some other way? And Sneakers was pretty private about t, I can tell you, just kicked in a wad of cash that we sure did need, without any public endorsement. I hate to tell you why, but the truth is the President had told somebody Old Sneakers looked like a French pansy with a hangover, and the word got back to Sneakers. It made him furious, particularly since half the Senate thought it was true, and the other half thought it was at least funny. After that, anything Sneakers could do to stick it up the President's ass and break it off, like giving Hunt money, he was happy to do—privately, that is. Pity there weren't more with the same grievance, because money was the big problem. We got along just fine without endorsements.

"Hunt had plenty of money for himself, of course, he could have lived well without lifting a hand; you don't want to forget he was a man who had all the advantages most of us never had. But he couldn't finance a presidential campaign out of his pocket, not even one of the big primaries. As a matter of fact—I know you won't pass this on—he did go pretty deep into capital. Against my advice, I can tell you. I always say a man doesn't really know what money's worth if he's always had plenty.

"Of course we got a lot of little money, ten dollars to a hundred at a crack, and with the bossism theme, naturally the big do-gooder groups and the Jewish liberals and the reform clubs and the rich man's conscience money all kicked in pretty good. But not a dime from Labor—the President turned those big-ass bastards right off. And not much more from business, except some of the real big money—some oil men, for instance, some of the mutuals, the highway interests, did come through, just to hedge their bets on the White House. And I guess they thought they were at least investing in a Senate vote after Hunt would get cut down at the convention. Which Hunt was careful to explain they were not doing, but those types, you know they always figure a little cash on the barrelhead can't do any harm, and what's a few grand to them? Hunt never wanted to take that kind of money. He was always a little holier-than-thou on money anyway, I guess because of his father's reputation. But I'd show him the bills, and if I had to I could call in Kathy to straighten him out. Kathy had about as much scruple as a pickpocket when it came to relieving some lobbyist of a wad, and never mind his motives. "Worry about that in the White House," she'd say. "They can't buy if you're not selling. Worry about our motives, not theirs." And Hunt would hold his nose and I'd put the money in the bank and she'd go out and squeeze somebody else. Everywhere she went she picked up a thousand or two thousand or ten from some local type she smiled out of his head, and when she made a money pitch to an audience, the menfolk just couldn't wait to throw their wallets in the collection plate. But money was still our big problem, even considering all she raised and talked Hunt into accepting.

"What we had we socked hard into TV. We had more TV than anybody and better, because nobody else had realized as soon as we had what TV could do. But it broke us flat; you have to pay for the tube in greenbacks and in advance, or no show. The little we had left went for travel and convention communications and organization, a little for printing. The heart of the staff was just what we'd had, Danny here and Ralph James dealing with the press, and Sprock & Berger grinding away in the townhouse on position papers, Curly on the road. I guess I was holding the whole thing together, more or less. That meant we had to have volunteers or die, which was where those Anderson for President clubs came in. The primary organizations came out of those clubs full of housewives and preachers and professors and young people who were shut out of the party, and then we just had to move those same volunteers, most of them as amateurish as we were, right on to the convention. Most of us had never even been to a convention. I remember reading a lot of books about the nominating process, and I can tell you, they turned out to be mostly baloney.

"And when it was over, I kid you not, those debts scared me. The phone company settled forty cents on the dollar, and airlines for half, but a lot of the landlords and vendors we had around the country never collected a dime. I used to worry about that, but Kathy always said to forget it. 'If we'd won,' she'd say, 'most of them would have canceled the debt before Hunt could take the oath. It was an investment to them.'

"But, one way or another, we scraped through the primaries without losing to anybody except down in Bingham country, which didn't matter much. Of course there hadn't been any top-flight opposition, but one way we knew we'd done pretty well, the President got on the horn and asked Hunt to come see him again. That caused some joking around the office, that if the Old Man was ready to come out for us, we'd have to junk the bossism theme and start talking about continuity. But when Hunt got to the Oval Office and they'd said hello, the President laid it right on the line.

" 'You're still going through with this all the way, Senator?'

" 'I don't have much choice, do I, Mister President?'

" 'You could hear yourself nominated, it's always a kind of a proud moment for a man. Then you could run up a respectable vote on the first ballot, just to keep the faith, and throw it to the Vice-President the next time around.'

" 'Our people won't throw, Mister President. Yours might, but not ours.'

" 'That's what they all say. You much interested in diplomacy?'

" 'Not that interested.'

" 'Well, you know you got to remember in this business, the big possums walk late.'

" 'Mister President, I really don't think we've got any choice now. We've made too many commitments and too many people got their necks on the block.'

" 'Well, I just thought I owed it to the party to bring it up.'

" 'Much obliged,' Hunt said. 'But anyway, you're not going into the convention with nobody but the Vice-President, are you?'

"The President chuckled a little, Hunt said later on. The Old Man reared back in his big chair, cocky, tough, smart; he'd done or seen everything in politics for forty years past. 'You got some of your daddy's blood,' he said. 'One of the meanest men I ever knew.'

" 'Mean enough he'd have blown the Vice-President over with one puff from his cigar. He smoked good Cubans.'

" 'Are you as mean as he was, Senator?'

" 'I don't think I'll need to be. Mister President, we'd still rather have your support than anybody's. After you count up heads and find out the Vice-President isn't going to make it, and neither is Stark, I hope you'll get back in touch with us.'

" 'Stark?' the President said. 'I wouldn't hit a hog in the ass with Stark.'

" 'And I know you haven't forgotten, Mister President, once the party nominates a man, we've still got to win the election.'

"Then Hunt gave him a lecture on how Senator Hunt Anderson had a better chance than anyone else to do that. The President heard him out politely, rocking back in the big chair. Then he stood up and shook hands, a little abruptly; Hunt said he never saw a harder pair of eyes on a man. 'Well, Senator,' the President said, 'if the cricks don't rise, I reckon we'll see you at the convention.'

"So Hunt figured, after that, it would have to be Governor Aiken. And it was about the very next day, I mean Hunt had hardly got out of the President's office, before that goddam prison revolt broke out in Aiken's state. 'Why, the sons-of-bitches must have paid off those cons,' Hunt said when he saw the headlines. It did seem that nobody could be that lucky, to have that kind of an opportunity handed to him on a silver platter two weeks before the convention opened.

"Looking back on it today, I guess that's when the game was lost, if it wasn't already. Because when Aiken went in that cellblock alone and faced down a gang of armed convicts and gave 'em amnesty if they'd come out in one hour with all their hostages unhurt, even Hunt had to admit it was am impressive performance; and when the convicts did come out on sched-ule and Aiken went right back and called out his legislature and said *now* would they pass the prison reforms he'd sent up that year and they'd buried six feet deep, they not only passed the reforms, they gave Aiken the one thing he hadn't had—with a little help from those damned convicts, they gave him a national name and a bold image that people recognized and liked.

"Of course Aiken wasn't formally in the race, but it was a going rumor that the president had been moving around to get him in it in the right way, and get him known around the country, and we saw right away what a tough break that prison revolt was for us. And when Kathy came back from wherever she'd been when she heard the news, she came straight to my office, sat down by my desk, pulled the phone over to her side, and said to me, 'If you ever say a word to Hunt about this I'll skin you alive. What's Dunn's number?' "

Which is the kind of thing I can just hear her saying, Morgan thought, amused, feeling a little like a proud father, the way men do when they discover a woman doing something they might have done themselves, or wish they might have done—except I didn't know then how large a part Kathy was playing in the campaign.

He had heard a hundred stories like Matt's since then. She had been in it so deeply that Joe Bingham's press secretary had told Morgan in confidence that he knew for a fact she was screwing her way systematically through the state chairmen, so that if Anderson got nominated he'd be the first man to win a convention flat on his wife's back. Morgan had laughed out loud, knowing that kind of crude rumor-mongering would backfire on those who spread it. Besides, he had thought, you only had to take a look at Kathy, then at most state chairmen, to know that she couldn't want even the presidency that much.

But even if he had known about the call to Dunn he wouldn't have been all that interested, because, then, he had been preoccupied with Anne. It still hurt to remember, he thought, scarcely hearing Matt ramble on; out of all the hurts, the humiliations, the heartbreak, that time seemed in many ways the worst. Not that he knew yet exactly what had happened, whether it had been some game of her own, some exercise of contrition of self-penalty or more likely mockery, or whether her strange sudden opening to him, that convention summer, might have been a last desperate reach for whatever it was that had eluded her, as something eludes us all—whether, perhaps, she had momentarily believed that in yielding, submitting herself, opening deliberately to penetration that tough core of resistance against which he had battered so often, she would find something ironically more bearable, as if willed and cynical submission would be at once more controlled and less punishing than the fierce isolation of self. Or perhaps, he sometimes thought, she had only been preparing rich ground for the seeds of his destruction, or hers, or both.

Never mind, he thought, never mind. But it came flowing back to him, as it sometimes did—the stupor of passion that had held him, the magical colors of a sudden life never before known or sensed. It came flowing back, borne perhaps on the memories being evoked around him, of that convention, that hotel, those crowded streets, those interminable hours in the howling, fogged arena—those days and nights forever linked in his being to the one suspended moment out of all his time when he had thought he was going to break through, pierce the walls around him, between them—when in the crisp, depraved, limitless connections of love-making, white and fusing as a welder's flame, he had believed briefly that he would conquer solitude and overwhelm death, he was at the end of isolation, the self would be transformed and reborn in unison.

"But the truth was," Matt Grant was saying, "that when the convention opened, Hunt may have been the big primary winner but he was in desperate shape. He had shot his bolt in the primaries. There weren't any more delegates to be had that way. Bingham's Southerners didn't offer much hope to us. Nobody quite knew how many delegates the President and the regular leaders commanded—that depended on for whom and for what—but the going guess among the columnists was about four hundred. So the President and Joe Bingham between them could put approximately half the convention out of Hunt's reach. The only way he could possibly make it was to deadlock the whole thing and play for the breaks or a deal—to swing Stark's liberals, maybe, and put together all the favorite sons, including that character Dunn was running. With his own delegation and some strays from surrounding states, Dunn was holding ninety-eight delegates for his man. I'm not likely to forget *that* number. So you see why Kathy called Dunn when Aiken hit the headlines. Dunn looked like the key to the jackpot."

And no doubt by then, Morgan thought—Matt's narrative weaving itself in and out of his own insistent memory like a car in heavy traffic—Kathy would have had her doubts that Hunt would call Dunn, because Hunt was essentially a candidate, not a manager; he liked to be on stage, not in the back rooms.

"A Boy Scout," some of the leaders had called Anderson, even if that hadn't quite fit with their denunciations of his "ruthless McCarthyite tactics" against Hinman. There was a rumor all over the headquarters hotel, about the time the convention opened, that the governor of an oil state had offered to put some oil delegations together for Anderson, second- and third-ballot strength, in return for a suitable guarantee that he would turn the tidelands over to the states, if elected. As the rumor had it, Anderson had disdained the offer, although accepting it might have cut a big slice out of Bingham's support and the White House bloc.

Morgan had tracked down Matt Grant and asked him about the rumor, and Matt had professed not to know, while suggesting smugly that he did. Then Morgan located Kathy—alone, as befitted the Anderson campaign style—at a mammoth cocktail party thrown by one of those Washington hostesses who trail political gatherings as the camp followers used to come along in the dust of armies. This particular crone had rented a ballroom and dozens of bartenders; in the middle of the resulting thousands of delegates, pols, gawkers, reporters, and wives milling noisily around, Morgan and Kathy were as alone as a couple on a liferaft. Kathy looked tired, a little edgy, but not bored; as she talked, her eyes kept roaming the heaving tide of faces around them. She was sipping something bland. A carpetbag button was pinned to her dress, which was cool, discreet.

"The story sounds like Hunt," Morgan said, "but it also sounds pretty blatant even for the oil types."

She nodded. "But we like it, don't you? It would spoil our image if it had Hunt actually making a sneaky deal."

"So the story's a plant?"

"Stop being a bloodhound, of course it's not a plant. It just didn't happen quite the way it's spreading."

"Then how did it happen?"

An elegant old busybody in pearls and a Stark button interrupted to talk a little civic uplift with Kathy, who promptly asked her to switch to Hunt —a hard, direct pitch. She got an arch promise to think it over.

"Just for your background and you didn't get a thing from me, that oil jackass did come to see Hunt." Kathy took the Scotch out of Morgan's hand, sipped it quickly, handed it back. "About as subtle as an elephant. Thinking of supporting Hunt blah blah blah. Good government umph umph umph. No question of any promises or anything raunchy like that. But what did Hunt think of higher education?"

"I'll bet he admired it."

"Well, the Governor admired it too. But it turns out the only way the Governor can possibly improve higher education in that poor little old state of his is to finance it with tidelands oil revenue. But the states just happen not to own the tidelands, not yet, and he wanted to know what Hunt as president would maybe be willing to do about that."

"I get the whole fascinating picture."

She leaned past Morgan to shake hands with a flustered delegate in a carpetbag button and to compliment his wife on her dress, which was large enough to cover a horse, and had to be. The huge, crowded ballroom was hot and airless; the rumble and shriek of voices rose like tobacco smoke toward the huge limp cloth portraits of the candidates drooping high above them. Aiken's was missing, and the more conspicuous for that.

"Of course Hunt gave him a brilliant lecture on state taxation," Kathy said, "so if that was a deal, I guess we turned it down, but we think the Governor was just playing big wheel, or at the most just sounding us out on his own, he isn't really anybody. I will admit Danny and Ralph have been helping the rumor along, since we're not likely to get much oil support anyway. Where's that little peach of yours?"

"Off somewhere. All this bores her."

"So I heard. There's somebody over there I've got to see, Rich." She started past him, stopped, looked up smiling, her eyes wicked. "Everything's all right with her now, isn't it? Since she's back?"

Morgan had faced it out; in his euphoria of the moment, he remembered, he had even thought he could afford to be smug about it. "Better than ever," he said and struck back. "Better than running for president." And for just a moment, as Kathy slipped away in the crowd, her lovely, still face looked back at him, not smiling any longer. For the first time since he had known her, he saw something hurt in her eyes, something inexplicably wounded, and knew he had reached her.

Perhaps that had been an omen, he thought, for both of them. Because later that exact day, in the dim, stale room spared a junior journalist by harassed convention managers, on the experienced bed where he had fallen with Anne, clenched and groaning in the haste that had seized him as he watched her dressing to go out, saw her drawing on her stockings with the effortless grace that never failed to arouse in him something yearning, hurting, that drove him as inexorably as the will to live or the fear of nothingness—suddenly, as he thrust himself desperately into her, as if into salvation and surcease, Anne had gone rigid beneath him; as if in shock, her whole body jerked, her head turned away, her forearm fell stiffly across it, and he felt her hard, abrasive, forbidding, where a moment before she had been soft, warm, enfolding. Like scalding steam from a pipe, words came hissing between her teeth: "Finish . . . finish!"

"What?" he mumbled thickly, out of control, hunched and rooting in stupefaction, his life drawing to an aching coil somewhere within the ever-threatening void that surrounded it.

"Finish!"

Desperately, calling out to her, he plunged on, until at the end she took her arm away and looked up at him with chill, foreign eyes while the coil unleashed itself and he moaned and shook and collapsed—alone again, and mortal.

"Here's Dunn now," Matt said. "Do you remember when Kathy called you before the convention, Dunn? Another drink?"

"Just a drop." Dunn sat behind Anderson's table again. "She called me a number of times before the convention."

Oh, she did, did she? Morgan thought.

"I mean about Aiken."

"Oh, sure, she asked me if I thought Aiken would be a candidate. I asked her if she thought the sun would come up. She said, 'Well, that won't force your hand, will it?' I said it wouldn't. She said that was a good thing, because Hunt would win if I didn't cave in. I was polite, and she said she and Hunt would appreciate it if I'd keep everything open for a while. That was what I aimed to do anyway, and once she was sure of that, she dropped it. She didn't try to push me where I wasn't ready to go, and she saw she didn't have to, because at that point her interest and mine were the same."

"But she had more than that in mind," Matt said. "She hung up and she said to me, "We've got to have Dunn and I think we can get him if Hunt won't be a fool.' "

"I guess she was trying to get the feel of me," Dunn said, "reminding me we had common ground. They couldn't win on the first ballot, so naturally they wanted to stop everybody else. I wasn't anxious for anybody to win on the first ballot, that wasn't hard for them to figure out.

"I had this bloc of delegates, nothing big, those from our state and a few more from the smaller states near us that have the same problems. We were all behind one of my associates as a kind of regional favorite son. He had some potential—some cabinet possibilities maybe. Some of my people could even see a vice-president in him but I never aimed that high. Besides, he wasn't the main thing.

"The main thing was that we wanted the party to know we were there. We wanted to swing weight when it counted, come in and put somebody over. Personally, I didn't much want the President dictating the nominee. Bad precedent, bad business all around. I like organization but not a closed shop. And some of the leaders with the Old Man weren't exactly my kind of people. So I had put together our bloc independently and I was floor manager, nothing big at all, but it had possibilities as long as nobody had the convention locked up. We didn't think anyone did. I remember Drew Pearson wrote a piece just before that convention opened; he said it was a mob looking for someone to tell it which leader to follow, and that was about the way we saw it.

"We had a good head count on Bingham, because you can always tell what the Confederates will do. My memory may be a vote or two off, but I think there were twelve hundred nineteen delegates that year, so six ten were needed to win. That's about right, isn't it, Matt? You're a detail man. I had Bingham pegged for two sixty-five on the first ballot, and he could hold most of them as long as he wanted. Which depended on how big Joe's delusions were, because the right way for him to play it was to throw the Southern delegations somewhere on the second or third ballot.

"Stark wasn't quite as easy to count, but our best reading gave him at least a hundred, maybe more. Nobody thought he could win, except on the outside chance that the President and the other leaders couldn't put anyone else over. I did think Stark had a shot at second place but I never fuss over second place.

"You could also tab the favorite sons, practically on the nose. Counting our man and the others, I put the favorite sons down on the first roll call for a hundred and fifty, of which we had ninety-eight. So Bingham, Stark, and the favorite sons were about a hundred short of a majority, but Anderson's votes meant the Old Man didn't quite have a majority either. Anderson was actually claiming over four hundred but that was kind of hollow; I didn't give him more than three hundred fifty, and I figured even that was probably a little high, because giving him that many meant the President and the regular leaders also would have only about that many. But I couldn't figure a first-ballot nomination out of that arithmetic, and that suited me.

"The big question in my mind was whether or not they'd bring on Aiken from the start, or produce him once the Vice-President had gone as far as he could. I thought the former, but, if that was it, somebody would have to cut the old gentleman off at the knees, and I didn't really think even the President was up to that. They had been close over the years. I thought the President would probably hire the assassin.

"But for a long time nothing at all seemed to happen. The platform committee got to work a week early. The credentials committee was already in a fight over some rival delegations from a couple of the hogjowl states. The press was in town by the thousands, and that was one of the first conventions fully televised; everywhere you turned you tripped over a cable or somebody put a mike in your teeth.

"By the morning of the day of the first session, the city was practically at a standstill. Hotel telephone service was a memory. If a man didn't know where a service elevator was, the only way he could get out of the headquarters hotel was to walk down thirty or forty floors. When he'd get to the lobby, he couldn't get to the street or the bar for the bands playing, the pretty girls pinning buttons on him, the rubberneckers standing around, and the delegates talking politics. And still, even that late, as far as I could see, the President and the regulars hadn't made a move. Everyone was talking about Aiken, but nobody seemed to be doing anything, and some of the boys were getting restless. They were afraid they were going to get left, and nobody seemed to have any word from the White House. But you have to expect that kind of treatment if you let somebody else do your thinking for you.

"The Vice-President had arrived the night before, in full cry. At the airport, naturally, they had turned out every city employee and his wife and children and brothers-in-law and *their* families. All the placards had union bugs and the torches were oil-fired. That rally was as spontaneous as grand opera, but there were a lot of people out there, and it never took more than that to get the Vice-President going. I was watching on television, and he made the kind of speech they hadn't heard since the Cross of Gold—an old-fashioned silver-tongued oration about the road ahead, the winds of freedom, and the blue skies of hope.

"The Vice-President had that airport crowd up and screaming, which was what they were there for, but those cameras weren't city employees. They were coming in tight on his sweaty face and his windmill gestures, and when you saw the jowls up close and quivering under the chin, and heard that high-pitched voice calling off those shopworn phrases, you knew he was finished. Maybe they'd turned out that big crowd to give him a last chance to show them something, but he didn't, nothing they wanted to see. Whatever style he might once have had, when they turned those cameras on him he was just a garrulous old man.

"Personally, I doubt if they even meant to give him a last chance; they must have known by then it was hopeless, even if he didn't. The first morning of the convention, as if in the flush of triumph, he grandly presided over a breakfast meeting of all the leaders—even me. I wasn't considered a team player any more then than now, but they could all count; my little bloc of delegates stood up for me. So I was there with the big movers and shakers—some city leaders, a few state chairmen, the top union chiefs, a handful in all, not counting the Vice-President himself.

"I went expecting fireworks. I'd been up early, reading the papers before the hike down the stairs, and had seen the tipoff far down in an article that quoted a lot of pols and hangers-on about what they thought would happen.

Just a paragraph quoting a certain Labor goon, not the kind who was invited to breakfast with the Vice-President or who conferred at the White House. He had too long an arrest record for that. Never mind who he was, he's been helpful to me. Might be again. I knew him well enough to know he had a sharp eye for what was happening in the unions. 'They'll never take the Vice-President,' he had told the reporter, or words to that effect. 'He's too old.'

"After I thought about that while walking down twenty flights, his willingness to tell the truth about the regulars' supposed candidate meant to me that the Old Man was ready to act at last, and Labor was going to put in the knife. That opening-day breakfast, I thought, would be a nice private place to do the deed. I doubted the Vice-President was expecting it. I wasn't sure the old gentleman even read the papers past the headlines, or that if he did, he'd know that that particular union character usually knew what he was talking about. Sure enough, the Vice-President was all bounce and joviality even at that hour. He'd always been a great yarnspinner, and before they poured the orange juice he was giving us a Herbert Hoover story.

" 'Stubborn as he was, stubbornest man I ever met, right in the depth of the Depression, with practically that whole state out of work and hungry, Hoover went out to Charleston, West by God Virginia, to dedicate some kind of a memorial. He got up to speak, and there was a multitude out there, all right, big as that crowd we had last night, and just as Hoover walked on the platform, the National Guard fired off a twenty-one-gun salute to the President. It made a racket like the Civil War, and when the cannonade died down and Hoover was still standing there, some old fellow in the back of the crowd rose up and hollered, "By gum, they missed him!" '

"Knowing what I thought I knew, I didn't laugh as hard as I might have in other circumstances. We were at a large table, seven or eight to a side and a couple at the ends. I was seated across from the Vice-President, down a bit, with a good view of his face. He was looking pink, healthy, and pleased with himself. He told another story or two; he had an endless supply for all occasions. So I was surprised when he fumbled in a briefcase, pulled out the morning paper, and laid it on the table—folded to the exact page I had been reading before I came.

" 'Now, gentlemen,' the Vice-President said, 'I invited you here for a little good fellowship, and to talk about how we'd handle things this week and then in the election. Maybe first I'd better ask you what our old friend Ed meant by what he says in the paper this morning. *Who* won't take me? '

"There was a long silence. The old gentleman looked up and down the table—I remember thinking he had a very clear eye for his age—and suddenly his face and jowls seemed not quite so pink, more nearly red with anger. 'Ed's usually clued in and I'm not deaf,' he said finally. 'I've heard all the Aiken talk, but not from the White House.' Again he looked up and down the table. 'But if no one's got anything to say, then I guess we'd all better agree that for once Ed's off base. Right?'

"I heard a chair scrape back somewhere to my right. The Vice-President looked quickly in that direction. It was so quiet in that room you could hear traffic echoes from outside, glassware ringing somewhere near. But there were, suddenly, no waiters hovering around us. A somber bodyguard with a Secret Service button in his lapel stood with his arms folded in front of the door, gazing over our heads.

" 'Mister Vice-President'—you can all guess which one of the Labor statesmen it was—'everybody in this room loves you and respects your record. But some of us *have* been talking. It's going to be a hard race. We don't know whether a candidate sixty-nine years old can take it, and anyway we wonder if we can win with anybody that old.'

"The silence fell again. Everybody knew the voice that had spoken was not to be ignored. But the Vice-President was game. These politicians will surprise you, time and again. You think there's not a vertebra in the bunch, and most of them are gutless wonders, on any reasonably hard public issue, but most I've known, in a personal crunch like that, they'll stand up to the end. That morning the old gentleman never flinched.

" 'After all these years you and I and the other boys here have worked together, I never thought I'd live to hear any of you talk about me as just a "candidate sixty-nine years old."'

" 'Now you know how we all feel about you, it's nothing personal, it's—'

" 'Well, if it's not personal,' the old gentleman said, 'it's not anything, it won't hold water at all. I'm nine years younger than the recent Prime Minister of England; they had one named Gladstone who was *eighty*-four. Goethe was working on *Faust* at eighty-two, and if any of you gentlemen haven't read it, I can say it's high time you did. If I mistake not, Oliver Wendell Holmes was up toward ninety before he decided he was too old for the Supreme Court. A man's as old as he feels, and I'm not a doddering fool, gentlemen. What's this all about? Aiken?'

"The great Labor statesman was silent a moment, then, in a voice that sounded as if he were choking on his eggs, 'I've heard you tell Lincoln's story, you know the one—about the man ridden out of town on a rail. When they asked him how he felt about it, he said if it weren't for the honor of the thing he'd rather walk. You and I are old enough friends, been through the wars together, you know I feel exactly like that man right this minute. But I'm afraid it's been decided—you can't win, Charlie, you're too old. We've got to find somebody else and that's what we're going to do.'

"For one bad moment I thought the old gentleman was going to break at last. He stared across the table, his face muscles working. The skin over his cheekbones was white, stretched, papery. But he still had to have it confirmed; after a lifetime of experience, he had to go for it one more time.

"He turned to me. 'You don't run in the pack, Dunn. What about it?'

" 'This time,' I said, 'I'm with the hounds. You can't win.'

"The old gentleman sighed and slumped a little. The room was silent as the grave; no one moved. Then he forced a weary, quick smile. 'Reminds me of the old fellow down home that went to town every Saturday night and indulged his taste for the bottle, which was considerable. Long about midnight the mules'd come clomping home and the old man's sons would come out and find him stretched out in the bed of the wagon, dead to the world. They'd put the mules in the barn and the old man to sleep till time for church. It happened so often that one Saturday night they got tired of it and only put the mules in the barn and just let the old man sleep it off in the wagon, to teach him a lesson. And he rose up around dawn and looked around him and then he says, "By golly," he says, "I've either found a damn fine wagon or lost a good pair of mules!" ' '

"I never heard any laughing as loud as what followed, relieving the tension and getting us over the worst of it. When we stopped laughing, the old gentleman had got himself together—he was still hanging on. 'Of course, I'm not withdrawing until I talk to the President. Wouldn't be proper at all.'

" 'Why, certainly, certainly, nobody could expect that,' the Labor states-man put in smoothly. 'I know I speak for everyone here, not a word's coming out of this meeting until you give us your decision. Right?' He looked up and down the table with his collective-bargaining glare.

"A general chorus of agreement hailed this cynicism, and then the old gentleman showed his age and the lifetime characteristic that had made him a politician. 'Maybe he won't agree with you,' he said slyly. 'Maybe he'll tell you boys something you don't expect to hear.' In the renewed light in his eyes I could sense the indomitable gambler's streak that runs in them all—the belief that God's hand might still be on the chosen man, and no matter how bad it looked at the moment, together they might still manage to win. I could see all that in his eyes and face and then I didn't look at him any more.

" 'Well, I'll just tell you what you're bound to know already,' the Labor statesman boomed heartily, confidently, 'if the President's with you, then *we're* with you!'

"Somehow everyone got through the breakfast. It was sumptuous but we ate little, and the talk was desultory at best. As soon as decency allowed, members of the group began drifting out. I stayed to the end; it seemed the least I owed the old gentleman was not to leave him alone at the table. Finally the last small knot of us left the room, the Vice-President among us, and moved into the sitting room of the suite that had been set aside for him. Just as we entered an aide rushed in from the corridor, clutching some newspapers under his arm. The old gentleman took the papers held out to him. I looked over his shoulder. It was the early-bird afternoon edition, and across the top the headline proclaimed brutally PRESIDENT BACKS AIKEN.

"The Vice-President's shoulders slumped a little; the headline could not have failed to extinguish the last vestige of the hope that had raged for so long in his thin old breast; but he stayed game to the literal end. He was smoking a cigar, and as I watched he rolled it once across his mouth and clenched it up at a rather jaunty angle, cocking an eye at me. 'So that little son-of-a-bitch finally sold me out too?'

"The Labor statesman was long gone, one of the first to leave, spouting undying affection; it would have been an interesting question for him to answer. I shrugged; the old gentleman knew I wasn't that much in the pack.

" 'I guess I am too old at that,' the Vice-President said. 'Otherwise I'd have seen what was coming.' He tossed the paper on a sofa and took the cigar out of his mouth. 'Anyway,' he said, 'I ain't as bad off as Uncle Joe Cannon when he was eighty-one and still in the House with me. Everybody knew old Joe couldn't get it up any more, and one day he got to debating with this lady member and Joe says to her, "Will the lady yield?" And of course she replies as nice as you please, "The lady will be delighted to yield to the gentleman from Illinois." And Uncle Joe in his white beard looks around, grinning, and says in a stage whisper you could hear in the gallery, he says, "My God! Now she's yielded, what can I do about it?" '

"Maybe the old gentleman could have done more about it than any of us thought at the time, but that's hindsight. Late that day, after Aiken had formally announced he was a candidate, the Vice-President went on TV and said he was in the race to stay, Aiken notwithstanding. The old gentleman would always pitch in that way for the party; sometimes I wonder if any disappointment or even outright betrayal can put a limit on his kind of loyalty. 'Hell,' he told me later, 'those fellows *did* make me Vice-President, didn't they?' So he stayed one more round that might have been the hardest of all. They only wanted some first-ballot votes for him so they could switch them to Aiken on the second, to make it look like a stampede."

"Exactly the way we had it figured," Matt said. "A lot of our people thought we had it made by the time the Vice-President was dumped. But Hunt and Kathy and I knew Aiken was the real McCoy."

"Maybe you fellows don't realize it," O'Connor said, apparently recovered from his Irish gloom. "but that was my first convention and it was artistically a bomb. Very bad TV. And the speeches! Christ, as we used to say in Boston, how the wind blew through that hall! Everything was going on, if anything was, off the floor. On the floor, talk, talk, talk, and thousands of people not a one of which knew from nothing, or had even heard anything you could believe, and lots of them asleep with newspapers over their crumby faces. Lousy TV.

"The only place worth seeing, which I mean is what TV is about, was the lobby in the headquarters hotel. Now down there you could get some pizzazz—bands marching through, snake dances, every now and then an honest-to-god fist fight. Great TV. Out in the middle they'd put up this big log cabin as the Vice-President's display, supposed to make you think he's Lincoln, I mean, but it didn't help a bit, did it? In one corner there were all these pretty girls with their boobs out for Stark. They ran his information booth, and that was some information! I think it was Kansas complained, and Stark made 'em cover up the cleavage a little. I always figured that sealed his political doom—I mean, any man that would do a cowardly thing like that. Anderson was too poor to afford lobby space, of course; we just hung up a big carpetbag banner and sign that says, 'Get on the Bandwagon,' Room So and So. Up there we had do-gooders that would twist your arm off before they'd give you a cup of coffee.

"But that cornpone, that what's-his-face—yeah, Bingham. He's got the biggest Confederate flag you ever saw hanging down the lobby wall and his girls passing out buttons that say, 'The South Will Rise Again.' I didn't think they ought to allow that kind of thing, I mean *I'm* no bigot. Although I got to admit those little Dixie cups giving out those cornpone buttons, they were something. Wearing these Confederate military outfits with short skirts and cowboy hats and little swords, really cute broads, and everyone a goddam bigot to the bone. I made some big time with one of those Confederate quail. Took her to lunch, bought her some drinks and what not, and maybe the second time I took her out, over about the sixth drink —they all got a hollow leg down that part of the world—I say to this stacked-up little bigot, 'Come on, General, enough of this idle chit-chat. Let's get down to brass tacks.'

" 'Why, what are you talkin' 'bout, sir? Where you tryin' to get me to go?'

" 'Up to my room to see the view,' I says, quick as a flash.

" 'Why, sir, I declare, I b'lieve if you was to get me up there, you just might try to get me to go to *bed,* I mean, all this whisky and all.'

" 'Exactly,' I says, 'but only to make love.'

" 'Well, sir, I don't know what kind of girl you think I am, but I just don't know if I ought to do anything like *that.*'

"Then I played my ace. 'General,' I says, 'don't y'all know I'm a Southern Irishman?'

"And those Confederate eyes lit right up till you could see the stars and bars on the whites. 'Well, I tell you, sir . . . whyn't you go right on up to yoah room, and we'll just meet up there in a minute after I change.'

" 'Change?' I says. 'But you won't need any other clothes, General.'

" 'But, sir . . . I just couldn't go to a man's room in uniform!' "

"Oh, for Christ's sake," Glass said, "I'm willing to believe almost anything but you're putting us on."

"Swear to God," O'Connor said. "Listen, that little bigot turned out to be my first wife. She was why I had to leave Anderson. She thought he was a Communist. Then the reason I had to leave her was because she wanted me to join the Klan. I only married her in the first place because she was non-political in the hay. Also non-stop. Sometimes I even miss that bigoted little twat of hers."

"Well, while you were having your fun," Matt Grant said a little dourly, "the rest of us were working our ass off. I'll have to say that for Hunt, he never stopped working from dawn to dawn. From one caucus to another, and if there weren't any caucuses to go to, he was up in his headquarters suite shaking hands, or on the phone talking to somebody, or getting himself on TV. I'm not sure when he slept, or if he did; I know I hardly closed *my* eyes for four days and four nights.

"Hunt would see the press every day and somehow he'd look fresh as a rose and confident as a banker, but it was tough on him. We'd known enough to hold back some announcements, so that every day we could produce some more delegates, or even a whole delegation, as if it had just decided to go for us. I don't know whether that fooled anybody, but it didn't fool us, of course; we weren't climbing the mountain at all. 'It's got to be in the roll call,' Hunt would say, 'we've just got to deadlock it and see which way the cats jump.' But I was afraid I knew.

"About that time Kathy got the idea they'd try to steal it from us. God knows, she had reason. Of course, the White House controlled all the convention machinery, and I don't need to tell you fellows, they didn't hesitate to use it either. They did their damnedest to throw out some of our delegations, but we were expecting that, it's old stuff, our people had credentials by the bale. Then we tried a cute one on them, although I was dead against it. Hunt wanted to put in a loyalty oath to drive the Confederate red-hots out; that would not only reduce the number of delegates needed for a majority, the way he figured it, but it might swing Stark's liberals to us. At the least, it would put Aiken on the spot to know what to do.

"But hell, we had an ironclad agreement for rights to the floor, they were going to recognize one of our delegation chairmen; and when the time came he was right down front waving his state banner ten feet from the rostrum. He might as well have been home watching TV. They never did recognize him or hear our resolution—which is what we ought to have expected in the first place. And when we got up a minority report on the platform, with a plank on migrants and another on bossism, they cut us off at the pass— gave us exactly five minutes of debate, which was hardly even time to read our report. I *had* expected that all along. Thank God, there was only a voice vote on that fiasco, because it didn't show how weak we really were.

"They just had all the muscle, even if we kept telling ourselves we had the people. And as a matter of fact, although they'd stuffed the galleries with city employees that yelled on cue for Aiken or the Vice-President, that backfired on them because we rounded up a real, honest-to-God crowd *outside* the hall and kept them stirred up, marching and protesting about not being able to get in the hall.

"That did just what Danny said it would do, it pulled the TV outside with our crowd, because the TV people go where the action is and there wasn't much inside; they kept thinking there'd be a riot or something outside. The result was that the whole country got the idea that the people were for us and the bosses were locking them out of the convention; in fact, that may even have been true. But much good that did us inside. In there, the people didn't matter a damn.

"So no wonder Kathy got paranoid about it. 'The bastards will steal it, I know they will,' she'd say. Kathy was cussing like a man by the time that convention was over, and I couldn't much blame her although I personally never like to hear a woman talk like that myself. 'Isn't there any law in this goddam country?' she'd ask me. 'Do we just have to *let* them steal it, the way they wouldn't even let us talk about the platform? Don't people have anything to say about who runs the country? Doesn't it mean anything we've been running all year too hard to take a breath and we're the only ones who've won any primaries and can show any real votes?' Kathy was really beautiful when she got mad like that, tired as she was and under all that strain; those blue eyes would flash fire, and she'd get a look on her face like a queen when they come to take her to the headsman.

"It all came to a kind of flash point for us the afternoon before the first roll call; I guess you'd have to say the pressure finally got to us. It was just before Hunt's afternoon news conference; he was still, technically speaking, the front-runner with all his primary victories but everybody knew Aiken was closing fast. He'd shown a lot of foot in the few days he'd been in it. Not that almost anybody under seventy without a jail record couldn't have moved fast, with the kind of power he had behind him. So we knew the questions were all going to be about Aiken—one of the troubles with a situation like that is the reporters always want to talk about the other guy rather than hear what you have to say for yourself. They bait the bear in hopes he'll fall on his face.

"Nothing personal, but if you ask me, nothing in this whole business of politics is as rotten and merciless as a bunch of damned reporters smelling blood and closing in like a bunch of wolves for the kill. I'm sorry, I don't mean you guys of course, but I've seen it so often, and they'd have stripped Hunt right down to the bone if he'd ever let them. That day the TV cameras were lined up like artillery and the writing types were sitting there just waiting to get their claws in so the cameras could show everybody the bloodshed and action. No way out of it, in this business, you live and die by the press; so while the makeup man was fretting over Hunt's face, I was filling him in on the latest we knew, which left us still ahead on the first ballot but not by much. Kathy was sitting on the bed, watching Hunt and the makeup man.

" 'Pretty ridiculous,' she said, just right out of the blue.

" 'What?' I thought she meant something in whatever I'd just said.

" 'Fussing over his silly face like a debutante.'

"There was a towel across Hunt's chest, under his chin, and he stood up and threw the towel on the floor. 'Well, do you think I enjoy any of this goddam play-acting and chasing cobwebs?' he yelled.

" 'Go on,' I said to the makeup man, 'and close that door behind you.' He went out, looking over his shoulder at Kathy coming up off that bed like a cat after a bird, charging right at Hunt.

" 'You love every second of it and you make me sick!' " she yelled right back at him. 'Pretending you're so fucking pure and noble and out there grabbing for it like your father!'

" 'Oh yes,' Hunt said, lowering his voice, but not gently, 'I know that's what you think, you snotty bitch, but who pushed me into this crazy thing anyway, who nagged and needled and told me how great I was till I didn't have any choice—'

" 'Now, now,' I said, 'you two calm down, you're tired, there's no—'

" 'Keep out of this!' Kathy said. She didn't turn her eyes from Hunt. 'If you think I'm going to stand here and let you make out the licking you're going to get is all my fault, think again, buster, think again! I never even wanted to leave New York and go back to that shitty state of yours. *I* didn't want to run for the Senate, *you* did. And if you hadn't acted so high and mighty, I could have had this thing won for you by now. But—'

"Matt," Morgan said, "don't you think this is a little too personal and private?"

"Well, no, goddammit. Frankly, I don't. Because if we're talking here about how it was, this is one of the truest parts, and besides I had something to say in the middle of that fuss that I think was important.

" 'Now, just a damned minute!' I yelled at both of them. 'You two just listen to me for once.' And I don't reckon either of those two poor little rich kids had ever heard Matt Grant or anyone else raise his voice at them before, and they looked thunderstruck. I was kind of mad at that.

" 'I've been hauling wood and carrying water for you two for four years now and I haven't been slaving away just so you could stand here screaming at each other and pulling the house down around our ears. Hunt, you wouldn't even know how to answer the mail if I didn't do it for you, and Kathy, maybe you'd rather be queening it up in some restaurant in New York, but you're here and the two of you managed to drag me with you. And you can both just damn well get hold of yourselves right now, if for no other reason because you owe it to me. In fact, you both owe me a hell of a lot more than that!'

"Well, they stood there staring at me like the world had gone crazy, that big fellow with TV powder on his face and Kathy with her lower lip trembling and tears in her blue eyes and so beautiful at that moment I just wanted to get down on my knees and take it all back.

" 'Matt,' Hunt finally said, 'you're right, and I'm sorry. I'm sorrier than I can say. And I've got to tell you now, Kathy's right. I don't think we can win this thing.'

" 'Oh, Hunt . . . ' " Kathy spoke just those two words, but I couldn't even begin to tell you how much was in them—how much hurt, and what a sense of how much they had expended of themselves, for it to come to nothing in the end.

" 'I just don't see how we can.' Hunt was looking at me, but he put one of those long arms of his around her. 'But, Matt, I owe you just as much as you say, maybe more. And I owe something to Kathy and maybe even to myself, whoever that is. So I'll tell you—we're still going to give them a run for the money, Matt. I promise you.' He pulled Kathy against him. 'They're not going to steal it either. I'm not Old Bull's boy for nothing, you know.'

"She kissed him on the cheek, nothing special, and pulled him toward me, and hooked one of my arms with hers, and we all three stood there in a little knot in the middle of the room.

" 'I'm sorry I said that about your father, Hunt. Matt's right, I'm tired, so tired, but listen . . . listen, you two! I don't think we're going to lose, that was just temper talk. We're going to win! I know we are, we've come this far together and we're going the rest of the way. Something's going to happen, it's going to break for us, we're going to make it break for us!'

"And you know what? I actually thought for a while that she was right. She gave me a feeling we could pull it off, somehow, and then it dawned on me that it was really the first time since we'd been in it that I had thought, Hunt's going to be president, maybe he's really going to be president. I looked over her head at Hunt, and he had a strange, faraway look on his face, something . . . hot in his eyes, and I just knew he was feeling what I felt. Suddenly I thought I could tell he was thinking about winning again; as late as that, he was still thinking about winning."

"That girl," O'Connor said, "in those days she could make a man think anything she wanted."

"Something the public doesn't generally understand," Dunn said, "is the kind of pressures on people like the Andersons."

French nodded. "Politicians, when they lose, they lose in public, don't they? Right out in front of everybody."

Well, not always, Morgan thought, not necessarily, not even Anderson. What he lost in public wasn't half of what he lost. Because among other things that story Matt just told shows another thing: as late as that, Hunt still had Kathy too. But when that convention was over, she was long gone, like Anne.

"Well," Dunn said, "he was as good as his word—he gave it a run for the money and they didn't steal it from him. That was the first year they tried to have the nominating session in prime time, and it was an unmitigated disaster. They got on the air on schedule, then there was an invocation and a speech from a superannuated govenor who recounted the glories of the party all the way back to the War of 1812—day by day, one of the columnists wrote. But when they began to call the roll for nominations the real trouble started, because of those little red eyes watching from the TV platform.

"The first state chairman that stood up had a voice full of grits. 'Mister Chariman,' he roared, 'the grett stett of A-la-BAM-uh . . .' and I knew right away it was going to be a long night. He went on about the grett stett's pure waters, unbounded opportunities, great traditions, and ditchdigger wages for two or three minutes before he got to the point: 'The grett stett of A-la-BAM-uh . . . passes!'

"Bingham wanted to be more than just a Southern candidate. He'd arranged for Arizona, where he had some backing from retired stockbrokers and descendants of pioneers, to yield to his home state for the nominating speech. Arizona yielded but not without a recitation of its entire history and a catalogue of all its glories, minus the smell of the Phoenix stockyards. When Bingham's delegation chairman got up to announce that his state would make a nomination, it took him three minutes by the clock just to identify which state he had the high honor and personal privilege to represent. When the cameras are on him, I'm sorry to say, every man is an orator.

"The nominating speech for Bingham was by a courtly governor who rolled his rs but that speech wasn't too bad, only thirteen minutes. What hurt were the five seconding speeches, which couldn't be delivered until after the fifteen-minute demonstration that followed the nominating speech.

"The demonstration featured replicas of Confederate cannon bombarding the delegates with wads of pingpong balls, each of which had Joe Bingham's picture stamped on one face and the word 'Never!' on the other. The seconding speeches were supposed to be five minutes each, but the five took just under an hour, with appropriate mini-demonstrations after each. All that put Bingham in nomination adequately, but the roll of the states hadn't even got to Arkansas and there were four major candidates and all the favorite sons still to go.

"I put my man in after Bingham. Profiting by his example, I lopped off two seconding speakers and cut our demonstration in half. Nobody else seemed to notice my lead. Stark had Connecticut yield, so his state could put him up next, and the speakers and the demonstration took an hour and a half. Then Aiken went in with the biggest demonstration of all because they had the galleries packed and were trying to show a public groundswell. The Vice-President didn't put on much of a show; he was loyal to the end, but I suppose by then his people didn't really have their hearts in it. Some other favorite sons were sandwiched in there, and finally the roll call came to Anderson's state. I tell you, I almost made up my mind to go for him when I saw he'd taken the same cue I had and pulled out three seconding speeches."

"My idea," O'Connor said. "We're sitting there watching Bingham's nothing-ball show in Anderson's room and we're pulling up our pants legs while the stuff rises and I was insisting it was too long, they were turning the viewers to stone. But Hunt kept saying he couldn't do anything about it, his seconding slate was as carefully balanced for geography, sex, race, religion, and ethnic groups as anything Tammany ever saw. Some of those speakers might go away mad if he backed out at the last minute. But finally the last bigot comes on and, Jesus! he starts out reading the same Jefferson quote about watering the tree of liberty with a little blood that the seconder two speeches back had opened with, and Hunt leaps up like somebody goosed him and yells out, 'By God, I can't stand it! We'll go with the black congressman and that old battle-ax in the pillbox hat. Forget the rest! We'll pick up a million votes just by getting it over with.' "

"Well, he might have done just that," Dunn said, "but at a convention the problem is the delegates inside and not the voters outside. Anderson didn't have much luck trying to mix the two. The Anderson crowd outside tried to rush the doors and join the demonstration when his name went in. The cops held them back, but the regulars put one more black mark beside his name. I thought it was bad form myself, but it was past midnight and a little melee at least livened things up. Besides, the TV watchers saw the fight at the doors of the hall rather than one more stale demonstration inside, and that probably helped keep them awake.

"There was only one favorite son to go in after Anderson's speeches, and everybody in the hall began to wake up and move around and the tension began to build—the excitement even television can't quite kill off at a convention, the knowledge that the biggest stake of all is on the table at last. There's a peculiar duality about it. The game is there in front of you, and yet you know something's probably happening somewhere else. The deck is being stacked out of sight of the players and the spectators. If you're holding cards, looking for delegates, or trying to put them in at the right time and place, it's a wracking experience. A convention is no place for quick nerves or impulse buying. There's too much happening, too many currents moving, no one can know for sure what everyone else is up to. Card files and computers are great, up to the first ballot; but after the roll call begins, a man better have an instinct for what's happening. He better have good connections and a settled stomach.

"That night, it was well past midnight before the convention came back to the grett stett of Alabama, whose chairman made his speech again, then threw the whole delegation in for Joe Bingham. The Confederates pranced around a little and fired off some more pingpong balls, just to get things moving. Back then, we didn't have a rule against speechmaking when a chairman announced his vote, or that a delegation would be bypassed if it had to be polled; those were put in later for the TV people. So every chairman made a Chamber of Commerce speech before casting his state's vote, and some of the delegations insisted on a man-by-man poll, so each delegate could get a moment of glory on the home screen. The roll call was slow as molasses. Nobody had expected a winner the first time around, and gradually it came clear that the thing was going just about as predicted. I can't call off the exact vote, but Anderson led with what I'd expected, about three fifty, and —"

"Anderson, three hundred forty-five," Glass said, handing Dunn a book from Anderson's cluttered shelves. "Here it is, right here in the *Information Please Almanac.* I just looked up the convention for that year."

"Which was a calculated gamble," Matt said. "You see, I wanted to go in lower and have a bigger swing on the second ballot, but Hunt said he had to run first or drop dead, and we couldn't be sure how many they were going to hold off Aiken and put on the Vice-President. So we went pretty near whole hog on the first ballot."

"Then Anderson was right and you were wrong," Dunn said, "because they brought Aiken in second at two sixty-eight. If Anderson had been much lower than he was, it would have scared the Nervous Nellies in his delegations—and he had plenty—to say nothing of the effect on some he'd won in primaries who were itching to desert to a winner. They panic quick when the roll's called. Bingham ran strong too, just five behind Aiken, but that was high-water for him. I don't remember Stark being so weak, but according to this he was fourth with only one twenty-eight and a half. The Vice-President had sixty-five, quite a comedown they set up for the old gentleman, wasn't it? My man and the other favorite sons totaled—let's see

—a hundred forty-nine and a half. So nobody was anywhere near a majority. I felt good about that because it was just about what I'd told my people would happen."

Yes, with that adding-machine brain, Morgan thought, watching the green lenses opaque and intimidating. It's too bad Glass found the almanac because I'll bet you'd have remembered every vote to within two or three. Not that it matters, but so could I.

Morgan had been working in the press area that night cramped between the teletypist and Hobart chewing his nails. It had been Morgan's first convention, too, as it had for O'Connor—for that matter as it had for Anderson. But Morgan had not let that be known. His paper was treating him as if he were a veteran political reporter, and he was letting it happen. Good cover. Morgan had done well for his editors, he knew that, he was proud to think how unusual it was to be assigned to write the running story for the leading newspaper, never even having set foot in a national convention before. But he was not sure they realized that; they only knew he could turn out the kind of copy they had to have—fast, above all; short graphs and short takes, full of details, long on the surface action, with just enough of the current underneath not to offend their sense of propriety. Morgan was a star in that galaxy, he knew it, they knew it—and never more so than that night.

The scene lay before him, that heaving sea of people, the rising tide of numbers, the banners and the bands. The memos were coming in from the floor men, the phone-set on his head brought its steady rasp of guidance from the hotels, the headquarters suites, the "torture chamber" behind the speaker's rostrum. All had to be pulled together, set down, made coherent, dispatched—as if in one motion, without hesitation or reflection. Morgan could handle it; he could even silence nervous Hobart with blank stares and insulting disregard of advice.

Oh, I could handle it all right, he thought, I was a professional.

Out of sheer professional instinct, out of his hard, gemlike talent for imitation and reproduction of everything burned into his brain through years of watching and waiting and reaching, Morgan knew what would happen, what he would write had happened, almost before it could come true; in the inspired rush of description as if it were prevision from his fingers to the machine to the eager, tearing hands of Hobart to the drumbeat keys of the imperturbable teletype to the immense humming night and on to the far machines and hardening lead, Morgan felt one long, perfect line of communion pulsing and unbroken, a lifeline—but to what end, what life?

And he knew with sick certainty that in this facility alone had he ever found himself, his meaning, his place.

Morgan could recognize himself, about the time he filed his third new lead in its crisp professional symmetry, with the same clarity that a few days before had disspelled the late-day dimness of his stale room, the evening flick and flash of headlight beams and street lamps reflected through the flutter of leaves and the limp drift of curtains at the window; he could recognize himself as he had at that moment when Anne had rolled from under him and stood stiffly by the bed . . . oh, Anne! white, luminous, tiny in the dusk, saying, "Not through me, you selfish shit, you're not going to reach through me like I'm not there. I'm not going to be just some kind of salvation for you . . . I'm going to live too!"

And in the bitter salt of seeing clear he was alone as always, knew he would be, but pleaded a last time *don't leave don't go I need* . . . but it was no use, he knew as he spoke.

"I'm going, Rich," Anne said. "I have to go."

But he had to stay, reach, get on, he knew that too. And it seems I did, didn't I? he had often thought as the years crept by.

So that night in the howling hall, with the galleries swelling down on him, and the faces swarming past the rail, and the headphones crackling with another life, in his fingers an absolute mastery, perfect control, oneness with his value—in that moment of his fullest being, Morgan saw himself clear, stripped the phones off his head, stood up abruptly, kicked the rough wood bench backward, and said to Hobart, "Breath of air."

Distress flooded Hobart's stubbled, harassed face, but Morgan said, "That'll hold ' em for the last edition. They'll have to replate for the late stuff anyway." How jargon soothes, he thought.

Morgan stepped up on the bench, to the top of the thin plank table, feeling it give and sway beneath him, and walked down its jammed length, above pounding colleagues sweating out their grinding copy, that stuff of their lives that in him flowed as easily as blood from an open vein. He leaped down into the crowded aisle, flashed a pass at a surly guard, and trotted down clacking steps to a concrete corridor running dankly behind the hall. Behind him, groans and shrieks went up at some senseless development. Morgan found a booth, slammed the door behind him, dropped in a dime for long distance. Anne was drunk when she answered.

"Jus' sittin' here thinkin' 'bout you, sweetie."

The booth smelled like well-worn shoes. "I've been writing my arm off. Haven't stopped all night till now."

"Jus' what I was thinkin', jusazackly what I was thinkin' 'bout you doin'."

"You got home all right, did you?"

"Depends what you mean all right."

"I guess it really is better," Morgan said. "I know you were bored out here."

"Bored there, bored here. Lone there, lone here. S'no diffrus."

"Can I do anything, Anne? Any goddam thing at all?"

"You wood't. 'Cause if you *would*, you would have. But you never did."

"Didn't *what?*"

"Jus' did't," Anne said. "And if you would, you would have. I'm drunk's hell, sweetie."

"I'd never have guessed."

"Not 'cause of you."

"I didn't think so."

"'Cause of my goddam life. You did't know I had one, did you? B'longs to me'n' nobody else . . . 'specially not you."

"Are you alone?" Morgan said sharply, meanly, nowhere else to turn. "Have you got somebody there with you?"

"Go back t'work," Anne said. "'S your thing." The phone clicked distantly, finally.

Morgan sat in the booth. It didn't smell like shoes but like a damp basement. Maybe he wouldn't go home at all, he was thinking, little Rich could survive, kids were tough. Or maybe he would take both of them somewhere else, change all their lives. But either way it would solve nothing. Morgan knew that.

He sat in the booth a long time. When he opened the door to go back to his profession, his place, his redeemer, they were already calling the roll again.

". . . tried to put off the second ballot to the next day," Matt was saying, "but you know how they had that convention by the balls. We couldn't even get recognized, and the first thing we knew they were balloting again, trying to stampede it for Aiken. The only thing we could do was put in our second-ballot strength and beg the uncommitteds to hold on."

"Dunn said, 'I was feeling a little pressure by then'— sounding as if he did not really know what pressure was or why it should bother anyone. "I had one of the biggest uncommitted blocs and of course they were all after it. They knew the Vice-President's delegates were moving to Aiken. That was a pretty good swing in itself, but they knew I knew it wasn't enough. Aiken's floor manager was a shrewd old ex-senator who played pinochle with the President. Pretty soon I saw him come pushing and shoving down the aisle like a truck. He got down on one knee by my chair and somebody shoved in behind me. It was one of the governors in our bloc, a fellow with big hopes. I hadn't asked him to listen in, but my guess was that Aiken's floor manager had.

" 'Dunn, you can count the hairs on a Siamese cat, I've seen you do it,' the floor manager said. 'Now, you know you got the chance of a lifetime here. We understand some of these other favorite sons got their ass in a sling, they got to move to Anderson on the second go-round, but not you. Stark and Bingham won't cave in this early. I'm leveling with you, Dunn, because with you we can crack the whole thing wide open. Now's your chance, just what you've been waiting for.'

" 'I believe I'll hold awhile.'

" 'But listen'—that governor of ours was jumping up and down—'don't you think—'

" 'Your man's nowhere near a majority,' I told Aiken's floor manager. 'I thought the White House had more muscle than that.'

" 'He's coming on. You know he's coming on, you been here before.'

" 'Show me some more.'

" 'Goddammit, Dunn!' That governor was itchy; he never did go anywhere. 'We'd hate to be holding the bag if Aiken goes over. Maybe this is the time.'

" 'Show me some more,' I told the floor manager again, and he bludgeoned his way off along the aisle, swearing like a sailor.

"The phone between my feet began to ring. Stark's people wanted to know indirectly what I wanted. I said I wanted a winner and hung up. It rang again, and a cabinet officer was on from downtown. I promised him to think hard about Aiken and the national security. One of the other governors in our little bloc came over and asked me if I was sure. I said no, but did he believe I was wrong? A man from Bingham came by and said they'd appreciate it if I held the line, and I said I'd appreciate it if they held the line. An Anderson delegation leader came by and told me about the will of the people. A state chairman who'd already put in his delegation for Aiken arrived to turn the screw; so did one of the men who'd been at the breakfast with the Vice-President.

"Then Curly Layton, in white linen and a hand-painted tie, strolled down the aisle. I stood up to shake hands, and he put his lips close to my ear. 'You understand our position, Dunn. We can't make it without you but maybe we can with you.'

" 'That's the way it looks to me,' I said.

"Curly squeezed my arm. 'You'll be hearing from us.' Then he strolled on, as casual in the crowded aisle as a sightseer on Fifth Avenue.

"Other delegation leaders just happened by, just happened to wonder. As the grett stett of Alabama began its Chamber of Commerce speech for the third time, opening the second ballot, the phone rang again. It was Kathy Anderson.

" 'You're a little late,' I said.

" 'I've got my spies. They say you're holding.'

" 'Even though I've only got one arm left.'

" 'What are you thinking of doing?'

" 'Backing a winner.'

" 'Then you must be thinking of us.'

"I wasn't yet sure what I was thinking and not just because of the long distance from three forty-five to six ten. I wasn't against Anderson just because the President and the other leaders were. I thought Anderson had style, and he obviously had more courage and brains than most. I liked the way he'd run in the primaries and handled himself in the pinches. He would run well in the fall, I could see that. As for the other possibilities, Stark and Bingham were clowns, but I could live with Aiken and I supposed the country could too. I just didn't have much to gain from an Aiken nomination, there were too many cooks to spoil that broth. If I could put over a long-shot like Anderson, there would be more in it for me and my people. But moving to Anderson would be a big risk, as far as he had to go and with as much power as he had against him. Besides, I was like a lot of others, I wasn't certain about him. I thought it was rather curious, for instance, that I was hearing from his wife but not from him. In fact, at that point I'd really only talked to him directly just twice.

"The first time was before he announced and before we closed our state with the favorite-son candidacy. Anderson came out for a speech to a civic group and called me. Late that afternoon I went to his hotel for a drink. I told him we'd go to the convention uncommitted past our favorite son, and he understood that; Anderson had as good an instinct for the right move and the right thing to say as any candidate I've ever seen. We got on —so well in fact that I opened up a little.

" 'Senator,' I said, 'Paul Hinman's nothing to me. I had no commitments to him. But weren't you a little rough on him?'

"He looked at me over a glass of Scotch. 'Rough as a cob. Do you think it was below the belt?'

" 'I'm more interested in what you think.'

"He nodded and thought about that before speaking. 'Maybe I'd have been more . . . precise, if it had been in a courtroom. But I'd have done it some way. I *saw* places like the camps he owned. I *talked* to the people he was gouging. I've seen some dead kids in places like that, lots of hungry ones. Hinman didn't care. Lonnie Tobin's identification was positive there's no reason to think he was lying. Hell yes, I'd do it again.'

"He reminded me of that the second time we talked, which wasn't until our caucus the second day of the convention. He'd made a good little speech —ripped right in on the bossism thing even with me sitting there. In front of our crowd he showed he knew about some problems that interested us. He had a good line or two on water problems, for instance, and a tough farm program that made sense, production controls. He said he would build up the national defense, which back then was good politics everywhere, and even better economics in our state. He wasn't as bad as some of the delegates had expected on the states' claim to the tidelands. So when he asked for second-choice consideration, there was a decent hand; anyone can do home work, but not everyone can sound like he knows what he's talking about. Afterward we talked privately, and I told him he'd done himself some good.

"That made him smile. 'With you?'

"I thought how tall he was, and how much older than when I'd talked to him a year before. We stood in one corner of the big room where the delegation had caucused, and the crowd was moving past us toward the corridor. There was a lot of pointing and talking, and a couple of photographers were snapping away. 'With all of us,' I said.

"That made him laugh out loud. 'In your delegation, they tell me, there's a constituency of just one.'

" 'You know better. I wouldn't last long if I asked them to do too many things they didn't want to do. But they liked you.'

" 'Good, I'm glad you think so. But are you still worrying about Hinman?'

" 'I was never worried about Hinman.'

" 'Then about me?'

" 'I own some racehorses,' I told him. 'If I waited to buy a perfect horse I wouldn't own any.'

" 'I'm a long way from perfect, Mister Dunn. But if they count me out here for what I did to Hinman, I'll still tell you the next day what I told you the last time I saw you: I'd do it again because I know it was right. There's no doubt in my mind; Hinman deserved what he got.'

"But in my experience a great many people deserve punishment, or might if you looked into it. That isn't an idea that inspires me. I'm more concerned about who does the punishing, and how, and with what right. So I wasn't certain about Anderson as the second roll call got under way; besides, the middle of the convention floor at that hour of the night is a bad place to have to think things through.

"So I said to Kathy on the phone, 'They're getting down to our state. Call me back after this ballot, if you're still alive and kicking.'

" 'We'll be alive and kicking so hard nobody will have to tell you.'

" 'Then call me back and tell me if Curly can do some business in those Bingham delegations.' Just as I hung up, the itchy governor stuck his face in mine, trying to look dangerous. He smelled of whisky and panic.

" 'Our boys are switching, Dunn, it's now or never.'

"The loudspeaker boomed our state's name. I looked back along the aisle a few rows to the itchy governor's delegation and signaled to a friend of mine, the man who had picked its members. He came right over.

" 'Your man wants to break your commitment.'

"My friend looked at his governor. The loudspeaker was calling again. So were some of my own delegates, trying to get my attention. 'Then I'll have to poll the delegation,' my friend said.

" 'Christ.' The itchy governor's tough face was beginning to fall apart, and he tugged his tie loose. 'We'll be left at the post—can't you guys see, the switch is on?'

" 'Let's poll the delegation then.'

"The loudspeaker called us again. I got up and cast our state for our favorite son, and a big cheer went rolling through the hall; a lot of Anderson state banners were waving at me, and Bingham's people peppered the crowd with some more pingpong balls.

" 'All right, goddammit,' the itchy governor said as I sat down. 'You know I can't swing it if you poll the bastards, they're all your guys, but I tell you, you're both missing the goddam boat.'

" 'Tell me later,' my friend said, 'when you learn to count like Dunn.'

"That was the kind of night it was. The place had sorry air-conditioning; it was jammed with people who were worn out and short-tempered. Rival-ries were strong and nerves were raw. Bingham's delegates constantly waved Confederate flags and that didn't help anything; when they started singing 'Dixie,' one Northern delegation with a lot of Negroes got up and began singing the 'Battle Hymn,' and it took the chairman a quarter-hour to restore some kind of order. Even then the noise was overwhelming; trying to move in the aisles was like going fifteen rounds. There was a dispute in one of the Midwestern states and the delegation had to be polled. The count came out wrong and they polled it again. The night began to look as if it would never end; some of my people were catching naps, sleeping in their chairs, and I had to keep a constant eye out that others didn't wander off and get lost in the crowd. I ate a plastic hot dog in a cotton roll and watched Aiken's floor manager come blundering back down the aisle.

" 'You dropped the ball, Dunn. Stark's going to move first. You better get with it.'

" 'If Stark's moving, you don't need me.' He glared at me and went away. I called over a couple of my people and told them to find out about Stark. Then I studied my tally sheet. The polling of the Midwestern state ended and the roll call droned on. Aiken was coming up all right, mostly with the Vice-President's switched-over votes, but so was Anderson with some pick-ups from favorite sons and a handful from Stark. Anderson was no push-over, that was obvious on the tally sheet. Those second-ballot gains must have scared Aiken's people, but Anderson was still in desperate shape; all that power behind Aiken was beginning to show.

"Listen to this from the almanac—here's the way the second ballot came out: Anderson, three seventy-eight. That was thirty-three over the first ballot, so he was still the front-runner but just barely. Aiken had picked up seventy-nine to keep second place with three forty-seven, and that made it tight as Dick's hatband. Bingham was running steady, up six to two seventy-nine lily-whites. Stark was the only one down but just to one twenty-three, unless you count the Vice-President, of course; all but three of the old gentleman's first-round votes had moved to Aiken, and I wondered what prodigies of loyalty or honor or stupidity or missing the word those three holdouts represented. The favorite son with the ninety-eight, that was our man. There was still no one anywhere near six-ten, not on paper anyway.

"But if Stark moved on the next ballot, then Anderson had to have our bloc to stay alive. The way I read the scorecard, if Stark swung to Aiken and I moved to Anderson, there'd be something near a deadlock, and the Confederates then could probably put over the man they chose, Aiken most likely. If I went to Aiken along with Stark, that would be the ball game but damn little in it for me. You don't get much for running in a stampede.

"On the other hand, if I went to Anderson first, what would Stark do? I'd seen him earlier that day, and his nerves were worn as thin as a sales man's shoes; besides, he had the clear intention of squeezing the vice-presidency out of somebody, and I thought Aiken would make that kind of a deal only as a last resort. But while I was trying to figure things out in the middle of that madhouse, I heard the gavel and somebody making a motion, and suddenly the whole mob was shouting aye for a recess to ten a.m. There was no objection even from the Aiken delegates.

"I looked at one of my people half asleep in the chair next to me. 'If they don't want to vote again right away, Stark must be holding on,' I said. 'Anderson's still alive.' "

"I almost got down on my knees when that happened," Matt Grant said. "Not just for the reprieve, but I was so tired I thought I'd drop if they went down that roll one more time. But Hunt stood up and turned off the TV and said to Kathy, 'Now it's time for the nut-cutting.'

"And she said, 'Call Dunn.'

"But instead, Hunt got his floor managers and delegation chairmen in, jammed them all in that room somehow, while he lay propped up on the sofa, and went around the circle. None of them was giving up or selling out, they weren't that kind, but every single one agreed with what Curly Layton told him bluntly. The word was out that Stark would be forced to Aiken, if not on the next ballot, then soon. So we had to have Dunn or throw it in.

"When they left to get an hour or so of sleep, Kathy said, 'Now call Dunn.'

"But Hunt said to me instead, 'Get Morgan.' "

"At the time," Morgan heard himself saying, "I could cheerfully have had him shot. I was almost literally dead on my feet. By the time I'd filed my last lead and shoved my way out of the press area, all our hired cars had left; the publisher and the managing editor and the columnists and their wives had got to them first, and the people who'd done the work had to shift for themselves. I was carrying a typewriter and an old briefcase, and I was so beat-up I couldn't have walked a block. So I hitched a ride on a beer truck into a part of the city where I could get a taxi. I remember the truck driver was for Bingham because he said Bingham would keep down the coons. But I was too tired to care. I went to sleep in the taxi, and again standing up in the service elevator going up to my floor. I was sitting on the bed with my pants off and wondering if it was worth it to take off my shirt, when the phone rang.

"Never heard a man swear with more feeling," Matt said, chuckling. "I remember saying he couldn't be any tireder than we were, which just made old Morgan cuss some more."

"But I'll tell you what I was really thinking while I put my pants back on," Morgan said. "It was *why me? what's up?* You know, to get a call from a leading candidate at the most crucial stage of a national convention, even if he was an old friend—at that time of my life, I reckon I'd have crawled up seven flights on my hands and knees. Which is damn near what I had to do, because I couldn't get the service elevator to come back and the public elevator lobby on my floor was jammed with drunks and delegates and wives and whores—hopeless. By the time I managed to haul myself up to the twelfth floor, from the fifth, I was leaning so far forward I really was balancing myself with my hands on the steps above me.

"Anderson's floor was quieter than mine—they had cops on the candidates' floors. Matt had given them my name, and after I showed them credentials there was no difficulty finding my way to twelve-oh-one. Matt let me in; the living room was blue with smoke and littered with glasses and overflowing ashtrays. I remember the sour light and all those stickers plastered on the mirrors, and the posters on the walls looked sad and ridiculous, like women sobering up. " 'Hunt's in the bedroom,' Matt said. 'I got to get an hour's sleep or collapse.'

"I watched, a little enviously, as he went off to bed. Then I went into the bedroom. A big bowl of chrysanthemums was half dead on the dresser. It was hot in there, as if the air-conditioning couldn't pump itself that high in the building; they had opened the two windows, so you could hear the engine mutter and the truck clatter from the early-morning streets. Kathy was moving around the room in her slip; Hunt was in his shorts on the bed, propped against the headboard, under a big 'Anderson's In!' poster taped to the wall. Danny here stuck that up over their bed for a gag on Kathy. The bed was covered with tally sheets and papers, a tray with the remains of someone's room-service hamburger and french fries, and from an open briefcase there was a spill of pamphlets and carpetbag buttons. Kathy looked tired, older even than the hour and the strain seemed to require. Her face was pale, unmade-up; her hair was in disarray, and her shoulders were slumped a little; a strap kept slipping and she would push it into place impatiently. I threw my jacket on one of the hotel's fake antique chairs and dropped into another, loosening my tie. We were a collection of zombies.

" 'To what,' I said, 'am I indebted for this delightful goddam surprise?'

"Kathy looked at me with undisguised disgust. 'Not for your wisecracks.'

"Hunt laughed, as he had so often come to do, without humor, a dry lusty sound in the room. 'We're on edge, Rich. I don't have to tell you that.'

" 'I'm sorry, I'm tired too. I was trying to be cheerful and I guess it's not he time for that, is it?'

"Hunt may have been as tired as I was, but he didn't show it anywhere out in his face and in the slouch of his shoulders; he had that incredible politician's inner steam still driving him beyond fatigue, toward the golden moment, and he seemed almost as alert and intense as if he had just risen from a good night's sleep.

" 'What do you hear about Stark, Rich?'

" 'Going to Aiken for sure.'

" 'Next ballot?'

" 'Or the next.'

" 'Then why'd they recess?'

" 'Now you,' I said with satisfaction, and wit that seemed to shine splendidly through the fog of my exhaustion, 'undoubtedly perceive some diabolical maneuver worthy of Martin Van Buren or maybe even Machiavelli himself or one of those old-time cats. But Richmond P. Morgan s of a simpler turn of mind.'

" 'I'll say.' Kathy pushed up the errant shoulder strap. She was still moving constantly about the room, as if unable to stand still or to rest— driven, reaching.

" 'So what simple-minded Morgan sees, and Morgan's spies confirm as absolute incontrovertible fact, is that that old razorblade in the White House sent the word out here he didn't want Aiken nominated like a thief n the night after everybody was in bed in the East and the TV turned off. So they went over to morning, figuring you for dead anyway.'

" 'That clicks,' Hunt said, 'that's exactly what they'd do, and it gives us our chance. Bingham's going to hold forever and they let us off the ropes. That gives us a last chance.' "

Morgan fell silent. He had forgotten nothing, the moment was as clear n his mind as if he had had before him a sharp photograph of the three of them in the stuffy bedroom. But some things he knew he could never tell; to do so would have been like exposing that inner core of self he had guarded all his life. Because it had been Kathy who had spoken next, and not kindly, and as if in the last throes of exasperation.

"I don't want him here, Hunt, he ought not to be here!"

"Tell him why," Anderson said calmly.

She had wheeled on Morgan then, eyes snapping, fists clenched, lunging at him slightly, the shoulder strap slipping down her slender arm and her hair flying unheeded, beautiful as fire. "Because you'll go out of here and spread it over your whole stupid front page. You may call yourself a friend, but there aren't any friends when it gets down to this point. You're a reporter first—Hunt, you know he's a reporter first, last, and always!"

Before Morgan could open his mouth, Hunt spoke again, the authority in his voice unmistakable and final. "No," he said. "No, Rich is the only one who doesn't want anything from me. Rich won't bullshit me."

And Morgan had stared at him a long time. Morgan had sat there lumpish, tired, sick with his own inadequacies, the fierce, relentless reaching of his life, of all the world he knew—Morgan sat there silent until Hunt Anderson said again, "Rich doesn't want anything from me is why I need him here."

Kathy stared at Hunt too, the fallen strap forgotten, a white slope of breast heaving with her open-mouthed breathing. A clatter from the street rose suddenly through the window as if trucks were racing down the block.

"Not from you," Morgan said at last, the salt sting of tears harsh in the corners of his eyes. "Not this time anyway."

He hardly even saw Kathy turn away. He saw only Anderson's slow smile, the single nod of his large, odd head. And Morgan had understood then and afterward too much of what he had said, done, meant, in those seven words ever to repeat them to anyone.

"But before I could tell him I thought Bingham's holding out was a pretty weak reed to lean on," Morgan said in a moment, hardly missing the beat of his story, "Kathy spoke right up. 'You *know* you've got to do it,' she said. 'What's the good of even asking him about it?'

" 'If Stark goes over, I don't see how you can hold out,' I told Anderson. 'Bingham talks like Stonewall Jackson, but I doubt he'll be far behind when the stampede is on.'

" 'Oh, old Joe might hold on two or three more ballots, he's got the fever,' Hunt said. 'What about Dunn?'

" 'To the highest bidder. And you can guess who that'll be.'

" 'Well, isn't that still the only chance left, even so?' Hunt was sitting up on the bed, his voice rising a little. 'If Dunn moves to *us* before Stark can do anything, won't that maybe stop Stark or even make him think about coming our way?'

"Then Kathy charged at him. 'You're just wasting time you don't have sitting here agonizing over it.'

" 'What does Matt think?' I said.

" 'He thinks we've got to have Dunn.'

" 'Well, Kathy's certainly making her vote clear. Why haven't you done it already, if you think it might work?'

" 'First, I thought about going to Bingham instead, but that would be dealing with the racists. You're a backslid Southerner too, Rich, you know I'd hold my hand in the fire before I'd do that. And besides, even if Bingham would give, which I doubt, dealing with him would undercut the whole image and idea of our campaign with the delegations we've got. It could be a disaster. So it really does come down to Dunn or nothing, and maybe even he can't pull it off for us by now. But there's a good reason, anyway it seems good to me, why I haven't called Dunn.'

" 'I'm leaving,' Kathy said. 'I'm not going to listen to this shit any more.' She ran out of the room; the door slammed behind her, its sound explosive in the silence, and I remembered a night years earlier, in this house, when she had slammed shut a window with that same furious crash, as if the hands in their anger had animated the wood.

" 'You see, there's something I could offer that green-eyed shark,' Hunt said, as if he had not noticed her departure. 'But Dunn's a real shark, not like these other characters that act tough and cave in. I've studied him. Dunn would take my soul as well as my entrails. Dunn lives on men's souls.'

"He rubbed his eyes for a moment. I noticed the hair on his chest had gone gray and straggly. Then he slumped back against the headboard. 'Kathy doesn't see it that way. She's had some lines out to Dunn's people. She thinks if I let Dunn know I'm open to reason on state claims to tidelands oil, he'd come over for that.'

" 'Does Kathy really think you might do something like that? After all the things you've stood for?' It was my turn to sit up straight. Sweat had dampened my shirt and I felt it clinging to my back.

" '*I* think I might do it,' Hunt said. 'I want to win, Rich, I've got the fever too. That's what I meant about my soul. That's why I haven't called Dunn.'

"I slumped back in the chair. It would have to be that way, I told myself, a man could never be sure what he would do at the moment of truth, at the zero hour. It was only natural that he would think about it, wonder how well his nerves and character would stand the test.

" 'It didn't start that way,' Hunt said. 'You know the first time the idea of running occurred to me, I told myself it was crazy. I told Kathy the same, the first time she mentioned it. I told Adam I had no intention. Then you had that story in your paper, and I thought you were crazy too. But I don't remember when I began to think maybe it wasn't so crazy. Even when I actually started moving around the country, I don't think I really believed in it, I'm not even sure I wanted it. But maybe it was in the first primary

—remember the way we shocked them? I began to want it. Not the presidency so much, nobody knows what that's all about until he gets it. I mean I began to want to win, Rich, to come out on top. But I was afraid of that. I knew wanting to win can be worse than booze, and I'd stop myself and I'd say, "Where you going, boy?" Only before long, I wasn't stopping myself. I was just wanting to win. And now I'm down to the last trick, Rich, and I guess I'm hooked. I'm lying here wanting to win so much I think I might do anything. I've just been stopping myself from calling Dunn.'

"He fell silent, sprawled long and angular on the bed. I was too tired to know what to say, what to think. The echoes of his voice seemed to ring in the room, and then I realized he was talking again, his voice so low I could hardly hear it.

" 'On the other hand, Dunn would see how, if he moved first, it would put the pressure on Stark and maybe turn everything around. And that's the kind of chance I figure Dunn wants, to make a big score by himself, not just part of one with Aiken. So if I'm right that's *my* chance, you see, maybe I won't have to make a deal, maybe I can get Dunn in here and make him see how it could work if he threw in for me. I just might be able to pull it off.'

" 'And if you can't . . .' The words hung there in the airless room, in the echoes I thought I could hear of the slamming door.

" 'In that case, I'd probably offer him whatever he wants,' Hunt said. 'That's what I might find myself doing if I call Dunn.'

"Neither of us said anything for a long time. Then, strangely, my exhaustion seemed to go away, and my brain surged. Everything was clear to me. 'I don't think you'll offer him . . . anything. I don't believe you want to win that badly.'

" 'I told you once,' Hunt said, 'you're a funny goddam kind of professional.'

" 'But you've got to call him if you want to stay in the running. The question really is whether to call him and take your chance, or to quit and take no chance.'

" 'Exactly,' Hunt said. 'What's your vote?' "

It had, of course, been foregone, Morgan thought, pausing again, enjoying the suspense of his listeners, how he would answer that question. He wanted to chance it, Hunt had said, the first night they had met. *I've got to do it, I was born to do it.* Morgan remembered thinking fleetingly of the Great Bull Calf Walk, of Hinman goaded and beaten, but he knew he had been in no real doubt of what he would say; just as he had believed in Hunt

Anderson at the start and through everything, he had believed in him still, at the zero hour. Maybe I had to believe in him, or in something, Morgan thought, and maybe I still do.

"I didn't even hesitate," Morgan finally said, "I just told him to call Dunn. " 'You can handle him.' I said. 'You're Old Bull's boy.' "

"And Hunt laughed and reached for the phone—"

"Mister Grant," Jodie said, from the doorway, "you better come out front iffen you don't mind. The old Senator's here."

"Senator?" Matt said. "You mean Senator McLaren?"

Morgan knew before Jodie could answer that of course it was Zeb Vance.

"That the one. They parking his car now."

"Well, for God's sake," Glass said, "you guys can't rush out until Morgan finishes telling us—"

"Never mind," Dunn said. "There's nothing else to tell. The dealer in souls went to Aiken on the third ballot and that was the end of that."

The Storyteller V

The services were held at the graveside after the hot sun slipped low in the sky. Well before then, a large crowd of mourners was on hand; the meadow in front of Anderson's house was covered with parked cars, and the state troopers were out on the private road, directing parking along its sides. By twos and threes, people were strolling across the lawn to the house, and some early-goers were walking through the woods to the little graveyard on the hill. The stream of viewers through the parlor held steady until, long after the luncheon had been cleared from the tables under the trees, Morgan saw Bobby Anderson come out the front door, march down the steps, and join his friends, his face thin, pinched, his head high and held as if his neck and shoulders were rigid. Morgan knew it was over then, the coffin was closed, Anderson had disappeared from mortal view and lived now only in memory and record. For a moment he wished he had joined the line moving past the body, but it would have been a chilling last memory. Then he wished desperately that Bobby had come to stand with him rather than with his school group. But that was as closed as the coffin and could no more be reopened. Besides, Morgan thought, you made your choices in life, and he had made his; he would not go back on them if he could, he told himself.

Still the crowd kept coming. After a while a sleek, noiseless hearse, faintly misted with August dust, nosed among the walkers on the road, with prudence, as if unwilling to create more business for its owners. The hearse backed near the door of the house, and a few young men went over to admire its fittings and kick its front tires. Bobby went back in the house, looking reluctant, at the side of an assistant undertaker in a shiny black rayon suit and a silver tie. In a few minutes eight United States senators emerged from the house, pushing Anderson's flag-draped coffin on its rubber-tired platform. The undertaker from the registration stand and his assistant expertly guided it and the senators down the steps; with efficiency, the coffin was slipped into the waiting interior of the hearse. Kathy came out, on Bobby's arm; just behind them was a silver-haired man with a flushed, solemn face, the governor of the state. He walked with his angular wife, and around the four of them the undertaker flitted like a black moth. The hearse moved a few yards; a black Cadillac slipped into its place, and Kathy and Bobby got in with the governor and his wife.

Several buses had been moving back and forth to the graveyard, carrying older people, distinguished guests, and the faint-hearted who did not wish to walk. Morgan saw Zeb Vance and Millwood Barlow entering one of the buses; it fell in behind the Cadillac, and the two vehicles followed the hearse in stately progression across the fields toward the line of woods. As the bus went past, Morgan saw the faces of senators, bored and impatient, looking down at him. He walked a few steps with Sprock & Berger.

"It's a strange thing," one of them said.

"The way your life works out." The other seemed to know exactly what had been meant.

"I mean when we first went down to testify to his committee . . ."

". . . we never thought we'd spend a good part of our lives working for him, the way we have."

"But we wouldn't have had it any other way."

"Not looking back on it. Not considering the things we were able to do in our work that he made possible."

"The fact is," they told Morgan, or one of them did, "working for Senator Anderson, especially those first years, we felt we were part of something."

It had been a gift of Anderson's, Morgan thought, to make people feel that way—to suggest to them that they all shared an enterprise equally. Which, as the hearse creeping through the dust and the long lines of people walking to the graveyard attested, was only the truth. Maybe, Morgan thought solemnly, the only truth. But it was best not to descend into such gloomy considerations, he thought, lest one become ponderous with wisdom. He held back in search of Dunn, while Sprock & Berger stepped out briskly.

Dunn came along with French and Glass. Matt Grant and Danny O'Connor had gone ahead to the graveside some time before, to make sure all was ready. Glass herded Morgan a little aside from the other two men.

"You were right, Rich. I'm glad I stayed."

"Why? You really didn't have any obligation, no matter what I said."

"Because I'm interested," Glass said. "I'm wishing I'd known him. Besides I got a look at *her* coming out of the house and I'm beginning to understand the way you talk about her."

"I'll introduce you if there's a chance." Morgan put aside for at least the funeral hour the thought that Glass probably was trying to retrieve previous indiscretions; it was a time for charity, and anyway there would be nothing reprehensible about anything so human.

Charlie French, mopping his brow in the afternoon heat, edged between them. "Considering the size of this crowd, I guess Anderson must have been a popular man with the home folks."

"You can't tell by the crowd," Morgan said, "because a lot of them are here to see and be seen, and a lot more just for protocol. Anderson actually got to be something of a mythical figure down here—the only politician we ever had in this state who really ran seriously for president. After that he dropped more and more out of controversy and out of sight. So at the end he didn't have any real enemies. Matt's been running a good tight operation to take care of the constituents. People knew Hunt was drinking a lot, but that got to be part of the myth—the man who was almost great, then gave it all up or threw it all away, Old Bull's boy in the bargain. Hunt had a sort of mystery about him. I think it was more that than popularity."

Dunn was walking slightly apart from them, head down, as if in deep thought. Morgan started to move to his side, then thought better of it. Dunn no longer looked in a mood for talking, and until he was, there would be no use trying to draw him out. The four men walked on, among the chattering, perspiring mourners. Not far ahead, the hearse, the Cadillac, and the following bus were moving not much faster than the walkers, partly for funeral reasons, partly, Morgan supposed, to raise no more dust than necessary. The procession moved through the narrow wood and across the branch, where there was a hastily built footbridge; the water ran as clear and swift beneath the bridge, Morgan thought, as one could wish of life. It was strange how deep and dark and oppressive the wood had seemed the night they had sped through it in Anderson's racketing jeep, when in fact, as he had long since discovered, it was only a narrow band of trees on either side of a sighing flash of water.

Dunn was walking close beside him now, and momentarily they were separated from Glass and French. Morgan felt Dunn's elbow touch his, although Dunn was still walking along with his head down. "I knew all along you were one of Anderson's people," Dunn said, still not looking up, his voice faintly accusing. "You never wrote anything about all that."

Morgan did not have to be told what Dunn meant. "Just that one time, and even that was a wrench for me. Even if I didn't have to lie or slant anything. I just wrote what everyone else did—that you two met that morning but you finally supported Aiken. Maybe I should have put in everything I knew about how the meeting came about and why. But he asked for my help as a friend and I gave it to him. I'd do it again but I never have. No one else ever asked me."

"A man doesn't make many friends," Dunn said. "That bit about the souls was a little rough, wasn't it?"

"I let that out without really realizing you were right there to hear it. It all came back to me so clearly. I was hardly even having to think what I was saying." But he had left out some other parts of the story easily enough; he knew he had wanted Dunn to hear what Anderson had said. Why should Dunn get off without penalty?

They came out of the wood, and Morgan watched the bus climbing the hill toward Old Bull's grave and the waiting place in the earth to which Hunt Anderson would be returned. "Actually," Morgan said, "I don't really know all that much more that I didn't write. Just about as much as I said back there at the house." He looked at Dunn without turning his head, keeping his voice casual. "I never really did know, for instance, how far you and Kathy went with that tidelands thing or what you and Hunt said to each other in the bathroom."

"Ancient history now." Dunn's shoulders lifted in the slightest of shrugs. "Kathy and I talked some about tidelands, I guess. It was a big issue in our state and I had to listen." The same small shrug. "Ancient history."

"But didn't you see a lot of her, more than anyone knew?" The words were bitter in Morgan's mouth.

"She came to see me once before the convention. We got together once or twice while it was going on." He turned his head, and the green lenses flicked at Morgan and away. "I was in love with her a little, I suppose— if that's what you want to know. But when she looked at me all she saw was delegates. So I got over it."

They walked on. "Another interesting thing," Morgan said, "was what you said about who does the punishing. What did you mean by that?"

Glass came blundering between them. "Look at that crowd," he said. "At least he's going out in style."

Morgan cursed silently, but he knew it was too late. Dunn had moved slightly aside and was walking along again with his head down; it was a miracle to have got him to say what he had.

Just above them, people were spreading out on the far side of the graveyard, beyond the big trees and the iron fence that guarded the worn white stones. All around the brow of the hill and far down its grassy slope they stood, with more coming from the wood to join them—men with their jackets slung over their shoulders, others wearing them and wilting in the heat, women in wide-brimmed hats, thin dresses, shoes not meant for walking. Making his way up the incline toward them, Morgan thought suddenly that it was a multitude. Not a crowd, because that suggested more nearly a collection of people, a group drawn together, while it seemed to him that a multitude was essentially a vast repetition—and there before him on the hillside was surely just such a repetition, a simple multiplication of the singularity into which life so deceptively seemed parceled. In the presence of the great unity of death, the diversity of life was as nothing, as the variety of days to the certainty of night; and in the antlike swarm of humanity on the hillside, there was none who did not move nearer by the moment to the ultimate earth. A multitude, Morgan thought again, not becoming but understanding himself a part of it, as he climbed the hill.

The hearse and the Cadillac went under the arched gate into the grave-yard, toward the people waiting on its far side. The bus discharged its passengers at the gate and pulled away to join two others waiting on the hillside; even its exhaust growl seemed subdued in the oppressive heat, the funeral air. Morgan veered left, not to enter the graveyard, but to find a better vantage point than the far fringes of the crowd. Dunn followed; in the stream of people hurrying up the hillside, Glass and French had disappeared.

Morgan went past the gate to a place at the iron fence from which, between tree trunks and past the mute reminding stones, he could see Old Bull's outstretched arms and blessing hands; they were spread toward a dark green tent standing above an earth mound primly disguised in a robe of tinsel grass. Beyond the mound, Morgan knew, would be Anderson's open grave, defaced in its simplicity by the last futile gesture of human vanity even his corporal remnant would have to undergo—the strap-and-motor contraption by which his coffin would be lowered mechanically, untouched by human hands, into the redeeming earth.

Morgan and Dunn stood by the iron fence, watching across the grave-yard, as the eight senators lined up in two rows and the coffin came sliding smoothly from the interior of the hearse. This time the senators actually had to carry it a few steps to the waiting grave. Ironically enough, Updyke was among them, grown senior and honored, a confidant of presidents; and so was Jack Styron, now the majority leader. But the big mules of the old days were long gone before Anderson—Old Ed in seedy retirement in Washington, where he sometimes appeared on the Senate floor, unrecognized in the forlorn rags of his glory; Adolphus Helmut Offenbach a vegetable in the Naval Hospital at Bethesda, where he had lain for years the wasted victim of a stroke; Judge Ward dead, as he no doubt would have chosen, of a heart attack while rigging a loophole during a closed session of the Finance Committee.

The senators placed the coffin beyond the earth mound with its fake-grass coverlet and retired to the second and third rows of folding chairs that had been set up by the grave. Millwood Barlow and Zeb Vance were already seated there. The undertaker scurried around the Cadillac and held open its door. The governor and his wife emerged first, the governor snapping automatically into an effective combination of firm political stance and subdued awareness of the sadness of the hour. Bobby Anderson came next, looking angry; rather rudely moving in front of the undertaker, Bobby held out his hand to his mother, who stepped gracefully—the way she did everything—from the car.

Kathy was in black, the kind of straight simple dress she always had liked; rather daringly for the occasion but sensibly in the heat, it was sleeveless. Despite the Southern funeral custom, she wore no hat or veil, although Morgan saw a black touch of some kind in her hair. With Bobby at her side, she moved directly to the front row of folding chairs and sat down; she seemed almost ostentatiously to pay no attention to the stout minister who came unctuously to her side, his black robe flapping in the hot breeze. The governor and his wife were seated beside Bobby.

The minister went to the head of the grave, paused while the crowd noises stilled. Suddenly Kathy rose, went around the rows of chairs to the fence, and held out her hands to Matt Grant and Curly Layton. She pulled them toward a smaller gate, and they came inside and sat with Zeb Vance and Millwood. The minister waited until all were seated, then spoke mellifluously into the silence of the hillside and the waiting multitude: " 'I am the Resurrection and the life . . .' "

Morgan had for years steeled himself against the ancient litanies of youth and belief; they could not be borne amid the ashes of life. Resolutely he searched the faces of those beyond the graveyard. Danny O'Connor's red Irish face—cholesterol would get him, Morgan thought, get him soon—was contorted, as if he were trying not to weep. Myrtle Bell was not even trying —she wept prodigiously, loudly. A thin face, no longer ferrety under graying hair, caught Morgan's eyes and took him back—A. T. Fowler dignified by age and a prosperity that had not, after all, been spirited off to Moscow or Peking. Morgan saw Sprock & Berger, as alike as the iron spikes of the fence; and beside them the pouty face of Gravel Roads Johnson, who had been volunteering to one and all on Anderson's lawn that he had no ambition at all to return to public service. French and Glass were not in sight, but Morgan saw one of his old editors from the *Capitol Times;* a college classmate with whom he had once planned a movie-theater business; faithful Geraldine, gone irreclaimably to fat and convulsed in grief; and the Honorable Billy G. Melvin, expelled by the voters from Congress but for years more honored as the paid executive of his church's populous Southern branch.

" '. . . brought nothing into this world and it is certain that we can carry nothing out. The Lord . . .' "

Morgan looked at Bobby Anderson; the boy's face was as stony as when he had sat upon the steps that morning and spat at Morgan his hurt and bewilderment. He stared unblinking at the coffin hidden from Morgan by the mound and the fake grass. In recent years, Morgan knew, Bobby had been exceptionally close to his father, far closer than was Kathy, who had grown steadily apart from Anderson.

"It's as if after the convention Hunt had nowhere to turn," Kathy had told Morgan in one of their endless discussions of Anderson, and themselves, and what had happened to them. "As if he was one of those all-American athletes in college, who after all that glory and all those cheers never finds anything else satisfying in life, anything else that matters. Or as if somebody smashed the lenses and prisms that he'd always seen himself through, so he couldn't see himself the same way. Am I making any sense?"

"You are to me." Morgan held her more closely. The winter night beyond her window lay on the land like the pale chill light of the moon; but they were warm together, close, and in the grate across the room the last embers of a fire glowed and popped.

Morgan had long since left Anderson being prepared for bed in his room on the first floor, after an evening's boozy discussion of the relative merits of the seniority system and all other forms of assigning authority, a subject in which Anderson had developed much interest.

"Just a question whether you admit it or not," he would say, "because in every organization senior men tend to exercise authority, no matter what the rules are. Rules don't make organizations, men do. Procedure controls substance, but there's the rub, Morgan, there's the rub—men control procedure."

But Anderson was long asleep, and Morgan said to Kathy, "You're making sense to me because I remember the way he used to look at himself, back in the beginning, how he used to say he wanted to take chances."

"That's it," Kathy said, "and now it's as if he's taken his chances and lost and won't take any more, doesn't even see any there to be taken. That's what I can't abide, the way he's given up."

Morgan luxuriated in the warmth and smoothness of her skin against his own rough and crackly consciousness of himself; he moved his hands on her body, acute sensual pleasure in the touch. But she was talking now, and he knew from experience that she would not slip lightly from one thing to an opposite—from concentration on a problem into the abandon of love-making, from fierce passions into commonplace talk. They had been lying spent between love and sleep for nearly an hour before he had ventured the remark that had set her talking, once again, about Anderson.

"He's getting worse," Morgan said. "Better than half a fifth by himself tonight before Jodie came."

"And yet . . ." She turned her head so that it ground a little against his collarbone, and she was looking up at the ceiling, on which the last flickerings of the fire reproduced themselves in long, wavering shadows. "Hunt's not an alcoholic, you know that. He'd like you to think he's in the grip of some inexorable fate pulling him down, but that's not it, he knows what he's doing."

Morgan saw that he had opened the door beyond which crouched her ever-present and corrosive speculation on the past, and her own part in it.

"I didn't force him to do it, you know that, Rich, that awful night . . . morning, whatever it was . . . I walked out while he was still trying to make up his mind. Isn't that right?"

"You were beautiful. Like a thunderstorm. And showing enough tit to take my mind off politics."

"So *I* didn't make him go to Dunn, although I knew that was the only chance. And even if I did, he was the one who talked to Dunn, he did that, not anybody else in the world."

"I think it was this one was flopping out."

"Stop it, Rich . . . now stop it, I'm serious. Whatever Hunt says now, he was the one who went in that bathroom and talked to Dunn. All by himself."

"That *is* what Hunt says, any time he ever talks to me about it. But I thought it was your idea."

"And if it'd been me in that bathroom, Dunn would have swung to us, I can tell you that. But Dunn just didn't believe in Hunt because Hunt was soft, wish-washy. Just not good enough. Even when Hunt could offer him everything he wanted."

Darts of jealousy pinked Morgan. "How do you know so much what Dunn thought?"

"Well, Dunn *had* to tell me. I was Hunt's wife, I'd had all the dealings with Dunn. He owed me at least an explanation."

Dunn must certainly have thought so, Morgan thought. Morgan cherished among his secret lifenotes, and embellished in his storyteller's heart, the account of an obscure colleague who had chanced, during the final balloting, to be cruising the galleries, high above the convention floor, as the delegations rose one by one to destroy Anderson and nominate Aiken.

"Of course, I knew Dunn had already voted early in the roll call and I recognized him right away by those famous green specs," the colleague said. " 'What a break!' I'm thinking, when I see him up there, but at first I just wanted to pump him for some comment on the convention for my sidebar; so I tried to push up close. But then I realized who he was trying to talk to so I just faded into the crowd a little and put my pencil in my pocket and tried not to look like a reporter.

"Dunn was standing by the rail of this box, not shouting or even raising his voice but I could hear him all right. 'Mrs. Anderson'—he said it several times, trying to get her attention, see? She was sitting there looking down at the delegates below, staring ahead of her just as steadily as if there wasn't another soul within ten miles. Oh, she could hear him all right—if I could hear him she could hear him; but she never let on, not that gal. I was watching her every second, and she didn't so much as blink or move a muscle in that good-looking face. And then he raised his voice, just a bit, maybe it was really only just a little sharper than it had been, and this time he called her Kathy. 'Kathy!' he said, sharplike. And still she never moved or let on, not a muscle, not a flicker. She cut him down as cold as I ever saw a man cut down in my life; she didn't even look at him to do it, she just cut him dead. And he turned around and walked off. I jumped out and tried to get my comment, and he pointed those green specs at me as if I was some kind of an insect and said, 'No comment, no comment.' And I looked back at her then, that great-looking broad, and she was just sitting there like something carved out of ice."

"Why didn't you write that story in your paper?" Morgan had said, when he heard it told a year or so later, on a long press bus ride in the wake of a candidate touring the Polish vote in Hamtramck.

"Story?" the colleague said. "My editor said there wasn't any story, since we didn't know what he'd have said if she'd talked to him. We did print the 'no comment.' "

Which was all anyone needed to know about the common practice of journalism, Morgan had thought, but in the immediate context of Kathy's compulsive recollections and his own small jealousy, the story also raised an obvious question.

"Dunn owed you an explanation," he said, "but when did you get it? I wouldn't call Dunn a non-stop talker."

"Oh, he talked to me. He was a little in love with me, you see. Not for sex—I don't think Dunn could get it up for anything but a rigged delegation or a convention deal, but he thought we were two of a kind and back then he was right, I never really cared a thing about sex either. *You* taught me to like sex. So he was a little in love with me until I . . . hurt him. But after the convention, a year or so later . . . it was some Washington cocktail party. In those mobs you can always talk privately. I told him I was sorry."

Morgan pulled her closer in his arms. He could imagine the scene—how the green lenses and the taut face would have concealed whatever satisfaction or resentment or resolve to hurt or absence of feeling the apology might have caused in Dunn.

"What it comes down to," Kathy said, her voice whispering in the dark, "Hunt wasn't good enough for Dunn."

"That's what Hunt says too."

"After all that work. After those years and years of working as hard as we did. To come so close to the top, to be able to *feel* how close we were, and with all the people that did so much for us . . . after *everything,* to have it all go out the window like that . . . at the last minute practically."

Her voice trailed off; she had stiffened in Morgan's arms. He sensed, still wracking her, across the years, the hurt, the outrage, the reluctance even in the face of established fact to believe.

"And *he* sits down there sucking his bottle like a baby," she said, her low voice savage in the dark. "Don't let him tell you he can't help it."

"He never has. I never thought so."

"It's just that he can't hold himself up high and mighty any more. He can't pretend any more to be all that much better than his father, or even as strong. So he's pulled back from everything. If he can't be the white knight, he'll be the tragic hero."

"Oh, it's all so many years ago," Morgan said. "Don't let it eat you up any more. Don't let it go on affecting you the way it has Hunt. Sometimes I think that's why this is all wrong, between you and me, I mean. If I hadn't come along, if you and I didn't have this together, maybe you and Hunt would have got rid of all those old ghosts."

"No." Her voice was sharp, hard. "After the convention, I could never . . . things had been bad for us almost from the start, particularly after Hunt went into politics. You must have known that, it was as if I was the hired consort. Look good, tend the kids, give the dinners, that was all I was supposed to do. We went to bed twice a year, if we were drunk enough. Then the hearings and the campaign—for a while there was a place for me, we could be together in that, you see. But after the convention I couldn't go back even to what we'd had before. What I couldn't take was his just giving up. *I* don't want to give up."

They were quiet for a long time before Morgan said, "All right, I'll stop feeling guilty."

"Not if I know you. Not the way you dramatize everything."

Morgan guided her hand. "Dramatize this."

"My God," Kathy said, "you must pump that thing up like a tire."

Standing by Dunn at the graveyard fence, staring across the mound that hid Anderson's coffin, seeing Kathy's firm bare arms that had held him so often in love and thrall, Morgan was not sure if he had been remembering one night or many. There had been many—much love-making, endless talk. Sometimes it seemed to Morgan that his whole life had been love-making and talk, and it became difficult to distinguish the bodies and the words, the bodies from the words, the waves of reaching and the eternal mutter of explanation; and so a storyteller could only sift the litter, ransack the past for his needs, take what fitted best for his rickety structures. But sometimes it was even more difficult to know who was storyteller and who was Morgan, at what point the sifter of old conversations and connections had been merely a mutterer of explanations for his own reach.

" '. . . therefore will we not fear,' " the minister was saying, and Morgan heard in spite of himself. " 'Though the earth be moved and though the hills be carried into the midst of the sea; though the waters thereof rage and swell and though the mountains . . .' "

At Morgan's side, Dunn moved slightly; Morgan turned his head and looked at the lean neck, the hard jaw. Of course Dunn had been perfectly capable—no doubt was even more so now—of deciding on the spot that Anderson was not good enough, strong enough, decisive enough, whatever it had been; Dunn would not necessarily have had a word for his instinct. That was what even Anderson had believed had happened, what Dunn had told Kathy, what Morgan had been for years turning over in his mind— edging it here and there, again elsewhere, still again at another point, as a particularly jagged piece has to be tried and tried until at last it can be made to fit in a jigsaw puzzle. But Morgan had never been able to make that piece join smoothly with the rest of what he knew or had concluded. It was a piece that fitted as a story about Dunn; it did not fit as a story about Hunt Anderson.

" '. . . I will be exalted among the nations and I will be exalted in the earth . . .' "

Which, Morgan thought, the words catching his ear, was about what Anderson had set himself to seek. *I just want to show the best in a man instead of the worst,* he had said, standing near the spot where now his long body lay enclosed in lead and the flag. Not exactly a modest goal, and no doubt the seeds of failure were in the wish itself.

Across the graveyard Zeb Vance craned his neck—scrawny now with his great age—to see around the massive form of a Midwestern senator who sat straining forward as if to miss a word might bring hellfire. Zeb Vance, Morgan thought, watching the old man, had never harbored such great notions about himself, or anyone, as Anderson had; Zeb Vance was a wiser man, had seen too much of other men, knew—perhaps—himself too well. Still, there he was, squirming on a folding chair, after a drive halfway across the state, when in such heat and at his age no one could have required or even expected him to have come to the funeral of the man who had succeeded him in the Senate.

Zeb Vance had been stumping firmly up the steps of the house when Matt Grant and Morgan had rushed to the porch from Anderson's room; leaning a little on a cane, he nevertheless looked stronger and straighter than Millwood Barlow, who was just behind him, as always. A black man in a driver's cap stood by ready to help.

"Hello, Matt, you're getting old," Zeb Vance said. "Where's the widow?"

"But you're getting younger every time I see you." Matt took the old man in a bear hug. "She'll want to see you right away."

With bright, snapping eyes Zeb Vance looked across Matt's shoulder at Morgan. "Be dog if it ain't our star reporter. Millwood, look who's here. How long's it been since we seen this scout?"

Millwood peered uncertainly at Morgan, apparently not at first recognizing him. Zeb Vance, freeing himself from Matt's clutch, put out his hand —still huge but thinner now—to Morgan.

"Senator"—Morgan squeezed his hand hard—"it's been too long, too damn long."

His voice apparently triggered Millwood's memory. He stiffened, looking more closely at Morgan, then at the handshake. "I'll be getting out of the heat," Millwood said and went past them into the house.

"The thing you always got to remember about Millwood," Zeb Vance said, "is what a good heart he's got even if not each and every one of the Christian virtues."

"Like forgiving and forgetting?" Morgan still grasped Zeb Vance's hand.

"Oh, Millwood's an ace on forgiving, but where he falls down is forgetting. Millwood's like the late Miss Pearl used to be; Millwood'll hold a grudge till his fingers cramp. Matt, I never thought it'd be me burying Old Bull's boy instead of the other way around, be dog if I did."

"Well, it's always sudden when it comes." Matt's voice descended to the appropriate sepulchral tone. "But these last years . . . he wasn't really well, you know . . . he . . ."

"Too much booze is what they say. Not that I didn't put down my share and still do, but seems like some can and some can't."

"Well"—Matt cleared his throat—"it was actually a heart attack, Senator."

"What I aim to tell the widow, I never got to know the departed well's I should, but I sure pulled for him that time he went for the brass ring. Always struck me as a kindhearted man, unlike his daddy. Matt, I expect in the recesses of this splendid mansion us old farts won't have to look too hard for a breath of life to retrieve the day."

"You won't have to look at all," Matt said. "Just follow me."

Before the screen door closed behind him, Zeb Vance looked back, bright-eyed, at Morgan; except for his neck and the cane, the old man showed few traces of his age or the passing years. The gray hair was as thick as ever and still fell in a shock across his forehead; he still planted large countryman's feet as if he were putting down fence poles. For a moment it was as if Morgan looked back across time, not so much at the old Zeb Vance as to the former Morgan.

"But you take me, Scout, I never had the time for a grudge in my life. How you been doing?"

"Same as ever," Morgan said. "Onward and upward."

Zeb Vance let the screen close; he was hazy, indistinct, as he moved away beyond it. "Only so far a man can go in that direction," Morgan heard him say.

" '. . . and as we have borne the image of the earthy,' " the minister was declaiming in a voice that easily carried to the multitude, " 'we shall also bear the image of the heavenly.' "

Morgan listened a moment, steeling himself against the emotion he knew would come flooding on the tide of King James's English, in the pounding rhythm of old hymns. They would bring back as nothing else could the cloudless, endless summer of the past, the bright, ordered world of youth where in the red-brick church and the starched Sunday School class and the cramped choirloft under the roaring organ there was no doubt at all, no question—none allowed, none sought—and the world lay out ahead, uncomplicated, serene, as clearly posted as Exodus 20—*thou shalt have no other gods before me thou shalt not kill thou shalt not commit steal covet thou shalt not thou shalt not.* It wrung Morgan to the core to be carried back, as he always was by hymnal, verse, organ, to that far brief summer of youth, to be made once more to see the old familiar mirage; but for once he listened anyway—struck by the certainty that in choosing the Scripture someone had known Anderson well.

" 'We shall not all sleep, but we shall all be changed, in a moment, in the twinkling of an eye, at the last trump: for the trumpet shall sound, and the dead shall be raised incorruptible, and we shall be changed.' "

Even Anderson could ask no more than that. He had only wanted to be incorruptible, Morgan thought, and probably that had seemed little enough to ask when it first occurred to him. Morgan straightened his shoulders, cramped from leaning on the fence, and saw far down the hill a figure striding toward the graveyard.

" '. . . thy sting? O grave, where is thy victory?' "

The blocky figure coming up the hill was as familiar as the ancient question. Adam Locklear had always moved with that purposeful stride, not so much as if he knew where he would come out but as though he had only one way to go, therefore no need to hesitate or wonder. He came on steadily, not hurrying, no doubt hearing the minister's voice roll down the hillside to meet him.

For a moment the voice ceased, the lesson ended; Morgan looked back toward the grave.

"We depart only slightly from the traditional service"—the minister swirled his robe gracefully, his voice as richly modulated as a viola—"so that Senator J. Spencer Burns may say a few words of love for the dear departed on behalf of his colleagues in the Senate of the United States."

It was splendidly senatorial, Morgan thought, to suppose that a member of the world's greatest deliberative body might add something to the burial service or surpass the poetry of the Bible; but as long as there was to be a graveside eulogy, Burns would do as well as anyone, better than most. Earnest and hardworking, Burns had little eloquence and less imagination. "Burns puts me in mind of the best advice I ever got," Hunt Anderson had once told Morgan. "I made this bell-ringing speech down somewhere in the sticks and I pulled out all the stops, I mean I had choirs of angels singing and the trumpets of the mighty sounding. I didn't leave a dry seat in the house. And when I was through the old editor of the paper down there came up to me about five sheets to the wind, got up close enough to knock me down with his breath, and said, 'Young man, never be a solemn ass.' I keep wanting to tell Burns the same thing." But just as a consequence of his earnestness, like Anderson himself for different reasons, Burns was neither a fraud nor a con man. He had the strengths of his painful limitations; he had had to make the most of a cast-iron character.

Morgan watched Burns trudge with sledgelike feet to the head of the grave and give an awkward half-bow to Kathy Anderson. "Mrs. Anderson," he said, "Robert . . . the distinguished Governor of this magnificent state . . . my able and distinguished colleagues and former colleagues . . . friends . . . I have few words fit for this sad moment . . ."

Morgan looked again at Kathy, who was gazing steadily at Burns, her hands in her lap, seeming as closely concentrated upon him as she had once been upon Matt Grant's description of his tobacco bill, or upon Paul Hinman's testimony. Morgan suddenly wondered if in the midst of the funeral preparations she had heard of Hinman's new position.

Burns bumbled along, speaking of Anderson's intellect, achievements, high standing among his colleagues. Bobby's angry face turned once toward the speaker; then the boy resumed his hard glare at the coffin.

Burns pointed out Anderson's concern for the downtrodden; the governor eased his ample haunches on the hard chair. Myrtle Bell was taking notes; so was Charlie French; Geraldine wept noisily; and the Honorable Billy G. Melvin stifled a yawn. Burns took note of the fact that Anderson had almost been nominated for president, "winning the people's hearts although another finally carried their banner."

A rough, strong hand seized Morgan's arm above the elbow, and he looked over his shoulder into Adam Locklear's swarthy face and warrior eyes.

Burns declared that no other senator had been as willing to advise the newer senators or to help with their problems. Morgan and Adam shook hands, although Morgan sensed something hostile in his old friend's manner. Dunn nodded at the newcomer to their place by the fence. By then the sun was far down the West and shadows were long and cool on the stones; Old Bull's tall effigy shaded his son's grave. The dust from the feet of the multitude had settled in the stillness, and there was no hint of a cloud in the darkening sky.

"And just this final word to his lovely wife and this fine son that's so like his able and distinguished father," Burns said. "I don't have to tell them they can be proud of him because of course they knew him better even than his distinguished colleagues in the Senate of the United States did. But as I was leaving my office early this morning, this young page said to me, 'Senator,' he said, 'what has happened? Where are you going?' And I said the able and distinguished Senator Anderson had passed on. And this young page was apparently rather new at his job because he asked me if that was the Senator who had been sick so much. I said yes, Senator Anderson had not been in good health lately." Morgan saw that Bobby was listening; Burns' plain-spokenness had caught him. "And so this little page said to me, 'Well, then, I hope Senator Anderson is feeling better at last.' And I thought I would just leave his family with that thought from his distinguished colleagues—that we all hope that at last Senator Anderson is feeling better."

A more subtle man would have seen the implications of the story, Morgan thought, and avoided telling it; but one so obviously well meaning and devoid of guile as Burns could have had no other intention than the one his unadorned words conveyed. And so the page's remark, so Morgan thought, became doubly fitting, in what it might suggest to those who had known Anderson well, and in the simple sentiment of comfort Burns had meant to voice. For the first time during the service Bobby Anderson's face contorted as if he were on the verge of tears.

"Look at her." Adam's voice was no more than a breath in Morgan's ear. "Like marble. Like stone."

Morgan's eye ran between the huge effigy of Old Bull and the still, taut figure of Kathy Anderson; there was a certain superficial likeness, he conceded, from that distance. And, knowing no more than Adam did, someone could have thought her lifeless, impervious as the carved features of the monument. Morgan's stomach knotted; he knew what life pulsed and stormed beneath that calm, that concentration. Suddenly, disgracefully, he knew he wanted this service, this day, over with, the friends departed, the multitude dispersed, the earth closed—anyway, Anderson would have hated this interminable attempt to hold on to something already finished. Morgan wanted it over so he and Kathy could be close, secret, alive together in their hiding place, that dark, exclusive circle within which he believed he might even—soon, any day now—come to need no cover.

Three boys in surplices advanced to the head of the grave under the minister's paternal eye. Morgan shrank within himself; he knew what was coming, and he debated silently whether he might not better walk rapidly down the hill, whether anyone, in any case, would care—certainly not Anderson, who would have been the first to understand.

The high, sweet voices, unaccompanied, rose raggedly, quavered, then steadied:

"Abide with me; fast falls the eventide . . ."

Morgan called upon all his powers of abstraction. He thought about his appointment with the publisher. He observed A. T. Fowler shooting his cuffs, Sprock & Berger rapt by the spikes they resembled.

"The darkness deepens: Lord, with me abide."

Kathy was staring into her lap. Now, she had told Morgan, she would have to think about the years with Anderson, the life they had made. Bobby Anderson's face had gone absolutely blank, like Old Bull's stone eyes. Morgan's mind leaped desperately. Keller should have a raise. He watched Myrtle Bell putting away her notebook in a handbag the size of a footlocker. The thing to do was to put Dunn against the wall before the day was over, somehow divine the truth, or wring it from him.

". . . helpers fail, and comforts flee,
Help of the helpless, oh, abide . . ."

Morgan gave up. There were four verses, one down and three to go, and he knew them all, knew them with the aching certainty of old lessons learned in the heart. He had not known his father tithed, would never have dreamed of such a thing from the hard, hurt authoritarian who had ruled his first life; but at the funeral, standing between his sister Estelle and Anne, he had been amazed to hear the minister tell the sparse gathering of Ed Morgan's unfailing tribute to the iron God he had feared and followed all his life. And while Morgan was still taking that in, even thinking a little bitterly of what the extra might have meant in ease for his mother, clothes for Estelle, books, the choir had begun to sing:

"Swift to its close ebbs out life's little day . . ."

Earlier, at his mother's funeral he had been too small to realize that she was not just gone away, but gone; still, the weeping around him, Estelle's arm on his shoulder, the blazing white, tearless face of his father, the old women clutching him to their kindly bellies, the sad, low croon of the minister—it was too much, he could not fathom it. There was a great mystery that did not fit the brilliant light from the open windows of the church, the sweet smell of the flowers, the treasures of cake and pie and chicken in the kitchen at home. He began to cry then, shaking and whimpering in Estelle's arms, not so much for his mother, whose total absence he had not for a moment supposed, but in nameless dread, a sudden hysterical sense, echoed by the reedy, uncertain voices of the Methodist choir, of the dark beyond the tiny circle of his life:

> "Change and decay in all around I see:
> O Thou, who changes not, abide with me!"

Morgan put his face in his hands and wept again. This time he cried so quietly that, all the way across the graveyard, he could hear the racking sobs of Bobby Anderson.

It did not take the minister long to conclude the service, and after the hymn Morgan was so lost in the reverie he had dreaded, so immersed in things and times past he scarcely heard even the most familiar words, " '. . . he cometh up and is cut down like a flower . . .' "

The minister went to Kathy with comforting words. Local Legionnaires removed the flag, folded it reverently, and handed it to Bobby. The senators filed past the family, shaking hands and patting shoulders. Beyond the fence, on the slope of the hill, the crowd began to break into its parts, move away toward the house and the parked cars. The buses rumbled into gear.

"Well, Adam," Morgan said ineffectually, feeling his eyes still red and stinging, "you got here."

"Had to start at dawn," Adam said. "My old piece of a car kept heating up."

"You haven't changed much. Oh, Dunn . . . Adam Locklear. From the old migrant committee staff."

"It looks as if all Anderson's old acquaintances came," Dunn said. "I'm almost expecting Hinman."

"Didn't I even see Updyke with the senators?" Adam said.

"Same old Updyke."

"Then that undertaker better guard his hearse."

"Did you see the news about Hinman?" Morgan asked.

Adam made a wry mouth. "Heard it on the radio. People like that always survive, one way or another. I'd better go speak to Mrs. Anderson, getting here late like this."

They made their way along the iron fence, stopping for Adam to chat a moment with Sprock & Berger, then through the arched gate and toward the waiting limousine. The hearse had crept away. Many people now had surged around the grave speaking to Kathy and Bobby and the minister, shaking hands with the governor and the senators, examining the banks of flowers.

Adam pushed stolidly through the knots of people, with Morgan and Dunn following. Suddenly Bobby Anderson appeared in their path. "Adam!" The boy's face was glowing, and he almost shouted the name.

"Hey, look at that boy!" Adam stopped, pulled back in surprise, and glanced at Morgan. "Did you know he'd shot up that tall?" He stepped forward and clasped both of Bobby's arms above the elbows. "I could still throw you up in the air."

Bobby's eyes were shining, and he was grinning broadly. "No, you couldn't. I'm taller'n you are now and on the wrestling team."

"I'm damned." Adam shook his head. "Never thought I'd look up to that little squirt bouncing around the office."

"I knew you'd be here, Adam."

"Sure you did." Morgan listened sickly. "Listen"—Adam touched Bobby's forearm with a blunt fist—"your dad was a big man."

Bobby's voice was choked. "*I* know that. Not everybody does."

"Never mind anybody else." Adam's clenched fist rose, shook as if at the world. "I'm old-fashioned, boy. I think a man ought to live up to his inheritance. Your dad's yours."

Morgan glanced at Old Bull's blank face. He thought of bodies scattered bleeding across a Georgia grade crossing, his father's old Ford crouched on its sawhorses in the weeds, Anderson in his underwear on the bed in Suite 1201. Not so much a legacy as a chain, he thought; not so much something you lived up to as lived with.

"Don't worry about me," Bobby said. "You wait and see."

"Why, Adam, I didn't know you were here." Kathy came through the thinning crowd to Bobby's side. She held up her cheek for a kiss, looking past Adam's head at Morgan and Dunn. Her eyes too were red, her face a bit flushed.

"My car kept heating up or I'd have been here sooner."

"Hunt would have loved this . . . so many old friends, so much of his life."

"It was a beautiful service," Dunn said. "I've never been to an outdoor service before."

"Bobby and I wanted it this way. We didn't want to act as if his father was a churchgoer. And Hunt used to walk out here, he always had the graveyard kept up."

"Who chose the Scripture reading?" Morgan asked.

Kathy looked at him, and he saw her eyes fill again, a pulse flutter in her throat. "It was the same reading Hunt marked in the prayer book for little Kate."

They fell silent. Then Matt Grant and Danny O'Connor joined the group, shaking hands cordially with Adam.

"I'm going to catch Senator Babcock for a word on the pipeline bill," Dunn said to Morgan. "I'll talk to him on the bus and see you back at the house." He stepped forward, holding out his hand to Kathy. "One way is enough walking for me so I'll catch the bus. Will I see you at the house?"

"Of course." She was all graciousness and propriety, not so crushed as might be expected of a bereaved wife, Morgan thought, but carrying off the scene properly. She would have been incapable, he knew, of acting as if Anderson's death had been an unexpected calamity putting asunder years of wedded bliss. "I've got to move along myself, I can't keep the Governor waiting much longer."

"He's improving his time." Adam looked at the governor busily shaking hands.

Kathy looked amused. "You don't like politicians any better than you ever did."

"I liked your husband."

"But not when he left your migrants and ran for president."

"Your game, not mine."

Kathy put her arm through Bobby's, drew him close. "It was Hunt's game too, Adam. I don't think you ever really understood that was one game Hunt and I played together."

He stared at her a moment, blocky and strong as the base of Old Bull's effigy. Then he touched Bobby's arm again and stepped back. "The Governor's waiting for you."

Bobby pointed to his school group. "I'm going to walk with my friends, they're waiting over there." His mother released his arm and he started off, stopped, looked back. "See you at home," he called—to Adam, not to Kathy.

Morgan observed the details with professional precision, as automatically as a camera; there was something ignoble about it, he thought, the skill with which he performed his observer's work no matter what the circumstances. Only a storyteller could redeem such heartlessness, by clothing detail in truth; and suddenly mortal terror struck Morgan to the heart. What if he was not good enough? What if he could never do it?

"That's a good boy," Adam said. "Takes after his dad."

"You don't have to worry about one thing." Kathy's cool blue eyes followed Bobby, then came back to Adam. "*He* doesn't want anything to do with politics." She put out her hand to Adam, then to Morgan. "We'll talk later, won't we?"

They watched her walk toward the limousine to rejoin the Govenor and his wife, to whom Myrtle Bell was pouring out what might, from her earnest appearance and flooding words, have been her life story.

"Hasn't changed a bit," Adam said. "Little older in the face but look at that shape. And still tough, huh? She gave it to me a little."

"Because you haven't changed either." Morgan resolved to think no more about himself, or his failures past and future. He put his arm through Adam's, and they strolled toward the grave. "If I didn't know better I'd say you weren't a day older." But then, he thought, in a sense Adam Locklear had always been old. There was no way for him to age much beyond what had happened to him in the beginning.

"Ten years anyway since I saw you," Adam said. "You're a big mule now."

Morgan laughed. "You always knew how to hurt a guy."

"But I like what you write. Most of it, when I see it."

They looked down at the coffin lying on the machine that would—when everyone but the undertaker's workmen had gone—lower it into the earth. Someone had put several floral sprays on top of the coffin; anything, Morgan thought, to dress up the truth, hide the raw facts of death and disposal from the living.

"Was it really whisky that did it, Rich?"

"I don't suppose it helped. He'd had a couple of little heart attacks, and it was another one that got him yesterday. The booze was a big part of what ruined his health, I suppose, but I'm no doctor."

Morgan watched the limousine move past them and through the arched gate. The governor was listening intently to Kathy, and on the front seat Myrtle Bell—right on top of the prey, as always—was half turned to join the conversation.

"He wasn't really an alcoholic, I mean the sick kind who can't help themselves. Kathy thinks he poured it down on purpose, gave up trying after he missed the big chance at the convention. Drinking was part of giving up, being a tragedy—that's what she says."

"Bitch," Adam said.

"Hey!" Glass and French were calling to Morgan from the gate. "You coming?"

Morgan waved at them. He did not wish to look a last time at Anderson's coffin or to make anything dramatic of leaving Anderson to the workmen.

He took Adam's arm again, and they walked slowly across the graveyard toward the gate.

"You saw it coming." Morgan resolutely did not look back, and Adam was listening intently. "You saw him getting further and further into the presidential thing, getting the feel of it, the taste of it. Listen, was Tobin lying when he put the finger on Hinman?"

Adam shook his head. "To this day I just don't know. What he said was plausible, it could have been true. On the other hand, Tobin could have thought it would do him some good because it was what he knew Anderson wanted to hear. I told Anderson that from the start."

Adam did not seem surprised by the question; he answered as readily as if it had all taken place the day before.

"So Hunt didn't know for sure if he was lying either?"

"Of course not. I didn't even want him to ask the question. But he was bound and determined."

"I don't know if I want to make that walk again or not," Charlie French said as Morgan and Adam came up. "Why don't we wait for the bus?"

Morgan made introductions. "I'm walking," he said, "I can ride buses in Washington."

"I'll come along," Adam said, and Glass nodded. French shrugged, and they started down the hill. Most of the crowd had left, except for a few waiting at the bus collection point. The afternoon was nearly gone. Some stragglers were wandering toward the woods and the little branch.

Morgan glanced incuriously at those waiting for the bus. One was Curly Layton, who looked up at that moment and caught Morgan's eye. Curly came over with his hand outstretched.

"Honor and pleasure," he rumbled in his beautifully modulated baritone, which had yielded not a decibel nor a tone to the advance of age. "Been hoping all afternoon for a chance to talk about old times although I guess I'm pretty far away from the art. I was just chatting over here with my delightful old friend, Senator McLaren. A great American. We were just . . ." Curly, his hair white and tumbling and his clothes as immaculate as if he had not spent part of an afternoon in the dust and hot sun, orated on. Zeb Vance and Millwood Barlow joined the group.

"Why, Millwood, as I live and breathe, here's our star reporter again." Zeb Vance let not a second of silence follow Curly's last word. "Millwood and me been gabbing on so long we missed that dignitary bus, which just goes to show it don't pay to get old and flannel-mouth. But they say the bus is coming back. They can't make Curly here walk, he's got the goods on too many people."

"That son-of-a-bitch," Millwood said rather loudly. He glared at Morgan.

"Now, Millwood, there's ladies over there." Zeb Vance pointed his cane at those waiting for the bus.

"I been waiting many a year to tell the son-of-a-bitch what I think of him." Millwood's voice rose again. "Any son-of-a-bitch that would go behind a man's back and write a story like he did is a *certified* son-of-a-bitch —no, I ain't going to shut up!"

"Now, Millwood, you got no call." Zeb Vance shook Millwood's arm not angrily. Far beyond them, the bus crept out of the woods and started up the hill. "You fellows just don't pay any mind at all to Millwood. Ever since the late Miss Pearl passed on, Millwood's got too broody for his own good. Now, Millwood, you just—"

"Well, the son-of-a-bitch put Buddy in jail, didn't he? Just so you'd have to get outten the way of his friend Anderson, and if that ain't a son-of-a-bitch trick for a dinky-ass reporter to pull on a United States senator that never done him a thing but favors, I be dog if I know what is!"

"Millwood," Morgan thought he heard himself say, "I'm truly sorry." He watched the bus grinding up the hill. He tried not to think about anything; he tried not to look at Zeb Vance, at the other gaping faces.

"Millwood, you're embarrassing those ladies," Zeb Vance said as if scolding a child. "What would Miss Pearl think of that? Now you just keep a decent tongue in your head."

The bus muttered to a protesting stop. The door swung open and people began to get aboard, glancing curiously at Millwood. Through the dust floating in the wake of the bus, the long, slanting rays of the sun struck curious streaks of orange light. Millwood began to mumble, and Zeb Vance took firm hold of his arm.

"All right, Millwood, let's get aboard. Scout, I reckon you can see Millwood ain't quite hisself, but a little breath of life back at the house and he'll be raring to go again."

Morgan nodded mechanically, suspending thought; but he could not suspend emotion. He wanted to hide, not from the shocked, curious faces around him but from himself. It seemed that every deception and meanness of his life, the lies and excesses and failures to see, the withering of Anne's expectancy—every hurt given, all the damage done, down to the tiniest blades of grass trampled beneath his striding feet, the least blow struck by his outstretched, reaching arms—the main events of his life paraded before im, hazy and mottled in the sunstruck dust. "But what was I to do?" he was sure he heard himself say.

"Let's just get on there now and get a decent seat," Zeb Vance said.

Charlie French took Millwood's other arm. "Come on, old-timer," Charlie said. "Let's you and me take a load off our feet." French glanced once at Morgan—it seemed to Morgan with a certain strange amity. Then Charlie and Zeb Vance maneuvered Millwood toward the bus.

"Didn't I tell the son-of-a-bitch?" Millwood demanded suddenly, loudly, of no one.

"You sure did," Morgan thought he ought to say. "You sure told the son-of-a-bitch, Millwood." But he knew by then that he had said nothing, nothing at all.

"I wouldn't say that old boy thinks so much of you," Adam Locklear said as the bus door closed.

"There was a man named Buddy Pruden," Morgan said, speaking rapidly once he started. "Zeb Vance's AA in the old days. I got a tip and looked into it and turned up a few things. Buddy was in with some other staff types —anyway, as far as I could tell he was. Doing favors. Using senators' names and stationery, including Zeb Vance's. Influence at the FCC, SBA loans, things like that. I wrote a story, and Buddy and some others went to jail. Zeb Vance took the responsibility for Buddy and retired."

"Hell of a story," Glass said.

"The duties of a free press," Curly Layton intoned, "are not always pleasant. I may say, however, that you newspaper fellows were always more than generous to me."

"Curly, you missed your bus," Morgan said, watching it creep down the hill.

"Do me good to walk. Besides I get a kick out of talking over old times in the art, now that I'm out of it."

Morgan nodded absently. "I'm not sure what else I could have done. But Zeb Vance never believed that story was true, maybe because it came just before he was to run again. He always said if I'd brought the facts to him before the story ran, he'd have been able to show me Buddy was framed or didn't know what he'd got into. I was never sure what Zeb Vance thought, except Buddy was his friend, and Zeb Vance stood by him."

"Hell of a story," Glass said again.

"Buddy only served a few months. But it broke him, he was never the same again. Died a few years back." Morgan started off down the hill and the others came along silently. "I got the state press award for that story.

Better still, I got a new job in Washington. My start in life, you might say. It really was a hell of a story."

They walked on. But I wonder if it *was* true, Morgan thought; and if Lonnie Tobin was lying, and if Hunt Anderson tried to sell his soul to Dunn, and whether anything at all can be said for sure. He looked quickly, furtively, over his shoulder; against the red arc of the sun beyond the rim of the hill, the workmen were shoveling dirt into the grave. Morgan stopped then, looking back; and the others stopped and watched with him. The workmen, black and sticklike against the sun, moved steadily at their work; Morgan imagined the sound of falling dirt against the coffin.

Adam Locklear, watching with him, spoke quietly. "I wonder if I let Anderson down. Sometimes I wish I'd stayed on, worked with him while he was running for president. I was against that, but I kept wondering what happened to him and if I could have done something, how it could have turned out so wrong when it started so right. Maybe if I'd stayed with him—"

"I doubt it," Morgan said. "No offense, but some things not even you could do for him. Nobody could have. Some things he just had it in him to do."

"Maybe I'd at least have understood what happened."

"I doubt that too," Morgan said. "I'm not sure anybody ever does."

Old Bull's Boy V

"In fact, there are a hell of a lot of things in this world not many people understand," Morgan said as they walked on. He felt himself talking against the dark, against the far, imagined rhythmic thud of falling dirt. It was important to keep talking, he thought, so that they could not hear the falling dirt. "Like, for instance, you'd maybe think to look at Curly here, he'd spent his life doing shampoo ads on TV. The fact is, if you don't mind my saying so, Curly, Curly was the best state governor I've seen in my time, and I've seen more than I like to think about."

"I'll defend to the death . . ." Curly looked pleased. ". . . your right to say that."

"Of course, Curly knows it isn't saying much, considering what governors mostly are, and maybe yesterday's politician is just yesterday's newspaper anyway; we're going down the superhighway so fast maybe there's not even any use looking back."

Morgan was talking almost to himself; he knew he could not really let himself think about the grave being filled, about Zeb Vance, Millwood, Bobby, what he feared he would find in his own life, his own disappearing years. "But we all keep looking back anyway, don't we? We all keep trying to figure out how we came to be where we are, wherever that is. So here's Old Curly looking like he's not a day older, looking just about the way he did at the convention—although even further back than that, they tell me Curly used to wear spats and swallowtail coats until they began to whisper it around that he wore his hair long to cover up a wart on the back of his neck—so why did he wear a long-tailed coat?"

"I used to tell'em there was only one way they could find out," Curly rumbled, beaming. "Those coats were part of my style for many a year. You see, Old Curly believed in keeping the voters entertained, if nothing else."

Like Zeb Vance, Morgan thought, but he said, still interposing memory against memory, "You're just covering your tracks the way you always did. You fellows will never get a word of it from Curly, but the truth is that he entertained them all right, but Curly's real style was to give the interests half a loaf and spread the other half around. Curly put up the sales tax and vetoed an income-tax bill, because that was what the money in his state wanted, and that's big money. Then he eased down the banking laws so central-city banks could put branches in the small towns. That was big money too. Curly figured that was about half the loaf, or anyway about what the traffic would bear; then he called his due bills. The next thing anybody knew the school appropriation was fifty per cent up, and there was a medical clinic plan for the countryside where they couldn't afford hospitals, a job-training program for dropouts, and a state civil rights commission with teeth. And all that was another kind of big money. Nothing revolutionary, you understand, not in Old Curly's state; nothing that really threatened anybody. That wouldn't have been Curly's style."

"Not by a long shot," said Curly happily, "because what a long and misspent lifetime in the subtle art of politics taught me, gents, is that the only thing that really scares the bejesus out of the fatsos is the idea of spreading the wealth, what they call redistribution of income in the fancy economics schools. So if a practitioner of the art stays off that kind of foreign idea, maybe even gives the bigger bankrolls a few more bucks to take to the grave with 'em, why, gents, the truth is they won't make too much trouble over some modest little social program. Frankly, the bastards are usually too stupid to know what you're up to."

"What he calls his modest little social program," Morgan said, "was what gave him his link to Anderson. He saw you for what you were, Curly."

Curly shook his mane. "But I couldn't see him until that fanged angel, the late Senator's good wife Kathy, laid a few measures of public opinion on me. There were times, I confess it in old age, when the spoiled breath of ambition escaped these nostrils. I'm afraid I had to be persuaded to go with Anderson. But I never regretted it."

"When Kathy got through persuading him," Morgan said, "Curly went in all the way and took over the pre-convention delegate operation in the non-primary states. Then he was Anderson's main floor manager. Like Matt said, it was Curly and his people that made the operation look halfway

professional. But not even Curly could pull it out for Anderson after Dunn
went to Aiken. Could you, Curly?"

Morgan had heard the news almost as soon as he was awake. He had
staggered, almost literally, out of bed, put on a clean shirt, and made his
way down the freight elevator to the lobby, which was already jammed.
Another reporter grabbed his arm and asked if he'd heard that Dunn was
going to Aiken. Morgan said it was news to him and pushed on. He ran into
an Anderson delegate who said Anderson would have to pull out now, the
shit had hit the fan. On the sidewalk, where Morgan stopped to get his
bearings, two characters in monogramed shirts pushed past, talking about
Dunn putting Aiken over. Morgan went around the corner and found his
newspaper's rented limousine, in which the managing editor and a couple
of other reporters made room for him. They all had heard the same thing.
On the way to the convention hall a radio voice reported importantly that
informed sources said it would be Aiken as soon as the roll could be called
again.

Morgan had spent a good part of his professional life discounting rumors,
but he doubted by then that this was a rumor, and by the time the rented
limousine left him outside the convention hall his wits were stirring, his eyes
had cleared, and he had it figured out that Hunt Anderson must have made
his pitch and Dunn behind his green eyeglasses had totted up the odds and
played it safe.

Inside, in his newspaper's makeshift quarters, the news was all over the
ticker, looking official but without any real confirmation from anyone.
Morgan bought a paper cup of asphalt coffee, then put a phone call through
to Hunt's suite—a minor miracle. Matt Grant came on the line; he'd heard
what Morgan had heard but knew no more. He didn't even know where
Hunt was, he said, but he did know that Kathy had gone to the convention
hall. When Morgan hung up, the chairman was banging the gavel, and
Morgan, carrying his steaming coffee, had to race for his place in the press
section.

Kathy had not been in the hall all week. He searched the galleries for her
box, while Alabama declared itself the economic bonanza of the age as well
as the foremost supporter even unto death of Joe Bingham; but the place
was too dim, the smoke of four long sessions hung in hazy planes over the
floor, and there was too much movement and color, too many faces and
bodies; it was impossible to pick Kathy out of the kaleidoscope. Morgan
concentrated on his coffee, tally sheet, and notebook. He could hear in his

headphones the voices of the other reporters, trying to pin down the rumor about Dunn, who apparently was giving nothing but no comment to anyone. But there was not long to wait until Dunn's state would be called.

The way that hall was laid out—Morgan would never forget—three aisles radiated from the rostrum through the delegates. The two outer aisles were at about forty-five-degree angles to the center aisle, which led straight up the middle of the hall; halfway along its length a wooden tower rose into the murk, which was occasionally pierced by a weak draft of air-conditioning to disclose the peering television cameras atop the tower. From where Morgan sat on the outer rim of the wooden platform that had been built for the press to the right of the rostrum—there was another like it on the left—he could look straight along one of the angled aisles, and by turning a bit in his seat he could also see along most of the length of the one nearest him. Halfway up that aisle Dunn's delegation had its place; as the name of Dunn's state screeched through the hall, Dunn rose slowly and adjusted the microphone in front of him. Morgan could plainly make out the lean jaw, the carefully combed hair, the green spectacles. Dunn scarcely waited for the silence that fell instantaneously, as if some great hand had turned a volume button all the way down.

"Mister Chairman . . ."

Unaccountably Morgan remembered that those had been the first words he had heard Hunt Anderson speak, five years earlier, when Anderson had been starting the long road that had brought him to this place—had brought Morgan there too. Morgan sat twisted in his seat, staring through the haze of smoke at Dunn; ever after, it was all arrested in Morgan's mind, frozen there forever, like the timeless, suspended life he had seen in the old wet-plate Brady photos of another day—the delegates massed on the floor with their upturned, waiting faces, the crowds jammed in the galleries, the wooden tower looming in the center, the banners drooping high above, the state standards atop their slanting stalks, and Dunn's tall figure with the microphone pulled near the green spectacles.

". . . casts sixty-one votes for Governor Aiken!"

The moment of silence was shattered by an animal roar. Delegates leaped into the aisles screaming like madmen; the galleries blossomed suddenly with Aiken banners and placards; and down the aisle that slanted away in front of Morgan, a brass band in red coats came thundering on cue, its drums pounding the march, its brasses shrieking "Happy Days Are Here Again!" Aiken's people had done their work well. Dunn had thrown in his whole state delegation, and everyone in the hall knew that meant thirty-seven more from the states following his lead—so the tide was running at last.

Aiken's people—mostly White House operatives and dependents—were ready for the moment with bands, placards, delegations primed to lead the snakedance, galleries packed with the faithful ready to shout and whistle. Someone also had brought a small siren, and as the mass of delegates shoved along the aisles in the sweating, screaming wake of the band, the long, piercing moan of the siren rose and fell through the uproar with curious, ominous insistence, an alarm more than a jubilation, as if to remind the snakedancers that triumph was brief and struggle long.

Morgan watched calmly—it must have appeared—as if under no pressure. That early in the day he was in no rush to file, and he sipped his coffee, ticking away in memory and notes the few details of color and scene he would later need to re-create the moment in his sure professional prose. He watched calmly, but not really even seeing. He had never realistically expected Anderson to win, and he had a professional cover within which to shelter from the ordinary involvements of men; yet there was a certain tart bitterness in his heart, a momentary raging resentment at the sheer inequity of life, the monumental unfairness of the world, that after so many long months of costly, wearing work, after so much investment of ambition, dreams, selflessness, in spite of the clear superiority he felt Anderson had offered—despite all that, mere power had prevailed again, and victory, however brief, had gone to one who had merely been at hand.

Morgan threw back his head to shout into the din, hurl his curse at Dunn, at fate, but as he did so his eyes, as if by magic, found Kathy in her box, alone in her familiar circle of intensity, still, aloof—Morgan thought indomitable. Then the whorls and planes of smoke closed again, and he could see her through them only hazily; but in that moment it came to him clearly that if power prevails, struggle goes on; because power, prevailing, could only accumulate more power, protect power, hoard power. That was the irony of victory, Morgan thought as the crowd shouted and stomped and swirled, that was the circular truth of drum, brass, and siren. Power prevailed and became powerless; struggle continued and was all.

So, as the snakedance began to wind down, the Aiken banners to flutter and fall, the placards to dip, the band to march out with a last happy blare of trombones, Morgan told himself that Anderson had lost only to the recurring prevalence of power, which, properly seen, was hardly to lose at all, since nothing save power could truly be lost to power.

His rage gone, Morgan felt hollow inside; he was shattered to find that it was an emptiness to have it over. He was not accustomed to defeat, for himself or for those he valued; usually he tried to avoid situations that threatened rebuff or rejection, but when finally challenged he had always been able to make his way, survive, sometimes surmount. He felt Anderson's failure somehow as if it were his own, and he disliked it fiercely. But there was nothing to be done; it was over.

As the roll call resumed and wore on, the delegations began to break, all but those for Anderson. State after state tumbled into place. The column of figures under Aiken's name lengthened on Morgan's tally sheet; he kept on putting down figures, looking up no more, making the entries stoically, raging again inwardly. He would see them in hell, he thought mindlessly; he would see them all in hell before he would concede defeat or let them know he was hurt.

Hobart touched his arm. A sudden feeble yell went up in the back of the hall. Morgan looked up along the slanting aisle that stretched in front of him. The yell grew into a wilder cheer, and some of the Anderson delegations surged to their feet, their state standards waving and dipping. A bass counter-chorus of boos swelled under the thinner sound of the cheering. Hunt Anderson and Curly Layton were coming down the aisle arm in arm, looking straight ahead. Even with his slight stoop, Anderson towered over Curly, and the odd planes of his head looked drawn, edged, pulling his face into a mask. Curly was immaculate in a white suit, hand-painted tie, and cotton hair. They came from under the overhang of the balcony, and the galleries caught sight of them. Another cheer went up, caught, held, until the booing rose beneath that too.

"Never been done!" Hobart was yelling. "Never been done before!"

The chairman was banging his huge gavel, his normally mottled face apoplectic, his bald, bomblike head wagging angrily. Officials were crowding forward on the rostrum to see what was happening; the roll call had stopped, drowned in the excitement. Photographers were rushing forward, their bulbs flashing, and the cameras on the tower were turning to follow the progress of the two men along the aisle. Morgan saw an Anderson delegation chairman jumping up and down and screaming unintelligibly; near him a whole Aiken delegation was booing in unison and turning its thumbs down. He looked up to find the box where Kathy was sitting and, through the haze and swirl, saw that Hunt's appearance seemed to have jarred even her iron composure. She was leaning forward, looking down at Hunt and Curly, her hands before her on the railing. Such a departure from the still and queenly attitude she had been maintaining suggested to Morgan that she knew no more of what Hunt was doing than anyone else did.

"What the hell's he think he's up to?" a reporter yelled from a nearby bench; he was glaring as if Morgan were the official Anderson interpreter.

Another, from behind, shouted, "Stampede! Bastard must think he can get a stampede going out there!"

Anderson and Curly were almost in the well before the rostrum by then, moving slowly, still not looking around or waving. Just then Anderson looked up, searched a moment, caught Morgan's eye. Morgan saw his shoulders rise in what might have been a shrug; then Anderson looked straight ahead, still coming on.

Hobart was tugging at Morgan's arm. "He's going to try to speak, I swear he is, he must be trying to turn it around!"

"He's going to withdraw,"Morgan said, guessing. "He's going to move to make it unanimous." I'd see them in hell first, he was thinking. I'd see the bastards in hell.

"In person?" Hobart was staring wildly, terrified by lack of precedent. "It's crazy!"

"Maybe *he* is," Morgan said. "He's never been licked before." But I'd see them in hell, he thought.

Anderson and Curly disappeared beneath him, into the tunnel that ran under the rostrum and to the waiting room behind it. The cheering died almost immediately but the booing went on for a while, defying the chairman's gavel. Then Morgan saw one of the party flunkies come rushing along the runway from the waiting room. Beyond him, through a gap in the curtained doorway, he caught a glimpse of Curly's white suit. The flunky whispered to the chairman, who was still banging the gavel to halt the last dying grumble of boos. The chairman's bald head began to shake vigorously. The flunky went dashing back along the runway, where Curly in his white suit was waiting; Curly's mane tossed angrily, and he called something back toward the curtains, beyond which Morgan knew Anderson must be waiting.

"They'll never let him speak," someone said in the row behind Morgan. "You can't speak during a roll call, it's the rule." But Morgan knew that rules at conventions existed to be set aside or broken by those with the power to do it.

"Never seen such gall," Hobart said. "Who's he think he is?"

"Goddam upstart," the reporter behind Morgan snarled, " 's' if he hadn't caused the party enough trouble already."

"Pride," Hobart said. "Wouldn't you think he'd have more pride?"

"Absolutely not," Curly Layton said. "No way. After that shitbird Dunn caved in so pusillanimously, Anderson had no more chance than a one-legged man in an ass-kicking contest. Not to take too much credit, Old Curly, for one, knew that right away. So I went to the floor quite early that morning, just to salvage what I could. I'd heard the evil tidings about that ass-hole Dunn from one of his own goons, and my sinking feeling, gents, was that the bird had flown the coop. But by then, frankly, Old Curly was —I'll own right up to it—emotionally involved, as even we practitioners of the art are apt to be.

"Anyway, it was never Old Curly's style to . . . ah . . . cave in too fast. After all, even caving in, I learned the hard way over a good many years, is a political act. If a sound tactician knows how to cave in, and when— why, he ought to be able to get a modest return on even such an unpleasant investment as that. Think no small thoughts, I say. So I wasn't just trying to hold our gallant forces together on the off-chance that the reports were wrong. I was raising here and there, I hoped judiciously and with some effect, the delicate question of the vice-presidency.

"Now, gents, I know the common view is that that office is not worth what schoolboys used to call a shit in your hat; but frankly some people tend to forget the fact that as the cynics say it's only a heartbeat away from the Big Casino. I was working without instructions, I confess it, because during the campaign Senator Anderson had graciously tendered me a certain welcome carte blanche. Even so, I knew I couldn't go too far; but I thought my principal had made a good showing against massed and relentless forces, and once the Leaders had punished him with a good swift kick in the ass, I doubted they'd be vindictive. Revenge is of small worth in the politician's art, friends, but in all candor Old Curly overestimated their practice of the art. But it didn't matter. We'll never know what might have come of my small efforts that morning, because before the hall filled up a messenger found me at my labors and said Senator Anderson wanted to see me. His wish was of course my command. He turned out to be just outside the hall, in a rented limousine with drawn blinds, stylish, I thought, in a roped-off area of the parking lot thoughtfully set aside for we VIPs. I could see right away when I got in beside him that he had not enjoyed, the night before, that sleep that knits the ravel'd sleave of care.

" 'Senator,' I said, elaborately cheerful, 'if you're going to be president, you got to have a better-looking pair of eyes than that in the morning.'

" 'Ah, damn it, Curly,' he said to me, 'you know we're down the pipe.'

"So I asked him if he was entirely certain about that green-eyed, double-dyed, motherfucking Dunn.

" 'He gave me the word himself,' Anderson said.

"There was only one other thing I needed to know then, to put even more wheels in motion than I already had rolling. I told him that in Old Curly's judgment there still was a splendid chance for Number Two, that in fact I had already laid a few lines in that direction.

"He recoiled as if I had handed him a snake. 'Scratch that,' he said immediately. 'I'm not a Number Two man.'

"There was a telephone in the car, and I immediately called one of my lads inside the hall and told him regretfully to cash in the chips. If I may say so without intent to boast, gents, I'd been around long enough to know when a man meant what he said and when he was playing ducks and drakes. Of course the Senator was not, I could rather easily detect, in the best of shape to make decisions of high policy, and I suppose that with a certain unscrupulous guile I might have gone back inside and put together a little something without his consent. But when he said he was not a Number Two man, it crossed my mind that for some people that really would be worse than anything—second best. And I didn't for a moment doubt that Hunt Anderson was one of those unfortunates.

"So we sat there chatting idly. It was sweltering inside that car with the windows up and the blinds drawn, but he didn't seem to notice. Pretty soon, on the radio, we heard them start the roll call, and we both listened, as I remember it, without a word. What were words at that moment?

"It came inexorably, gents, down to that limp prick Dunn, and that settled it. I let the radio have one good blast of Old Curly's choicest vocabulary. Anderson just sat a moment, then opened the door and got out. As if with a certain relief—almost gaily, as I recollect—he peered back in at me and said, 'Let's go, Curly.'

"I was struck almost dumb. 'You're not going in that den of thieves!' I remember crying out while I scrambled out of the car. But I had trouble catching up with him, the way he was moving across the parking lot on those long legs of his. I remonstrated all the way, and when Old Curly remonstrates, gents, he remonstrates.

" 'I'm a delegate,' he kept saying, as if that mattered. 'I've got a badge to prove it.'

"I endeavored to tell him there was absolutely no need for him to enter that noxious hall.

" 'No need for anything I've done so far,' he said. 'They've tried to make me play their game from the start, but I haven't yet, and I won't now.'

"I explained, rather patiently I thought, that a candidate's appearance on the floor was generally considered bad form. And what the hell was he going to do when he got there?

" 'I'm not a candidate any more. I just withdrew. I'm going in there and tell them so in person and tell all my people to get behind Aiken. That'll show the bastards who's a good party man.'

"Well, gents, there I was, like a cowboy in a rodeo hanging on to one of those bucking steers, and I had about one minute, I'd judge, going across the parking lot in the hot sun, to hit on a course of action. Now let it not be thought that Old Curly is one to discount gestures; because life instructs us all, if we heed it, that sometimes a well-conceived and well-executed gesture has more effect on men than anything else. But for my principal to go personally before the convention—well, I could hardly help seeing right away that it was going to look grandstand at the least, and at the worst like one last desperate riverboat gamble to stampede the convention. In short, it was going to look bush league and like anything but what he intended, and I'll have to confess to you gents—on the day we've buried him I'm almost ashamed to own it—but just before we got to the VIP entrance the thought did occur to Old Curly that maybe the good Senator really did have down deep somewhere a lingering shred of the hope that springs eternal. Maybe he was fooling even himself. It wouldn't have been the first time that had happened to a practitioner of the art, and believe me, gents, I got better reason to know than most.

"So I caught him by the arm at the door and looked him in the eyes. They were not going to like it, I told him rather firmly I believe.

"He shook his head and said to me, 'I haven't run away from the pricks yet, Curly, and I'm not going to start now.'

"Once again, with some desperation, I assured him that no one expected him to withdraw in person. He didn't *have* to go in there. But then he settled it for me.

" 'Yes, I do,' he said, and of course that was it. If I could have seen my way clear to deflect him, I certainly would have. I had tried hard, but then I could see his mind was made up. After that, why, gents, I had signed on, hadn't I? For the duration."

"We had a hell of a time getting past the gate. One thing life has taught Old Curly: on every gate, at every gathering, there is some squinty stupid-ass guard who knows only one phrase, and not even a submachine-gun planted in his belly can get another word out of him except 'I got my orders.' Well, he was there that morning, naturally. Anderson delegate badges were a dime a dozen and the guards on that gate had been turning away crashers all week. Even when I vouched for him, I still had to get one or two of my lads to come out of the hall and back me up, one rather physically. And after we got past that obstacle and into the lobby of the hall, Aiken's lousy demonstration was just breaking up. We were just in time for the band to come out of the hall and deafen us, and for a rush of the hoi polloi to the refreshment stands, and the first thing we knew we were surrounded by a mob of people who'd recognized Anderson.

"Naturally, most of them were Aiken fans, and I suppose seeing their major opponent in the hall scared them, so they started yelling at him. A few were shaking their fists, and we were getting shoved around rather brutishly. Some son-of-a-bitch even spit on me. And I began to notice something I thought strange—Anderson had always been good in crowds, you know, he was what we call grabby, he'd always seemed to love touching and being touched—but that day as we tried to push our way through the louts he seemed to shrink away from them, almost, I might have thought had I not known him better, to be afraid of them. The smile on his face was frozen; there was something rather blank in his eyes; and the strangest thing of all was that before long I could tell *I* was leading *him*.

"It was a little better after we got into the hall itself; there weren't so many people right around us, blowing their breath on us. Everybody was up yelling and booing, but nobody seemed to be trying to get *at* us—a fact that Old Curly, for one, viewed with profound relief. So we went right on down the aisle, and by then it was almost as if I had a blind man at my side, depending on me to lead him along. It was too late to turn back, but in all candor, gents, I was worried as hell. I thought my good Senator might have gone into some kind of shock.

"And then, when that bald-headed old tub of shit with the gavel refused to let my principal speak, why, gents, I like to blew my stack. There Old Curly was, in full view of God and everybody, with a shell-shocked candidate on my hands, and enough due bills out on that cueball cocksucker to send him to jail, and he still wouldn't break into his no-good son-of-a-bitching roll call. I knew it was against the rules—practically everything is against the rules, gents, but practically everything gets done too, one way or another, and you know that as well as I do. *He* knew Anderson only wanted to withdraw, there wasn't any danger to Aiken or anybody else. Frankly, just in all candor, not to speak ill of any man, it ain't my style, I never really understood before what small-bore shits they were, how they hated Anderson, how far they were willing to go to pay him out for showing them up so often, for not practicing the art by their rules.

"So we just had to sit there while the roll call went on. We even had to sit through another Aiken demonstration when he finally got his damnable majority. Just before the roll call was over, Old Curly finally had had enough. I went over to that slick-headed bastard myself and put a load right in his ear. 'Anderson speaks now,' I said, 'right now, or Aiken can forget about carrying my state this fall.'

" 'You can't do that,' says Skinhead. 'You wouldn't dare!'

And I told him the hell I wouldn't. I told him that two could play his kind of chickenshit game. And I told him that when Aiken lost my state with all those electoral votes, I was going to make damn sure everybody from the President on down knew just exactly which shiny-headed prick was responsible. And that did it, gents, because before they announced the totals, he finally called my principal to the rostrum."

"And after all that," Morgan said, "Hunt only gave them about four or five sentences, not even memorable sentences. 'Friends, you've picked the best man,' he said, or something like that, 'and I guess I ought to know, because I learned it the hard way.' The Aiken people were in, by then they could afford to cheer, and they did. I'm not sure what else he said, because I was thinking of that first sentence and what it must have cost him. I didn't know then that he'd told Curly he wasn't a Number Two man. But I knew what Hunt Anderson had thought of himself, had hoped for himself, and I thought the empty words of a 'good loser' wouldn't have come easily; they had had to be learned 'the hard way' indeed, and I remember wondering even then what that would finally mean to him, what it had done to his image of himself."

Morgan had looked up again at Kathy's box: it was empty. Morgan wished he were not there either, but he had to be; he was a professional and it was his work; he could not evade the last measure of Anderson's defeat.

". . . so, all of us working together, friends, let us move ahead to the great victory we cannot in unity fail to win!"

That brought Anderson an ovation, and he stood there a few moments and took it, grinning, waving back at them, while Morgan thought of the irony of the dashing Anderson campaign, with its emphasis on a new kind of politics, finally coming to its end in that hot and smoky hall, with the delegates half listening to a few wheezing old lines out of the limitless rhetoric of all the politics and politicians of the past. And the last straw was that appearing on the floor in person was just the kind of unorthodox thing Anderson had been doing and profiting from. In that sense it had been just a continuation of the campaign—one last step too many.

There was, after all, a thin line between a brilliant exploit and bad judgment, and Morgan wondered if Anderson had had the golden touch for so long, had become so accustomed to its magical results, that he could no longer recognize when he had slipped across the line. Or maybe they had taught even Old Bull's boy that he had to play the game. One way or another, it had come to an end in those last ritual words, the brilliance gone in the blue smoke that hung over the hall, as if from burnt-out fires.

Some time later, Anderson told Morgan that when he and Curly had come into the hall and found themselves surrounded by a mob, and then when they were walking down the aisle and heard the booing, he realized he had been wrong to think that the crowds, at least, would never go against him.

"All through that campaign," Anderson said, "I was the popular favorite, or that's how it seemed to me. Maybe I was just reading my own press clippings. But I was the one running against the bosses, claiming they couldn't dictate to the people. I suppose I got to thinking of myself as the good guy trying to beat the bad guys. At least that's what I thought the people thought. Then when Curly and I went in there, I saw that that crowd thought *I* was the bad guy. It was a shock. I looked at all those angry faces and all those shaking fists and suddenly I thought to myself, Maybe I'm the one that's gone wrong. Maybe I've been fooling myself right along."

But that had been years after the event; at the time Morgan had tried to get to Anderson behind the rostrum, but Curly had hustled Anderson out right after his brief speech. There had been a short recess while Aiken got himself together and conferred with the President and the other leaders, but after that the convention went right ahead with the vice-presidential nomination. Morgan had to sit through a staff meeting during the recess, then was busy at the phone and typewriter until far into the afternoon. Finally, during another recess before Aiken's evening acceptance address for the prime-time audience, Morgan had time to go back to his hotel for a shower and shave. First, he went straight up to Suite 1201.

A cyclone might have hit it. The litter of the campaign was everywhere —posters askew on the walls, pamphlets and photos and badges and press releases strewn over the furniture and floor, in one corner the forlorn soft-drink machine that had pumped out cups of the only bribe Hunt's headquarters had had to offer. A few workers hung around, disconsolate. In one bedroom Morgan found Matt Grant, ever the orderly bureaucrat, pulling together the files in cardboard boxes.

Matt riffled a stack of index cards with his thumb. "Delegates," he said. "I could give you the color of eyes and credit rating on most of them, but it's old stuff now. Two years of work in these boxes, and it wouldn't bring you fifty cents at the junkyard."

"Hunt can get an income-tax deduction. He can give his papers to some library and deduct the dollar value."

Matt's saturnine face frowned. "Maybe we'll need them next time around. Maybe we aren't ready for the grave."

"If you've got the stomach for another go, you need a doctor. Where's Hunt?"

He'd already left the city, going off someplace to lie in the sun. But Kathy was still around, Matt said, waving vaguely toward the farther rooms of the suite. Morgan found her in a bare little room beyond the one where he'd talked to Hunt early that morning—by then it seemed a year or so before. They had used the room as an inner sanctum; all the hotel furniture was out, replaced by a metal desk, a telephone, a few chairs. Beyond the open windows there were street sounds; far off, a brass band was playing. Kathy was at the desk, a stack of notepaper at her hand, looking tired and a little disheveled.

"Are you holding the bag?" Morgan asked from the doorway.

She smiled faintly and sat back. "Getting off some notes to a few people who went out of their way for me during the convention." She did not say "us." Then she added morosely, "A very few."

"Why didn't you go off with Hunt? The note-writing could wait a few days. Forever, for that matter." Morgan slouched low in one of the metal chairs; suddenly he was tired again, almost as tired as he'd been in the next room early that morning.

"Hunt wanted to go. I didn't. I don't like lying in the sun." She looked at Morgan steadily. "I don't like running away either."

"Is that what Hunt's doing?"

"You saw that scene in the hall this morning, I could see you on the press stand."

"There are those," Morgan said, "who might think your walking out on his speech was a kind of running away."

"Not anybody I care about. Not anybody who knows me."

"It was a bad idea. He ought not to have charged in there." Morgan decided to press her a little. "But I'd have thought you'd want to be there to the bitter end."

"See him there as if he were down on his knees and that bald-headed old prick gloating over him? After all we've been through? I couldn't stand a minute of it." She tossed her head angrily, ran a hand through her hair. "That wasn't really the bitter end anyway. The bitter end came this morning when Dunn was here."

"What happened?"

"I wasn't in the room."

"But didn't Hunt tell you?"

"Just later that Dunn was going to Aiken. Hunt doesn't tell me a damn thing." It was an evasive answer, but at that point Morgan had no reason to believe he would not be able to learn what he needed to know from someone, in time. And he had another, to him more important, question to raise.

"You remember the day Hinman testified? You remember what I said to you?"

She thought a moment, pursed her lower lip, shook her head slowly.

"Well, then," Morgan said, not tired any more but suddenly as angry as he'd ever been, "fuck you. Adam Locklear was right after all. He said you were a cold-blooded snatch, and you are." He got up, kicked back his chair, and started out, not looking back. See her in hell too, he was thinking. I'll see them all in hell.

"Rich . . ."

She said it so softly Morgan almost didn't hear, almost kept on going. When he looked back she hadn't moved; her eyes were steady.

"Tell me what you said that day."

He told himself to keep on going out of the room but he stopped. "I said when you and Hunt got wherever you were going, if you needed me, I'd be there. Or something sappy like that."

She looked around the bare room, at the scattered chairs. "And this is where we're going, isn't it?"

Morgan felt a certain large triumph; his anger was gone. "But this morning," he said, "you didn't even want him to talk to me, you were so sure I was just a goddam newspaper snoop."

"Adam *was* right," Kathy said.

"Well, forget it. I was angry, the way you always seem to make me. But forget anything I said."

"No," Kathy said. "You *are* still here, Rich—like you said you'd be, even if I didn't hear you say it." Her face began to crumple. She hid it in her hands, and he could just hear her say through her fingers, "I do need you, Rich, I do!" before she leaned slowly forward, put her head on the desk, and began to cry.

"But what really happened?" Glass said. "When Anderson met Dunn, I mean."

"I asked him that morning." Curly Layton was beginning to puff a little as the walk turned uphill toward the Anderson house. "While we sat there sweating in that closed car, listening to the roll call, I said, 'For Christ's sake, Chief, wouldn't that ball-less bastard hold on even one more ballot?' Anderson just shook his head as if he was still puzzling it all out. Just shook his head and didn't say a word."

"And you heard Dunn this morning," Morgan said. "As far as I know that's all he's ever said about it."

"It's morbid," Adam Locklear said, his deep voice carrying clearly in the evening stillness, "this prying back into something that happened all those years ago, with Anderson just now going cold in the grave. We've all got our own lives to live, haven't we? Cotton to pick and taters to hoe, the black folks say. But I have to admit I'd like to know myself what happened to Anderson. He was one man I believed in. Even when I saw him going off the track, getting those presidential ideas in his head, I thought it was a mistake, but I never thought it would finish him. I never thought he'd wind up a sort of gentle has-been, if that's what he was—much less a drunk. You and he always did drink too much whisky, Rich, and I used to think you were both really wasting yourselves that way. That stuff never did anybody any good. But back when I was working for Anderson, the drinking wasn't so bad, no worse than with most people in Washington. What shocked me was a couple of years ago when I was up there for some hearings at the Civil Rights Commission, I dropped in to see him and he got plastered at lunch.

" 'Goddammit,' I remember telling him, 'those hearings you ran on the migrants were the best thing anybody's done around here in years, but what have you been up to lately?'

"He just laughed. 'We got some bills through for you,' he said. 'I promised you that, and I came through, didn't I?'

" 'And good bills at that. Actually working. That's why I hate to see you sitting on your ass when there's so much else to do.'

"And then he said a kind of funny thing: 'Maybe it's not good to take on too much, Adam. Maybe a man like me is only really good for one job like the migrant business.'

" 'Bullshit,' I said. 'If I believed that, I'd of gone on welfare ten years ago.'

"Well, he sat there awhile with one leg over the corner of his desk, thinking about it. 'We're all different, Adam,' he said at last, as if that might be news to me. 'You saw your life a certain way, a long time ago, and as far as I can tell you've never doubted it was the right way, and you've always been able to meet the commitment.' And then he said another funny thing: 'I think you've been lucky,' he said.

"Now that got under my skin a little. I don't poormouth myself, you know that, Rich, but on the other hand, where I come from and what I do aren't exactly what you'd call the good life either. So I hit him a little. 'Oh yeah, I've been lucky, Senator,' I said. 'I never got started on the social life, I've been too busy; so I never had to break any bad habits or scald my innards with booze. That's good luck all right. And all my life I've been so busy keeping what you call a commitment, I never had the time for a lot of big talk about it or a lot of crap about changing the world.'

"I thought that would get his dander up, but he just nodded at me. 'Exactly,' he said. 'That's just what I mean about luck.'

"I actually thought he was just joking me along, and anyway he was always a hard guy to stay mad at. We talked awhile longer and then I left. Never saw him again. Now I wish I'd pressed him more. I wish I'd tried harder to get at the root of what was wrong. Or maybe I never would have understood how a man could just waste his life that way."

That was a judgment Morgan was not sure Adam Locklear or anyone else was entitled to make, although to some extent he shared it—or had shared it.

When Anderson had returned from his rest in the sun after the convention—the Long Island woman had lent him her beach house, Morgan remembered—he had looked tanned and healthy, and he had gone right back to work in the Senate, almost as if nothing had happened. He made some speeches that fall for the Aiken ticket, not too many because the leaders still didn't like or trust him and didn't want him to get any credit. Hunt also had a Senate campaign of his own coming up two years later, and he once quoted to Morgan something Judge Ward had told him, that a senator's six-year term was like All Gaul, divided into three parts.

"The first two years," the Judge had said, "you can be entirely a statesman. The next two years, my boy, be half-statesman and half-politician. But the last two years, your ass better be all politician or you can start looking for work."

Anderson laughed about that. "I guess I got into the all-politician phase a little early," he said.

Anderson was in no trouble in his home state, even though Gravel Roads Johnson and one or two others kept wondering out loud how he'd managed to run for president and still represent the state's interests. That was a backfire line, as it turned out; because a primary reason Anderson had so little trouble was the prestige he'd built by running for president. Every time anyone mentioned that even critically, it just increased the effect.

Morgan had wondered since if it might not have been a good thing if Anderson had had a tough opponent for re-election; that would have given him a new challenge, kept him running hard, left him no time for brooding. But Anderson hadn't been pushed; only some small-town mayor had finally jumped into the race against him, just to keep Senator Anderson honest, he said, but in fact to make a name for the congressional race he was planning for two years later. Against such a soft touch Anderson hardly had had to run at all—a couple of O'Connor's leftover TV spots had been all he needed —and with Matt operating the Senate office efficiently, there was plenty of time for looking back—too much, Morgan had come to think.

Anyway, the drinking had not been the main thing, not at first. What Morgan noticed first was the time Anderson began to spend in his home state, and his lack of real interest in the Senate action. Ironically enough, that helped rehabilitate him with the Judge and the other Leaders. He was no longer pushing controversial matters or holding embarrassing hearings or putting the arm on senators for tough votes. He wasn't competing for good committee spots or preferences. He was available for pairs, to co-sponsor innocuous bills; he was always willing to preside or to sit on the floor while windbags on the other side of the aisle talked banalities. He made cracking good fund-raising speeches for just about anybody who asked him, and he was always willing to call for a quorum or to ask to have his vote announced, if it meant some late colleague could get to the floor in time to be recorded. He was, as the Senate measured things, a good senator.

He spoke seldom—"the sound of my voice," he once announced rather slyly while toasting, after too many martinis and too much wine, a colleague who held the one-man filibuster record, "is not a music that entrances me as in my youth." When he did take the floor, it was for the kind of brief and pointed remarks that earned for him in the press gallery the reputation of an intellectual, since he was believed to write his speeches himself, which he often did. The press gallery, of course, was a poor judge of intellect, but, among senators, Anderson also earned a certain rare distinction; when he spoke he was regarded as worth listening to, rather than as habitually getting off something "for the record" or "for the folks back home" or "for the media."

But it didn't take those—like Morgan, or Matt—who knew Anderson long to see that there was no purpose in him, no guiding notion, no sense of activities coordinated toward some coherent end. Before long it had been impossible not to notice that his drinking was getting worse. Anderson would call up a friend for lunch and it would turn out to be a bottle bout into the afternoon; or after a dinner party he'd drag someone home with him, or follow someone else, and then keep him up till dawn, drinking and yarnspinning and replaying his presidential campaign or the Hinman hearings. By the time of his next re-election, two years after the convention, he had an absentee record that might have killed off anyone else in another state or with a strong opponent. As the years went along, when he'd show up at committee meetings or hearings, he often made the most incisive comments or raised the most penetrating questions, but there was seldom any follow-through, or action built upon the insight. Then he began to show up with decreasing frequency and, worse, sometimes not in the best of condition. The sight of Senator Hunt Anderson, lately the front-running presidential candidate, snoozing gently at the committee table, became all too familiar—if not quite as familiar as the empty place where he was supposed to have been.

Before long the extent to which he was being protected by colleagues who had once feared and disliked him was remarkable; but that was the Senate. Colleagues covered up his absences, kept his staff posted, looked after his interests and his state's on the floor. When he had come charging into the Senate, seized an issue and a place of leadership, and within one term made himself a leader with a national following and a chance for the presidency, they had thought him pushy and unprincipled; but now that he appeared to them as something of a wasting genius, a self-destructive figure with some tragic flaw, they admired him for what he might have been and sympathized with him for what he was.

There had been something rather brooding and mysterious about Anderson at that period; Morgan believed Anderson's colleagues thought he had been to a strange place they had never visited, had seen something of its terrors and beauties, and had come back set apart, and properly, from the ordinary struggles of men. Morgan himself believed something like that, particularly after Anderson had said to him, in the course of a boozy luncheon at Dirty Martin's, "You're getting to be a big man around this town, Rich. There's a lot of talk about those articles of yours, and I know why."

"Because I discovered you."

"Flattery gets you nowhere." Anderson shook a long finger with solemn emphasis. " 'Cause you're a romantic son-of-a-bitch."

"What's that got to do with my increasing fame?"

"Means you keep looking for something. Means you keep expecting things'n' men to be more'n they are. Including Richmond P. Morgan. A very decent fellow but no paragon. So you look at 'em closer than most, again including this R. P. Morgan chap. And when none of 'em turn out as good as they appear—well, they never do, do they?"

"Including Morgan."

"Including Anderson. Including ev'ry damn body. Oh, it comes through in what you write. A disappointed quality. Some of those goddam whistling sentences of yours take the ass right off some poor son-of-a-bitch."

"Well, what about you?" Morgan said. "You were the one who was going to change history, remember? I guess you're a hardheaded realist by now."

But it had become very hard to get Anderson to talk about himself, except for his campaign. "Oh, I remember," he said. "I remember ev'ry goddam thing."

As a surly waiter set the third round of martinis in front of them Anderson held up a warning finger. "Morgan," he said, "why are martinis at lunch like a woman's breasts?" Morgan shook his head. " 'Cause one's not enough and three's too many. God bless 'em."

In fact, whatever professional success Morgan was having in those years was like most—the product of luck and good timing. He had done good work, first on the migrant hearings, then on the Anderson campaign and the convention. His newspaper had hired him after he had written the congressional scandal piece for which Millwood had upbraided him, but it was his connection with Anderson that had earned him a shot at the convention; and not too long after that, the national political writer had retired, opening that desirable job at the right time.

The result was that while Anderson had been sinking into his protected obscurity in the Senate, Morgan had been working what Anne said was twenty-five hours a day, on the road so much his son hardly recognized him when he came home. "I'm getting to know every half-ass politician in the country, not to mention his half-ass state," he told Anderson, and he was piling up front-page bylines, points with his editors, and pay raises. Sometimes, in those hectic years, Morgan had imagined himself head down, arms pumping, tongue hanging out; he knew he was going to be bureau chief, sooner or later, if he could only keep up the pace, and after that—well, back then, it had looked like tomorrow the world.

It was then, Morgan knew, when he let himself think about it, that he had become a kind of stranger, not to himself, not so much to the Morgan he might once have been, but to the Morgan he had always thought, in the end, he surely would become—that Morgan who in the blinding purity of art and truth would set down for all time the product of a life, and so wrest from darkness the tiny flame of immortality.

In his own house, in the strained silences of atrophied love, he had become still another kind of stranger, father in his spare time, married really to his work, swordsman on the road, lost and chilled in the indifference Anne wore with the same cool style she displayed in the latest clothes or coiffure—that indifference with which, in the few grim nights when lust and rage overwhelmed his shame, she would lie white and contemptuous, unmoving beneath his desperation lunges.

"But he ran again," Glass said. "He couldn't have been all that far gone if he could try to do it all over again four years later."

"Never understood it," Curly said, shaking his cotton hair. "That time around, the only way Aiken could have lost that nomination was if he'd got caught raping a nun in Massachusetts. I told Anderson that. But he jumped in at the last minute anyway. Never understood it at all."

"Only just that one primary, remember?" Morgan said. "I guess just that one opened his eyes in time."

But Morgan could not be sure of that either. He did not believe Hunt Anderson had ever lost his political acumen, so Anderson must have known that the second time around Aiken had the nomination locked up before the fight began.

By then Anderson didn't have O'Connor to do his TV—or anybody for that matter. Kathy wouldn't touch the campaign. Anderson had no issue, no money, no backing—just a few nostalgic voters and faithful followers.

Morgan went up there once, during the first primary, but left after two days of the campaign. It made him angry to see Anderson doing so badly, where only four years earlier he had so unexpectedly triumphed. But Anderson kept plowing ahead, even when everyone else knew it was no use.

Kathy had managed to talk him out of going up there the night the primary returns came in; they had holed up in his Senate office to get the news, which was all in by ten p.m. Aiken had rolled right over Anderson, who soon went out in the hall where the cameras were set up. The issue had been settled so quickly, he'd only had time for one or two drinks after dinner, but, to Morgan, Anderson appeared strangely relaxed, almost content.

"I want to congratulate Governor Aiken," he said. "It's getting to be a habit with me. I want to say also that I'm not going to enter any more primaries. If nominated, I will not run. If elected, I will not serve. If drafted for the vice-presidency, I'll support the other ticket."

"Senator," one of the TV reporters said keenly, "does this mean you've given up national politics?"

"Yes, and vice versa."

Kathy, who had been standing beside Morgan, turned and went back into Anderson's office.

One old-timer was there from a wire service; he was gruff at best, and Morgan knew he thought correctly the whole thing had been a waste of everyone's time. "Senator," he growled, "why'd you enter this primary in the first place?"

"Oh, I suppose old politicians never die, Jack. And then I thought I ought to give the people who supported me so generously the last time another shot at it. Turned out they didn't much want it."

When the bright lights were out and they had wandered back into his private office, past the rooms where Matt and a few staff members were closing things down, Anderson looked at Morgan rather wistfully. "I know you think I was a fool too, Rich, but don't be too hard on me. I really did want to see if anybody still cared . . . particularly if I did."

"And did you?"

"No. Which was the main thing I wanted to find out."

"As for anybody else," Morgan said, "you can't really judge by this one result, can you?"

"Doesn't matter," Anderson said. "*I'm* free of it now."

"I'll tell you why you really ran," Kathy said from the other end of his private office. She was sitting on the sofa where Hunt took his long afternoon naps. "If you don't know. It was just one more scene in the great tragedy. Like Barrymore falling off the stage into the bass drum."

"It was politics that ruined him, not whisky," Adam said. "You know that, Rich, you just won't admit it. It was politics that got him to thinking he could do more than a man can do."

Morgan had become used to the thinly disguised hostility that had grown between Hunt and Kathy, especially when his presidential campaign was being discussed. Morgan went often with them, in the years after the convention, to the Anderson place; he and Hunt would walk the fields for hours, then go back to Hunt's room and talk and drink into the night. They were men who wanted nothing from each other—anyway nothing more than conversation and company and silence—although Morgan occasionally raised the subject of what had happened at the convention. Most of the time, he thought, Hunt seemed to have a certain contentment Morgan didn't want to disturb. In the convoluted way of life, it even seemed to be Hunt who had become detached about politics, issues, power, where once it had been Morgan who had questioned their efficacy. There were times, Morgan sensed, when Hunt showed a certain protective feeling about Morgan, although it should have been the other way around.

"Don't take politics too seriously, Morgan, don't be a football coach," Hunt liked to say. One of his favorite quips was that politicians were like football coaches, combining the will to win with the belief that the game was important. Morgan always refrained from saying that it had been he who had first given Anderson the saying, years before.

Or Anderson would say, "For Christ's sake, Rich, life's too short, take some time off, go South, give Richie and that sexy gal of yours a chance to know you."

Once or twice Hunt had insisted that Morgan bring them to the Anderson place; but the few times Anne came, she and Kathy didn't get on; they would always make it a more formal occasion.

The last time Anne had made the trip she had turned to Morgan rather suddenly on the flight home. "You're screwing that hard-nosed bitch," she said. "Don't expect me to go down there ever again."

"What in hell are you talking about?" Morgan glanced nervously at Richie, who was sitting across the aisle, reading *Mad Magazine,* and oblivious.

"I'm not a fool, Rich. I can see what's between the two of you."

"Oh, come on, Anne. So sometimes I get a little hot and bothered around Kathy, most men do, but that's all there is to it." It was true at the time; Morgan thought how likely it was that imaginary sins would exact their penalties before the real ones.

"Well, if you're not screwing her," Anne said, "you're slipping. Anyone can see she's panting for you."

"How would you know anything about panting for me? God knows, you never have. And what do you care anyway?"

"Just don't ask me to go down there any more," Anne said. "I've got more pride than you have."

Morgan knew she did; she had had to. On the night before their wedding —Morgan had found her teaching school in the town where he had done his first newspaper work—after Anne had cheerfully repelled his customary effort at advance consummation, they had indulged in late Cokes and barbecues at The Castle, a drive-in with a parking lot so dark that the whole establishment was known as The Rassle.

"Your last chance," Anne said. "Any regrets?"

Morgan considered the question gravely, as in those days he had considered most things. "Some," he finally said.

Anne sat bolt upright. "You *bas*tard!"

"Well, I just meant . . ." Too late, Morgan perceived the enormity of his error. "Like I always wanted to go around the world, just for instance. Or own a yacht. Things like that. And with a wife and responsibilities and probably children, I mean it's just not as likely anybody can do anything like that."

"You can have your damned cheap ring back this minute," Anne said, wrenching at her finger.

"Aw, come on," Morgan said. "You know I didn't mean . . ."

But Anne had known no such thing, he soon understood, and he had taken half an hour trying to mollify her. The ring would not come off, and she had finally given up tugging at it and sat stiffly against the far door, staring straight ahead while he tried vainly to persuade her that none of the vague dreams of youth really meant anything compared to her. Until at last she had jerked her head toward him as if it were that of a toy; and even in the dark of the car Morgan thought he could see the fierce whiteness of her face.

"You listen to me," she murmured, so low he had to strain to hear. "I don't care about your silly dreams. I don't want to hear about your responsibilities. I'm not going to be some kitchen drudge and sexpot for you—if I thought that, you'd never get near me again. Listen . . . if you marry me, Rich, you'll *go* around the world. You'll have a yacht if you want it. You marry me and you'll do anything you want. Do you understand that?"

"Oh, baby," Morgan said. "God, yes, I never meant . . ."

"You'd better understand it. Because I'm *somebody,* Rich. And if you don't understand that, you don't understand anything."

But Morgan had not understood, not until years later; he had only wanted her and what he conceived of as Marriage and Life. Even when it was too late, it seemed to him that his obvious desire to love her as she wished should have been enough to outweigh with her his inability to do so. He knew Anne was proud all right—proud and hurt and indomitable, and still reaching.

So she had never gone back to the Anderson house, but something kept drawing Morgan back. He believed it was there that someday he would learn what had really happened between Dunn and Anderson—what had been said, what they felt, and how they reacted at that moment when Anderson's expectations for himself had come to their peak.

One night in the fall before Anderson made his brief, farcical jump back into the limelight, he had finally talked about Dunn.

"A very sharp man," Anderson said.

A fire was leaping in the grate; Kathy had put some splendid ham on the table an hour or so earlier; and late that afternoon they had pulled four fine lunging largemouths from the shaded pond in one corner of the Anderson

place. Two had gone back into the water, but two were cleaned for breakfast. The two men were relaxed, with a bottle of Scotch and the fire between
them. Anderson was musing, mellow. What the hell? Morgan thought, and
asked him again what had happened with Dunn.

For a long time after Anderson's quick, short reply, Morgan thought he
would say nothing more, and he resigned himself to the usual frustration.
Then:

"Those green glasses put me off," Anderson said. "I thought at first that
was an affectation, a little edge Dunn gave himself. But I checked and found
he'd really needed them since childhood. And I hadn't spent the first hour
with him before I saw he was a different breed of cat from most pols. He
scared me a little. I thought he was looking right through me with those
lenses. Maybe he was. Maybe he only thought he was."

By then Morgan's work had forced him to know Dunn at least superfi-
cially, although after the convention he'd had to work at being open-minded
about it. "You never can tell what Dunn wants," Morgan said. "I think
that's what's so scary about him."

Anderson thought about that and drank Scotch. "Maybe so. The way you
judge a man is what's important. It governs everything. I mean, for example, I judged Hinman right; I figured I could crack his shell and make his
arrogance do him in. Everything turned on that, and that's the way it
worked out. But I judged Dunn wrong."

"Dunn him wrong," Morgan said, careful not to sound too serious, and
there was just enough Scotch in Anderson to make him laugh.

"I was wrong about Dunn," Anderson went on, "because . . . maybe you
remember what I said when I called you in that night, Rich . . . I believed
he'd take the gamble. I didn't think he'd take the easy ride with Aiken. I
didn't think he cared about just winning as much as he did about pulling
off a big score. But in judging him that way, you see, I figured he'd judge
me the way I wanted to be judged, thought I ought to be judged. So the
real question is, what was his actual judgment of me? What kind of a fellow
did he think he was dealing with?"

Anderson drank more Scotch. Morgan held his breath until Anderson
spoke again.

"The first thing he said that morning, he came slipping in like a thief,
looking behind him through those goddam green glasses, and he said right
away, 'Are you bugged?' Christ, I was so dead on my feet—I get tired all
over again just thinking about it—I snapped at him a little. 'How would I
know?' I said. And he just nodded and said, 'You probably are. That old

man can get anything done he wants.' I guess he meant the President, and I guess he was right.

"Kathy came in just about then and shook hands. But I could see Dunn wasn't going to talk in there, whether in front of her or not. So I said what about the bathroom? 'Yeah, great,' Dunn said, and Kathy gave me a look that would have stunned a mule. She's always thought it was just a scheme to get away from her. She flounced her ass out of there, and Dunn and I went into the bathroom, and he actually turned on the shower. I got one of these long legs over the sink and sort of half sat on it—it's a wonder I didn't fall asleep. Dunn turned down the lid of the john, put his foot on it, leaned on his knee, and looked at me through those green lenses.

"That's when it got through to me, Morgan—when I saw he was waiting on me to take the lead—that it mattered as much whether he'd judged me right, saw me the way I wanted to be seen, as it did whether I'd judged him right. The truth was, I didn't have the faintest notion what he thought of me, and it was too late to find out."

Morgan, his writer's imagination leaping the years, could picture them in that bathroom, with its massive tub and the sink on which Anderson was perched rising on its thick stem like a marble toadstool from the old-fashioned barbershop floor, the dawn light gray at the frosted window.

"I still don't know how I did it," Anderson said, "I was just about out on my feet. Hadn't slept in, I believe it was three nights. But I pulled myself together that one last time, or anyway I thought I did, and tried to lay it on the line for him. I started by outlining the way I saw the situation. That the Leaders hadn't got the mileage they'd hoped for by swinging so much to Aiken on the second ballot. Maybe they should have waited one more. So the next time around, I said, if everybody held tight, Aiken would start to look bad and the thing might begin to slip away from them after all.

"Dunn just nodded once. So then I said, 'That's if everybody holds tight. But that goddam Stark, he won't hold, the way he looks to me. Stark's got the butterflies in his belly, and he's going to Aiken if what I hear is right. You still with me?'

"Dunn gives me another nod. 'So if it gets to Stark and the son-of-a-bitch goes over, that'll break the dam. But you come before Stark on the roll call.'

"That time Dunn didn't even nod, so I began to pour it on a little. 'Stop me when I get to be wrong,' I said. 'You stand pat and Stark jumps to Aiken, you're holding the bag, right? We all are. If you go to Aiken first, Stark does too, and that's the ball game, but what's in that for you? That's no score, to put over a guy who's going to get the marbles anyway.'

" 'Better than holding the bag,' Dunn says, just a whisper I could barely hear above the running water in the shower.

"So I came back at him quick. 'But what about the other possibility?' You better believe I was selling like a son-of-a-bitch. 'You're ahead of Stark on the roll call,' I said, 'so suppose *you* swing to *me*. Meantime, I send Curly Layton over there to stir up Stark's butterflies, and you know Curly can do it. When Stark hears you're going to me, and the demonstration Curly's boys will set off, that's going to put the squeeze on him till his balls ache. At the worst, he'll go on to Aiken the way he figures to do, and we've got a deadlock. Or maybe he won't go anywhere, and then we're really in business and Aiken's in a sling. It's even possible Stark'll come all the way to us on the same ballot—I wouldn't bet against it once you crack the whip over his head. That would be the big score for both of us.' "

And then, while Morgan sipped his Scotch, his feet stretched casually to the fire but his mind as alert as it had ever been to every nuance of what Anderson was saying, to every recollected detail—then Anderson fell silent. The fire snapped in the grate; outside a little wind had come up, rattling the shutters; and somewhere in the house Morgan could occasionally hear Kathy, or maybe it was Jodie, moving around.

The silence began to stretch out, bear down. Morgan had never been so close to knowing; it seemed to him that no less than the riddle of life was about to be answered for him. He feared to put in even a prompting question, lest he shatter the moment.

Anderson was slumped in his chair, his chin down a little on his chest, his eyes staring unwinkingly at the fire, his hair in its usual cowlicks and sprouts, light and shadow moving softly on the odd planes of his face. Morgan took the empty glass out of his hand and went silently to the bar in the corner of the room.

"I not only judged him wrong," Anderson said at last, while Morgan was still pouring drinks, "but I guess he judged me right."

"How's that?" Morgan capped the Scotch bottle, careful to jar nothing, make no unexpected sound or movement.

"Not the way I wanted to be judged."

Morgan went almost on tiptoe across the room, handed Anderson his drink, and returned to his own chair.

"Dunn not only didn't go for the gamble," Anderson said. "He knew I would offer him a deal if he didn't. And if I would offer him a deal, after that high and mighty campaign against the bosses, then of course I wasn't any better than any of the rest—maybe I was even a worse hypocrite—and there was no more reason to put me over than any of the others. Maybe not as much, if he didn't really care about the big score."

Morgan felt a mixture of relief at knowing and shock at what he had learned. It did not square, he thought; it went against all his own judgments, against all those instincts about men on which he had to rely in his work. It shook him to have been so wrong.

"What did you say, Hunt? I mean when you offered him the deal?"

Anderson made an expansive, dismissing gesture with his long arm and shook his big head. "Stop asking so many goddam questions, Rich—I'm not a bloody reporter like you. I don't remember what I said or he said or anybody said. We weren't in there long enough to say much; it was the hot water he was running and we didn't even steam up the mirror. How the hell should I remember what was said when I don't even want to think about it any more?"

"Well, damn your eyes," Morgan said, angered by the suggestion that he was intruding, frustrated again at this new curtain rung down in the midst of the play, shocked still at the unexpected nature of the scene he had glimpsed. "You remembered what you wanted to remember, or what you wanted me to think you remembered, and now you chicken out of the only thing I ever asked you for."

Anderson chuckled. "Which happens to be the one thing of mine you or nobody has a right to, not even if I remembered, which I don't for one second admit I do. Besides, I keep trying to tell you, what matters is how Dunn judged me, not what I maybe think I said or he said three years after the fact. And I know how he figured me, because he told Kathy and she told me, you can bet on that. Do you think he was banging her?"

"Don't be a damned fool," Morgan said, furious. "Even if that were true, and it isn't, you ought not to ask me or anybody anything like that."

"I know it, and I don't really think that. Kathy's too careful to screw around, and she doesn't have to find out things in bed, she's got her own methods. But she was close to Dunn, she talked to him a lot at the convention, you know. He's told her everything that happened—and she's rubbed it in so hard, sometimes I feel like striking back. But I guess it was a shitty thing to say." He lifted his glass to the ceiling of the room. "I apologize, Kathy, you win again."

"It wasn't easy on her," Morgan said. "She wanted to win that nomination. She wanted it as badly as you did."

Anderson's mouth twisted in faint irritation, and he took a drink before answering. "You put that just right, Morgan, just right. I don't reckon I'll be allowed to forget what happened either."

"Forget what?" Morgan was still trying but without hope.

"What I told you a minute ago, about Dunn. Morgan, whyn't you put some Scotch in all this branch water you poured in here?"

And no amount of booze or blandishment got any more than that out of him, then or ever. When Jodie came that night, Anderson was half asleep in his chair. Morgan was still fuming, and not at all drunk.

"Well, I for one just don't like to think of Anderson as being ruined," Curly Layton was saying. They had walked quite near Anderson's house. Most of the cars were gone from the meadow, but the faint odor of exhaust and the dry prickle of dust hung in the warm evening air. "But if he was, I'll tell you one thing I've never understood and never will. He was married to about the strongest and smartest woman I ever knew, and a looker at that. How could she let him ruin himself, if that's what he did?"

After Jodie had taken over in Anderson's room, Morgan went into the hallway and up the curving stairs. As his head came up to second-floor level, he could see a thin strip of light, dim as a candle's glow, falling across the corridor ahead. He had come up those stairs many a night and stopped in front of Kathy's door, listening, hearing nothing, only the hard pounding of his heart, his shallow breathing, the shudderings and creakings of the old house. He had often put his hand on the loose knob, told himself to turn it, longed for the soft, devouring darkness beyond it. He knew the door would not be locked, was there for him to open. Since that day in the bare little room at the convention hotel, when he had first held her in his arms, Morgan had known he had only to act. The fierce attraction that, subdued or thwarted, had made them clash like natural forces, had needed only the merest recognition, a comforting word, a first tentative touch of bodies, Kathy's hair soft as breath on his lips, to flare unmistakably between them.

Yet Morgan had waited. Something had kept him going past the unlocked door. Not Anne—that part of his life was an empty chamber, peopled only with occasional remembered sighs, kept neat and untouched deep within him, as a long-departed child's room might be kept immaculate for his imagined return.

And not Hunt—Morgan knew Hunt and Kathy had lived for years an arranged life, made intimate only sporadically by the death of a child, the shared struggle of the campaign, and now spiraling, on her part, into smoldering hostility and, on his, into an indifference seldom broken by the bitterness toward her that Morgan had seen that night.

Certainly not Kathy—sometimes, Morgan knew, she watched him with puzzlement, and in the secret clasp of a hand, the flick of an eye, the casual brush of an arm, once in the tension that rose tangible between them as the dust motes in the silent, sun-stabbed air of a taxi in which they were riding from Capitol Hill to Georgetown—in a thousand ways, Morgan knew she was waiting for him.

Himself, then—for he had not acted, nor had he come up the steps even that night intending to act. He stared at the dim strip of light a long time. It lay there on the floor as if drawn by a determined hand, a barrier, a warning, and he knew if he stepped over it and on to the familiar guest room at the end of the hall he could never come back. So the decision was forced, and there had never been in his mind any doubt of what he would do if that were to happen. He would reach once more, as he had always reached.

Morgan went up the steps, seized the loose knob, pushed her door farther open, went in, and closed it behind him. The light came from a small lamp near the window; it left the bed in shadows. Kathy was not in it. She was sitting on the little sofa, just outside the brightest circle of the light.

"I've been waiting," she said. "A long time."

"It's going to be complicated."

"Everything's complicated."

"No, it was simple not to come in here. It was easy to know you wanted me to come in that door, that I wanted to come in, and still not do it."

"It wasn't easy for me." She stood up. She was wearing the kind of full-length robe he came to know that she always wore—never anything coquettish.

"Wait and see how much easier than it's going to be now," he said. "Because I'm not just coming in here this once, you know, and never again."

"You'd better not."

"And we're not going to have some sneaky little two-bit affair for a little while until we get tired of it. You know that too."

"Why don't you stop telling me what I know?" She came a few steps toward him, reached down, clicked off the light.

"Did you ever have anything in your mind," Morgan said in the darkness, "that was just right, just perfect, that you wanted to do?"

"Yes."

"That's why it was easy for me not to come in. It was just perfect—it was almost a pure vision—to *think* of coming in here."

"That's why I thought you wouldn't ever come. I know you, Rich, I've known you a long time. You don't want to admit that nothing's pure in life."

"I know," Morgan said. "Everything gets complicated."

In the dark they had come close together. He put his arm around her, and they went to the window and looked over the fields silver in the autumn moonlight. There was a sound in some far corner of the house, a door closing. Morgan closed his eyes, put his face in Kathy's hair, saw in brilliant subliminal flashes Anne's tight scornful mouth, CHICK'N STEAK DINER flashing red in the night, beautiful long tanned legs, fire shadows dark on Anderson's face . . .

"Maybe it was like in television," Glass said.

They had stopped beneath a tree on Anderson's lawn. A few figures were moving near the house. The governor's limousine waited grandly at the foot of the steps. More lights had come on, including a dim one in Kathy's room.

"I mean, in television," Glass explained as they looked at him, "the most successful guy finds a role to play. He comes across on the tube as a particular kind of person, you know what I mean? Maybe this Anderson was that way. Like Doctor Kildare. Or Perry Mason. Everybody thinks of a guy like that in a certain way. And if he gets out of that role, he can lose it all. People who saw him one way can't see him any other."

"But they can turn the dial," Morgan said. "The guy that plays the part is stuck with it."

The Professional II

They walked across the lawn to the porch. Just as they reached the steps the governor and his wife, closely followed by Matt Grant, came out of the house.

"Oh, Rich," Matt said, "I'm glad you got here." He met Morgan at the top of the steps. "Riding in with the Governor," he whispered; then, aloud, "There's a message—you're to call Keller at your office. And you just missed Danny. He went off with Sprock and Berger. They said they'd probably see you on the eight-thirty plane."

Morgan thought glumly of the redhead and glanced at his watch. It was six-thirty; he would have to hurry to make it.

"Kathy's already said good-by to the Governor, and now she's upstairs talking to Dunn," Matt said. "She wants to see you before you go."

The governor loomed up beaming over Morgan. "I just want you to know your home state's mighty proud of you, Mister Morgan. Follow every word you write down here. Don't always agree, of course."

"I bet not," Morgan said. "Much obliged, Governor."

"Come see me while you're here." The governor winked massively. "Might even have a story for you."

Over the governor's shoulder Morgan could see Matt's pleased face. "I'm supposed to get out tonight, Governor. If I miss the plane, I might take you up on that."

"Any time, any time at all. Well, come on, Alice Mae." The governor seized his wife's arm. "Let's get over the creek before dark. Y'all come see us at the Mansion."

Matt shook hands again, whispered hurriedly to Morgan, " 'Preciate anything you can do." He gave Curly Layton a hand, clapped Glass on the shoulder, held out his hand to Adam. "Hasn't been the same around the Senate since you left."

Adam nodded. "I can believe that."

"Can't keep the Governor waiting, Adam. Wish we had more time to talk." Matt hurried down the steps and into the limousine. It pulled away, with a flurry of waving hands at the rear window.

"Poor Matt," Morgan said, "I don't think he's got a prayer."

"For what?"

"He wants Hunt's seat."

"Jesus," Adam said, "they haven't got the dirt in the hole yet."

"My friend," Curly Layton put a fatherly arm around Adam's broad shoulders, "when I was governor I had a senator die on me once, with five years to go on his term. It was the foulest period of torment I ever went through while practicing the art, I don't mind telling you. Running for office was Valentine's Day by comparison. The first six hours after we got word the distinguished Senator Daughtry had cashed in—he was on a Foreign Relations Committee inspection trip to the French Riviera, rest his soul—I had twenty-one applications for the seat and eighteen nominations from people that wanted their man appointed. By the end of the week I had over a hundred fifty names on a list, and every one of 'em an honor to the state with a lot of clout. Hell, my friend—hell, I say—is as Eden compared to what a practitioner goes through when he's got a list like that to weed the culls out of down to one."

"What'd you do?" Glass asked.

"Appointed myself with a promise to the people to serve out the term and never run again. Only way I could see out of a bad spot. Besides"—Curly's jowls shook with mirth, and a curl tumbled across his forehead—"I decided I was the best man."

"Maybe this governor'll do the same thing," Morgan said. "I don't see what he'd have to gain by even thinking about Anderson's AA."

Curly shook his head. "No mileage in that."

"While you guys talk politics"—Adam rubbed his stomach—"I'm going to scrounge something from Jodie in the kitchen. Not a bite since breakfast."

"I'll come along, I'm starving too." Glass said.

They went into the house. Curly and Morgan stood looking out at the darkening sky, listening to the crickets. A black man whom Morgan recognized as Zeb Vance's driver came across the lawn. "Lookin' for Senator

McLaren." His voice was soft, slurred, and it took Morgan back to many an earlier evening, many another summer, and the crickety sounds of youth. He knew he had to be on guard against nostalgia; if he let himself, he would wallow in it, not so much in memory of what had been as in despair at what was, and would be, in their hard contrast with the soft colors and gentle voices of the recollected past.

"I'm not sure . . ." Morgan said, wary of confronting Millwood again.

Curly picked up the vibrations immediately. "Tell you what," he said to the driver, "you come along with me and we'll find them inside somewhere. Maybe the Senator will even give an old friend a lift to town."

The driver came up the steps and they went into the house. For the first time in hours Morgan was alone. He went out to the lawn and sat under a tree, away from the lights on the porch, around which moths were beginning to cluster and flutter. The sun was far beyond the edge of the earth and, that late in the summer, night was falling fast. The sky was cloudless, purple, limitless. A single star hung brilliantly over the house, over the dim light in Kathy's room. Morgan wished he were far away, farther than the star; he wished he were shining and alone in a heaven too vast to imagine, where nothing could be complicated.

The black driver came out of the house and helped an unsteady Millwood down the steps. Curly and Zeb Vance followed. As Morgan got up and went toward them they stopped, watching him come into the light. "You fellows leaving now?" he said awkwardly.

"Got to get on, Scout." Zeb Vance clapped Morgan on the shoulder. "Long drive for the old folks. I reckon you won't hold it against Millwood he spouted off a little back there. Millwood's got a good heart."

"I know he has. And I don't think I'm the one that ought to hold anything against anyone."

"Rrrumph," Curly said. "I'll just shake hands and get on down there to the car and chat with Millwood."

"Curly"—Morgan took his hand—"I'll be on the road soon, and I'll look you up." But he knew he would not; he knew Curly knew he would not; they both knew there would be no need.

"Always glad to see old friends." Curly held Morgan's hand a moment, then went toward the car. Morgan saw that the handsome head was not so erect on the broad shoulders as it had been earlier; the day had been hard on everyone.

"Fine man," Morgan said.

Zeb Vance nodded. "One of the best I ever knew, and I did know some in my time, Scout. Only Curly went off on purpose, gentleman that he is, so we could chat, and there's nothing to chat about, far's I'm concerned. I told you I don't bear a grudge. I always left that to Millwood and Miss Pearl."

"Well, then, would you mind not calling me Scout?"

Zeb Vance peered at him in the failing light. "Why not?"

"Because it's what you used to call me, and now it breaks my heart."

"Well, if it breaks," Zeb Vance said, "it goes to show you've got one, Scout. Maybe more of one than you think. Walk with me to the car."

They moved along a few steps, then Morgan stopped. "I don't want Millwood to chew me out again."

"Millwood's not but barely compos mentis, if that. I poured enough bourbon down his gullet, I expect that driver had to hoist him into the back seat with a crane."

The engine was running, and the door was open for Zeb Vance. He turned to Morgan and held out his hand. "You might as well come see me sometime."

"I'd like to, you know that, but I don't know if I'm coming down here any more." That was a little dramatic, Morgan thought, but he vaguely wanted sympathy—he was not sure for what.

Zeb Vance shook his head vigorously, letting go of Morgan's hand. "Now you don't want to take too much after that fellow we just buried," he said. "He always looked to me to take things too seriously. What I think is, a man ought to do the best he can and not believe in too much."

"So he doesn't get hurt too often?"

"So he don't have to waste too much time bleeding and moaning." Zeb Vance got in the car laboriously, closed the door, and peered at Morgan from the window. "Come on down and see me anyway, Scout. It's hard to go back but it's harder to get away. Hum-up, driver."

Morgan watched the car move away. That was all right, he thought, not believing in too much was fine if a man could be that way. It was good advice to give. Still, he felt better, having opened himself to Zeb Vance as he had seldom opened himself to anyone. It had not quite been sympathy he had received in return, but there was a certain relief in having shed some of his burdensome cover, as if he had dropped off a heavy coat. Or perhaps he was only dramatizing himself again—Morgan Over the Hill, or The Twilight of Life, great scenes from The American Drama.

He turned toward the house. All the lights in Kathy's room were on; her unmistakable outline moved momentarily across the shade. As close as they had been, he thought, had he ever truly been open with Kathy?

Inside—with relief Morgan noticed that the white spray was gone from the doorway—he met Dunn coming down the curving stairs. Now or never, Morgan thought, but before he could speak Dunn asked if he wanted a ride into town.

"When are you leaving?" Morgan asked.

"In a minute or so. Those friends of yours from Washington are coming along to catch the eight-thirty flight. Mine goes the other way a little after nine."

In the car with Glass and French would be no place to challenge Dunn. Besides, he would have to see Kathy; he wanted to see Kathy. "Well, I'll get a ride some way a little later on. Jodie can drive me if nothing else. I've still got some things to talk over with Kathy."

"She's holding court upstairs."

"There was something I wanted to ask you too."

"I've got a minute or two." The green glasses turned toward the parlor where Anderson's coffin had been.

Morgan fancied there was still a faint funereal odor of sickly flowers coming from it. "Not in there," he said and led the way back to Anderson's room and closed the door behind them.

Morgan went to the bar cabinet and poured vodka over ice, raising his eyebrows at Dunn. Dunn shook his head, private behind his green shield.

"Anderson's in the ground, Dunn. I guess he was the nearest thing I had to a friend, anyway one that I kept. Those few minutes you spent with him in that damned bathroom all those years ago turned his life around somehow. Everything built up to that meeting and everything went downhill from there on."

"Figuratively speaking. What's up and what's down could be a matter of judgment, don't you think?"

"I'd like to know what happened in there, Dunn. I can't make you tell me, but I can ask you."

"But if you have to ask me, it means that Anderson never told you. So why should I?"

"Because Kathy told me what you said had happened. What you told Kathy had happened."

"You don't believe it?"

"It never sounded like the Anderson I thought I knew." Morgan understood that he was clinging, not just to Anderson's integrity but to some vestige of his own.

The green lenses turned, moved slowly, as if Dunn were peering at the pictures and cartoons on the wall. But they were in shadow. The only light in the room was from an old floor lamp near the bar; it cast a small yellow circle around them. For a moment Morgan thought Dunn would step out of the circle, toward the door.

"Tell me what Kathy told you," Dunn said.

"That the reason you thought he wasn't good enough was that he tried to sell out to you on the tidelands, and so you thought he was soft and a hypocrite."

Dunn came forward into the light. "I take you for a friend, so I'll say this much. Anderson and I agreed that if Stark went to Aiken, particularly if Stark and I both went to Aiken, the game would be over. He thought there was a chance if I moved first, to him, it would scare Stark into holding fast or following me, and I'd make what Anderson called a big score by putting him over. That's what he wanted me to do, swing to him on the third ballot. I don't know if he was prepared to pay a price or how high, because I told him straight out, and in so many words, no dice. I had decided to go to Aiken and put him over if I could."

Morgan set his empty glass down with a small crack. "You mean he didn't offer you a deal of some kind?"

"He looked stunned. He looked like he'd been hit between the eyes. He stared at me with his mouth open—"

"Lost the golden touch," Morgan said almost to himself. "Anderson really thought he could persuade you, he really thought he could pull it off."

"They all do, if they're any good."

"But that was all? He didn't—"

"He was almost mumbling. He was dead for sleep, I could see that, and then I'd hit him where he lived. It was like he was in shell shock. The water was running in the shower—I'd heard the White House had him bugged —it was hot in there, and don't forget, we were both about out on our feet. He was mumbling something about writing my own ticket, I heard that all right, but it wasn't coherent. And then he did a strange thing. I've never forgotten it, Morgan. I can see him in there now with the steam beginning to come out around the edges of the shower curtain. He was perched up on the sink and slumped against the medicine cabinet while he was mumbling and staring at me. And then he stood up. He unfolded himself off that sink and stood straight up, towering over me, and with just the light in there from the frosted window, he seemed even taller than he was. 'Of course, Mister Dunn,' he said very formally and clearly, 'of course you understand I won't be able to accept your terms unless they're compatible with the positions I've taken.' "

The words fell heavily, one by one, into the silence of the room. Moving carefully, Morgan poured more vodka into his glass. I must miss nothing, he thought.

"I didn't know what he meant," Dunn said. "I'd already told him I was going to Aiken, but I told him again."

"Because you thought Anderson wasn't good enough?"

Dunn shrugged. "Maybe we could have put him over and maybe that would have been a big score for me, but I wouldn't have done it if I could have. I didn't give a damn for Paul Hinman then and I don't now, but Anderson gave me a problem. I was afraid of a man who thinks he's got a duty to punish people he thinks deserve punishment, particularly those that are in his way. I'd decided to put Aiken in the White House because I didn't think I'd have to worry about the way Aiken would use his power."

"That sounds great," Morgan said, "just great. But it's bullshit. Dunn the protector of liberty. Let me tell you what I think, Dunn. You're lying in your teeth. You chose Aiken because he was a conventional pro with the powers on his side. Putting him over at the convention was a safe bet; and you knew you could break bread at the White House table with him. Anderson told me one time he'd figured you wrong, and now I see he really did. You didn't have the guts to risk it either way with him, at the convention or later in the White House. And you didn't even have the guts to tell me the truth, much less tell Kathy the truth."

Dunn took off the green glasses and rubbed his eyes with his knuckles. Blinking weakly in the dim light, he looked at Morgan, and Morgan knew then that Dunn saw no more clearly than anyone, and could be no more certain of things than anyone who dealt intimately with men.

"Maybe you're right," Dunn said, putting his glasses on slowly. "I was afraid of Anderson, I wasn't afraid of Aiken, that was the nub of it. Maybe I just rationalized my reasons and you're right about them. Maybe I went to meet him that morning hoping he had some better idea than just asking me to chance it with him. And when he didn't . . . I don't know, it was a long time ago. But one thing I know you're wrong about, Morgan—I told Kathy just what I've told you."

"Then why would she—" Morgan stopped, set his glass down again. A door slammed somewhere in the house. A car started up and left.

"You'd better ask her. She knew Anderson never offered me any kind of a deal. 'We *could* have won it then,' that's what she said to me, and I asked her what that meant, and she looked right through me and said, 'Because you'd have changed your mind if he'd offered it—if *I'd* offered it.' But he didn't."

It seemed like hours to Morgan that he stood with Dunn, silent in

Anderson's room. Then the door opened and Glass appeared. "You fellows ready to go?"

"Coming," Dunn said.

"You'll have to go on without me." Morgan was numb. He knew he was going to be angry, he was going to rage and curse; but for the moment he was numb. "I have to talk to Kathy."

"Christ," Glass said, "I was just yakking with her, and I've got to say now I see what you characters mean. A little past the prime but what a shape on her. You won't make the eight-thirty if you don't come now, Rich."

"I'll catch a flight in the morning.

Dunn put out his hand. "Look me up next time you're out my way, Morgan. Lots of other things to talk about, you know."

Morgan shook hands mechanically.

Glass came into the room, grinning, hand outstretched.

"I'll do that," Morgan said to Dunn. "Someday."

"S'long, Rich," Charlie French called from the door.

Morgan waved to him, then took Glass's soft hand.

"Terrific meeting you," Glass said. "I always say you're tops in the media."

It might be the nearest thing to an epitaph he would ever have, Morgan thought, raging inside; in the end, his cover story—tops in the media—was the only mark he would ever make, and at that only upon Glass's swift and shifting world. And that was an ironic justice indeed, the more maddening because Glass himself seemed to have no need for cover. Could it be possible that Glass had no concepts to meet, therefore no failures to hide?

Morgan watched Dunn leave the room. Glass still was gripping Morgan's hand.

"You know, I learned a little something from you," Glass said. "I mean the way you handle yourself."

Morgan laughed harshly. "Better not look too close."

"Well, you showed me a lot of class, and so did the lady upstairs. And I guess the way you both felt about Anderson, he must have had it too."

A lot of class, tops in the media. Suddenly the phrases seemed no more meaningless than anything else that might be said of a man, or a life; because who could be sure how another had conceived himself, how far he had fallen short?

"I guess that is as good a way as any to put it," Morgan said. "I appreciate that, Larry. I really do."

Glass released his hand, clapped him on the arm, and went out of the room. The tape on his neck peered back like an unwinking eye; it seemed to be staring at Morgan long after Glass had gone.

Morgan went to Anderson's table, sat down, put his head down on his arms, clenched his fists and began to pound them on the table. Something suffused his brain; he felt for a moment as if the top of his head might fly off. His fingernails bit deeply into the palms of his hand, and his back teeth were clenched so tightly he could hear them grinding, feel the pressure stabbing up his temples.

After a while the rage passed, as he had known it would have to, and he began to think calmly about Anderson. *Dunn not only didn't go for the gamble. He knew I would offer him a deal if he didn't.* Except she only let you think you offered it, Morgan thought. That cold-blooded snatch.

He stalked out of Anderson's room, then into the hall beyond. From the pantry at its end he heard the loud voice of Myrtle Bell. "Got it all? Okay, big boy, I'll be in tomorrow." A receiver was banged on its cradle, and Myrtle came charging out. At the sight of Morgan, dismay touched her face, then she barked at him. "Who's eavesdropping now?"

"Not me, I'm just coming from the john."

"And I'm just kidding." But he could see the relief in her face.

"You do remind me I've got to call my office," Morgan said.

"Well, I'm off the phone, it's all yours. Aren't you catching the eight-thirty plane?"

"No, and you won't either if you don't get moving." He gave her a distant peck on the cheek, patted her ample bottom and went past her toward the pantry.

"You're staying here?" There was a certain edge to Myrtle's voice that Morgan had heard before. He looked back quickly and thought that her nose was actually quivering, like that of a hound on the trail. Goddammit, he thought, but said, "Oh, sure, upstairs. I'm shacking up with Kathy already, didn't you know?"

"Go to hell" Myrtle relaxed visibly. "Not that you don't probably have your plans. So long, big boy."

He would have to be doubly careful, Morgan thought, dialing. All such trivia went deep into Myrtle's limitless and unerring memory banks, and now it would take but the slightest hint to send her rummaging like a computer's whirling disks through her vast stored treasure of gossip, observations, implications, possibilities, until inevitably the connection was made. If—he thought grimly, thinking of Kathy, Anderson, Dunn—there were anything again to be connected. And would it matter anyway?

Janie gave him Keller right away. In the background, Morgan could hear the typewriters clicking out their nightly fancies.

"Nothing crash," Keller said.

Morgan braced himself. The more Keller underplayed it, the more important the event. A famous story had it that one day the finiancial writer had rushed into the office, livid with excitement, to say that the world monetary system was at that moment collapsing. "Take four hundred words," Keller was supposed to have said, but he denied it: "I offered him five." It was the way Keller tried, with small success, to keep things in perspective.

"Cockcroft's office called," Keller said. "They want you and only you, and they want you to call tonight, no matter how late."

"Big deal." This was a message Nat could have delivered, so Keller had something else on his mind. "I'll call the bastard," Morgan said and waited.

"Yeah, well, one other thing," Keller said. "I hear by the grapevine up there . . . " Keller spent his days on the phone to the home office, in all its nooks and crannies; the intelligence he vacuumed from his endless conversations was nigh infallible. ". . . the little prick's going for you this time."

Decoded, that meant the managing editor was after Morgan's neck, and mortally, as compared to less serious knifings in the past. Morgan knew he did not have to tell Keller about the meeting scheduled with the publisher. Keller would know.

"I thought he would. What's the scenario you hear?"

"Boot you upstairs with a big title and nothing else."

"Well, keep your ears open," Morgan said unnecessarily. "I'll be in tomorrow."

"Yeah." There was a moment of silence on the line before Keller said, "If you get it, Rich, you think maybe I could talk 'em into early retirement?"

"Christ," Morgan said, "the bureau would fall apart if you did that."

"Well, it would be the one goddam dirty deal I couldn't stomach if they stick it to you."

Morgan turned his head momentarily from the receiver; he thought Keller might hear the choking sound in his throat. "Ah, hell," he finally said, "if you're with me, the hell with them."

"See you tomorrow," Keller said and hung up.

Morgan stood a moment in the pantry. He was beginning, he thought a little drily, to feel stretched; but he could not worry about the managing editor now. He dialed zero, recited his credit-card number, and asked for 202-456-1414. Naturally, Cockcroft would be working late.

"White House," said a brisk operator's voice, as if ready to put the unknown caller through to the President.

"Mister Cockcroft, please."

"Just a moment, sir." There were clickings and buzzes; a bored English accent finally came on the line. "Mister Cockcroft's office heah."

"This is Rich Morgan, returning his call."

"What was the name, sir?"

"Morgan."

"Could you spell that, please?"

"Cockcroft knows how to spell it," Morgan said patiently. "He called *me*."

"Well"— the English accent dripped dubiety—"I'll see if I can locate him."

"Try his desk," Morgan said. "I happen to know he spends a lot of his time there when he's in the office."

The English accent giggled. "You must be one of those newspapermen."

"Put the bastard on," Morgan said. "But tell me first, what's a nice girl like you doing in a place like that?" At long range, he felt suddenly witty, masterful, in charge of things.

The English accent giggled some more, but Cockcroft came abruptly on the line. "Yes?"

The brisk impatience of the word, its unyielding assumption of greater priorities elsewhere, struck Morgan bluntly. He was, in spite of himself, not so much intimidated as made wary; it would not do, he thought, to give this man an opening through which to demean him.

"Rich Morgan," he said. "You wanted me?"

"Well, damn your eyes, Morgan," Cockcroft said merrily in his Ivy League tones. "You slipped us the shaft again." It was condescending, insulting, Morgan thought, that Cockcroft could manage to suggest that the Hinman exclusive had been no more than an amusing incident.

"No thanks to you," Morgan said, reminding Cockcroft that, having done his best to prevent Morgan's story, he had after all been outwitted. "I must say you guys got lousy taste over there." His Southern accent was becoming deeper, his words were more slurred, as he burrowed into his cover.

"How so?" Cockcroft sounded amused again, certain his taste was one thing that could never truly be questioned.

"Paul Hinman."

"Well I, for one," Cockcroft said, "rather resented your dredging up all the old twaddle in your piece this morning. All that's old hat."

"So is Auschwitz."

"I can't accept that at all." Cockcroft was now dismissing Morgan from decent considerations. "Paul Hinman is one of the ablest men in the country, I think that's conceded. Look here, Morgan . . ." Briskly he put aside the one question as beneath notice and called Morgan to the real point. "I called to ask you to a small backgrounder in my office at eleven tomorrow. Paul and I want to brief you and two or three of your . . . ah . . . compatriots on some of the things we have on our plate. Nothing about dirty tricks, of course, but I think we can underpin you a little on some of the trouble spots and pass on our evaluations."

"Hinman'll just love having me there."

"We've discussed that. Paul's too astute to blot his copybook before he starts. He's very fast off the blocks."

"I'll bet," Mogran said. "Off the record, I suppose?"

"Deep background."

"Just once, why don't you characters lay it on the line?"

"Not one of our options," Cockcroft said crisply. "This is a dangerous world we live in, Morgan. Paul's going to be our man in the back alleys. I don't think the American people really expect him to . . . ah . . . lay it on the line."

Morgan knew he faced the ultimate trap of his calling. He could go and be told what they wanted him to know; or he could stay away and his paper would learn only at second hand whatever it was they wanted him to know. Morgan had long since lost any sense of thrill or superiority at being included among those so selectively admitted to the higher levels of national calculation; he knew the more he operated on those levels, the less he was likely to penetrate the deliberate presentation of things to their actuality. But whether or not he went, Cockcroft and Hinman would have their say, and neither would have to take responsibility for it. And at least, if he went—so Morgan always rationalized—he could cross-examine.

"I'll be there," Morgan said.

"Good, good. And . . . ah . . . Morgan, just in the national interest, I hope . . . ah . . . well, whenever Paul's name comes up in the future, is it really going to be necessary for you to rake over the coals?"

"You're goddam right it is," Morgan said. "See you at eleven." He hung up, knowing it was hopeless. Hinman's new activities would erase within weeks any lingering memories of his past. It was the genius of America that all time was present time; the past existed only in the shadows of the soul, where even in its invincibility it need never be acknowledged.

Going up the stairs to the second floor, Morgan could hear Kathy's voice. As he came into the second-floor hall, she laughed, the rich pleasant sound of it carrying through the house, attacking its funereal silence. She was in her room with Adam Locklear and Bobby.

Morgan stopped in the doorway. "Looks like we're about all that's left," he said.

"Well, I can't say I'm sorry. It's been a long day. Come on in, Rich, where've you been?" She looked tired, but calm, in control.

"On the phone. It's my fate."

Morgan had not missed the sullen glare that had appeared in Bobby's eyes. The boy stood up, unfolding his long body with a certain familiar angularity. "Come on, Adam, I want to show you what I've been doing in the workshop on weekends."

Adam looked at his watch. "I've got to get started before long, but I guess I've got a few minutes."

"Plenty of room if you'd like to stay over," Kathy said. "You too , Rich."

Adam shook his head. "I'd love it but I've got to get back. Okay, Bob, what's this great project?"

Morgan could hear Bobby talking rapidly as they went down the steps. The coffee pot was on the table before the sofa. He poured himself a cup and sat down.

"It's a scale-model sailboat," Kathy said. "You'd think it was the China Clipper, the way Bobby's worked on it." She went to her closet, took out her long robe. "Adam was always good with Bobby. I guess I was the only one in the family he didn't like."

Morgan watched her unzip the black dress behind her neck, her hands and arms graceful as birds. She stepped out of the dress, hung it in the closet, slipped on the robe, and, sitting on her dressing-table bench, began to peel off her dark tights.

"It was so hot, I started to shock the populace and not wear these, but some things even I draw the line at."

He looked at her long legs, tanned as ever, but felt nothing, not a tremor. Then she stood up, pulling the robe around her, and came across the room.

"I saw you crying," she said. "I wasn't surprised. I know you're a sentimentalist. I wanted to cry, I really did, it opens a person up. But I just got some silly tears in my eyes, nothing that did me any good. I cried a lot last night though. When those children sang 'Abide with Me,' I thought that was when I'd come apart, but I didn't. And when Bobby started bawling I had to pull him together. So I didn't cry. Sometimes I think I'm not like other people, Rich. I seem to be harder inside or maybe I'm more selfish, I don't know what's the matter with me. If anything is. Of course, these last years with Hunt some ways were hell, but we'd been together a long time, done a lot of things, there was a lot of just plain familiarity between us, whatever else. He was generous as he knew how to be, and he was good when little Kate died, really good. I've always been grateful for that. So you'd have thought I'd be more broken up than I am, just at the time gone by and spent together, if nothing else—I mean the sadness of the way things turn out."

"No, I wouldn't have expected that."

"You know me better than anybody, I guess. Hunt never really did know me at all. As if he didn't really care to, or think it mattered." She sat on the sofa by him, touched his leg, put her forehead momentarily against his shoulder.

"Maybe he should have got to know you better."

She laughed drily. "It might have helped at that. But I guess I'll have lots of time now to think about Hunt, where we went wrong. Where I went wrong maybe. I don't want to talk about it tonight, or think about it." She got up, walked toward the bed, turned back to him. "Rich . . . it's not quite positive . . . I think the Governor's going to give me Hunt's seat."

Morgan's first thought was professional: *I ought to have my ass kicked, that's why Myrtle was here.* Then he thought: *Kathy could have told me.* Kathy did not wait for him to speak.

"It makes sense, you see, because the Governor doesn't want to appoint himself—he thinks that'd be fatal in this state. But he may want to run for it when the special election comes up next year, so he's thinking first about a seat-warmer, he's frank about that. On the other hand, a lot of people might want to run then, and he may decide it's best to stay out. So he can't think about *just* a seat-warmer, he might need someone who can win. He wouldn't want his appointee beaten, that would hurt him too."

"But what about Matt?"

"Hopeless. The Governor says staff types never make it. and I must say I agree. No, he needs someone who's got a claim—they put in Huey Long's widow, you know—but also somebody who could run well if it comes to that. I told him frankly I thought I could. Danny O'Connor spoke to him and promised to do TV for me or the Governor, whoever runs."

"You've been a busy little bee."

"That state chairman's a problem though. That clod, Brock. He's got some assemblyman he wants appointed. Rich, do you know anybody who might get to Brock?"

"Zeb Vance. He put Brock in years ago."

"Just the man. I'll call him in the morning."

"Not that it matters"—Morgan put down his coffee cup—"but since we spent a pleasant little hour in here this morning, you might have mentioned all this to your faithful lover, mightn't you?"

"Well, I had to promise the story to Myrtle Bell. That way, she was willing to tell the Governor she was going to give him a big ride in her column tomorrow, on the likelihood he was going to name a woman to the Senate."

"Bullshit," Morgan said. "You're a lousy liar."

She had been pacing the room, the tails of the long robe sailing behind her. She whirled toward him. "Well, you'd only have tried to talk me out of it, you know you would."

"No, I'd just have told you not to be a cold-blooded snatch, the day you buried Hunt. I'd have told you to think about it tomorrow."

"But that might be too late, and everybody was *here*. Spencer Burns promised him I'd get the best possible committee seats. Even Dunn—Dunn spoke to the Governor about it. He said he thought the time had come when a woman could win."

"God," Morgan said, "I'd be the last to doubt you could win anything you went for."

"Well, why shouldn't I want it then? Why should I wait till tomorrow when the opportunity was today? I sat around all these years since Hunt quit. Before that, I played the game with him. I almost made him president, if he'd listened to me. I never once let him down in any way that mattered. Why shouldn't I go for something myself, now . . ." She stopped.

"Now the way's clear. No reason. But for somethings most people don't need reasons."

"All right, it's cold-blooded if that's the way you want it, but I've got a chance for *my* life now, Rich, not some echo of Hunt's or something hidden in a dark room with you. You'll leave here and go back to that round-heeled little peach of yours, and what good will that do me?"

"Anne's not round-heeled," Morgan said. "She's only reaching like the rest of us." But there was, he conceded, a certain brutal justice in what Kathy was saying, even if he believed it was mostly Richie, and not Ann, he would keep returning to. Why should Kathy not call it a dark room? Why should it be more to her than something furtive, fleeting? It certainly could not be called a life. And he knew before she sat down on the sofa beside him what she would say next, and what he would answer.

"The Governor admires you. He said you were our leading journalist." Her finger traced a line from his knee to the middle of his thigh. "If you'd call him . . . better still go see him . . ." The finger moved back to his knee.

He looked into her cool blue eyes. "And say what?"

"Well, he said he respects your political judgment and besides . . . if he thought you were going to write something good in your paper about his appointing a woman . . ." The finger moved again.

"I'll tell you like one of my first editors told me. In my business, you have to be a prick but not a whore."

The blue eyes never faltered. "You're so high and mighty. You're like Hunt, you think you're above things."

"But Hunt didn't think he was above things when you got through with him, did he?"

She leaned away from him, sinking into a corner of the sofa. A tiny line appeared between her brows. "What's that supposed to mean?"

"I've been talking to Dunn about what happened at the convention. Hunt never offered Dunn a deal."

"He didn't have the guts," Kathy said. "When it mattered, Hunt didn't have what it takes." She got up and went to the window, looked out over the meadow.

"But you told Hunt—hell, you told *me*—that Dunn went to Aiken because Dunn thought Hunt was soft and a hypocrite."

"That's what Hunt was."

"But that's not what Dunn thought he was, just the opposite."

"It doesn't matter what Dunn thought. I know what Hunt was. Who should know that better than I do?"

Morgan got to his feet. He wanted to kick over the coffee table. He wanted to put his hands under the bed and upend it. He went to her, seized her arm, and turned her to face him.

"So you persuaded him he was what *you* thought he was. And you let him think Dunn thought so too. You convinced him he'd tried to sell out and botched the job."

"Take your hand off me," Kathy said, her eyes hard as slate. He did, but he did not move away from her. "I didn't have to convince Hunt of anything. Long before I ever talked to Dunn about it, Hunt came blubbering to me in the middle of the night, right here in this room; he was drunk, but he was sober too, and he woke me up and said, 'I was going to do it, I swear to God I was going to do it, I *wanted* to do it, and that green-eyed bastard never gave me a chance.' I told him to go to bed and sleep it off, but he wouldn't; instead he sat down on my bed and kept talking. Over and over again he told me—he was going to give Dunn anything Dunn wanted for those ninety-eight delegates. 'I'd have given him the Grand Canyon,' that's what Hunt said to me, 'I'd have given him your sweet ass, baby, I wanted those delegates so much, but the bastard never gave me a chance. His mind was made up.' And pretty soon Hunt passed out over the end of the bed there, and slept till morning. It was the only time we were ever in bed together after the convention."

"I see," Morgan said. Until that moment, he realized, he had believed in his heart that somehow Anderson had been good enough, that it was all a mistake, a misunderstanding, proper historical research would someday amend the record.

"So when Dunn told me what he'd thought, it made no difference to me."
"I knew what had really happened, whatever Dunn thought." Her clenched fists came up in front of his chest, trembling. "I could have done it. I could have persuaded Dunn. But the only time it really mattered, Hunt failed. *That's* what happened. And if you mean I reminded him of it any way I could—all right, that's true."

"Not so much that he failed himself," Morgan said, "but that he failed you."

"You asked me once, Rich—the first night you were in this room with me—you asked me if I'd ever wanted something that was perfect, that was just right for me to do?"

"A pure vision."

"And I said yes. Well, mine was what Hunt ruined for me. Mine was winning that nomination, doing what they all said couldn't be done. Beating them, every one."

And something else, Morgan thought, something else you said that night: *nothing's pure in life.* "What were you going to do with it all?" he said. "If you'd won."

Kathy put her hands on his chest and her head between them. "I never thought about that. I just wanted to win. Your heart's beating like a triphammer."

"It always does when I'm anywhere near you."

"Then you're not so high and mighty after all."

Because nobody can be, Morgan thought. "I'm just wondering," he said, "if a reporter is allowed to make love to a senator."

"Nothing against it in the rules. I've already looked."

"Even if I don't go to see your goddam governor for you?"

"I knew you wouldn't all along."

"Then why'd you ask?"

"I just thought I might persuade you. I just thought maybe I could."

"And suppose the Governor should decide he wants to run in that special election?"

"The first thing's to get the appointment. But I'll bet if he picks me it'll turn out he won't want to run at all."

"Especially," Morgan said, "if it has to be against you."

"One reason I love you," Kathy said, "is you take the trouble to know me so well."

They heard Adam and Bobby coming up the stairs and moved apart.

"You got a real shipbuilder here," Adam said from the doorway.

"He showed me some things on the lathe." Bobby's voice was excited. "Adam's a whiz on the lathe."

"Adam's a whiz," Morgan said. "And I'm going to bum a ride to town with him."

Bobby protested Adam's leaving; Kathy, suddenly looking exhausted, said good-by to them in her room. Bobby, scarcely polite to Morgan, left them on the front porch, and they went across the lawn.

It was dark; from the moonless sky a few stars winked at them, and across the meadow a breeze moved against the treetops. Morgan could smell the earth, the animals in the fields, honeysuckle. He walked slowly; he was not particularly anxious to return to the world of the managing editor, Anne, Hinman, the Blakey Show. And then it occurred to him that he had not quite finished with Anderson.

Adam's car was parked on the road, a few minutes' walk from the house. It was a dusty old sedan with a crumpled fender, a cracked window, one door that wouldn't open; the top of the dashboard was littered with maps, paper cups, envelopes.

"This old buggy's practically my office," Adam said.

"And you're off tonight?"

"By breakfast I can be in Asheville, if the mountain roads don't get me. I've got to be in court tomorrow."

"Then I hate to ask you, but if you can spare ten minutes, let's go back to the graveyard."

In the dim light from the dash Adam's face was expressionless. "No problem." He followed Morgan's directions into the road that would take them through the wood. "Bobby only partly wanted to show me his boat,

Rich. He told me what's been going on between you and his mother. He knows all about it and it cuts the kid up."

Morgan stopped himself from the rapid invention of a cover story; he was going to come out, he told himself, out into the open. "I know it does. I wish it could be some other way. But sometimes things just cut people up."

The car nosed into the wood. "That woman poisons what she touches," Adam said.

"You don't know her. You don't know anything about her at all."

Adam drove cautiously through the brook, and Morgan remembered how the sheet of water had risen above the jeep and fallen in a cool spray on their heads, his and Anderson's.

"And to be blunt about it, Adam, no criticism intended, you didn't know much about Hunt either. He was right that you've been lucky. I tried to tell you something like that once. I said you knew who you were. All Hunt knew was that he was Old Bull's boy."

Far above them on the hilltop, the lights of the car fell dimly on the trees underneath which the carved and dated stones rose from the earth, vainly marking lives.

"Call it luck," Adam said, "but try it some time."

Morgan went on relentlessly, watching the lights brightening on the trees, the fence, the arch. "Call it character if you'd rather. You were born as practical as a pair of pliers. Or maybe life just put so many practical things in front of you to do, and gave you so many tools to do them with, that if you'd let yourself be pulled off in some other direction, you'd have known you were ducking out, wasting yourself. Anyway, you knew what to do and you could do it well, and you did. I don't think Hunt Anderson had that kind of luck. Or character."

The car went on up the hill, through the arch. Its lights shone on the stone effigy of Old Bull, the flower-covered mound under the canopy. Morgan got out and walked between the stones. Adam followed, leaving the engine idling, its whine blending with the whisper of wind in the leaves. Morgan went past Anderson's grave to Old Bull's stone feet, set forever on their solid base.

"There was a lot of Old Bull in Hunt," Morgan said. "It was at war with everything else in him, with what he expected from himself and wanted most." He felt in his inside jacket pocket, where—reporter-like—he always kept a pencil safe against emergencies. "He wanted to show the best in a man rather than the worst." Morgan went down on one knee and began to write on the stone base, under the carved words ALWAYS A MAN. "Maybe that standard was too high, but he set it himself, and better that way than too low. I think he gave Old Bull a run for his money."

"What're you doing?"

"What Hunt told me once he aimed to do. Only he didn't believe then it was going to include him."

Morgan stood up. Under the carved epitaph he had scrawled in thin, wavering letters LIKE YOU.

"Should you mark up a man's gravestone like that?"

"Don't worry," Morgan said, looking up at the stone hands, the marble eyes. "Time will wear it away."

Adam dropped Morgan at the Bright Leaf and drove off with what sounded to Morgan like a disapproving clash of gears. Morgan went straight to his room, called his home office and—just before deadline— dictated a story that the governor was likely to appoint Hunt Anderson's widow to the United States Senate. Take that, Myrtle Bell, he thought, and slept soundly.

He arose early, took a taxi to the airport, and caught a breakfast flight north. It was a clear day for flying, but the plane made two stops before Washington National, and by the time he was on the last leg over Virginia, Morgan's stomach and jaw muscles ached from the tension of takeoffs and landings. But he felt ready to cope with the managing editor. He knew he was a professional, a valuable property; he might even get tough, put it on an either-or basis, see how they liked that. Old Barstow had a good fight going inside the Pentagon, which was about to break, and maybe he'd put that in the managing editor's eye for good measure. Keller was damn well going to have a raise. As for Anne and Richie, he would take Anne out to dinner that night and see if a new leaf could be turned, although he knew from countless previous leaves and dinners that the prospects were dim. There was a doubleheader with the Yankees on Sunday; Richie would enjoy that—he was the only fan in the world who considered the Washington Senators a great team.

The seat-belt sign went on for Washington. They were coming in from up the Potomac, low over the Key Bridge, with the gray spires of Georgetown University on the left, Theodore Roosevelt Island just below. The classic white pillars of the Lincoln Memorial, pure as dreams, stood at the head of the Reflecting Pool; beyond it the Washington Monument thrust tall and severe into a clear blue sky. Morgan could see far down the Mall, past the red-brick toy castle of the Smithsonian and the stone sprawl of the

National Art Gallery, to the Capitol on its hill, serene beneath its dome and beautiful as hope. The plane trembled a bit in the hot rising current. Directly beneath him, the Jefferson Memorial stood by the Tidal Basin and beyond the wingtip he could see the White House and the elliptical park before it.

For a moment, and from that altitude, it was all in Morgan's window— a pure vision of America, the great stone façade of the Republic, the romantic ideal of man. It shone in the morning sun, and from the air the grass looked green and fresh. Then the plane dipped lower, and he could see the long gleaming lines of cars on the Fourteenth Street bridge, carrying humanity to its strivings, peopling the vision with men and women.

Morgan had a glimpse, across the fouled brown river, of crowded streets, beehive buildings, demolitions in progress. He had just time enough to see that everything was going on as usual before the plane settled to the earth. With luck in traffic, he could be in his office in time to read the mail before Cockcroft's backgrounder.

AN ACKNOWLEDGMENT

I am indebted for much information about the facts of migrant labor to a brilliant series of articles by Kent Pollock, published October 5–12, 1969, in the Palm Beach, Florida, *Post,* and to the authoritative documents and hearing transcripts of the Subcommittee on Migrant Labor of the Senate Committee on Labor and Public Welfare. There are, however, no such places as Agri-Packers, Inc., and Saugus Number Two, however typical they may be. Both are imaginary.

Except for a few historical personages to whom I found it necessary to refer, all the characters in this novel are imaginary.

Tom Wicker